HEAVEN'S JUDGE

a Novel by
ARNDT SCHORR

Second Book of the
Fourth Angel War Series

ABSOLUTELY AMAZING eBOOKS

Published by Whiz Bang LLC, 926 Truman Avenue, Key West, Florida 33040, USA.

For information contact:
Publisher@AbsolutelyAmazingEbooks.com

ISBN-13: 978-1949504286 (The New Atlantian Library)
ISBN-10: 194950428X

HEAVEN'S JUDGE

FORWARD
PART ONE
INDEPENDENCE

YORKTOWN, Virginia
October 19, 1781

The Archangel Gabriel watched General Cornwallis surrender. The defeated British commander was hemmed in on horseback, by French troops and cavalry on one side, and those of General Washington on the other. Lord Cornwallis and his soldiers would be held until the government in London negotiated an acceptable peace, withdrawing their forces, and denying any further claim to sovereignty over their former colony.

The British had lost the battle for America.

The forces of Heaven were greatly pleased.

Gabriel turned away. He was bound for Philadelphia, to ensure things in the capital were going smoothly, based upon heavenly alliances made with a number of angels involved in founding the United States. These were fallen angels in human form, determined to throw off British rule and sever their long-standing ties with the devil.

Lucifer, with his stranglehold on Europe for centuries, had made a mistake that would haunt him for two hundred years. Fearful of the spiritual forces ranged against him on this side of the Atlantic, he set up shop in Westminster, siding with parliament and their mad king.

The devil lent them his considerable powers; until it was clear the British cause was lost. The slaughter had angered Heaven. Seasoned Red Coat regiments marching in full formation, firing musket and cannon as they came, churning their enemy to blood, meat and bone. An enemy made up of young boys, tradesmen and farmers, thrown into scraps of blue uniform to represent the Continental Army. Casualties were catastrophic, and the war seemed already lost. But the Americans had other fighters, older men who had brutally defeated the French and their Huron allies in the mountains and trees of the North. The French had no talent for forest fighting. They were too proud to surrender and fought in the open to the last man, shooting any of their native mercenaries who tried to run away. It was a historic defeat, and the American colonists returned home to great acclaim and resumed their former existence. Now, a decade later, it was these experienced veterans, along with their sons and nephews, who saved the American Revolution with flintlock rifles and raw courage.

Like the French, the British Army fought in formation, out in the open, and when they did they were unstoppable. However, after Charleston fell the American strategy changed. There were no more blue uniforms, no more battlefields, and no more British victories. As they had in the Canadian War, the rebel army became a free-ranging militia of sharpshooters. Shadows in the shadows, spread out in a ragged line at the edge of pasture or woodland path. All enemy forces on the move were now met by withering gunfire, mowed down without mercy by riflemen they never saw.

In less than two years the war was over. The final

battle was decided today, with the redcoats throwing down their arms. Now they made a raggedy column, headed for temporary imprisonment. Humiliated and defeated. Proud, strutting peacocks no more.

The Angel Gabriel, flying low and invisible over Pennsylvania, smiled with satisfaction. A long-awaited miracle had finally taken place. A land where Lucifer had no influence now existed. A land ordained by Heaven to decide the destiny of the whole world.

Today the devil was every bit as defeated as General Cornwallis.

Gabriel's laughter echoed through the clouds.

FORWARD
PART TWO
THE DEFEAT

Little Bighorn, Montana
June 26th, 1876

THE SCALPING BEGAN AT NOON.

It was the huge Cheyenne called Wing-Shirt, who urged his equally large pony up a low rise in the prairie to survey the carnage. The beast balked at the smell of blood, snorting and pawing the ground. Soft words from his rider were needed to quiet him.

The warrior named Wing-Shirt was Gabriel.

The horse was an illusion.

A ghastly sight greeted them both. The slaughter had turned rich green grass into a sticky red lake. Bloody, hacked chunks of human flesh lay everywhere. The squaws of the village attacked by Custer had already passed through, gouging out eyes, severing genitals and hacking the white men into small pieces. Now came the warriors: Sioux, Cheyenne and Arapaho, darting across the sticky ground, sawing with knives at decapitated heads in final insult, taking topknots of hair, seeking to destroy the victim's eternal spirit. A victory dance had started. Thousands of feet pounded the ground. Thousands of throats whooped with joy.

It would go on for hours.

Gabriel turned sadly away.

Lucifer had finally arrived in this new, thriving America. His influence in Washington was strong, and this cowardly, ill-fated Custer campaign was all his doing. For a full year, peaceful villages had been put to the sword, usually women and children, while the men were off hunting. The 'Boy General' had made it his personal technique, blind to the hatred he was stirring up among his victims. A hatred that had exploded into fury today.

Custer's corpse was unrecognizable

Stripped and chopped up like the others.

Gabriel's sadness was not for the cavalrymen or their commander. A bunch of bully-boys who got what they deserved. The angel's heart wept for the doomed tribes who had sealed their own fate. Not many would survive the winter. Revenge for this massacre would be harsh.

The tribes were doomed.

And the devil was still in Washington.

Unless and until Gabriel could drive him out.

FORWARD
PART THREE
FIRE AND FURY

Hiroshima, Japan
August 6th, 1945

THE DUST CLOUD, TOXIC WITH RADIATION, was still rising and spreading to form a mushroom. The bomb called "Little Boy" had done its work. An ancient city built of paper houses was gone. Seventy thousand Japanese died in the initial impact. A figure that would soon double, as radiation burned through living skin and bone. Hiroshima's army garrison was undermanned, most of its soldiers sent to the front. As a result military losses were minimal – but women and children died by the tens of thousands.

A million angels hovered above the scene.

Many of them wept.

This bore the mark of Lucifer.

Germany had tried saturation bombing and suffered a humiliating defeat at the hands of the Royal Air Force. British and American retribution, when it came, was terrible. Berlin, Hamburg, Frankfurt and scores of other major cities were leveled flat. Families digging in the rubble for food were shot by S. S. units sent in by Hitler to maintain public order. Russian artillery and infantry, advancing from the East, destroyed everything with rockets, cannon and shells. Within weeks the German surrender left Japan standing alone.

American bombers turned their fury on Tokyo and other dense population centers on the larger Japanese islands. A million paper houses were set ablaze, but the Sun-God Emperor and his generals stood fast.

Japan would fight to the bitter end.

And now, with Hiroshima on fire, they refused to change their mind. "Little Boy" had not persuaded them.

Two days later, at Nagasaki, a second atomic bomb did. Its nickname was Fat Man.

Gabriel moved another million angels into place.

They were going to be busy.

CHAPTER ONE

April 1st, 2025

HE TOOK HUMAN FORM at Kennedy Airport.

That is to say he entered the body of a living mortal. There are those who call it possession, but to the Angel Gabriel, it was more like hitching a ride without asking the driver. Gabriel's host this time was an international terrorist: a plump, Lebanese arms trader operating out of Jerusalem for Al Qaeda, Hamma, Hezbullah, and several other Islamic terror organizations, their supporters and sympathizers, including top members of the Saudi royal family, and, of course, the rogue states of Iran and Syria.

This particular weapons dealer also had an obsession for indecently young girls.

He liked to deflower them.

His name was Amir Affhad.

He happily served Sunni and Shiite alike; although the two factions were at war in Iraq and fighting a subdued battle across the entire Middle-East. Amir Affhad made vast profits for himself in the process – his expertise so great and widely respected that both sides tolerated such double-dealing without complaint.

Only two forces in the universe could overcome the hatred between Sunni and Shia: the first was Amir Affhad; because in the world of military supply and demand he was the grandest of grand wizards. The second was Al Qaeda, whose interests he represented; because Al Qaeda was dedicated to the downfall of the United States, and even historic enemies, like the Sunni Saudis, and Iran's Shiites, were united by their hatred of America. No Arab state had ever said this publicly, or admitted supporting Al Qaeda. That would be politically foolish and dangerous. However, despite years of diplomatic hand-wringing and denials, no Arab state had spoken out against Al Qaeda, either.The Angel of Death entered Amir Affhad with some distaste, but he had not chosen him lightly. This was a key figure in events about to unfold in the Afghan hills that could destroy America, a man poised to commit a great evil, which put the angel in no mood for mercy. Gabriel had already decided that the arms dealer was not long for this world. It was not a hard decision to make.

Man and angel entered the luxury of a first-class cabin, settling their shared bulk onto plush, velvet upholstery. Gabriel stared out of the window through the eyes of the Lebanese, seeing the still gaping wound in the New York skyline where the twin towers once stood, still around despite the replacement structure, and the years that had passed since the catastrophe. Gabriel felt Affhad's twisted pleasure at the sight, the pride he took in the sacrifice of those who hi-jacked the planes. The Arab had no pity whatsoever for the innocent thousands who died.

A great anger arose in the Angel of Death. It was not an anger he could control; nor would he ever wish to.

For this was the anger of God.

Gabriel made a mental shift. The Arab's heart contracted, causing him violent pain, as the angel squeezed. At least, it was something akin to a squeeze, and Gabriel kept it up for several seconds.

Reluctantly, he relaxed his grip and returned Affhad's heartbeat to normal. The man sagged with fear and relief, certain that he had escaped a full-blown heart attack. Gabriel was disgusted by the decay of this creature's soul, or rather, what was left of it. The demon living inside Affhad was taking over, and before long nothing human would remain. This demon was Gabriel's real prey. It's very presence was offensive, and he felt an overpowering urge to kill it now. But if the demon died, so did the Lebanese arms dealer, which must not happen until tomorrow. That, and only that, saved the demon for now.

But Gabriel could sense its fear.

It knew who he was.

And so this flight promised to be worse than usual, not only due to the atrocious service on American airlines, but because Gabriel was trapped with this evil creature inside the body of a psychopathic Arab.

The shared hearing of all three of them absorbed the announcement for take-off. Four engines rose to a high-pitch; then became subdued. The passengers in First Class tilted gently with the fuselage as they climbed out of JFK airspace. Gabriel sensed the Arab's fear as the plane tore down the runway with a disturbing rumble; then lurched into the air. Amir Affhad was afraid of take-offs and landings, and the Archangel took some pleasure in that.

At the front of the cabin, a stewardess demonstrated how to die safely in an orange life-preserver.

Gabriel always found that amusing.

Having overcome first a heart-attack scare, and now a fear of flying, the Lebanese mopped his brow and opened a brown, leather briefcase. He glanced out of the window again. The scene of the World Trade Center was still in plain sight, and Gabriel felt the Arab regain his composure, smirking once more at this memorial to

Palestinian suffering that America would never forget.

Gabriel decided to let it go.

Until tomorrow.

Affhad took some papers from his case and set it down beside him on the seat. He crossed one leg over the other, balancing the embossed sheets, as he added up their face value in dollars. These sheets were international bearer bonds, and Gabriel, also doing a calculation in his head, was amazed at their total worth. It was blood money, paid in full, and the angel knew how Amir Affhad had earned it. The Lebanese was beaming with pleasure, but hid the papers quickly, when a young stewardess asked politely if he would like something to drink.

He demanded tea.

When it came, he sent it back, insisting it be served in Mid-East fashion, which involved a glass, a tray and a lot of cubed sugar. The poor girl retreated and returned with the necessary items, relived to have them on board; then escaped as swiftly as she could, despite Gabriel having forced the arms dealer to smile and thank her, as she put down the tray.

The Archangel savored the tea.

He savored it, and considered world affairs. The attacks of 9/11, and subsequent events in the Middle-East – the mountain of American and Iraqi casualties, followed by widespread sectarian slaughter – had caused anger and disgust everywhere; not only on Earth but also in Heaven. For the first time in several centuries, Gabriel, Angel of Death, was sent for and dispatched, and here he was, more than a decade after the twin towers went down – still killing anybody who threatened to unleash Armageddon. Gabriel was charged with preventing, by direct intervention, the colossal world-ending catastrophe that seemed more likely every day. Iraq never became democratic, the Americans never really left and the fighting eventually resumed as before. Iraq, Iran and Syria were now the greatest threat to world peace; their leaders seething over N A T O Soldiers in North Pakistan and Afghanistan, and increasing American drone attacks – with Saudi Arabia stirring the pot behind the scenes. In Afghanistan the picture changed as soon as vast mineral wealth was discovered. An ocean of precious ore lay beneath the rock-strewn terrain like a previously undetected treasure. The geography of the war quickly shifted. US troops started to fight from the center, defending American mining operations as they set up shop. Nowadays the ore-rich area was protected by America, while Taliban forces held on fiercely to the border-regions at the edges.

Enraged by all this foreign intrusion, seen as the greatest blasphemy since the crusades, Fundamental Islam was poised to inflict further punishment on the United States, and the Angel Gabriel was flying to Jerusalem inside this overweight Lebanese for that very reason.

One hour ago, Gabriel squeezed the life from the heart of a US senator, a man demon-possessed, like Amir Affhad. The senator, James Orville, had been bribed on a regular basis by the Lebanese for various favors. Last week, Affhad had asked for and received, a letter of introduction to a most valuable weapons connection in New York. Today a deal for black market nukes had been struck, a shipment to Iran involving a massive payment through offshore banks. This deal cost Senator Orville his life a few hours later. Gabriel administered a heart-attack on the golf course where Orville was teeing off instead of casting a Senate vote.

Now the nuclear purchase was in motion. It resulted in a heavenly death-sentence for Senator Orville and Amir Affhad from Gabriel, currently a case of one down and one to go.

Even when not killing the wicked, Gabriel traveled a lot, often crossing the world several times a day, and it drained his powers. By inserting himself in a mortal like Amir Affhad, he avoided all that. For Gabriel to zoom from London to Paris or Los Angeles, and back again, took only a snap of his fingers, but it used up enough divine energy to part the Red Sea. He had come up with alternative forms of travel: Gabriel could become a human of his own creation, and pay for a flight with fake cash or credit cards, or let a real human provide the body and an airline ticket. And using Amir Affhad today served another purpose: Gabriel could monitor the arms dealer's movements, and keep an eye on him right up until he died.

There would be no reprieve.

Gabriel found no joy in taking life; it was a heavenly adjustment; nothing more and nothing less. He tended to do it painlessly, with a heart-attack. Not out of pity, but because it was widely accepted that it could happen to anyone, at any age, and such a death was rarely investigated.

And the Angel Death would hardly be blamed if it was.

Still in daylight, the plane crossed the European coastline. The angel looked down at choppy waves through Affhad's eyes, wondering if they would arrive in Israel on time. He thought of more about to die, listing in his mind those to be dealt with first, starting with the Lebanese and the well-hidden fugitive he was probably returning home to see. Gabriel concentrated hard, committing several names and faces, and their locations, to memory. It made an unholy list.

The fat Lebanese was asleep.

On impulse, Gabriel moved the sleeping Arab's hands to put on headphones, and found a channel of progressive Hip-Hop. That should upset Affhad nicely when he woke up and wondered how it happened. Meantime Gabriel relaxed inside the bulky frame of his host and enjoyed the music.

It drove the demon crazy.

Afternoon became evening. The First Class compartment filled up with flight attendants, cold drinks and hot entrees. Affhad woke up, ripped off his headphones and ordered dinner, once he had recovered his composure, from the same young hostess as before.

Dinner arrived on a tray divided into two sections. The Lebanese bent down and sniffed, to assure himself that no pork, alcohol or other forbidden ingredient was present in either the food or the sauce. Once satisfied, he devoured a whole grouse and washed it down with Perrier.

The water congealed the fatty food in his stomach.

Gabriel was revolted.

Hours later, darkness was pierced by runway lights as they landed, Jerusalem lay huddled around them, its tiny airport bustling with armed Israeli men and women in uniform. The Arab arms dealer went through line after line of security checks, and was eventually driven home in a Rolls Royce by his chauffeur. There was no traffic, and the journey was less than a mile.

His fake papers had worked just as well here as in New York, but Israeli cameras were turning, and their data base would soon spit him out, exposing his true identity, but by then it would be too late. No one had discovered the fortune in bearer bonds, hidden in a secret compartment in his briefcase. This was still the Middle-East, and it was nobody's business to rip such cases apart, especially as anyone whose business it might have been had received a huge bribe as soon as he encountered them. Amir Affhad knew what was necessary, and happily paid. Several customs officials would soon be buying brand-new, luxury cars.

Affhad was home by midnight.

Of course he had a penthouse. His wives and children occupied a tenement hovel several districts away. Thus he enjoyed opulent luxury, freedom to indulge in forbidden sex, and an extremely low overhead.

A typical Arab husband of his class.

The hour was late. Two servants bedded Affhad down. Gabriel sensed the man's drowsiness, despite that nap on the plane. The Arab's thoughts, as he fell asleep, were of victory and triumph over America, the Great Satan, and of the gratitude that would be heaped upon him tomorrow, for a job well done. Also thoughts of his generous financial reward, earned in the most despicable way. It was paid in advance, and redeemable in hard currency all over the world.

Perhaps he would buy a private jet.

And a Caribbean island..

Before long he began to snore.

Gabriel waited while he slept, as did the demon, which by now was fully unnerved by the Archangel's presence and frantic with fear.

Breakfast was eaten late and seemed endless: Fruit, yogurt, figs and olives with flat, unleavened bread, and a bottomless pot of treacle masquerading as coffee. Finally the Arab left the house, taking both angel and demon with him.

They were soon leaving the prosperous area of the city, headed for the slums and bomb-sites of the Palestinian quarter. Quite a walk for a portly Arab in the midday heat. His pounding heart confirmed this, and Gabriel detected fear, mingled with anticipation. With some satisfaction the Angel of Death read Affhad's mind and realized they were on their way to the big meeting.

Loose rocks skittered on what passed for a road, as the fat Lebanese trudged in his chosen direction. Children in rags played barefoot in the dust. The only adults in sight were the beggars, seated at intervals, hawking various ailments, which they announced as one passed, rattling a battered tin cup or other receptacle, asking for alms in the name of Allah. There were, however, plenty of adults out of sight. And they were watching. The sweating Lebanese turned a corner and called out a greeting. Gabriel saw a house with P. L. O. Graffiti on the walls and above the door. The roof was missing tiles, displaying shell-torn rafters, and a sad-looking donkey was tethered to a rail, next to the crumbling well.

Flies buzzed lazily in the heat.

Nothing else stirred.

It seemed they had arrived.

Two armed men approached Affhad, surveying the street with flinty eyes. They patted him down, not very thoroughly, Gabriel thought. That meant they knew him, and he was here by arrangement. This was indeed the crucial meeting, the reason Gabriel came from New York.

The voice from inside the house, as the door opened, was clear, resonant, and had authority. It said: "Mr. Affhad?"

Amir was ushered in.

The guards took position outside.

The interior was hardly lavish, but furnished with enough good taste to be strange in this setting. The angel recognized their host on sight. This confirmed his judgment in choosing the Lebanese. Few obtained access to this particular safe house. Amir Affhad was clearly one of them.

Gabriel smiled to himself.

Oman Ben Salim, the host, was tall, elegant and handsome, dressed in an Italian-styled suit. He had a rakish, close-trimmed black beard and wore his hair in a gleaming ponytail. A reporter from Time magazine had once called him a Movie-Maker's Dream. Ben Salim was proud of that.

He was, in fact, a very powerful demon.

Not a possessed human, like Amir Affhad, but a fully-fledged demon in his own right, posing as a human being.

His good looks made him exceptional.

Most demons living among mankind could only be described as ugly, and some were downright hideous. They covered this by masquerading as humans in advanced old-age, and this worked quite well; although they would not be called Movie stars in Time Magazine. Evil acts cause further physical deterioration, and so they looked even worse as time went on. Ben Salim, however, was so powerful that he kept his attractive appearance, despite the brutal crimes he committed on a daily basis. Ben Salim was a ruthless butcher.

He was chief warlord in this region, acting as a liaison between Hamas, the main Shiite force behind Palestinian and Lebanese causes, and Al Qaeda, the Sunni terrorist organization sponsored and funded by the Kingdom of Saudi Arabia. Omar Ben Salim was the gatekeeper. Omar Ben Salim was all-powerful.

He shook hands with Affhad and said: "Greetings, Amir," in a cultured Egyptian accent, although Ben Salim and his charming manners were not very welcome in Cairo these days. Not that Cairo had any problem with terrorism – she was one of its largest backers. Cairo hated Ben Salim for branching out on his own, and doing it better than them.

He gestured to a low table covered with Damask cloth, laden with grapes, iced water and two ornate glasses. The men sat on cushions, facing each other. Ben Salim sat ramrod straight. He stared at his guest with a haughty look, displaying aloofness and interest at the same time.

Here was someone utterly in command, and this was his command post. All his enemies were either dead, or on death-lists. Gabriel was meeting him for the first time, and sensed his malevolence. Ben Salim was making ready to attack his greatest enemy: the United States of America. It was why Amir Affhad was here, and why Gabriel had come with him. Ben Salim fully intended to unleash the wrath of Islam, and fulfill the worst prophecies of the Koran.

Although he, of course, believed in none of it.

Gabriel read Ben Salim's mind, becoming aware of how much the demon needed this Lebanese visitor, the obscenely perverted and grossly overweight Amir Affhad.

The only reason Affhad was still alive.

Ben Salim was mindful of the man's importance in the scheme of things, smiling with great politeness as the stirred the iced water before pouring. Refrigerators were not common hereabouts, due to power problems from the constant shelling, and iced water was a tribute to the value of Amir Affhad.

The Lebanese was vital, as was the journey he had just completed. Not to mention his business contacts, which spanned five continents, and were essential to the greatest attack ever conceived against America. In short, this deviate was an embarrassment in a devout Muslim world, but he was irreplaceable.

Ben Salim's memory revealed to Gabriel how the Egyptian had despised the Lebanese at first, a fat abomination who fondled little girls, who lisped when he spoke, often giggling in mid-sentence, and who was above all a coward, afraid to take risks. Unless for a huge profit.

Surprisingly, this opinion was overcome.

Amir Affhad's first assignment, awarded grudgingly, involved a large amount of plastic explosive. In those days Semtex was rare, and available in terrorist circles from limited sources. Ghadaffi was one, but being difficult, having gone to ground after his near-death experience with the jet fighters of President Reagan. That left one other serious supplier: the Irish Republican Army, who'd been General Ghadaffi's biggest customer, but now had little use for Semtex, due to peace talks they were having with the British. Obligingly, Ben Salim offered to take any surplus explosive off their hands. After some debate, the Palestinian purchase was approved by Belfast, to be regulated and finalized in America. Which was where Amir

Affhad came in. The fat Lebanese, it seemed, was a requirement, having been asked for by name.

Thus he became Trans-Atlantic.

It transpired that the man was a master of his craft. He spoke the language of murderers, and drove a hard bargain. In short he exceeded beyond all expectation in the Irish dominated city of Boston, even reducing the price by a third and securing free delivery.

This redeemed him.

And made him a necessary evil.

And so it was ever since. Ben Salim's disapproval was buried, at least until the Lebanese was no longer of use. Until then he would be treated with great civility, and honored like a prince. Because, Ben Salim told any doubtful colleagues, Amir Affhad might be a pig, but he was a most valuable pig.

He was Al Qaeda's pig.

Gabriel found these thoughts amusing, especially in view of heavenly opinion on Oman Ben Salim. Compared to him, the Lebanese was a knight in shining armor. Ben Salim was the demon King.

He topped Gabriel's list.

Affhad was halfway down it.

Talk began in earnest between the two Arabs. A lot more than Semtex was involved. Negotiation for the nuclear devices, six of them, was concluded. The source was that recommended by Senator Orville, who sadly made news yesterday by dying of a heart attack.

It still dominated every channel.

A well-placed demon was no more.

Both Arabs regretted his loss. He had long been a director on the board of the Newcastle Group, and international company that fronted for American and Saudi oil interests, and his influence in a world of interconnected wheelers and dealers would be sorely missed, but the demon world had replaced him already. There was no shortage of corrupt senators in Congress.

Or demons.

Orville's successor was a woman. She had just been elected for a third term, and was demon-possessed like Amir Affhad, the difference being that she knew it; Affhad did not.

Suddenly Gabriel heard Affhad telling Ben Salim that Senator Orville's nuclear weapons supplier turned out to be perfect. This made the angel pay attention. It was the kind of thing he wanted to hear. Apparently, said Affhad, this supplier would broker the entire transaction, interfacing with North Korea and China on behalf of their customer, the crazy radicals in charge of Iran. Orville's American contact lived in New York, of all places; the first US city successfully targeted by Al Qaeda. It seemed there were indeed Americans who would do anything for money.

This one was betraying his country.

No one had expected to obtain nuclear hardware from such a source. The price, however, was colossally high. There was an intake of breath from Ben Salim, as Affhad named a final cost of twelve hundred billion dollars. But the price was fair and both terrorists knew it. And the money was readily available, as long as there was oil in the deserts of Saudi Arabia. Affhad's cut, in the briefcase he had with him, was fifteen per cent, deducted and converted into bonds yesterday, when he made the initial payment via Chase Manhattan Bank. His share alone amounted to some eight hundred million, and he was worth every penny, at least in the eyes of Ben Salim.

Whose cut was ten per cent.

However, Affhad's portion included a commission on two similar deals, in which Ben Salim had played no part, and one of which had gone sour. It irked the Egyptian demon slightly, but made Amir Affhad extremely rich.

One of the guards ducked in through the door. It was Elajah, the intelligent one, alert and looking concerned. In time of danger he was always first to spot it. Now he said: "Israeli troop carrier."

"Ben Salim nodded. "One is scheduled."

He had contacts at a nearby military barracks.

Elajah cast a longing look at the remaining water, most of the ice having melted. Ben Salim ignored him and refilled both glasses to the brim.

Elajah vanished.

A cell phone rang, shrill and demanding. Ben Salim drew it from an inside pocket and snapped it open. If the CIA was listening, they were wasting their time, because this cell phone had been made secure at enormous expense by Russian experts, using the latest technology.

Ben Salim gave a curt greeting, then talked at length while the Lebanese politely pretended not to hear, although he and Gabriel were both listening intently. It seemed one of Ben Salim's militant groups was under fire in the Gaza Strip; there were heavy losses, and the Israelis had the upper hand. The Arab force could be wiped out. But there were reinforcements, if Ben Salim gave the word. There was still time. He asked which Israeli units were deployed, and in what strength. The answer caused him to grimace and cover the receiver. He said: "A dozen tanks and scores of infantry. We have thirty dead, and they want me to save them with men I have no intention of sending. Even worse – they want more Stingers."

Affhad put on a sympathetic face. He remembered those hand-held American "Stinger" Missiles. He himself had arranged the sale. It was part of President Reagan's "Arms for Hostages" deal that caused a great scandal in the United States. Some were used to humiliate US forces by bringing down two Black Hawk helicopters. One dead pilot was dragged naked through the streets – to the cheers of madly dancing crowds. Strangely enough, President Reagan was never blamed for this, but President Clinton was.

Ben Salim ended the phone call with a curse-word and hung up. He resumed conversation as if nothing had occurred. Men were dying for him in Gaza, while he sipped daintily at his water.

Gabriel knew Ben Salim to be ruthless and cruel: Jewish children lined up at a school bus stop; a chorus of machine guns spraying them with bullets. Jewish pilgrims in prayer at the "Whispering Wall", then a bomb-blast scattering their arms and legs. These and countless other lives squandered by Oman Ben Salim over years, for a cause that demanded carnage; not justice. A cause that was evil, supported by this demon, a cause that desired corpses; not a homeland. Gabriel was repulsed by what squirmed in the demon's mind; Ben Salim was determined to exceed his worst crime thus far: The Twin Towers in 2001, coordinating the attacks, and overseeing the operation. Now he intended to do even worse.

Gabriel had other ideas.

The Angel of Death stopped reading the demon's thoughts and focused again on the conversation between the two Arabs.

Amir Affhad was speaking: "A transfer to an offshore account in the Cayman Islands. He insists on that."

The American, he explained, owned a vacation home, one of many, in the State of Florida. But the nuclear weaponry promised lay far to the North; a restricted airbase in a lonely region of Utah.

Ben Salim toyed delicately with a grape. He said: "Are you certain that this man can deliver?"

Affhad nodded. "He is behind the Free Patriot Militia. His name is Beck." Neither name meant anything to Ben Salim.

Affhad said: "He hates his government."

"His own government,"

"Yes."

"An American."

"He hates us even more."

Ben Salim was clearly intrigued. Even the poorest Arab would never betray his country, and money was worshiped here. He said: "Then why sell to us?"

"To finance his own war."

"Americans fighting their own people with our money. Let's hope they win."

"Our own action will destroy them first."

"If Allah wills it."

Affhad shrugged. His faith in Allah was limited.

And Ben Salim had none at all.

The Hamas leader produced a note book. "You have the account number?"

"Yes." Affhad recited it. "You agree: Another hundred billion now?"

"By way of Zurich; the rest upon delivery. All

Americans are liars, cheats and rogues. How is this one different?"

Affhad smiled. "He's worse than any of them." Then the smile disappeared, and he suppressed a shudder, having known who Beck really was, when he looked into the eyes of this rich New Yorker with nuclear weapons for sale.

Gabriel knew this fellow Beck only too well. His more common name was Scott Anderson. Both were identities used by Lucifer, the fallen angel. The devil's main source of power was Scott Anderson's ownership of a vast, international media empire. Century News Corporation was a household name, with dozens of national newspapers, and even more TV cable companies and networks, with a magazine division bigger than Time-Life. Scott Anderson was a modern-day Goebbels, propaganda minister for Adolf Hitler, except that Scott Anderson was a thousand times more effective. Every media outlet he owned preached the same things: International hatred and strife – driven by phony patriotism, resulting in warfare and bloodshed.

Lucifer ruled the world from Century Corporate Headquarters in Manhattan. The Anderson persona was the one he used most, but there were others with which he was equally successful, furthering his various interests. One of these, the Free Patriot Militia, was vital to his plans for the future, with a membership of thousands, devoted to the overthrow of the United States government.

This was Lucifer's Hammer.

And he was getting ready to use it.

Gabriel knew all about this paramilitary group, spread across the United States, hidden away in mountains, forests and deserts, with stockpiles of weapons and explosive, funded by Lucifer, who channeled a fortune into their coffers, as only a billionaire like Scott Anderson can. This ensured that they got the latest in sophisticated weapons and technology. As their Commander-in-Chief procuring weapons was easy for Lucifer. For many centuries now he had been the leading world arms supplier.

As for this sale of warheads to Ben Salim, the Angel of Death was about to make sure it came to nothing. Gabriel found it ironic that Ben Salim, the foremost demon in Jerusalem, had no idea this convenient offer of nuclear weapons was coming from the devil himself.

Although the Lebanese seemed to have guessed.

Ben Salim smiled at Affhad. "Your American is just the kind of friend we need," he said.

The arms dealer smiled back, and Gabriel read his thoughts. It was now several years since the World Trade Center collapsed. That had shaken the world, and Affhad was proud of the part he'd played: Meetings on the Pakistani border with Afghanistan; the trips to Iran, shaking hands with Khomeini; the overnight sessions in Jordan and the United Arab Emirates. But mostly, of course, Amir Affhad had been a bag-man for the Saudis.

And he still was.

Amir Affhad had arranged secret agreements between Syria, Iran, Egypt, the Palestinian, Libyan and Lebanese militant factions and the Kingdom of Saudi Arabia. The Saudis were in control, with a yearly income counted in trillions of dollars from every developed nation hooked on oil, which meant all of Europe and North America, and most of Asia and the Far East.

Saudi Arabia ruled the world.

Although no one ever said so.

China was their newest, biggest customer.

American domination was over.

Now America could be destroyed.

Amir Affhad was reporting to a certain Saudi prince next, at a private meeting scheduled for tomorrow, in Karachi. Prince Kamal was the Saudi's money-man, and a cousin of the King. A cousin responsible for finance, and the planning of terrorist acts through Al Qaeda and other organizations. Prince Kamal would be delighted by this purchase of nuclear weaponry, although probably aghast at the price. A flight had been booked for Amir Affhad tonight, and he would be in Pakistan, talking to Prince Kamal, by morning. It only remained to procure payment for the devil, posing as General Beck, and finalize that back here, with Oman Ben Salim.

The Lebanese began reading aloud from his notes.

It was then that Gabriel chose to withdraw, exiting the body of Amir Affhad. The angel became himself again. Neither the demon-possessed Arab, or the demon posing as an Arab, noticed anything. Gabriel prevented that, as he drifted outside, taking human shape as he went.

Gabriel "touched" Ben Salim's bodyguards before they saw him, and both men collapsed to the ground in an unconscious tangle of arms, legs and automatic weapons. Alive, but doomed to die.

It felt good to be free of Amir Affhad.

Gabriel's attire was now suitably local, consisting of a simple white robe and a turban of the same color. A dark beard, chiseled cheekbones and a slight hook to his nose completed the picture. Even for an angel, he was exceptionally tall, and made an imposing figure. He sighed at the prospect of what he must do next, and how he would probably have to do it.

He began to walk along the empty street.

Gradually he formed a plan.

It was somewhat primitive, but it would hide Gabriel's involvement here, at least for a while, from Lucifer. That the plan was brutal could not be avoided. Gabriel had not thought to use actual weapons – he rarely, if ever, did; but now he needed to leave a false trail. Those who found his victims must believe this was murder, and most likely an act of terrorism. Gabriel had little time to arm himself. Those two bodyguards might awaken, or the other two might finish talking and leave the house.

He barged into a house just like it, and cleared out the occupants with one single, Angel of Death look. He searched room by room, and came up with an amazing amount of guns and knives, even a curved-blade sword. He selected a handgun, to find it lacked ammunition. The only thing with bullets was an old Winchester repeater, its stock chipped and most of the temper stripped from the barrel. Gabriel was afraid it would blow up in his hands. In the end he grabbed a wicked-looking knife and the sword.

He hurried back.

Elajah and his partner were still lying there. Gabriel beheaded them as he went by. Then he entered the house.

He was inside less than two minutes. Both the deaths were violent and painful. The demon calling itself Ben Salim went first, with a severed head. Then Amir Affhad, easier because he was still part human, dispatched with a stab to his ailing heart. Then Gabriel chopped both bodies to bits. This butchery was for the benefit of Israeli Security forces, the Palestinian Police and the world press – a great deal of which was owned by an evil entity in New York who hated Gabriel's guts.

When the angel emerged from the house, he looked as he had at JFK. He wore a fedora, a lightweight suit and carried Affhad's leather case. He stepped over the two dead bodyguards and sauntered along the street as if he owned it, an unusually tall European tourist, clearly not intimidated by the fact that he was in an extremely bad neighborhood. As a precaution, Gabriel spun a mind-block from his hat-brim to the ground. Those who saw him would not remember him if questioned. Some would remember the tall Arab in white, and that made a perfect smoke screen.

A wallet materialized in the inside pocket of his linen suit that materialized a few minutes before. The wallet contained a driver's license, denoting a Hans Behring, aged thirty-five, resident of Hamburg, Germany, a senior sales executive for Mercedes Truck Division. Gabriel also had a passport, in the same name, hidden in the briefcase, next to a small fortune in monetary bonds.

There was also an airline ticket to Hamburg, although Gabriel's final destination was Kiel, some Kilometers away. He had something to do there, and would continue to use airlines and airports, to conserve his power. He walked on until he was in a better neighborhood, and took a taxi to the airport.

It was evening in Germany by the time he rented a car.

The ancient city and seaport of Kiel, like its sisters, Hamburg and Bremen, had survived several hundred years of storms along this cruel stretch of the North

Atlantic coast.

Its history was dark with secrets. Few citizens remembered today, or chose to remember, that its largest employer, the firm of Krupp, was linked to the worst crimes of the Twentieth Century. Krupp workers, marching into Krupp factories in wooden clogs on cobblestones, injected enough iron and steel into the German war machine for their Kaiser to start the First World War. The Second World War was financed by the fortune made by Krupp during the First. They backed Adolf Hitler, an obscure fanatic with just the ideas they needed, bringing him up from a political nothing to leadership of the German Third Reich. In those same factories, Krupp manufactured everything Hitler needed: from cannon, tanks and battleships to the giant ovens used in the death camps. Krupp's founders did not survive the war-trials at Nuremberg, but the Krupp fortune did. They still owned the largest shipyards and steel mills in Germany. Today's Krupp workers, headed home on those same cobbled streets, gave no thought to this as the Angel of Death drove by in a rented Audi.

Gabriel killed Krupp directors, on a regular basis, but it didn't seem to do any good. Krupp still made warships and still made armaments – and, because Germany was no longer a world power, and America took the cream in legitimate arms sales, Krupp's big market was the third world and its crazy dictators. The bloody civil-wars raging everywhere were made possible by Krupp, who happily supplied both sides, as long as they had the money.

Nowadays Kiel, like many other north German cities, was a hotbed of terrorism imported from the Middle-East. Immigrants from all over the region abounded: Turks lived alongside Iranians, Syrians, and other Muslim transplants. Mostly working people, waiters or laborers, with a few businessmen and merchants thrown in, but the vultures of Holy Jihad fed on them, taking their money in donations and their young men as recruits. Sometimes there were bombings, sometimes a shooting or a stabbing. Sometimes German police made an arrest. Sometimes they didn't. Either way Islamic terrorism was a growth industry here, and the German authorities were concerned – especially after fresh bomb plots in London and renewed rioting in France. Gabriel was also concerned, although that was not why he was here.

But he did have a strange feeling.

The Audi drove smoothly with great precision, despite the uneven, cobbled road surface. Gabriel drove for some time before realizing that he was lost. Then a green and white Volkswagen flashed its blue light behind him.

It was the Polizei.

He pulled over and an officer approached him in a white cap and green uniform. Gabriel wondered what he had done wrong. He reached for his papers. They were in the glove box. There should be no problem. He was Hans Behring, and able to prove it, but you never knew with Germans. They never ran out of rules, and loved to enforce them. A traffic ticket was most likely, but Gabriel had no time to waste on being questioned, or even worse, being taken into custody. He hoped his crime was a minor one. Had he run that red light?

A car screeched to a halt at the opposite curb.

A very tall man got out and came over to them, except that this was not a man. It was Michael, another Archangel who just happened to be Gabriel's brother. He wore a long leather coat and flashed a badge: It said he was Kriminalpolizei, an Inspector. He really looked the part.

His German sounded local. "Was der Teufel ist hier los?"

(What the devil is going on?)

The cop was young, but inspectors did not intimidate him. "This driver ignored a red light."

Michael nodded. Gabriel groaned. Quite a serious offense. No on-the-spot fine, as he had hoped. There would be a court-date. But worst of all, this patrolman's next move was a background-check of Hans Behring, using the computer installed on board every "Streifenwagen" as German police cars are called. Unfortunately Hans Behring would not be in their data base. That might cause trouble, unless the two angels used friendly persuasion or hypnotism. Michael said: "I know this gentleman. He's from Hamburg."

The officer stepped back. The two angels shook hands and smiled at each other. The next few seconds were crucial. They should soon be on their way if this went well. Gabriel was lucky. Michael had known his brother was coming and sensed that he was in difficulty.

Michael regarded the young policeman. "Leave this to me, Officer. I'll escort Herr Behring to his hotel."

Both angels willed him to comply.

The cop realized he was outranked and outnumbered. There would be no ticket, no court summons and no fulfilling his daily quota. "Have a good evening, Herr Inspektor," he said with a politeness not entirely polite. He saluted and returned to his car.

The name Behring somehow vanished from his head.

Michael looked anxiously at his brother. "Oh, my, you

look worn out. He indicated the Audi. "Just lock that up, and I'll phone Hertz later."

Gabriel opened his mouth to argue; then closed it again. There was no point. His brother was right. Hans Behring and the Angel Gabriel were both exhausted. Being in human form was extremely tiring. It made you wonder how they put up with having to sleep all the time.

He locked the car and pocketed the keys, realizing that Jerusalem had taken its toll on him. He had not enjoyed what he had to do there, and now he had Lucifer to deal with in New York. He shrugged and got into Michael's black B M W, a car apparently favored by Kiel's detective inspectors. Gabriel had rented from Hertz, but Michael had conjured up this vehicle to rescue his brother from the German legal system. It whipped along like a street racer. As they drove, Gabriel relaxed and became a tourist, sitting back to enjoy the ordered Gothic that was Kiel. The neon streetlights had come on, giving everything an eerie glow.

Jerusalem was behind him. Michael needed him here and now. Gabriel began to calm down. This was not the war-torn West Bank. It was Germany, and he was not here to kill. He was here at Michael's request, to help with a potential demon. Gabriel had to deceive some brutal, money-grubbing mortal with an angel version of the truth. It should be easy. It was pretty much what angels did for a living.

Michael pulled into a hotel parking lot and eased into a vacant space. "Two rooms with bath," he said. Gabriel realized again how much he needed to cleanse himself, and sleep. Taking Affhad's briefcase out of the car, he said: "Do they at least have hot water?" It was a joke. European plumbing is notorious in Winter. But this was April.

"They do." Michael held open a heavy glass door and juggled two room keys out of his pocket without dropping his luggage. He handed one over to his brother.

They went to their rooms for a shower and a nap.

Gabriel slept for a day and a half.

Two days later Michael took him down to the dining room and they pretended to eat lunch as they talked. "Look now. He's on your right," said Michael. He spooned up some soup; then carefully spooned it back, when no one was looking. It was swimming in bacon grease.

The Angel of Death glanced across the room. A bullish German; late thirties; hard faced. Dark, cropped hair and a faded tattoo on one arm, partly visible due to the rolled up sleeves of his rumpled black shirt. He sat alone, with the marked air of a man waiting for his check.

Other diners avoided his eye.

Gabriel said: "And his name?"

"Karl Jaeger." Michael set his spoon down in the plate. "On the way to check on his girls. He always eats here at Midday." He smiled. "Jaeger's your TV-stereotype German: quite predictable. That's why I booked us here, and why we're pretending to eat this dreadful concoction. He's the one I brought you here to see. Maybe you can make him listen to reason. It's more your kind of thing than mine."

"No demon in him?"

"Not yet. Some have been sniffing around."

Gabriel said nothing, wiping his mouth before looking again. "So you say he runs prostitutes. He looks like a tough customer."

Michael dropped his voice to a murmur. "Oh, Karl's a very tough customer. He owns all the brothels in the old harbor district and makes fifty million euros a month, all in cash." Michael paused, then he leaned forward, speaking even more softly: "Also involved in drugs. Large shipments to America."

Gabriel had a sudden thought. "Drugs coming from where?"

Michael saw that his brother understood. "Certain people based in the region you just left," he said. "The kind of people you visited. He has access to their funding. He has started making huge payments for them – to your old friend in New York."

Gabriel's odd feeling returned. "Scott Anderson?"

Prince of Darkness and media Kingpin.

"None other."

A waiter stopped at the brothel keeper's table.

Karl Jaeger was paying his bill. By any standard he was strongly built, with wide shoulders, a deep chest, and muscles that said he worked out. He was well over six feet, although Gabriel or Michael would dwarf him standing up. Gabriel stared at the man, then caught himself and looked away.

Angels do not excel at math. But Gabriel knew that fifty million euros a month, from Jaeger's girls, would never produce the twelve billion dollars for Amir Affhad's nuclear warheads. Even if each girl slept with a constant stream of customers for the next ten years.

But the poppy fields of Afghanistan would.

And Saudi petrodollars.

That was where Karl Jaeger's money was coming from.

And Lucifer's money – the full sale price.

Karl Jaeger was a front for Al Qaeda. There it was: The terrorism connection. And the Lucifer connection. Gabriel recalled sensing something when he first arrived here, two nights ago.

Now he had the whole picture.

"We need to pay our bill," said Michael. "We'll follow Karl on his rounds. He drives a red Ferrari."

Gabriel signaled to a waiter. "Wir Zahlen." Both angels pushed their untouched soup away, despite the man's accusing stare.

Gabriel was still thinking about those drug shipments. It all tied in together. A deal cut in the Middle-East, but financed from here. Massive Arab payments being passed on to America. It was a perfect and untraceable arrangement.

Karl Jaeger was routing money to Lucifer. This was money laundering at its most devious. Just as sophisticated as it was clever. If things went belly-up, and the deal was discovered, Karl Jaeger was the fall guy. Authorities would be overjoyed at making the biggest drug-bust in history, and even if a connection was made, no one would guess this was payment for Al Qaeda's nuclear arsenal.

Brothels must be a good cover. Gabriel realized Jaeger must be bankrolling other operations for Ben Salim and the Saudis. Their middleman, Amir Affhad, had recently been in Moscow, negotiating with the Red Army staff officer in charge of Russia's nuclear surplus, which was more cause for concern. Jaeger would also channel hard cash for that transaction.

The red Ferrari led them through busy, narrow streets.

The unmistakable smells of the ocean grew stronger: The tang of salt; a musky, mixed odor of seaweed and seabird droppings; the spillage from all manner of boats; then sand, seashells, the stench of fish, and an occasional whiff of leaked fuel. Karl Jaeger stopped before a row of high, block-style buildings. The surrounding ground was concrete, with grass growing through the cracks; littered with garbage cans and their spilled contents. A seagull strutted pompously on the bone-dry surface. Small boys were playing soccer with a worn-out ball, and darted in and out of it all.

The angels parked some way back.

Michael said: "This is where we part. I'll leave you the car, and meet you back at the hotel." He stepped out of the B. M. W. And prepared to vanish into thin air. "Drive back more safely than the other night and remember this about Karl Jaeger: He's violent. The police don't intervene. He owns all these buildings, and many more in this area, all filled with working girls. He's paying off a lot of cops. It makes him a law unto himself, and he thinks God is a joke."

Gabriel opened his door and got out. "I can handle this."

Michael's eyes twinkled. "And beware the temptations of the flesh. Some of his women are quite beautiful."

Gabriel said, "Must be. The kind of money he makes."

Michael laughed. "Do your best. Put the fear of God into him."

"I intend to," said Gabriel grimly.

His brother vanished.

Meanwhile, Karl Jaeger had also disappeared.

Now where had he gone? Taking human form was so

aggravating. Gabriel did not want to search every building, as if he were mortal.

The soccer players saved him the trouble, pointing with grubby fingers, as soon as he asked. First stairwell in the first building. Each youngster received a brand-new five euro coin, manufactured in an angel's pocket.

Gabriel approached the first high-rise.

The entrance-way was blocked by a pretty red-head in a see-through negligee. She was clearly naked underneath, as she shifted in the bright, afternoon sunlight. She spoke in soft, French-accented German. "You want me, Liebchen? One t'ousand euro for one hour."

Ten times her actual price.

And twice as long as she expected it to last.

Gabriel declined, looking regretful. "I'm here to see your boss. He's expecting me."

She sighed, making room for him to pass. "Boss, 'e upstair."

"Merci, M'amselle." He took out his wallet and gave her a hundred dollars. "Now, this is for you; not Herr Jaeger. I can find my own way up."

She snatched the money like a cat. "Merci, M'sieu. Top floor. First room on right."

Gabriel nodded his thanks and started up the stairs. As he climbed he thought about Michael's description of this wealthy pimp, Karl Jaeger. All attempts at "saving his soul" had resulted in failure. Michael had even tried direct contact, speaking to Jaeger more than once, trying to talk sense to him. Michael was not only rebuffed, but told flatly that angels did not exist, and then threatened with his life. It seemed nothing more could be done, but Michael had asked his brother, the more formidable Angel of Death, to give it one last try.

Gabriel was unsure of the outcome, but he certainly knew how to get a mortal's attention.

Karl Jaeger would believe in angels in about two minutes.

The lighting was extremely dim, as Gabriel reached the end of the stair and stepped through a low archway onto the top floor.

The first bedroom was locked. Moans and grunts could be heard from the other side.

Gabriel was in a hurry. He had to fly to New York tonight and he had no time for knocking. It was not intimidating enough. He drifted through the paneling of the door.

Jaeger was naked on the bed. So was a thin black girl who screamed out as soon as she saw Gabriel emerging through solid wood. She scrambled onto the floor and fled into a corner. Then she sat, wide-eyed and trembling, hiding her nudity with arms, hands and knees. Her nostrils flared with fright.

She knew Gabriel for what he was.

Jaeger studied Gabriel with narrowed eyes. "Who the fuck are you?"

He spoke the heavy dialect of the docks.

"We haven't met," said Gabriel.

"How did you get in here?"

Gabriel shot a look at the girl. "Ask her."

The prostitute whimpered, but Jaeger ignored her.

The room was cheaply seductive: A king-sized waterbed with black silk sheets and a fake, zebra-skin bedspread, all reflected everywhere by smoked glass mirrors that covered the walls and ceiling. Black light lamps gave it all a purplish-bluish glow. Gabriel turned back to the girl. "Perhaps you should leave us. Herr Jaeger is going to be a little busy."

She went gratefully, crossing herself as she grabbed a robe and unlocked the door.

She believed in angels.

Karl jaeger did not. "I said who the fuck – "

"Look into my eyes," Gabriel suggested softly. "It will come to you."

Karl Jaeger stared into a nightmare: A depiction of his future, prepared just for him. It showed the consequences of his life, unless he changed his ways. Jaeger found the concept of angels and heaven absurd, so Gabriel sent him briefly into the pits of hell, complete with scorching fire, eternal agony, and the bodies of the damned, twisting in torment forever,

No such place existed, but Gabriel's version was very convincing, and it had never failed him.

The Archangel halted the vision. "That's who I am."

Jaeger sat upright, fumbling for cigarettes, nearly knocking over a night table. His forehead glistened, and his face looked pale, even in this kind of light. He stared wildly about, looking at anything but his visitor. He still seemed unlikely to crack, but Gabriel was not finished.

The best was yet to come.

An apparition floated in the air between them. It was the girl who just left, still naked, but shown in death, her corpse half eaten by worms and maggots, her skull shattered and oozing slime. In reality she was downstairs, terrified but unharmed, pouring out her story to other girls from rooms like this one.

Karl Jaeger was convinced, and he began to stammer

in fright. Gabriel made her vanish. The rest should be easy. "Well," he began, "You need to . . ."

"You're like that other one," Jaeger blurted out. "The one who said he was an angel. I don't understand any of this."

"Yes, you do," said Gabriel dryly. "And I have a few questions for you." The angel needed information, if it could be had.

"What questions?" Jaeger said defiantly. Some of his confidence was returning. "I have nothing to ..."

The door flew open.

"Otto!" screamed Jaeger, "Shoot this bastard."

Otto was a huge troll. He held a Mauser automatic in one huge fist. Either Karl Jaeger had pressed some silent alarm, or the girl downstairs had alerted Otto. It didn't matter which. This was the result. Now Gabriel had little choice.

He decided to leave a message for Lucifer.

The one he had not left in Jerusalem.

Otto started to squeeze the trigger. That was as far as he got. His eyes began to bulge, and his free hand went to his heart. "Mother of God," he said hoarsely. "What's happening to me?"

It crossed Gabriel's mind, as he killed him, that Otto was only doing his job, like Ben Salim's guards in Jerusalem. But this German thug was as lacking in innocence as they were.

Now was a good time for Otto to die.

The angel turned back to Karl Jaeger, who had somehow produced a gun of his own: Probably from under his pillow. It glinted dully as he aimed it at Gabriel's head. This was a moment of truth.

The Archangel threw a thought, hard and fast.

Jaeger flinched, then froze. He mouthed an oath as he felt paralysis setting in. Then the darkness passed over him and he was gone. His remains sank to the bed-sheets. The weapon slipped from his fingers and crashed to the floor. Karl Jaeger would not be firing it, or answering any questions. He was meeting his maker.

Gabriel felt cheated.

CHAPTER TWO

IT WAS 7:00 AM, and the Washington Beltway was jammed with traffic crawling in either direction. Sweating at this early hour, Bo Clement wondered if a Hybrid V. W. Convertible without air-conditioning was a big mistake — even with the top down, and even if he did get a good deal on it. Most women found it cute, as they did Bo (short for Beauregard) — but this pre-Summer heat was a killer. Planetary Warming was getting worse. He drummed on the steering wheel and looked in the mirror. His neck had a bite mark on it. Bo had been on a blind date the night before, the very first of his life. His secretary, Jean Holloway, had set him up with the friend of a friend's daughter. An old money family, Jean had whispered in awe. Clement had played along — buying flowers, booking a table at a pricey Greek place and skipping lunch to get theater tickets — all to avoid offending a secretary he really liked.

The never made the theater at all. They barely made it out of the restaurant and into a taxi. The girl was insatiable, and found a moving vehicle sexually stimulating. Bo Clement was in reasonable shape, but he ached all over this morning. Jean Holloway's high-bred debutante not only sapped his strength on the way to her place in Georgetown, but wanted more when they got upstairs, and then wanted more in almost every room. And it was no small apartment her wealthy parents had leased for her. Bo Clement did not get home until two this morning.The car radio was playing Pink Floyd, and

Clement began to sing along in a fair imitation of the original. He often sang in the car, even with the top down, oblivious to the startled looks of other road users. Ten years before, Clement had sung with a series of struggling bands to get through college, while he studied international affairs. Now he was a senior agent in the Homeland Security Division of the FBI.

Even before the Twin Tower attacks, Clement's field had been airport security and improving airline operating procedures. He was seen early on as a man to watch, exposing security hazards, which he fixed with low-cost, common-sense decisions: beefing up such things as ceiling cameras and on-the-spot computer checks at passport control. In those days he worked out of Miami, enjoying the girls and the sunshine, traveling all over the country as a counter-terrorism consultant. After the assault on the World Trade Center, he transferred to a little known section of Homeland Security in the nation's capital. Now he worked to keep suicide bombers, hijackers, or anyone else with bad intentions, out of the United States.

He was very good at it.

His bosses were impressed.

They also despaired of him.

He never wore anything authorized. Usually he was in blue jeans, sometimes with sandals and bare feet; sometimes with high-heeled cowboy boots, but always with the same, ornate, turquoise studded belt. Today was no exception, and Clement wore a blue denim jacket, with those snake-skin boots poking out under his jeans. This flamboyant attire – and a tendency to speak out at the wrong time – often set management teeth on edge, but he was generally accepted as an eccentric genius. Other agents admired him, and this made him a minor celebrity.

Clement thought he was normal.

Fortunately his department head rated him highly, and saw him as one of his best operatives, and that protected Agent Clement in an environment where mavericks were not generally welcome.

His Volkswagen lumbered after the car in front, which never seemed to exceed ten miles an hour. But now Clement saw the familiar figure, standing at the roadside. It was Mason. Clement saw him. And refused to feel guilty. This might be the second time he had been late this week, but Beltway traffic was hardly his fault. He flipped on his turn signal and moved onto the hard shoulder. Clement drove slowly along it; then stopped beside his colleague.

Mason clambered into the passenger seat. He was an ex-cop with a bland face and receding hair – car-pooling with Clement because they were temporarily working the same hours on the same floor. Jim Mason was an undercover agent who spent long stints in the field as an infiltrator. However, this was his month to collate his own findings and those of his peers, complaining his way through mounds of reports and other paperwork. People in the building tended to ignore him. Clement was someone who didn't. As a result he had a friend for life.

Clement said: "Did Richter call?"

"Sure did. He'll be at the Alexandria exit."

Clement nodded. Good. That would entitle them to use the faster moving lanes reserved for car-pools. For now, he was still trying to re-enter traffic that had hardly moved at all. A battered pick-up was passing. Clement revved the Volkswagen and got ready. He finally cut in front of a Chrysler van driven by a soccer mom, ignoring her angry horn as he set off at turtle speed for Alexandria.

Richter got in the back and said: "Morning, guys."

Clement spoke over his shoulder. "Morning. Charlie. Sorry we're late."

Richter carried doughnuts and a thermos of coffee with some polystyrene cups. They all chewed and slurped as Clement eased into the car pool lane and left the rush-hour traffic behind him. Richter worked in Foreign Liaison and Overseas Ops; which meant he interacted with Clement, whose job was knowing which terrorist group was doing what to whom, and where they were doing it, with emphasis on those headed for the United States.

People compared Richter to Clark Kent, and it was easy to see why. He wore the exact style of horn-rim glasses, kept his hair slicked down and wore a blank look on his face most of the time, as if the world defied comment. People thought he did it for effect; to seem more intelligent than he really was. Clement knew they were wrong. Richter was a mental Superman.

Clement had always liked him. Not that he had anything against Jim Mason, who was a nice enough guy, but Charlie Richter had a quiet humor, and a way of summing up any situation quickly and accurately. Clement warmed to him early on, and enjoyed his conversation, even when it was political, which Clement usually hated. Anything Charlie Richter said was worth listening to, which was uncommon, at least in a senior member of the D. C. Intelligence community.

In the parking lot, Richter and Mason got out and waited for Clement to back into his space. He joined them, carrying his lunch in a zipped, plastic case. The two of them made jokes about it, as they always did, and Clement said: "Okay, guys. Let's go and kill terrorists," as he always did.

His Homeland Security office was south of Alexandria, a modern complex of brick buildings. It resembled a small industrial center with armed gate guards and anti-vehicle barricades. They all went inside.

Clement's cubicle was one among scores of others on the ground floor. An incoming e-mail was flashing on his computer, to be opened as soon as he logged on. He took off his jacket and draped it over his chair. Then he sat down, rolled back his sleeves, clicked on his mouse and began to read.

The e-mail came from Charlie Richter, and at first Clement wondered why his friend had not mentioned it in the car. It was pure routine: Israeli intelligence reporting the assassination of two heavy-duty names on their most-wanted list. The pair had been discovered yesterday, along with two dead unknowns, at a Hamas safe-house in the bad part of Jerusalem. According to the report the two better known corpses had taken some identifying. All four were butchered like sheep, two beheaded, but the other two had been cut into pieces.

If Tel Aviv had it right, and it usually did, the pair of major interest were Oman Ben Salim and Amir Affhad. The names rang a distant bell, but Clement could not put his finger on why.

Anyway both men were now in multiple, bloody bits.

Hamas and Al Qaeda had sworn revenge for the killings, which was unusual. Typically such announcements were not made. It meant these two men were important enough for their deaths to matter. It also showed that terrorist leaders had no idea who did it. So it wasn't them.

Palestinian police were investigating on behalf of Israeli Security, but based on the Palestinians' track record, no one expected an arrest very soon. Clement opened a data base and cross-matched those two Arab names. Then he understood why Charlie Richter had kept quiet in the car.

Ben Salim was bigger than Elvis.

Up to his neck in 9/11 – and a whole bunch of other shit. No wonder his name rang a bell.

But here was the kicker: Whoever the second guy, this Amir Affhad might be, Israeli Intel had him flagged as having just returned on a flight from New York, using a high quality forged passport. Tel Aviv found this serious enough to inform the Americans by means of a signal classified "Immediate! Urgent!"

That did not happen every day.

Clement frowned and read some more. Amir Affhad was no slouch, either. Another World Trade Center player but more on the fringes – a go-between for Ben Salim and others, for years. Both men were high up in terrorist circles, and Clement felt the world was better off without them.

Then the thunderbolt struck: Israeli sources, some reliable, some less so, agreed that Amir Affhad had been actively shopping for nuclear material in any form available. That meant he would buy anything from a dirty bomb to a ballistic missile. And he was buying for Oman Ben Salim, who in turn represented Hamas and Al Qaeda. Suddenly both men were dead.

Clement pursed his lips, thinking.

They wanted nukes. So who killed them?

And why?

Finally he picked up the phone and called Yosuf Abrahams. The switchboard at the Israeli Embassy took seconds to put him through. Yosuf was expecting the call.

Clement said: "So . . . Who killed these two superstars?"

"No idea."

"And what the hell was one of them doing in New York?"

"Isn't that for you to find out?"

That was true enough.

"Come on, Yosuf. Then give me the assassin at least."

"We found a knife and a sword," said Yosuf. He and Clement had worked on many cases together. "Not a common method."

"I'd say not. What else do you have?"

"Nothing. No prints. Unreliable witnesses. We've got bullshit."

How can that be? They were chopped up. Two of them beheaded outside, in full view of the neighbors."

"That's what I said," said Yosuf. "In fact, to be honest, it's hard to credit. But you have to remember what kind of neighbors you get on that kind of street. And this thing has caused quite a stir. Some saw an Arab, not a Jew, walking about in white robes. And it was only one killer, from the angle of the wounds.

"And New York? Do you have any connection between these murders and Affhad coming here?"

"Nothing, Bo. Absolutely zilch – you can take my word for that. We would tell you right away."

But he's huge in black market armaments, right?"

The hugest. Highly wanted by us, and you. That tells us nothing."

"Known to be shopping for nukes."

"All our sources agree. Yes."

"But trying to buy in New York? Are you kidding?"

"We truly don't know. But it does seem unlikely, given that the Big Apple, and everyone in it, is a number one nuclear target. We thought it scary enough to give you what facts we have. Amir Affhad's trip to America caught us on the wrong foot. So far it's a dead end."

"Okay, I got it." Clement's stomach twisted into a knot of worry. Give me the murder details, then."

"The weapons came from a house nearby. We got gibberish from the owners. They mentioned the guy in white. They say he was tall, and scared the shit out of them. Nobody remembers his face; only his height. That's one of few verifiable facts. The angle of blows puts him at close to seven feet."

"An invisible giant."

"In robes and turban, according to what we have. This killer was not a city dweller. More like a desert tribesman, or nomad, or farmer from some outlying village. Out there they fight one another over goats and camels, and they use blades. This kind of primitive slaughter is their trademark"

"Anyone else see anything?" Clement was not buying this Lawrence of Arabia crap for one second.

Yosuf hesitated. "One old man claims he saw the Angel of Death, wielding a knife and sword. The locals say he's simple minded. Their cops agree. He insists the intruder was an angel, but this witness is over eighty; he sees angels all the time and tells anybody who will listen. He's famous for it."

"Hardly a reliable observer," agreed Clement. "So, that aside, you've given me everything, right?"

"Correct."

"Can I count on you if anything else comes up?"

"As always."

Clement thanked him and hung up. He did not share Yosuf's vision of some goatherd butchering two top terrorists. He didn't think Yosuf believed it, either. That meant the Israelis had another theory. Clement decided to take this up to the top floor. He headed for the elevator, taking his notes with him.

From the outset the Department of Homeland Security was a strange thing in the mind of most Americans. It's duties were ill-defined, at least publicly. It came in for a lot of ridicule for petty issues; like taking scissors from old ladies at airports while seagoing container traffic went unchecked, and nobody seemed to know who was in charge, or which law enforcement agencies it replaced, or what exactly was its scope. The White House wasn't sure either – their answer changed from one administration to the next, according to who was asked. The Secretary of State might give an opinion, only to be contradicted by another cabinet member, or by the Head of the FBI or the Director of the CIA, or by Homeland Security itself. Several Presidents had made statements, most of them conflicting – and allegations of unconstitutional behavior refused to go away. On top of everything else it remained a mystery where this lavishly funded department got its intelligence support.

No one was answering that question.

Understandably the D. H. S. benefited most from government's knee-jerk reaction to 9/11. World terrorism became the bogeyman that haunted America's already paranoid Intelligence Kingdom. Response from the top was to hurl unlimited money, personnel, resources, and a calamitous amount of bureaucracy at the problem. A staff in excess of eight hundred thousand was soon assessing terror-threats for newly birthed agencies that sprang up like grass. A lot of this funding, people and resources bounced into the open hands of Homeland Security.

D. H. S. Leadership knew exactly how to use it.

A massive expansion began.

No one noticed the increase in Homeland Security's power because it happened so slowly and they hid behind an undeserved reputation for incompetence. But the turning point was the early years of Iraq's occupation, as American casualties advanced steadily. First two thousand; then three, and four. George W. Bush stood firm, refusing to accept that things were going badly, and refusing to take responsibility when proven wrong. His answer was to accuse the CIA of starting a war with false information.

One by one, White House advisers got a free walk and perhaps a medal, but the CIA got blamed for everything – from the lies about weapons of mass destruction and nuclear capability, to Saddam Hussein's involvement in the New York attack. The troop surge in Iraq saved George Bush to a degree, but not the CIA. Then there were further mistakes, like the Benghazi attack, and the drone attack revelations, involving the killing of American citizens, during the Obama administration, with the CIA running the show. None of this helped. The agency was further discredited when Bush and Cheney walked away with heads held high, leaving the CIA holding the bag

By 2016 Langley was in disgrace and falling apart at the seams. It was now that Homeland Security came into its own, by seizing more power and going international. The CIA was powerless to stop them, and the D. H. S. leadership was smart enough, and political enough, to get away with it. They started off by slipping FBI agents into other countries where the line between foreign and domestic threat was blurred, which was pretty much everywhere. And many FBI agents, when the immediate mission was over, never came home. They took up residence and remained. Over time, this became a river, and then the river became a flood. Before anyone really noticed, the FBI had its own spy network all over Europe and the Middle East. Homeland Security had become the new CIA.

They treated the CIA's regrettable fate as a warning. History and the media had always judged D. H. S. by success or failure. The World trade Center was regarded as the failure that outweighed anything else, which was utterly unfair because the D. H. S. had not existed at the time. But this was politics as usual, and the D. H. S. hierarchy reacted with stealth and cunning.

And they built an overseas empire.

Nowadays their successes went largely unclaimed, because those agents involved were still in place and had to be protected. Any victory they did make public, usually the thwarting of suicide attacks across the Atlantic, was met with cynicism, or, even worse, totally ignored. The American media was never won over by the D. H. S. Neither was the American public.

One success involved Bo Clement and got him promoted to senior agent. Dutch police detained six Saudi nationals with firearms at Amsterdam's Schipol airport. The Saudis had boarding passes to destinations all over the United States. Washington was informed, and wanted them for trial. Extradition was agreed upon, despite weak legal precedent, and vehement protest from the Saudi Ambassador in Holland. Clement was one of three operatives sent to pick them up.

Everything was fine, until the FBI men were on their way back and arrived at the departure gate with their prisoners. Although shackled, one terrorist slipped his chains and ran, punching a Dutch detective and pushing an old lady to the ground when she got in his way. Clement was faster than anyone else. He sprinted after the man, tackled him, and brought him down.

Then he pressed a gun to the man's temple, and held it there while the chains were replaced. The other agents said he should have shoved his gun up the guy's ass and pulled the trigger. In Holland Clement was celebrated as a hero and awarded a medal. At home he was thanked by the FBI Director, given a citation, and promoted five years early. The US media overlooked the whole thing. But in Europe, Clement got his fifteen minutes of fame.

Now he knocked on Heathcote's door and went in.

Bradley Heathcote was head of Clement's department: a raw-mannered man of fifty-eight with a weakness for bow-ties and suspenders. His reputation for honesty and integrity was as legendary as his ribald sense of humor. He had thick iron-gray hair, kept short. A habit left over from his twenty-five years as a US Marine. He sat at a rosewood desk, picking at the keyboard of his computer. There was no visitors' chair, so Clement stood, clutching his notes. Heathcote sat back and reached for his cigarettes and lighter, oblivious to the government ban on smoking.

He grinned at Clement. "You look like a shark sensing blood in the water."

"It may be nothing," said Clement.

He chose caution, which always worked better with Heathcote. These murders in Jerusalem might well be something – one of the victims was red-list and recently in New York under a false name. But the worst thing for Clement was to push this too hard. His boss viewed hasty conclusions with suspicion and always rejected them, but if left alone he formed his own opinion quickly, and acted upon it, caring little for any backlash. One reason why Clement liked him.

Heathcote lit a cigarette. "Just a second, I want to catch the early news update." He leaned across to turn a television for them to watch. Obviously there was a news item he was interested in. Audio came first; then hazy pictures on satellite feed . . . "latest in a series of suicide bombings," said the voice-over in a broad London accent. "it caught this ancient and holy city of Bethlehem completely by surprise. The bomber was female, and the only terrorist to die. The one hundred and thirty-seven victims were all Christian, including twenty-four Americans – and a bus-load of British tourists visiting the Holy Land."

This was a new Jihad tactic, and Clement felt his stomach flip. "This could start some shit," he said.

"Yes, it could. I've already had a call from above. We're on full alert, along with our armed forces all over the region. Christ, it could drag us into another war, which is what the guys who sent that bomb want. It's an invitation. They think we'll be more upset if they don't just kill Jews."

"Christians – Brits and Americans."

"They're pushing our buttons." Heathcote looked angry. He said he had heard an initial report on the radio, driving to work. Now he switched of the television and put out his cigarette. He looked at Clement. "So what have you got?"

Clement handed over his notes. "I think Yosuf is holding back."

"Why would he do that?" Heathcote scanned the page and looked up. "Looks straightforward enough. They're dead. Who cares? My question is, why was one of them here?"

Clement nodded. "It's my question, too."

"And . .?"

"This was a professional hit, but who ordered it?"

"I agree. What's your best guess?"

"These kind of guys don't tolerate rivals – and this was clearly not the Israelis," Clement said. "Also out of the question: Yosuf's theory – some tribesman killed them. Rode in from the desert to do it."

Neither man smiled, although it was quite ludicrous.

Heathcote frowned. "Who does Yosuf really think it was . . . or rather, who else is there? Us? I think the Israelis suspect America did it, and they couldn't be more wrong. But that's why they inform us, then tap-dance around. The culprit is secondary as far as I'm concerned. Our main interest has to be this: Amir Affhad traded in weapons. So was he buying or selling in New York? If he was looking for nukes, and he probably was, did he succeed? Are the bad guys getting missiles from Americans? We'd better find out, and quick."

This was Heathcote at his very best, thought Clement.

Calm and analytic, never blinded by the light.

"Sir, if those murders were us, it would be on CNN, and you would have known about it in advance. But you're right, that's what Yosuf thinks. Why else bullshit me? So who was it? Who's left? Nobody I can think of; not even Russia. They wouldn't take on Hamas or Al Qaeda. No, I think there was a nuclear deal in New York and these killings are linked to that. A double-hit, because someone disagreed. Ben Salim connected Islamic factions that hate each other. Acquiring nukes to attack us is right up his street. That's why Affhad was visiting him – the ruthless Hamas leader connected to everybody. It tells me more than one Arab faction is involved in buying these weapons. Maybe some Islamic government was against this attack and took these guys out."

"That's certainly plausible." Heathcote paused and read the notes again. He was engrossed, and fumbled for another cigarette. He couldn't find his lighter. Clement spotted it beside the computer and handed it over. Blue smoke formed a wispy cloud around them both.

Heathcote folded the notes and gave them back. "No answers there," he said. "I can't believe a nuclear arms sale to major terrorists taking place on American soil. But why else would Amir Affhad risk everything to come here? That's the key question, and it must be answered. I'll put you on this for a couple of weeks. Find out whatever you can. Ask in all the usual places, and some unusual places. Ask around in Washington, use your diplomatic contacts. Go to the Middle East. Get out there and ask the right people, but don't let anyone know what we suspect, in case we're right. The press would jump on it; so avoid reporters. We don't want to start a panic."

"Thank you, sir." Clement made for the door. From this moment it was an official assignment. A lot of resources became available. Heathcote's power reached up to the sky, or at least as far as the White House.

Clement turned, and said: "Okay if I use a pool-car, sir? Mine has no A/C, and it's that time of year."

"Sure, Something sporty." Heathcote never shortchanged his people. He started typing again, one key at a time. "Listen, sign out a weapon, too. You never know who's out there, and you might ask the wrong question."

"Okay, sir."

"And only shoot terrorists."

"Yes, sir." Clement went out.

~ ~ ~

On his way back downstairs, Clement wondered if he should have requested a credit card; then realized he could authorize it himself. His father, an intelligence veteran, often said: If you don't ask, they can't say no." It was true years ago, and still true today. Heathcote would approve Clement's gold card, because asking questions, that might or might not be dangerous, was expensive if you wanted answers. Clement would be buying drinks and lunches all over the diplomatic map. Not to mention the bribes. He would also be talking to criminals and terrorists, taking overseas flights all over the place. Heathcote knew it wouldn't be cheap.

Heathcote was very successful, and expected success from those under him. When he interviewed Clement, building a new team, with Homeland Security still in its infancy, Heathcote had said, "Your job is to make me look good. Do that, and I will always back you up."

~ ~ ~

There was a message on Clement's voice mail when he got back. He recognized the voice of last night's date. It sounded sultry, and heavy with sexual energy. No name was given. Clement dialed her number and remembered that she was called Destiny. Some parents expect more from their children.

She answered on the first ring, even more husky than before: "This better be Bo Clement."

He laughed and said it was. Women were a serious weakness with him, and he knew it. As busy as today promised to be, here he was, calling right back. "Destiny." he said. "Nice surprise." Clement needed to delay this conversation until later. After all, as he reminded her, he was at work.

She chuckled. "You worked hard last night."

He chose the easy flattery. "You wore me out."

"That's what I do." Her tone was inviting and Clement's good intentions began to fade. She said: "Can I see you tonight?"

Sounding sultry had morphed into sounding hot.

He knew he was being reprehensible. "What time," he said.

"Seven. My place."

"Fine." He had to be crazy. This girl was going to give him a heart attack, and his Ben Salim investigation was supposed to start tonight. Clement should be in the Bunch of Grapes, plying well-placed foreign sources with drinks; not shagging his brains out in Georgetown.

But she was incredibly . . . incredible.

He heard himself say: "Sounds good. What should I bring?"

"Come naked."

All thought of his new assignment was momentarily forgotten. "I'll be there," he said.

"Super. I'll expect you." She hung up.

Super? Clement looked at the dead receiver. Was that really him? He had just made a date he could not possibly keep. He sat motionless, renewing his grip on reality. Clement hated it when his libido interfered with his life. Unhappily that seemed to be much of the time.

He focused on work. No more distractions, or thinking about Destiny or her fatal charms. He usually had no time for those with inherited wealth. And starting a lasting relationship now was impossible. This woman seemed determined to be an exception. Did he really want to see her tonight?

Yes, he decided. But he knew he wouldn't.

He phoned Yosuf Abrahams again, and asked for a secure-line fax of the original reports in Hebrew and Arabic. Nothing made much sense. Yosuf had made it clear, but translators vary, and a second opinion wouldn't hurt. Clement had interpreters of his own.

He called FBI Headquarters, to confirm that no known American hit-men were out of the country, and none were known to use swords or knives. He also asked for a similar check on European assassins.

He told Finance Department he needed an open credit line on one of their Amex cards.

He filled out requisitions for a car and a gun.

He asked cell-phone surveillance for anything picked up over the next few days that mentioned Ben Salim or Amir Affhad, and wondered if Heathcote would sign that requisition. Satellite time was mega-expensive.

Finally he visited Jean Holloway, dodged all her

questions about his date with Destiny, and dictated a memo to all field agents, telling them what they needed to know, and what they needed to look out for. He told Mason and Richter in person, and added the bad news about not giving them a ride home.

It was seven o' clock when he was done.

He called Destiny and said he couldn't make it.

Then he headed for the Bunch of Grapes.

~ ~ ~

It was also evening in New York.

The devil stood at his window.

Lucifer lived in a vast, luxuriously appointed brownstone, shrouded by trees, opposite Central Park, where, at the moment, his view of splendid oaks was ruined by the sight of some black, homeless man sifting through garbage cans in search of food, despite the failing light.

Being immensely wealthy, posing as an American media mogul with more influence and power than any head of state, the evil one, currently known as Scott Anderson, found the poor extremely irritating. He was composing an editorial in his head, voicing anger at the homeless roaming freely where they had no place. Lucifer's words would be headlines tomorrow, and Mr. And Mrs. America, and the rest of the world, would eat them up with breakfast. The masses, as Lucifer knew only too well, like to be told what to think, and he was happy to oblige, having built his global media empire for that very purpose. What Century News said today furthered Lucifer's plans tomorrow. But a lot of people defied him, either Christians or other religions. They believed in helping the poor and weak, in loving your neighbor, and a whole lot of other stuff Lucifer hated. Scott Anderson, by way of Century News, rejected that as nonsense, on every channel he owned, and every page he printed. His political commentators and pundits stated publicly that they were "people of faith", but most of them were lying, because they were either demons, or demon driven. Lucifer rarely hired anyone else. Century News was anti-liberal, and anti-gay. It despised foreigners, and it hated gun-control. Century News was also a last hold-out supporter of American military action in the Middle-East. Century tolerated Republicans, but only if they acted tough, and it condemned Democrats, no matter what they did. And as part of its overall message, with very little subtlety, Century News was anti-Arab, anti-Hispanic and anti-black.

The devil was an equal opportunity bigot.

Scott Anderson was Lucifer's cleverest creation so far: An irresistibly grouchy old entrepreneur, a self-made man with a reputation for hard work, unshakable vision and plain speaking.

Who, everyone believed, came from Philadelphia.

He turned away from the window, cradling the glass of Burgundy in his hands to sniff its aroma.

This room, his banquet-sized dining hall, contained a long, oaken table carved by monks in the Fifteenth Century. Its current owner sat down at one end and began turning the pages of his best-selling US daily. A single paragraph in the overseas column on page seven caught his eye. Oman Ben Salim and Amir Affhad were dead. The devil set down his wine and re-read the item twice.

A passenger jet passed low overhead, causing the windows to vibrate, but the noise did not break Lucifer's concentration. Those two Arabs should not have died.

One was a high-ranking demon, and the other demon-possessed, ready to become equally powerful, given time. Not to mention that both were vital to Lucifer's nuclear scheming.

Two top Jihadists, ready to destroy America.

He opened his humidor, took out an illegally imported Monte Cristo, lit it and blew smoke rings along the gleaming table-top. He held up the cigar to admire the perfection of its ash.

Not much detail in this news item, he noted. Even in an America with little interest in overseas events, this piece lacked hard fact or information. Only the names were given, with no background for either man, other than their link to world terror. That, decided Lucifer, was a good thing. The less the public knew about these two the better. The deaths had been excessively violent according to investigators, with no further detail except for a hint that terrorist rivals did it. All in all, the devil decided, it could have been worse. On the plus side, Hamas and Al Qaeda were not mentioned, which meant his nuclear arms deal was still alive, its security not threatened, because Islamic plans to nuke America would hardly be on page seven. Not in one of his newspapers.

Still, these two deaths came at a bad time.

Direct contact was broken.

Lucifer wanted to scream aloud – it was vital his plan be carried out now. The planets were in conjunction. The world was on the brink, with nation against nation. Battle lines had been drawn, aided by his biased news coverage and slanted editorials over the years, creating strife along political and religious lines, while all over the world,

Century News turned aggressive patriotism into a fatal, spreading disease. Now the end was here. Those two world wars were nothing, compared to what came next. Mankind's stupidity guaranteed it.

Just thinking about this cheered the devil up. This Second Millennium was hailed as a giant leap forward by those believing in the future of humanity. They hoped that the breathtaking strides in technology and information would set the world free. They also believed in the basic goodness of people everywhere. The devil knew they were in for a bitter disappointment.

The stage was set for his final game.

And of all the balls in play, the Middle-East was the most important, and must be kept bouncing.

Lucifer had already initiated the procurement of nuclear weapons for Amir Affhad. Two five-man Patriot-Militia teams were in Utah ready to go. They had Air Force pilot uniforms and genuine paperwork authorizing them to fly the missiles out of the state, and later out of the country. They had military transports, authenticated orders, and getaway tickets to Switzerland, the Bahamas or anywhere else they desired. Unfortunately these tickets would never be used. Once delivery was achieved, ten American graves would be dug in the Sahara desert.

Amir Affhad had thrown that in for free.

On the Utah Air base itself, senior officers had been bought off at great expense to authorize movement of nuclear material. These men, too, would vanish, with the ink of their signatures barely dry, their bodies buried in the sandy expanse of Utah. Of course there was a General involved. There had to be, because no one of a lesser rank could give protection to such a scheme. The one working for the devil in this case commanded the Utah base, and they often worked together, because this General was a demon. General Bertram would live – but his money-grubbing subordinates would die. The devil liked Americans because they loved money so much. They would always do anything for the right price. They would betray their country, or each other, for a quick buck. Lucifer adored the savagery of it all.

Like a dog-pack, tearing itself apart.

But in case Utah failed, Lucifer had a Plan B. In fact getting nuclear weapons, and getting them on time, was so important that he also had a Plan C. The problem was, only one mechanism existed for payment. So much money could only be raised once, no matter how many plans Lucifer had. This money was coming from Muslim extremists, the only ones insane enough to do it. And so much money had to be filtered through a middleman in Europe. This chain of events had already been set in motion by the buyers, Ben Salim and Amir Affhad, but while the transaction had not been compromised, both buyers were suddenly dead. This created a huge problem for the devil, a problem he must solve right away, because Armageddon's clock was ticking.

Nuclear arms were not the problem. Plan B. was in action now. The devil had Lung Chiang with a firm deal in China, ready to provide weapons of mass destruction to Iran, as long as the North Korean leadership kept its word, and delivered the plutonium cores on time. That was Plan B.

Plan C. involved Moscow. But the Russian transaction was on hold. The Red Army General in question was about to be arrested. The Kremlin was Lucifer's Plan C., and would be again, once a new General was found. Russians were expendable. They always had been; it was their curse.

But the cash was a problem.

Because it was Arab cash.

Now Lucifer needed some new Arabs, and quickly. He must be able to revive his agreement with Amir Affhad, and agreement which secured him a deal with Oman Salim and whatever governments and terrorist organizations he served. Those with the power and the money. They were what counted. Scott Anderson needed to confirm that he still had a deal with them.

Such people are not easy to contact.

And time was short.

On top of everything, Scott Anderson was aging rapidly by the day, like the villain in a Dracula movie. This didn't matter in the long run; because he had already selected a young mortal for permanent possession, but breaking in a new body right now would be inconvenient, and setting up this successor was taking a lot of lawyers and a lot of time. The attacks on America came first.

And their world-wide impact.

Scott Anderson, deteriorating or not, must simply stay the course, but now things had suddenly ground to a halt, and the devil could see no quick solution. He relaxed his rigid control, banged a fist on the table and cursed aloud. Everything was at stake here, a sequence of events that could not be delayed. Planets do not stay in alignment forever. His entire operation had a limited shelf life. Now it had lost its terrorist connection. At least it had lost the ones he knew by name.

Who else was out there?

The answer eluded him, floating in a part of his mind

that refused to give it up. A few names trickled into his consciousness. It took time, but he managed to conjure them up, rejecting them one after the other, until he had the name he wanted:

It was not an Arab name.

Karl Jaeger.

Karl Jaeger was the answer.

The German. The rich pimp with all that drug and oil money. Hundreds of billions of dollars filtering through the banking system – from Afghan poppy seed and Saudi oil profits, laundered for them by Karl Jaeger. This German must be highly thought of in terrorist circles, and extremely well connected, for anyone to trust him with that much money. Yes, decided Lucifer. Karl Jaeger was mixed up with those two dead bastards, and he must know other bastards just like them.

There was a phone number, some seaport in northern Germany. That was where Karl Jaeger lived. Lucifer was certain it was stored somewhere in Scott Anderson's data base.

He stood up and left the dining room, crossing the paneled and richly carpeted hallway and went into the study. He retrieved Jaeger's number on his lap-top, picked up the phone and dialed, starting with the international code for Germany. He heard a ringing at the other end.

In Kiel it was three in the morning, and a sleepy voice answered in German. The devil saw no need to apologize for the hour, and demanded Karl Jaeger in the same language. Lucifer understood, and spoke, every tongue on Earth. It was the one angelic power he retained.

The news that Jaeger had died was a shock.

Lucifer digested it, and a warning flashed in his mind

like a bright, red light. The rest of the story, coming over the phone in a flood of guttural dialect, was worse. The bright, red light became a screaming siren. A young prostitute was saying an angel had visited Karl jaeger. Visited him and killed him in cold blood, along with a bouncer and enforcer named Otto, who tried to intervene.

The girl believed in angels.

So did Lucifer. He slammed down the phone and swore.

Even louder than before.

CHAPTER THREE

GABRIEL STOOD ACROSS from Lucifer's brownstone and heard the devil cursing.

He fleetingly remembered Lucifer as a brother angel, long ago. The universe had been young then, and all of them young with it. Every day was a new day, each flower a work of art, each blade of grass a valued treasure. The life of this new world, Earth, was based on happiness and joy.

Then had come the fall. Lucifer and his followers had rebelled against the rule of Heaven, and all that was beautiful began to decay. The power of love was suspended. Jealously, violence and cruelty were introduced to mortals who knew no better. The laws of creation cut in, which brought violent extremes of weather, and the onset of disease and ignorance everywhere, due to the lack of heavenly guidance. Then Lucifer introduced the art of war.

All that was thousands of years ago.

And things since then had gone from bad to worse.

The devil replaced the last of Heaven's power with technology, during what man called the Twentieth Century, and he had everything he needed in place by the Twenty First.

Now Mother Earth itself was ruined, her tree depleted and her oceans and skies polluted. Warfare, hunger and disease were rampant, and every day it got worse, and the fallen angel named Lucifer was to blame. So were the million or so angels who defected with him, and the countless number of demons who joined them. The devil's legions had perverted the course of mankind beyond all expectation and now he was ready to destroy everything.Gabriel saw the evidence everywhere. Fish hatched with cankers on their scales. Whales, octopus and dolphins beached for no reason, and tidal Tsunamis tore into vast tracts of coast, killing populations deep inland. Everywhere cities were destroyed by fire, wind and flood. Hurricanes bore down on Ireland, disastrous killer earthquakes from Mexico to Uzbekistan. Sea levels kept rising, many vital glaciers were already completely gone.

Invasion, occupation or civil war were taking place in a dozen countries, ready to spill over into a dozen more. Half the world was suffering from famine, or losing their homes to natural disaster, while the rich industrial nations ignored it all, spending money on cell phones, lap-tops and wide screen TV's or on gas-guzzling cars, S. U. V.'s and the fuel to drive them. Billions were wasted, as the greedy nations destroyed the environment and each other's armies. Another World War was little more than a phone call away. Mad politicians ranted and raved in political hot-spots. Atomic weapons were owned by insane dictators ready to sell them to their insane allies.

World leaders were in denial. Everything was under control. Pollution was a hoax. Climate Change was debatable, and arms control must be maintained through negotiation and sanctions (making the victims angrier). Speaking out for reason had no effect. In fact it hardly slowed things down. With some irony the starving and disease-ridden Continent of Africa was rarely mentioned.

And the mad dance went on.

All to Lucifer's tune.

It was why Gabriel was here. He still had the ability to read Lucifer's thoughts, although the devil could no longer read his, or those of any other angel. That was a power he had lost. But now Gabriel knew everything, and what he overheard in Jerusalem made more sense. Amir Affhad had indeed made a pact with the devil, to rain down destruction upon the united States.

Nuclear weapons for Al Qaeda.

For detonation in America.

Lucifer, and his various back-up plans, must be stopped from fulfilling the worst prophecies of all time.

Gabriel was no longer Hans Behring, a top sales executive for Mercedes Benz. He was now one of New York's homeless, and an African-American who spent the past hour rummaging in garbage cans to annoy the Prince of Darkness. Lucifer had been looking directly at Gabriel and not recognized him.

Down-and-out is a great disguise. No one really looks at a street person, especially in New York. Making your way across slum neighborhoods on foot here was dangerous, unless you were dressed like Gabriel in filthy cast-offs and sneakers, with a tattered baseball cap worn back to front for good measure. People left Gabriel alone, from street muggers who scorned him, to the well-to-do, crossing the road to avoid him, faces turned to hide their guilt. A taxi had dropped Gabriel off at Times Square, where Hans Behring ceased to exist and Artis Brown was created. Artis belonged to the age group that went to Vietnam, and always carried his disabled Veteran's card, in case he needed some kind of identification.

Gabriel had come here with scores of other angels. A few, like him, were in human form and dressed as he was, scavenging garbage near Lucifer's house, and mingling with the street people who always sent the devil into a rage. Still more angels hovered unseen, surrounding the brownstone and screening it from above. Lucifer was not to be destroyed or even harmed, but his power could be contained, his ability to cause major problems restricted. That was why so many angels were here, and why they would be staying. The devil had brought this on himself.

Gabriel decided it was time for him to go.

Stooping slightly, he moved away, shuffling his feet.

Leaving angels here in force made him feel better.

Lucifer's power was still formidable, but it would be harder for him to use it. For example, he interfered with the weather more and more, destroying entire regions with hurricanes and earthquakes. This would no longer be so easy; it would exhaust him, and slow him down. Nor would he be able to flip around the world, as he normally did. He would be reduced to airline travel, like Gabriel, except for emergencies, and that, too, would wear him out.

Gabriel began heading back to the airport, and decided to remain Artis Brown a little longer, in order to reach an area better serviced by taxis without drawing unwanted attention.

Reading the devil's mind was helpful, but now other matters required Gabriel's attention – the black market in nuclear weaponry from either Russia or China. Russia was nearest, so he'd fly there next, once he was Hans Behring again. This time it would be Artis Brown who ceased to exist in Times Square.

He crossed Central park and walked faster. The sidewalk was not so full now, with the workday over, but there were still plenty of tourists, shoppers and pleasure seekers. Gabriel heard everything from rapid-fire French, Italian and Spanish, to the slower pace of Dutch and German, and a smattering of Russian and other Slavic languages. He also heard Chinese and Japanese, but these speakers were American born, and came from Chinatown and Little Tokyo.

To Gabriel's amusement, most Europeans stared at Artis Brown, but none of the Americans did. A kindly family from London sent a little girl running to give him a dollar but all Artis got from New Yorkers was a thousand yard stare.

There was a disturbance at the next corner. People were shouting excitedly, some of them pointing at something behind Gabriel, or at something above his head. A woman sat on the ground, an empty purse open beside her. Suddenly it was clear that the crowd was not pointing above or behind Artis Brown. The fingers were pointing at him.

That was how Gabriel got arrested.

There were too many witnesses for him to vanish, no time for hypnotism, and too many of them were convinced that Gabriel was the thief, although he had been nowhere near her, and did not have the contents of that purse. Artis was a street person, and the only suspect in sight. The victim was too shaken or confused to speak, so the police took him in.

The police station was worse. The desk Sergeant took one look at him and found him guilty. Artis was homeless and black. Either one meant a night in the cells. They put him in a holding tank. It was filled to capacity, and the noise was deafening and the smell unbearable. There were scuffles for space, and those with seats looked lethal enough to keep them. Street hustlers, drunks and vagrants rubbed shoulders with junkies, break-in artists and transvestites. Gabriel saw one man with a knife up his sleeve, and two others sharing a syringe in a corner.

And then, naturally, he was attacked.

Two thugs in swastika jewelry decided Artis Brown was fair game. They beat up blacks and street bums on the outside. Artis was both and in here. One man seized him from behind. The other aimed a vicious punch to the head. No one could explain what happened next. There were two screams. Both men flew into the air, then crashed to the ground, knocked senseless.

Artis was now allowed plenty of room. One tough-looking prisoner offered him a cigarette, which was politely refused.

Names were called at intervals by a guard, and those chosen were led off to night court. They did not return.

The holding cell was slowly emptying out.

Gabriel's turn eventually came.

He got six months.

He had plenty of opportunity to escape: While exiting the courtroom and as the prison bus was being loaded; then as it drove to the jail, and finally from the jail itself. Gabriel allowed each chance to pass; until they arrived at the prison yard to be checked in, because the jail was close to an airport.

They hosed him down and fingerprinted him, which would do them no good at all, and then they numbered him and locked him in a cell for the night. It was the early hours of the morning. His cell-mates were already asleep.

Gabriel raised one finger.

An air duct cover opened, slid wide, and stayed that

way as if he had crawled out.

Then he drifted through the stone wall.

When he materialized at the airport he was no longer Artis Brown. Minutes later Hans Behring bought a ticket to Moscow, having retrieved his money-packed briefcase from a left luggage box in the Departure Hall.

He could see the river before he saw Moscow itself, golden onion towers gleaming in the sunlight. The Russian pilot made a perfect landing. Women in the streets were wearing summer dresses.

Gabriel's hotel was a large, sprawling cavern that once hosted royalty, but more recently, anyone important in the Communist Party. Nowadays it served as a dormitory for rich foreign visitors. No red-star hung over the main entrance, but a big, star-shaped stain showed where it had been.

A hall porter rushed to assist Herr Behring with his briefcase. It was the only luggage Gabriel had. He was resigned to sleeping like a human, but he had no need of their travel accessories, pajamas, toothpaste or razor blades. The briefcase made him more human. He kept it close, unwilling to part with that much cash for a second. He would need it when he got to China. New York had been exhausting, and Gabriel soon found himself falling asleep in a Tzar-sized bed.

Next day six guards stood at the foot of the Kremlin steps. Gabriel drifted by unseen, as two of them began their strange, goose-stepping march back and forth. The angel had no time for credentials, or making an appointment, but round the corner he materialized as a

Russian Army Colonel with a map-case full of money clutched in one hand.

Now he could afford to be seen.

He stepped around a marble pillar, and a sentry sprang to attention. "Good morning, sir." No one said Comrade any more.

The soldier's tone sounded polite but guarded.

He was probably wondering where Gabriel came from, and looked too young to be away from his mother. Gabriel saluted. "Good morning. Is General Renkov's office along here?"

"Yes, Colonel. At the end."

Another Russian Colonel, a genuine one, strode around the corner towards them, and Gabriel hesitated, unsure whether to salute someone of his own rank. He really must study-up on the military if he meant to get away with this sort of thing. He was still trying to decide when the problem resolved itself. The other officer passed by without a sideways glance. Perhaps he had been too deep in thought to notice Gabriel or the sentry. Perhaps the new Russia did not require salutes.

"At the end," repeated the corporal helpfully.

Gabriel thanked him and moved on.

He felt extremely irritated with himself. Maybe he should have inhabited the body of a real Colonel who knew all the rules and regulations instead of faking it. But a suitable Russian Colonel had not been available until just now. All the same it was not a very good start.

Gabriel's footsteps echoed on the glossy, tiled floor.

He approached General Renkov's office. The general was always a Communist hard-liner, but notoriously corrupt. His latest misdeed, the one of setting a price with

Amir Affhad, attracted not only the attention of Renkov's superiors, but that of the Angel Gabriel, who consulted Heaven. The judgement was harsh, even harsher than that of the Russian High Command. Today marked Gabriel's first visit to this part of the Kremlin.

And General Renkov's last day alive.

Gabriel wanted this to go smoothly. He shuddered at what happened four days ago in Jerusalem. His grisly handling of those deaths might have been necessary, but it would not be repeated.

The general's name and rank were stenciled on his door.

Gabriel opened it without knocking, and spied a solitary figure at the desk. The general looked up. He should be expecting someone, probably more than one, to haul him off for court martial and disgrace. That had been promised him. Gabriel conjured up an arrest warrant and stepped forward as if to serve it. That would get him in close enough to deliver a heart attack without unforeseen complications. He pointed a finger at the Russian's chest.

It was not to be.

General Renkov had the drawer open, and a gun at his temple before the phony colonel could react. Gabriel groaned inwardly. This reminded him of Karl Jaeger. Was a bodyguard named Otto about to appear? The angel almost looked around to make sure. But he realized there was nothing he could do here. Events were taking their course. The Angel of Death had made a wasted journey.

There was a crashing explosion.

Gabriel looked down at the dead general, coming to the conclusion that this was probably a fitting end. A self-inflicted death fitted the crime. This Russian had been ready to cause the death of millions. A week ago Al Qaeda sent its representative, Amir Affhad, with a deal for Renkov – senior officer in charge of an obsolete but still deadly nuclear arsenal.

The general accepted, but then he got caught. The young captain guarding a stockpile of warheads in Murmansk not only refused a hefty bribe, but reported it. No one could have foreseen that kind of idealism, and it sealed the fate of General Renkov, as surely as the bullet that killed him.

Gabriel knew some of the rest of the story. Once accused, the general had known what to expect: a guilty-plea in exchange for a lenient sentence. Things had changed since the Iron Curtain came down.

Next, Renkov contacted the terrorists, to explain his situation and make them an offer: He would still see the deal through, if they paid the previously agreed amount to his family, after the trial.

That was why General Renkov came to work today, knowing he was about to be arrested, and why he had been signing a transport order for ballistic missiles when the Angel of Death arrived at his door.

But ten minutes before that he had received a phone call, explaining that his plea-bargain had been disapproved at the highest level. A trial would indeed take place, but a life sentence lay ahead.

In Russia, life means death.

Gabriel had not known about that phone call.

The angel stepped up to the desk and saw the order was already signed. It was neatly typed, and called for six projectiles to be delivered to an undisclosed destination. Now there was blood on the paper, making it blotchy and wet.

There were rapid, running footsteps outside.

That gunshot had been loud.

The arrest warrant in Gabriel's hand vanished as quickly as it came. He leaned forward to take the bloody transfer papers from the general's grasp. They quickly disappeared. Then Gabriel, too, vanished.

He drifted out of the Kremlin.

Outside, on the flagstones of Red Square, he was again Hans Behring, citizen of Hamburg. He was soon back at the airport, having paid his hotel bill in phony, angel-fabricated rubles. He took an Aeroflot flight to China.

~ ~ ~

Beijing a colorful maze as always: streets jammed with trucks and cars, hampered by peddlers, housewives, bicycles, rickshaws, old men and young men, and children of every age and size. Everyone seemed to be wearing blue suit, or gray cotton dungarees with a cone-shaped hat. Such outmoded clothing was a stark contrast to this futuristic, sky-rise metropolis, where impressively tall buildings were still springing up – like trees made of shimmering glass, concrete and steel.

And the noise. The noise of construction was everywhere.

Hans Behring's dilapidated old taxi inched along. Gabriel knew it was quicker and cheaper to walk, but he rode anyway. Most Chinese are spiritually attuned, like the black girl in Kiel, or the old man who recognized Gabriel in Jerusalem, and if anyone here saw an angel walking about, the whole crowd would take up the cry.

The taxi dropped him at a Buddhist temple.

Chinese Communism has an odd relationship with

Chinese religion. Christianity is banned completely. Buddha is also banished but tolerated. Gabriel said a few words to a young priest standing at the door, and was allowed in.

Everyone here knew the Archangel Gabriel.

Most of them were angels, too.

He stepped into a great room, a lacquered-wood haven of calm and tranquility that defied Chinese Communism and made the world seem very far away. He walked across bamboo flooring, amid low, muted chanting that vibrated in the air. He passed monks, and angels dressed as monks, all in yellow robes, praying.

Gabriel came to a beaded curtain that divided off a small area, and knelt. The curtain only partially hid a large, pot-bellied statue of Buddha, covered in flaking gold leaf.

Someone softly approached Gabriel from behind.

He turned, and saw Kang-Wei, an old-looking and wrinkled Chinese angel wearing priestly robes, and whose aging and wrinkles were fake, to avoid a hullabaloo each time he ventured out of the temple.

Kang-Wei was Gabriel's main contact in China.

They went off together, to drink green tea out of delicate porcelain, and to speak Mandarin, a dialect they both learned six thousand years ago, when it was in common usage.

By the time the tea had refreshed them, Gabriel knew where he had to go, and who to see:

The master criminal, Lung Chiang.

~ ~ ~

That evening, Gabriel went.

Lung Chiang was tall and fat, a broad-faced Shanghai

Tong leader who lived on the fringes of Beijing. Lung Chiang ran Beijing. He also ran this rambling, rickety, open-air restaurant looking out on the river, its decaying bamboo construction strangely defiant of gravity. Chiang sat at a low table, with water lapping under the floorboards, surveying his kingdom. A mound of empty oyster shells grew in size as he ate. He seemed to grow taller and fatter, even sitting down. A cup of Japanese Sake sat by his hand, and he used it to swill down a mouthful of food.

Nearby straggled a line of local underworld figures, some of them with their mistresses, all hoping for an audience once the oysters were gone, and the evening's entertainment was over. Most were here to curry favor, or to repay debts, and others merely to pay homage.

Every one of them had already placed their bets.

Tonight was Fight-Night.

Gabriel stood in a crowd packed against the rail surrounding a large, bamboo cage. He had an appointment with lung Chiang.

Both rail and cage stood in an area cleared of tables for the evening. Gabriel was now Chinese in appearance, but too tall to fool anyone around here for long. He was grateful for both the crowd and the darkness. Behind him, a sallow-faced woman was saying: "Never wait for the start. The odds are better now."

Lung Chiang wiped his mouth and clapped his hands. The first event was about to begin. One of his henchmen pounded on a gong. This caused an instant reaction. The spectators cheered and started to stamp their feet. The air was hot and humid, and people soon began to sweat. And now they became restless, when no contestants appeared,

Some shouted for the animal trainers. There were hisses and boos.

Then a man stepped into the light around the cage. He had a long pole over one shoulder, with a flat basket dangling from it. He removed the lid, and pushed a black cobra through the bars and onto the cage floor. It wriggled furiously, and the audience roared with delight.

There was a further delay, and people became restless and impatient again, as the minutes ticked by. The snake had coiled itself in a corner, and was striking at thin air. It whipped forward each time, with vicious speed.

Then another trainer appeared, dragging a small cage on wheels. A wildcat threw herself at the bars, spitting hatred at the crowd. People backed away as she passed, her teeth grazing the bamboo that encased her.

As the two cage doors opened, silence descended, and the cobra slowly raised its hooded head.

The wildcat burst in, goaded with an electric prod, and the snake reared up almost its full length. It swayed slightly, eyes not moving, fixed upon its prey.

The wildcat froze, tufted ears twitching, her legs braced.

There was total quiet.

Gabriel looked over at Lung Chiang, who was smiling faintly. Now the Tong leader rose and entered a separate room at the rear.

The creatures in the cage stirred.

The wildcat bellied slowly forward, front paws splayed, back stiff, her muscles tense. The cobra ceased swaying. Its eyes shone like dark gems. Every inch of its body was poised to strike. The wildcat sensed, as did everyone watching, that this was a crucial moment. She lunged so fast, her body was a blur. Her claws raked the serpent's belly, but her jaws snapped loudly together, as she missed his spine by a hair. The snake slithered rapidly away, leaving a bright red trail, then reared up again, dangerous as before.

The wildcat screamed its rage.

The feints, probing attacks and counter-attacks began, both fighters striving for advantage – until the floor, daubed everywhere with snake blood, became slippery and treacherous, and both creatures seethed with anger, hatred and frustration. Five minutes became ten, and ten fifteen.

The crowd was hushed.

Finally the cat lunged, and missed – again.

It was fatal. The cobra's head descended like lightening. Its fangs struck the cat perfectly, at the neck.

Those watching were as one, transfixed.

It was over. The poison acted instantly. The wildcat let out one final, hideous scream, then sank down, legs buckling, eyes glazed. She held up her head for a last, agonized moment; until her chin drooped, and as it touched the floor, she died. The contest was decided.

There was a roar of applause, and the thunder of stamping feet.

Wagers were paid off.

The bloodied cobra was removed, hanging limp.

The cat was thrown in the river.

Gabriel backed away from the rail. It was easy to force a path through the throng, due to his size. He made for the door where Lung Chiang had disappeared, and spoke to one of the Tong-leader's bully-boys. Before long another bodyguard led him past the line of gangsters and hangers-on still waiting for an audience.

Chiang's man knocked at the door.

"Who's there?"

Gabriel entered.

Chiang was eating again, squatting like a coolie, attacking a bowl of rice with swiftly moving chop-sticks. He looked up and saw Gabriel. A quick shadow crossed his face, and was gone.

Gabriel said: "Greetings, Chiang."

Lung Chiang smiled broadly. Setting aside his food, he came to his feet.

"Ah, the Angel Gabriel."

Lung Chiang never changed.

He was the only fat angel. His glossy, jet-black hair was swept back in a queue. He had created for himself a face with slightly slanted almond eyes, and a wide nose above thick lips and double chins. He had the faintest wisp of black mustache, which gave him the look of an ancient emperor, and won him the respect of the kind of gutter trash waiting outside. His entire body rippled when he laughed, and with Chiang's huge girth and welcoming smile, it was easy to forget that this angel was a vicious thug who ruled by murder and extortion.

He also consorted with demons.

Lung Chiang was a fallen angel.

And there were nearly a million like him.

Gabriel once asked him: "Why does no one recognize you as an angel? You're always in plain sight."

Chinag had laughed his fat man's laugh. "I don't act like an angel. I'm a well-known criminal. No one ever suspects."

Every renegade angel taking part in Lucifer's rebellion,

so many years ago, was in a similar situation to Lung Chiang today. They made up most of the rich and powerful on Earth, and had done so for thousands of years. Most were political giants; many of them led nations, as presidents, prime ministers, or as kings and queens. From Nicaragua to Sri-Lanka; from Russia to Cambodia and from America to Australia, they were there, fighting to hold on to power. Europe's larger nations were dominated, as were those on every other continent. Not all of the fallen rose that high. Some were elected to more modest forms of government, or ruled smaller nations, which offered the same luxury as any superpower, but had the added advantage that the right to rule was less fiercely contested. Many were only mayors, councilmen or other civic leaders. This depended on how much spiritual potency they still enjoyed; because it was slowly draining away. That was affecting them all, just as it did Lucifer, as the final days drew near. But success was also determined by how much position and power they craved, and some were just happy with less.

Many posed as leaders of industry, making untold fortunes for themselves and their stockholders, out of oil, drugs, alcohol, guns, tobacco and meat: anything vital to human existence in a misguided world. Others were master criminals, like Lung Chiang, having started ill-gotten empires centuries ago and turned them into profitable industries. Lucifer's million disloyal angels covered every part of the small, inhabited rock called Earth. Other positions of power, not held by them, were filled by Lucifer's demons. His combined forces exceeded those of Gabriel.

All that was about to change.

Gabriel had been so commanded.

He had angels in correspondingly high positions everywhere, although most of them were unaware of their celestial status. This counter-army would soon be awake and thrown into action.

Lucifer knew this and feared it.

So did Lung Chiang.

Now Chiang sat down and Gabriel did the same. Two over-sized Chinamen, sitting cross-legged with a few feet between them. Chiang resumed his meal. The rice had been stirred in oil and soy; it glistened on his chin, and some dripped on the green silk of his robe. "Are you hungry?" he said.

"I rarely even pretend to eat."

And the rice had been cooked in animal fat.

As Lung Chiang knew very well.

They studied each other. Gabriel still regarded Chiang as an angel, but did not trust him. The fat bandit, like all the fallen, existed on the dark side, allied with the forces that opposed Heaven. Gabriel knew how Chiang became so powerful among the Tongs over the years. Lung Chiang seized control by betraying allies, ordering untold deaths and unleashing the bloodiest street-fighting in Chinese history. Gabriel also remembered Lucifer's thoughts in New York, and had them confirmed today at the Buddhist temple. Chinag had promised Amir Affhad, a week ago, to broker a deal between Iran and North Korea for nuclear warheads. That meant three purchases were being made, or attempted, if you included whoever replaced General Renkov in Moscow. All of this said the devil had the initiative. But was Chiang's transaction completed, or was he still working on the Koreans, or his own government, or both? Kang Wei, at the temple had not known, but Gabriel hoped to get the answer from Lung Chiang, and sat wondering how to go about it. The fat angel was cunning. He appeared relaxed and friendly, but he knew why Gabriel was here. How would he react? He and Gabriel both knew Chiang's very existence was threatened. Should Gabriel come right out and say that, or ignore it, as if nothing were wrong?

"You're in trouble," he said bluntly.

Chiang's smile stayed in place.

"The Lebanese was here," Gabriel went on. "He fronts for the Saudis, who are bankrolling for Iran. They've also been to the Russians, but that fell through, for now. You are their link to North Korea. You have to refuse them, if it's not too late. And you must refuse them, even if it is."

"They pay me in gold. All parties have secretly signed."

That told Gabriel he was too late. Arab drug and oil money had won the day, and the Chinese and North Korean wheels were in motion. He said, "But Chiang, you know what's at stake."

"I do. One ton of gold is quite a stake."

"And this world is destroyed?"

"This world is worthless." Chiang belched and placed his bowl between them, chopsticks balanced neatly on top. Gabriel knew Chiang did not mean what he said. It was an opening move. Chiang's first offer was simply this: Nothing. It was going to be a tough negotiation. Lung Chiang turned towards the closed door and yelled: "Bring us something to drink!"

Gabriel resolved to stay sober.

Knowing Lung Chiang was doing the same.

Chiang sat back, and wiped soy sauce and oil off his

face and onto his sleeve. "You will drink with me," he said to Gabriel.

"And have you dispose of my drunken corpse. Like one of your rivals? I'm no threat to you, Chiang." Gabriel wished it were true.

"I know better," said Chiang, but there was no tension in his voice, and that smile was still there.

Gabriel considered. His objective here was to stop an arms deal; not to play cat and mouse. Both angels knew neither of them would drink anything. Lung Chiang was just buying time to think.

Gabriel decided not to let him.

He said: "You know I was in Jerusalem, and Amir Affhad is gone."

"Yes."

"And Ben Salim."

"Yes."

They were your money supply."

Chiang shrugged. There were plenty of Arabs.

Gabriel said: "Your fate hangs in the balance.'

Chiang's eyes flashed. "My soul you will not take so easily."

Gabriel knew that was true. But it might have to happen. He went on: "I took something from the Lebanese. A briefcase filled with business papers: Notes of meetings, balance sheets and sales budgets; to show Israeli customs. Under that was a significant amount of money, hidden in a false bottom. I still have it."

Currently in the safe-keeping of Kang-Wei.

Lung Chiang became fully alert, sensing the bribe being offered. Gabriel saw the greed in his eyes.

"Inside the false bottom the case is stuffed with

bearer-bonds in every hard currency, issued by Swiss, German and other European banks. I've kept them with me since I found them. Large, unidentifiable amounts are always useful. If you and I could come to . . ."

"What are you saying?" said Chiang calmly. "I can have some of it?"

"All."

"How much, exactly?"

"A lot." Gabriel was not quite ready to disclose the amount. "Affhad made a deal with Lucifer, after seeing General Renkov, and after seeing you. A large commission was paid to Affhad, on each occasion, in advance. The Lebanese was smuggling it home when I bumped into him."

Chiang was hooked. Gabriel played his trump card. "It comes to eight hundred million dollars."

Chiang quickly totaled three sales like his own, and calculated a finder's fee. "Exactly right," he said. "Your honesty is refreshing."

Someone knocked at the door. Lung Chiang gave permission to enter. His man had a tray, with a jug of chilled rice wine and two cups. Looking at Gabriel, he asked his boss, "More cooked rice?"

"No need," said Chiang with dry amusement. "He never eats."

The man left them to it. Outside there was an outburst of cheering, as another event started up in the bamboo cage. Two dogs would spend the next fifteen minutes fighting for life and limb.

Chiang poured the wine, filling both cups, and handed one to Gabriel. They both sipped sparingly, tongues barely wet.

"Listen," said Gabriel. "Lucifer won't win this, one way or the other. Heaven will never allow it. Save yourself while you can. Drop out of this Korean sale."

"If I do, you pay me off?"

"Yes."

"And if I don't?"

Gabriel shrugged.

"Are you threatening me? Is Heaven threatening me?" Chiang unexpectedly downed his wine as if it were water. He didn't need an answer. The threat was out in the open.

Gabriel put down his wine cup. "Chiang, you know I don't make threats. If you choose Lucifer, you're damned. That's for you to decide. I offer an alternative. Affhad's bond money will take you into the next century. It's from a regrettable source, but no one will hold that against you — if you give up crime and intrigue. Turn your back on Lucifer, before it's too late."

Gabriel paused. He was not winning Chiang over. He tried another approach. "Lucifer hates you."

Chiang lowered his eyes. "He needs me now."

Gabriel wasn't about to say so, but this Chinese angel was Lucifer's best bet so far. Chiang couldn't be stopped without destroying him, and Gabriel wouldn't do that unless North Korea delivered and Chiang was responsible. Until then he had a chance to redeem himself. He was, after all, an angel. The bribe-taking General in Utah, on the other hand, was a demon, and more easily dealt with, and Gabriel would be taking care of him soon. Unfortunately that gave Lung Chiang his best chance ever to impress Lucifer. The devil would be grateful, and pay a huge bonus.

That was how he did things.

Gabriel pushed his wine away; then pointedly got to his feet. Chiang looked at him, realizing the discussion was ended. Courtesy made him heave himself up to face Gabriel. "I'll consider your offer," he said formally. Gabriel could see he almost meant it. Chiang's style was to take the pay-off; then go ahead with the North Korean nuclear sale, and that was precisely what he intended to do.

Gabriel shook his hand anyway.

Chiang showed him out. "I'll send word," he said.

~ ~ ~

By next evening Gabriel had been summoned, and was mounting the gangplank that led onto Chiang's river-moored junk. The Chinese Gabriel was no more, replaced once more by a German named Behring. He carried Amir Affhad's briefcase, and wore the same suit and hat as in Jerusalem.

The marshy inlet was private and deserted. The clamor of the city was lost, far across the flat-lands. The stale, greenish water of the estuary showed hardly a ripple as the junk pulled against wind and current on thick, tarred ropes. Chiang's floating home was a refurbished antique, decked out in black red and gold lacquered paint, hung with oiled paper lanterns, giving a faint glow in the early dusk.

The deck was freshly scrubbed, and Gabriel took off his shoes as he boarded, watched by surly-looking crew-members, stripped to the waist to haul up the mainsail, which rose black and stark, against the pale wood of the mast. He was directed to the main cabin, and went in stocking feet down some steps to the lower deck. The smell of incense rose to meet him.

The main room was delicately and sparely furnished,

with an elegant smattering of priceless vases, varnished tables and carpets that once graced China's Imperial Court in the Sixth Century. The walls were decorated with equally valuable paintings, and rare, screened prints. At the far end of it all was the inevitable statue of the Lord Buddha on a shiny black plinth.

Beyond that sat Lung Chiang, cross legged on the floor. There was the faintest of sensations, as the junk slipped its moorings and got smoothly under way, but Gabriel had no need to steady himself, as he made his way between the works of art to join his host and sit down, In a few minutes the junk would reach the mouth of the estuary and be ready to put to sea.

This was the heaviest of vessels, and it would remain lumbering and stable, even in the worst of storms. Otherwise Lung Chiang would never risk his Ming vases. Although if stability failed, there was always angel magic. The obese Chinese angel was still capable of that.

They faced each other, sitting cross-legged, as they had last night.

Gabriel removed his hat, opened the case and began stacking paper bonds into neatly ordered piles in front of Chiang. German Bundesbank; Credit Suisse; Banque Lyonnaise; the Mercantile Marine of London and a couple of exclusive institutions in the Duchy of Luxemburg.

Chiang looked on in surprise. "You are paying already? . . . I have not given my decision."

Gabriel smiled. "I decided an act of faith would do no harm."

"And Lucifer?"

"Does not know I'm here, or my whereabouts at all. He has business elsewhere. Please do not enlighten him."

There was not much hope of that.

Chiang seized a sheaf of bonds and counted it. "One hundred million," he said. He checked more piles of similar size and value, adding them up as he went. "With this much I can ..."

"Escape Lucifer's clutches," finished Gabriel. He stood up abruptly and brushed imaginary dust from his hat. "If I leave now I can reach shore without using much of my power."

"Return with us, on the tide."

A feeble delaying tactic, Gabriel thought. He had no doubt the devil could arrive in seconds, if summoned by Chiang. To get at Gabriel, Lucifer would not care how many angels surrounded him in New York.

"There's no time," said Gabriel. Then, also from Affhad's case, he took a Century newspaper, overseas edition, published overnight by Lucifer's Far Eastern branch. Its headlines screamed of atrocity in Bethlehem, and of twenty-odd Americans among those killed by a suicide bomb, and inside, on page two, an editorial clamoring for vengeance. Gabriel said: "The American public is about to be whipped into a frenzy, with Lucifer doing the whipping. This catastrophe in Bethlehem may cause the tension he needs to get something started."

Gabriel tossed the flimsy newspaper to his host.

"Inflammatory," agreed Chiang, when he had read it.

Gabriel made a face. "The devil wants to exploit American fury. He's hoping for a missile response, although it's a long shot. US bases in Britain have the capability, and I wonder just how furious America is."

Chiang walked him out of the main cabin. "Does this mean you're going to New York?"

"No. Lucifer is best avoided. He's busy trying to identify the successor to Amir Affhad." Gabriel's voice tailed off, and he frowned. Best not to say too much. Lung Chiang was treacherous and cunning, and Gabriel might as well be talking directly to Lucifer. The Angel of Death thought quickly: The devil had minions in both Senate and Congress, although not the White House itself, and those minions would be mobilizing for Armageddon on Lucifer's orders. Gabriel had to keep abreast of what was going on. Better go to Washington immediately. He had no time for airlines and airports. He would simply have to waste spiritual power; then stay in the American capital long enough to recuperate. At the same time he must also take care of Lucifer's accomplice in Utah, the satanic General Bertram.

Chiang said, "What does Lucifer want?"

He meant: How much do you know, Gabriel?

The Archangel had no intention of revealing that. He answered only in a general way, as if he had misunderstood. "What he's always wanted," said Gabriel. "To end the world. Just to prove how powerful he is. He wants the final Armageddon, and the human race obliterated, or close enough to it that they run to him for leadership. The devil wants them to worship him. Lucifer dreams of ruling the world. He's either too blind, or too stupid, to realize that he's been doing that for centuries." The two angels climbed the wooden steps and walked out onto the open deck. The sky was by now a deep, purplish blue, transformed by a myriad of stars into the perfect backdrop for Chiang's darkly silhouetted junk, as it glided through swells of water.

The two angels said farewell, and then Gabriel walked

to the wooden deck rail. He drifted upward and cleared the rigging, only too aware that he had not won over Lung Chiang.

~ ~ ~

The portly Chinese angel watched him disappear, then made his way down to the small rear cabin where he slept. He opened a desk-top computer and got on-line. There was a ten-hour time difference in New York. He hoped the devil was at home, sober and occasionally checking his e-mails. Typing in stilted English, Chiang gave brief details of both meetings with Gabriel, predicting that the Angel of Death would indeed avoid New York, as he had said, but guessing that he was still heading for America. Most likely to Washington DC.

Lung Chiang clicked on "Send" and signed off once transmission was confirmed. The Chinese angel chuckled to himself. Gabriel might not have said where he was going, but he was, and always had been, quite predictable.

Chiang was not finished with the internet. He gathered the bonds left by Gabriel and contacted his various brokers, first in Tai-Wan and Hong Kong, and then London, Frankfurt and Brussels. The total, based upon face value, was more than eight hundred million dollars. Chiang quoted their serial numbers, denominations, and the names of the issuing banks. He tasked his brokers with establishing that the bonds were genuine. If so, Lung Chiang was rich enough to buy a Chinese province, and Gabriel was a misguided and utter fool.

Stockbrokers in key cities are permanently on line, and Chiang's all promised to reply within a few hours. The ocean can be very calming, and he decided to stay at sea overnight.

As Chiang logged off, he glanced down at the stacks of bearer bonds. Something strange was happening to a certificate on top of one pile. He picked it up to examine it closely. The print was fading, and had almost vanished. He frantically grabbed more, and saw the same thing. With a sinking feeling, Lung Chiang leafed through more piles: they were all turning blank.

Chiang sat, unmoving: Gabriel had done this, because he had known all along that Ching would betray him. The Angel of Death had cast a spell, and it went into effect the second Lucifer was contacted.

Now Chiang knew the price of sending that e-mail: Eight hundred million dollars.

~ ~ ~

The White House lawn was immaculate, and fringed with trees and flowers that made it a picture in the spring sunshine. The President looked down as the garden rose to meet him. Helicopter One, a dark blue Westland – emblazoned with a crest that told everyone who was on board – dipped down gracefully, rotors spinning in a reduced, low toned rhythm. Helicopter One touched down, and President Christiansen stepped out onto the grass.

A tough first year in office was about to get worse.

The sun was mid-high, the humidity choking. The aircraft had been cooler, even at low altitude, even with one door open. Down here his clothes were sticking to him and his skin felt clammy. He hated perspiring on camera. The battery of flashbulbs was already going off, and he was not yet in proper range. An Aide murmured something at his side, but the President brushed him away.

Edwin Olson, his Press Secretary, came towards him across the grass, his leather soles slipping on the smooth turf. He seemed ill at ease. "The entire Press Corps is here," he said. "Asking the same old questions: When will you keep your promise, and pull out of Iraq and Afghanistan? And why did we ever go back in? And if we're staying over there, why don't you try to win? But this thing in Bethlehem is taking over. They want to know what you intend to do about it."

"Of course they do," said the President. "We'll play it cagey." He meant that they would say nothing."

The White House Press Corps, one of the few things Christiansen disliked about being in office. The Right-Wingers acted like a band of vultures, eager to gnaw at his corpse: Elites in a society made for the elite and the wealthy, the well-educated and the superior. Nowadays they required kid-glove treatment, having become extra hawkish in recent months. It did not help that US casualties around Baghdad and Kabul were once again at record highs. They blamed the new President, and portrayed him as a buffoon. "Goody One-Shoe," a reporter had recently called him. "Half-assed about withdrawal, and lukewarm about victory," and it had become a battle cry.

The Left Wing, if anything, was worse.

Liberals and the liberal press, now calling themselves progressives, were outraged that the country was still at war; although he had spent only five months in office. And it was not only liberals, and not only about the war. There were peace marches, and hunger and poverty marches, with the economy still tanking, wholesale unemployment, bankrupt industry and millions of people left with nothing to do but march. Some of these protests had turned into riots, with citizens beaten, kicked and shot at by police and the National Guard. Mercifully, no one was maimed or killed, but the new administration was blamed. The Left said Christiansen was too tough. The Right said too lenient.

He made a great target for both sides.

The President had not yet come up with a good counter-strategy, or a way to shift the blame. He was being allowed no time to settle into the job, and getting little or no help from either the Congress or Senate, and his popularity was falling away, while the Armed Forces leadership blocked him at every turn.

Bethlehem could only make things worse.

He pushed through the press corps, walking fast, with Edwin Olson and the Secret Service blocking for him, while the subject he expected was raised again and again – the War, the War, the War! This was simply ignored, and slowly a path was beaten through the crowd.

Then came the other expected question: "President Christiansen!" bellowed one, unseen reporter. "What about Bethlehem? Are you and the Chiefs of Staff considering military options? Will the American dead be avenged?" Then came a flurry of shouted questions, all in the same vein, some from voices he recognized; others not. Bethlehem was indeed the new hot issue.

"We are considering everything," he said grimly. He was completely drowned out by their clamor, and heard Edwin Olson, gallantly telling them in a loud voice what the President had said.

Christian's group reached the entrance: an arched, colonial affair with decorous French doors. There was cool air inside. Air that beckoned. Christiansen ducked away from the barrage of microphones, and one of his guard detail opened the door just wide enough to allow the presidential party in.

The President stepped inside. Edwin Olson turned at the threshold. "No more questions," he said silkily; then followed his retreating boss

The Chiefs of Staff, the Secretary of State, and several members of the cabinet were waiting in a conference room. Edwin Olson accompanied the President inside, and closed the doors behind himself as he left. Christiansen took his seat at the table, next to George Garret, his Secretary of State. "The Press is after my blood," said the President. He did not need to explain that it concerned those Americans killed in Bethlehem.

"So are they." The Secretary of State indicated the Generals, Admirals and other Staffers arranged before them. "They also want a commitment from you to stay in Iraq and extend Afghanistan again, just as they always do."

"I won't do that. The country is going bankrupt. So what do these guys expect me to do about Bethlehem? Start another war?" His microphone came on unexpectedly, and the question boomed.

A heavily decorated Marine General in his late fifties answered. He was a Four-Star, and his face looked as if it were carved out of wood. "We propose, sir. To make this right in the name of the American People." The President closed his eyes. Whenever the "American People" was invoked, his gorge rose. It had become an overused and cheap political trick. He hated the phrase, and mistrusted those who used it."

So did the Angel Gabriel, who hovered invisible, just below the expert brushwork of the ceiling plaster.

A female voice interrupted the silence.

A woman in naval uniform was speaking.

Christiansen, still thinking about the Four Star General and the American People, had not heard what she said, and asked her to repeat it.

"Our suggested response to the attack in Bethlehem, Mr. President."

She was the Commander of the Sixth fleet, Admiral Branch, just having flown in from her Headquarters in Naples, Italy. She was here to give the briefing. Kathy Branch was responsible for entire Mediterranean theater of operations, with special emphasis on the counties around the Red Sea.

Bethlehem was therefore her bailiwick.

Secretary Garret knew and respected Branch, and was pleased by her recent promotion. He scribbled a quick note to that effect, and passed it to the President, who quietly read it, as he said: "Yes, Admiral. Please go ahead."

"We have two tactical subs on standby." Kathy Branch looked around the table, allowing the word 'tactical' to sink in. It was insider-talk, meaning armed with short-range missiles. The President controlled his emotion. Some in this room were seriously considering a nuclear response. He almost pointed out how few Americans were killed, but the thought of a press leak stopped him. He'd be accused of insulting those who lost their lives.

His Secretary of State intervened masterfully. "None of our allies will go for this, Gentlemen." He smiled at Admiral Branch to acknowledge that she was a lady. "You're kidding yourselves. The French, the Germans – even our best friends, the Brits – would condemn it. My God, Russia and China would throw a fit!"

The marine General pounded the table. "Maybe it's

time to tell them all to go to hell, sir."

The President grunted. There was more of this crap coming, he was sure. He did not intend to tolerate the same old arguments. He needed a serious solution to a serious dilemma.

The Marine was in full flight. These aren't true allies, Mr. President. They're all in cahoots with each other! Moscow sells Russian oil to every one of them, making a killing with bumped-up prices. So do the Saudis and the Arabian Gulf countries. The Europeans stiff us on Iraq; so they can run to the Rag-Heads, and say: "See? See what we did? We dumped on the Americans. Can we please have cheaper oil?" He paused and sipped some water. "Take the Germans – still up to their old tricks by new means. Why was Rommel in the desert, all those years ago? Trying to get oil, same as the Brits, and when he didn't, Hitler invaded Russia – trying to get the same Russian oil Germany is happy to pay for today. Then the French: They need oil, so they won't touch us, or our foreign policy, with a ten-foot pole, and as for the Brits – well, now they dump on us, too. The Europeans are a bunch of crooks. They ass-kiss the oil producers, muscle in on our oil supply and try to shut us out. And now there's India and the Commies in China – both clamoring for more oil!"

Most of this was undeniably true. Ironically the international oil embargo on Iran, imposed after America's long and weary struggle to get it adopted, had benefited Russia. It gave them a hugely increased percentage of the world oil market, and let them charge whatever they liked.

Secretary Garret did not disagree. He said: "Well, Russia is certainly happy that we're bogged down in Iraq, and not them. The same in Afghanistan and the Pakborder region. And with us spending billions a day; including troop occupation, re-building and paying off militia on both sides to stop them killing us and each other; they love what it's doing to our economy. It allows Europe to outspend us on oil, and drive the price beyond our reach, and that represents a huge economic problem for us. Any one of ten European currencies is murdering the dollar."

Someone snorted. "They're killing us! Europeans pay twice as much a gallon, and they have since forever."

George Garret again addressed himself to the crusty Marine General: "You're partly wrong about Russia. Our number one enemy is Iran. Far more dangerous than Moscow knows how to be; now, or in the future. When Israeli planes bombed the Iranian nuclear program out of existence, the Ayatollah blamed us, and he still does. They buy enriched uranium from some crack-pot dictator in New Guinea; then our closest Middle-East ally, Israel, obliterates it, wiping out every nuclear facility they have. You bet Iran blames us, and hates us more than ever, if that were possible.

"Oh, sure, Russia hates us. They remember Ronald Reagan secretly funding the Afghan Guerrillas, to the tune of a billion dollars – driving the Red Army out, toppling the Soviet Union into bankruptcy and collapse. And now, in Kremlin-think, it's pay-back time. They make billions from all, and finance our enemies, in Iraq, the Afghan hills and the Hindu Kush – letting them fix oil prices and kill our soldiers in Baghdad at the same time. It's a second cold-war, and Russia is winning. But Iran hates us more; they want us obliterated, as revenge for losing their nuclear program."

There was a subdued murmur. Losing US soldiers was one thing, but no one was going to fix oil prices except the men in this room. Oil meant Saudi Arabia and Iraq. They were the main source. Everything else was small potatoes. Now the Saudis were an ally in name only, and they could pull the plug at any time, but Iraq was in American hands, effectively an American possession, and most people in this room intended to keep it that way. Too many battles had been fought. Too many Americans had died. Besides, it had been agreed after 9/11, in marble hallways and smoky back rooms, by Republican and Democrat alike: Iraq should be invaded and taken, for a guaranteed oil supply, and as a permanent military base in the Middle-East. Congress was tired of being jerked around by Arab dictators and Kings. They went in, and stayed there. All political arguing since then had been pure theater. This was, after all, the age of scrutiny, and voters had to be told something.

So they got fairy-tales about democracy and freedom.
And the spreading thereof.
When it was really all about oil.

~ ~ ~

President Christiansen was from Wisconsin, and not an oil man. One reason he got elected. The average American wanted out of Iraq and Afghanistan so badly that Mickey Mouse could have won, by not being a hawk, and by promising to bring the troops home. But as soon as the new President arrived in this building, it was made clear he was not in charge, and both wars would go on. Those truly in power laughed in his face: From their point of view he was perfect. He could take the blame for Iraq for four years, at the end of which he'd be dumped by the electorate, making room for a President more to the liking of the Pentagon. Most likely a retired General, or other military leader. America had not built those multibillion dollar Green Zones in Baghdad for no reason. US troops were never leaving.

Now the military establishment was here in this room, trying to tell him what to do about Bethlehem. And now, as he had back then, President Christiansen felt frustrated, but he was not going to let them tell him anything. He was about to take this meeting in hand. He cleared his throat. "You will not fire any missiles in response to this incident in Bethlehem, gentlemen. Let me make that clear. We need a better game plan, and we need it right now. Admiral Branch?"

"Yes, Sir." The Admiral prepared to deliver a back-up plan which did not involve nuclear weapons. There was always a second plan, and the top brass always brought it along. Their first option always called for aggression, and always got denied, at least by this Commander in Chief.

Admiral Branch tapped an intelligence folder in front of her. "We know who was responsible, Mr. President, and we know where to find them."

"Your battle plan?"

"Ground troops. Helicopter support."

The President felt the walls closing in. This sounded a lot like past disasters. He sometimes wondered if Democratic Presidents, like Carter and Clinton, when attacking Iran or Somalia with troops and helicopters, had been set up for failure by their own, Republican-voting Generals.

Now he wondered that again.

Because he was a Democrat.

He decided, as he always did, that it was an unworthy thought.

He might as well hear the Admiral's plan.

"So whom do we attack?" The President was asking this question of the room at large; well aware that Kathy Branch was speaking for everyone. The General Staff had put her in a tight spot.

"A training-camp in Syria, hidden off the beaten track," said Admiral Branch. "Mostly ex-patriot Saudis, with a few Pakistanis and Afghans thrown in. Syria thinks we don't know; but we do."

The President said: "How good is your Intel?"

"Solid," said Admiral Branch. "We have someone in the camp. He made contact yesterday, with his CIA controller. That girl who blew herself up in Bethlehem – she trained in this camp, with our guy."

Her words floated up to Gabriel.

For several minutes now, he had relaxed a little. There was to be no bombing. The President had said so. Gabriel had been ready to leave, satisfied that the worst danger had been averted; but now he pricked up his ears. An attack on Syria was putting your hand in a nest of rattlesnakes. The President's decision was crucial. Gabriel strained to catch every word that he said.

The President asked about the staging area.

"Turkey," said Admiral Branch.

The President was unimpressed. "They have terrorist problems of their own, they can't give us real support. Going from Turkey into Syria is high risk, and prone to leaks in security. Find a better ally to help us out."

Christiansen himself was thinking of Israel, although he would not say that out loud. Bethlehem was, after all, an Israeli city. What if Tel Aviv agreed to carry out the reprisal on Syria themselves?

The Secretary of State had no idea what was in the President's mind, but as a life-long diplomat, he was appalled by what he was hearing. "My God, Mr. President – if anything goes wrong, a strike against Syria is madness. We're still trying to disengage from Iraq!"

There were more than a few scowls at the mention of disengagement, and Garret reddened with anger. He had a lot of enemies in this meeting, because, largely due to his stance, and the public speeches he made to defend it, public opinion was still in favor of troop withdrawal. American troops, Garret kept saying, could be home by the end of the year.

He added defiantly: "An attack is the last thing to consider."

"It won't be from Turkey," said Christiansen. "And we are unlikely to do it at all. I'm simply asking for options."

George Garret was equally direct. "Our Intel might indeed be good here, but our strategy is not."

The President leaned close, to speak only for his ears. "We can hand this over to the Israelis. Bethlehem is their town, and they like to play tough guy. Let them take care of it. At least they won't screw it up."

Garret nodded. This would throw Syria off balance, reminding them that they had another powerful enemy with troops in the region, experienced troops that were fresh and ready to fight; not exhausted and overstretched, like American soldiers after twenty years in the field.

The President stood up. "Thank you, everyone. I'm sure the Chiefs of Staff will come up with something better by tomorrow."

"I doubt it," muttered the Secretary of State.

President Christiansen sat back down and said, just as softly: "We'll call Tel Aviv, as soon as we're alone." The Secretary nodded and remained seated.

There was a noisy movement of chairs, as everyone got up and left. The President sat talking to Secretary Garret for a long time, in the silence of the empty room. Finally they phoned the Prime minister of Israel.

Gabriel listened carefully to what was said.

CHAPTER FOUR

THE BAR ON CAPITOL HILL was almost empty.

Shahanna Dufaux checked her watch again and thought, It's nearly a quarter to nine, and I'm drinking alone.

She shifted on her stool, to see herself better in the bar mirror, above a sparkling row of glasses. Her make-up was fading. Liquid brown eyes looked tired. Her hair hung in straggling, black curls. But the classic beauty of her sculpted brown features still shone through, with a hint of French-Moroccan stubbornness in every curve. She recognized the look on that face. Shahanna had seen it often. It was the face of a woman without a man.

She re-read the memo in her mind.

It was in French.

Dear Mademoiselle Dufaux,

Your assignment in Washington D. C. ends next month. Our Embassy in Tehran has need of a Vice Consul. You are promoted to this position, and will transfer to Iran once your replacement is trained. Travel arrangements will be made as soon as you advise this office to that effect.

Washington D. C. Secretariat

Corps Diplomatique Français

Goodbye, America, said Shahanna to herself.

She downed her scotch, ordered another and tried to feel like she had something to celebrate. It didn't work. Her job here may not have been exciting, but America excited her, and D. C. was the capital, the hub upon which the wheels turned, and the restaurants were not too bad. True, there were very few interesting men here, but that would certainly be so much worse, in Tehran, of all places.Of all hell-holes, thought Shahanna.

She had sweated through her degree; then changed majors, and earned another. She had endured Paris, with its insane, anti-Arab prejudice; its crippling university fees and high rents, and its dreary weather most of the time. Her years in Paris had been a prison sentence, as far as Shahanna was concerned, and she had missed everything about Morocco every day: a dazzling blue sky above bleached white beaches, the hubbub of the street markets, and the tiny boats putting out from the shoreline where her village had stood for centuries. It was a long exile, but Shahanna finally achieved the impossible and entered the French diplomatic service, like her French-born Arab father before her. Her mother had been so proud.

Now she was thirty-five, unmarried and overseas.

Which drove her mother crazy.

Shahanna shrank from marriage. She didn't even have affairs any more. That was her choice, here in Washington, with such a limited selection of men. The diplomats here were all the same: snobby, ambitious fools, with very few exceptions, and she had little opportunity to meet any other kind of male. Shahanna had long ago decided that most men saw her, or any other woman, as little more than a life-support system for a vagina. She was holding out for a man who didn't.

Shahanna realized that being well-educated and accomplished didn't help. She had nothing but contempt for a world where one sex ruled. If men were so superior, why was everything in such a mess? At least if she remained single, and alone, she still had her job. Getting married would mean saying goodbye to her career.

A husband who was an Arab, should she finally go home, would be the worst. She would be hidden away, and forbidden to display her beauty out of doors, like being sent to the French Embassy in Iran for life. In Washington D. C. the problems were different, but just as serious in other ways. Women ventured out alone here at their peril. The clubs and bars were a hunting ground for every kind of male predator. And so, because the Bunch of Grapes was a hang-out for her profession, Shahanna came here most nights to avoid unwanted strangers.

And never met anyone new.

She drained her glass and ordered again.

An American might not do, either, she decided morosely. They rarely left their own country, and would never follow a wife who worked overseas. Most Americans hated the French, and hated Arabs. That hardly looked good for Shahanna or her chances of a job in America. She'd be trapped here, being little more than a household appliance during the day; expected to provide dinner and sex at night. Quite a step down for a woman of her capability. International politics was her field. She had a degree in that, and another in physics, which had always fascinated her. But in American terms this counted against her. She was an unpopular majority and a woman. No, if she married an American, she would wind up at home, doing chores, or watching T. V. and eating one box of candy after another. So she might as well be in Morocco, married to a rich man's son, which was her darkest fear.

But Mr. Right was out there.

An American, or a Chinaman, or whatever.

Wouldn't you think?

Shahanna knew roughly what he was like. Where was a man who wanted a long, committed relationship without the shackles of matrimony? Where was a man whose way of making a living did not conflict with hers? A man who could share wealth, happiness and her body without going overboard in one way or another? Did such a man exist? He did not seem to be in Washington D. C., but wherever he was, he certainly did not live in Tehran.

The clock was ticking.

Hurry up, American or Chinese man.

I leave in three or four weeks.

Tehran meant back to Islamic life, even as a senior member of French Embassy staff. It was a dismal prospect: Having to wear the veil in public places, living as a second rate human being again – any trace of Western-style equality stripped away by religious fanatics.

The French were promoting her, and she was glad of that. It meant more money, and increased respect, but mostly from Frenchmen who would spend a lot of time trying to get her into bed. Shahanna was used to that, and knew how to fend them off. She just wanted to guard her virtue anywhere but Iran.

It was no use moping. She reminded herself that Iran counted as hazardous duty, and a tour there ended after one year. Her next transfer would be due before she knew it. Shahanna would leave Tehran, and be every bit as young, attractive and successful as she was now.

And God knew where.

Probably not America.

Her eyes caught movement, and she watched a figure appear in the bar mirror. It was a man about her age and quite good looking. He wore tailored denims with cowboy boots and a turquoise studded belt. Shahanna realized she had seen him in the Bunch of Grapes before. Had he been unattractive, she would have paid her tab and left when he took the seat next to hers. But then she would never have met Bo Clement, fallen deeply in love with him or become an FBI undercover operative. And the world would not have been changed forever.

He introduced himself.

She let him buy her a drink.

She answered all the usual questions:

"Yes, I come here most nights."

My name's Shahanna. From what used to be French Morocco."

"At our Embassy, on Wisconsin Avenue. But I'm leaving Washington soon."

"No, not the Moroccan Embassy. The French."

"My last name is Dufaux."

"My father is half French."

Close up, she found Bo Clement exceedingly hot.

She kept that to herself.

~ ~ ~

Their waiter in the upscale burger place on K Street was yawning as he handed them menus.

Shahanna was impressed, but not unduly, by the sleek, electric-powered Jaguar Clement had borrowed from the motor pool. He admitted right away that it was not his own, as he opened her door to drive over here, and that impressed her more. Forgetting herself, Shahanna had squeezed his arm with an unexpected familiarity. She put it down to all the whiskey she'd had.

She felt a little tipsy, and squinted at her menu

through a hazy three-dimensional fog. Clement didn't seem to mind. He had steadied her at the door, and told her she was beautiful. That was a very good start. Now he closed his menu and said: "Want to split something? The portions here are too much for me."

"Good idea," she said. This man was showing signs of perfection. She hoped the bubble didn't burst too soon. After all, she'd only known him for about an hour and a half. Why were his eyes so dreamy? She said: I don't really eat meat. Just give me some of your French fries." Shahanna ate meat all the time. She just couldn't bring herself to eat hamburger meat."

He ordered and gave back the menus. The waiter returned with two glasses of water and a carafe of Merlot with glasses. Clement sat back and regarded Shahanna. "So what do you at the French Embassy?"

She couldn't be bothered to explain. "Oh . . . a bit of everything."

"And your first language is Arabic?"

"That's right."

"And you have two degrees: World politics and Physics."

"Yes."

She caught his facial expression. He seemed impressed. He said: "And next month you go to Iran, with a promotion."

"Not out of choice. Without that promotion I would kill myself."

"That bad, huh?" he fiddled with his napkin. "Think Iran supports terrorism?"

She snorted. "Are you joking? The Iranian government is a terrorist regime. Of course they support it, and talk out of both sides of their mouth to the Western powers. The Ayatollah, who made himself "Supreme Leader", is good at that."

She wondered at all these questions. Clement's demeanor indicated that she had passed a test, and now she saw what he was doing. He must be some kind of diplomat, or in espionage. Who else ever came to the Bunch of Grapes? Suddenly she realized this was more than a date; it was also work. She said: "The Iranians are bad news, and they still want nukes, at whatever cost. Everybody knows that. But why the third degree? Are you with the CIA?"

"Nothing so grand," he said sheepishly. "I'm attached to an obscure unit of the FBI in Homeland Security. We monitor the Arab nations. Counter-terrorism by another name."

"Nice time to tell me," she said waspishly.

"If I said so before, you'd have dumped me at the bar . . . and . . . I didn't want to be dumped. You're stunning."

She was angry, but pleased. "I see no reason not to dump you now, but you are also . . . stunning." Shahanna could hardly believe she said that. More proof that too much alcohol had loosened her tongue. She hated sounding so eager.

He apologized. "Don't go. I really like you. We won't talk shop."

"Okay, then."

Stunning beats angry every time.

So does a good looking charmer.

His burger came and they divided up the fries. Shahanna recovered her good mood. So he was in Intel and maybe wanted to use her for some undeclared purpose. Well, she was in intelligence, too, and could just as easily use him. And if they had an affair that would be an added bonus. But he must hurry on both counts, she told herself, almost giggling aloud; because very soon she'd be gone. Anyway, she decided, looking at him as a cheetah looks at an antelope, why pass up on a superb American male, just because he's become part of your job?

The yawning waiter was back. "The bar is closing," he said. "Would anyone like something else to drink?"

He offered champagne on the house.

That should get anyone into bed, Shahanna thought. She gave Clement a brazen look, but then heard him say: "No, just the Merlot, thanks."

They ate in near silence. Shahanna thought the fries did not taste very French.

She washed them down with plenty of wine.

She noticed Clement drank sparingly; only two measly glassfuls by the time it was gone.

Was that to preserve his sexual stamina?

Shahanna hoped so.

She was ripe for seduction.

He eventually asked for the check. It came, and she let him pay when he insisted. Shahanna felt too befuddled to argue, or even work out the tip. And his gold card was government issue, he said; so her feelings of guilt went away.

As they left, he said, "There's a man I'd like you to meet; if you're not too tired. Her bedroom fantasy evaporated. She was not too tipsy to realize he was talking about someone important, and work related, at this late hour. Ordinary people do not receive visitors in the middle of the night. "Okay," she said. She might well regret this, but she was curious, and still attracted to Clement.

Maybe he'd seduce her later.

He helped her to the car, although reality was sobering her up. They left the city, taking the White Street Bridge, and joined a jostle of traffic going north, with Clement sticking to the speed limit. He passed signs for Northern Virginia, and Maryland; then turned onto a winding, country road.

Shahanna was feeling even more sober and awake, and a thought popped into her head.

"She said: "You want me to spy for you."

"We might." he took a bend fast, the Jaguar humming quietly. "That's not my call. I was at the Grapes tonight, looking for gossip on something that recently came up, but once I started talking to you, I saw your potential."

Her heart sank. Was he attracted to her or not?

"What makes you think I'd do it."

"There's a fire in your eyes."

"You mean, I might be stupid enough."

"That's not what I think at all. Look, you need to speak to my boss. He will explain everything."

She nearly said, Turn the car around and take me back. But she had come this far, and besides, she was flattered, and intrigued. All the same, she was glad she was sobering up, and would stay on her guard.

She said: "Who are we going to see?"

Clement shook his head. "Introductions later. I phoned him from the Bunch of Grapes, before we went to the restaurant. He said to bring you no matter what time it was."

"Why are you recruiting me?"

"I can't really say. But you'd be undercover."

"Oh, and risk all for America?"

"You're the perfect Arab woman." He turned and gave her a look that was purely personal. A look of such obvious longing that left no doubt Bo Clement was attracted to her.

She smiled. "I'll do it; as long as you think I'm perfect."

He didn't answer. They passed a sign in a hedgerow that said "Private Property", and the car slowed down. They turned onto an uneven driveway and bumped along for some distance, then stopped at the barred gates of a large gabled house. A speaker phone was attached to the mail-box. Cement's electric window wound its way down.

"We're both here," was all he said.

The gates swung open. The Jaguar crunched onto pale gravel and stopped in a circle of light near the front door. A man came out of the shadows and peered through Clement's open window at Shahanna. "Hello," he said.

Clement looked up at his boss but spoke to the woman. "I want you to meet my boss, Deputy Director Heathcote."

An imposing figure, Shahanna thought. Tall, with broad shoulders and a military bearing, even in a tie-less shirt with the collar unbuttoned. This was further emphasized by the cropped gray hair and shoes that shone like new, even in the limited porch lighting. He had an open, honest face, as a certain type of American does, and her instinct said she could trust him.

She already trusted Clement, so she relaxed a little.

Heathcote came around the car, opened her door and helped her out. He led them into the house, pointing out rooms as they passed, like a host receiving guests for dinner. His home was flawlessly neat, and seemed never-ending, furnished with unexpectedly modern taste. He finally sat them down at a marble table in the kitchen, which was an austere arrangement of stainless steel and countless ebony cabinets. It was equipped like the kitchen of a space-age gourmet chef, with gadgets and knives, iron pots and crockery of the very best.

He served fresh coffee.

Shahanna found him adorable.

Helping himself to cream, Clement said: "Anything from the Israelis, sir?"

"No, nothing on Bethlehem. Or your Jerusalem murders."

Their openness surprised Shahanna. Her French colleagues spoke in more guarded terms, even among themselves, and never said anything in front of outsiders. Clement's question, however, like Heathcote's answer, was no great surprise. The whole world was talking about this bomb that killed Americans in Bethlehem. America was expected to react strongly, and even the French were sympathetic. Shahanna also knew about the killings of Amir Affhad and Oman Ben Salim, but not in much detail, because compared to Bethlehem it was of little or no importance. At least, that was the opinion of the French Embassy, and rightly or wrongly, they considered themselves expert in matters of this nature.

She decided to play it dumb. "Murder in Jerusalem? Isn't that a normal, everyday occurrence?"

Clement said: "This was different."

"Oh, different how?"

It was Heathcote who answered. "Don't bullshit us. You're in French consular Intel. You know all about this."

Shahanna reddened. They were bound to have a file on her, and he had read it, probably tonight.

Not quite so adorable.

He refilled her coffee cup and slid an ashtray closer to his side of the table. He was already on his second or third Camel.

Clement stood up. I'll leave you both to it. If you need me, I'm asleep in front of the T. V." He yawned convincingly and headed off for the living room. Shahanna guessed this was a prearranged, tactful withdrawal."

She looked expectantly at Heathcote, awaiting his next move.

He asked her bluntly: "Why did you agree to this meeting?"

"Oh, no," she said. "You talk; I listen."

Heathcote looked at her, slightly amused, as if seeing her for the first time. Now he knew she was nobody's fool. "Okay," he said finally. "America is under siege by men who have no names. I don't mean the leaders. They have household names, and you see them on T. V. They couldn't deliver a bomb, or fire a gun, if you paid them. They're rich, old men who were educated here, or in the U. K. — then decided we're satanic, and have to be destroyed. No, not them. I'm talking about those they persuade to do the dirty work for them. Angry young men and women, victims of the time they live in, and victims of those old men, who exploit them. Terrorists are created in camps, like a product. They have no names or faces, and we don't know who they are until they strike. Those unknown names and faces are what we're after. We have to go over there and find them, before they do America harm. But that's something we can't do for ourselves, because we can't pass for native. We need you for that. You and others like you."

"You have Arab immigrants. Why not use them?"

Heathcote said frankly: "It took too long for us to learn to trust them. Some are being recruited, but an American upbringing is hard to hide, and those from overseas, like yourself, always do better."

"So you want genuine Arabs. You need me to turn traitor."

No, of course not. France is not an enemy."

Don't be so sure, she thought.

But Shahanna would not be betraying France. She was not French; that had not been what she meant, and Heathcote knew it. Her job, if she agreed, would be to betray her own Kind. Heathcote pretended to think she meant the French, and she decided to let him get away with it. Because betraying the monsters he described, monsters she'd hated all her life, was no betrayal at all.

"So why are you here?" he repeated.

She had a sudden urge to tell the truth. "I hate the French. And I hate extremist Islam, because of what it does to women like my mother. I detest their stupid preaching; their stupid rules, and the way they poison the minds of our young people. I can't stand the idea of being in Iran, and having to put up with French bullshit and Islamic bullshit at the same time. And you know, as I do, that Islamic terrorism is simply a violent extension of Islamic bullshit. They're waging war in the name of God. All religions do it. Ours is worse than most."

He didn't speak, but she had his attention.

Shahanna said defiantly: "Well?"

"Well, what?"

Shahanna wondered what he was thinking. Had she blown any chance at this job, to escape the French, and avoid going to Tehran? But then, she realized, Heathcote just intended to use her in some other Arab country, and put her life in danger. So who cared what he thought? Finally, she said: "Mr. Heathcote, I don't think I'm really what you're looking for."

"Clement does. And I agree."

She looked at him. She was seized by an impulse to shock. "He looks like a great fuck – or I wouldn't be here."

He raised his eyebrows. She arched hers. There was complete silence; then they both burst out laughing. The interview was briefly suspended, and they were two people with the same sense of humor, sharing a joke that either one of them could have made. When their laughter subsided, he raised his coffee cup, toasting her gravely. They had found a common bond. Heathcote lit yet another cigarette, and the atmosphere between them was greatly improved.

He finally spoke. "Clement is street-smart and tough; not just a pretty face. He's also extremely experienced. So when he breaks off an investigation to tell me about you, I know enough to pay attention. He says you're just what we need: bright, self-reliant and used to getting your own way. In other words, a survivor. I see that in you, too, just since you've been here. No, Miss Dufaux, I'm afraid you have it wrong. You are exactly what we're looking for."

She was flattered. For some reason this prompted her to say: "And I'm beautiful, too."

"Right. Men are distracted by that. You don't know what an advantage that is; or, more likely you do. And you're fluent in the language of those who want to attack us. And you have the right education. We can pass you off to the bad guys as a nuclear physicist; which makes you highly desirable. Now ... you can stick with the French, handing out hors d'oeuvres in yet another embassy, or you come over to us. But I warn you: We are desperate for Arab undercovers; so when we find them, they fight on the front line. Are you ready for that?"

Shahanna laughed. "In a trench, with a machine-gun? I was hoping for something less stressful."

"Like What?"

"I don't know . . . Seduce the Supreme Leader, and prove he's a terrorist with a tape-recorder hidden in my bosom."

Heathcote laughed again. Shahanna thought, Listen to me – joking my way into a suicide mission."

Heathcote said: "Our front-line has no trenches. Those fighting for us have no supply lines, and very little support. They fight alone, or in small, isolated teams. Can you do that, Miss Dufaux?"

Oh, yes. Just give me the chance, she thought. I'll fight like a hell-cat, against the pigs you're talking about. I hate the very sight of them – and with your help, I can kick them in the balls.

Heathcote said: "Clement would go, too, due to your inexperience. I assume you have no objection?"

"Of course not," she said. "A safety net."

And a sexual reward, she promised herself.

"Fitting him to your cover story will take some time. He's American. You, on the other hand . . ."

"Are a foreigner," she said. "And need a watch-dog."

"Not true. I was going to say you are no problem, but hating all things American is the norm where you're going. Clement will stand out like a neon sign. It won't be easy but we'll come up with something convincing for him. We have experienced people who do nothing else but create credible backgrounds – then plant so much evidence that the new identity can't be broken."

"Portray him as an American terrorist?"

Heathcote nodded. "Even Clement won't recognize himself."

She decided to ask him outright. "So have I got the job? When do I start?"

"You'll have to give up French citizenship."

"No problem. If you make me American." Was she was pushing too hard? He might say no.

"A US passport – tomorrow."

Her heart leaped in her chest. Oh, they wanted her badly.

Heathcote's eyes became serious. "People die, working for me."

"Do I get buried in Arlington Cemetery?" It was a terrible joke. But the danger of all this was just sinking in."

"Not buried at all, if I have anything to do with it. Let's get back to your most impressive feature from a terrorist standpoint: Your degree in physics. We upgrade it with a crash course in atomic weapons, and give you a background in nuclear physics. Next we add marksmanship training. Once we turn you loose, if it's all done right, Al Qaeda will snap you up."

"You had this planned already."

"Yes, we did. Waiting for someone like you."

Shahanna was hardly surprised. She knew that terrorists with nuclear capability was America's worst fear. She felt a sense of satisfaction at being picked for this. If this was her destiny; so be it. Better than evading ass-grabbing Frenchmen until she got her pension.

She smiled at Heathcote. "Where do I sign?"

For an answer he stood up and called to Clement that he should take her home. Then, with quaint good manners, he stepped round the table to shake Shahanna's hand. He welcomed her to the team, whoever they were, and confirmed that by tomorrow she would indeed be an American citizen. Then he excused himself, saying he had a lot of phone calls to make. He left the room as Clement came in.

Shahanna guessed that a security check was undoubtedly under way on her. FBI phone, fax and e-mails would be heavily employed, especially if Heathcote was in a hurry. People in France, Morocco, and here in Washington would be asked about her – about her political beliefs; her social background; her financial standing; and last but not least, her sexual preferences. Shahanna did not mind; she had been through it all before with the French. But deep down, it made her uneasy, and she hoped it would be done quickly and cleanly. A lot of the questions asked would be embarrassing, for her, and her friends and family who were asked; although the answers would be exactly what the Americans wanted to hear.

She closed her mind to it and stood up to thank Clement for bringing her here in the first place.

She said: "What do I tell the French?"

"Goodbye, basically."

"But not about tonight."

He laughed. "Well, no. Just your resignation will do."

"This is a big thing for me."

"Oh, I know it is."

"I'll make you proud."

His face was serious. He looked at her as if they had known each for other forever. "We know you will. That's why you got the job."

Then he explained a few things about Heathcote. Having served in Viet Nam, the Deputy had been one of the first to accept the futility of hundreds of thousands of troops trying to defeat a few Muslim fanatics. He shot to prominence with a memo that found its way to the White House. "It's a gang war," he wrote bluntly. "We need gangs of our own, highly trained in counter-intelligence and killing. And we need a lot of them, planted in any country where Al Qaeda hangs it hat."

Shahanna was joining Clement's gang.

She thought: I'm an American. How marvelous. She said: "I have you to thank for this."

"You're welcome. You'll be the best, I know it."

She gave him her sexiest look. "Darling, you have no idea."

He laughed again. "Come on. Let's drive you home."

Tonight's show was over, she decided. A not-so-romantic drive into the country, two cups of coffee, one pledge of total allegiance and no sign of lovemaking to come. At least not tonight. Well, there was plenty of time. They would be working together, even if it was as dangerous as hell.

They got in the car and drove back the way they had come.

She began making up lies for the French.

~ ~ ~

Lucifer, as Scott Anderson, wore a tuxedo. It was adorned with medal ribbons he did not earn or deserve. But this White House function, a buffet dinner for five hundred guests, demanded such formality. Besides, people had tolerated Lucifer's bad behavior for two thousand years, due to the spell he cast over those who came into direct contact with him. He could wear whatever he liked.

Most of those invited were high-ranking military, which was one reason why Scott Anderson had made every effort to be here. Six other reasons were warheads from Utah. Lucifer's relationship with armies of every nation, and with one empire after the other, had sustained him for centuries. The devil could not exist without conflict. He thrived on bloodshed and death.

America was tailor-made for his needs. A young country founded upon the highest ideals of mankind. Ideals that were only too easily perverted. Lucifer was quick to turn the sin of pride into excessive patriotism. He had kept them at war, or on the brink of it, since they freed themselves from British rule. Now, beginning a new century, they found themselves dealing with all four Horsemen of the Apocalypse: War, Pestilence, Hunger and Famine.

A powerful nation on a hair trigger.

And the world quaked in fear.

Lucifer couldn't have been more pleased.

~ ~ ~

That notwithstanding, he had come to the White house in a bad mood. He received a message from Lung Chiang before flying here on the shuttle from New York. Lucifer was furious to learn that Gabriel knew about the operation in Utah, and knew so much about his plans altogether; to a point where the devil wondered how much was leaked by Lung Chiang, whose weakness for money, like his fondness for rich, stir-fried food, was well known.

The news that General Renkov had shot himself made matters worse. Now Lung Chiang and the Koreans were in an even stronger position. On top of that, the Iranians never shut up. Their hate-crazed President came yapping on the phone every day, always asking the same thing: Where were the six devices he and the Saudis had been promised? He was never rude or disrespectful to Scott Anderson, because this Iranian leader was a demon, and knew who Anderson really was. But his phone calls were a nuisance. And a nuisance that could not be ignored, because without him there would be no nuclear attack on America.

And no Armageddon.

And that was not all, Lucifer thought angrily. It seemed the Angel Gabriel was also in Washington, according to Lung Chiang, and that was more cause for concern. Lucifer came here tonight to meet his Air Force General, the demon providing missiles from his command in Utah, and having Gabriel in town was unsettling.

To say the least.

The devil helped himself to salmon from a silver tray. The food, like everything in the White House, was the very best. Lucifer circulated, listening to the talk of Generals, Admirals and their staff officers as they ate and drank. He heard nothing of importance. Not even the dumbest of them wanted to reveal secrets here, but Lucifer hoped alcohol would soon intervene and change that. If not, he could always read a few minds, but he was not yet in the mood.

He needed a drink.

On the nearest table was a Burgundy imported from France. He poured himself most of a glass, and smelled its bouquet. He sipped. It was good, seeming almost chewy, with a richness that pleased him. Lucifer drank more deeply, filled his glass to the brim and moved away.

Everyone clapped as the President entered. It was a peculiar custom, having begun in the Nixon years, but Lucifer was used to it by now, and he joined in, The applause went on until the Commander-in-Chief raised his hands to stop it. Then he vanished from view, as those nearest to him swarmed around.

A certain stiffness was in the air, due to Christiansen's arrival. It seemed unlikely that alcohol would loosen any tongues for a while. The devil sighed, It was time for some good, old-fashioned mind control.

He took his wine into the throng, greeting people he knew, and shaking hands with those to whom he was introduced, smiling as he went. He flattered some, to make them talk, and set traps for others, asking cleverly phrased questions which had the hypnotic power to extract truth. Lucifer soon had a growing stash of secrets that would make the whole evening worthwhile.

He possessed all the power of Gabriel, or any other angel, although he was unable to direct it at angels. His power had been perverted, to make it stronger, and it was based on evil. The devil used evil to confuse and control people. Those meeting him for the first time were charmed. He often made them believe they had known him for years and owed him favors. Some of the things he demanded as repayment were unbelievable. Murders were committed, great fortunes were stolen and nations were betrayed. It depended on Lucifer's needs at the time.

There was a string-quartet playing softly in an alcove, but no one paid them much attention. Lucifer found a

Colonel with an Airborne Cavalry unit, and started pumping him. This man soon revealed a new wave of secret drone attacks in northern Pakistan, a wonderful lead story for tomorrow, but the devil found himself listening with only half an ear and wondering why his Utah commander had not yet arrived. The cavalry officer was dumped, rudely left in mid-sentence, as soon as he'd told Scott Anderson everything he knew.

The devil made his way out to the reception area and entrance. A spit and polish Marine Sergeant stood by a card table littered with discarded invitations and half empty drinks. Lucifer said: "Did General Bertram arrive yet? He's coming from N. O.R.A.D." The sergeant ran a finger down the list on his clipboard. Then he shook his head. General Bertram's name had not been checked off. He was either late or not coming.

Lucifer went back inside and fumed with frustration. He nodded and smiled as before, but he felt distracted, and no longer in the mood for human beings. They spoke to him but he hardly heard. He was swept away on a wave of fury. How dare General Bertram simply not show up? Lucifer was specifically here to speak to him face to face; there were aspects of the Utah plan that were too sensitive to be handled any other way. Moreover the two of them had reservations at a stylish, out of the way place with private rooms and expensive girls, for later this evening. So where was Bertram, and why had he not sent word if he was delayed?

Lucifer's thoughts were interrupted when someone addressed him by name, and he turned to look, realizing they did not use the name Anderson, but actually called him Lucifer.

It was Gabriel, in an Air Force uniform.

The angel said dryly: "Not getting any younger, I see. Evil shenanigans do take their toll, don't they?"

Lucifer controlled his anger. "Well, what a surprise!"

"Come now. Lung Chiang practically directed us both to Washington with his warnings. We both knew we'd meet."

"What if I just destroy you? Here and now."

"You'd also destroy the White House."

"That, too, has a certain appeal."

"Not underhanded enough for you. Besides, someone would be sure to notice. It's quite an important place."

"You're making jokes? The Archangel equivalent of fiddling while this modern version of Rome burns? This whole city will soon be gone, and you know it." The devil kept his voice low, not wanting to be overheard, still controlling his anger. Here was Gabriel, his most detested enemy, openly mocking him in the presence of the President and the cream of America's military. Not only was that infuriating, but why was Gabriel so cocky?

Gabriel answered that. He smiled. "General Bertram had a heart attack on the Freeway. His driver took him to the emergency room, but there was nothing to be done. Your home-grown missile supply won't be coming. Tonight or any night. I'm letting you know, in case you want to send flowers."

"I hope this is another joke."

"Your N O R A D Connection is dead." Gabriel was still smiling, but Lucifer felt the angel's anger; it matched his own.

Gabriel said: "Autopsy will show advanced symptoms of angina. No one will be surprised; I added it to the

General's medical file. He suffered little pain – at least the human part of him. Your demon was another matter. It had been in Bertram for a long time, and it went screaming into the darkness, in agony from the shock, when I yanked it out of him."

Lucifer was devastated but concealed it. "How did you know about Bertram?" he said. He and the General had been very careful. No public meetings, no word uttered by phone and nothing written down.

"His adjutant works for me."

Another fucking angel. Lucifer silently cursed the heavens. He tried to recover by saying: "I'll get nukes by other means. You can't win."

"That's what you think," said Gabriel.

Then he vanished.

Lucifer was left standing there. He looked around, afraid the angel may have been seen by everyone else. But everything was as before. No one paid the devil – or the place where Gabriel had stood – any attention. Lucifer regained his composure and melted into the crowd. He had no wish to attract attention; especially not in front of the President of the United States.

The President was an unawakened angel, protected in the general sense by a screen of his wide-awake, heavenly brothers; flitting around the White House grounds during the day, and forming a giant canopy, screening off the entire building, to keep him safe at night.

Which was why Gabriel never approached him directly.

And why Lucifer didn't dare.

The President was guarded night and day by a young female angel named Effra, She'd been fending off demons and Lucifer's fallen angels since the latter stages of the election campaign, when she thwarted an assassin. Effra had extraordinary strength and powers, even as guardian-angels went, and was regarded by her kind as ready to take on Lucifer himself.

Another reason the devil kept his distance.

There was no point in staying at this boring White House function any longer, or going to a high-class brothel alone. Lucifer decided to go somewhere he had planned to visit later this week. It was a long time since he committed any serious mischief in Israel, and some hot sun and palm trees might soothe his nerves. He snapped his fingers and transported himself to a ticket counter at Washington's Reagan Airport. He could still make the last shuttle back to New York, with a connection to Tel Aviv.

No one at the White House missed him.

Or remembered he was there.

At JFK Lucifer's tuxedo transformed into a lightweight outfit for the climate he would encounter tomorrow. He added an overnight bag for appearances; although, like hand-luggage carried by Gabriel, the contents would never be unpacked. The devil had little use for such things.

He was incapable of sleep.

Lung Chiang had said Gabriel was using air travel to conserve energy. It made sense for Lucifer to do the same. Angels were all over the outside of his house, sucking his power. That meant the final battle with Gabriel, which was starting, would take everything the devil had.

~ ~ ~

Fortunately El Al had an overnight flight.

Lucifer was a major enemy of Israel, but he flew with their airline all the time. El Al's seats were always full, because they had dealt with hi-jacking, and worse, for years, and hardly ever got attacked any more. They were safer than anything else in the air. It amused Lucifer to use them. Besides, a jam-packed plane gave the privacy he preferred, although he also relied on hypnotism to avoid attention. This was partly because Lucifer was developing an old man's tendency to think out loud, and much of it was obscene, or homicidal.

The jet-liner whisked the devil past the Statue of Liberty and swung out over the scrappy, sunken islands that surround the city's eastern approach, chasing after the next sunrise but doomed never to catch it. Lucifer sat in reduced lighting, amid those sleeping or trying to sleep. His thoughts focused on Gabriel, Lung Chiang and the Prime Minister of Israel. Both angels must be destroyed; Gabriel as soon as possible, and Lung Chiang once America was reduced to ash. Israel's Premier would also be exploited, but he might well survive, depending on performance. It was never too late for Lucifer to slip a demon into any world leader who showed promise.

El Al Flight 507 droned on through the night.

No one on board seemed to notice that a hideous old man in Tourist Class spent the night muttering, smoking cigars, and blowing clouds of foul-smelling smoke down the aisle.

They landed twelve hours later.

~ ~ ~

Tel Aviv was not Jerusalem. It was modern and cosmopolitan, with artistic office blocks, wide boulevards and designer clothing stores. It had all the chic of a European fashion center, with the bustle of a Bazaar as its driving force. There were armed police and soldiers everywhere, but mostly in the shadows. The parliamentary buildings of the Knesset towered high, in contrast to the stubby architecture all around it. People on the street were well-groomed and affluent-looking. The entire city was a showcase, showing the world that the State of Israel was alive and kicking, and it intended to stay that way. If a terrorist bomb went off, special construction crews arrived with the fire, rescue and ambulance services. Broken glass was replaced, new paving stones were laid, and any scorched walls or street signs were re-painted – all in less time than it took to evacuate the dead and wounded. Nothing was left to show what had just happened. Life went on as before.

Lucifer knew why the tiny Hebrew nation did this. It was a defense mechanism, caused by two thousand years of persecution, most of which had been inspired by him. Thousands killed for sport in Europe by Crusaders on their way to the Holy Land, and later, the obscene spectacle of the Spanish Inquisition – torturing and burning Jews in the name of the Catholic Church. Another six million butchered in the Nazi Holocaust; yet they kept coming back for more. Since rebirth in 1948, the Jewish State had taken on all-comers, from a dozen hostile Arab neighbors to Idi Amin, deranged dictator of Uganda, who fed his political enemies to crocodiles. Even Lucifer found that impressive. Actually the devil never minded Israel's refusal to submit to his will; it made a worthy adversary. But, of course, he would destroy them in the end.

Their own prophecies said so.

~ ~ ~

Lucifer rode into Tel Aviv on a bus, cigar in hand, watching the sun climb slowly between the darkly silhouetted buildings of the suburbs, sharing a jolting ride with sales clerks, cleaners, office workers, waiters and waitresses, making their way into a city soon to be consumed by overpowering heat. Some were eating breakfast, despite the lurching of the vehicle. Some dozed in their seats. The rest chattered loudly in Hebrew, Arabic and all the languages of central and eastern Europe. The devil amused himself by giving most of them smallpox. It was time Israel had something else to worry about beside their Arab enemies. A widespread and deadly epidemic should add nicely to the coming chaos, once Lucifer got his claws into the Prime Minister.

He got off near the Knesset. At this early hour no politicians would be here, so he found a cafe and ordered coffee and a newspaper. The waitress brought both. The paper was full of articles and opinions on a forthcoming referendum on education, noting that the Prime Minister would be opening a new high school this morning, somewhere on the edge of town. Lucifer read slowly and drank sparingly. By eight o' clock the streets were full to overflowing. Pedestrians risked their lives, dodging cars and taxis driven with a ferocity that defied imagination. The devil joined the throng and headed for the ministry buildings. Halfway there he stepped into an alley, to become a wraith of gray smoke that floated off in the direction he had been going. Lucifer could no longer become completely invisible.

It was part of the price he paid.

~ ~ ~

At nine o' clock, as electric gates swung open for the Prime Minister's limousine and escorting convoy to leave his heavily guarded enclosure, a smoky shadow floated unnoticed into the roomy lead car. Israel's elected leader, Mochel Arayan, was talking on his cell phone, with a cigarette burning unevenly in the door ashtray beside him, as he jotted notes on a large yellow pad in his lap. Two Mossad men sat opposite, with Uzi automatics across their knees. They were routinely scanning the streets and rooftops on either side of the car.

The Prime Minister was a heavy-set man of sixty-two, with silk-like hair that had been white for years. He thanked the caller, whoever it was, said a courteous goodbye and hung up; then finished his notes in a neat Hebraic script. He sat back and lit a fresh cigarette, stubbing out the first. He seemed deep in thought.

The thoughts came from Lucifer, a smoky shadow in an empty corner, projected into the mind of Mochel Arayan so expertly that the Premier accepted them as his own. And as the gleaming black car, and its cavalcade, gathered speed, Lucifer fed him one idea that was an absolute zinger: In revenge for the slaughter in Bethlehem, why not a nuclear strike? Israel had the weapons but never thought to use them. What Syria had done was extreme provocation. Wasn't it time for a change of policy? Furthermore the rumor was that Syria had improved chemical weapons. The implications were horrific: Missiles carrying a virus like smallpox, for example, could wipe out the Jewish State in months. A preemptive missile launch was the only answer to that. Lucifer made this last idea the most attractive.

Prime Minister Arayan was surprised at himself: Ideas he always found repugnant seemed suddenly to make good sense.

The limousine reached the high school and its

passenger mounted the front steps with security detail and hangers-on close on his heels. He was immediately greeted by local dignitaries and their hangers-on. Mr. Arayan shook a lot of hands, made a moving speech and planted a tree.

Lucifer floated away unnoticed.

He, too, had planted something.

It would bear fruit very soon.

~ ~ ~

Within hours of Mochel Arayan's return to parliament, he and other members of the Knesset debated hotly around a table in a spacious, sunlit room with bullet-proofing applied to its windows.

But windows are no defense against the power of suggestion. Beyond the glass, the hazy cloud that was Lucifer hovered in mid-air, sending warlike thoughts into normally balanced minds. Harsh courses of action dominated conversation inside the room. The devil pumped rashly insane ideas into one speaker after another – aware that the effect would last no more than a few days. Hypnotism has its limits. But the main thing, Lucifer knew, was for these men to commit to a hot-headed plan before they had time to think. It didn't matter if they regretted it later. The devil saw it as a good sign that this political wrangling, consisting of little more than one aggressive speech after another, had lasted for almost two hours. Eventually, however, it seemed that enough had been said, and a vote was called for.

A young secretary passed out slips. She had pretty dark eyes. None of the voters smiled at her. There was a heavy silence, as pens wrote on paper, and then the slips were collected. They were counted and checked twice.

It was unanimous.

A nuclear strike against Syria.

CHAPTER FIVE

GABRIEL WORE THE SHABBY CLOTHES and baseball cap of Artis Brown and stood next to the security barrier at the installation in Alexandria where Clement worked: A black man handing out pamphlets on veterans wounded in Iraq and asking for a donation. Most people gave him a dollar.

The situation with Lucifer had heated up. The angels at his New York residence remained in place, but there was little sign as yet that the devil's power had in any way diminished. Angels in Tel Aviv reported that Lucifer had been there. As a result Israel convened a war-council, and the Syrian camp involved in the Bethlehem bombing was to be taken out by a limited missile attack. There was also talk of wiping out the Syrian capital of Damascus.

Gabriel expected America would prevent that.

He was here to find out.

He needed a human body to get him inside this complex. The angel could enter by going through walls, but that would not log him on to the computer system. You needed passwords for that. Passwords that changed daily. Gabriel wanted an FBI operative with a top secret clearance or better. What had happened at the Israeli Knesset would either be in the data banks here, or at CIA headquarters. Gabriel usually found the Feds more up to date. That was why he was trying them first.

A car stopped at the security gate. The driver was a graying man with the air of a retired soldier who now pursued a more intellectual existence. He had eyes that had seen violent death, and a set of the mouth that said he was tired of it. His face was open and honest, under hair so short his scalp showed. The identity card he showed the gate guard bore the name Heathcote and he was a departmental director. Gabriel moved closer. He became invisible, blanking out Artis Brown in everyone's mind. It was time to rock and roll.Gabriel shifted into the American's bulky frame.

And looked out at the world with Heathcote's eyes.

An ugly, frightening world, inhabited by those who cared for its safety, by those who fought off despair every day, forcing themselves to believe that good wins over evil. They did not enjoy what they did. They were driven by higher ideals. It made Heathcote perfect for Gabriel.

The angel knew just how he felt.

And Heathcote had the very highest security clearance.

Gabriel had none at all.

Angels gather information by various means. They watch and they listen, and that produces most of what they need to know. Some things are heard in high places, Gabriel had just visited both White House and Kremlin, but sometimes a remark from a factory worker is enough. Today a medical orderly in Tel Aviv whispered to his wife that an entire hospital wing had been cordoned off – to conceal a fast spreading outbreak of smallpox. An Israeli army major told his mistress that all leave for missile units was canceled, and Gabriel's people in Tel Aviv said the Knesset was still in emergency session. The Minister of Health had been summoned, and asked some serious questions.

So now Gabriel had to deal with a plague as well as the

threat of nuclear warfare. Lucifer had been busy.

Gabriel had to take action, and needed more information. The odd spoken word was no longer enough. He needed the big picture.

Inside the FBI building were computers that held secrets. Some of these were today's secrets. The daily reports, messages, satellite-feeds and domestic and foreign intelligence that was systematically decoded, analyzed, collated and filed. They made a complete graphic of current events, and Gabriel needed to access it. The only thing keeping him out was iron-clad security.

That was where Heathcote came in.

Once logged on, he would look where Gabriel told him.

~ ~ ~

Heathcote's office was a wasteland of neglected paperwork and sparse furniture cluttered with top secret files. It smelled of tobacco smoke and recycled air. Heathcote sat down at the keyboard and typed in his log-on code with one finger. Fifteen minutes later, Gabriel had what he wanted.

Tel Aviv was under quarantine.

Knesset members were evacuating.

America had vetoed the missile attack on Syria.

But they had given Mochel Arayan the go-ahead for a conventional attack on the offending terrorist camp by Israeli ground troops.

For Gabriel, that was graver and more immediate than a smallpox outbreak. Any form of attack on a Muslim country by Israel would put the world in crisis. What was the American President thinking? This was the same nonsensical idea that he concocted after that cabinet session in the White House, with Gabriel listening in. Why was Christiansen so determined to go this route? The answer, realized Gabriel, was very simple: This way America's hands stayed clean, but Christiansen looked strong for backing the operation. Everyone knew such an attack was impossible without Washington's approval. Gabriel admired the President's subtlety.

Not so surprising, in an unawakened angel.

All this meant that Gabriel must save Syria first, although people were already suffering and dying in Tel Aviv.

There was no time for air travel.

Gabriel snapped his fingers.

~ ~ ~

Seconds later, his brother Michael fell into step with him on a street in Damascus, ancient capital of the Syrians.

The Archangel Michael knew without asking what Gabriel wanted to know. "One hundred are coming, and they'll be here soon," he said. "I pulled all the guardian angels from an ocean cruise liner."

Gabriel grunted. "That's more than enough."

Michael was now a bearded Arab with stained teeth. He and Gabriel wore much the same clothing. Not the smartly creased linen suits of Europeans, but the rough robes of street peddlers or pick-pockets. They blended in like Artis Brown in New York. They wore down-at-heel slippers, their hair thick and unkempt under ragged head-cloths, and both had knives tucked into their belts.

Two criminals on the prowl.

Or insurgents at a Syrian training camp.

The plan for tomorrow was Michael's. It was calculated to curb violence and save life, both Arab and

Israeli.

Gabriel's talent lay more in the other direction.

Michael headed a vast army of guardian angels, a celestial presence spread across the world to protect mortals – mostly from themselves. The hundred he was bringing, to prevent outright slaughter tomorrow, were all old hands. Tonight, here in Damascus, they would wear clothes like Michael and his brother. But tomorrow in the desert, only half of them would dress that way, mixing with real terrorists in the confusion, while the other half became part of the attacking force, wearing Israeli uniform – and firing Uzis loaded with blanks. That was Michael's plan in a nutshell.

The two angels followed narrow, winding streets, the sun setting behind them, until they came upon what remained of the old city wall.

Michael said: "Who do we save?"

Gabriel had thought about this. He had considered letting any demons on either side die. Then, of course, there were Islamic extremists, and men on the other side, who were guilty of evil acts and deserved to die. They would hardly be missed. But that would do more harm than good. In the feud between these two cultures, death only led to more death. Gabriel knew this was just what the devil was counting on. He turned to look at Michael. "Save them all," he said.

"Both sides?"

"Yes."

"Thank God." Michael was clearly relieved.

They came to an old, ruined buttress. Angels began to materialize out of thin air, still wearing the odd-ball clothing of shipboard tourism, which transformed into local garb as they touched the ground. Like most angels, they looked like ordinary men and women, except they were rather tall.

"We seem to be ready," said Michael.

Gabriel looked around, recognizing some of the faces, briefly sharing his brother's sense of relief. "Choose your two groups," he said.

~ ~ ~

The Israelis attacked at daybreak.

The campsite was an isolated spot, excellent for concealment but not easy to defend from a commando-style raid. It stood on gritty, rolling sand dunes, broken by a stretch of flat terrain dotted with scrub, upon which the tents had been pitched in ragged rows, for the most part coated with dust. It was as far from water as from Damascus, and that far again from the nearest oasis; so clear plastic barrels of water came in by truck every day. The Jihad could not have found a more remote location.

The concept of discipline is unknown in desert lands, which is why transgressors are often maimed or beheaded. This camp had no discipline, either. No guards had been posted, and a boom-box was playing outside, having emitted pop-music, loudly, all night, breaking security and all the laws of Islam.

This radio served as an electronic beacon for the six Israeli 'Stealth' helicopters as they came in.

There would soon be audible engine noise, as they swooped in to land. That was inevitable. The Israeli commander realized this, and dropped off a pair of Humvees at one thousand meters out, to race ahead and cover his approach. The two ground vehicles jolted into rapid motion, throwing up plumes of sand.

Each had a light machine gun mounted on its hood.

Gabriel and his angels hung invisible above the crooked tent lines, squinting to see the hovering black aircraft as they came forward with a gigantic desert sun rising behind them.

The only sounds came from the camp:

There was the music and a drone of mixed snoring.

And somewhere a goat bleated.

No movement at all. Except the wind blowing sand in clouds across the campsite.

The helicopters drew nearer, and pilots and gun-crews could be clearly seen, faces blurred by their dark helmet-visors.

More sand whipped up from the beating of the rotor blades.

And now there was incoming noise:

Whupp . . . Whupp . . . Whupp . . . Whupp!

It grew louder until it seemed deafening.

Still no one in the camp stirred.

Gabriel hoped no news-teams were flying in to capture the action on film. The last thing he needed was T. V. coverage. Angels can't be seen or recorded on camera, but what they were about to do would be clear enough once the footage was analyzed; because the action of angels can be seen but not explained, and that was a problem. Gabriel cringed at the thought of millions of viewers watching the events about to unfold, then the so-called experts, and the T. V. pundits and religious cranks, all churning out explanations until one of them came close to the truth.

Gabriel shrugged. If a camera crew was here, so be it. Cameras overturn onto the sand, exposed film cannot withstand desert sun, and satellite feeds are easily disrupted. Nothing would get back to the network. He called over a couple of angels and told them to take care of it if necessary.

At that moment the stark shape of a Humvee breasted a rise. Its gun swiveled left and right, seeking a target. It was joined by the second Humvee, also scanning the area, its machine gun turning with the rhythm of an experienced gunner. Both vehicles were now very close. The early sunlight glinted on their camouflage paint. They slowed at the fringe of the camp All six helicopters dipped and formed up behind them, hovering at about thirty feet.

Gabriel saw dozens of airborne troops sliding down weighted rope lines to the ground.

More kept coming.

Angels materialized among them.

None of the Israelis noticed.

The Humvees revved up. Soldiers and angels jumped aboard, clinging to every handhold. An order was given. The two transports raced forward, the rest of the ground force following at a fast run.

Someone in the camp finally heard them.

There was a panicky shout.

Heads popped out of tent flaps, and Gabriel thought, A good thing we came; this would have been a massacre. What we need is a lot of luck and no nasty surprises. God help us all.

The Humvees had slowed, disgorging men.

Those coming behind were fanning out.

The first Humvee passed the outer tent line.

Arabs poured into the open, yelling warnings and curses and pulling on clothing as they ran. Most had weapons in their hands, but were unable to bring them to bear. They stumbled at the enemy like slow-moving targets.

One of the Humvees fired a burst, but shot high, as a uniformed angel nudged an Israeli elbow at the right moment. The bullets sprayed harmlessly into the air. A few feet from Gabriel, terrorists began fighting back. Angels on the opposing side stepped into the path of every bullet. Some fell, convincingly dead, and others played wounded, while still more ran forward to take more shots, or return fire with blanks.

More angels came out of Arab tents in Arab clothing, carrying bogus weapons. They sprinted forward to mingle with the defenders, who were at last recovering from their initial shock. Their gunfire became heavier and more accurate, for many of these terrorists were excellent marksmen.

Their bullets magically ceased to exist.

Now in a wicked crossfire, the Israelis advanced with amazingly low casualties, none of whom were Israeli. A few more angels had fallen to the ground, making things look authentic.

A young Pakistani in a flak jacket threw a grenade at point blank range. An angel threw herself down on it. The impact threw here into the air, but of course without harm. She fell back to the sand, another obliging corpse.

Gabriel saw that a Century News team, the cream of Scott Anderson's empire, was indeed present. They filmed only briefly, however, then realized that their equipment was failing to function.

The cameraman said it must be sunspots.

Meanwhile the two sides of combatants met like clashing cymbals, and the fighting became hand to hand.

There was feigned stabbing with knives and bayonets, as angels pushed mortals aside, to block danger to human life. Automatic weapons and pistols were discharged, but missed. The only victims in this battle were those Gabriel had brought with him. To disguise this, more and more angels went down.

Between two tents an Arab cook was setting up a heavy, rapid-fire machine gun on a tripod. Gabriel solidified into human form beside him, pointed at the gun, and shouted above the noise: "Hold your fire!"

The cook ran off. Gabriel let him go, snatched up the bulky weapon and heaved it aside as he ran towards the fighting. Several terrorists who heard him shout at the cook were staring his way and let their weapons fall. They thought Gabriel had ordered their side to surrender.

Gabriel and another angel saw something at the same time: Two Arabs holding one Israelis, one of them about to slit his throat. They were forced off him by two figures dressed as they were, but with unbelievable strength. The victim staggered off. The knife and two guns were wrenched away.

Meantime other Arabs were shouting: "Stop firing!" with no idea who Gabriel was, or why he had shouted. Those within earshot had thought he was in charge, and begun to obey to a man, yelling to their comrades to do the same. The attackers, who had barely broken a sweat, saw this and began to take prisoners. More terrorists surrendered. Then more. Very soon the battle was over.

With the Bethlehem bombing fresh in their minds, the victors were not gentle. Prisoners were beaten and clubbed, knocked to their knees with gun-butts, as they were herded into groups. Angels posing as Israeli officers ordered this to stop. Other angels handed out cigarettes to friend and foe alike. The very thought of tobacco made Gabriel cringe, but tensions were high, and the lives of the prisoners hung in the balance. The Israeli commander had a decision to make: Either to transport them back to Israel, or settle this now, with shots to the back of the head. It depended less on cargo space than it did on the mood of the captors. Gabriel was banking on nicotine, and a little hypnotic suggestion, to calm things down.

And a strong angel presence.

Suddenly someone yelled out a warning. All eyes turned to the sky. Three Syrian MIG-18 fighters were flying low over the campsite in close formation. Heat from that exploding hand-grenade had shown up on local alert systems.

The MIG's were here to investigate.

They overshot the camp and peeled upwards in a high, graceful arc. They would be radioing in what they had seen. Gabriel guessed what would happen next: Their base would tell Headquarters. A decision would be made. The order would be given. Within seconds, missiles would rain down, wiping out not only everyone here, but any evidence of terrorists on Syrian soil.

Everyone began shouting in two languages. Some prisoners broke away and ran for cover; others dropped to the ground. At the same time their Israeli guards tried to stop them. There was more clubbing, and a lot more kicking and punching. Arab fought against Jew; while angels fought to separate both.

When the chaos finally subsided, it was too late; the screaming jets were overhead, closing in for the kill.

One missile was launched.

Another followed it.

Empty tents evaporated, as if they had never been.

The ground quaked.

Nobody moved. Everyone was petrified with fear. Gabriel, who had diverted the first two missiles, pointed a finger at a third and detonated it in mid-air. The force of the shock-wave was like a blow from a mighty hammer. Then came the sound, so intense that it hurt the ears.

The planes passed so low that sand rose up in thick dust swirls, smothering those on the ground and blocking out the sun. It also gave everyone temporary cover. Gabriel was grateful for that. He turned his attention to the unseen aircraft, and the pilots that flew them. He and those with him pointed at the sky. The results were both satisfactory and immediate. One flier ejected from his cockpit for no reason.

One believed his fuel was gone and broke off the attack.

The third lost all sense of direction. He landed in the desert, a mile away.

At the campsite, sand and dust began to settle. Things normalized. A commando raid with few casualties, and little resistance from the captives. These were marched under guard to the Israeli helicopters. Gabriel saw that there was to be no massacre, as he had feared, but time was limited. There might be more Syrian MIG's at any moment. Gabriel silently instructed the Israelis and their commander to hurry. Michael's angels began to withdraw. One by one they vanished, and suddenly there were less combatants than before on both sides, but nobody noticed. They were all too busy, their minds consumed with other matters.

Gabriel stayed behind. He threw up a mind screen to stop enemy aircraft from coming within several miles.

The Israeli cargo transports were loaded up and prepared for take-off.

Gabriel floated unseen into the command helicopter.

Once the Humvees had been stowed away, every available inch of deck space was taken up by men and women; either standing with their weapons cocked, or on their knees, hands behind their heads. Winners and losers side by side.

Coded phrases were exchanged with Israeli headquarters, and the return flight began.

The campsite reduced in size and disappeared.

As Gabriel expected, more MIG aircraft were detected nearby, but all six Stealth helicopters lived up to expectation, remaining invisible to enemy radar, and nothing came of it.

Gabriel watched the flight computer and instrument panel from behind the lead pilot. There were no mishaps or navigation errors, and no regrettable incidents; except for a young Saudi who threw up on his guards during a steep turn. When they came to the Syrian border, Gabriel's anxiety began to ease, and by the time they saw the Red Sea and touched down in Haifa, he stopped worrying.

The Century T. V. crew was on the same aircraft as Gabriel, and among the first to disembark, arguing fiercely and blaming each other for the failure of their equipment. They all knew their jobs were lost. A few, knowing for whom they worked, feared worse than that.

Medics waited in the landing zone to treat the wounded, but the only injuries were cuts, bruises and one dislocated wrist.

The solitary death, when the terrorist threw the grenade, had been witnessed by a lot of people, but the body must have been left behind, and nobody could remember who it was.

Oddly, no one seemed to be missing.

So no paperwork was filled out.

When the debriefing started, a count was taken, there were considerably less prisoners than previously reported. This was attributed to the confusion and the heat of the moment.

No one pursued it further.

Some said their own force seemed larger in Syria.

Nobody could explain that, either.

~ ~ ~

Early the next day, Gabriel felt relieved, making his way through the old town district of Haifa, disguised as a larcenous looking street vendor. Yesterday there had been the very real danger of a bloodbath in the desert. Now it was gone, and the part played by him and Michael and the others went undetected. The best outcome they could have hoped for.

He turned a corner and reached his destination.

The street cafe was like any other in this part of town. Its striped, ancient awning was raggedy, worn through in places, and provided limited shade. The patio was strewn with unpainted tables, their umbrellas and basketwork chairs. Gabriel wended his way over to where Michael sat over untouched coffee, every bit the American tourist, wearing a loud print shirt and a floppy-brimmed canvas hat. Gabriel joined him and pretended to offer cheap trinkets for sale.

The owner came to chase him off. He looked like his

restaurant. Old, seedy and worn out, and in need of a complete renovation and clean-up. Michael handed him a few banknotes and assured him he was indeed interested in fake gems mounted onto inferior brass-work.

Gabriel was allowed to stay.

Three men in dust-stained overalls took a table next to the roadway. The owner went across to serve them, wiping his hands on a grubby towel. A single woman, dressed like a secretary, walked in and sat down next to the two angels. In Israel there is no class distinction, and this blend of customers was by no means unusual.

Michael pushed away the shoddy merchandise and said discretely to his brother: "Well, we did it. Thanks to you."

Gabriel held up a cheaply made amulet. 'It was your team," he said. "And you picked them."

"Well, we were lucky. That grenade going off, with no one hurt, and the attack planes, the way we got everybody out..."

Gabriel suddenly saw what his brother had been doing besides ordering coffee he didn't drink. On the table was a hand-written list with a pen beside it. To the mortal eye, it showed tourism-sights in Haifa, but for Gabriel, it listed the names of demons to be dealt with in the near future. They all had the name of a city beside them, and some an actual address. One name, it was the leader of Austria's Neo-Nazi Party, had a circle round it. Gabriel wondered why. "What's Bruno Schwenk up to?" he said, picking up the list. "Besides running for office?"

Michael looked away. "We sent the Angel Mordecai as a reporter, to interview him."

"To interview Schwenk?"

"Yes."

"One of Lucifer's top Generals?"

"Yes, Gabriel."

"At the peak of his career?"

"Gabriel, he is about to be elected, and we all know what Lucifer has planned for him. I thought it might be helpful to have someone go to Vienna. Maybe Schwenk could be stopped."

Gabriel had a feeling. Something had gone wrong. Michael was trying to break it gently.

Gabriel said: "Why don't you just tell me?"

"I will," Michael said. But he remained silent. After a strained pause, he finally said: "The Austrian destroyed Mordecai, with a demonic curse."

Gabriel sat and let this sink in.

The proprietor brought fresh coffee, with an extra cup for Gabriel, who paid the man, over-tipping as if he, and not Michael were the rich American tourist. The message was understood: This fool is about to buy something. Leave us in peace, or be cursed as an unbeliever."

There was a lot of head-bobbing, smiling and fake friendliness, and the owner went back to his kitchen.

Gabriel envisioned the Austrian demon's face in his mind. Schwenk was already an old man before the demon world took him over. His wizened features and sparse silvery hair were standard for anyone in their seventies. But this goblin-like creature had satanic strength. He was running for President of Austria and certain to succeed,

Gabriel felt anger. An angel was no more; killed by this Austrian monster meaning to imitate the Austrian monster before him – Adolf Hitler. Schwenk had long been seen as a problem, and this Mordecai incident underlined that. Gabriel took the pen and crossed off the Austrian's name.

"I'll visit him next," he said.

On the street a newspaper vendor walked by, hawing the midday edition. Gabriel beckoned him. It was a local paper, but in Israel they all covered a substantial amount of world news.

He read the front page. Their lead story was the raid on Syria, and an editorial praising its success, because of course the commander and his men were stationed here in Haifa. Then another front page headline, lower down, caught Gabriel's eye. It made him look up at Michael, who looked back with a questioning expression. Gabriel said, "We have work to do."

Michael frowned. "What's happened?"

Gabriel handed him the paper.

Michael spotted the headline even quicker than his brother. "Lucifer has a lot to answer for," he said.

Their sense of well-being over the Syrian raid faded away as they both digested what was happening in Tel Aviv.

The small-pox outbreak was rampant, and the city had been cordoned off. People were dying like flies.

~ ~ ~

Clement discussed it with Heathcote, although, strictly speaking, this was not a Homeland Security matter. But small-pox was terrifying, especially if it was delivered chemically from beyond Israel's borders, as rumor insisted; then it certainly became the business of Heathcote and his people. Any chemical attack on Tel Aviv could be duplicated in New York or San Francisco.

Heathcote had thought it urgent enough to organize a

meeting of experts in the various fields involved; which might take day or two, because they were coming from all over the country. For now, both Clement and Heathcote wondered aloud where chemical warfare might have originated. Most Arab countries were potentially guilty. Then again, most of them had to be innocent. A guessing game seemed unlikely to bear fruit, so the two men let the matter drop for now; or at least until Heathcote's emergency conference took place. Their conversation switched to other matters.

Now Clement broached the reason he was in his boss's office. "Something big is brewing in the hills between Pakistan and Afghanistan."

Heathcote sat back, tucking his thumbs into his suspenders. "No great shock," he said. "That place is crawling with bad guys. What have you heard?"

Clement said: "One of my undercovers – a guy we thought to be missing in that sector . . ."

"Your Iraqi."

"Yes – he's alive, thank God." The man, whose name was Jhalal Ben Rashid, had been jailed and tortured by Saddam Hussein; and then worked for the Americans since the first Gulf War ended. "He surfaced briefly in Pakistan, and mailed a coded letter to our consulate, which they forwarded to me."

"What's it say?"

He's been recruited by some Saudis. They've had him out of sight on the Afghan border, being trained at night, living and sleeping in caves during the day. Getting him ready for Baghdad."

"And that's something big? They're been churning out trained insurgents in those hills for years."

"They pulled Jhalal out of training. He's a volunteer."

"For what?" Suddenly Heathcote was interested.

"Something in America, but they've said very little so far, and there's a selection committee – a Tribunal, they call it. Oh. Yeah – and it's been made clear this is a suicide mission."

"Are you kidding?" said Heathcote. He gave his visitor a grudging smile. "Good work, Agent Clement. You may just have won the lottery. A Tribunal organized 9/11 for Bin Laden." He lit a cigarette and inhaled deeply.

"I don't know Jhalal's role in this. He might be carrying a message, or smuggling cash – something low-key."

"Volunteers don't do that stuff," said Heathcote. "Nor do Tribunals. They want him for something dangerous and important."

"They might reject him."

"Why should they? We didn't."

"I'll flag this red, then."

"You bet. Nothing was ever redder."

"Okay, sir. And I wanted to ask . . ."

Heathcote's phone rang. He answered it, giving Clement a chance to collect his thoughts. The hard part, he knew, would be talking Heathcote into anything high-risk. The man never gambled – at least not with the lives of his people, and if that included Clement, it certainly included Shahanna, because she was a raw recruit with no field experience. And what Clement was about to propose meant danger for both of them. Clement thought they should find Jhalal, and gatecrash his special mission – a direct attack on America.

Clement wanted to exploit Jhalal's incredible luck, for that was what it was, and this chance might never come again. Clement was about to suggest something his boss might think insane. But if anyone was ever in the right place at the right time, it was Jhalal. Clement thought Heathcote should capitalize on this by sending in two more agents. Not to do so was unthinkable.

Now Clement must persuade Heathcote.

Shahanna's training was going well. Everyone said so. They all agreed that her main strength lay in character, intelligence and a feel for this kind of work. Apparently she was also a dead-shot with a pistol. All this was good enough for Clement. He hoped it would be for Heathcote.

Heathcote was saying: "Yes, Mr. Secretary. "We'll check into that."

Clement knew he hated dealing with politicians. Heathcote hung up.

He grimaced. "That was the same old bullshit. Okay, Bo – you were saying?"

"Suppose we really have won the lottery," Clement said," "And this Jhalal thing is a nuclear strike against the United States, courtesy of Amir Affhad, and we have someone on the ground."

"I'm with you so far. What's your point?"

Here goes, Clement decided. Taking a deep breath, he said, "We insert a team to back up Jhalal. At least two people. Capitalize on this as fast as we can. It sounds like a Jihad."

"Skip the crap, Bo. Just tell me what you want. You have that look in your eye. That blood in the water look – and you want approval for something I won't like. Am I right?"

Clement took another deep breath. "Sir, I want to go, and take Shahanna. All her instructors say she's a natural, and I would like to ask her, with your permission. This is the big one. I'm sure she'll agree."

"Shahanna might, but I won't."

"Sir – "

"Are you out of your mind? You're a perfect choice – except you don't speak the language or know the area, and she's a raw beginner with a good chance of getting you both killed."

"I've got to convince him, thought Clement. "Sir, I've come up with a scenario: She's an American-hating bitch, a self-styled terrorist we arrest for subversive acts: a bomb plot, or something. We tie it in to her nuclear physics – and you've said yourself: that's a major selling-point for the guys we're after."

"How do you fit in?"

"I'm in love with her and follow her around like a puppy-dog. I'll do anything she tells me. For her or for Islam. I've talked myself into everything she believes in – and she treats me like shit. The bad guys love to exploit misguided Americans – I think they'll buy it."

"How do you get to Jhalal?"

"You deport her. The puppy-dog follows. The Jihad finds us. We find Jhalal."

"Now the look in your eye says "Bullshit"."

"No, sir. "It's a chance.""

Heathcote snorted. "If I endanger a good man, and a rookie, for bullshit based on a chance, I need my head examined."

"Sir – "

"You're not going, son – either of you. That's final."

"She's so perfect for this – "

Heathcote's voice was firm. "I don't waste lives, Ever. You know that, Senior Agent Clement, and you're pushing you're luck. You and the woman will have orders soon. But it won't be this assignment – and I don't want to hear another

word about it. Do I make myself clear?"
    "Look, I just think – "
    "Bo – you hear me?"
    "Yes, sir."
    "Okay, then. Get lost."
    Clement retreated.

CHAPTER SIX

MY NAME IS ASUTO KENYATTA. I was born in the years of no rain in a Kraal, far south of the white man's big town, Johannesburg. I am a grown man, who has killed a lion, and killed men. Yet these Pakistanis and sand-dwellers call me monkey boy. They say this to my face, thinking I don't speak their tongue. I was born a Muslim and live by the Koran. I came here to fight, and they paid my fare."

They call themselves warriors. We hide in caves. We don't even hunt. Our food is what starving villagers can spare. There is no honor here. Our training is high standard, but it is carried out in the dead of night, and we have no ammunition I pray every day to Allah – for a glimpse of the sun, or a live bullet.

My mother and grandmother raised me. My father was shot by the white police, for supporting Nelson Mandela. No one in the new government remembers my father's name. But they do support the Muslims.

My father was a Muslim hero.

I grew up tending goats and cows. I drank blood mixed with milk like the other boys. My favorite book was the Koran, and I stopped such drinking when I was twelve and I read that it was against Allah. When I was eighteen they sent me into the bush to live off the land for a month. That same year I was horsewhipped by some Afrikaners for fighting, when one of them called me Kaffir. When I was twenty, Mandela was released and we danced in the streets. He was elected president, and we Muslims were the only ones in our village who did not get drunk. Alcohol goes against the laws of the prophet.I volunteered ten years ago. The wait was long. Finally they sent me to fight in distant places, sometimes in Africa, sometimes in the sand countries, and I killed many men for them.

Now I am a hero.

And they call me Monkey.

American drones flew above us yesterday and the day before. They hunt for us and sometimes drop bombs that explode and kill. Yesterday we stayed in the caves and stayed alive. One of our youngsters was scared and ran outside to aim his gun at the planes. Our squad leader shot him in the back. It was the right thing to do. He gave away our position. Now we have to move away from here.

If the Americans don't bomb us first.

Our leaders seek men for a special mission. I have volunteered for two reasons: To get away from these dung-eaters, and because the target is across the sea – in America. I hate all Americans.

Volunteers must go to Waziristan, to the Tribunal. I don't know what a Tribunal is, but I have to go. The truck will come in a day or two, once we are in a safe place. The Tribunal will say who goes to America and who does not. Jhalal has told me this. Jhalal is my friend. He never calls me Monkey, or laughs at my mistakes in their ugly language. But Jhalal does not say what a Tribunal is, either. I think it is someone rich who can pay for airline tickets.

The Afghan boy who ran outside was buried in disgrace. His parents will be held responsible. That is wise and just.

I am glad to go to the Tribunal. If chosen, I will not

panic, as he did. I will die if I must, and enter Heaven, as is promised.

Praise unto Allah.

I pray to be chosen.

I have never been to America, but I know it is evil.

Our names shall be written in blood. The Great Satan will be destroyed.

It is Allah's will.

~ ~ ~

Prince Kamal adjusted his cuff-links. Emeralds glinted briefly. He was sixteenth in line to the throne, and wore western clothing, as always. His red, checkered headgear identified him as a Saudi Royal, but also underscored his authority on this Tribunal. Kamal had that authority, not only because he represented the crown, but because he was Saudi oil money, which made him god-like in this gathering of peasants, Of course he was also low-ranking enough to be sacrificed if exposed as a member of Al Qaeda. He looked around with disdain, at his two fellow chairmen, and at the roomful of thugs who controlled this Afghan hill country all the way into Pakistan. Prince Kamal disliked these Tribunal meetings. They meant contact with lower castes and killers, and never failed to set his nerves on edge.

For their part, everyone in this room detested him. Kamal was cruel, tyrannical, impulsive and treacherous, even by their standards. But he had the King's favor, which meant he also had the King's trust, and no one dared speak out against him. Jihadis are blindly obedient by definition.

Most here were not Saudi, but they answered to Saudi power. Prince Kamal was an extension of that power.

His accent was jarringly snobbish when he spoke: "My

King greets our brothers in arms against the Great Satan." Kamal treated them all to a royal stare, calculated to put them in their place and keep them there throughout this proceeding, which seemed to be about recruitment and finance, but was really about Saudi control. "First – Good news: The Americans agreed to six hundred dollars a barrel."

It was true, but hardly good news as far as this group went. It would not improve their funding by one penny, but it sounded very impressive. They responded with grave nods and murmurs of appreciation.

Kamal went on: "As for today's volunteers, we have two hundred candidates sent by training and resistance groups from several countries. We expect less than half to be suitable, and another third to fail or drop out. I'm authorizing Twenty thousand dollars per head for upkeep and training, and another fifty thousand for each one who takes part in the mission. Fifty million is assigned to Logistics – over and above the price of arming the attack." The danger of his position never left Kamal's mind as he spoke. Here he was, isolated from the royal family, breaking international law and bankrolling a massively lethal act of terrorism. If it went wrong, he would be alone. The King, his cousin, would disown him, just as he disowned Osama Bin Laden. And yet, Kamal reminded himself, the Americans must be stopped. They were bleeding Saudi Arabia dry – their oil policy was ruthless, and their military unbeatable.

Terror was the only answer.

Six hundred dollars a barrel was nowhere near enough for your only natural resource, when it was fast running out. America must now be forced to pay a different price altogether.

An attack on America required the mass killing of innocent civilians. American drones were doing that, in Pakistan, Syria and Afghanistan. Therefore the Great Satan had to lose major cities, for it to make any impact.

The old, and women and children would die.

Millions of them.

This was a sin against Allah, but Prince Kamal saw no other answer. Besides, the Ayatollah said that America was cursed by God. They deserved this.

Kamal cleared such thoughts from his mind. He was a Prince of the Crown, and had his duty to perform. The King had sent him personally, having formally embraced and kissed him.

Kamal was here to choose martyrs for the cause.

The two other chairmen, seated either side of him, were General Bahat Makhud, from the Saudi Army High Command, and a Pakistani named General Haffrir Rameesh. Both were top Al Qaeda members. Each was a powerful man in his forties, with a large belly and black, pitiless eyes. Each wore a graying beard. They were the military face of Al Qaeda, dressed in khaki uniform with blue turbans. The others around the table were of little consequence. They just made up the crowd. Half of them could not read or write. They were basically hill bandits.

The first candidate was led in, a youth of barely twenty. He stood tongue-tied and awed before them.

It was General Makhud who spoke. "Are you ready to die?" he asked. The boy hesitated, then nodded.

Makhud smiled, as if satisfied.

In fact, this one had already failed. First, he was too afraid to speak, and they had no use for cowards. Second, the boy had hesitated, and would do so again, if called upon to give his life. This question and the response was the only real test. This interview was already over. The Tribunal would dismiss this boy quickly. There was no time to waste. This operation must be carried out when Americans celebrated the Fourth of July, just three months away.

Prince Kamal thanked the young man – who had still not uttered one word – and said they would let him know. The buffoon actually took this for acceptance, bowing and nodding, mumbling in gratitude as he made for the door.

In came another, and this time General Rameesh asked the question. Again the reaction was found lacking, and the interview cut short. A burly Afghan with sinister eyes slouched from the room.

Others came and went. Not a hero among them. Prince Kamal started to despair. He must find at least fifty, but at this rate finding half that seemed unlikely. These idiots would be happier scrubbing toilets. None of them had what was needed. They were all too stupid, without courage, or both. Kamal seethed at the prospect of sending for more volunteers, and the expense of getting them here and the time wasted. Everything done in these parts took a river of cash.

True, cost was no real problem, but time was, and in any case, when it came to money Prince Kamal had no tolerance for waste. One reason he was given this job. He began to get a headache.

Then an Iraqi named Jhalal walked in and everything changed. Jhalal showed great eagerness when asked if he was ready to die, and even seemed ready to die right now, at this moment, if so commanded. He had an almost sad, hard-bitten look, a man not given to boasting or bravado, and Jhalal's file said that he was already a seasoned soldier. "Allah is great," Jhalal assured the entire room. "He who loses his life for Him awakes in His arms." Then, for good measure, the Iraqi added: "It is my vow to die for Islam."

Until now each interview was fruitless, but this man had everyone's attention. He said everything they wanted to hear, and had the attitude and bearing they were looking for. Prince Kamal sent an approving look in his direction. This was seen by others, and a wave of approval flowed around the table.

~ ~ ~

Jhalal himself was satisfied with his performance. He also knew that Clement and Heathcote would be delighted, once a message was sent to them.

The Tribunal questions became more personal. Jhalal rolled out his cover story, just as he had many times before: passing himself off as a former member of Saddam's elite Palace Guard who refused to accept the defeat of American invasion, and refused to lay down his arms. Like many others, Jhalal Ben Rashid had been smuggled out of Iraq and spirited away to Afghanistan.

There he joined the Jihad.

This could also be verified from his file, but the Tribunal wanted to hear it from him. He retold it just as it happened, without mentioning that when the war ended, he had been planted by the CIA – wearing a Republican Guard uniform – among other Iraqis who had just surrendered. Back then Jhalal told his fellow prisoners his name, rank and cover story, to fix it in their minds for when Al Qaeda came asking. Then he escaped, with plenty of witnesses to his heroism in eluding the guards. Naturally this getaway was arranged, with American sentries looking the other way. Prince Kamal and the Tribunal believed the entire story. Its ending was predictable but also true. Jhalal told it very well:

His recruitment to the cause took place almost immediately. A Syrian network found him wandering around in his guard uniform, and adopted him. Jhalal was fed, watered, given new clothes and weapons, and taken by secret mountain passes, over several weeks, to Kabul.

He had been in action ever since.

Today his story matched his appearance, and both made a powerful impression on the Tribunal. No one doubted him for a second.

Jhalal passed the Tribunal.

~ ~ ~

Prince Kamal felt renewed hope.

His headache receded a little.

The next volunteer came from the same camp as Jhalal: a black South African: Asuto Kenyatta. His story was different again. This Kenyatta was no untried youth or defeated soldier. And as he insisted on saying himself – rather surprisingly – he was no monkey. He had fought in Angola, Mogadishu and Yemen before assignment to Kabul. Once there, he joined up with the Afghan rebels, fighting the American forces. He had moved around a lot, and finished up in the borderlands.

The Pakistani cave dwellers were hostile and treated him badly, he said. Asuto would be honored to be chosen for what promised to be a suicide mission. He hated the Muslims here almost as much as he hated the Americans. He asked only one question: How soon could he leave

Pakistan?

Asuto also told them, with prompting, of what action he saw with the Taliban in the North: His unit marched through the desert for five days without food or water. The Americans surprised them at a wadi with a dried up well, where they had been driven by thirst. Asuto Kenyatta was the only one to fire back, the only one who did not put up his hands, and the only one with enough sense to run into the desert and hide in some brush. He kept moving south, alone, for ten more days, and was near to death when found by a passing camel caravan.

Asuto Kenyatta was also accepted.

Kamal breathed easier, encouraged by the score of two. He hoped this was the turning point, and for the next few hours that certainly seemed to be the case. Suitable men, and suitable women, kept coming in an uninterrupted stream. A few rejects went almost unnoticed. Selection was adjourned when they had thirty – more than half the total needed altogether – and this was only the first day.

Now Prince Kamal decided he might be home earlier than expected, to play in the King's birthday polo match after all. It was a great honor to be chosen for this event, and the prince had been furious at having to miss it.

His headache was completely gone.

He sent for his car.

It was there in seconds.

~ ~ ~

Shadowed by men in dark suits and sunglasses, the prince and his two Generals were driven to an exclusive night club in the hills. Food had been ordered; along with a local band, and a trio of talented belly dancers.

Their table was the best, and laden with delicacies.

"So we don't have a single missile, and Amir Affhad is dead?" General Rameesh was speaking. Traces of roast lamb fat glistened on his chin. Kamal was horrified at the General's indiscretion – blurting out the word missile, in a public place. Rameesh was a well-known figure, and people around here were not stupid. Any waiter, belly dancer or tambourine player could put two and two together. The countryside might soon be alive with the news that the Jihad was going nuclear.

General Makhud chose to ignore Kamal's warning look. "And our New York supplier? No contact?"

"Not yet," admitted the prince.

But he did have Amir Affhad's diary.

And it contained an E-mail address.

"What are you going to do, Highness?" General Rameesh wore a sullen look. He resented the Saudis and their wealth and arrogance, and he resented this hawk-faced Prince in particular. Rameesh came from a republic, and did not hold with royalty. He had already made it clear that he blamed the Saudi King for the death of Amir Affhad, which was ridiculous. Even more huffily, the General said: "Why not contact New York through our bankers in Geneva?"

Kamal dismissed this suggestion with an impatient shake of the head. He clapped his hands.

A slim young woman with a jewel in her nose brought them water in scented bowls, for their greasy fingers. No one spoke until she left. Now General Makhud asked: "What does His Majesty say?"

There was a hookah loaded with hashish on the table. Prince Kamal took a long pull at it, inhaling deeply. The effect was almost instant, the other two receding in his vision. He experienced a warm, liquid feeling. Finally he said, "I am to go to New York myself."

Makhud's eyes went wide. "You are to replace Amir Affhad?"

"No – more than that. I am also to direct this mission. When training commences, I shall be running the camp."

It was true. The King had announced the promotion himself. Kamal said quietly, "Do not doubt my success."

Makhud looked away, and Kamal realized the King's favorite General was eaten up with envy. Prince Kamal was already in the secret inner circle, but to be entrusted with Affhad's job meant a bestowal of the highest rank – let alone to be in charge of this crucial attack as well.

It made the prince Al Qaeda's top man anywhere.

Kamal saw himself more as a drone target.

"Let us set missiles aside," Rameesh said angrily. He was watching the stage. A scantily clad was writhing to the music, arms entwined over her head, breasts moving seductively. "We have other problems. One: No place to train those we selected today. Thanks to Israel, the Syrian camp has been exposed and destroyed. Two: A shortage of staff and equipment, also caused by the attack on Syria. Three: No one to intimidate or bribe foreign officials. Ben Salim died with Affhad. Four: The plan is incomplete. How will our teams get through increasing airport security?" With a sneer, he said: "I think we must postpone this venture." There was silence. His list of problems boiled down to one question: Can we still carry out simultaneous nuclear strikes on the United States? General Rameesh didn't think so.

General was a loyal Saudi patriot. He sided with the

prince. "Nothing must divert us. The King insists on that."

Kamal hastened to agree. "Any problem can be solved. Funding has already been released to me."

"You have the money?" Even Rameesh was impressed.

"More than anyone could ever spend."

The Afghan General became even more respectful. "Your King must be optimistic. How did you convince him?"

Rameesh was saying: Now convince me.

"Airport security. I know how to breach it."

"I can hardly believe that," said Rameesh levelly. "May we share this secret?"

"Yes, please tell us," said General Makhud.

Kamal said: "Later, in the car." He had meant to tell them anyway, but not here in this place. The Prince knew that in this night-club, walls really did have ears. Hidden microphones everywhere, put in by the Taliban. Many sinners or dissenters were prone to condemn themselves over hard liquor. Kamal dropped his voice. "We won't have to train pilots, or fly the planes," As he spoke, he looked nervously around. But no one had heard. No one was sitting or standing nearby.

Kamal clapped his hands for the check.

Abruptly changing the subject, Makhud asked him: "And the insurgency in Iraq? The Afghan fighting – Iraq, Syria and Pakistan?"

"The struggle must go on. The best way to recruit our young, who are by now our third generation of unemployment and unrest. What else do our jobless and angry young men have to do? Better they join a militia, and hate America – than turn that hate on us; because we are so rich and we keep them so poor. The Iraq and

Afghan-Pakistani wars must never end. That's vital to both sides. For America it's about oil, but for us it's Sunni against Shiite. All Shia are dogs. They must never prevail; no matter what. Islam will not be safe until they are eradicated. As for the Americans, they are just too spoiled and lazy to give up gasoline and their leaders lack the will to make them do it. Prolonging this war is a mutual need. Good for us, and good for the American military industrial complex. Without our oil; they're paralyzed. You cannot run that massive arsenal of ships, tanks and munition, or move motorized divisions, without an ocean of fuel. They don't have enough themselves, so they buy it from us and fight on."

Makhud frowned. "Yes, quite so. Unhappily there is more to it than that. America now has permanent bases in Iraq, a foothold in our midst that they have always wanted and which they will never give up. As I have said before, this infuriates Iran and Syria, making it increasingly difficult for me to get their support – recruits, funding, weapons and so on. They have more manpower and equipment than we do. Without the insurgents they supply, we would lose."

Kamal was unimpressed. "Anything that upsets Iran, or Syria, is a good thing. They are our enemies. Nothing can ever change that. As for them supporting us in our fight with America, what choice do they have? First and foremost, we are all Muslims. They must take our side against the Great Satan. That's why they tolerate Al Qaeda, allowing it to operate freely here in Taliban country. Also why, although they detest my presence, they let me come here. Iran and Syria have no choice."

All three men knew something else: something they

could not say out loud. Israel, with American backing, had rendered a huge favor by bombing Iran's nuclear program into oblivion – first in 2019, and then again in 2020. The second time, every laboratory and missile silo in the country was reduced to dust and rubble. Since then Iran was seen in Arab eyes as something of a whipped dog and they knew it. That was why they agreed to buy six nuclear bombs from North Korea and trans-ship them to North America for Al Qaeda, knowing any attempt to keep the weapons would be betrayed to an ever-vigilant Israel by Saudi informers.

Kamal ended by saying: "Our biggest advantage is this: American troops on our soil for twenty years, and their many crimes against Islam: Hundreds of thousands dead each time they bombed Baghdad. Women and children still being slaughtered, just miles from here, by unmanned drones. That brings us more recruits than we could buy with a year's oil revenue. And it brings a continuing alliance with heretic enemies, like Iran and Syria."

His listeners knew this was true, and kept quiet.

Now the check came and Kamal paid it begrudgingly.

Each of them took an exotic dancer to a private room. They did not leave for quite a while.

On the way outside, General Makhud could not resist asking again how European and American security systems were to be overcome at dozens of international airports. Makhud was told to be quiet.

But in the car, Prince Kamal told them.

Their eyes gleamed with satisfaction.

Airport security was no longer a problem.

~ ~ ~

Two days later the Prince crossed Central Park West at noon, in the direction of Lucifer's house.

Prince Kamal was confused. He had expected to hear from a man called Beck, the leader of an absurd, underground army described in the diary of Amir Affhad, but Kamal's invitation to come here had come from someone else: A well-known American media-mogul, dripping with wealth, and the last person you would expect to be selling part of the American nuclear arsenal.

Scott Anderson had said on the phone that he'd been trying to winkle out Prince Kamal for more than a week. He did not sound pleased.

Why had the Saudi's E-mail to Beck taken so long?

It seemed like a rocky start.

~ ~ ~

Kamal was using an assumed name, and was now on foot, having got out of a taxi some while back. His passport, issued by Jordan, a favored American ally, said he was Abdul Rashid, and entitled to diplomatic immunity. The Prince believed this made him only reasonably safe. He was not sought in America, or listed anywhere as a terrorist, but his picture appeared in society magazines. So today he was not dressed as a Saudi Prince, and both his passport entries were genuine, purchased at great cost from the Jordanian Ministry of the Interior. An hour ago, American Customs and Immigration had waved him politely through, but the Prince still worried, and he would do so every time he used that passport. He could not afford to be arrested in New York.

Or recognized anywhere.

Kamal was assuming the duties of Amir Affhad. Like everyone else, the Prince had despised the man, but respected his expertise. The fat Lebanese performed miracles on demand, financial miracles which Kamal was now expected to duplicate. The Prince did have a Harvard degree in economics, and he felt equal to the challenge, but Amir Affhad's shoes would not be easy to fill.

Then there was Scott Anderson, the American Kamal was here to meet. The man was a billionaire, and bound to be a tough negotiator. Would he try to squeeze out some extra profit, now that Affhad was gone? Prince Kamal decided it didn't matter. He, too, was a tough negotiator.

And his whole family were billionaires.

Something made Kamal look behind him. The street was surprisingly empty for this time of day, but a black homeless man was following him, staying about fifty yards back. Prince Kamal kept walking. He ignored the intruder and concentrated on bank transfers and finance. That was his mistake.

Fifty yards behind him, Gabriel quickened his pace until Artis Brown was only thirty yards behind. Then twenty.

Kamal didn't notice. He was figuring amounts of cash and reciting memorized offshore account numbers. Sixty billion had already been transferred, being the profit from a month of oil and drug shipments. That had gone to a bank in the Cayman's, as stipulated by the mysterious Militia leader, who now seemed to be out of the picture. Presumably Scott Anderson had access to this payment. If not, it could be a problem. Prince Kamal had no idea it was all the same person.

What he did have was a cashier-check for five hundred and forty billion in the inside pocket of his jacket. It was untraceable, laundered through an exclusive private bank in Dubai. He had nervously touched it several times, on the flight. The King, his cousin, had handed it to him personally and wished him luck. Prince Kamal hoped this staggering amount of money would buy him a smooth ride with Scott Anderson, even if the news baron was super-rich. It was tax-free, and unaccounted for. That kind of cash, in such a chunk, was hard to come by.

And still only half the purchase total.

Without knowing why, Prince Kamal glanced to his left. The homeless black man had drawn level with him, and now he raised one finger, pointing at the Prince. At the same time something cut into Kamal's mind with the precision and abruptness of a knife. It became hard for him to see, speak or think. A voice suddenly spoke in his head, and it came from the dark-skinned figure beside him.

"Turn back, Prince Kamal."

The Prince had a vision: A dark, winged figure swooping downward.

It was the Angel of death, coming for him.

Then all reality fell away.

The prince was back at home.

He stood alone, on the royal palace wall – with loud explosions and the screams of running people, far below him.

Kamal was watching the final battle for his country. Missiles rained down on the capital, Riyadh, and American planes filled the darkened sky. Bombs turned buildings to vapor. Flame and ashes rose up into the air.

Now the sky overhead was turning black.

This was Saudi Arabia being obliterated, explained the voice in Prince Kamal's head – all because of the deal

Kamal was about to make with the devil, who wanted America laid to waste. This disturbing vision, said the voice, was a preview of the revenge of the most powerful nation on Earth.

Of course, the extensive Saudi oil fields, still largely underground, would remain undamaged. Later, when the sands cooled down, the victors would plunder the oil, as a final insult.

Now with a jolt, Prince Kamal's mind cleared. The terrifying images were gone. He was back on an almost empty New York thoroughfare, with no one else in sight. Had it been a dream?

No homeless black man.

No Angel of Death.

No nuclear aftermath.

It took Kamal a moment to recover. He stood trembling. He had no idea what was meant by a deal with the devil. No idea about any of it. How could a voice have spoken in his head? He slowly shook off his fear. This was his imagination, all the doubts he'd had for months, expressed in another way. Finally he shook his head to clear it and continued down Park West. He was entering New York's ritziest neighborhood, where only the rich and powerful could afford to live.

The Prince had Scott Anderson's prestigious address written down, but he had memorized it high above the Atlantic, having nothing better to do. The in-flight movie had been atrocious.

There was a break in the buildings, and Kamal knew he had found the place: an imposing brownstone set off on its own. Four floors with a modern-designed penthouse, just visible at the top. It had a virtually private view of the park and its magnificent oaks and flowers, all coming into bloom with the early Spring.

The steps to the front door, at the end of a short drive, were topped by on either side by heavy stone gargoyles – giving the impression that demons were guarding the house. The oaken door was fitted with a high-tech intercom, and scanned by infra-red cameras, and all the gadgetry one might expect.

The intercom was slim-line and matte black. Prince Kamal spoke his name clearly, acutely aware of being alone and on foot. He wished he was in a stretch-limo, letting his driver handle this.

Seconds went by.

The front door swung wide open.

Prince Kamal had his first, unwitting sight of Lucifer, Prince of Darkness. A tall, imposing figure, yet with wizened features far older than his erect stance would indicate. He wore a dinner jacket, and had a cigar in the hand that was not holding the door. He greeted the prince with great friendliness, and stepped aside to let him enter. Kamal was immediately struck by the magnetic charm of Scott Anderson. He drew you in, as if to share a secret you already knew.

Anderson led the way up a broad marble stairway. He said, "So you're the new Amir Affhad."

"Yes." Prince Kamal was proud to admit it. They went up to a paneled room that obviously served as a study. There was a Goliath of a wide-screen T. V. – surrounded by countless shelves of books and opulent, leather armchairs. The television set was showing stock market closes – of course, on Century News.

They sat down. The devil flipped a remote control and

Wall Street went off. Kamal said: "I am of the royal blood. The King's cousin."

"I know who you are, Prince Kamal." There was something chilling, in the way this was said.

Kamal was taken aback. He said: "I bring final payment for the first phase, drawn on a Zurich account, as agreed. Did the Cayman's deposit arrive safely?"

"It did. I have already put the money to use."

This was a relief for Prince Kamal. At least there were no complications in that regard. He said: "So when can we expect shipment?"

"Very soon. There will be some delay. My source in Utah has dried up. The initial supply will now be coming in from the far East. North Korea will ship to Iran, brokered through a trusted colleague in Beijing. It's simply a logistics problem. Nothing to worry about."

"How much delay?" Prince Kamal was alarmed. We have a schedule. Iran is only the staging area, a diversion. They must ship the cargo here, to arrive well before your independence Celebration. By then our teams will already be on the move. The deadline is six weeks."

"No problem. North Korean ships are docked and waiting. It only remains for the material to arrive in China. A week at most."

Kamal was beset by doubt. If the Utah scheme had failed; then why believe in this one?

Anderson said: "This will all go smoothly. It shall come to pass, as the so-called holy books say. I guarantee this – absolutely."

Prince Kamal met the devil's opaque gaze.

And his misgivings slipped away.

~ ~ ~

With the practiced ease of the angel he once was, Lucifer slipped into the mind of Prince Kamal. There was no demon as yet, but that would come soon. The devil had just the right one in mind.

But Prince Kamal's thoughts were something of a shock. The devil sat, unmoving, with a long ash on his cigar, and saw what had transpired since Kamal's landing at JFK First, a yellow cab; then Kamal deciding to walk from Times Square – apparently for no reason. Lucifer knew better. The Prince's mind had been manipulated by Gabriel, who then accosted the Saudi visitor, and scared him half to death with visions of a black man and nuclear payback.

Lucifer was livid. The Angel of Death was everywhere, like a plague, popping up whenever anything significant was going on. There was nothing to be done about it, and knowing what Gabriel did was better than not knowing. The devil consoled himself with that. He looked across at the Prince, and said: "I shall have Armageddon." His voice was icy cold. And he wasn't speaking to the Prince.

Kamal paled at both the words and tone.

"That black bastard was no angel," said Scott Anderson. "It was just a penniless beggar. We have them here, just as you do at home." He spoke as if knowing about the homeless black man was perfectly natural.

Kamal nodded dumbly. He rose from his seat, moving in a trance. He reached into his breast pocket and handed Scott Anderson the largest check he had ever seen his King issue and sign.

The media man accepted it with his former charm and composure, and suggested a glass of whiskey. They drank together, standing on the sumptuous rug. Anderson asked

Prince Kamal to be patient and wait, making himself scarce in the wide-open spaces of America. Lucifer also promised a new, and firm, delivery date. The Prince should have it within a few days.

In a daze, Kamal agreed to everything.

Then he phoned for a cab.

He couldn't get out of there fast enough.

CHAPTER SEVEN

GABRIEL ASSUMED BODILY SHAPE in Tel-Aviv, a city by now choked with horror and death. Hospitals overflowed with victims of smallpox and their corpses were piling up in morgues that simply couldn't cope.

The Angel of Death became Hans Behring.

Gabriel didn't rush here from Haifa, which had been his first thought. Instead he had transported to New York, so as to spook Prince Kamal, who was on his way to meet Lucifer for the first time.

Gabriel's break from airline travel – which took him to Washington, the Syrian desert and Haifa and New York – had exhausted him, and drained his power. That was why he had confronted Prince Kamal and not Lucifer, because terrifying a mortal used little or no energy at all.

Most of them were paranoid to start with.

What Gabriel did to Prince Kamal might not have been very effective today, but it would prove extremely valuable later.

Now Gabriel was in Tel-Aviv, his energy gone. It would be hours before he was able to take serious action. Frustration overwhelmed him as he took in the scene around him. There had been so many deaths! He forced his mind to take over,, choosing a strategy for when he recovered. Somehow Gabriel had to wake the dead – hundreds of thousands of them – without anybody noticing. Gabriel was able to countermand death, although he rarely did it, but death was his specialty, as much as

Lucifer's, and for now there would be no more of it in Tel-Aviv. Reversing the fatalities that had already occurred came next. Once Gabriel decided how.And got his strength back.

He had landed in a residential area. Loudspeakers were blaring from the trees and lampposts.

They'd been hung hastily to deal with this crisis, and boomed their message from street to street, and building to building. It could be heard in every home or office block, and could be heard regularly, once an hour.

It was the same message that had played all week. Gabriel heard it echo all around him. The words first in Hebrew, then Arabic, then finally in English: "Stay inside! Anyone on the street will be detained. Drink only bottled water. Our mains supply may have been contaminated by subversive outside influence."

"If you or any of your family become sick, do not try to contact the hospitals. They cannot help you."

Infected buildings must display white bed sheets, or other large cloth as a warning. Isolate the sick, and keep away from them. Stay in another room, a cellar, or a basement. May God have mercy on us all. Further announcements will follow."

Gabriel looked around. Every house in sight had a white sheet hanging somewhere. Some had more than one. He started walking. The apartments on the next street, and the street after that, had even more. White sheets dominated for several blocks. White sheets spreading macabre trails across the city.

There was a numbed silence everywhere.

Gabriel was worried about breaking curfew. He had no energy for vanishing, but he dare not risk being arrested.

Escape without killing would take too long. After some thought he climbed into a parked car and went to sleep.

Scores of angels moved unseen, over the spot.

~ ~ ~

When he awoke it was dark. He was not at his best, but he felt ready enough, and he had to get started.

Gabriel rarely performed miracles. They were flashy, and they caused too much attention. This one was quite simple, but it required a vast amount of power, which was why so many angels were in the city – some of whom still hovered over him to ward off danger.

Gabriel must now bring the dead to life.

And heal the sick.

And put things to rights.

He drifted out of the car and sped, invisible, high over Tel-Aviv. He finally came down and manifested as himself, the Archangel Gabriel, still tired but refreshed enough, standing in front of the beleaguered city's largest mortuary. Gabriel concentrated, head bowed, drawing on the angels all around him, and those all the way up to the skies and beyond. Thousands of pairs of wings beat softly, beyond human sight.

Gabriel felt a surge of warmth.

It went on for some time.

The feeling subsided.

Heaven had answered.

The miracle was complete.

He knew instantly that it had worked. He heard the cries of surprise, and sensed human joy, seconds later. Soon after that people were shouting everywhere and running through the streets.

Gabriel turned away.

He began looking for the largest and foremost of their hospitals: The one recently established and sponsored by the University of Israel in Tel-Aviv. He had to walk halfway across town, but he found it.

He must act swiftly.

While memory could still be erased.

He vanished.

~ ~ ~

Gabriel materialized in the main corridor leading to the laboratory wing. He wore a set of pale green operating overalls and matching cap, and had a blue-covered file under one arm. There was a laminated name-tag on his chest. It gave his name as Doctor Lev Shimon.

He walked up to the reception desk and said: "I have an appointment with the head of Medicinal Chemistry."

The duty nurse was a slender brunette. Her telephone was silent, her face devoid of any hope. News of the miracle had not yet come. That might well work to Gabriel's advantage.

The nurse looked in her diary. The entry was there, but in a handwriting she did not recognize. Gabriel had added it just before she opened the book. The girl looked at him with tired, red-rimmed eyes. No one here had slept in days. "Yes, Doctor. That would be Professor Zhorabek. Take the second left as you go down the hall. There is a sign on his door."

Gabriel said: "Thank you. You've been most helpful." Oddly, this reminded him of his ill-fated visit to General Renkov, in the Kremlin.

The professor was in his fifties, exhibiting baldness, a weight problem, and all the signs of considerable mental strain. He looked as tired as the nurse, after days of battling small-pox. His handshake was firm. He invited Gabriel inside, and offered coffee as they sat down. The angel thanked him but declined.

The professor had his hopes pinned on this meeting, or so he now believed.

He looked enquiringly at Gabriel's blue folder.

The phony Doctor Shimon opened the file. "The figures and calculations on the first pages might not be clear; they're in my own writing. But the rest is typed and easy to read. The formula works. My test results are at the back. Extensive local dosage, here in the city, has already taken place. The crisis has passed."

He handed over the documents.

It was a breakthrough cure for smallpox. Not a preventative vaccine that had to be used before contact with the disease, but an outright cure for those already afflicted. Such a thing had never been dreamed of. Gabriel found it most ironic to introduce it because of Lucifer, to reverse an epidemic that he had started. That surely made it the devil's gift to humanity. But no one would ever know.

Except Lucifer. He would hardly be pleased.

Zhorabek did not speak. Gabriel knew the Israeli physician felt like a condemned man granted a second chance. A condemned man who seconds ago had been part of a condemned nation. No one had hoped to confine this outbreak to Tel Aviv. It would have devastated the whole country.

Zhorabek read it all twice. Gabriel watched him examine figures and symbols with an expert eye. He would lean over a page, tapping at it with one finger, as if checking for accuracy. Finally he sat back with a satisfied expression.

"You've saved us," he said.

Gabriel said: "Not me but God."

Professor Zhorabek shrugged and looked up at Doctor Shimon. "Let's say you, with God's help," he said.

Gabriel could not argue with that.

The professor walked him to the door.

When they shook hands, Zhorabek was smiling. "Our labs and private factories will speed production. Other hospitals will help, of course. So will medical organizations all over the world. Even Iran has offered assistance. They're seriously afraid we suspect them of starting this plague."

The professor was babbling.

Gabriel sent out a general thought-scan.

All recent memory was erased. History was changing in an instant, as millions of angels reshaped events in minds everywhere. People in Tel Aviv, Israel at large – and all over the world – simply forgot that anyone had died. They remembered only that a great catastrophe had been averted.

Everyone infected had only been sick.

And then cured.

That left Gabriel with the rumor that somehow the smallpox had originated from enemies tampering with the water supply. Professor Zhorabek had just demonstrated the problem. Iran now feared Israeli vengeance, and was doubtless readying for war. Gabriel knew this rumor had to have come from Lucifer, and it must be refuted. Gabriel needed a powerful transmitter.

~ ~ ~

The broadcast went out on all channels.

Viewership was off the charts.

Gabriel had become a female news anchor with a starchy Hebron accent:

"This is Barbara Vella, reporting from Tel Aviv."

The camera cut to the University hospital, a broad shot of the frontal facade and the steps leading up to the entrance; it showed Professor Zhorabek, standing at the top with his staff. They were surrounded by reporters, cameras, and jubilant patients who had unknowingly returned from the dead. There was no sound; just the voice-over in the silky tones of Barbara Vella:

"All Israel celebrates tonight – as our capital is saved from smallpox by a near miracle."

A near miracle was acceptable in people's minds.

A miracle was not.

The picture shifted to a recovery ward inside the hospital. Gabriel, as Barbara Vella, continued:

"It was thought at first that victims had died in the outbreak. Luckily that turns out not to be the case . . ."

Barbara Vella went on at some length in the same vein. Little would be recalled about her later, and in a few days no one would remember her at all. But for now, the television audience hung on her every word.

Gabriel was nearly finished. He came to his last point: "Intelligence sources now say chemical warfare was not used in any form. Some airborne strain of the virus seems most likely – given the speed at which it spread . . ."

The Angel of Death smiled into the camera. He imagined Lucifer, seeing his own media tactics used against him. The images of a healthy Tel Aviv were irrefutable. The devil had lost another round. He was not the only one who could manipulate people with television.

~ ~ ~

Heaven's Judge

One hour later Gabriel booked a flight back to Washington. When he came out of the TV studios in Tel Aviv, two names had floated into his mind. One was Beauregard Clement; the other Shahanna Dufaux. As was often the case, Heaven had not chosen the most convenient time to tell him something. Gabriel had intended to go to Austria. Now he was on his way to meet two mortals whose destiny was to help him.

Gabriel had mixed feelings.

Destiny did not always work.

~ ~ ~

The Bunch of Grapes was packed. It was Saturday night, and a live band was playing loudly upstairs.

Gabriel had chosen his disguise with care. The white shirt was silk and imported. His tie was from an upper crust English school, and would match his manners, accent and a slightly arrogant style. His dark blue blazer bore the hand-stitching of a London tailor, and would have cost a tidy sum, were it not an illusion. His slacks were dove gray and slim-cut, with a crease sharp enough to slice bread. Everything about Gabriel said British Secret Service, and that was his intention.

Henry Archer was Gabriel's most charismatic character, someone that had flitted in and out of British and American Intelligence activities since Kennedy was President. Whenever this man showed up, he was accepted instantly as a trusted colleague by even the most hard-bitten professionals. Women found him attractive, and men admired his expertise and long record of success; all of which existed only in their minds, inserted by Gabriel as needed. Everyone was agreed, both men and women, that Henry Archer had a certain hypnotic quality.

James Bond had nothing on Gabriel.

Henry Archer paid off a cab, walked past the line waiting to enter the Bunch of Grapes, and smiled gratefully as two thugs at the door let him in because they thought they knew him.

The Bunch of Grapes had three bars: The one blaring heavy rock, the only one to charge admission, and a sports bar, with enough slots and video games to bankrupt the line outside if they ever tired of noise and dancing. The third bar was equal in size, but high-priced and lavishly furnished. This was the one favored by Washington diplomats where Clement and Shahanna first met.

They were here now, the last two of a party celebrating her departure from the Corps Diplomatique. Their French hosts had left over the past hour, some of the men sulking, once Clement was announced as Shahanna's rich American fiancée, and the reason she had quit her job.

Clement had colored his hair, wore a pair of glasses and grown a wispy mustache; all of which prevented recognition by the French, but did not fool the Angel Gabriel, who easily spotted Bo and Shahanna. They were listening to piped jazz and drinking vintage champagne – the only thing Shahanna would let Clement order, saying scotch always got her into trouble. It was a joke between them, she having consumed a massive volume of whiskey the night they met.

Gabriel sat down with them without being asked. He took some champagne, using a glass that appeared in his hand; then topped up his two companions. Henry Archer was acting as if they all came here together – which was exactly how Clement and Shahanna now remembered it: They had all been to the Englishman's favorite Indian restaurant for an early dinner; then come here for a drink, to talk shop and gossip like old friends. The two mortals would remember correctly tomorrow, but for now, it was just as if no French diplomats had been here this evening – and Clement and Henry Archer had known each other for years.

Clement's disguise simply disappeared.

Neither mortal noticed.

Gabriel looked at them. They were like a boy and girl – all humans were children to him – on a first date. They were falling in love, but Clement didn't know it. Of course the woman did. Clement was wearing a suit for a change, cream colored, in a light-weight cotton, with a pink shirt open at the neck. He made a convincing rich man's son, which he really wasn't, but the French had bought it. Shahanna had on a black silk gown stitched with white and silver orchids. It was halfway between a sarong and a sari; except for the low neckline front and back, showing off sculptured shoulders, and, by Washington standards, a scandalous amount of bosom. She looked as beautiful as any woman does in the perfect dress. To Gabriel's mind, she and Clement made the perfect couple.

The angel had a sudden vision:

Shahanna, hands tied above her head.

A man screaming, spitting in her face. Several powerful slaps, and her head bouncing sideways each time.

Hands pawing at her. Clawing at her breasts. Tearing her shirt.

Gabriel could not really see the man's face, but he knew it was Prince Kamal.

The vision changed:

Now he saw Clement, arrested and beaten bloody.

There were torture implements. Screaming and a flow of blood. Men in fur hats moved around the prisoner. A breaking of bone, and then a sickening crunch, as the fracture was struck with a hammer.

The image was vivid; then it faded away. Both the visions had been vivid. Now they were gone.

Gabriel looked at his two companions, and understood why Heaven wished him to protect them.

Shahanna, between hefty swallows of champagne, was describing Muslim culture to Clement:

"The vast majority of our people are just like Americans, or any kind of western European. They don't believe in violence – they believe in hard work and raising their families. They also believe in Democracy and deciding things for themselves. That's why so many flee to America and elsewhere."

Clement said: "I studied your Muslim theology in college. Islam is based on peace and reverence for God's creation. Not too different from Christianity. At least that's what I was taught. Mohamed was another Messiah."

Shahanna snorted. "His words have been distorted. He preached the same values and teachings as your Jesus. Our holy men couldn't wait to change it, twisting things to suit their purpose. To wage war, to enslave people with insane religious dogma while the high priests live like Kings. Every religion has done this. People like me hardly believe in God at all. It's a miracle that we do. Your Jesus sounds wonderful, but nobody follows his teachings, do they? Turn the other cheek? Your enemy is your brother? Pooh! Your True Christians and our True Believers would wipe each other out if given the chance. What's the religious basis for that?

"Jesus spoke out against conflict; so did Mohamed, but the priests on both sides are right-wing conservatives. They hate free thinking. They hate change. And most of all they hate every other faith. Especially those with more followers and more money in the collection box. They are in the God-business. Money, and the power it brings, keeps them in a life of luxury. Everything else is smoke and mirrors. The bottom line is all that cash. That's why all religions insist theirs is the only true God. They wear fine robes, sit on gold thrones and eat and drink of the very best. Most of their followers don't.

"I reject all of them. I accept only God. I hope He's more like your Jesus than the Christians and Muslims believe. Their angry, punishing version of God is the fantasy of angry, punishing old men. The world needs a God, or an Allah, who doesn't require us to obliterate each other."

Gabriel thought that was well said. It sounded like the world he'd been sent down here to put in place. A world Lucifer hated with every fiber of his being. Only time would tell who won or lost. But Gabriel could certainly see why Heaven had brought Shahanna to his attention, and it seemed likely from the look on Clement's face, that he was of a similar mind.

A waitress came up, stopped next to Gabriel's chair and asked if the champagne was cold enough. He nodded politely, and told her it was fine, a very good year. "Please put another bottle on ice," he said. "This one won't last too long."

The waitress smiled, captivated by a well-faked English accent, and headed back to wherever she came from. Gabriel toasted Shahanna and pretended a sip. But he leaned in closer to Clement, to read the American's mind.

A mind full of information:

Al Qaeda was recruiting in Afghanistan for a nuclear attack on America. Clement worked for Heathcote, whose desk-top computer Gabriel monitored daily, and it seemed they had an undercover on the ground. The agent's name was Jhalal, and Al Qaeda loved him. He was in the right place at the right time. Heathcote had refused Clement's request to insert himself and Shahanna into the operation to back-up Jhalal. Gabriel could sense the young American's disappointment and frustration. The angel knew something would change Heathcote's mind soon, but he could not say that to Clement.

Instead he said, "I'm off to foreign parts."

"Oh, where?" asked Shahanna.

"Our Embassy in Karachi," he said, then dropped his voice. "I have a man in Taliban country; the part of the Afghanistan border they still control at great distress to Uncle Sam."

Gabriel knew Pakistan was a place from which such an agent could be supported. These two would know it, too. He said: "His name is Hassan."

It was an astonishing thing for Henry Archer to say, violating a cast-iron rule: No one ever revealed or identified an undercover, even by code-name. In fact Hassan was a human disguise Gabriel used, and he wanted that name fixed in these young Americans' minds. Hassan would protect them.

As ordained by Heaven.

Clement's thoughts revealed that Jhalal was Iraqi, and

Hassan was now Iraqi, too, Gabriel decided. Hassan would show up at Prince Kamal's training camp and convince Jhalal they were lifelong friends. Clement and Shahanna should join them both shortly after that.

That was Gabriel's plan.

Now Hassan would come as no surprise to them.

Henry Archer looked quickly around the room, as if to ensure that no one had overheard. He was actually checking for demons, a species well represented in both the diplomatic and espionage communities. There were a score of tables, mostly unoccupied, but a few had people sitting at them, or someone sitting alone. No one was paying much attention to Henry Archer and his companions, although most shared their occupation. But in one corner, sure enough, sat a group of demons, posing as North Koreans. They were talking with a Chinaman who looked vaguely familiar. Gabriel couldn't remember where he knew him from.

He wracked his brain, leaving Clement and Shahanna to their own devices for a moment. Their interest in each other was taking an upturn, fueled by champagne. They were getting tipsy. Gabriel pretended to do the same. He swiftly sent for another bottle. But his own glass remained untouched.

Tipsy is one thing. The woman who now showed up was out-and-out drunk. She was attractive, but some ten years older than Shahanna and swaying slightly when she walked. Apparently she had decided to turn this trio into a foursome. Her eyes had the brittle glaze of those used to getting their own way, and her expression said she liked the look of Henry Archer, which was why she was here. Her dress was tight-fitting enough to emphasize a buxom figure.

When she sat down she showed a lot of thigh.

Gabriel sensed danger.

She was a novice demon; that was clear to him right away. But that wasn't all. He sensed there was something else, something connected with the North Koreans and their Chinese guest in the corner. Their role wasn't clear, so Gabriel ignored that problem and focused on her.

She helped herself from his glass, one hand on his shoulder, and announced that she found him very attractive.

Clement and Shahanna looked completely nonplussed.

Gabriel suddenly knew why she was here.

This was a message from Lucifer, a reminder of what Gabriel did to him at that White House get-together. The devil was saying he knew where Gabriel was, who he was with and why. There was no other reason to send a demon to this table, and she had been sent, Gabriel realized, by the bogus North Koreans across the room. Gabriel felt foolish for not having noticed them earlier, and again asked himself why that Chinaman was so familiar.

Then he remembered: A week ago, this man served wine to him at Lung Chiang's restaurant. That explained everything. Not only had their white, female demon accosted Gabriel on Lucifer's behalf, but a Chinese-Korean weapons deal was taking place under Gabriel's nose – doubtless very amusing to the devil and those involved. This was Lucifer having the last laugh. Gabriel was not sure what might happen next, but doubted that it would be pleasant, or a coincidence.

The waitress came, bringing a new bottle and checking

discretely if they were okay with that strange woman at their table. She seemed to decide they were, and replenished the ice bucket after refilling everyone's glass.

Gabriel's admirer, whose dress was still riding up, ordered a new bottle without asking anyone, and added: "Let's snap it up there, Honey."

The waitress stalked off.

The female demon gazed at Gabriel. "I'm Leah. Who're you, handsome?"

She slurred most of the words.

"Henry. Henry Archer," said Gabriel. There was no point in not telling her. It was what she was told to ask, although those who sent her recognized Gabriel, so why would they care what name he called himself tonight? The intoxicated woman lurched in her seat and almost lost her balance. She was getting fearfully drunk. Gabriel was sure she had no idea what her masters wanted.

She would have blurted it out already.

"Well, Henry Archer," she said, with a faint hiccup. "Here's to your health." She toasted him with his own glass. It seemed unlikely that the waitress was going to bring her one.

"And to yours," said Gabriel, glad to be rid of his drink, hoping that he'd soon be rid of her.

"Ooh, I love that accent. You're a Brit, huh?"

"Yes, that's right." Well, he was for now.

"What do you do?"

it was a standard Washington question.

The one everybody asked.

"I'm attached to the British Embassy."

"Attached? Hell, I work for an Embassy. Attached means you're some kind of spy, am I right?"

Henry Archer smiled. "Ask me something else."

"Won't talk, huh? Don't you love me, Henry?"

"Madam, you make my knees weak." His upper-class vowels underscored the sarcasm.

It made Clement laugh.

Leah scowled, and drank more champagne.

"More?" Gabriel tapped the bottle. His instinct was to sedate her. Then escort her back to the North Korean table.

"Sure. Champagne is yummy." She stuck out her glass.

Shahanna intervened. Very loudly, she said: "You've had quite enough, and you need to go away."

Leah's eyes swiveled like search-lights, her mouth forming a reply. But someone came behind, and put a hand on her shoulder. It was the recently installed North Korean Ambassador himself, and Gabriel realized, seeing him close up, this was an incredibly dangerous demon. He had been in the consulate since his predecessor was murdered, a few years ago, and spent most of his time passing on nuclear threats in the name of his crazed national leader.

Leah looked very uneasy, and tried to rise. The stocky Korean held her in place with no effort.

"This is my boss," she said nervously. "Mr. – "

"They know who I am," said the Ambassador coldly. He looked over at Gabriel. "But who is this?" It occurred to Gabriel that perhaps this was all she had been told to find out. The information the North Koreans were really after remained a mystery for now.

She hesitated. "Says his name is Archer."

The Ambassador raised an eyebrow. Gabriel saw something flicker in his eyes, then it was gone.

Gabriel was at a loss. Why would they persist with this nonsense? They knew who he was – had known since he arrived. So what did they want? Maybe the Archer identity after all? Gabriel doubted that. He tried to probe the Ambassador's mind, but a shield was firmly in place.

Gabriel stared hard at the Korean's eyes. If he saw anything at all, it was panic, contained, but undeniable.

Gabriel waited, but the Ambassador said nothing. Then he released the woman and helped her from her seat. His face was wooden. "Time to go," he said. The two of them departed.

It was only when the Ambassador rejoined his party and sat down, and Gabriel saw him exchanging glances with Lung Chaing's bodyguard from Beijing, that it fell into place.

Of course! They'd got caught. They did not know Gabriel would be here, and were not, as he first thought, trying to rub his nose in the weapons deal. To the contrary. They were trying to hide it.

The deal was being finalized in D. C. to protect Lung Chiang and his reputation. Gabriel had blundered into it. No wonder they wanted to be sure who he was. They sent the woman so the Ambassador could come and get her. He wanted to get close enough to see if the Angel of Death was indeed here. Now he knew he was mortified. How to explain this to Lucifer? The Koreans should have fled when Gabriel arrived. The Angel of Death smiled broadly. He could only imagine what they would tell the devil. Or what the devil would say to them.

The waitress brought the check. Gabriel insisted on paying, despite the protest of the others, and left a handsome tip. All in money of his own making, each bill a perfect forgery, and good at any bank.

The three walked out together.

The Koreans watched them go.

~ ~ ~

It is always raining in Austria during Spring and Summer, but it had stopped for a short time, and the mountains were free of cloud.

The sun shone on grassy slopes.

The band played loudly: A patriotic accompaniment. Bruno Schwenk looked out over meadows filled with supporters. Half a million throats roared out a Neo-Nazi hymn that he himself had written. Years of work and planning were paying off at last. Schwenk swelled with pride.

A once small political movement was now a blockbuster. Victory at the polls was only days away. Schwenk envisioned the Nazi Party re-instated, not only in Austria, but Germany, too. He saw a sea of Swastikas, heard the tramp of marching feet. Soldiers in gray uniforms would once again make all Germans proud. Nazi armies would conquer, just as they had before, but posing at first as N.A.T.O. Members, blasting through with their tanks, infantry and planes, firing missiles, backed by cannon. Bruno Schwenk felt almost as if it had happened already, and he sensed the same feeling in this crowd. Their fervor washed over him.

Now the singing, and the band, faded away.

It would take three years to dominate Europe militarily and politically, but only if Lucifer kept his promise to eliminate the United States, thus taking them out of the game. And he must do it now, this year.

Three years was nothing.

Then another five to defeat the Chinese.

Schwenk had waited for this moment for over sixty years, since he had been a boy in post-war Vienna, and his personal astrologer was promising. that Schwenk would live long enough to achieve all of his goals.

Barring any accidents.

Or the Archangel Gabriel.

He began his speech. Schwenk had no prepared words or phrases. He did not need them, he just followed the mood. It was the mood of the mob, but somehow it came from Schwenk himself. A wave of frenzied excitement rippled through them. He absorbed it, and used it as a tool. He brought them to the edge of hysteria, knowing what to say and how to say it, and exactly how far to take them. He used his hands. He used his voice, letting its tone rise, and become strident; until he was yelling at them in fury, and they hung on his every word. He had to keep stopping, allowing them to howl their approval. It all went on for over an hour. Schwenk finished with a passage from Mein Kampf. Then it was over.

He looked out at them, and raised one arm in a stiff salute. Every right arm out there responded. The applause was deafening and prolonged. The band struck up again, and played to echoing cheers.

Then he left the stage.

That was how it was done.

As another speaker took his place, he descended wooden steps and went back to the tent behind the platform. He shook hands with everyone he passed, smiling as he thanked them for their help. They were cattle. None of them worth any more to him than the grass upon which they stood. After the election, many such hangers-on would be pushed aside. Later on, once the machinery was turning, some would be arrested. Their loyalty to him, and to the Reich, was questionable.

He changed his shirt and had a campaign worker shine his shoes. He made some notes and sent for his car. Schwenk gulped down two bottles of mineral water one after the other. He always did this after a speech, to soothe a larynx which suffered when he abused it as he had today. Bruno Schwenk always protected his vocal cords. Face and body could age and decay, he didn't mind. The Dark Lord in New York had said that would happen. But Schwenk knew his voice was his secret; the melodic beat to which Austria marched. To which the whole of Europe would soon march. Today Vienna, its weak government and nation were his for the taking, thanks to that golden voice. Next came Germany; it was only fitting . . . and then France . . . and then all the rest. Even those American puppets, the British.

Bruno Schwenk would save them for last.

A united Europe was already crushing America monetarily, tearing apart her weakened economy which would never recover from the Chinese stealing her vast manufacturing base. Europe had its own serious financial woes, but it was ready to march, and in far better economic shape that the United States. German industry had saved its bankrupt neighbors repeatedly; which weakened America further. Once the Nazis were in power, all this would grow steadily worse; then accelerate after the final assault: the devastating attacks promised by Lucifer, wiping out New York and half the country.

There would be no more America for Germans to fear anymore. No hands across the sea. No second front. Bruno

Schwenk's Europe would have a free hand. This time Great Britain would toe the line with all the rest. Otherwise a modern, Stealth-equipped version of the Luftwaffe would bomb London out of existence. Then they would wipe out China in a thermo- nuclear war.

With mountains of dead on both sides.

Pulling on a green, Tyrolean jacket, Schwenk remembered his father: Just a photo in uniform with an Iron Cross. Heinz Schwenk never returned from an American prison camp outside Frankfurt. Nor had anyone else. The allies had not planned for capturing three million prisoners in the depth of Winter. The camps they built were square, open enclosures bounded by chicken wire, with no buildings, no heat – and hardly any food. Freezing cold, and starvation, killed the German prisoners, placing all three million in massed graves by that Christmas. They died as skeletons, walking on spindly legs in the snow, begging for food from well-fed American troops. They died cursing their captors. They died for the Fatherland, at least in the mind of Bruno Schwenk, whose black heart, after all these years, still burned for revenge.

The victorious allies kept it quiet; both at the time – and during the fifty years of cold war that followed. Worldwide horror at Auschwitz and Dachau had not diminished, and the victors feared the obvious comparison to what happened to the remainder of the German army.

Including an Austrian called Heinz Schwenk.

Who might just as well have died in Siberia.

As a guest of the Soviet Union.

Bruno, his son, remembered the Russian occupation of Vienna as a child. First the Cossacks, looting and raping. They killed at random out of twisted revenge and pleasure.

Then the tanks of the Red Army, rolling over living and dead in the streets. Even now, in his seventies, Bruno Schwenk saw their fiendish shapes still, running through the rubble, swigging at bottles of vodka and firing at anything that moved. Austrian civilians, mostly women and children who had survived six years of war, were shot like rabbits. There was not a single pane of glass, not a window unbroken anywhere. The Austrians called it Soviet kisses.

Then the miracle occurred. There were talks in Geneva, and in Vienna, where an aging Volksminister bombarded the Russians with honeyed words and pretty women. The vodka flowed and they agreed to petition Stalin for a full withdrawal. Stalin talked to Roosevelt and Churchill, and was promised anything he wanted. He never got it, but his troops marched out of Austria without firing another shot.

It was a miracle, nothing less.

Then came the Americans. They behaved better, in accord with the standards set in other liberated countries. This meant they behaved like schoolyard bullies – buying anything or anyone they wanted for a pack of cigarettes or a bar of soap. A pair of nylon stockings turned an American soldier into a millionaire. Small luxuries became currency, and people were merchandise. It was as simple as that, Austria tolerated it, for the same reason it was tolerated everywhere else; because, after all, these soldiers were not killing anyone, at least not often – which was a big improvement on the Russians.

Bruno Schwenk, aged eight, did not accept it. His mother became a whore like all the others; she had no other way to feed herself, or him. Her son seethed with hatred and resentment, as a succession of grunting foreigners took their pleasure on a blanket in a corner of the cellar where he and Mama lived. Sometimes he wished these soldiers would shoot her afterwards – for the shame of it.

Sometimes he wanted to do it himself.

Being a child, Bruno had not known how fortunate his country was. To the North, the Germans had to contend with far worse. Almost half the Third Reich was occupied by Russia with all the ferocity, violence and depravity seen in Austria. Sadly for the Germans no Austrian-style miracle ever came. East Germany became a Communist country , and sixteen million souls went under Stalin's yoke, sacrificed by Roosevelt and Churchill to appease Stalin over allied occupation of Berlin – which he considered an affront, having taken the city single-handed. So it was for fifty years, until that wall in Berlin crumbled and fell. And it was during those years that Bruno Schwenk became what he was today: A vengeful monster who hated the world.

The boy grew into a man but never forgot. He held a burning grudge, for a father dead and a mother dishonored. When his mother died, during his teens, Bruno horrified everyone by refusing to attend her funeral. But at school he was a gifted pupil, and went to university on merit, paid for by the state.

He had only one goal – Politics. When he graduated, Nazism was still banned, but small groups had re-emerged under a variety of assumed names. Bruno Schwenk joined one, and was soon a rising star. His gift for making a speech did not go unnoticed, and it was put to good use. Ten years later the law against Neo-Nazis was relaxed.

Twenty years after that, Bruno Schwenk led the most frightening political machine in Europe. It won elections in several Austrian provinces.

It brought him to Lucifer's attention. Austrian and German T. V. Stations, those affiliated to Century News in New York, covered Schwenk's every move, recording his success. He received a personal visit from Scott Anderson, the head of the network, and Bruno Schwenk's destiny became a foregone conclusion. Demonic possession followed, and he became an unstoppable force.

Austria was his for the taking.

Lucifer's bargain was simple: Schwenk must rapidly assume power in Germany, no matter what. Then the economic war on America must be intensified, with Schwenk leading the giant power bloc that was Europe.

Schwenk was confident. Germans were sick of Socialism, and sick of laws being passed in Brussels; not in Germany. They would listen to him: "Why allow France and Holland take part in our future," he would ask, "hating us Germans, as they always have, because they fear us! Germans unite! Throw off this foreign influence! All Teutonic people together! " It was a proven formula. It had worked before; it would work again, with the economy in a slump, unemployment rising, and industrial growth at zero. That made a perfect storm. Schwenk knew it wouldn't take long.

It was already working in Austria.

It would work in Germany.

There was a discrete cough outside the tent. Schwenk called out: "Eintreten!" – the military version of "Come in!"

One of his secretaries came in with a note. Schwenk

smiled at her in dismissal and read the message. It said simply: "Edelweiss Hotel. Eight o' clock." The note was signed: Gabriel.

He folded the paper and put it in his pocket. The Edelweiss Hotel was in the heart of Vienna, half an hour's drive away. And of course Gabriel was the name of the Angel of Death. Surely this note was not from him.

Of course it was.

It had to be.

Bruno Schwenk had destroyed an angel.

Schwenk feared Gabriel, for good reason. The Austrian could read a newspaper. Demons were dying everywhere in recent weeks, mostly from a heart attack, Gabriel's stock in trade; although he had beheaded and chopped up those two in Jerusalem. Now he had sent for Bruno Schwenk. The Austrian's belly crawled with fear. It was one thing to destroy and angel with a curse.

Quite another to face Gabriel.

Yes, this message was from him, Schwenk was sure of it; the Angel of Death wanted retribution. There was only one punishment to fit this crime. Gabriel could kill a demon with a single thought. Bruno Schwenk was doomed.

But only if he went to the Hotel Edelweiss.

So he wouldn't go.

He shivered, despite the sunshine, on his way to the car. He instructed his driver, Fritz, to take the Salzburg Autobahn and avoid Vienna altogether. Schwenk would go to the mountains and hide. He owned a small hunting lodge in the Arlberg that belonged to his father. He could not imagine that the Angel of Death knew about it. The Mercedes, a large, black 500 S L, started to move.

Schwenk sank into the luxury of the back seat. He opened up a hidden cabinet in the arm-rest and poured schnapps into a small metal cup. He quickly gulped it down, feeling better as it burned through throat and chest. Gabriel could wait forever in Vienna. It would do him no good.

There was something unusual about his Chauffeur from the back. Fritz didn't look quite right, from what little could be seen of him with a head-rest between them. Schwenk stared hard for a moment, and shrugged it off. That note from Gabriel, and all it implied, was making him jumpy.

Their speed increased once they got on the Autobahn. Schwenk gazed out at fir trees dying of years of exhaust emission, as the Mercedes cruised at a hundred and fifty kilometers an hour. The limit was one hundred and ten, but Bruno Schwenk, soon to be leader of the Republic, was not likely to get a ticket.

A mist enveloped them as they reached the Arlberg. Objects appeared eerily as the large car approached, then vanished as it swept past. Every now and then, a Swiss-styled Chalet added to the air of enchantment. All the same Schwenk felt a stab of fear. He had no idea why – there was no danger here. Vienna was far away, and getting further away by the minute, making him even safer.

And the Arlberg was a second home. He spent a lot of time there, once his mother died and he learned of its existence. Why had the stupid woman not moved them there after the war, avoiding the horrors they both experienced? Bruno Schwenk would never know. But he enjoyed the seclusion out here. Even the smallest town or village was known to him, and every trail in every forest.

He knew he was safe around here, but his anxiety was returning, just the same. He reached for the schnapps.

Again it did its work.

Eventually they approached the Kitzbach exit and slowed down. Fritz said, "Herr Schwenk, should I look for somewhere to buy food, or see if the Gasthaus is open?"

It was Monday. The Gasthaus would be closed.

Schwenk grunted. "Find something, I'm hungry."

When the driver answered, Schwenk noticed that his voice sounded odd. "I'll stop in the village. That place on the Hauptgasse."

Schwenk knew it – a family-owned Delikatessen, but that voice was bothering him. Something was wrong.

Maybe the man was tired. Fritz was not young anymore. Schwenk had employed him for thirty years and they had been on the road this morning at dawn, to drive to the Rally. Maybe fritz's health was finally failing. It mattered little. There was no friendship or familiarity between them. For Schwenk, his driver was just a means of transport, and a butler. Maybe it was time for a new one.

The Delikatessen Lendl was open.

They stopped and Fritz got out and opened the rear door. Schwenk stayed where he was. He said: "You go in. Here's some money. See if they have any French bread, and get some Leberwurst."

"Yes, sir." Fritz took the offered bills and closed the door. He did look different, perhaps in the way he held himself. He also looked a lot taller. He saluted as he walked away.

And don't take too long, thought Schwenk. This recurring fear of his had to be a warning, and he felt exposed out in the open.

Don't be so stupid, he told himself – you'll soon be in father's lodge. Gabriel is in that hotel, still waiting.

Schwenk's courage had returned by the time Fritz came back. The driver's door opened and closed and the engine restarted. The journey resumed without a word from either of them.

The village of Kitzbach was left behind.

The chauffeur finally spoke. "A friend of mine is dead."

That voice no longer sounded just wrong. It was another voice. This was not Fritz sitting in the front. Schwenk suddenly knew, with dreadful certainty, that Judgement Day had arrived.

Gabriel was driving the car.

Fritz, alive or dead, was back in that meadow.

Schwenk realized he'd been outguessed. The Angel of Death had known he would run, and had simply come with him. And by not going to Vienna, Schwenk had made it easier for him. Vienna was overflowing with witnesses. Kitzbach was only a dot on the map, way off the beaten track, with a tiny population. Hardly anyone knew Schwenk's hunting lodge existed. He had gone to a lot of trouble to ensure that. By coming here he had dug his own grave, and Gabriel had let him. There was no more remote of secluded place in the whole of Austria. Schwenk stared at the winding road in the headlights, with a growing sense of dread.

His life, like his world-conquest, was seriously under threat.

Fear was joined by dismay. It was not meant to end this way. His greatest victory was at hand. Election, and all that followed, had been guaranteed. All the polling said so.

Then Schwenk realized: That was why Gabriel had acted now. It was not just vengeance. It was a brilliant, shattering blow against Lucifer's grand design. That was what made it so final and depressing. Bruno Schwenk knew there was no arguing with Gabriel and no way out. The old Austrian shuddered. The demon in him knew this was the end. He had murdered an angel. His punishment might be a lot worse than a heart attack. The Angel of Death had gone to a lot of trouble on Schwenk's account. He must have some dreadful form of torture in mind.

The thought froze Bruno Schwenk's blood.

He tried to invoke the devil. He had done it before, several times, and it worked. For example, when he killed that angel, and got into this situation. Schwenk muttered the necessary incantation, his voice low, and waited expectantly. But there was no upsurge of power and no unity with Lucifer, as usually happened. From the devil, in his New York apartment, there came a bleak wall of darkness.

Lucifer was ringed by angels.

Schwenk was a rat in a trap.

"Angel Gabriel," he stammered. "You tricked me perfectly. I did not expect you here."

Gabriel said nothing.

Schwenk blundered on. "It was a mistake,' he said. "The curse was far stronger than I thought. A mistake – I swear it."

Gabriel's hands gripped the wheel. "It was a death curse, applied with Lucifer's help. You tried it again just now. They only have one purpose."

"Well, yes. But it was a mistake. Just trying to protect myself. Then and now." He decided to try begging. "I never meant any harm. Please spare me!"

Gabriel turned off the main road. They were deep into the mountains, with sharp rises and hairpin bends. Their speed dropped to a crawl, and the engine howled a protest in second gear. Schwenk began crying and babbling one excuse after another, most of his words drowned out by the Mercedes.

Gabriel stared at the road.

They labored up a rocky gradient. The fog grew thicker as they got higher, and the temperature got lower. Schwenk shivered, and his knees were knocking, not entirely from the cold.

They stopped at the hunting lodge.

It was served by a narrow path. Gabriel parked, and turned to stare at Schwenk until the Austrian opened his door and got out. They left the car and walked in the chilly mist. The angel stayed on Schwenk's heels. The old man slowed to an awkward stop, as he fished for his keys, and said: "Look, don't do this. Please don't . . ."

"Just open up," said Gabriel. "We'll talk inside."

"Yes, yes. Of course."

Schwenk led inside, switching on lights until they reached the kitchen. Gabriel had brought in the groceries. He put them on the table. "How very modern. Everything looks brand new."

"Want some bread and Leberwurst?"

"No. Nor do you."

Schwenk realized this was it.

He said: "Can't I at least sit down." He had decided that only a heart attack could be administered in that position.

There was no answer.

The room began to spin. A distant voice, sounding like Gabriel echoed in his mind, saying that nothing could save him. Schwenk groaned. Then he cried out for forgiveness and a second chance. Gabriel thought otherwise, and squeezed the Austrian's heart, very hard.

Schwenk staggered, and grabbed at the table. He missed, and collapsed to the floor, striking the table with his forehead.

He did not die easily. Gabriel toyed with him, squeezing and releasing. Schwenk screamed with pain. Finally he could scream no more and his breath came in gasps. He lay in a puddle of urine; his lips trickled blood. The payment for killing an angel called Mordecai. And wanting to imitate Hitler.

Gabriel snapped his fingers.

The darkness descended.

CHAPTER EIGHT

IT MADE HEADLINES for a week.

There was a flood of tributes to Bruno Schwenk from his supporters, curt regrets at his death from opponents and critics. Excerpts of his biography were splashed over the internet and shown on T. V. around the world. A memorial service was held, and the city of Vienna was swamped with Nazi mourners.

But without Schwenk the election was lost.

The discovery of his body marked the end of a manhunt instigated by his driver, one Fritz Kohler, who had reported his employer missing.

The genuine Fritz had awoken, the day after Schwenk's triumphant speech in the meadows, in his own bed and in his own apartment, with no idea how he got there. In a panic, he had telephoned Party Headquarters – to hear that not only Schwenk, but also the Mercedes was missing. Party wisdom was that Schwenk had probably taken a short, unscheduled break, with or without female companionship, and there was no cause for concern. Fritz Kohler knew better. In thirty years Bruno Schwenk had not dallied with either sex, and he did not take vacations – especially on the brink of the most important election of his life. The chauffeur was alarmed, and called the police. It was days before anyone thought of the hunting lodge near Kitzbach.

Austrian police found no trace of a break-in or struggle. Groceries on the table indicated an intended short stay in Schwenk's mountain hideaway. His car was parked outside, proving he must have driven himself. Only one set of footprints (Schwenk's) in the snow – from the car to the house. Medical evidence pointed to a massive, coronary stroke. The victim was not young. No grounds to suspect foul play. Bruno Schwenk had died of a heart attack, not surprising for a man who ate bread and Leberwurst at his age. The coroner in Vienna confirmed those findings the very same day.Lucifer's rage, when he heard, was uncontrollable.

The very phrase 'Heart Attack' screamed 'Gabriel'.

Everything was deteriorating into a battle with this fucking Archangel! Lucifer smoked one cigar after another, pacing his penthouse floor, and had tantrums at every news editor and producer that worked for him. It wasn't the first time he blamed them for news that angered him, but this was worse than anyone could remember, and few of them knew why.

Those who did kept their mouths shut.

Pure spite was Lucifer's next reaction: He fired just about every staffer he had in Austria; he fired their reporters, and screamed at the head of his Austrian network for half an hour, at the transatlantic phone-rate, then fired him. Now the devil felt better. So did Century investors; because the huge empire that made up Century networks was not confined to the United States, and it was less harmful to corporate interests if he lost his temper overseas.

~ ~ ~

Beauregard Clement was also having a bad day.

All investigation into the removal of Oman Ben Salim and Amir Affhad had come to nothing; despite his having consulted every informant he had – not only here at home, but by flying all over the Middle-East to talk to some of the scariest people on the planet. That all ended now. Word had come down from the D. H. S. Director: Money and man-hours were being wasted – and today the case was officially dropped. Clement had run out of gas.

And that was not the only reason for Clement's bad mood: There had been a lot of high-profile deaths across the world in recent weeks, and the common factor was nuclear weapons. Those killed were either trying to buy them, or supply them, rather like Oman Ben Salim and Amir Affhad, who died plotting an attack on America with atomic devices on behalf of Al Qaeda. Clement believed all these deaths were connected, and had been hoping to tie all the facts together. But now with his investigation canceled, there was no way to do it.

Part of Clement refused to let go. He sat at his desk, determined to give it one last try, making a list of linked murders that could go to Heathcote with a request for taking further action:

A brothel owner and drug financier in North Germany, with connections to Oman Ben Salim and Amir Affhad. Heart attack.

A Russian General accused of trying to sell missiles to Amir Affhad unexpectedly committed suicide.

The Commander of N. O. R. A. D. died. Heart attack. No cause for suspicion, but the General was responsible for most of America's nuclear missiles.

Two of the same General's strategic squadron pilots were murdered. Their bodies were spotted by a truck-driver in Utah. The wind had disturbed a freshly dug grave-site at the side of the road, exposing arms and legs when the trucker stopped on a deserted highway to relieve himself. Nuclear bomber pilots are highly trained, highly valued and highly privileged. How did these two get themselves killed?

Earlier that same week, on the same highway, a dozen or so crazies from all over the country – members of a paramilitary group called the Free Patriots – were burned alive in their motel. Charred body parts revealed that they were tortured with electrodes before they died. Two local men confessed, and were in custody. Both psychotic criminals who recently joined the Utah chapter of a Satanic cult. Clement could make nothing of this incident, and crossed it off his list.

He sat staring at his desk-top for a long time. He had to admit that nothing really meshed together. The connections were thin, the incidents too spread out and the detail too skimpy. Hard evidence of any link eluded him. Clement knew it was not enough to take to Heathcote.

He erased the list from his document file.

The next item for attention was a message from Jhalal. It was a classic mix of good and bad news.

The undercover Iraqi had been chosen for the Al Qaeda Attack on America, but he was still in a cave in Pakistan. The proposed training site in Syria was wiped out by that Israeli Commando raid. However, the best part of Jhalal's coded text was so good it was priceless, outlining details of the plot:

Everything was funded and led by Prince Kamal, an up-and-coming Saudi Royal. Clement knew about this prince – he had a reputation as an international playboy who liked to hurt people, including women, in his spare time. A man ruthless in his financial dealings. Word on the

Arab street said it was unwise to get in Prince Kamal's way. Also known to be something of a drinker, sex-fiend and womanizer – a habitual smoker of hashish, equally addicted to luxury hotels and cars. But this was the first mention of any involvement with Al Qaeda.

Jhalal said the Prince was rumored to be visiting the United States, and before he returned, a new training camp would be available. Clement made a phone call when he read this. US Immigration had no trace of Kamal for several months; which meant the Saudi had used a false name. If he was here at all.

Clement decided he was.

It meant Al Qaeda had a big-shot on the loose in the United States, working on a large-scale, terrorist attack. And not only that, but Clement's nuclear-related body count indicated that such weapons might well be involved.

Recent footage from airport security cameras would have to be played back and gone through face by face. There was no great likelihood that Prince Kamal would turn up on film. If he was smart enough to use an assumed identity, he knew enough to avoid being photographed. Clement would have the tapes reviewed anyway. This Saudi was a clear and present danger wherever he was.

Jhalal had indicated the United States.

That was good enough.

Suddenly Clement knew what to do, and what to say to Heathcote. This Prince must be found before he went back. On the surface that was a tough proposition, given the size of America and the thousands of foreigners visiting at any time. But as Clement saw it, this Saudi made an easier target while he remained on American soil. His Royal Highness shouldn't be too hard to find.

This was no trained terrorist, skilled at evasion. This was a pampered rich-boy, used to the best of everything and going first-class when he traveled. His background and upbringing said he would not hide out in some small town in Tennessee, Idaho or Oklahoma. He did not have enough sense. The prince was addicted to a life of luxury. He would doubtless stay in four-star hotels in big cities, rent fancy cars from exclusive companies and act like a typical big-spender. He would dine at the best establishments, ordering fine wines and delicacies in the company of expensive women. If his picture were sent to top caterers and hoteliers, it should be a matter of hours before somebody gave him up. Then the FBI could grab him, and deport him or throw him in jail. That would be up to Heathcote.

Clement pursed his lips in thought.

There was another way to handle this.

Maybe the prince should not be arrested; merely watched. Follow Kamal back to whichever airport he chose to go home from, and watch him during the flight. He could Chiang planes, doubling back, or even switch identities en-route. It didn't matter. Once they had Prince Kamal, they must never let go.

He would lead them to Jhalal,

And to the new camp.

And the quicker he did this the better.

Clement gathered his thoughts and his notes together, getting ready to go upstairs to his boss. But before he could get out of his chair, the telephone rang.

He picked it up. "Agent Clement."

"Afternoon, sir. This is Sergeant Dunne in satellite surveillance."

Clement sat up. "Yes?"

"Your request, sir, some time ago, to search for new terrorist camps. Well, we have one."

Stay calm, Clement told himself. It might be nothing. "Where?" he said.

"Iran. In direct line to the Afghan border." This was certainly not nothing. Jhalal could be there already.

Clement said: "I'd like an aerial scan, as soon as possible."

"I'm emailing it now, on a secure lap-top."

"Looks like a training site?"

"Matter of fact, it does. Just setting up, and we have a high-definition telephoto series of close-ups – some faces for you to look at. I'll send originals later by messenger; for better clarity."

"Great! Sergeant, you just made my day. However this turns out, you get a case of scotch – single malt."

"Well, thank you." The Sergeant sounded pleased. "Glad to help, sir."

They both hung up.

Clement sat back in his chair, feeling better than he had all day. The Iran border. That made sense. Another mountain area, full of nooks and crannies to hide in. Not far from where Jhalal and other recruits were hiding in caves. Clement was not surprised. Iran was up to its neck in terrorism and always had been. Prince Kamal could hardly ask for a better host than Saudi Arabia's bitterest enemy. But as a Sunni, he would be deep in the most hostile of Shiite strongholds. Clement decided that this ought to weigh heavily on Kamal's mind.

That was something to think about.

Maybe it could be used against him.

Jhalal could say things, stoking a furnace of paranoia.

Twenty or so work-spaces across the room, a secretary stood up and yelled: "Fax for Agent Clement!"

"Coming!" Clement yelled back.

Her name was Alice, and she was a tough cookie. Clement would have to sign a security log. And it was she who would unscramble the transmitted material. Clement put on his humble look.

He headed for her desk.

He called over to Jean Holloway, who sat across the aisle. "I'm seeing Heathcote at two. Let him know I'll be late."

She said she would.

Clement signed for his Fax and received a small sheaf of shiny pages, He made his way back to his desk.

One of the first pages he looked at showed Jhalal, cross-legged on a blanket, eating from a tin plate with his fingers. The detail was good enough to show pieces of chicken and the pattern and coarseness of the blanket; so Clement had no trouble recognizing his man.

The next shot was of a black face, new to Clement, so he fed it into the computer. The name came up as Asuto Kenyatta, a South African known to have fought for Hamas and Al Qaeda on several fronts during the last five years. The photograph showed a guy who would fight the entire world single-handed, and couldn't wait to get started. Asuto Kenyatta was a hard-bitten killer.

There were a lot more photos, showing a lot more faces. A few were on file, who were easier to track, but most were not, being raw recruits, and that was a bad thing, these unknowns could slip through Clement's fingers that much easier. Of course these pictures would be in everybody's data-bases, including Immigration at every American entry point, but no system is foolproof, and one photograph, taken by satellite, is hardly the best way to spot somebody who might be disguising their appearance. People like that could sneak in every day.

Clement set aside the personal pictures and thought: Right, let's see where they've taken Jhalal.

The aerial views were detailed, and extremely clear, made up of digitally enhanced satellite shots taken from the outer hemisphere, and enlarged until you could count large rocks as they lay on the ground. Clement arranged the various segments on his desk, like a Jig-Saw puzzle, for a full overhead view.

He jotted some notes.

Total area of camp – less than two acres. Tent lines both sides; latrines along the southern fence. One large wooden hut for instructors (or the camp leader?) One on-site water tower on a brick foundation; two vehicles in plain sight: One a battered Jeep, the other a run-down truck, both with their camouflage nets still on the ground. Obviously Prince Kamal did not plan on any long distance travel.

Clement had to admire the efficiency of Sergeant Dunne: Numbered arrows on this picture-map showed where the recruits in those close-up shots had been found by the eye in the sky.

Dunne's satellite source was a high-flying module leased from an Anglo French Aerospace company. Clement imagined it with antenna fully extended, capturing the camp on film before sweeping on through the dark atmosphere. Clement was lucky to have satellite access, and hoped it would continue. Heathcote was warning that budget concerns might shut him down soon. This sort of thing devoured money, and the search for one Iraqi must not be allowed to bankrupt an entire department. But now Clement had to believe that finding this camp, and finding Jhalal, would save him. Nothing gets funds quicker than success.

That reminded him of his appointment with Heathcote. The time was Two Twenty-five. Clement would be at least half an hour late. He began working on his apology as he ran for the elevator.

TAPED   MINUTES:
CLEMENT/HEATHCOTE/MUNROE
> May 5th, 2: 50 pm.
> (Door closes.)

CLEMENT: "Sir, I'm sorry for the delay . . ."

HEATHCOTE: "It's okay, Bo. Your secretary called, and Alice sent me a copy of the stuff you just received by e-mail. Take a seat. I had chairs brought upstairs for you two gentlemen. Now, Senior Agent Clement, let me introduce Doctor Eugene Munroe. He runs NASA's satellites, including the magnificent bird you're hooked into. His folks took your camp pictures, and he's got something else that will blow your mind. Filmed a few days ago."

MUNROE: "I want you both to look at this – footage taken over northern Iraq during the last daylight sweep. These prints are grainy, but what we need to see is quite well defined."

CLEMENT: "It's some sort of armored transporter."

MUNROE: "Yes, it is. And if you look at this later shot, you'll see the open doors, and workers in protective clothing. For over two hours, they followed the procedure for unloading a neutron core – the heart of any atomic bomb. They unloaded six of them. Iran just went nuclear."

HEATHCOTE: "And where did the truck come from?"

MUNROE: "We ran the license plate, and got lucky on another sky-cam. This shot, taken two days ago, shows the same truck getting loaded in Dubai from a North Korean freighter."

HEATHCOTE: "Christ – North Korea. I guess we can say this material is not for some nuclear power station."

MUNROE: "I think we need to act quickly. What else do you think?"

CLEMENT: "We have to assume this is for Prince Kamal. It might not be, but the odds are good. Six devices is too much of a coincidence."

HEATHCOTE: "Well, it's clear, Bo, your guy on the spot just became worth his weight in gold, and your other mission just went top priority."

CLEMENT: "My other mission, sir? You mean I can go?"

HEATHCOTE: "Yeah, you're going – you and Shahanna. These nukes in Iran are a stone's throw from where your guy, Jhalal, is sitting with a plate of rice in his lap. And you can bet your ass on this: They will turn six cores into viable bombs in no time, bombs that are coming here to America. That's why you're going there, Bo. Your Iraqi is going to need help. If you can find him."

CLEMENT: "You're approving my undercover insertion plan? Me and Shahanna as star-crossed lovers? She evil – me stupid."

HEATHCOTE: "Well, I don't like it – but this situation is red hot. I can't think of anything better, or quicker. I have to use you and Shahanna. I must have someone with your capability on the scene. Once those bombs are ready and delivered to this camp, I need you and Shahanna as well as Jhalal. God knows how quickly those terrorists and bombs will disappear. Christ! They can be here in a month!"

CLEMENT: "How soon do we go?"

HEATHCOTE: "Whoa, son, you have to prepare, Your cover story is a good one, as far as it goes. But it's got some holes and it will take time to get it right. Then there's background and documents. People in places you never lived have to swear they went to school with you and went to your granddaddy's funeral. You also need fake parents and a birth certificate. Same thing for Shahanna Dufaux, once we decide where she's from. I'm saying two weeks."

CLEMENT: "Two weeks is fine, sir. I was afraid you'd say four."

HEATHCOTE: "Then there's passports, credit cards, bank accounts and all that. Two weeks is rushing it – and here's something else: To get past Prince Kamal's crowd alive, your character has to be more than some lovesick fool. They don't like us messing with their women. Hell, they'd cut your throat – then eat breakfast."

CLEMENT: "We'll come up with something, sir."

MUNROE: "How about a background in nuclear physics, like hers? That ought to make him more attractive."

HEATHCOTE: "Damn, Eugene. I like that."

CLEMENT: "So do I . . . it fits. It's the only reason Shahanna had anything to do with me in the first place. We're in the same field – she saw my potential, and she's been stringing me along ever since."

HEATHCOTE: "And she treats you like crap. It does fit."

CLEMENT: "I'll need a crash course from someone really good; just the basics of how a bomb works, and how to make one. These guys aren't looking for someone to run their national nuclear program. We also need a convincing way to meet Prince Kamal, or one of his underlings. We think he's in America right now, and I'm already after the son of a bitch!"

HEATHCOTE: "Okay, that's a start. Now I want an air-tight plan, or nothing doing. Understand, we have our work cut out. This has to be as safe as we can make it. Eugene, keep that bird of yours aimed at that camp any time it's in range. We have to know what these lunatics are up to, with as few interruptions as possible. The lives of three agents depend on it."

MUNROE: "Will do, Brad."

HEATHCOTE: "Right, we know what to do. Let's get to work."

TAPE ENDS

Lucifer gloated when his nuclear program was solved by North Korea, despite his rage at being told that Gabriel had somehow witnessed the entire proceeding. On top of that the devil had suffered a substantial setback – returning Karl Jaeger's deposit to Al Qaeda, along with Prince Kamal's six hundred billion, and that was only a fifty per cent down payment. Lung Chiang and North Korea would split the rest, as well, but Lucifer had decided he could live with that.

And gloat.

Armageddon was now in motion.

That evening he dined with Lewin Smith – President of Century Cable News – in the executive suite of their corporate headquarters in New York, an edifice dominating the skyline and known as Century Tower. If Century Corporation was Lucifer's crowning achievement, then Century Cable News was the jewel in that crown. Lewin Smith was a Londoner, and worked there for Century, until Scott Anderson moved him up the food chain and across the Atlantic. In London, Smith's nickname had been "Hard Bollocks", an obscene British testament to his take-no-prisoners management style. Here in New York, he was known as "The Crocodile", in an American tribute to the same thing. He was rumored to be bi-sexual, and was equally hard on male and female employee alike. Lewin Smith was ruthless, utterly without scruples, and the best scandal monger anyone had ever seen. It made him the perfect News Director. But the devil, when he brought him over, had wanted a change of direction: All news coverage was to become pure politics; no more sex-scandals, rapes, child molesters or celebrity murder-trials. None of the old material that was Lewin Smith's stock-in-trade. Lucifer wanted to home in on the dirt and scandal of major-league American politics. Century News would stay in the gutter, but only the gutter in Washington D. C. – a gutter that overflowed with filth and slime, most of it concocted by him.

It was a novel concept when century launched it, but other networks followed and it became a blue-print for the entire industry, a format so effective that American T. V. news was changed forever. Lewin Smith's job was its own reward. He now had more power than the White House.

The devil had made him President of something far bigger than America.

Then came war: Invasion in the Middle-East. Covering political scandal suddenly took a back seat. Century News poured patriotism into American living-rooms, and both Generals and politicians must be seen without blemish. Breaking this rule had ruined a most promising war in Viet-Nam. So Lewin Smith's team went back to child molesters and rapists. America hungered for lewdness, and Century News was expert at serving it up. The devil was pleased, and showered Smith with generosity. Over the years, the Brit had become rich, sleek and fat, and liked nothing better than a gourmet meal. To dine here tonight was the highlight of Lewin Smith's week. It would also put more unsightly pounds on his midriff.

Only his credibility was thin.

This evening Scott Anderson had ordered braised lamb. It was served on a large, silver salver by a white-clad chef.

As they were eating, Lucifer said: "Think this wine sauce has too much garlic?"

"Not a bit," said Smith.

The devil knew it was sincere, reading the mind of this man who, after all, came from a nation of sheep-eaters. Smith's compliment was genuine.

Lucifer said: "I like to have that tang; to offset the heavy flavor of the meat."

"Absolutely delicious, sir."

Lewin Smith was good at ass-kissing; besides all his other qualities, and the devil never tired of it.

Lucifer prodded at a potato with his fork. "I'm informed that Iran has obtained enough atomic material for half a dozen suicide bombs." He applied his knife without haste.

Smith looked up from his plate. "Are you serious?"

"Absolutely."

Lucifer was pleased by Smith's astonishment, but also saw that the professional in him was hooked. This was how a T. V. Audience would react: Lewin Smith was horrified, but fascinated at the same time, and craving for more. America would respond the same way. This meant sky-high ratings for weeks to come; worth far more than any money lost to North Korea. It was why this dinner was taking place. No one could instinctively drive ratings like Lewin Smith.

Smith was just the man for this: A master at media manipulation. He knew how to fill Americans with terror; then take that terror and exploit it. And the best part was that this time the fear was justified; because Iran did indeed have the weapons – and Century News could shout it from the rooftops. And while this was going on, Lewin Smith would analyze, dissect and rearrange American public opinion. He would run opinion polls and focus groups, taking the nation's pulse like a doctor. And from that Lucifer could decide how to shape this story – knowing in advance what viewer-reaction would be. It worked even better than hypnotism.

And used virtually no satanic power.

The devil began his sales-pitch to Lewin Smith: "Remember those two terrorist big-shots, the ones who got chopped to pieces in Jerusalem?"

"Vaguely."

"Well, I had an odd feeling about that and I've looked into it. It seems those two were cooking up a nuclear attack on America – buying weapons and recruiting suicide squads. Others have carried on where they left off, and now, with this Iran thing – do I need to draw a picture?"

Lewin Smith hated all things Arab. "Bloody Hell," he said. "Are you sure?"

"I pay a lot for this type of information. More than one source gave me this. Our intelligence agencies know, and are saying nothing. That allows us to leak the story and blame the leak on them. We break this as a Century exclusive, quoting unnamed White House insiders."

Smith nodded thoughtfully. "That's definitely the way to go."

The devil felt invigorated. He loved the way Lewin Smith was sucking all this up. Of course there were no paid informers – in Washington or anywhere else. Lucifer had far better sources than that. His information came from those who had sold the neutron cores to Iran. Having it confirmed by a renegade angel in China was like the cherry on the cake. The corruption of Lung Chiang was Lucifer's greatest triumph. And the best part was sticking it to the Angel Gabriel.

"The news story of a life-time," said Smith, envisioning not only high ratings, but also a healthy bonus from Scott Anderson. "Does our competition know?"

"My sources are exclusive. Trust me."

"Oh, I do."

Spoken like a true believer.

Lucifer was amused. Lewin Smith was not a demon; nor was he possessed by one. Yet. But he'd make a good candidate when the time came. Lewis Smith was a thoroughly evil man, with no idea who his employer really was.

The devil resumed eating with great relish.

His dinner guest, on the other hand, put down his knife and fork, dabbed at his lips with a napkin and got ready to voice his thoughts.

Lucifer swallowed, grimaced and reached for more wine.

Smith said: "We break this on the evening broadcasts, as you say, but without too much detail, quoting White House and Intel sources. If they know about these nukes, as you think they do, their denial will be useless. They look bad for keeping it quiet. Then, for maximum impact we release full details on our breakfast news and talk show. They never quote sources. They usually don't have any; they just make it up as they go along. We can tell this any way you want."

This breakfast show was a blockbuster – the Century News juggernaut that had wiped out all its competition, including C.N.N. And Fox News. It was a strict, talk-show format, with a typical Lucifer slant, and it had topped the ratings for five years straight. Advertising revenues were sky-high.

It was called American Dawn, and combined the successful aspects of every other show of its type. It was Lucifer's prized creation, an opinion-shaping monster based on lies and propaganda. It was hosted by two women and a man. All three were household names. All three of them held right wing views. And all three were unflinching in their Patriotism. There the similarity ended. Two of them were rather stupid, the man and one of the women, while the other woman – the show's virtual star, was intelligent; ruthless; and had the instincts of an alley cat.

Her name was Kathy Lester.

A Century News Powerhouse.

The show itself was mean-spirited and took no prisoners. Its hosts criticized the President at every turn, just as they criticized any Democrat. Their material came from Scott Anderson himself: the topics to discuss, what issues to raise, and who to admire or politically assassinate, of course, and the man in the White House was constantly being roasted on a spit. The program was in its seventh year, and Lucifer had already chosen it to launch the Iranian nukes story.

He found it gratifying that Lewin Smith had done the same thing.

The devil stopped eating and pretended to consider. "I think you're right," he said. "The breakfast show. That's a great idea! We need to remind people just how scary Iran really is. This is just the right show for that. It's target audience are paranoid sheep who hate all foreigners – with Muslims topping the list. We bring out old coverage of Iran, its leaders spewing hatred, denying the Holocaust, calling us the Great Satan – and shaking their fist at the world. We show Iranians burning the American flag, storming American Embassies and Consulates; that sort of thing. We blame the White House for not fighting back, and being afraid of a terrorist regime that hates our guts. People will simply eat it up."

"How long do we run it?"

Lucifer said: "This will run for weeks. Make it your main feature until further notice on the morning show, and headline it on our news updates for the next few days. By then it will dominate the news, and we milk it to death.

So will the rest of the media industry. Morning, evening, late-night – you name it. This story is going to change the world."

"And then there's your PAC's."

Lucifer smiled. It was almost as if his News Director had a crystal ball. Century's financing of their own PAC's, or Political Action Committees, was Lucifer at his most inspired. It was also very effective. Century News remained a silent partner while these action groups advertised, delivering their right-wing political message, on every Century channel. It was incestuous, and brilliant – one wolf feeding the other. In the case of the Iranian Nukes, they would take on the President one-on-one, repeatedly telling viewers in thirty-second spots, that Christiansen was weak on terror – and completely unable to deal with Iran and this nuclear threat.

The best part, for Lucifer, was that his PAC. Advertising revenues exceeded what Century spent setting them up in the first place, because other billion-dollar corporations were lining up to contribute. Another pleasing factor was that Century News did not have to defend this most convenient political loophole. It was signed into law years ago by the Congress, and upheld by the Supreme Court.

For a while Lucifer and Smith ate in silence. Finally Smith asked the big question: "Where did Iran buy the nukes?"

The devil grinned and waved his knife and fork. "That's next month's story. You don't have to tell them everything at once. North Korea did the deed – another country that Americans love to hate – and we'll run with that, just like we're running with this. We, you and I,

Lewin, are about to own public opinion outright. And that will become a continuing situation for months to come."

But Smith was only half listening. His brain was ticking, as he worked out game plays and what order to execute them in – thinking and planning like a major-league coach. The ability that got him this job.

Lucifer's glass was empty. So was the bottle. He rang a small silver bell to summon his stooping demon butler.

The servant appeared.

"What do we have in a good Bordeaux?" the devil asked.

The answer came in dreadful, hell-spawn gibberish, but the wine offered met with the devil's approval, and the butler went off to fetch it.

"How soon can you start?" the devil asked Lewin Smith.

"Late tonight. And American Dawn tomorrow morning."

"Good. Introduce it on the morning show as breaking news. In-screen headlines, with a supporting crawl underneath, the whole nine yards. Which of our three attack dogs will you use?"

Lewin Smith considered. "The star, I think. To do it justice."

"I agree. Pretends anger well."

Again, Lucifer's choice. Kathy Lester, his empress of evil. Besides being lead-host on American Dawn she had her own recently established Sunday political commentary program: "Century Compass" (Find Your Way in Politics.) The format was as right-wing as Kathy herself, who was currently Scott Anderson's spoiled favorite. She was attractive, well-educated and came from Chicago. She was clever with words and wielded American patriotism like a sledgehammer.

Kathy Lester was a no-bull-shit straight shooter from the Mid-West with just the right know-how to exploit America's fear of Islam. She would talk tough, harking back to the World-Trade Center; then blame Iran for everything from that to the Shiite rebels in the Gaza. By the time Kathy got to the Iranian nukes, America would be screaming for blood. No doubt about it: Lewin Smith knew his work. Kathy Lester would spin this story like a top. The devil need look no further, This news campaign would be a work of art. Then newsmen from other networks would take it and spread it across the air-waves like rancid butter.

Lucifer smiled. He said: "Have Kathy introduce it as an unconfirmed rumor. Our competitors will swoop in and run with it, unconfirmed or not. Then she confirms it on her next show, attributing the story to those same networks. She protects my sources by denying we broke the story. Kathy's very good at this sort of thing. Our viewers believe any lie she tells. Sacks of fan-mail, every day."

The butler returned, and poured a little wine for them to taste. It was judged to be adequate, and both their glasses were filled.

Lewin Smith said: "Kathy's visiting her children for a few days, in Connecticut. Her ex-husband lives out there. He has custody. She got most of his money."

Lucifer knew all of this. He grunted into his wine glass. "Ask her to return early. Use my name if you have to."

"Yes, sir," said Smith. "I'll call her now." He got to his

feet.

"Sit down," said Lucifer. "Jonathan's made desert, and we haven't had coffee yet. Another half hour won't make any difference. Kathy Lester gets a few more minutes with here brats."

~ ~ ~

New York police did not find Prince Kamal at any of the better hotels in their city. Clement's red-flag was worthless, with half a million visitors at any given time, and not enough manpower to widen the search. Patrolmen with photographs could not try every front desk in Manhattan. The NYPD already had more listed possible terrorists than they could handle. They told Clement they were sorry.

It was soon a familiar response.

Police departments all along the Eastern Seaboard said the same thing. They were too busy. No sign of Prince Kamal under any name. It was a dead end.

Clement tried the West Coast with little hope of success. This was quickly proved correct, and he was running out of cities and states.

He decided to try the heartland.

The Midwest had very few ethnic Arabs – few of whom were considered radical, and none of whom were considered a threat. As a matter of fact, police there were taken aback by the question.

Clement became desperate.

He requested airport surveillance tapes, and Manhattan street observation-tapes. He was getting ready to ask for the same thing from other major cities when the miracle happened. One tape, from JFK three days before, showed Prince Kamal coming into a baggage hall and going through Customs. He was a Jordanian called Abdul Rashid. And he was gone.

No record of where he went.

But it was something.

Prince Kamal was here.

Clement called NYPD. again. They agreed to send out men to ask cab drivers about incoming flights that day, and show Prince Kamal's photograph. There were a lot of taxis involved. It was several days before Clement got lucky, and they found the driver called Kiro Yovkov.

The driver who remembered Prince Kamal.

Now help from other agencies came springing out of the woodwork. Among other things, an anti-terrorist unit that New York noticeably did not offer before was suddenly put at Clement's disposal. Clement said thanks; but no thanks. Just put the taxi driver on a plane.

Kiro was flown to Washington at government expense. He'd arrived this morning, and was seated beside Clement's desk, a cup of coffee in one hand, doughnut and napkin balanced precariously on one knee. Kiro smelled of cabbage and tobacco and his clothes were greasy. He did not speak English very well.

His green card said he was Bulgarian. Clement, like everyone else, was struck by how tall he was.

Because Kiro Yovkov was Gabriel.

In Washington the angel had taken to looking at Heathcote's computer every day, reading encrypted traffic and anything sensitive concerning the Middle East. It was how he learned of Clement's search for Prince Kamal. That caused a cab driver named Kiro Yovkov to show up at JFK and tell a cop that he took the Prince downtown one week ago.

That got the Angel of Death on a plane to Washington.

Agent Clement was pleased to meet him; every bit as pleased as he was to bump into his old friend Henry Archer a week ago, just as Prince Kamal was smuggling himself into the United States.

Clement treated his unexpected guest like an idiot-savant. Kiro had an easy-going, friendly manner, a wide gap-toothed grin – and the thickest Slavic accent anybody ever heard. You had to strain to catch what he was saying. He wore a fake designer watch and a cheap red tie. Everyone on Clement's floor treated him like an astronaut preparing for a spacewalk.

The interview had just started. Clement said: "Exactly where did you last see the Prince?"

Gabriel answered in English that sounded Russian. "Sir, I already say to police in New York: He get out Time Square."

"What about before that?" said Clement. "While you were driving. Did he speak? What kind of thing did he say?"

Gabriel shrugged. "Not say much. Say only: Go downtown. Then he say, when I driving: Go Time Square. All this I say them in New York." Kiro's story fitted the facts. Prince Kamal chose Time Square when the Angel of Death drifted into his cab and made a mental suggestion. Just before the Prince walked across a park and had his momentous experience with Artis Brown.

Clement groaned inwardly. Kiro Yovkov was right – everything he was saying was in the police transcripts sent from New York. But the ground had to be covered again. Go back to the start, hear it told again from the beginning, and keep repeating the process. If there was anything of value, it would eventually emerge. It was out of a text book, but it worked, as long as you had the time.

Clement wasn't sure he did.

But Kiro was his only chance.

Clement said: "Let's go back to basics. Six days ago you pick up a Saudi Prince in your cab. Did you know he was a Prince?"

"Yes, sir . . . recog . . . nize. Kiro recognize him, okay?"

"And he's in your cab. Didn't that seem strange? Why wouldn't such a man use a Limo?"

Kiro spread his hands and looked confused. "Sir, I cannot know this. Prince say go downtown."

"Okay. Was he dressed like a Prince? Try and remember what you thought at the time." Clement knew that if Kamal was posing as a middle-class Arab they would never find him.

Kiro bobbed his head theatrically, causing movement of his whole body, and almost spilling his coffee. The doughnut and its plate teetered alarmingly on his knee. "Yes, he wear very fine clothes. I know Prince from magazines – he look like my brother, Gregor. Prince very same like him."

"Was he rude, or polite? How did he treat you?"

Kiro Yovkov flashed a wide smile. "Oh, no. Prince not rude. He very polite. But he cheap. He say how much downtown? Before we drive. He not get in car, until he know. He tell me, go Time Square. Then say no pay tip, only pay fare." This was true. Prince Kamal had been bullying the real driver, when Gabriel entered the cab.

None of this helped Clement. "Remember anything else?"

It was time to mention Scott Anderson, but not too

quickly. Gabriel screwed Kiro's face into a frown. "I don't –
"

"Give it a try," coaxed Clement. "Was anyone else around while you had him as a passenger? Was he with anyone?"

"Someone else? No . . . wait, yes! – cell phone. Prince call someone he know, from my cab."

"Who did he call?" Clement held his breath.

"Was like . . . big boss. Important man."

"Really? What makes you say that?"

"Prince Kamal polite me . . . I say you already . . . but this person he call sir, and make his voice different – much respect. He speak like this man King."

"The name," said Clement. "Did you hear a name?"

Gabriel paused – as if in thought. "Maybe Allison. Maybe . . . something else. Yes, wait . . . Name was Anderson."

"You're sure?"

"Yes. Remember now."

"The Prince called someone named Anderson?"

"Yes, is correct. Anderson."

"Okay. How about a first name?"

"Ah – not sure."

"Think for a second. Take your time."

"Okay. Prince get in car – say, how much downtown?"

Clement snapped his pencil. Kiro looked startled. Clement said: Don't worry. I know it's hard. Take it easy, you're doing fine."

"Maybe name was . . . Scott. Maybe, not sure."

Clement wondered why that name sounded familiar. Scott Anderson? Then he got it. Surely there was only one man of that name to demand respect. There couldn't be two. And Anderson probably lived in Manhattan.

And even Prince Kamal would have been respectful.

No, decided Clement. It was preposterous.

He said: "Scott Anderson? The billionaire? I don't think so, Kiro. Prince Kamal might even know him, but he's not here to socialize. He's here secretly, to hurt America, and Scott Anderson is a huge patriot. The last man Kamal would go to for what he has in mind. Believe me. You must be mistaken."

A Lucifer tie-in wasn't going to work.

Gabriel reluctantly let it drop.

He tried another approach. "Kiro good American, too. Police ask everyone about Prince Kamal. I say, Yes, I drive him. They say go Washington. I say, Yes, I try to help. Now I thinking maybe I see Prince when he go home. Prince must go home, yes? Maybe take my cab again."

That knocked Scott Anderson out of Clement's head. Finally this cabby had said something brilliant: the Prince had to go home! Most likely from JFK, where Kiro could be waiting for him. Clement said excitedly: "That's exactly what you'll do. You're going to spot him for us when he tries to leave."

Gabriel was glad to finally get there without planting it in Clement's mind. It was more honest this way. He said: "You think idea good? Wait airport? Wait until Prince Kamal come?"

Clement nodded. It was a good idea. A cab driver lurking in wait for someone was far less noticeable than a cop – or teams of cops, which might be necessary. A lurking cab driver was not noticeable at all. Someone who would not spook the Prince, when and if he showed up. Hardly a great idea, but like Kiro Yovkov the taxi driver, it was really all that Clement had.

Kiro was barely drinking his coffee, and grimaced each time he took a swallow. Maybe it was too hot. Clement walked across to the water cooler and filled a paper cup. He went back and gave it to Kiro. The Bulgarian smiled.

Gabriel set the coffee and doughnut aside and drank water.

Clement said: "Your suggestion is a clever one: We find the Prince without him knowing. Extra policemen might scare him off. You can spot Kamal and deliver him to me, just by sitting in your cab."

Kiro's smile became wider.

Gabriel was smiling because he could do a lot more than deliver the Prince. The Prince was on Gabriel's list, but fairly low down.

Nobody lives forever.

Prince Kamal would not live much longer.

Clement said: "I won't lie to you. There is some danger. The Prince is a violent man, traveling alone without bodyguards. There's no telling what he'll do – or if he is armed. We don't want him spotting you."

"Kiro not afraid." Gabriel found the Prince laughable. He had decided to drive Kamal to the airport personally, in a yellow cab that would materialize when the time came. This was better than Clement's plan, and Clement didn't have to know about it. Until the time came.

Clement smiled reassuringly. "You are a good American, Kiro. Prince Kamal is a very bad man. Finding him is important."

Gabriel nodded obligingly.

Clement continued: "We have cameras in departure halls, but we only got a quick glimpse of him coming in, and he may be more careful going out. He'll be trying to avoid them."

Gabriel's work here was done.

"I go back New York today?"

"Yes, you do. We'll book you on a flight. I'll join you tomorrow or the next day. Do you have a cell phone?"

"No, sir. Expen . . . sive. And Kiro not know how they work."

"We'll buy you one today, on the way to the airport, and someone will show you how to use it."

"Phone belong to Kiro?"

"Sure – it'll be bought in your name – and that's how I'll contact you when I get to New York. I'll call you on it, okay?"

"Yes, sir. Thank you, sir."

"Don't call me sir. Bo is fine. Please excuse me while I make a phone call. It won't take a moment."

"Please . . . more water?"

"Of course. Help yourself. There are magazines by the cooler."

Clement called FBI travel section. "This is Senior Agent Clement, in D. H .S. I'll need a one-way ticket to New York, next available flight. Yes, Ma'am. Business Class, at government rate – top priority. Name is Yovkov, Kiro." Clement spelled them both. "I also need two top priority standbys' for the next two days, at the same rate. The names are Clement and Dufaux."

Once Clement had Kiro's flight number and check in time, a lot of things went into motion . . .

. . . and Gabriel was freighted back to New York.

~ ~ ~

Prince Kamal was in Las Vegas.

He had never been here before; but it was well known in terrorist circles as a place with very lax security – except where gambling was concerned. As long as no Casino was robbed or cheated, no one cared who you were or what you did. Al Qaeda agents in the United States had recommended it as the perfect place to hide. Kamal was no gambler, and dubious, but prostitution was legal in Vegas, and that persuaded him. He decided to sample the fleshpots and take advantage of this unexpected terrorist haven. He needed somewhere safe while his deal with Scott Anderson was finalized. The Prince became an unregistered guest in a luxury hotel owned by Arab investors.

He had flown here in the Lear Jet of an oil sheikh, a family friend with a mansion and private airfield in Rhode Island. The taxi ride from Anderson's place in New York had been overlong, but instinct told Kamal to stay below the radar: No rented limousine, and no Rolls Royce from Rhode Island to pick him up.

Once here, his spending had sky-rocketed. High class call-girls and exotic dancers do not come cheap, and Kamal had opened his wallet. He had come to America loaded with cash because a shopping trip for nuclear arms – under an assumed name – was no time to be flashing his gold card.

Kamal lay on the rumpled sheets of the King-sized bed in his luxury suite. Last night's plaything, a fiercely strong brunette with implanted bosoms and pierced nipples, had just left, although it was almost noon.

The bedside phone rang. Kamal picked it up.

Khalid Hassimi was in the lobby. Could he come up?

Twenty minutes later Hassimi was dressed and having

coffee with Hassimi on the balcony.

Khalid Hassimi was a lowly member of Al Qaeda's Las Vegas cell and a bearer of messages. The rest avoided contact with the Prince to protect their cover. Nobody outside the cell knew who they were. Kamal assumed they were a band of thugs and killers, and he had no desire to meet them.

Khalid wore a tropical shirt and white jeans. His hands were weighted down by gaudy rings with absurdly large jewels. He looked like a cheap thief, which was exactly what he was in Islamabad. Here he was a playboy like everyone else. Khalid was twenty, drove a Porsche – and regularly lost big at the gaming tables.

He said: "A fine day, my Prince, I trust you slept well."

Khalid was a fawning piece of shit, reflected Kamal, but it was wise to surround oneself with such people – they will do anything to climb the ladder. However, Prince Kamal had little use for a boot licker today. He resolved to find out what he wanted and be rid of him.

"Why are you here, Khalid?" His tone was gruff and impatient, and he saw anger flash in the boy's eyes. But only for an instant. This punk knew better than to offend his betters.

Khalid told him: All six weapons had arrived in Iran, a ploy to trick the American satellite – a trick that gave Iran more leverage among the Arab states, and more prestige than ever before. The trick was also this: The Americans expected some time to be spent making finished bombs before shipping; but all six neutron cores were reloaded during darkness and sent to the Port of Aden, where they were put on two Korean freighters like the one that brought them – each boat to go by secret and separate route to America. All six devices would be assembled en route to arrive in the United States that much quicker. Custom-made detonators would be coming later, out of Europe. The Great Satan would be destroyed on the appointed date.

Within minutes Khalid was in the elevator, and Prince Kamal was packing to go home.

He almost phoned Scott Anderson, but decided against it. Let him wonder where the Prince had gone.

Half an hour more, and Kamal took a taxi out into the Nevada desert, where the Lear Jet was waiting. It took him back to Rhode Island and another overlong taxi ride to JFK.

~ ~ ~

That evening, in New York, Clement knocked on the door of Shahanna's hotel room. He had theater tickets, and reservations at a top French Bistro. The irony struck him as he waited for Shahanna to let him in: Tonight was a replay of his blind date with Destiny, the Washington debutante he took out a month ago.

It seemed like a year.

This hotel was run by the FBI And used for housing agents in transit or terrorists being deported, although both categories were never here at the same time. It was a five star safe- house, which was just what Clement and Shahanna needed until Prince Kamal came out from whatever rock he was under.

They were both excited by New York.

Clement forced his mind back to the mission. Their cover stories were watertight, carefully studied and rehearsed, and they were ready to go. Clement had decided a night on the town might do them good – letting them forget for a time where they were going, and the danger they faced.

Shahanna was not expecting to go out tonight. Clement suddenly thought he may have acted hastily. She might be walking about naked. He waited nervously at the door, deciding this was a mistake. Their flight had been delayed twice, and he had noticed her yawning, as they landed.

Perhaps she was asleep.

Then again, she could be in the shower.

Her door opened.

She had on a black silk evening dress, rather low cut for Washington, but perfectly acceptable in New York. The sheen of it was enhanced against her skin. She let him look for a moment. Then stood back opening the door even wider.

She said: "Won't you come in?"

"Are you going out?"

Her eyes shone and she grinned impishly. "Yes, with you."

He entered and she shut the door.

"How did you know I was coming?"

"We're in New York; just off Broadway. I'm gorgeous and you can't resist me"

Clement longed for a drink. He hadn't been expecting that dress.

"Wait while I get my wrap and purse," she said.

He crossed the room and sat on the bed. It was either that or a spindly love-seat with lace frills. Her room was surprisingly feminine for a government funded operation. It was decorated in pink, cream and gold, with more lace at the windows and a maroon carpet. It reminded him of strawberry-swirl ice cream. His room was not like this at all, but decked out in black and gray with chrome and leather furniture. It had matching metallic lamps and modernist painting.

This hotel could surprise you.

There was a rose pink coverlet on Shahanna's bed that looked like silk. Clement ran his hand across it and felt the mild, electric crackle of nylon. He had a sudden and unexpected vision of himself and Shahanna on this bed, naked and kissing passionately. This aroused him beyond belief.

He directed his thoughts elsewhere.

On the floor was her open suitcase, partly unpacked. Shahanna's fake passport lay beside her fake student I. D. from a University in Chicago and a canceled US Residency visa, all resting on some blouses, a pair of jeans and a colorful assortment of T-shirts. The Passport was Moroccan. Clement picked it up. The picture showed Shahanna, but the name given was Sorya Kharaman. The owner of that name was in a high-security cell, somewhere in Texas – and would be until this operation ended.

Sorya Kharaman – the real one – had just been arrested for terrorist activity. She had been studying physics. Now Sorya was being deported, or so anyone checking would soon discover.

But the one expelled would be Shahanna.

The genuine Sorya had been detained for good reason. She hatched a plan to plant a bomb in a student dormitory, and got caught as she tried to carry it out. Another Arab girl had given her away.

Now the new, counterfeit Sorya stood before Clement, wearing a lacy shawl. It was silver, embossed with black flowers to match her dress. She said: "Do we have time for a drink?"

"Sure. The theater is two blocks away."

"Good. A play. How about Vodka Martinis?"

"Please, but no olive." He glanced at his watch. There was plenty of time. It was a ten minute walk and they had an hour. He looked down at his rather ordinary pants and jacket. "Who knew you'd be so . . ."

"Stunning." There was flirtation in her tone, and Clement remembered their first meeting, when each agreed the other was stunning, in that trendy burger place. He had intended tonight as a light diversion; nothing more. Now he was fast losing control. He was shocked by his reaction to her physical beauty, and the way she kept looking at him since he arrived. He imagined her naked, arms stretched toward him. This was doing no good. He blinked, and the vision receded.

Shahanna brought Martinis in misted, frozen glasses.

He held out their tickets. "I hope you like Tennessee Williams."

She bent to look, revealing even more of her breasts. "A Streetcar Named Desire. "

Clement wrenched his eyes away. "Ever see it?"

"Only the movie, on French T. V. – but I loved it. This will be marvelous."

"I was afraid it might bore you." He looked into her eyes and saw that flirtation again. "I've booked a table for later. I hope the whole night will be marvelous."

Damn, he had said 'Night'. Now he was flirting.

"It will," Her eyes flashed at him. She handed him his drink and eased down onto the love-seat. She gave him a seductive smile, raised her glass and said: "Here's to finding that prince."

She didn't mean Kamal.

Clement sipped his drink. It was potent. So was Shahanna's effect on him. Subtle lighting made her sultry and mysterious. Her eyes and lips were gleaming. Clement felt the undeniable lure of her attraction – they could stay here and make love. She was only waiting for him to say it.

He willed himself to think of something else.

They could fall in love later.

If they returned from Iran.

But he imagined how their lovemaking could have been, and hated the decision he had just made.

"What are you thinking?" she asked.

"Uh, nothing."

She chuckled. She knew exactly what he was thinking. "We'll talk about it after dinner," she said.

Clement thought: Get a grip on yourself! Two women have done this to you inside a month. Destiny was pure lust. This one has you falling in love and lust. For God's sake, remember why you're in New York.

He decided to change the subject.

He said: "I have my cell phone – in case Kiro calls."

"Suppose we're between acts, or something?" In the theater, or was her meaning ambiguous, sexual?"

Clement played it straight. "Kamal's flight is held. And we break the speed limit."

"Ah. That could ruin everything."

Definitely sexual.

She continued to avoid directness, talking in veiled innuendo, until their drinks were gone and it was time to leave. She kissed him on the cheek, as they exited into the hallway.

She locked the door behind them.

They walked slowly, and still arrived with time to spare. The lines were long. They joined one. He said: "I hope we live through this."

"Tonight?" Her eyes twinkled.

"No, tonight we'll be fine."

"I hope so. It's looking good so far."

"Are you going to keep teasing me?"

"Oh, I'm not teasing. Remember I said that."

"Not teasing is worse. We have to be ready if Kiro calls." He thought: Why am I fighting off the woman of my dreams?

The line moved and they soon took their seats.

She sat close and held his hand. He fought against staring at her cleavage. She was slender, but well-endowed; like a movie-star, he thought. No, like a Greek goddess. He felt her hair brush his cheek and wondered if they might indeed end up naked in her bed. He looked down, trying to concentrate on her shoes; they were silver, chic and expensive. She might not like the French but she had very French taste.

He suddenly wanted to know more about her. "What made you go to Paris?"

"My parents," she said simply.

How long were you there?"

"Five miserable years."

He'd known all that – it was in her file. Her father's name was Marmut Dufeaux. French-born son of a mixed colonial marriage. He had returned to Morocco as soon as he passed the diplomatic exam.

"And where did you study?" Clement did not know that. He must have missed it, although her file was not very thick.

"Why are you so interested?" she said.

He grinned. "You're still stunning. I want to know everything."

For God's sake. Now he was flirting with her again.

Her laugh was low and throaty. "That was the right answer."

She turned her head and kissed him lightly, brushing his lips with hers, the whole thing as natural, and sexual, as making love to the right music. She said: "No one can know everything." She turned away again, as if in dismissal. Then, to his surprise, in the time before the curtain went up, she told him.

Her father was still a junior diplomat, and suffered for it when the French Empire fell and the French left Morocco, leaving him too, because he was an Arab with a family he would not desert. He was beaten bloody by a mob that was ransacking the embassy when he arrived to clear his desk. "All this happened before I was born. My parents had four other children before me," she said. And her father, half crippled now, became an outcast, exiled to his country house in poverty, his family eating only what a barren plot of land produced, which kept them half-starving much of the time.

Papa finally got smart and went to the money lenders, to buy more acres, add more crops and invest in irrigation and farm equipment. Things soon turned around. Food was scarce and prices rose, and a few good harvests made the Dufaux family prosperous once more. Their standing also rose. They were invited to parties and functions again. Life was back to normal. Shahanna was the first child to go to a private school. She excelled there, and graduated with honors. She was the impish favorite of her father. He spent a fortune on her higher education, that included four years at the Sorbonne, and a three-year post graduate degree. She studied international politics and physics and ended up with a full doctorate in both.

She also became fluent in French, Italian, German and English – in addition to the Arabic she grew up with.

Clement knew the rest: Accepted by the Corps Diplomatique, and sent to Brussels for two years. Then Rome, Berlin and London. Everywhere she went, each embassy saw the same thing – an attractive female who spoke four languages. They treated her like an air hostess. Shahanna was assigned to Protocol – arranging official parties, state dinners and all forms of entertainment, from dress balls to front-row opera seats. Her work was highly rated, and got her to Washington, where she was finally promoted to Vice Consul for duty in Iran. But she would remain trapped in Protocol. All this fueled a slow burning anger in Shahanna. She had not attended the Sorbonne to create banquet menus for the French. She was keenly aware that her talent was completely wasted, and Iran would be no different. The belated promotion had, if anything, made things worse because it would have worked out fine if she was a man.

So know she worked for Heathcote.

And America.

Bo checked his watch. "It should start any time."

Shahanna smiled. "This is wonderful. If the FBI Thing doesn't work out, you have a big future in theater bookings."

"You mean, if the Prince Kamal thing doesn't work out."

She looked at him. There was a rigid tension, that seemed to encompass his entire body. Clement strove to relax. The last thing he wanted was her thinking he was nervous. He stared ahead, hoping the subject was dropped. But Shahanna broke the silence. "You think Kamal might have gone home already?"

Clement came jolting back to reality. His weakness for this woman simply must be set aside. He reminded himself to act like a case officer. "Prince Kamal's coming straight for us," he said. "I'm sure of it. Our Kiro will reel him in."

She kissed his ear this time. "Then, lovely man, stop worrying."

So much for professionalism.

Clement gave himself a short lecture on mixing business with pleasure. It didn't work. "That taxi driver," he said. "is vital in this. I have a good feeling about him, too. He's an immigrant, determined to serve his new country. It's very American. Clement didn't say so, to avoid sounding corny, but Shahanna was technically also an immigrant, and doing the same thing. Before she could answer, the orchestra began to play, and the rows of ceiling lights went out, one by one.

~ ~ ~

"More wine?"

They were in the French restaurant. The food was up to Shahanna's somewhat unforgiving standard, and the champagne equally good. Both their faces were slightly flushed. Clement tipped the bottle. Twin crystal glasses both bubbled up once more to the brim.

"So you liked the play, he said for the tenth time."

"I adored the play."

"You don't think Brando was better?"

"He probably was. But that's not the point. We had front seats on Broadway. The atmosphere was electrifying. The actors gave it all they had and they were very talented. Even Brando couldn't have beat it when that young guy stepped up and yelled "Stell-ah!" It was magical."

Clement grinned. "I guess you did like it," he said. "I just feel nervous; like being on a first date." He regretted saying that, and quickly pulled himself together, determined not to go down that path again.

Her eyes smiled at him. "Relax – We're having a wonderful time."

"Oh, I'm fine. Really."

"Good."

Of course he wasn't.

There was a pause, as they both sipped champagne.

"I had an idea," said Clement. "I thought of it during the second act: Why not go undercover now, right away. Take on our new identities and get used to them. Better here than at the airport."

"You mean, be terrorists?"

"No. Radicals will do for tonight. We don't want to get arrested."

They both laughed.

"Let's do it," she said. "No more Bo and Shahanna. From now on we're the wicked Sorya and her dumb, American boyfriend . . . Oh, no! I've forgotten your new name. Thank God Prince Kamal isn't here!"

"No harm done," said Clement, and stretched across the table to shake hands. "Hi, I'm Robert. Robert Henry Keller. I come from Utah, and my whole family are Mormons. I hate all that religious crap. Call me Rob."

"What are you doing here, Rob? Why do you hate America?" She said this with a humor that Clement found slightly jarring.

The political machine in Washington that exploits ordinary Americans. That's what I hate," he said flatly.

"Oh, a modern revolutionary. Isn't that a bit extreme – for a rich boy who doesn't know what hate is?"

She still looked and sounded quite flippant.

Clement drew a deep breath and spoke as himself. "Listen, Shahanna my character has enough hate to join his own country's enemies. Your character hates everybody except Islamists. She even hates my character. Now you remember that and get serious. This is not a sit-com for television. You and me, we're a couple of psychos ready to kill everyone in this room – then shoot our way out. That's how we have to think and feel. That's what we have to make Prince Kamal believe. It's no exaggeration to say that our lives depend on that. Okay?"

"Yes. You're right to start this now."

Now she's getting it, thought Clement. He said: "Pleased to meet you. May name is Rob Keller."

"A pleasure. Sorya Kharaman."

They had both watched the real Sorya's interrogation through a two-way mirror. Sorya Kharaman was tough, and a piece of work. Her captors regarded her as mentally unstable. Clement realized it was difficult for Shahanna to play that role, but it had to be done, and done perfectly.

Shahanna reached out to fill her glass, ignored his. He realized she was purposely breaking the mood. There would be no more flirting. And her face seemed to change, as she said: "Why did you take me to see that dreadful play? It was vulgar, decadent– and disgusting."

Now she sounded angry. But at the same time, it was astonishing how dangerous she suddenly seemed.

He remembered what she had said about Sorya: "I know her. I grew up with girls like her – they lived in my village, and on my street. They spouted fundamentalist bullshit to get the attention of boys, and wound up believing it themselves. The worst of them got recruited."

Now Shahanna's imitation of Sorya was spot-on.

"Had no idea what the play was like," said Clement. "I'm sorry, Sorya."

She gave him a withering look.

Clement became himself again. He said: "Okay. That's very convincing. Obviously you can do it. But let's stop for a second – I have something to show you." He gave her a piece of paper from his wallet. It was two columns of numbers, with the decoded message written underneath. Clement said: "This came in today from Jhalal. It's very brief, and disturbing."

She read it:

NO WORD OF PRINCE. MISSION TAKES PLACE
4TH JULY.

Clement said: "Our biggest holiday. America's birthday. That means we have nine weeks." He dropped his voice. "Deduct travel both ways – and we have eight at best. Not very long, is it?"

"We'll manage."

"That was the right answer."

She laughed.

He smiled. "No laughing. Stay mean – for about nine weeks. Remember, you have nothing but contempt for me."

"Careful what you wish for. I'll be a bitch."

"Good. Then do it."

She grinned. "I shall be vile," she said.

They had finished eating. Two French waiters cleared the table, deftly picking up everything and stacking it on trays.

Clement nervously seized the chance to speak French. He had been rehearsing one phrase all day, and now he said: "Maintenant du cafe, s' il vous plait." He knew his accent was probably awful, but she was beautiful, and he wanted to please her. He also knew this might be a dreadful mistake."

One waiter asked him something in French. Clement groaned inwardly. Seconds slipped by. As he frantically tried to guess the question. He felt his face turning red. This had been a bad idea.

The Frenchman shrugged and spoke to Shahanna.

She said: "Do we want cream and sugar?"

"Yes," he said. "I mean – Oui, s' il vous plait." He felt ridiculous, and wanted the carpet to swallow him up. Cream and sugar, for God's sake. How dumb was that? What else would the guy say, when you ordered coffee? Clement looked up, and saw Shahanna smiling at him.

~ ~ ~

She smiled, because he was superb. He had tried to speak French, just for her, and she was crazy about him.

It went against all reason. He had picked her up in a bar, got her into what seemed like a bad movie – and now they weren't going to have sex because of this stupid mission. They were cursed. Thinking this, Shahanna realized some of it was not that funny. It was infuriating.

Her smile vanished,

Sorya was back.

But Shahanna was not too far away.

She practiced being awful to him while thy drank coffee. He was met with a stony silence if he tried to speak, but the look she gave him said it all. And if she spoke at all, it only resulted in some cruel criticism of him.

Shahanna was not enjoying this but she did it. She had imagined things differently. Before that drive to Heathcote's house in the Jaguar, she thought she and Clement might date, as people did – going to the theater and a restaurant, like tonight, or going to the Zoo, or holding hands and watching old movies on T. V. from her couch. Instead she had to be cruel to him all the time, in a region where one or both of them might well wind up dead. And not only that; for weeks she had longed for an evening alone with his man, and now it had come, she was a nagging bitch from hell.

He paid the check and they returned to their hotel. His room was on a different floor to hers. They did not kiss at her door. This was their new, cold relationship, and she hated every part of it.

He said goodnight and walked away.

She went inside and slid the bolt.

Her heart was pounding.

She had loved him from the start. He was handsome and intelligent, and amusing honest and endearing. This was finally the one: The man you waited for all your life. She loved him. It was as simple as that. She knew it tonight when he spoke stumbling French in a French place he had chosen just for her.

She had treasured his company tonight; especially his reaction to this dress. When he sat on the bed she knew he wanted to make love to her. She'd been tempted to undress, and ravage him on the spot. Why hadn't she? Shahanna was still asking herself that. But tonight had been fraught with tension, which might spoil it, and their first time must be perfect. Once it happened, she knew, they would be joined for life. That was why she kept her clothes on and went to the theater instead.

But she wanted him badly.

And there was something else. From that first night; as they drove along a country road to meet Heathcote.

He had asked: "Who's worse? The French . . . or Muslim radicals?"

She had thought of her father, and said, "Bankers and lawyers."

He had laughed. "Don't forget politicians."

It was that laugh.

She had been hooked then.

That laugh did it.

And thinking that, she went to bed.

~ ~ ~

Clement sat on his own bed, staring out at Manhattan and wishing he had a drink. Why wasn't he on that ridiculous powder puff of a bed, making love to Shahanna? Then he felt guilty. His thoughts should be on the job he had to do. As he thought this, his cell phone, which was on charge, rang loudly enough to make him jump.

It was Kiro, voice close to a whisper. He was on his way to the airport with Prince Kamal in his cab. How this came about was not explained. Kiro kept it short, and ended abruptly. Clement was left holding a dead phone. But he had heard another voice, quite loud, in the background, That must have been the Prince.

Clement sprang into action.

He ran to the elevator, dialing Heathcote's number as he went, and punched the number for Shahanna's floor. He got there and rang her bell. She opened up looking tussled, and he told her to grab her deportation kit, leave everything else and be ready to go in ten minutes. Kiro had got them in the game.

He ran back, using the stairs, talking in panting breaths to Heathcote; then said goodbye and put on blue jeans and a stained sweatshirt with a hood. He pulled a heavy, denim jacket over that. He knew that Heathcote was now making one phone call after another: Police departments, customs officers and immigration officials must be alerted, informed, or warned off, depending on their part in this drama. The airline would be asked to hold Prince Kamal's flight, no matter what, until Clement and Shahanna were on board.

He looked around the room, in case he was leaving anything important behind. He did a mental check: Passport, false documents, including a driver's license, registration of a non-existent automobile, credit cards and a pleading letter from Rob Keller's parents in Utah, begging him to come home, or at least write.

Clement had everything. He locked the door behind him, knowing an FBI team would sweep the room clean.

They made JFK Inside half an hour.

The plane was waiting.

It went very well. Shahanna was driven onto the runway with sirens and flashing lights, attracting the attention of everyone on board Arab United Airlines Flight 447, including Prince Kamal. Then she was led to her seat in handcuffs – in case anyone had not got the message.

Clement went to the ticket desk, playing his role of the faithful dog who follows his mistress in her misfortune. The FBI, acting on Heathcote's orders, had put out the word on both of them. As a result, once Clement was given a ticket and went to the departure gate, he got cold stares from the ground crew who issued his boarding pass and walked his luggage to the loading ramp. His suitcase was thrown contemptuously on the damp ground, his carry-on thrust at him in sullen silence.

Heathcote would have been delighted.

Strings were also pulled by Heathcote at Orly Airport in Paris, where a half hour layover became a two hour delay. Passengers were allowed to disembark, and by chance Sorya Kharaman and Prince Kamal spent that time in a tiny waiting room, with only a handful of other passengers. Shahanna's looks persuaded the Prince to introduce himself as Abdul Rashid. And her cover story, fed to him like candy over the next two hours, did the rest.

When Kamal heard she studied nuclear physics and attempted to blow up part of her college, his face didn't change, but he was clearly hooked. And when she mentioned Rob Keller, a young American nuclear physicist she had dangling by a string, Kamal was hooked again. When she added that this dangerously naïve young man had followed her onto Flight 447, Sorya and Rob Keller were invited to stay at the Saudi royal palace for a couple of days.

CHAPTER NINE

BY MID-DAY THE AIR-CONDITIONING in the American Consulate in Islamabad was proving unequal to its task.

Gabriel was glad he didn't have sweat glands.

Pakistani clerks and secretaries were perspiring as badly as the American spies and diplomats that Henry Archer had come to visit. This conference room was cramped and stuffy, and too many people, American and local alike, were in it.

Gabriel projected here from Kiro Yovkov's fast vaporizing cab, after he dropped off Prince Kamal. Once again the angel was a highly respected British intelligence agent, and most in this room believed they knew him, at least by sight. Henry Archer looked exhausted and drained, due to Gabriel's whizzing around the world, but his American hosts put it down to jet-lag.

Regional satellite pictures, complete with white-lettered map co-ordinates, were flickering on the screen of more than one lap-top, each new image accompanied by a soft, electronic ping from the orbital down-link.

Actual maps, and actual photographs, littered a trestle table, around which those not pacing or standing were seated.

Coffee cups were everywhere.

Gabriel had spent two hours in this room, filled with men who headed the fight against the rebels in the Afghan hill country, trying to stop them crossing into northern Pakistan, without resorting to the use of drones. Part of a campaign to improve America's tarnished image. Henry Archer was looking at close-ups of Prince Kamal's secret camp in Iran, and other close-ups of people there – including an American-planted Iraqi named Jhalal, and a black South African friend of his called Asuto Kenyatta. Gabriel committed both faces to memory, as they would be important to Clement and Shahanna, when and if they reached the camp.Among those at this briefing, there were some who wanted to take out this camp immediately, given Prince Kamal's intent. Others argued against it for various reasons: The U. N. Was still debating the legality of destroying that camp in Syria, and a further attack could lead to censure for Israel and America at the same time. Worse, wiping out this Iranian installation might spark off a war. Next: Jhalal could not be sacrificed with the camp, because he was CIA, and an irreplaceable asset. Destroying this camp and its inmates was pointless. Prince Kamal would simply recruit more people and set up shop somewhere else. This new location would be heavily guarded and secret and harder to find. In other words a step backwards. The Prince's plan would continue without Jhalal working against it from the inside.

And without Clement or Shahanna to help him.

Gabriel listened, sipped coffee and nodded at everything that was said. He smiled, or looked serious, depending on the topic. If asked for his opinion, he read the speaker's mind to get it.

Yes, inserting Clement and the woman was good thinking.

Yes, allow Kamal's terrorists into America.

No, do not detain them until they go into action.

That was the key to intercepting the bombs.

No, other nations should not be alerted.

No, not even the Brits.

Yes, the President must be informed.

It went without saying that Henry Archer would not leak this to his own people. He was known and trusted. Otherwise he would not be present. Everyone in this room was on the same side. Gabriel happily agreed.

He had no people to tell.

Only angels.

He looked up as the door opened and Heathcote walked in.

The angel was not really surprised – Heathcote had his Iraqi agent at risk already, and two more trying to join him. Naturally he wanted to know what was being decided. He had a lot at stake.

The Homeland Security executive shook a few hands; then took a seat opposite the Angel of Death. Like everyone else, Heathcote assumed he knew Henry Archer from past occasions and nodded politely. He was given institutional coffee, and soon had a cigarette burning on the table edge while he read the notes on this meeting.

He eventually looked up. He said: "This is the main event, ladies and gentlemen. The mother of terrorist attacks. The one we've always feared; the one most of us have spent a career preparing for. Now it goes without saying, everything I tell you, and what we discuss here, stays in this room."

Some of them looked bored. They had all heard similar speeches before.

Heathcote seemed to sense this. He took on the look of a prize fighter facing a challenge, his hair bristling defiantly. "Now listen up," he said. This is stuff we can't officially tell the President, although he gave the order. It's against State Department policy, and against Federal Law."

They were no longer bored. Heathcote said: "We're going to hit this Prince Kamal. Just eliminate him. Well away from the public eye. Not on his way home, but at the camp, once our shooters are in place – or outside the camp, if he leaves. We had considered a self-burying bomb, to obliterate this campsite completely, but your reasons against that, in these notes, were also my reasons. Sacrificing three of our own is out of the question. I spoke with the President, and he agreed."

A CIA Man raised one hand. His shirt looked damp, and sweat glistened on his forehead. "So when do we take out this dude?"

"As soon as our snipers are ready. It will slow his program down; give us a chance to organize. And it sends exactly the right message: We know what they're up to, and we won't tolerate it. They'll move camp, which slows them down more, and Jhalal will tell us the new location. We're using Special Ops marksmen. A team has been assigned. They're being flown out this week."

The man nodded. "But is Prince Kamal the only problem? Do they have anyone to pick up where he left off?"

Heathcote shrugged. "There are two others. We'll be taking them out, too?"

"Who are they?"

"One's a General in the Saudi Army, a troubleshooter for the King, and the other's a warlord who calls himself a General. Their names are Makhud and Rameesh. You have them on file."

There were nods around the table. Both names were A-listed.

"These three are the Tribunal. We have this from Jhalal, and from a belly dancer who works in a club they go to up in the hill country. This girl doubles as a hooker. She says General Rameesh talks a lot after getting laid. She told us what he talks about for a large amount of cash."

An orderly brought in a tray of cold cuts – the meat half buried under mounds of rolls and bagels. There were potato chips, and mustard and mayonnaise. Gabriel helped himself to some, like everyone else, and soon abandoned it on the paper plate that came with it.

Heathcote spoke through a mouthful of ham. "Killing those three will buy us time, but Iran still owns the nukes. Their attack plan will not go away while that remains true. We have to track, find and destroy those bombs. That's job one."

Someone said, "That's some fucking job."

Heathcote stopped chewing and swallowed. "It's why I have people on the ground. Jhalal, of course, and Clement and Shahanna, assuming they make it to the camp. Those three will cross the Atlantic, with the nukes doing the same thing. Destroying the bombs will be their prime responsibility. I wouldn't risk the lives of three agents for anything less."

Someone else spoke. "Destroy them. How exactly?"

"Blow all of them to Kingdom Come," said Heathcote. Nuclear devices can be blown up like anything else – there's no danger of a nuclear detonation. The bits simply evaporate."

Gabriel said: "What if the bombs don't go to the camp?"

Heathcote looked at him sharply. "They almost certainly will. Kamal needs a way to get them to the United States. Who better than the teams that use them? That's what our analysts think."

Gabriel knew the analysts were wrong. He had been inside Prince Kamal's mind, during the taxi-ride to JFK – and discovered that the bombs had not remained in Iran. That was apparently to dupe the American satellites. Shipment to America was already under way by sea.

He said: "Do you have a backup plan?"

Heathcote scowled. "Understand one thing," he said. "There can be no back up plan. If Clement and the others fail, no one else will get close enough to try again. Six nuclear devices, and our advantage over the perpetrators, will be lost to us. This is our best shot."

He had used the word fail.

Instead of die.

But that was the only way they could fail.

"I see," said Gabriel. The flaw in Heathcote's strategy could be overcome. Over the years, Gabriel had learned how to out-think American analysts.

Heathcote looked at him. "Do I know you – Mr. . . . ."

"Henry Archer." Gabriel made a lengthy hypnotic suggestion.

"My God!" said Heathcote. "The Brit sharpshooter – in Cambodia!"

Gabriel shrugged. "A long time ago."

It would have been had it ever happened.

Gabriel said, "I'm here as local British liaison. Nice to see you again, Mr. Heathcote."

Heathcote drew on a false, implanted memory. "This guy saved my ass," he said to the room in general. "I was out on my own, in the D. M. Z. – and just got snake-bit, when I was found by a squad of North Vietnamese. Henry here shot 'em all – from a thousand yard treeline. Then he gave me anti-venom toxin."

"I was Australian then," said Gabriel.

They all laughed. The British were never officially in Viet-Nam.

Heathcote leaned across and shook his hand. "We've never really met, Mr. Archer, but you were in all the reports, and our side and yours both gave you a medal. I think of your name with gratitude."

Gabriel half rose, to grip a beefy hand. He felt a twinge of conscience. Heathcote was a good man, and Gabriel hated deceiving him, but this group played a vital part in coming events, and they needed to be won over. "It was nothing," he said modestly. "A telescopic sight did all the work. I just pulled the trigger."

There was an approving murmur. It subsided as Heathcote began questioning the department heads seated around the table. The answers came in a variety of lengths, and things settled into something between a pop-quiz and a security briefing. Everyone here knew what was at stake for Heathcote, and for America, and a lot of thought went into what was said.

Gabriel sat thinking as it continued. He had no idea when Clement and Shahanna might get to the camp, if they made it at all. Angel observers had them pinpointed in the Saudi palace; but for the mortals in this meeting, the whereabouts of the two agents was unknown. Both were last seen at a French airport with the Prince, as a cavalcade of cars whisked them away. The FBI Report said Kamal's mood seemed upbeat upon landing in France. That was all.

Gabriel could not hope to explain how a member of British Intelligence knew not only where they were but what they were doing; so he said nothing; leaving those in this room, particularly Heathcote, to grapple with the question.

The Angel of Death's energy was low, but he was about to expend some more. His best move was to go to Prince Kamal's camp now, establish himself there, and await the arrival of the Prince and his two latest recruits. Gabriel looked about him. This meeting was winding down. Anything important appeared to have been dealt with. People were swapping jokes and war stories. Cold beer had appeared, and much of the conversation was getting raucous. No need to stay any longer. Henry Archer stood up, making excuses about a meeting at his own consulate, and left.

Minutes later he hovered high above the rocks and gullies that lay on the northern reaches of Iran.

~ ~ ~

The new campsite lay forty miles from a broken-down oasis called Sidi Ben Affra, where the only industry was the farming of dates, and shaping bricks out of camel dung to light fires. Growing poppy was frowned on by local clerics. There was no civilization for a hundred miles in any direction. Poppy seed was nevertheless transported through in vast amounts by local Fedayeen.

Gabriel materialized as an Iraqi named Hassan, just inside the barbed wire fence surrounding Prince Kamal's personal patch of desert.

The camp bustled with activity: Recruits were putting up tents. Others practiced with small arms, shooting at targets made to look like American soldiers; or marched in step on a square of sand that had been raked flat, then hardened by pounding feet. A few men were eating, picking at metal plates with their fingers, dotted about cross-legged by the kitchen fires, where cooks stirred at big, black iron pots, or ladled rice and lamb onto more metal plates. Lunchtime had come and gone; so those eating now were either early for dinner, or stragglers, or had the good will of a cook.

Gabriel wore recycled military clothing and a dirty Fidel Castro style cap, which made him look like everyone else. He walked around until he had seen everything. The heat was oppressive.

He went to the front gate and asked about Jhalal. "There are three of that name," said the sentry. "Which one?"

"He of Iraq."

"Ah, that Jhalal. He will return soon. He and that African monkey took the supply truck to Sidi Ben Affra for water. They also pick up the last of the newcomers. Who are you that seeks him?"

Gabriel had a decision to make – was he a terrorist, or a trainer of terrorists? He chose the first. It offered better access to Jhalal. "I am Hassan, also of Iraq. Jhalal and I are friends. We served Saddam together, in the Guard."

Gabriel started to walk away.

The gate-guard called after him. "I shall tell him, Brother. Go with Allah."

Hassan was the tallest man he'd ever seen.

Gabriel couldn't just walk around doing nothing. He went over to help pitch tents, thinking about what he had just heard. These newcomers the sentry mentioned. Could they include Clement and Shahanna? Gabriel doubted it. There hadn't been enough time. They had to sell themselves to Prince Kamal and get invited to join the program. That had to take three or four days, or even a week or more – if Prince Kamal didn't unmask and murder them first. The sentry said today's recruits were the last. Well, sentries don't know everything, and this one may have made that up to seem important. Gabriel had not thought him very bright.

Clement and Shahanna would either show up or not.

Hassan put up tents for two hours.

Tightening the guy-ropes to a canvas shelter that would serves as a classroom, Gabriel watched the supply truck drive away from the camp gateway. It bucked and swayed over uneven ground, until it reached a row of tents and stopped. The tailgate dropped, releasing twenty or more men who dropped to the ground. They shouted to one another excitedly, as they were divided into groups by armed guards who bellowed hard enough to raise the dead. These groups were then marched to their tents. Most of them passed within a few yards of where Gabriel stood.

There was no sign of Prince Kamal, Clement or Shahanna.

Apparently princes did not arrive in battered trucks.

The driver and his companion got out of the cab. Gabriel recognized Jhalal from Heathcote's computer files, and guessed who the African beside him was: The one they foolishly called Monkey. To Gabriel's experienced eye, this was a battle-hardened killer, ready for demonic possession.

It was only a matter of time.

Asuto Kenyatta was not yet infested with a demon, but

Gabriel saw, even at this distance, that several hovered around him, and given the man's part in coming events, one of these wraith-like creatures was bound to step in and take control. The spawn of Lucifer were always ready.

Gabriel walked over to the truck, slipping himself into Jhalal's memory as he went. They were now lifelong friends, and whatever the gate sentry had said to the driver would make more sense. The angel forced a similar memory into Asuto Kenyatta; except that it was short term – beginning here at this camp, a few days ago, when they met for the first time.

Asuto's demons were outraged.

But there was nothing they could do.

They flapped invisibly around him, hissing at Gabriel.

The truck was an ancient, wheezing Chevrolet; its engine was still running, every piston-turn causing a giant shudder: A vehicle dating back to the Shah; which made it over forty years old, its large bulbous hood rich in patches of scab-like rust. Underneath, the exhaust system was badly holed. It belched noise and black smoke in all directions. Jhalal had not switched the engine off, because trucks this old were hard to restart once they overheated. This one was already running hot, with steam spurting steadily from leaks in the radiator.

Gabriel was surprised that Prince Kamal was stingy enough to settle for such a dilapidated wreck, although mistakes of the same kind were evident all over the camp. Cheap wood was being used for construction. It was untreated and would warp in the sun. All the tents were second-hand, their canvass faded and soiled. This Prince must be something of a tightwad.

Jhalal saw Gabriel and his face lit up.

Here was his best friend.

Hassan.

The two men embraced, one so much taller that it made a comical sight. The angel and the undercover spy. Gabriel sensed a deep sincerity in Jhalal. The South African was another matter.

Jhalal suggested they get rid of the truck. All three squeezed inside the cab, with Gabriel hunched on the transmission cover; then they bumped back across the sand to park the vehicle in an open area near the entrance gate. The same guard nodded as they walked off.

It was time for the evening meal.

Jhalal pocketed the keys, and led the way to the open air kitchen. The smell of roasting meat wafted on the air. Other men joined them, heading in the same direction, hungry after working in the hot sun. The smell of cooked flesh grew stronger. Gabriel stifled a groan. Here in the open, watched at close quarters, he would be forced to eat meat and then throw up later. And even worse, the way this camp was being run, he'd have to do this twice a day.

They lined up before two sweating cooks.

Everybody received spicy chunks of lamb dripping with juices, topped with flat, rounded bread. Gabriel was nauseated. He followed Jhalal and Asuto, and sat on the ground to eat with his hands like everyone else. He knew this was the custom, but his fingers would smell disgustingly for hours, even after he washed them. Asuto Kenyatta dipped a hunk of bread in his plate and said: "May Allah bless this food."

Jhalal echoed him.

Hassan did not.

He shot a look at Kenyatta, and decided to try

something. How skilled was this man in Iraqi dialect? Gabriel said: "Thy mother was a cheap whore."

There was no response.

Jhalal laughed. "He doesn't understand. Just a few phrases."

Gabriel chewed, swallowed and fought off the impulse to gag. He inched closer to Jhalal. "I have something to tell you," he said. The angel looked around. No one else was in earshot, and there was no knowing when the two of them would enjoy this amount of privacy again. Jhalal waited expectantly.

Speaking softly, Hassan said: "I, too, work for Langley."

It was a lie, but a good one, because it could not be disproved, and would serve Gabriel extremely well in the long term.

Angels told lies to mortals all the time.

Gabriel was very good at it.

The Iraqi was thunderstruck, but his face didn't change.

He said: "You are saying the Americans sent you?" He spoke carefully, murmuring into a cupped handful of food.

Hassan nodded. "Clement, too, is coming here."

"How can that be?"

"Clement and a Moroccan woman."

"You scare me, Brother."

The four of us are a team. We must be as camels in the desert, fitting in – as if we belong here and nowhere else. All four of us must be chosen for this madness in America. It will be up to us to stop this attack in the final stages. We have to be part of the assault team."

Jhalal was silent, as he struggled to take all this in. He

said quietly, "You are the bravest of lions, Hassan."

Gabriel shrugged. "No braver than you, Brother. What you do for Heathcote and the Americans is beyond belief."

"I do it for me, and for what Saddam's son did to my family."

Gabriel understood: It had begun with Jhalal's brother. He had been tortured to death, a cattle-prod inserted in his rectum, by Uday Hussein, who had tried and failed to seduce the man's wife. Then the entire family had been arrested, including the wife and her children. Then Jhalal, his wife and newborn baby. The brother and his family were executed. Jhalal was tortured and lived. His infant son died in a cell, of malnutrition, and the distraught mother hanged herself the same day. A few years later, at the conclusion of the first Gulf War, Jhalal Ben Rashid offered himself to American forces as a spy against the regime of Saddam Hussein.

A job that restored his will to live.

They finished eating, and Asuto took the plates back. Jhalal called after him: "We go to the tent."

The African grunted.

As they walked, Gabriel glanced at the sun. It hung low, a dull orange color, and about to set. The faithful began scurrying past, each carrying a prayer mat and wearing expressions of devout concentration. Others ignored the hour, strolling idly along and doing nothing. Hassan and Jhalal latched onto that group. Asuto Kenyatta came trotting by with the faithful.

Angels do not need to pray.

Nor does a man whose baby was murdered.

Gabriel refused to even pretend, not with this collection of cutthroats.

Jhalal never gave it a thought.

~ ~ ~

Four days later, at noon, the Prince arrived.

He looked commanding and cool, stepping out of a customized white Range Rover. He wore tailored jodhpurs, a khaki shirt and gleaming leather riding boots. The red and white checkered head-dress was shading his neck. He barked orders, and soon everyone was assembled on the hot sand to hear what he had to say.

His reputation spoke for itself.

Half of them feared him on sight.

The other half admired him.

"My brothers," Kamal said loudly. "We are the Revenge of Islam!"

"Islam!" came the response. They were not all his brothers, but they knew what was expected, and they obliged him with a mighty roar. Then someone shouted "Allah U Akbar!" and that became the cry; and the noise went on for some time. Bunched fists were waved in the air.

Gabriel peered over the crowd, and glimpsed Clement and Shahanna, standing in the background. That was a great relief. They had at least made it this far. Gabriel saw it as nothing short of miraculous.

Now it fell silent. Prince Kamal's voice was calm and controlled, seconds later, when he called: "Sorya."

The woman approached.

With everyone else, Gabriel heard Prince Kamal introduce Sorya as his personal assistant.

Her resume was not given.

Her background was not explained.

The Prince was obviously a man of few words when

addressing what he regarded as low-class scum.

But there was a murmur of acceptance. No one showed the slightest resentment. Terrorism is blind when it comes to gender.

The man who came with Sorya, however, was not introduced. Many in the crowd were aghast that he was clearly American.

Gabriel saw the humor in this. For years, one of Al Qaeda's top goals was the recruitment of non-Arab Americans, who could slip in or out of the country, or move across it as unquestioned citizens. The project largely failed. Americans do not betray their country often, and they shrink from suicide missions. They are far too shrewd to believe virgins await them in Heaven. Rob Keller had been packaged as the exception. Gabriel was sure this influenced the Prince when 'Sorya' showed up with a man ready to leave a mushroom cloud over six American cities. Such an infidel was a great prize. Prince Kamal had recognized that.

His slow-witted listeners did not.

Gabriel glanced at Jhalal, standing beside him. The Iraqi's face showed no flicker of recognition, although Clement was unmistakable at this distance. Jhalal was too well trained to react, and Asuto Kenyatta, on the far side of Jhalal, had no idea who Clement was. His eyes were on Prince Kamal. Like everybody else, the African was straining to hear what their leader had to say.

What they got was a pep-talk.

Gabriel was reminded of Bruno Schwenk, beguiling hordes of Austrian fanatics, shortly before he died. Gabriel had watched from beneath the peak of a chauffeur's cap, having put the real driver to sleep in his home. But this speech of Kamal's, on behalf of Al Qaeda, was different.

This speech was about suicidal death.

The Prince spoke of sacrifice, honor and a holy cause. This group was the Revenge of Islam, he said. They would rain down nothing less on the Great Satan – godless enemy of the righteous. America would cease to exist because of those here today. He did not say that many would die here in this camp, executed in the most horrible manner for failing this training. That was for tomorrow. Today he told them they were hand-picked, an elite group chosen for this special purpose, and they should be proud. For their part they believed every word of it. It was exactly what they wanted to hear, and they were proud. Gabriel could see it in their faces.

Pride is a Deadly Sin.

"Allah U Akbar!" shouted the Prince.

"Allah U Akbar!" They thundered back.

Gabriel smiled. He had heard it all before. In different ways. In every country on Earth.

Prince Kamal ended with a brief outline of the mission. He felt quite safe in doing so, Gabriel was sure. No security leaks were expected. The Angel of Death was familiar with the training methods of Al Qaeda: The only recruits leaving here alive would be those going off to die in America. Potential informers would be staying here, under the desert sand.

Six US Cities were to be destroyed, said the Prince, and this would take place on the Fourth of July. It was just another date to this audience. No one here had ever heard of Independence Day. But they were thrilled to learn that nuclear weapons were involved. That made them stand taller. A gigantic blow would be struck for Islam – and this camp had the honor of delivering it.

Suddenly the speech was over.

The Prince was leaving.

"Allah U Akbar!" he said one last time.

It was shouted back from the crowd.

After a few words of dismissal, Kamal bent down to pick up a lap-top in a case at his feet. He walked off with Sorya. Rob Keller hurried after them, and they all drove off in the range Rover, circling to another part of the compound, where accommodation had been built for them, in the form of an elongated wooden hut.

Gabriel stood thinking.

He wanted that lap-top.

The Prince had kept it close, by his feet.

That made it important.

~ ~ ~

Gabriel spent his days training, eating, and secretly throwing up.

This morning's class was English. Most Arab's speak and understand it well, often to the point of fluency. A small minority don't, and today they were paying strict attention because failure to do so could prove fatal. Prince Kamal had let it be known that only the highest standard would be tolerated, in every class, and every subject – on pain of death. This was not considered an idle threat.

What kind of death was not explained.

Everyone in the classroom Gabriel found himself in today was making every effort to speak perfect English.

They sat on the ground, under an awning. Only the tutor was on his feet, walking occasionally between students.

Asuto Kenyatta was reading Hemmingway aloud. He

was hardly eloquent, but up to standard. His accent and race were seen as an advantage, because very few Americans would think him a Muslim. That was a considerable advantage when it came to entering the United States. The tutor expressed approval and satisfaction, and told the African to pass the book on.

Gabriel read next, scoring high marks with the Canadian teacher, who was taking names and making notes. The book soon went to Jhalal, whose English was near perfect. He read less than a paragraph from "For Whom the Bell Tolls", before he was told to stop. The next pupil read, and then the next . . .

Gabriel was thinking about that lap-top.

It went everywhere with Kamal, and stayed with him when he slept in the wooden structure that served as office and living quarters for him, Clement and Shahanna. The three of them spent every night there since their arrival. Kamal's unusual attachment to this lap-top made Gabriel want it even more.

Gabriel sensed that Clement suspected the lap-top, too. But it was too dangerous, at this early stage of his relationship with the Prince, for the American to do anything about it. Even if Clement took that chance, and looked at Kamal's data-base, he had no way of telling Heathcote what he found.

That was where Hassan and Henry Archer came in.

Gabriel could drift into Kamal's bedroom and shake loose the computer's secrets. Hassan would tell Clement he had hacked-in, and that Henry Archer would report the contents to Heathcote through British channels, using the secure system set up between London and Washington. Gabriel knew from past experience that playing both roles at once – Hassan and Henry Archer – made such things very easy.

Gabriel's thoughts returned briefly to the classroom, where someone with a low life-expectancy was murdering the words of Hemingway in a tedious, heavily-accented stammer. The Canadian was writing furiously.

Gabriel decided to visit the Prince's room.

This English lesson was boring.

Raising one hand, he summoned the Canadian. The language teacher came over with an inquiring look. Jhalal and Asuto Kenyatta had noticed, and turned to look. The awful Hemingway recital came to a stop. All this created more attention than Gabriel intended. He asked for permission to leave, blaming it on stomach pains, and meat that may have been rotten.

Within minutes he was crossing the parade ground. As soon as the coast was clear he vanished.

~ ~ ~

He materialized in the British Consulate in Kabul.

Stepping through a wall into a corridor, he became Henry Archer, and instantly familiar to anyone who might see him. He needed a coding machine, and somebody to make it work. He sauntered down the hall. People greeted Henry Archer as he passed their open doorways. Gabriel knew where he was going. He had been here before. He recited Heathcote's security-signal code, as he walked.

At the far end he made a right. A shorter corridor led to a room that stood on its own. It was marked "Message Centre" with British spelling. An armed guard sat behind a Plexiglas screen. He recognized Henry Archer and let him pass through the electronic gate.

The message room was in semi-darkness. A dozen

operators kept their blue-tinged faces staring up at the up-link and transmission screens. Gabriel heard a female voice say, "Mr. Archer. What can we do for you today?"

Henry Archer reached for a message pad. With a pencil he inscribed three lines of numerals, the code that identified Heathcote. Then he wrote in plain text: Confirm safe arrival of two airmail shipments (Clement and Shahanna). Effectiveness of previous delivery (Jhalal) continues.

Gabriel finished by saying that more data would soon follow, and signed it. Then he handed it to the woman who had spoken.

There was a clicking from her keyboard, and one thousand dollars a minute was drained from British government expenditure. The lady operator finally sat back, and said: "Transmittal confirmed."

Gabriel thought, So far, so good.

He thanked her and said he'd be back soon. He left the same way he came. The narrow street outside was deserted, allowing him to dematerialize unseen. His power was still weak; he felt that as he transported. He must try to conserve for a day or two. The lap-top was next – fortunately the energy used would be negligible.

Kamal's training camp appeared in misty form below. He slowed, and vision was clarified. He remained invisible as he descended.

The ground rose gently to meet him.

Sand crunched under his feet.

The angel breathed a sigh of resignation.

He was back among the damned.

Just in time for another disgusting lunch.

~ ~ ~

Hassan attended two lectures that afternoon. The first on handguns made out of Kevlar and other non-scan material. All of these weapons were over-light and prone to jamming. Their recoil was tricky to control, making it hard to hit the target. But Prince Kamal's instructor, a Belgian weapon designer, emphasized that no airport in the world had equipment to detect such firepower, and assured everyone that with enough practice the accuracy problem could be overcome – and once this happened, the kill-range was twice that of a normal automatic. Jamming was acceptably rare, with the odds against, particularly during a short action, as contained in Prince Kamal's plan. Those going to America would be expert with long range pistols that could fool the most sophisticated security system.

Many camp instructors, like this man, and the Canadian, who was from Quebec, spoke French. It was a lifeline from Prince Kamal to trainees who grew up as Shahanna did, in the former colonial regions of North Africa. When the language crunch came, as Kamal said it would, then poor English with a French accent, or fluent French, would be accepted and bring a stay of execution. No reason for this had been given. The Prince was not famous for explaining things.

The second lecture took place in Kamal's makeshift office building. Sixty or more people crowded into the largest room. The Prince described the next lecturer as vital to the success of this entire undertaking. A man who would teach them what they needed to know about nuclear technology. Now Prince Kamal stepped back and asked that someone to enter the room.

Two figures appeared in the doorway. One was

Clement, playing his role as Rob Keller, an expert in nuclear physics. The other was Sorya, who was in the same field, and would act as his interpreter. Of course, Shahahanna was the true expert here, and would not be translating as much as expanding on the fairly limited knowledge of Clement – to increase his credibility. Shahanna had sold the translation idea to Prince Kamal, pointing out that many in this class would not accept a woman as expert in anything, at least in the beginning. She and Clement stood by, while the Prince told everyone that Rob Keller was, in fact, a renegade American, totally devoted to Islam – and to the destruction of the land of his birth.

This was met with more surprise than resentment toward the American. That was largely due to the way Prince Kamal emphasized Keller's qualifications, rather than his nationality. Of course, that was exactly how Shahanna sold Clement to the Prince in the first place.

Fans whirred on the ceiling, generator-powered to combat the stifling heat. An air-conditioner was impossible; because one powerful enough to cool this hut in Mid-Summer would collapse its wooden walls like paper. Rob Keller's first class started with the Prince still present. This served as an unspoken guarantee of everyone's full attention. Not one pair of eyes strayed from the front, as Clement spoke – with Shahanna transforming his words rapidly into Arabic.

Nuclear physics is a complex subject, and Clement, with the help and expertise of Shahanna Dufaux, gave the impression that he knew a lot about it, reinforcing Gabriel's theory that they must have somehow demonstrated this to Prince Kamal, which doubtless saved their lives and got them into this camp. Gabriel scanned a few minds sitting round him, and found them trying hard to absorb what was being said. Everyone was feeling anxious – well aware of what happened if they failed this or any other class. The Prince knew a thing or two about motivation.

They grew even more anxious when the Prince began asking questions at random. Now the whole room reeked of fear.

Those who answered correctly sagged with relief. Those few who did not looked devastated.

"Not good enough," said the Prince eventually. "Mr. Keller, how long to whip these half-wits into shape?"

The American said: "About two weeks, your Highness." He did not need to add that some would never make it.

"Good," said Kamal, in a tone that implied it had better be the case. "We have no time to waste. Have them fully-qualified by Mid-June."

"You can be sure of it, your Highness." It was quite a concession from the Prince, thought Gabriel. That gave Clement more than six weeks.

"Excellent," said Kamal. "Then carry on. I'm off to inspect the camp."

The Prince inclined his head and gave Clement a thin smile. Then he left the hut and stepped into the hot sun outside.

Gabriel saw his chance. No need to wait until tonight; Prince Kamal was without his computer, which meant it was unattended. The angel blocked everyone's memory of his being here, then drifted into the room next door. It was a makeshift office, filled with cheap furniture and little else except cardboard boxes overflowing with what looked like stacks of files. The lap-top was not here. And it was not in either of the next two rooms, one of which was completely empty but for two nylon sleeping bags. This must be where Keller and Sorya slept. The fourth room had one table four chairs and a small cooking stove. There were cans of coffee, dried milk and packages of processed food. This was the kitchen.

That left the Prince's bedroom.

The door was locked, so Gabriel drifted in, leaving it locked. That way he would be alerted by anyone turning the key.

The bed was freshly made.

The lap-top case sat at the foot of it.

Gabriel materialized as Hassan.

The case was locked with the same caution as the bedroom. Kamal was consistent, if nothing else. Rumpled bedding and a wide-open door would have been a lot less effort, making it impossible to tell Gabriel was ever here. As it was, he must take care to disturb absolutely nothing, and leave the computer just as he found it.

The sound of Clement's voice, and Shahanna translating, carried faintly from the classroom. Gabriel listened for a few minutes. The Prince was clearly absent, or he would have interrupted by now; which was clearly his unwavering style. His absence worked for Gabriel. The coast was clear.

A locked case was no challenge.

Gabriel looked at the tiny brass lock, and conjured up a key. He fitted it into the case and turned it gently.

The computer was revealed.

A Toshiba.

He lifted it out and plugged it in before delicately raising the lid. Gabriel hoped the Prince, like most people, used his birthday to log-on. He did. Document-Files and e-mails came swimming to the surface; some in English, some in the looping curves of Arabic script. Gabriel understood both, he just hoped he had enough time. He sat on the floor, to avoid ruffling the bed. The lap-top gave up its secrets, as he typed at angel-speed. Fingers a moving blur. He struck gold with the third document file he opened. It had a promising title:

OPERATION: REVENGE OF ISLAM

Part I: Finance, Recruiting and Training.
Part II: Planning and Operation.
Part III: Target Cities and Defenses.

Gabriel couldn't have asked for more.

Good, he thought. The lunatic has written everything down.

They always do.

Gabriel skipped Part I, paging down rapidly. Finance and recruiting had already taken place, and training had begun. Parts II and III contained plans and attack zones, making them far more important to read. Gabriel did so as quickly as he could. Kamal had made the Planning section detailed and lengthy. Gabriel skimmed it, and soon had what he wanted. He noted that every word on these pages had been sent by e-mail for approval by the Saudi King. His comments and replies were everywhere, filtered in between those sent by Kamal. Gabriel suspected involvement of other members of the royal family, and a quick look under "Finance" proved him right. Here were more notes and replies, from some of the higher-ranking Princes. Now Gabriel wondered how the world's leading oil producer could play this double-game with its biggest customer? And how could American Presidents, one after another, pretend not to know? Gabriel had no answer, so he started on Part III.

He noticed a section headed: "Airports and Security". Thinking: Now, that looks promising. He was not disappointed. The international airports of six densely populated American cities were listed, with a full analysis of security measures at each one, and the way to beat them.

Now Gabriel knew the six targets.

Part II had already told him the rest: A nuclear detonation was to take place at each airport, calculated to disrupt transportation on nationwide scale, wiping out the cities concerned – and creating an even worse economic crisis than the September 11th attacks. This time, as before, each target had been selected for maximum impact, most being financial arteries. America's economy would again be paralyzed for years, and almost impossible to repair, if it recovered at all. In the best traditions of Al Qaeda, this was an act of evil genius.

Gabriel looked up from the screen.

No wonder Lucifer had embraced it.

This plan was too comprehensive, too massive in scope, to be stopped by simply eliminating Prince Kamal. He was just a front, a monster whose barbarity made him a natural to run this camp. There were plenty more where he came from. The Saudi clan positively bulged with Princes, plenty of them psychopathic. Eliminating Kamal would have virtually no effect. This fact must be conveyed to Heathcote. His sniper team must be withdrawn.

Gabriel read on:

Six twelve-man teams to leave European departure points, boarding jumbo-style aircraft as off-duty crew. Suitable airlines had been selected, and each team would have uniforms and credentials that were the real thing. All six teams to include fake pilots – in case their authority should be needed. Nobody argues with an airline captain. No nuclear device to be present at take-off or landing. Those would travel by other means. There was simply no way to get even one on board a plane. Six devices on six planes was completely out of the question. They would be shipped by sea.

This was not news to Gabriel. Angel watchers reported that all six bombs were on North Korean freighters bound for Canada and Mexico, and, whatever route they took, would be in America when needed.

Gabriel heard a scraping of chairs that said Clement's lecture was over. The angel quickly returned the lap-top to its case and locked it. Gabriel put everything back just as he found it.

Then he vanished.

~ ~ ~

Clement stepped out of the hut and crossed the compound. He went to where the main refrigeration units stood, hooked to their generators. The noise they made was a low, vibrating hum. Four industrial-sized refrigerators, where ten-gallon containers of water, totaling a week's supply, were stacked high inside each one. Clement could have drunk it all. His mouth was dry, every nerve was taut with adrenalin, but he felt elated. Prince Kamal was completely fooled.

With Rob Keller less than halfway through his lecture, the Prince had been won over. Prince Kamal was not only taken in, his vanity was satisfied. Choosing Sorya and Rob Keller demonstrated his excellent judgement.

It had been the same in Paris.

They had landed, and a delay was announced before Shahanna's handcuffs had been removed. Soon Sorya was free everywhere except the United States, trapped in a waiting lounge with a top member of Al Qaeda. During the trip, she had no contact with the Prince or anyone else. But she got lucky with the layover. The delay lasted for hours, and at the start, shaking his hand, Sorya had smiled invitingly and said, "Your Highness, such an honor to meet you."

Clement had kept his distance, waiting to be introduced if the Prince was indeed captivated according to plan.

Captivated was not the word. Shahanna wowed him, although he remained calm and dignified, due to his upbringing and background. He responded with a cool smile. "My dear, I'm flattered. But surely you have mistaken me for someone else." Then the Prince had introduced himself as Abdul Rashid, Jordanian businessman, and Shahanna pretended to believe him.

It was easier than expected. Sorya had been deported wearing a daringly low-cut tank-top under a denim jacket. Shahanna now removed the jacket. Prince Kamal spent two hours gazing at her breasts and hanging onto her every word. He was introduced to Clement, told his background and fed every detail of their cover story. The result was a four-day stay at the Saudi Palace, during which Kamal soaked up every word they told him, evidenced by his recruiting them both for Revenge of Islam. They had passed with flying colors.

Reaching this camp was the pay-off.

Turning the spigot on a ten gallon plastic bottle, Clement bent his head to drink. Then he hefted the container on one shoulder and started back for the hut. He decided too much confidence was foolhardy, and made a mental adjustment. Better to focus on staying in character, and pleasing this maniac Prince.

Clement carried the water into the kitchen.

Shahanna was waiting with plastic cups.

She began speaking loudly, for the benefit of electronic bugging that was almost certainly in place. "Don't stand there gaping. Put it on the table, you idiot. The Prince is waiting."

Clement obeyed, grunting. "Shit, Sorya! Don't be such a bitch."

"Watch your mouth. Profanity is forbidden."

"What the hell isn't forbidden, for Christ's sake? Why can't you just be nice for once?"

"We're not here to be nice. We're here to destroy your vile monster of a country. Try to remember that."

She filled two cups and a glass jug, placing everything onto a bamboo tray. Then she swept out of the room.

~ ~ ~

Clement caught half a glimpse of Kamal, seated on his bed in a red silk robe with Gucci slippers dangling loosely from his feet.

Then the door closed.

Sorya said: "Shall I make tea, Your Highness?" She always spoke in English to him. Her version of Arabic was different enough from his to justify it, but she did it mainly for Clement's sake. Luckily the Prince believed his own English to be flawless, and he loved to show it off.

The walls were skimpy enough for Clement to hear them. He smiled, because if Prince Kamal had bugged this oversize garden shed, he had wasted time and money. Clement and Shahanna knew better than to ever say an incriminating word. At least indoors.

Box springs creaked, as the Prince either stood up or shifted his weight. He said: "Tea would be nice. Do not call me Highness."

"No, Kamal."

"I have told you before."

"Yes, Kamal."

Her tone was soothing, but not the look on her face as she re-entered the kitchen.

Clement wanted to laugh out loud.

She heated water at the stove and made tea in silence. Then she poured it into two tall glasses with fancy handles. Prince Kamal went camping with great style. Sorya put both glasses on the same tray as before. The Prince answered her knock curtly, and she went back in.

The bedroom door closed behind her.

There was a prolonged silence that eventually became awkward, even through the wall. Clement pictured them both, drinking tea and ignoring each other. Then the prince said coldly: "You can go."

This time, as the door came open, Clement saw Kamal reading something from the lap-top, which sat at his side. He sipped his tea as he did so, and acted as if Sorya did not exist.

She closed the door behind her, looking at Clement with a finger to her lips. She finished her tea and rinsed the glass in the sink. Then she led Clement into the room with sleeping bags. They had only a fan for ventilation, and it was doing a poor job. Shahanna stripped down to her underwear, and sat on one quilted bed.

Clement did the same. He could not help marveling at her beauty, but also at her courage. Since they got here, she seemed at ease with the danger they were in, and with being in Sorya's skin. Clement could not believe how good was at this. The woman was a natural-born undercover.

He winked at her and blew a kiss.

She grinned, but when she spoke her tone was angry and impatient. "I asked for a glass of water. Where is it?"

All three people in this acoustically challenged hut knew she had said nothing of the sort.

Clement grinned back, and padded off to the kitchen.

~ ~ ~

Henry Archer was back across the Pakistan border, visiting the British Consulate once again.

His female encryption clerk was as friendly as ever. "Top Secret?" she asked with a breezy smile.

"Highest level," said Gabriel apologetically, and waited while she went through the computerized rigmarole that this involved.

He gave her a heading: "Washington. Code Name: Iron Man." (Heathcote.) Then he gave her the daily cipher numbers and she was ready.

She commenced rapid typing.

Henry Archer began dictating:

"The Operation named: Revenge of Islam."

Now Gabriel laid it all out, saying the lap-top was found by Hassan, another Iraqi recruited by Heathcote around the time he found Jhalal. The American would vaguely recall doing so, although the details might be hazy. The two Arabs were lifelong friends, it had turned out. How very smart of Clement's boss to let them work together. Such things made all the difference out in the field.

Heathcote would be pleased with himself.

Gabriel liked the symmetry of that.

Henry Archer transmitted Kamal's material complete, even down to the comments of the Saudi King and his brothers, cousins and uncles. The Angel of Death listed all six targeted cities, and gave Al Qaeda's security-rating of each one. He added the name and description of anyone in the camp likely to be qualified for the actual mission. Their fake identities and photos should follow soon. The rapid-fire clicks of the keyboard went on for some time, this being possibly one of the longest messages Gabriel's obliging English lady had ever sent.

And she was giving Heathcote plenty to do.

~ ~ ~

By morning, Gabriel was back with Jhalal and Asuto Kenyatta. Their class was studying the layout of six US Airports. Next they learned how to say English words and phrases in a variety of European and South American accents. In a few weeks, when the airline uniforms were issued – few sitting here would look or sound as if they came from the Middle East.

Next day they were joined by Sorya and Rob Keller, both of whom were already cleared for the final mission, the American due to his nationality and nuclear expertise. And the woman because she pestered Kamal unceasingly until he gave in. Of course her own education in physics had played a role, but men in the Arab world will always look down on women, and it amused the Prince to toy with her. What

Shahanna, with her western ways, viewed as persistence, he saw as having to beg.

Either way she was bound for America.

Their next class was a surprise, and an important one. A small, sealed container had arrived, in the keeping of a Saudi palace guard, yesterday, when Jhalal and Asuto brought water in the supply truck. The courier treated Prince Kamal with great respect, as he handed over the object. It contained blue-printed schematics, showing the workings of a nuclear detonator. There were also leaflets on how to make one explode. These bore lettering with bold Korean strokes.

The courier went away in the truck.

This class was immediately assembled.

The schematics were laid out on a trestle table at the front of the room. Trainees were permitted to study them in small groups, returning to reproduce the drawings and instructions as best they could, on yellow pads of paper handed out by the Prince, who watched them as a dog watches meat.

That evening eleven men and women disappeared from their tents. All had done badly in one or more classes. Some had shot poorly at the pistol range. Some still spoke English badly, after extensive coaching, with no chance of ever being taken for anything but a terrorist suspect. Most damning, not one of them had understood the detonator blue-prints at all. That was their worst crime, and it brought a death sentence. At dawn eleven heads made a grisly spectacle on sharpened stakes in the sand, their sightless eyes filled with the horror of their death.

Gabriel had been saved some work.

CHAPTER TEN

HENRY ARCHER'S MESSAGE, and its dire warning, made a few stops on the way to the White House and the Oval Office. It arrived there only sixty five days before the Fourth of July.

It had spent two day's spread across Heathcote's desk and floor, being scrutinized by analysts from every branch of America's espionage services, most of whom believed they knew Henry Archer personally, and took him at his word. Everyone else knew this Brit at least by reputation, and accepted that this transmission was worth its weight in gold, and unlikely to have been intercepted because it came from the British Consulate in Pakistan. The safeguards between America and its top ally were unbreakable, even to the Israelis and the Russians.

These codes had never been cracked.

Besides Henry Archer's alarming news, other reports had come in from the Far East: The China watchers and those on the North Korean border were saying that their contacts – rice merchants who visited frequently, fishermen who came and went as they pleased, and drug-pushers who heard whispers on the street – were all telling the same story: An unnamed Chinese Tong lord had secured a deal between Iran and Communist North Korea. Six nuclear cores, suitable for building short range missiles. All of this had the blessing of Red China.

The Dragon of the East was out of its lair.

Like anyone of his profession, Heathcote was relieved to have something to go on, even in circumstances as grave as these. Being ignorant of facts, and waiting, wore away at the nerves, and this information gave him something to do. He had been a foot-slogging Marine officer, used to getting down in the mud and giving orders. Now he was a master spy, sifting details, clues and assumptions, before assigning men and women to sometimes deadly tasks. He knew it came down to the same: Now he'd been catapulted back into battle. And this promised to be the toughest battle in American history, with Heathcote acting as a General on the front-line. But it was also the greatest crime story of all time, casting him as a detective.

He must excel in both roles.

Once examination of Henry Archer's account was concluded, copies went to FBI Headquarters, CIA Headquarters and eventually to the President's Security Adviser, who was furious at the delay, and demanded to know why the President had not seen it first. A nuclear attack – for God's sake!

The Washington two-step began.

Heathcote did not take part. He busied himself with issuing directives to those he trusted most: "Warn all airlines that a shut-down is likely for Independence Day." and "Seize all flying school records for the last five years. Re-check foreign students." and "Request evacuation plans from civic authority in all states – those with their cities and airports under threat to be contacted first." There was no mistaking the seriousness or purpose of these instructions.

Nine weeks to a mammoth crisis. This Revenge of Islam, if only partly successful, would decimate America.

It struck at her population, economy and air transport system on an unthinkable scale.

A solid defense was near impossible.

Heathcote knew that.

But he was going to try.

With faxes and e-mails circulating his offices everywhere, he made appointments with people in power who knew his track record. He talked personally to those who ran the country. Most of these meetings were inside the Beltway, but Heathcote also flew to Chicago, Miami and Los Angeles. After some transatlantic telephone calls, he visited his counterparts in London, Paris and Munich – where he was received with courtesy and promises of support.

Back home he went to see the senators who ran the finance committees; then the industrialists who ran the senators, and then the stockbrokers and bankers who ran the industrialists and everything else. These were the money people, and Heathcote needed a shitload of money.

Hundreds of millions were pledged immediately. Heathcote told them that was not enough. He told them that if this went badly, American money would be worthless, with the world bank offering ten cents on the dollar, and leaving those he was talking to with nothing. The Great Depression would be nothing compared to what happened next. He had made his point. Pledges rocketed into the billions, and massive deposits went into a secret fund at the Chase Manhattan Bank.

But Heathcote had other things to do. According to Henry Archer, two freighters were underway, bringing the bombs to America by routes kept secret even from Prince Kamal. These ships were overseen by angels at all times, and their location was known, and would always be known, but Henry Archer could hardly tell Heathcote that. The Americans must intercept the deadly cargo unaided, but it would not be easy. Heathcote already realized that. These freighters would not be flying the North Korean or Iranian flags. They could be registered in any of a dozen terrorist-friendly countries, and they could be cruising anywhere. The US Navy had neither the time, the ships or manpower to stop every vessel on the high seas. Nor did any other navy.

Heathcote decided to use them all anyway. He consulted the list kept by Lloyd's of London; then contacted Shipowners, Cruise lines and Naval Admirals and captains from all over the world. No one refused to help, but several pointed out that finding any two vessels among tens of thousands, scattered across all oceans, was practically impossible. Heathcote asked them to try.

Then the President sent for him.

Heathcote was to give the Revenge of Islam briefing . It involved standing on what he called the American Eagle carpet for only the second time in his life. He spoke in his gruff, ex-Marine voice, and did not waste words. He left out unconfirmed reports, and related only what he knew for a fact. Most of it came from Henry Archer. All of it made your hair stand on end.

The interview was relatively short. The President took off immediately afterwards on Air Force One. He was to attend fund-raisers in several Mid-Western states, where he was still doing well in the polls.

He was doing poorly everywhere else.

An hour later Heathcote was contacted by an Army Colonel. Their special unit had pin-pointed Prince Kamal, using voice-prints and cell phone traffic; the Prince was in the camp in question, and in charge of it. Special Forces Command was asking if the hit team should go straight in.

This confirmed Hassan's information on Prince Kamal, but the Iraqi undercover had cautioned against this hit, and he was the man on the spot. Clement and Jhalal had doubtless also been consulted.

Heathcote told the Colonel to hold off for now.

This was relayed to the squad on the ground – a four man detachment of the 101st Ranger Division, who were dug into a pit in the sand which fried them by day and froze them by night.

They were to stay put and wait. They were seventy miles out, watching the camp using long range infra-red imagery, which they matched to photographs they had. They knew the whereabouts of Prince Kamal at any given moment. Heathcote now asked them to keep an eye on the well-being of his four people in the camp. The sniper team signaled back that they had pictures of Clement, Shahanna and Jhalal, but no likeness of Hassan, and no idea what he looked like.

Heathcote suspected a glitch in the computer system and made a note. Tomorrow he would have someone look into it.

Strangely, that did no good.

Hassan was a gap in the universe.

But that was tomorrow. This was still today, and some surprising events were still to take place.

One hour later, Heathcote was at his desk, eating a hot dog from the canteen. The red scrambler light flashed on his telephone. He picked it up. The caller was the CIA Controller for most of the hot spots in OPEC. He quickly told Heathcote to watch CNN and hung up.

Heathcote switched on his set.

A compelling long-shot came into focus.

Something all too common had happened in the Persian Gulf, beyond territorial waters.

A Saudi supertanker was ablaze. The flames were a towering orange mist that ran its entire length, beneath a column of black smoke that hung in the air for miles. Even as Heathcote tuned-in, the ship was sinking like a stricken sea monster, twisted shards of the stern slipping slowly below the waves.

The crew was surely lost.

A CNN reporter swung in a harness under his news helicopter. He was shouting into a hand-held mike, flanked by lakes of blazing oil as they spread across the sea. He outlined the developing story:

A gunboat stolen from the Saudi military had been packed with gasoline drums. These drums did not contain gasoline. Bogus sailors in Saudi uniform had got in close, detonating enough explosive to wipe out an entire fleet. They died with their victims. No one on either side had any chance to jump.

The tanker was the Nexus Star.

Almost a quarter-mile in length.

Eight hundred million dollars in oil, bound for the United States.

Heathcote knew exactly why this had happened. It occurred more and more. Al Qaeda was keeping the Saudi King on track, in case he became tempted to waver. They needed both his blessing and unrestricted financial support. These tanker atrocities were a reminder. The King presented such attacks to the world as undeniable proof he did not support these outlawed, terrorist villains. It confirmed him as their sworn enemy. Was he not losing billions in these raids?

Heathcote knew that was bullshit.

His phone rang again. This time it was the White House.

An hour later he was on his way to meet Air Force One in a two seated C-12 jet.

Four hours later he was having a light supper with the President and Secretary of State, feeling somewhat out of place. Air Force One had left the Eastern time Zone with Heathcote on board, and was now flying high over the Great Lakes. The President was attending a Farm Show in Wyoming tomorrow, hoping for corn-fattened donations. He looked quite young for his years. An ocean of cloud stretched into the darkness beyond the portholes of the main cabin. The three men sat loosely arranged around a table that folded out of one wall.

President Christiansen was eating a Caesar's salad and drinking bottled spring water. He oozed energy for a man who had been on the move all day. Heathcote found him too good looking for a President: almost angelic, with blond hair that refused to go grey, and pale blue eyes devoid of guile. His suit was impeccable, his tie perfect. He set aside his plate and used a napkin to wipe his lips; then he looked directly at Heathcote and asked about the Saudi oil tanker.

Heathcote stopped eating and focused. He explained what happened and what lay behind the bombing: Al Qaeda was keeping the Saudi King, and their cash flow, on the right path.

The President accepted this reasoning, interrupting

only to ask if all the tanker attackers were Saudi. Heathcote said no one would ever know – except the sharks that ate them. When Heathcote finished, the Secretary of State said: "Are you sure the King won't see the light here, and turn to us?"

"He will not, Mr. Secretary," said Heathcote firmly. "He's pouring millions into Prince Kamal's operation as we speak, a nuclear strike at us is the King's top priority. The Saudis are a lost cause. Payment for those six nukes will buy enough rice and grain from China and Russia to feed North Korea for years."

The president said wryly, "Maybe we should shoot the King, instead of Prince Kamal."

Heathcote paused, then realized it was a joke. Then he explained his hold-off on the assassination of Prince Kamal, and the reasoning that made him do it. He did not mention Hassan, or any source.

"Are we certain about all this?" said Secretary Garret.

Heathcote knew it was the President asking.

"We are, Mr. Secretary."

"The Saudi King, personally involved."

"Yes, sir."

Garret said: "It's one thing to accuse him of conspiring against us. Quite another to prove it."

The President said: "I accept Mr. Heathcote's judgement. Our covert networks all agree that the Saudis secretly work against us. Always have."

Heathcote regarded both men. They had been friends for years, and he knew they were double-teaming him – playing good-cop and bad-cop to see what his reaction would be. Well, Heathcote was a real cop and he would not react. His job was to deliver the facts so these two could make the decisions. Heatchcote guessed that confronting Saudi Arabia was the last thing they wanted. Relations with the Saudi Kingdom were delicate at the best of times – and had always dominated American foreign policy. The First Iraq War took place because the Saudis saw Saddam Hussein's invasion of Kuwait as a rehearsal for invading them. They repaid America with ten years of cheap oil, and by keeping the dollar as the world currency for oil payments. When Saddam eventually threatened to turn to the Euro, dealing a deadly blow to the American economy, he was attacked again, thrown out of power and executed – an unmistakable warning to Iran and Syria, who were also considering the Euro. Shock and Awe did their work, and Iraq was conquered twice, to save the American dollar.

Half a million Iraqis died.

Most of them civilians.

If Saudi Arabia ever switched to trading in the Euro, instead of dollars, the US economic structure would collapse completely, one more factor that forced America to ignore the treachery of the Saudi King.

Like his predecessors, President Christiansen was caught in this trap. Saudi oil was America's lifeblood. For road transport, air travel and heat in Winter. There was no home grown or viable alternative. Not even natural gas, seen by many as America's ace in the hole. Natural gas could not fuel cars, trucks, planes or ships to meet the massive energy demands of America, either civilian or military. Wind, solar and electric cells were taking longer to develop than expected. So was the electric car. There was still no substitute for Saudi Arabia and its oil wells. All this meant the Saudis ruled the United States, although nobody ever said so.

Drilling accidents in American waters had only made things worse. Since the BP disaster there had been dozens more, until an urgent act of Congress brought offshore operations to a standstill. That forced the price up on world markets, with Saudi Arabia and Russia making obscene profits, resulting in the unimaginable $600 a barrel cited by Prince Kamal at his recent Tribunal meeting.

It meant President Christiansen, like every President since the First World War, had to walk a crooked line.

Those desert pipelines must keep flowing.

The President thanked Heathcote for his assessment, then said: "I'm moving two more carriers, the Truman and the George Washington, through the Suez Canal. They will serve as an unspoken threat. Mr. Heathcote, you're right. Keep Prince Kamal in the land of the living unless I say otherwise. Keep your sharpshooters there, but tell them to play cards and drink a lot of water. We must be very sure of our ground, before we kill a Saudi Prince of the Crown. I see that now. On the other hand, let's track down the two Generals who work with Prince Kamal, and take one of them out. Probably the Saudi. He's easier to find than an Afghan, and it tells the King we're onto him. Make it nice and public and blame it on Al Qaeda, before the King can say anything. It will weaken him in the eyes of his subjects. And it sends another message. From me."

The Secretary of State broke in, addressing Heathcote. "Listen, if all else fails, one of those two carriers will drop a cruise missile into Prince Kamal's camp, and that will be the end of it."

Heathcote nodded dumbly, refusing to think about the

chain reaction that might set in motion.

The president read Heathcote's mind. "It won't come to that, I'm sure. Prince Kamal's operation will be stopped on its way here from overseas. You, Mr. Heathcote, will see to that."

It was a pat on the back, a threat and a dismissal. Heathcote understood and got to his feet.

He was shown to a sleeping cabin.

~ ~ ~

In the morning he got a Presidential memo, and a ride in another C-12 jet back to Washington.

He read the memo on the way:

It said that the White house intended to move diagonally against Prince Kamal by deploying aircraft carriers to threaten the Gulf States – but not to move directly against the Prince with snipers. This officially reversed previous policy. Heathcote was to consider pulling his hit squad altogether. It was a request; not an order, so Heathcote was expected to ignore it, but now the American President was covered. Wiggle-room for White House denials now existed.

Heathcote was acting alone.

Heathcote was also warned against sharing information with the Brits, although everything worthwhile so far had come from Henry Archer. The British press was always like a wolf-pack on the scent, and much of the time their government no longer supported American policy, which often led to press leaks. An American operation inside a camp in Iran would make a juicy scandal – especially as it included a four man hit-team who had no right to be there. British Intelligence was to be shut out. Heathcote must carefully vet anything revealed to Henry Archer.

Heathcote thought it a stupid order, so he would ignore that as well. Henry Archer was a Brit, but trusted. He was also running Hassan on Heathcote's behalf, and would be told anything he needed to know.

Finally Heathcote was to make verbal reports, to the President, twice each day.

In the Oval Office. In person.

There was a hand-written note from the President at the end. It said: Everybody I've talked to says you're the best, which makes you the man I need. Please contact me personally if anyone gets in your way, or you run into any red tape.

Many thanks, Christiansen

~ ~ ~

Heathcote returned to Alexandria and got back to work. He was soon eating more frankfurters in between cigarettes. If the smell of tobacco and grease was overwhelming, he didn't mind. If his few visitors found it objectionable, there were no complaints. Word travels fast: Bradley Heathcote was the President's chosen one.

He worked all day.

He worked all night.

Heathcote worked to keep four agents, and one nation, alive.

On the third morning a janitor shook him awake. "Sir, would you like some coffee? We just made it fresh."

"Yes, thanks. Please leave it on my desk."

He went off to shave.

The buzz of the electric razor brought him gently back to life. He must not fail. He told himself that every morning at this time. The millions of lives he was now responsible for weighed on his mind. This had become far more than spies in a camp, or that Special Forces unit in a baking hole in the sand. Now it embraced every American man, woman and child living in half a dozen cities, each with a population well over ten million. These cities spanned an entire continent, and defending them from Prince Kamal or Al Qaeda, or anyone else, was proving a nightmare. Governors and Mayors varied in character, but first and foremost they were politicians. Heathcote spent two days on the phone without getting a clear answer or commitment from any of them. No one wanted to spend money on the kind of defense he needed. His funds in Chase Manhattan Bank were substantial, but not enough to cover this. Heathcote envisioned corpses under mountains of rubble, because no one would put up any cash. Had they forgotten what a hurricane did to New Orleans? Texas? Florida? Puerto Rico? What another one did to New Jersey? This would be far worse and multiplied by six. A hurricane is a surprise, Revenge of Islam was not. Prince Kamal had named a date and listed the targets, but the civic leaders Heathcote had spoken to didn't seem to believe it.

They didn't want to.

Heathcote cleaned his teeth and left with his toiletries, willing himself to somehow get political America's attention.

He thought of asking the President for help.

Heathcote drank coffee and decided that would not work. The President's approval rating said they probably wouldn't listen to him, either. Politics run on success, and poor opinion-polls reek of failure.

Voter loyalty in Wisconsin was not enough.

~ ~ ~

But Heathcote wasn't thinking about opinion-polls, a day later, when he asked for an urgent meeting with the President, instead of waiting for their evening appointment. They last met just hours ago, but this matter could not keep until tonight. Heathcote had growled that at a White House staffer by phone.

The President met him in the Rose Garden, and had a pair of pruning clippers in his hand. The midday sun beat down on the two men, and on the best tended top-soil in America.

The President looked relaxed, and wore no jacket, but a floral cravat that made news when he first wore one in public. You could probably put him in a fashion-show, thought Heathcote, as the slim-built world leader cut a yellow rose from the stem and smelled its fragrance.

Heathcote said: "My Brit says you're in danger."

That evoked a thin smile. "Comes with the job."

But Henry Archer's warning was urgent, and alarmingly worded. An attempt on the President today. Method unknown. It was certainly alarming enough for Heathcote to rush over here like this.

It seemed Hassan had learned something of such concern that he sent it straight on to Henry Archer, by-passing security procedure. Neither Heathcote or the President would ever know both roles were played by the Angel Gabriel, with no communication involved.

Heathcote said: "One of my Iraqis heard Prince Kamal talking on his cell phone. He was telling someone to assassinate you today. Apparently the plan has been in place for some time. No idea how it will happen."

"You're sure of this?"

"Yes, sir. Or I wouldn't be here."

The President sniffed the rose again. "Well, I can't run for cover. I'm too busy and it looks . . . cowardly."

"Take precautions, Mr. President. Stay inside. Down in one of the shelters."

"No, I'm sorry. I'll say it again. An American President should not hide, or run away."

Heathcote glanced over at the Secret Service detail – four young men standing at a respectful distance. "Sir, this is not an attack on New York or Washington. They are coming directly for you." Heathcote held his breath and hoped that his words would be effective.

Christiansen gestured at the four agents, having seen Heathcote's look. "That, Mr. Heathcote, is all the protection I need. The First Lady says, and I agree with her, that the world hates a yellow-belly. Going to ground in time of danger means danger for others. I won't do it. That's it. Understood?"

Heathcote nodded, seeing this man with a new eye.

"Sir, I still think – "

"The President cut him off with a hand-chop.

"I said that's it."

This was obviously a closed door.

Suddenly there was the angry buzz of an aircraft engine, causing both men to look up.

The incident was timed at 12: 03 pm.

The intruder was a small Cessna aircraft.

It was three minutes late.

The Sunni pilot, inserted in America years before, had turned the wrong way over Pennsylvania Avenue, then flown on for one and a half minutes and had to come back. He may have mistaken some large monument for the

White House. Whatever the reason was it killed him.

That three minutes saved the President's life, and saved a lot of others from injury, death or hideous burning from a dirty bomb. That three minutes gave the Air Force time to respond.

Heathcote saw right away that the private plane, looping sideways and flying at a crazy angle, was not alone. It was drawing thunderous fire from the trio of F-111 fighters that came in behind it.

A dark plume of smoke billowed from the back of the Cessna's cockpit; then, with a sharp crack, one wing ripped completely away. The crippled plane dropped like a stone to explode in a far off corner of the White House lawn. Flames shot out and scorched the grass.

The blackened bomb, unarmed and unexploded, would be found later, beside the pilot's equally blackened corpse.

Heathcote stared incredulously at the wreckage. The President did the same, his fists bunched and his hair disarrayed.

Police and ambulance sirens were already wailing.

There was a blur of bodies, and the Secret Service ringed both men in a defensive stance. The agent in charge, gun-drawn like those of his men, spoke into the mouthpiece on at his throat.

Heathcote turned to the Chief Executive. "Best to move from here, Sir. There may be a second aircraft."

It didn't seem to penetrate. Heathcote felt at a loss. The President's right knee was visibly shaking.

The Air Force had performed superbly, thought Heathcote, and he sought to ease the tension by saying so.

The President didn't answer.

But he did begin to move.

He leaned on Heathcote's arm. One of the Secret Servicemen supported him from the other side. The President was in shock, not responding to anything, as they led him to safety. The plane was still burning, surrounded by fire engines and yellow clad firemen with gushing hoses and extinguishers. Around them the grass was already ankle-deep in foam.

A presidential aide waited inside with a stiff drink. The Secret Service had sent a man ahead. President Christiansen threw it back in one swallow. One agent said: "Sir, please sit down. We've sent for a Navy doctor, he needs to take a look at you."

The President shook his head. "Are you kidding? The Press Corps will say I'm not fit to govern."

He summoned up an engaging smile.

Heathcote saw he had recovered.

Bethesda was called again, and the doctor canceled.

Someone stepped across a lush carpet to press an elevator button.

Heathcote was relieved. An assassination had been averted, and the President was in one piece. There need be no American response; and for now, no missiles fired at Iran from the sea. The world as everyone knew it was safe. Henry Archer's warning had come too late, but fate had intervened.

Heathcote needed something to say. It didn't seem appropriate to get emotional, so he smiled, and said: "Mr. President, you were right about the Press Corps, and you don't need that doctor."

The President gripped his hand. "Thanks for what you did today. And for being so tactful. We'll make a politician of you yet."

"No thanks. Too many enemies."

"I deal with that. So would you. People rely on me, but they're relying on you as well. We can't let them down."

The elevator doors sprang open.

Heathcote watched the President and the others step inside, thinking that America could indeed rely on this man who refused to run away. President Christiansen had won an admirer.

"This evening," said the president. "Eight o' clock – see you then."

The doors closed.

That was when it dawned on Heathcote that this foiled attempt could work in his favor. After this news broke, every phone call he made to a city or state official would be taken seriously.

Prince Kamal had actually helped him.

~ ~ ~

Close to a hundred angels, the Angel Effra in particular, relaxed and breathed a little easier. They, too, had been alerted by Gabriel and played their part in keeping the President safe from harm. They had watched and waited for days, having been warned immediately when the Archangel, in the form of Hassan, first heard of the plot that had just failed.

At the first sighting of the tiny plane, Effra had unfolded her wings and launched herself at it, tugging unseen at the undercarriage, forcing it into the devastating shellfire from those defending fighter-jets.

At the same time, President Christiansen was surrounded by an invisible band of angels who normally screened the White House. Both tactics succeeded in a perfect blend of celestial and human action, as Heaven always intended. In Iran the Archangel Gabriel was quickly informed.

~ ~ ~

A day later Lucifer, as Scott Anderson, called Prince Kamal on a secure phone and said: "Your suicide-pilot failed."

Kamal already knew that. It had taken him a day and a night to accept it. He had broached the news, bitterly disappointed, to Sorya and her boyfriend, Rob Keller. Their reaction, however, was subdued, as if they were pleased but afraid to show it. The more Kamal thought about it, the more this bothered him, and he realized how little he really knew about them. Perhaps his first impression had been wrong, and too impulsive. These two would bear watching, just in case.

He had assigned watchers accordingly. A Somali woman called Mahata, and the African, Asuto Kenyatta. Both already stood head and shoulders above everyone else, in ability, aggression and cold-blooded evil. They proved this a few nights ago, by executing the condemned.

This phone call from Scott Anderson was unnerving.

It struck fear into Kamal's heart.

The prince dwelt in a dark place, trusting no one, and normally such a call from New York would arouse only suspicion and anger, but for some reason Scott Anderson terrified Kamal, as had that nightmarish visit from the Angel of Death. Prince Kamal constantly had dreams about that black man in Central Park, and felt the same terror every time. Because of this, or maybe in spite of it, he clutched the phone tightly and resolved not to show his fear of this long-distance caller, although the mere sound of Lucifer's voice was chilling.

Kamal thanked him for calling. He confirmed that six packages were even now on their way. That meant the nukes. Lung Chiang had done his work, said the Prince. That meant China, and Prince Kamal added that both suppliers had played their part, which referred to North Korea and the Iranians. The American, of course, knew all of this, and had only called to vent his anger over the bungled attack on the White House. There was a silence; then Lucifer said goodbye and the line went dead.

The Prince sat and brooded. He had sensed from the beginning that this powerful media mogul could destroy him, and would do so without a thought. Prince Kamal had that feeling now, and it ate away at his soul. He sat there feeling helpless, until he finally did what a bully always does.

He took it out on others.

First he worked himself into a simmering rage. Then he went into action, powered by that anger. He sent for guards and instructors and asked for names. Who was failing the course? Who had offended against the laws of Islam in the past week? Who ignored the call to prayer? Prince Kamal soon had a list in his hands. Not as many as he wanted. He added some names, some of them at random.

Then he waited for nightfall.

His men went from tent to tent in the early hours. The condemned were dragged screaming from their sleep. They were made to kneel and garroted with wire and their bodies thrown in a heap, doused with gasoline and set alight. An ominous glow covered the campsite. The stench put a stop to outside eating for days. Everyone watched these brutal murders from the tents, but no one spoke of it later, or made a sound while it was happening.

Prince Kamal's mood improved.

His appetite was fine.

Next day he ate breakfast in the kitchen with Sorya and Rob Keller. They talked about anything but the mishap at the White House, or the Prince's death-dealing fit of temper last night.

They were eating lamb and rice again. Sorya pulled a face, and said one of the cooks, a skinny, one-armed man who rarely stopped talking, had seen a flock of birds flying overhead and was asking for a hunting party to go out.

She gave Rob Keller a contemptuous look. "Aren't you supposed to be a crack shot? I find that hard to believe."

The American looked at her, hang-dog, but said nothing.

The Prince intervened. "Our experts say Mr. Keller's scores are excellent. They have a higher opinion of him than you do."

"I shoot better than him," Sorya said nastily.

Arguing was pointless, decided the Prince. He said: "You'll both go. A hunt is a good idea, as long as you keep together, and take reliable guides. I don't want anybody lost in this wasteland. Sorya, you will postpone your feuding with Mr. Keller, and obey local hunters of my choosing. They will not be deceived by the shifting sands. You could wander off and not know where you are, even with a compass. You can have the keys to the Range Rover."

He turned to Rob Keller. "Take cartridges for whatever rifles and shotguns we have. I want everyone heavily armed, and be sure to take a rocket launcher. You never know."

Keller paused in his eating and nodded.

"It shall be as you say, my Prince," said Sorya, in her slightly French and slightly Arabic sounding English.

She did not call him Kamal, and she ignored Rob Keller completely.

Then she stalked out of the kitchen.

~ ~ ~

Prince Kamal stayed in his office, making phone calls, and sending e-mails and faxes. The one incoming call concerned his abortive attempt on the American President. It was the King, his cousin, who had known nothing about it, and had been explaining that to the White House for over an hour. The King screamed hysterically for fifteen minutes before slamming down the receiver.

Kamal descended into one of his darker moods. The headache that came with it made him consume a bottle of painkillers, and he soon became resentful and drowsy at the same time.

It was impossible to work. He gave up, and went to his bedroom by way of the kitchen, where he made things worse by consuming a tumbler of vodka. Somehow he made it onto the bed, but was unable to undress before passing out. Before long it was noticed that he was missing, and not long after that, his door opened, and was quickly closed again. Word soon spread that Prince Kamal was unconscious, flat on his back, and smelling strongly of alcohol.

In a stupor, the Prince revisited his childhood. Most of his memories had been happy ones, of a gentle loving mother, of costly toys and games and fawning servants, but these were not the images that came to him now. Ghosts and monsters that once terrified him as a small boy in his sleep returned to haunt him. His long dead father appeared. The old sheikh grew the head of a jackal and snarled. Flies crawled on the chunk of meat between his paws. His mouth opened and yellowed teeth tore at rotting flesh, sinew and bone. Prince Kamal looked more closely, and recognized his own half eaten carcass.

His screams carried across the compound.

The scene changed, and his mother danced naked before him, her hands moving obscenely over her breasts and private parts. The Prince was revolted and attracted at the same time. Suddenly it was no longer his mother who danced. Instead a long line of the dead. Those he killed for Al Qaeda, and those he executed this week, and the week before – dancing through flames at the gates of Hell, beckoning him with charred claws. Now the Prince screamed so loudly that Hassan and Jhalal burst into the room, against the advice of everyone else.

Hassan was holding back his laughter.

All these dreams were courtesy of Gabriel.

A combination of guilt, drugs and alcohol overwhelmed Prince Kamal. As did the spell cast on him by Gabriel in New York. The Prince was in a serious coma. More people ventured fearfully into the room. No one could wake him, and after many attempts and much discussion, he was loaded onto the battered supply truck and taken to the nearest hospital, some hundred miles away. This took a long time, and until the truck returned, most of the camp believed he was dead.

~ ~ ~

Meanwhile Clement and Shahanna were hunting

desert fowl and concealing their true relationship from two of Prince Kamal's most devoted followers. This was harder than they had imagined.

Today they were getting plenty of practice.

Nodal and Khafar were Fedayeen, and fiercely loyal to the Prince. Guards on loan from the local chieftain they served; he was also fiercely loyal to the Prince, in return for gold from the Royal Saudi coffers. The two hill bandits guided Sorya and her American to a tiny oasis not shown on the maps in the Prince's glove box, but only after Sorya tired of driving crazily across ravines and rocks at the risk of both axles. She almost overturned them several times.

Eventually the Range Rover was safely parked.

Palm trees, water and a light breeze made a welcome change after the arid heat, and tensions, of the terrorist camp. Nodal and his companion unloaded food, guns and ammunition. Minutes later all four hunters huddled around these items in a bushy area that would serve as a hide.

Both guides, and of course their tribe, were directly involved in smuggling poppy cake over the border. A small, brass hash-pipe was nestled in Khafar's hand now, as he sucked quietly on its stem. The smell, heavy and sweet, hung in the air as he released it from his lungs. Clement and Shahanna inhaled sparingly, when the pipe was passed to them. Saying no seemed unwise.

The next few hours were spent crouched, fighting muscle cramp, in what felt like refuge in a stormy sea. Midday became afternoon – until shadows lengthened, bringing the cool of early evening.

Shaded, and hidden by leafy fronds, the hunters waited in silence for approaching prey. They had already shot several hares, two falcons and most of a small flock of desert grouse. Nodal had brought down a wild fox as it fled with one of the falcons. Khafar said the flesh was good to eat.

Clement was first to see the next creature lured in by water. It was a deer, the size of a greyhound, its antlers stubby and short. Clement raised his rifle and pressed it to his shoulder, the metal sight cold and hard against his eye.

The deer drank. Its neck was bowed and its ears twitched, chasing away the cloud of mosquitoes at its head.

As Clement began to squeeze the trigger, something made him stop and lower his gun. The harmony and perfection of this scene was simply too much. He could not bring himself to fire.

The others were looking at him, but no one either spoke or took a shot. They were all thinking the same: With last night's killings fresh in their minds, and plenty of game already taken for the pot, there was no need for this deer to die. Meat did not keep long in this climate, and what refrigeration the camp had was used for water. Common sense and mercy prevailed. They would not take back venison and see it wasted. Not today, or any other.

It was a rare moment of harmony.

Sorya said: "Let's load up what we have and go. We can be home before the sun goes down."

She drove them back, following directions. First the sun was behind her; then in front. Sometimes they drove in a wide circle, with the orange ball sliding to the right or left. Shahanna had no idea when she was skirting quicksand, because the two tribesmen didn't tell her. It was their secret; and that secret was Kamal's hidden trap, in case any failing trainee tried to escape. Not knowing the way reduced Sorya's speed a little, but it was still in keeping with her reckless image.

Back at camp, they learned about Prince Kamal.

That same night, General Rameesh was killed by an assassin's bullet on his way to a brothel where he was a regular customer, in the part of Afghanistan regarded as a safe haven for him and his kind. One of Heathcote's teams shot him in the heart, as he left the premises. Another team had failed, despite days of waiting, to dislodge General Makhud from the Saudi Royal Palace, where he seemed to be in hiding; so Rameesh had died instead.

Heathcote thanked the shooter via satellite phone.

CHAPTER ELEVEN

THE PRINCE WAS BACK in three days.

The doctors had pronounced him fit, with a caution that his liver, after years of abuse, was at the point of no return. And a holy man had visited his bed, delivering the same warning and preaching hell-fire and damnation. None of this put Prince Kamal in a good mood when he returned. Nor did the fact that a particularly ill-tempered demon had slipped into his being while he lay unconscious.

Shahanna was the first victim of this demon, but also its last. No one could have foreseen what happened except Prince Kamal himself, although strictly speaking, he was no longer himself. All the same, what he did to Shahanna had been inevitable since their first meeting in Paris.

Finding her alone in the tiny office, he embraced her, slid one hand down inside her jeans until his fingers brushed her groin, and kissed her fiercely on the mouth. He seemed completely out of control.

Shahanna decided to let it happen to some extent, which may well have saved her life. With a convincing groan of pleasure, she kissed him back with a simulated passion that encouraged him to cup one of her breasts before she broke free, pushing him gently away.

Not now, she told him shakily.

He took it quite well: An uncomfortable few seconds with not a word uttered. And it hung unspoken between them that today was only the beginning. Almost immediately, Kamal sat down at his lap-top, while she busied herself with the shoe-boxes and wooden crates that made up her filing system. There was actually very little for Shahanna to do, and each minute seemed to drag. When the Prince finally announced that it was time for his morning rounds, she was greatly relieved. The memory of kissing him lingered still, totally repugnant.He took her with him.

For an hour they visited assorted training sessions, and the Prince watched, and asked questions:

"How does an Italian pilot pronounce 'altitude' in English?"

"What is the weight of a loaded 8 millimeter clip?"

"How do you hide it from a metal detector?"

"The distance in miles between Boston and Chicago?"

Each answer was written by the name, with a note of whether they got it right or wrong.

The Prince was hard to please. When a young Libyan tried to tell him the latitude of San Diego, its prevailing winds for the past week and standard approach patterns to counter them, Kamal yelled at the youth for taking too long. In another class he lost his temper because someone forgot that Lisbon was the capital of Portugal. Shahanna knew this was more than impatience. Not just the Prince being his overbearing and obnoxious self. This was sexual frustration. Shahanna was only partially right, because she did not know about his newly embedded demon – and did not believe in such things in the first place.

Hassan did. he was sitting at the back.

Shahanna decided to exploit the Prince's hunger for her. She drained her mind of emotion and considered how best to achieve this – likening Kamal to every Frenchman who ever tried to seduce her. Compared to them he was boorish, clumsy and unskilled; despite his good looks and considerable connections. Kamal's success with rich women, royalty, movie stars and celebrities was astonishing to Shahanna. More than that, Prince Kamal might be a brash pig, but by pursuing her so recklessly he left himself wide open. If she played her cards right, he would remain a slave to his sex-drive, and his weakness for Sorya.

Careful, she thought. He's physically stronger. But careful was hardly her style and she knew it. Especially when it came to beating this potential mass-murderer at his own sex-game. Shahanna decided to take whatever measures needed, if and when this got ugly.

They all ate out in the open.

The cooks prepared it over a pit of red hot coals. Everyone sat round in a wide circle. Shahanna ate sparingly. It was spitted desert fowl – dozens of which had been shot in recent days, but it was too gamy for her liking. Wild fowl was even worse than lamb, she decided, when it came to repetition. The Prince sat at her side, smacking his lips over roasted legs, wings and breast. He cleaned off the bones, tossed them aside and called for more.

He ate a second and third helping.

Shahanna moved nearer to him, concealing her uneaten portion. Waste was a sin Prince Kamal did not tolerate.

Finally he set aside his empty plate, and she inched closer, touching his thigh with her own. He reacted to her instantly. She thought: Oh, yes. You're mine! Then it crossed her mind he might grab her again, but that was impossible in public. This emboldened her, and overcoming her revulsion, she loaded her voice with sexuality as she said softly into his ear: "Let's go hunting for better meat, just the two of us." She intended to keep him at arm's length, and pump him for information. Clement would never approve, but Heathcote would.

The Prince's face took on a look of pure lust.

She took that for agreement.

There was a sudden hubbub on the other side of the fire. People craned to look. Asuto Kenyatta was on his feet and shouting. Shahanna could see him, but not who he was shouting at, and she couldn't understand him, because he was so agitated, and his Arabic was very bad.

The Prince called out: "Asuto, what's wrong?"

Kenyatta was fast becoming a favorite.

The African turned to point. "This bad person, he spit in my food. He say I am monkey, and my mother is goat."

The culprit was a giant Arab in a Kaftan. He pushed Kenyatta in the chest. "You are a monkey – but you had no mother!" There were howls of laughter, and onlookers began to jostle the African, who stepped back and went into a crouch, clearly ready to fight. He snarled with anger, and the men backed away.

"Enough!" said the Prince, getting to his feet. "This is no monkey."

He described Asuto Kenyatta at the Tribunal: A man totally unafraid, and the most experienced fighting man interviewed that day. And for that matter, the best fighting man here. It was probably true.

They listened with growing respect. Some were agreeing. Even to them, despite his poor Arabic and accented English, Asuto Kenyatta stood out. He had strength, cunning and agility. He was unflinchingly brave, with the reactions and senses of a jungle cat. Now Asuto

Kenyatta drew even more respect from this crowd, simply because the Prince had praised him.

Asuto scowled, still ready to strike.

Shahanna told the Prince quietly: "Promote him. And fix this problem."

Kamal seemed about to argue, but was probably mindful of her invitation to go hunting. He said loudly: "Asuto Kenyatta is now leader of this camp, reporting only to me."

There was a murmur of consternation.

But no one objected. They feared a soaking in gasoline.

"Now disperse!" ordered the Prince.

The crowd began to break up, taking away the scraps of food that were left, some muttering in protest.

Holy God, thought Shahanna. Now I have to go hunting with this son of a bitch. What was I thinking? But she had to go through with it. After all, she was the Femme Fatale determined to seduce him and steal his secrets. And the key to those secrets was Prince Kamal's over-active libido.

She said, "So, Your Highness. Shall I fetch the guns?"

"There's so much to do . . . the training . . ."

"Yes, but you need a break." She knew the hospital had told him that. The doctors had insisted he needed relaxation and a lack of stress, with absolutely no alcohol allowed. Kamal was on the verge of collapse, and his mental well-being was in jeopardy. They told Jhalal the same thing, when he went to pick up the Prince.

She said: "We're going."

"Oh, very well. For a short time."

Shahanna felt exuberant, having proved she could talk him into something against his better judgment. That was something to develop. Someday soon she might talk him out of a nuclear attack, or at least talk him into making a mistake which made an attack impossible. Shahanna grimaced at the thought that today she might have to talk him out of sex in a Range Rover.

"A shotgun for you?" she said.

"Bring two – and my Remington, in case of a deer."

She walked away.

~ ~ ~

Ten minutes later she was loading the Land Rover.

The wooden box of shotgun shells cut into her fingers. She shoved it into the back of the car and closed the tailgate. The Prince stood and watched. He had grown up with rooms full of servants.

Slightly out of breath, she said: "Plenty of wildlife this time of day."

The sun was at its worst, making the compound a furnace. The sand beyond the wire would be unimaginably hot. Nothing could live out there without water. Last week Shahanna hated that beautiful oasis becoming a slaughterhouse for birds and animals lured by thirst, and she hated it again today, but she smiled at the Prince as she walked to the front of the car. This hunting trip showed her ability to manipulate the prince. Next time she'd put his life in danger.

He handed over the keys. "You drive," he said. "Abdullah will be our guide."

Abdullah showed up as he spoke: Another hill tribesman hired on as a guard. This one had bad teeth.

He was told: "You ride up front, with Sorya."

The Prince got in the back.

They zig-zagged and circled certain dunes as before,

avoiding hidden quicksand and confusing Shahanna until she was utterly lost. If Abdullah suffered a heart attack, she and Prince Kamal would never get home.

"Not a bird in the sky," grumbled the Prince.

Abdullah shrugged. "Too hot to fly." He said no more, but that shrug conveyed everything. It was also too hot to hunt, but this fool had commanded it, and Abdullah would soon be sweating. He said: "Turn left now."

Sorya swung the wheel.

The Range Rover tackled a steep, shifting gradient against all odds, and raced down the other side. Prince Kamal said: "Bravo! British engineering."

Abdullah snorted. "Better we ride camels. The foreigners want the gasoline. Let them fight over it. The old ways are best."

"Look, a hawk!" The Prince ducked over sideways, squeezing head and shoulders out of the car.

He waved one arm blindly at Abdullah, inside. "Quick, a shotgun!"

"Here, my Prince. Both barrels are loaded." Abdullah thrust it hurriedly into his hands.

The Prince aimed and fired; then fired again. There was some cursing, then he said: "Reload," and shoved the gun back behind him.

Shahanna braked, and stopped. "You can't hit anything, moving over this bumpy ground."

Stopping made sense. It prevented her being blamed for whatever shot he missed next. Shahanna flinched as he fired again, twice in rapid succession. This time something fell to the ground with a thump, some distance away. It sounded too heavy for a hawk. The Prince's shout was triumphant. "Got you, you swine!"

Sorya said: "Ah – a flying pig."

Prince Kamal laughed uproariously and sat down, opening up the gun breech and releasing twin spirals of smoke. Shahanna drove toward whatever he just shot, thinking: You'd shoot me too, right now, if you knew who I really am. She slowed down enough for Abdullah to open the door and scoop up the kill.

She said: "Ugh, a buzzard, We can't eat that!"

Abdullah said of course they could.

"Isn't it tough?"

He looked sullen, and said of course it was.

She thought, You oaf, but you have saved my virtue just by being here. Even Prince Kamal won't try anything with you here. Thanks to you, Abdullah, I won't have to fight him off, but now we all have to eat buzzard-meat."

Shahanna realized her thoughts were rambling. She felt decidedly lightheaded, and put it down to the heat. Dehydration was a problem in the desert. She reached back for a canteen.

She gulped water as she drove. Abdullah told her to keep heading West, and they would come to the oasis.

He showed the buzzard to Prince Kamal before tossing it into the back, The Prince was pleased, and reloaded the shotgun as they drove on. "A tasty stew," he said, glowing with pride.

Not for me, thought Shahanna.

She would rather starve.

~ ~ ~

While the Prince was gone, others were in his hut.

It took "Hassan" only seconds to get into that lap-top again.

Jhalal and Clement were impressed, unaware that

Gabriel was using magic to save time. He had gone from office to bedroom, opening three doors, a steel box and a writing desk on the way, all at a speed that made them blink. Breaking and entering was a useful skill, but his two partners had not expected this level of expertise. But so far they'd found nothing. Searching Kamal's data-base again was their last option.

At least for now.

Clement stood by the window, keeping watch through a narrow slit in the blinds. Occasionally someone hurried by, but no one came too close – even with Prince Kamal known to be absent. Jhalal was stationed at the bedroom door, but it was more a gesture than anything else. The likelihood of anyone entering this inner sanctum of the Prince's world was not very high.

Bringing these two had been unavoidable. Gabriel could not keep hypnotizing the entire camp as a regular thing. It was exhausting. The last time drained him for hours. Searching the prince's hut with these witnesses helped his credibility with Heathcote, and a simple spell to open a few locks didn't tire him at all.

He logged on and accessed a new text-file.

The Prince, the Saudi Palace and Al Qaeda had been busy. It all took some time to read. Most of it concerned funding, or the transfer of funding, but there was one item of special interest.

Hassan tapped the screen. "Our Prince has become careless, or foolish," he said. "On the 3rd of July, mini-vans will be rented in all six cities. In every case they're using genuine credit cards, issued in false names. That's asking for trouble."

He let them both read it.

Clement looked skeptical and Jhalal looked blank.

Hassan said: "You saw the list of card numbers. We send that to Heathcote. He tracks their usage, then arrests everyone who has one."

Clement went back to the window. "Transporting bombs and paying with plastic? Doesn't sound like Prince Kamal to me. That was done before, in Oklahoma City, and he knows it. Our Prince is laying traps. Heathcote should stay away."

"This is false information?" said Hassan.

Clement nodded.

That did sound like Kamal. Tracking the cards would act like an alarm signal. So would a series of arrests. It made sense to all three of them. Gabriel put the lap-top away and they got ready to leave.

Clement held up a hand and stopped. "What's that sound?" he said quietly.

They all listened. A peculiar whirring came from the bed. Jhalal found a miniature recorder under the pillow, spewing tape in all directions. It had broken down just in time to tell them it was there. Jhalal reached over and switched it off before Gabriel could stop him.

That told Kamal they had been here.

Clement knew what to do. He pressed "START" and let the tiny machine continue to self-destruct.

Jhalal opened the bedroom door and they filed out.

Gabriel wiped the tape clean with his mind, just in case Prince Kamal had a spare recorder and a talent for rewinding tape.

No one saw them leave.

~ ~ ~

The Prince and Sorya returned with enough fresh

meat to feed a regiment. He had bagged two deer, a dozen more grouse, a multitude of assorted birds of the air, and what looked like a large yellow dog. This turned out to be a jackal. They were common in these parts and considered by Abdullah to be even better than buzzard. At least so he said, and Sorya held him to it.

The buzzard did not make it back.

Driving back, the Prince sat next to Sorya, who made him ditch the thing. To the disgust of Abdullah, who sulked. Kamal finally said the guide could keep the jackal, and its considerable meat, for himself.

Abdullah had thanked him, still sulking.

Cooks were soon plucking feathers, and hacking venison into grill-sized chunks. Large pots were heated on the fire for stew, and for boiling rice. When the time came, they added onion, spices and bay leaf. Chili and coriander were used. More herbs went in later, as they poured in rice from sacks marked "Product of China". The salt-rubbed deer meat was cooked on a dozen spits over glowing coals. The smells and the sizzling of juices and fat were tantalizing, and a long line formed for plates. Prince Kamal and his staff were served first.

It grew dark as they ate.

Suddenly there were flashes of light in the distance, like gunfire; then a crackle of small-arms, to confirm it. Heavy artillery joined in. Not too far away a battle was being fought. People stopped eating, and stood up, listening to the thunderous noise. Gabriel watched with everyone else, and hoped this had nothing to do with Heathcote's sniper team, although the direction said it did. Eventually both flashes and gunfire died down, and everyone drifted off to bed.

Gabriel felt ill at ease.

~ ~ ~

Iranian army trucks showed up shortly before dawn. The compound glared with their lights, there were so many, and the camp filled with soldiers jumping down from the vehicles, shouting wildly and brandishing weapons. Some of them fired into the air for effect.

Four prisoners were dragged out of the lead truck. The US Flag showed on their uniforms, and Gabriel's fears were confirmed. The shouting grew louder and blows were struck. Then a furious Prince Kamal stepped in. He asked for the officer in charge, who turned out to be a lean, scruffy-looking captain. The Prince told him to control his men. Then Kamal asked what four American soldiers were doing here, and the explanation took a while.

The intruders, clearly an elite unit, had been spotted three days ago by Bedouin horsemen whose keen eyes can identify a hawk one mile away, and who are not deceived by camouflage nets or desert uniforms. The riders told their story at an army post a few days later and a full-scale offensive was mounted.

The Americans were not easy to capture. They were hardened veterans, and the firepower they put out, and its accuracy, had been beyond belief. It took half a brigade to put them down, and even then, Iranian losses were so severe that those in command were facing court-martial. It ended when the G. I.'s ran out of ammunition and were overrun. The Iranian captain ended his report by asking Prince Kamal for somewhere to interrogate the prisoners.

The Prince was furious. His security was blown, and the whereabouts of his camp now common knowledge, but Iran was his host, and he had little choice. He offered his hut. Clement and Shahanna were rousted and told to leave. Then files, sparse furniture and Kamal's bed were shoved aside to make space.

The captives were separated and put in different rooms, including the cramped entrance hall. The bruises and dried blood on their faces showed up clearly in electric light, and the fresh blood seeping through their clothing where they'd been wounded. They had plainly been mistreated, and were in need of medical attention. Prince Kamal would not provide it. He decided to inflict the wrath of Allah. He and the captain saw it as revenge. The water-boarding and torture of Muslim prisoners was still taking place in CIA-sponsored locations around the world. Here was a chance to get even. These four Americans were a gift from Allah.

Rob Keller was sent for. This gave Prince Kamal some form of control. The Iranian captain spoke English, and he would ask the questions, but having an American on hand made sense. He might get something out of the prisoners, and besides, Rob Keller was the Prince's man.

That was not lost on the captain.

They began in the hallway with the most senior and most seriously injured man: a top sergeant with years of service, evident in the hard lines of his face. He was tied onto a wooden chair. One knee had been shattered by a bullet, and blood dripped on the floor. His teeth were grinding with pain.

Clement was horrified, barely able to credit such an awful turn of events. Then he looked into the prisoner's eyes and saw a message. The Sergeant knew who Clement was, and his eyes said he could handle this.

The Iranian captain started speaking.

The questions began routinely. Name, rank and serial number. This was normal, and the Sergeant, whose name was Doyle, answered them all. Then they changed subtly. How long ago did you enlist, where did you serve, why did you join Airborne? This was a maneuver to get Sergeant Doyle talking about anything but his current mission. The real questions would come later, once he was loosened up, and they would be asked expertly. The captain knew his work. This surprised Clement, until he realized this officer was not here by chance. As the interrogation went on, it was clear he had played no part in capturing the Americans. He was sent here to get answers. The man's competence and skill spoke for itself. He was a member of Iran's notorious Secret Police. The Ayatollah's fingernail pullers.

He gave a masterful performance.

But Sergeant Doyle was tough. Through swollen lips, he repeated only name, rank and serial number, and kept repeating them until the captain finally gave up. Now two soldiers took turns punching Doyle, having untied him and thrown him to the floor. The American rolled away whenever he could, but in the small space, with him injured, most of the blows landed. The beating went on for some time. On the captain's command they rained kicks on Doyle's shattered knee. He screamed, but still said nothing, even though his pants-leg became saturated with blood.

The captain grew ever more impatient. He told them to stop and put the prisoner back in the chair.

They used electrodes next.

It seemed to go on forever.

Clement came close to throwing up.

Finally the captain stood over the prisoner, repeating his last question for what he assured Sergeant Doyle was the last time: "Why were you issued with high-tech satellite equipment?"

The American looked at him but refused to speak. He'd never talk – it was written on his face.

The captain struck him viciously. Doyle's head rocked sideways, and a tooth was shattered. He spat it out in one dark, red sticky mess that clung to the floor. Clement did not move, knowing he must not react.

An interrogator came in from the next room. His knuckles were raw and his arms, beneath rolled up sleeves, were spattered with blood. He was a corporal. He saluted the captain and shook his head. Clement took that as a sign things were going no better next door. That prisoner was not talking, either. This was confirmed when his commander told Clement what the corporal had said. The second American had not cracked in the face of continued brutality. Several bones were broken, and electricity run through his genitals, all of which was standard procedure. Finally the man had been half-drowned in a bucket of his own urine, all to no avail.

That interrogation, like this one, was going nowhere.

They had, however, found something. He tried to swallow it, but they forced his mouth open and seized it. It was a small piece of paper – part of a message in code. He looked alarmed when it was discovered, and that made it important. There was no way of cracking the code, but a message meant only one thing:

These G. I.'s were in touch with their base.

Prince Kamal was sent for. He agreed that no matter what the message, it was bad news, whether being sent or received. It meant that his camp was blown wide-open some time ago, even before the Bedouin came across these intruders. This had been Kamal's main fear since the army trucks arrived. Now it had become a reality. He lost his temper completely, yelling at Clement and the Iranian captain, calling them morons with no idea what a catastrophe this was. When they had him calmed down, he explained it in simple terms:

It all added up to one thing. Now the American military machine knew the camp existed, the camp must relocate. It was the last thing they needed, he said. The burden of moving far enough away, and finding a new place, could not come at a worse time, with the launching of the mission so close. And it was going to cost a stack of money. The King would have to be told.

The King would not be pleased.

Saudi Arabia had strained relations with Iran at the best of times, and this camp was a costly favor, granted in the united Muslim struggle against the Great Satan. Now the King would have to go begging, checkbook in hand, to some other government, quite possibly another traditional foe, as greedy as Iran had been. Meantime Kamal had four American prisoners to dispose of.

He and the Iranian captain put their heads together, having sent Clement away, and they soon had a solution.

All interrogation ceased. Assuming full authority, Prince Kamal pronounced it a failure, and the captain agreed to put his captives back in the trucks. They would set out for the main road, and have a fatal traffic accident on the way. Four dead bodies would then go on display in Tehran. Their dog-tags gave them away. America's guilt would be exposed for all the world to see.

The captain saluted. He gave orders to his N. C. O.'s, who began assembling their men. As in any army, a whisper went from one man to the other: These Americans were to be killed, then burned to disguise their injuries. Then the same whisper began to spread throughout Kamal's camp.

One who heard it was Hassan.

Gabriel thought quickly. How to prevent the deaths of four American servicemen? When he had the answer, he ran over to a truck that still stood empty. A quick look over the tailgate, and he saw two sniper's rifles and grabbed one in each hand.

He carried them to Kamal's hut, went inside and asked for permission to speak to His Highness.

He showed the Prince the weapons. They had the latest technology, with digital, infra-red scopes, and rapid-fire, multi-shot capability. They could shoot a man from a mile away, or cut the same man in two at closer range, firing as a machine gun. Prince Kamal was fascinated. He took one and looked through the sight.

Hassan had his attention. He said: "My Prince, these were found in the American dug-out when it was taken. They came here to assassinate you. There is no other possible target."

The Prince looked shaken. "It cannot be," he said. "No one knew I was here."

Then he realized they did.

Just as Gabriel knew he would.

Hassan said: "It seems to me this puts you at a huge advantage. Washington took a huge gamble and lost. Their men have been caught. The world's press will make a meal of this."

Kamal considered. "Perhaps, but the camp is compromised. We still have to move everything."

"Regrettable but necessary, and our activity can still be kept secret. You can say this American hit-squad was captured anywhere. It doesn't have to be here, in Iran. Tell reporters it happened in Egypt, near a friend's villa, where you were staying. The press never check anything."

"Washington will deny that."

"It doesn't matter. No one will believe them, because there's no denying these are their soldiers, once you put them on television. I suggest you go to Cairo right away and call a press conference."

The Prince looked at Hassan. "It appears you have qualities I did not expect," he said. "Find our Iranian captain and tell him to clean up the prisoners. We'll have to film them here and pretend we're in Egypt."

~ ~ ~

But there was no press conference and no fake Egypt. The Prince had no intention of doing that. He knew exactly who to call, regardless of the time difference in New York. He called Scott Anderson.

The devil answered immediately.

Kamal gave him the story. He could imagine the effect his words were having, but the response caught him by surprise.

"Are you insane? This is a direct line to my house!"

"My apologies, but —"

"Our government wire-taps terrorists. You're on their list."

It was a sore point. Tracking such calls had to be how the American military got so close. The Prince said haughtily, "I'm using an unregistered cell phone that cannot be monitored. It's absolutely untraceable."

So was the devil's.

Scott Anderson grunted. He seemed satisfied with that. "So you want me to run this? Assassins in Egypt?"

"That is the idea, yes."

"Well, it's crap. No one has ever heard of you. I can't make a headline out of this. The world won't care."

The Prince saw the truth in that. He said: "Then they were not in Egypt after me. They were somewhere else after a more – shall we say, better known target?"

"Possibly. Depends who you choose."

"Well," said Prince Kamal thoughtfully. "We choose someone of great importance. Not only for press attention, as you say, but to get world opinion on our side for a change. Maybe a religious figure. Somebody who represents all that is holy to Islam. Now who is that?"

Anderson said it for him. "The Ayatollah."

"Ah, yes," said the Prince. "And we are in Iran. How perfect."

"You have this hit squad in custody?"

"Yes."

"In Iran."

"Correct."

"At least we don't have to lie about that."

Prince Kamal laughed. "Only about everything else."

"That's a terrific story. Your name will be kept out."

"Thank you, Mr. Anderson. I can't thank . . ."

But the line had gone dead.

CHAPTER TWELVE

HEATHCOTE SAT ON A COUCH at home, watching his captured soldiers on T. V. They were being hauled through a jeering, fist-waving crowd, outside the high-court building in Tehran.

They looked in very bad shape.

Two of them were on stretchers.

Heathcote imagined the President in the White House, watching this embarrassing story that broke with no warning. No heads-up from Clement's group, and nothing from the Englishman, Henry Archer. America blind-sided, by a breakdown in communication. The United States was caught red-handed, there was no denying it. The President himself had ordered the hit. But the President had covered his ass with a memo. Now it would be Heathcote's ass that got fried.

That was how Washington worked.

The Ayatollah, for Christ's sake!

Prince Kamal was very good.

Or he was getting good advice.

The Ayatollah was revered by every Arab leader, at least publicly, and admired in the West, where he was seen as a moderate. An attempt on his life would be condemned as a clumsy act of stupidity – and there was no way to prove this allegation false. No one would believe it.

Gabriel's reasoning had been somewhat different. The American President, angel or not, had strayed from the path of the righteous. Murdering Kamal in cold blood would have stained his soul, and the very soul of his country. America had clear laws against such killing – laws put in place over two centuries, by the will of angels and wise men. That was why Gabriel made no attempt to warn President Christiansen of the media avalanche that was now coming. Heaven was allowing its servant to reap what he had sown.Heathcote knew nothing of that. He was not, in any case, completely downcast. America's image was damaged but would survive. Heathcote was not concerned about appearances. Furthermore Heathcote was old and experienced enough to save his job, and any public outcry, here or abroad, would only last a few days. Heathcote could cope. But the fate of his Special Forces detachment was something else. As things stood now, according to Tehran, they faced the death penalty. But that, Heathcote promised himself, would never happen.

They were coming home.

He muted the volume on his T. V. And dialed Richard Powell. The newly appointed Head of the FBI was in his office and watching the same broadcast. He was angered by what he saw, and blamed Heathcote. This was clear the moment he picked up the phone. Brand-new in the job, Richard Powell was not familiar with Heathcote, his record or his reputation. The FBI Director resented being out of the loop on Revenge of Islam, with Heathcote briefing the President twice a day. None of this made for a good working relationship.

It didn't help that Powell was a demon.

If anyone had known, this would have explained his ruthless ambition. He was a hang-over appointment from the previous White House, which President Christiansen had thought long and hard about honoring, although he eventually did. The doubts had emanated from Powell's history of betraying those beneath him, be it to survive or get ahead. A sign hung on his office wall: "Be a Team Player. Suck Up!" Richard Powell was something of a rarity: A highly-placed demon who owed neither his position or his loyalty to Lucifer. He had got this high on his own.

Heathcote knew only that he hated calling him, but he had no choice.

"What are you gonna do?" said Powell.

Have our U. N. Ambassador deny the Ayatollah thing – it's just a crock of shit to discredit us and keep Prince Kamal out of it."

"Who will believe that? If I wasn't talking to you, my phone would be ringing off the hook! And not just reporters. The first call will be from the man in the Oval Office. What do I say to him?"

Heathcote smiled. "I'll be briefing the President, sir. I see him in just over an hour, unless I hear from his Chief of Staff. That's a standing instruction. I'm over there twice a day."

It felt good to rub it in.

"Fine," said Powell stiffly. "What will you say?"

"We get them home. Whatever it takes."

"Well, good luck with that project."

"Sir, it can be done."

Powell laughed. He began to see the advantages of not having to deal with this himself. "That's good news. The President will be thrilled to hear how you'll manage that. I myself can't wait to see them get on that plane."

Heathcote swallowed his anger and stayed calm. "We can do it," he said quietly.

Powell snorted. "They wore American uniforms, they

had satellite feed and they had cutting edge, high-tech rifles. They were in there illegally – and Iran has them and their equipment. We were caught red-handed. Iran's going to make a show-trial out of this, for God's sake!" Powell and Heathcote both knew it was retaliation for years of American drone attacks, water-boarding and torture.

Heathcote was unmoved. "We offer a deal."

"Oh, sure. I can't wait to hear this."

"An exchange."

"That's hardly a winner. Who do you have in custody that they would swap for what they have right now?"

"Three hundred terrorists on ice."

"Who? The last of the Taliban guys. Al Qaeda guys? The others we're holding without trial? Half of them are in jails overseas – and most of the big fish are Sunnis. Iran won't lift a finger for them. You don't have enough of their nationals to make it worth their while. You're pissing up a rope. But go ahead, Heathcote, suggest it to the President."

"The Ayatollah will agree," said Heathcote. "I arranged it last time. I can do it again. Those four men are not going to die."

"Last time? They had one CIA Officer. You handed them a hundred detainees from Gitmo – before it closed down. For just one of ours! They stole you blind on that deal."

"It only seemed that way."

"How's that?"

"Our man was a Senator's son, and they never found out."

The phone went silent.

Then Powell said grudgingly: "That may be. This is not the same."

"It will be, once we talk to the other side, and they talk to the Saudis, and they all think it through. An exchange will happen."

"You mean there's a twist."

"We create one."

"If you can . . ."

"Sir, you need to understand. This is not a bunch of crazy thugs who hate us for our freedom. We're talking ten thousand years of intelligent and sophisticated culture. They had street lighting when we were scratching ourselves in caves. Their mentality is based on respect and pride, and they take world opinion very seriously. Anyone can see our men have been mistreated – they've been wounded, probably tortured. None of that has been mentioned yet, but it will be soon. It won't make Iran look good, any more than a suicide bombing does. Look how quickly they condemn those. We kick up a fuss about brutality – and they'll be ready to negotiate."

Powell sounded tentative. "You think that'll swing it?"

"Sir, they have accused us. A lot of people won't buy it, and this can only get worse for them as time goes on. They have nothing else to show, and nothing else to say. I point this out to the Saudis – and they will soon persuade the Ayatollah. Can you imagine if one of our guys dies in their custody? The press will scream bloody murder. Suppose all of them die? That's why executing them is such nonsense. It's a bargaining chip. Believe me, there will be a deal. The Swiss Red Cross can handle the whole thing. I have a contact who helped us last time. He knows the right people."

Dick Powell reluctantly agreed and hung up.

Heathcote dialed a number in the Swiss Alps.

An hour later he was explaining it all to the President.

~ ~ ~

The Red Cross representative jetted straight to Tehran.

He was professional and experienced. Jean-Claude Porchet came from a small village on Lake Geneva, at the foot of the mountains close to Montreux, in the French portion of Switzerland.

He had learned Arabic as a child, in Algeria, where his family had traded in spices for generations. He further studied the language at the University of Geneva, after their return to take over his grandfather's lakeside vineyard. Jean-Claude also spoke English, German and Russian. He was therefore able to converse with a great many people for the Red Cross. Some of these people were world leaders . . . some were international bankers and financiers.

And slightly behind them . . . came Heathcote.

Jean-Claude was one of the best negotiators in Europe. That, and his influential contacts, made him Heathcote's first choice for this exchange in the Middle East that simply must not go wrong. Another reason was that Washington paid Jean-Claude three hundred thousand a year for doing things like this.

It was time for him to earn it.

There were no hitches so far. A good beginning had been made through diplomatic channels, which meant shady contacts in the Arab world who owed Jean-Claude Porchet a favor or two. America was virtually clearing out Gitmo. In return Iran agreed to release their prisoners after permitting a doctor from the World Health Organization to examine them under the watchful eye of

Jean-Claude. All four American's were in prison, having been denied hospital facilities.

That examination was where the Swiss was going now. He had no medical training, little more than basic first aid, but Jean-Claude worked for the Red Cross, and he could tell if someone was going to die. This morning he had interviewed the doctor who gave blood transfusions to the American sharpshooters before they went to their cells. This doctor had attended them every day, and said they were stabilized enough to fly home. His one stipulation was that they go in a pressurized cabin, luxury class, and not in some military cargo plane that would shake a fit man half to death.

Jean-Claude relayed this in every detail to Heathcote, who in turn passed it on to the American media. Reporters were told that talks were going well. All four men should soon be released.

~ ~ ~

Scott Anderson ignored the good tidings. Century News focused instead on those blood transfusions, and the source of the plasma being a third world country. Without any evidence, Century newscasters suggested the material may have been tainted – and the HIV virus was mentioned repeatedly. Century kept leading with this story, until the other networks pointed out that the blood in question was supplied by the Swiss Red Cross, sent ahead by their representative, Jean-Claude Porchet. Century News reacted as they always did, simply switching to another story.

Heathcote phoned four anxious military wives, to assure them that their husbands were AIDS-free.

~ ~ ~

Today, Jean-Claude was halted at the prison gates. He was taken to a stone cell and told to strip to his underwear. He was searched, and a detector passed over his clothes, his keys, wallet and briefcase. He wondered why the guards were so on edge.

The reason was soon quite obvious.

When he entered the cell of Sergeant James Campbell, he was appalled at the sight that greeted him. The man lay upon scraps of straw upon cold flagstones, with no bedding or pillow. His bandages were encrusted with dried blood that had flies crawling on it. There were rat droppings everywhere, and fecal matter that may or may not have belonged to the occupant. The smell was terrible. The Sergeant was unconscious, eyes rolled back in their sockets; his breathing came in raggedy gasps. His heartbeat, when Porchet took his pulse, was irregular and weak.

And this man was in stable condition?

The guard, standing in the open doorway, seemed unabashed.

Jean-Claude held his tongue. He was here to get them out; not to make a scene. He waited for the third-party doctor to arrive as promised. The prisoner rolled slightly, and blood oozed around his abdomen. Porchet suspected that he had been sedated. That was probably a good thing. The Swiss negotiator looked at his watch. He urgently needed a second opinion. Could this man travel or not?

If there was a Hell, Jean-Claude decided, Sergeant Campbell was in it. The broad valleys and brightly painted houses of Switzerland seemed very far away. Porchet wished he was home, having coffee and cream-cake with his wife.

The doctor turned out to be Swedish. The guards thought him a fellow-countryman of Jean-Claude's; although both Europeans explained the difference with great patience. The guards shrugged. Swiss and Swedish sounded the same, if your language was Farsi. And all infidels looked like gangsters in a movie. Who could tell one from another? And what would a man gain by it, if he could?

The doctor took Campbell's vital signs, and said his temperature was a little high, but that and the blood-loss were acceptable, and he prescribed more plasma. Everything else was satisfactory. Drugs had been ingested, but the patient was asleep – and not in a comatose state. "You're going home," he told the unconscious Campbell, patting his arm as he fastened a new bandage.

One of the guards spat on the floor.

"Take us to another cell," Porchet told them. He did not try to hide his disgust at what he had seen in this one.

Arnold Johnson was a black man from Arkansas. He was awake, and grinned at his visitors through cuts and bruises when they said he was being released. He spoke in a deep voice through split lips. "Give me five minutes with these guys, man. And a baseball bat. That's all I want."

Jean-Claude gave him a cigarette instead.

Sergeant Dean was heavily medicated.

But he got approved for travel.

Sergeant Doyle was the leader, the prisoner whose torture had been witnessed by Clement. More teeth had been knocked out, and he had a serious stomach wound as well as a gunshot knee. He shook hands with both men, but didn't speak or smile. It seemed unlikely he would smile for some time; though his eyes gleamed, when they said he would soon be back with his wife.

He was a Cajun, from Louisiana.

Jean-Claude thanked the Swedish doctor and they left the jail, each in a separate chauffeured car, and to a different destination. The Scandinavian was flying home, but his Swiss colleague was not.

Jean-Claude had a lot to do.

The Red Cross station in Tehran had cleared him an office, where he and several assistants tied up the phone-lines for most of the day, at the end of which an agreement was on his desk, exchanging the four American Sergeants for two hundred questionable terrorists in American hands who could never be brought to trial. This freed the White House from an embarrassment that had lasted for years, and got Heathcote's wounded heroes onto a plane.

The signature on the agreement was that of the Grand Ayatollah. Jean-Claude approved the terms and signed, then he picked up a phone and made one last call to Heathcote, whose quiet thanks said it all.

~ ~ ~

That evening the President was told, his gratitude evident, as Heathcote summed up Jean-Claude's considerable achievement. All four soldiers were safe and getting the best medical care, and a nasty political crisis was over. The President admitted honestly that the whole affair was his fault. Sending in special forces was his idea. It had fallen to Heathcote to get them out. Heathcote was surprised and pleased. He wished that Richard Powell, his boss, was here listening to this.

Heathcote returned to Alexandria, where another garbled message from Henry Archer was waiting for him.

Parts of the transmission were missing, other parts

unreadable; even to the expert hackers who toiled for Heathcote in the basement, three floors below. The portion that was legible concerned credit cards – and the renting of passenger vans in the six targeted cities. Heathcote sent a message back, asking Henry Archer to try again.

The Brits in Pakistan complied.

What came flawlessly back was everything Clement and Jhalal had helped Hassan to steal from Prince Kamal's increasingly valuable data-base. This was the second time it had given up its secrets.

But some secrets couldn't be believed.

The credit card numbers were thought by Clement to be planted. They should be checked out, and circulated, but no other action taken. Any investigation must be kept low-key, because it seemed likely Prince Kamal suspected he had an informer, or more than one, and this was an attempt by him to flush them out. Each credit card was a trap, and if inquiries were made, or people arrested, the Prince would know that he had been right.

That might lead him to Clement and Shahanna.

Hassan had come up with something else from Kamal's lap-top, and it was not a trap; at least, Hassan did not think so, and Clement agreed with him. According to one email Kamal had received, two North Korean freighters had picked up the six nuclear weapons from the Port of Aden, as soon as they arrived overland from Iran. The ships had split up, charting separate routes. and were now somewhere on the world's oceans, moving slowly towards the United States.

Heathcote sat, thinking, for a long time.

Then the phone calls began.

He telephoned his secretary. "Get me someone high-up in patrolling the Canadian border. Our people; not theirs.

"Yes, sir."

He waited.

Then there was a clicking on the line.

The next voice he heard had a Minnesota lilt. "Commissioner Johannson."

"Do you have any helicopters?"

They did, and occasionally borrowed from the US Air Force and the Canadians. Heathcote introduced himself and explained his dilemma. The northern border topped the threatened mass that was the United States. This mass was about to be penetrated, probably at two opposing points, possibly more. The threat was still at sea for now, but could come ashore anywhere on the North American continent, crossing the Canadian or Mexican borders, or land anywhere on nearly twelve thousand miles making up the US coastline. Heathcote asked one question: How much of that border could Commissioner Johannson protect, using every vehicle and helicopter at his disposal?

There was silence at the other end.

"Commissioner?"

"Well, sir, we have manpower shortages, not enough cars, and thirty thousand square miles that can't be guarded due to budget cuts. On top of that it's hard to find pilots; even when we rustle up enough machines between ourselves the Canadians and our own military. Things have actually got worse since 9/11 – but no one wants to hear about it. Least of all the Senate Finance Committee."

Heathcote was growing impatient. "So what are you saying?"

"Sir, if you want the border sealed for a given time-frame, we can just about do it, but it's got to be funded, and I'm not talking chump change

. Your costs will be sky high. The fuel bill alone will kill us."

"How much?"

"Four – five hundred million."

"That's for how long?"

"About a month – and that's just the dirt border between us and Canada. We do ground traffic only. Anything offshore, or coming on to shore – that's the Coastguard. We're not involved. You'll have to talk to them."

"Oh, I'm covered there, Commissioner. The Commander in Chief will be taking care of that personally. I'll telephone him, and he'll telephone them. And your funding will not be a problem, believe me. You, too, can expect a call from the President – most likely tomorrow. And we need three months."

Johannson sounded flustered. "Our American President? He's going to telephone me?"

"Yes, he will. And I'll get you all the money you need – I promise you that."

That seemed to do it. The Commissioner said he would start preparing for a large scale operation, and they both hung up."

Heathcote stared at the wall. He thought, I'm halfway there. Now he had to enlist the help of the President, to commandeer most of the Coastguard fleet, and then perform the same conjuring trick at the Mexican border that he just got away with in Minnesota. He prayed it would work.

He called his secretary again.

He was soon connected to another border patrol chief; this time in San Bernadino, Texas.

"Hello, this is Commissioner Decker . . ."

~ ~ ~

Lucifer was livid.

Four Americans swapped for two hundred rag-heads who should still be in US hands. No show trial; no censure at the United Nations; no admission by the President that he sent assassins into Iran. No scandal of any kind; just empty cells that used to be full. It made Lucifer sick. Every time a world-crisis looked promising, it crumbled into dust.

The Angel Gabriel was doing a great job.

It was 7: 00 am. Scott Anderson was chairing his daily news-meeting. The nobility of Century News occupied a long conference table, notepads and coffee in front of them, waiting for him to speak.

The devil manifested a thin, deadly, black and red snake. It slithered and hissed along the gleaming tabletop.

Everyone took care not to notice.

The room bristled with editors, writers, producers, and the morning and evening news anchors, and anyone of importance from a dozen Century studios tucked away in the glittering high-rise that was by now a corporate landmark in Manhattan. And all of these people were ambitious. You had to be insane with ambition to rise this high. It was a requirement.

And being a demon helped.

Lucifer said: "So what's tonight's lead?"

For his own amusement, he made the snake nothing, as if it had never been.

Everyone began talking at once.

They had stories from correspondents everywhere. Some good, potential leads, worthy of the devil's consideration – others that were vetoed as quickly as they were suggested. It went by a nod or shake of Lucifer's head. No one around here ever called him that, but they all knew or suspected who owned their souls. Stupid and ambitious rarely mix.

Evil and ambitious usually do.

There had been an earthquake in Karachi, causing great loss of life. Lucifer was slightly inclined to go with it, but such events were commonplace, largely thanks to him, and he said no.

There was a hostage-taking in Tokyo – again, no.

Two children abducted raped and murdered in Atlanta. A suspect had fled the scene in his car with a line of police vehicles hot on his trail. That was more attractive than the other two stories, but Georgia law forbade the filming of car chases, except by police cameras – so there would be no pictures for Century viewers as they downed their evening meal.

Another no.

There was silence. Everyone knew he wanted some dirt on yesterday's release of two hundred terrorists, something that would reflect badly on the administration – but there was no such dirt to be had. It was a lost cause in any case – Century News always portrayed itself as fiercely patriotic, and the whole country was celebrating the return of four heroic American fighting men. How could anyone, let alone Century, go against the flow on that?

The silence became uncomfortable.

Then one news editor cleared his throat.

"There's a new slant," he said. "On the North Korean nukes to Iran story."

People stopped fidgeting and turned to look.

""Let's have it," said Lucifer.

The editor's name was Robert Oliver.

"Luxembourg," he said. "A lot of money, we're told six hundred billion, laundered in Luxembourg through a bank no one ever heard of." Interest in the room heightened, as did that of Lucifer, and Robert Oliver grew bolder and more confident. "The Chinese government is involved in this – going through a Chinese tong leader to keep Communist Party hands clean – and they wanted payment in Euros. The Saudis refused at first, they only deal in dollars. But then it became a deal breaker. The Chinese insisted on Euros for their cut, which by the way was fifty percent. The Tongs took another twenty off the top. Not much left for North Korea, once everyone got a slice, including Saudi banks, brokers and so on. And of course, more deductions were made in Europe – as soon as the money arrived."

The mathematicians in the room calculated rapidly. The North Korean share was still colossal, and they were not likely to complain.

Oliver added that this was only a down-payment.

Lucifer said: "Where's your headline?"

Oliver did not hesitate. "Saudi involvement. One of our reporters in London has access to the transfer documents. America's biggest oil supplier is caught red-handed. A story to kill for!"

Lucifer thought for a moment. Saudi financing of terrorism was not news. It had been an open secret for years; kept under wraps to protect a succession of oil-deals and price negotiations. Lucifer's question was this: Was America at a point where long term suspicions could be confirmed? If such a world-shattering revelation were made, public acceptance was crucial. Should Lucifer tell viewers what so many of them half believed already? After some thought he decided the time was right.

"Run your story," he said.

There was a stirring among those present. Not only were they jealous of Oliver's success, but the leap in ratings caused by this revelation would keep them all busy and make them rich at the same time. There would be denials and counter-denials; political spin and counter-spin. The number of Senators, Congressmen, political pundits, lobbyists and strategists to be interviewed would back up like an old toilet.

This was where huge bonuses came from.

Robert Oliver asked outright. "How do we twist this?"

Spinning was for other networks.

Twisting was more vicious, and more painful.

Lucifer said: "Leave out any Euro against the dollar crap. Our viewers can only take one pending disaster at a time. And blame the money-laundering on someone else. No one in America knows where Luxembourg is."

Oliver shrugged. "Mid-east, Venezuela, Russia? Who do we want them to hate?"

"Always the French."

Everybody laughed.

"Muslims, of course," said Lucifer, more seriously. "Throw it back on them. Either Dubai, or the United Arab Emirates. Let their banks take the heat on this." A murmur of approval swept the table.

No one minded that the story was now a pack of lies.

"That's settled," said Lucifer. He sat back. He could see the relief etched on their faces.

The devil said, "All our T. V. News networks: Tonight's lead headline. As for our newspapers and magazines – the dailies can ride it for as long as it lasts; the monthlies can editorialize it to death for at least two issues." He lit a cigar and blew smoke rings. Lying was such a beautiful sin.

Kathy Lester and Lewin Smith sat to his left. They had recently become an item, having worked together on the "Iran Goes Nuclear" story-line, since she broke it on her top-rated morning show.

Kathy now spent most nights in his West-Side apartment. The devil knew Lewin Smith was bi-sexual, and this was how he operated: I advance your career – you sleep with me until I find someone else.

Apparently that hadn't happened yet.

Kathy Lester gave Lucifer her best smile and asked brightly as to the whereabouts of the Iranian nukes – as casually as if asking the way to Pizza Hut. Her voice was syrupy with respect.

Lucifer smiled back. She wanted to upstage Robert Oliver's bank disclosure by scoring points with the boss and grabbing a headline for her next show. It was the right question to ask. It would not be answered honestly, but this helped Lucifer protect his two Korean cargo vessels – by lying to a roomful of liars.

He said: "My sources say the material is in bunkers, deep underground in a vast tract of desert, to avoid detection and for safety. The North Koreans admit their fusion techniques are unstable, and that makes Iran nervous. They don't want to vaporize half their country.

These bunkers can withstand a lot of megatons – and were built for good reason. That stretch of sand is brimming with untapped oil reserves. Iran is always afraid of America destroying those fields with airstrikes. It would bankrupt the entire country. An accidental nuclear explosion would produce the same result. The Korean nukes will resurface when the 4th July bombers are ready to fly."

This was the perfect lie. And it would start to spread as soon as this conference ended. Century networks would not touch this story. The devil would forbid it, and be obeyed. But in the bars and restaurants around Rockefeller Center, where newsmen ate, drank and swapped gossip, the whispers would begin.

Other networks would steal the story in no time. So would all the news media not owned by Scott Anderson. There would be a call for more action from the White House. With luck, pressure on the President might result in direct action against Iran. At least an air-strike, if not an all-out nuclear attack. Meantime both nuke-bearing freighters were protected at sea, believed by the whole world to be deep under the sand of some Iranian desert.

Lucifer could not see a downside.

He told Kathy Lester that the Iranian bunkers were off-limits. No one at Century, including her, was to report their existence. Lucifer made it sound as if he was in direct contact with the White House. This impressed Kathy Lester, and told everybody present to keep their mouth shut. Lucifer said anyone pursuing this story would be fired. Some believed him. Some did not.

Then they got on with the meeting.

Two editors offered stories to accompany Robert

Oliver's money-laundering headliner – One a juicy Hollywood murder, the other a young American girl missing from a cruise ship in the Caribbean.

The Tinsel-Town story was perfect: A prostitute, drugged, abused and strangled by a movie-star nominated for an Oscar. The dead woman was black, so Lucifer wanted the coverage to depict her family as gold-diggers, the girl herself as an addict. The Hollywood actor, Century would insist, was the victim of a despicable scam. Releasing details of her arrest-record (they all had one) would seal her fate. Thus a most talented artist's career, and racism in America, would be protected.

The missing teen story wrote itself. The ship had docked in Jamaica and stayed overnight; she never came back on board. Local police had come up with nothing, and blaming them would be the focus of the piece. It mattered little if the girl had fallen off a cliff or been stabbed in an alley. What America wanted to read was that all foreigners, including foreign cops, were stupid, and inferior to Americans. Never mind that unsolved murders in America were breaking all records.

Lucifer approved both stories for front-page treatment.

But below the fold.

Next he approved continuing Century coverage of America's growing anger over illegal immigration – principally from Mexico and the Southern parts of the continent. Another hot-button issue was America's massive 'Private Security Firms', and their role in the Middle-East fighting. They now had half a million armed-to-the-teeth boots on the ground. President Christiansen was signing an executive order to restrict and eventually stop this. Lucifer wanted all of tonight's news shows to say the White House was going to put regular US troops in mortal peril.

Of course the mercenaries were also American.

Just greedier and more vicious.

The meeting wound down. Lesser issues received attention. National stories that had almost run their course, or items of regional interest covered by Century affiliates. International or overseas local stories would be decided later today in another meeting, based on what happened in the world, and what particular slant the devil decided to give it.

Lucifer became bored with it all. Even conjuring another snake – this time a four foot rattler, coiled and angry – failed to entertain him. He rushed through the rest of the agenda; then he cleared the room.

Except for Kathy Lester.

She was going to interview the President. And if it went well, she might bring down not only Christiansen, but the entire American system of checks and balances. The devil certainly hoped so. The American Republic had caused him nothing but trouble since it was founded. He took Kathy Lester up to his penthouse, and explained exactly how she would bring this tiresome presidency to an end.

~ ~ ~

Clement steered the supply truck through darkness and desert, bringing up the rear of a straggling convoy. Dust smears on the windshield forced him to squint, as he fought to keep the truck in front of him in his headlights. Nobody would stop if he fell behind.

Churned-up sand clogged everything, and the

windows were firmly closed. The humidity steamed them up further, and visibility was next to zero. His turn at driving had lasted an hour so far. Shahanna sat between him and Jhalal in the cab. And they were not alone. Hassan and Asuto rode in the back with a dozen others, squatting on top of loosely stacked equipment and baggage.

They were going, unbelievably, back to Afghanistan.

No!"

Prince Kamal had screamed it down the phone at General Makhud, but the king was adamant, and his general backed him completely. Afghanistan it had to be. No one else would take them. Talk of a multiple-strike on US soil had spread following news of Iran's recently acquired bombs. Not even the most belligerent Muslim state wanted to be linked with that.

Except Afghanistan.

The Taliban there just hoped the rumors were true.

As a result Prince Kamal had commandeered half the Iranian army trucks in his compound. And as the captain drove off with the remaining half – to hand over the four prisoners to the Ayatollah, for a trial that soon became an exchange – Prince Kamal had begun his evacuation.

They dismantled Kamal's hut and took down the tents. Water and rice were loaded with weapons and bullets. Uncooked meat could not be transported in this climate, and had to be abandoned. Everything else, whether needed or not, was heading east with this column.

Clement skidded violently into a tire rut, cursing and praying together as he pulled on the steering wheel. The truck lurched, straightened, and kept going straight. Clement was sweating, and not only due to the heat. The sooner they got to a paved road, or even a flattened cart-track, the better. The driver in front was now out of sight, and Clement put his foot down, to catch up. Breasting a slight rise he saw tail-lights again, and accelerated hard. Shahanna touched his cheek. Jhalal stared ahead, saying nothing. If he had worked out their relationship he was playing dumb.

Clement looked up at the sky and wondered if his expensive satellite was tracking them on infra-red. He hoped it was.

The Prince was up front in the Range Rover.

Clement swerved to miss a clump of palm trees; then throttled back, as he saw they were entering a small village. The trucks ahead of him had stopped. He braked to a halt, killed his lights, but left the engine running. Jhalal had trained him well. Dark figures moved in the gloom, and some of Kamal's drivers jumped down to talk to them. Hands gestured, and harsh words were exchanged. Jhalal opened his door and went to see what was going on. He was back in a few minutes.

This was a hide-out for Fedayeen mercenaries, over a hundred strong, one of many groups who roamed freely from frontier to frontier, committing acts of war for hard cash. These had been in Northern Iraq, blowing up pipelines, convoys and unarmed civilians. They also killed members of the occupation forces – or those who co-operated with them. Now they were here, raiding into American-held territory, blowing up American-built schools and killing families unwise enough to send their children to one. These so-called warriors were truly merchants of death.

Without lights, the village was dark and threatening.

More people descended from the vehicles, some arming themselves, all staring into the gloom. Shahanna went with Jhalal to find Hassan. Clement watched them go and put the hand-brake on, but still allowed the engine to idle. Winding his window down, he felt isolated, completely surrounded by enemies. Suddenly the vehicle-littered street seemed empty, except for him and his truck.

He wound the window back up.

His eyes adjusted more to the dark.

A stranger stood looking at him, head and face hidden by a black burnoose wound tight, leaving only a slit for his eyes. As Clement registered this, the man called softly into the shadows.

More men, dressed the same, came to stand with him.

One used the Arabic word for American.

Clement tensed, and locked the door.

The truck was now his coffin. He braced both arms around the wheel, and forced his back against the door, using all his weight. This caused the Fedayeen to rush towards him, and one of them fired a shot. The cab window shattered, and Clement was showered with glass. Now there was a hot, burning pain in his side. The bullet had struck a rib and bounced off. Clement felt faint, but reached across with his other arm, to clamp the door firmly shut.

A head encased in black appeared where the window had been. The man's eyes glittered at Clement. There was a muttered curse, then the click of a rifle bolt, and the barrel came into view.

The man was taking aim.

Clement numbly awaited death, but then came an outbreak of shouting, most of it in Prince Kamal's voice.

Things happened fast.

A pistol fired, at close range, and the Fedayeen fell back and away from Clement. The shouting intensified, as people came running. Clement looked down from the broken window of the cab. His would-be killer was on the ground, lifeless, a dark pool spreading around his head. Prince Kamal was bending over the body, reloading his revolver. Every gun in sight was trained at anyone with a gun.

Clement felt a jolt of fear.

Suddenly Hassan was center-stage. He moved through the two opposing groups, hands raised in appeal and talking persuasively. Then with one hand he made a strange motion. Gun barrels were lowered like magic. At the same time lights in the village came back on, and increased visibility made the scene less oppressive. It appeared the danger had passed.

Clement was losing blood at a rapid rate. He could feel it, throbbing through his veins, and imagined dying here. He glimpsed the stricken faces of Shahanna and Jhalal. Hassan came close, saying something to calm them, but Clement couldn't hear for the rushing in his ears. The Prince hovered in the background and holstered his gun. Then he, too, walked towards Clement with an anxious expression.

The truck door opened and they got him out. He felt drained, closed his eyes and surrendered himself to fate, wondering if he would open them again. The image of that Fedayeen pointing his rifle was burned into his brain. He was unconscious by the time they got him onto a stretcher.

~ ~ ~

He awoke a week later.

He saw unfamiliar shapes. Fish swam all around him, and a bloodless, cold fin brushed his cheek. He kicked violently, swimming for the surface . . .

His eyes opened.

Shahanna held his head in her lap, washing his face. It was daylight, and he could sense the strain in her. Then, noticing that he was awake, she removed the cloth and her body relaxed.

With a perceptible act of will she became Sorya again, giving him a scathing look. She rose, picked up a shallow bowl of water and tossed her cloth into it – before leaving the room with a flounce.

He lay on a camp-bed in Prince Kamal's re-assembled hut. Obviously the move to somewhere had been completed. Clement imagined Shahanna watching over him, and he hoped no one else noticed her obvious concern. His getting wounded had to be the worst coincidence ever, but with him in Kamal's bed and Shahanna walking around free, their cover had obviously not been blown.

That made up for the searing pain in his ribs.

He healed fast, but it still took two weeks. The bullet had glanced away from the bone, tearing through flesh to drop beside him. It was now on a string around his neck. He had trouble standing for very long, but he insisted on attending and giving classes, which earned him Kamal's respect. That brought him respect from everybody else, and secured him a place on the final mission.

~ ~ ~

They were not quartered in caves, as he expected, but in the bed of a high-walled quarry, dug out of rocky desert floor, centuries before. The camp stood on flattened-out layers of granite and slate. This pale stone floor, mixed with shingle, made a broad, flat rim about two hundred yards wide, surrounding a small lake filled with water so deep it was blue all the time, even if clouds blocked the sun. How such a thing existed in a world devoid of moisture was not explained. It had advantages however. Despite being back in Afghanistan and far from civilization, the lake gave them water. It no longer had to be brought in by truck. They had plenty of rice, and a living supply of meat every day, lured into rifle range by the bottomless lake. The new compound was self-contained, having no need of the outside world.

Prince Kamal was a happy man.

Local radio had announced that the quarry was re-opened, and from the air, or from a satellite, this appeared true: Tents pitched around a hut that probably housed management, or served as an office, and people scurrying on the ground, digging out fresh stone slabs after years of neglect.

Clement doubted the deception would last. America's eye in the sky was operated by the very best, and then there was Hassan's amazing connection to British Intelligence. He would tell Henry Archer soon enough and the secret would be out. Heathcote would have them pinpointed before long.

On a day when no classes were held, Clement was woken by Asuto Kenyatta, who came directly from the Prince. The two of them were to set up a hide on the slopes not far from the quarry, to improve and regulate the meat supply – shooting anything edible that wandered by. Hunting for the kitchen was better than sweating in a wooden hut with one cheap fan to cool it, so Clement got dressed and the two hurried outside, taking care not to wake Shahanna.

They doubled back along the wall of the structure they just left, and Clement saw the Prince at his office window, watching them as they ran by. Their eyes met, and for a second, a look came over Kamal's face. It was satisfaction: the expression of one who has defeated a rival. It was also the look of a sexual predator. Clement was fleetingly scared for Shahanna. But he let the thought fade, caught up in the moment, as he and Kenyatta loaded themselves up with rifles and ammunition.

~ ~ ~

Prince Kamal's desire for Shahanna had not gone away. It consumed him, and got worse by the day. He often fondled her when they were alone, managing more and more to bring that about, making her work early in the morning and late at night. Both times when no one else was around. Shahanna handled it with great tact; now breaking away, now leading him on. Thus far she had said nothing to Clement. It was a bizarre situation. Her mission included possible seduction, and as repulsive as that might be, she kept it in her mind. Her closeness to Prince Kamal was crucial, and he could not be simply put in his place, which was her first instinct.

It made her an easy victim.

On the morning it all went wrong, she was at work early. The Prince had not yet appeared, although he had asked her to be there, and usually showed up once he heard her moving about. It seemed odd, but Shahanna guessed he had overslept. He would be here when he was ready.

She was wrong. He had risen early and gone briefly

outside, sending a sentry to fetch Asuto Kenyatta. He told the African to set up a hide some way from the camp, and take Rob Keller to help him. They were to leave right away.

That took care of the boyfriend.

The Prince was no fool. With the instinct of a lifelong womanizer, he was under no illusion that Sorya's relationship with Rob Keller had ever ended. The woman was a good actress, but it showed in Keller's eyes. Prince Kamal stood in his office and watched the two hunters depart.

Then he went for a walk, humming to himself.

~ ~ ~

An hour later, Shahanna considered waking him, as she went through a cardboard box, looking for the address of a P. L.O. Sympathizer in Libya. Suddenly Kamal rubbed against her from behind. Shahanna sighed, and got ready to pull away if he didn't stop. But the Prince had other plans.

He reached around her with one hand, and something metallic circled her wrist; it snapped shut with a click.

Then she realized – he had handcuffed her!

He wrenched her hands up high, passing the chain over a metal rafter above her head; then her second wrist was cuffed.

His hands went to her breasts. Today she wore no bra; it was laundry day. Kamal ripped her shirt away, exposing them, then grasped one in each hand, and squeezed her nipples, hard, between finger and thumb. At the same time he closed in to kiss her on the mouth. Her movement was restricted, and Shahanna could not break free, so she kissed him back, writhing against him in exaggerated passion.

He kept kissing her and hurting her breasts. In between, he ripped off the rest of her clothes. Once she was naked he stepped back, taking out his gorged penis. His breath came in heavy gasps.

Then he raped her, and it was not necessary for Shahanna to fake anything. Her screams were real.

That was good enough for the Prince.

Her pleasure was not required.

Shahanna lost track of time; the pain was unbearable. She closed her eyes and went to a far off place in her mind, not responding or thinking. She retreated from the world, like an animal being beaten.

He finally left her, sickened and dazed, a pile of crumpled and torn clothing at her feet. She hung limply from the chain, unable to free her wrists or hide her shame. He did not untie her. This was aimed at Rob Keller, or whoever else found her, and told Keller about it.

Prince Kamal was making a point.

And Gabriel's vision had come true.

CHAPTER THIRTEEN

THE PRINCE STOOD IN HIS BEDROOM and washed all trace of Sorya from his private parts. He had stripped, and now he proceeded to cleanse the rest of his body. Then he went back over his groin area, scrubbing furiously.

He stared in the mirror, and thought, What was I thinking? Anyone could have walked in. It would have been disastrous. A scandal. But that was no problem now, he reasoned. Sorya was a tough customer. The act of leaving her just hanging there would spread fear throughout the compound. And if her American boyfriend complained, his head would look good on a stake. Kamal threw the sponge in the sink and took a clean shirt from his closet. He pulled it on and buttoned the front. He emerged from the hut fully dressed, nodding curtly to those nearby, and set off on his rounds. He had not gone far before disturbing thoughts of what he had done returned.

He imagined the execution block, a muscular man by it, stripped to the waist, a long curved sword at his side. Standard punishment for ravishing a woman, according to Islamic law. Public beheading always drew huge crowds, especially if the condemned was a Prince of the royal blood. The courtyard would be spotlessly swept for the event, and swept again after the blood was washed away.

Prince Kamal – dead and disgraced.

His life would end to a roaring of the common people. The sword would come swishing down; his head would drop to the sand; then roll away, leaving a gluey, red mess on the ground. Kamal felt the blade slicing his neck, severing artery, cartilage, windpipe and bone with savage speed; then his brain performing one final, lurching somersault as he died.There would be no funeral. His body would be butchered and fed to the dogs. He envisioned his shinbone in the mouth of a bull mastiff. The creature shook its head and growled, teeth gnashing as it tore at his flesh. This last image made the Prince whimper with fear.

Now the demon in him came awake, making every effort to harden Kamal's resolve. The Prince must pull himself together. At first it worked, and for a time at least, some of the fear was dispelled.

Kamal told himself, No one would dare accuse you. Your word is law here. Sorya can do nothing. If she has any sense she will say nothing. He realized that people were staring. He went and checked his reflection in the water of the lake. His eyes looked wild, his face pale and sweaty. His hair was askew, giving him a slightly crazed look. He had been talking aloud, something he did when distraught. Those watching may have heard. The demon's power over him receded. His guilty reflection in the water revealed a deep fear of being punished, depressing him even more.

The pleasure of sex with Sorya was gone. He had forced himself on women often, and the sense of triumph, of conquest, always excited him long after the act itself. This time was different. His sense of power over Sorya was short-lived. Now it evaporated. He thought, She's so beautiful, and I took her. I dominated her to prove I'm her superior. So why do I feel this way? Prince Kamal turned and walked away, leaving the lake to answer that question.

Once more, the guilt receded.

His demon was working overtime.

Prince Kamal became himself again. Sorya was an arrogant bitch and a tease. No wonder he had snapped, to teach her a lesson. She had no one to blame but herself. She had used sex to meet Kamal, and flaunted Rob Keller in his face, pretending their love affair was over. She had taunted the prince with her sexuality. An evil temptress, never saying no, but never giving in. Well, he had put a stop to that. After today Sorya would know her place.

Returning to the hut he did not set her free. He honored his decision to leave her chained, her body swinging and increasing her pain. A Prince does not owe any woman kindness. He searched his mind for a way to disgrace her further, and he found it. Asuto and Keller would be gone all day, and she could suffer, hanging naked, until they came back and discovered her. To ensure it was them, and only them, Prince Kamal posted a sentry to keep others out.

He returned to the hut. Once inside he ignored the woman as if she wasn't there. He walked past her and went to bed.

~ ~ ~

But it was not Clement and Asuto who found her.

It was Hassan.

Kamal's sentry did not prevent Gabriel drifting in through the roof.

She hung there, in shock and crying, turning quickly away to hide her nakedness when she saw who it was. She was unable to speak. Nor could she bring herself to look at him.

Gabriel knew instantly who had done this.

He had never been more angry.

He responded with action. First he put her into a peaceful trance. Then he undid her shackles and took her down gently, carrying her to the cupboard-sized space where she and Clement slept. Once she was in her sleeping bag, Gabriel invoked a spell to make her sleep the rest of the day. He cast another spell to make her forget what Prince Kamal had done. That memory was erased forever.

So were any physical signs.

Shahanna would wake up and it had never happened. And there was no chance of the Prince telling anyone.

He'd never get the chance.

Gabriel went back to find her shredded clothes, and repaired them with magic. He left them folded beside her on the floor.

Then he went looking for Prince Kamal.

~ ~ ~

The spell Gabriel cast in Central Park was still working.

The Prince was in a restless sleep, having one bad dream after another, filled with things he'd done to those unlucky enough to have crossed his path. A housemaid he had impregnated in his youth stared sightless from a pit, where she was stoned to death after her eyes were put out. Kamal moaned. "Father threatened to disown me! Sixteenth in line is better than being cast out!"

The scene changed to show his best friend at age fourteen. A boy called Mufti, a Mullah's son. He and Kamal were schooled in the Koran by Mufti's father. After study and prayers the youngsters were allowed to play: Kicking a soccer ball, practicing with slingshots, or just horsing around, as boys do when they are about to become men. Then the green-eyed monster came into play, as a beautiful girl entered the picture. Her name was Charrah, and she was sixteen, which made her light-years older than either of them.

She flirted with the Prince.

But she slept with Mufti.

When this came to light, Prince Kamal's reaction was swift, dishonest and cruel. He accused the Mullah's son of homosexual advances, and said it occurred not once but often during their friendship.

Mufti's father, a harsh and unforgiving man, tried the case himself. The boy got a railroad hearing and rough justice. The Prince was believed; the son was not. Sodomy is tolerated by Islam; if it remains private. This had become extremely public and the result was automatic. Mufti's genitals were exhibited on the ramparts. The boy was thrown out into the desert where loss of blood killed him.

Now his pallid corpse spoke to Kamal – asking why he ever told such lies, over a girl he had long forgotten. In the dream, a horrified Prince had his own private parts hacked off. He bucked in agony – as the blade sliced, and blood gushed over his thighs. This was Mufti's gift to him.

It was at this point that Gabriel, still in the form of Hassan, entered the Prince's bedroom.

The angel monitored Kamal's guilt-ridden nightmares and decided to wait them out. To wake the Prince now would be a mercy, and that was hardly Gabriel's intent. He stood at the foot of the bed to watch. The dreams grew more horrific. Gabriel enhanced the spell, making them last longer.

Then he left the room.

~ ~ ~

The angel returned some hours later, as things were coming to an end. He stood by the bed as before and raised a hand to stop to the torture. This caused the ghastly images to fade, and a sweat-soaked Kamal woke up.

He started, recognizing Hassan.

Was this some new nightmare, or was he awake? The Prince seemed uncertain.

Then his demon-generated guile returned. He said: "Hassan, my brother. What brings you here? Is something wrong?" He peered slyly at Gabriel, his eyes showing a trace of alarm.

He wondered if this involved Sorya.

Hassan was close to her.

The prince came half upright, easing onto his elbows, and prayed the subject of rape would not come up, knowing it was a forlorn hope because for Hassan to come this far into the hut he must have seen her. Kamal became wary. His demon was twitching in terror.

Gabriel said nothing.

Prince Kamal pretended anger. "What is it that you want?"

"Your soul," said Gabriel impassively.

The Prince stared.

Gabriel stared back. Then his face began to change. Suddenly he was Artis Brown, and then Hassan again. The Prince gasped, recognizing the homeless black man in New York who said he was the Angel of Death, a memory that chilled Kamal's blood even now. Imagining the destruction of the Saudi Kingdom had been bad enough, but this abrupt threat against his mortal soul was worse. Suddenly the Prince knew who was standing there.

It was not Hassan.

Gabriel said: "You are hereby damned."

The words struck Kamal like bullets. Words he had dreaded all his life, and it was the Angel of Death who uttered them, pronouncing final judgement. The Prince shrank back on his pillows.

Now he was desperately afraid.

"I found Sorya," said Gabriel. "What you did was vile. For you, the end of a long history of vileness. You're an animal, and will die like one."

"No, please," stammered Kamal. Part of him still refused to accept it. This was only Hassan after all, very angry, but a serious man, dedicated to the Revenge of Islam. Kamal could wriggle out of this.

"You're a patriot . . ." began the Prince.

Gabriel looked at him. "I'm far more than that,"

He made a swift, striking motion with one hand. Kamal's chest burned with fire.

The sensation intensified. The Prince screamed. Gabriel made another sweep with his hand and it stopped. Gabriel said: "You are dying, but not as badly as you deserve." Now he let the pain flood back.

It was now that the demon abandoned Kamal's body, flying several feet before it was stopped by Gabriel's pointing finger. It was hideous, scaly and covered in slime. The angel's hand moved slightly. There was a pain-wracked screech and a flash of light. Then nothing.

The angel turned back to Kamal.

Excruciating agony followed.

Until Gabriel was satisfied and stopped it.

The prince groaned. Suddenly he knew he was really

going to die. He said: "Allah is great." He was drenched in sweat.

"Wise and compassionate," agreed Gabriel.

"All seeing; all knowing," croaked the Prince."

"Blessed are the meek."

The Prince had no answer to that.

And he died.

Stepping into the hot sunshine, Gabriel felt better than he thought possible since finding Shahanna.

~ ~ ~

Driving the supply truck with one hand, Asuto Kenyatta lit a cigarette and offered the pack to Clement and Jhalal, who shared the seat to his right. Jhalal took one, Keller did not smoke, but Kenyatta believed that might change, and kept trying. Their hunting trip was postponed, due to a recent upsurge in such trips, and the resulting shortage of rifle cartridges They were on an ammunition run, across a hundred miles of barbarous country, making for Khyber al Makrit, a border town in Taliban hands, and well inside the region closed off to American and N. A. T. O. Forces.

Khyber al Makrit had bullets to spare.

Clement said: "Non-filters are plain stupid. You guys will die young."

Asuto's eyes narrowed to slits. He was easily insulted, and not sure of Keller's meaning. His dislike of Americans certainly extended to this one. He said: "My life is nothing, and soon we all die in your country. Look to your courage, my friend. If you smoke or not – your life ends with mine."

"I'm sorry," said Clement. "I meant no offense."

Asuto grunted. "I hope not, Mr. Keller. You would regret it."

Clement looked at this man, dressed in the same dungarees and cap as most of the camp residents, and wondered what made him so full of hate. Asuto was as strong as a bull, and fearless – but like a bull, he was stubborn, hostile and mean. Terrifying as an enemy. Little better as a friend. Especially now he was camp leader. He threw his weight around, and didn't hesitate to use his fists. Asuto's promotion had not improved him. but he was as surly as ever, and the only person he tolerated was Jhalal. Since becoming top dog, the big African did not care who he offended.

Clement tried again to smooth his ruffled feathers. He said: "What you smoke is your affair. I was joking."

"Not funny," said Kenyatta. "And the Koran tells us that time spent in laughter is wasted."

But Clement, too, had studied the Koran. "It also says: Laugh with your brothers. All scripture contradicts itself."

Asuto glanced at him in surprise. "You know the teaching. Very good, Mr. Keller. He was silent a moment; then he said: "I begin to see why the Prince is so impressed by you. Your power lies in the wisdom of the Prophet. Please forgive my anger. I spoke in haste."

"Anger is your main strength,' said Clement, and he meant it, although not as a compliment.

Jhalal had been watching the road. "Barriers up ahead."

Asuto wrestled with the gear-box, shifting to slow them down, because the braking system was virtually non-existent.

Clement said: "A roadblock? Not the Fedayeen." He fingered the tender side of his rib-cage, recalling that gunshot.

Asuto said: "No. Taliban auxiliaries. They keep the passes free."

Free of us Americans, thought Clement. He gritted his teeth, dreading the thought of taking another bullet.

"Don't worry." said Jhalal.

But he looked worried, probably for Clement.

There were armed men in their path.

Oil drums had been upended to block the narrow track. Kenyatta drove up to the men by the barricade, and stopped. He kept his words simple, but this made his Arabic sound even worse than usual. "Greeting, my brothers. We go Khyber al Makrit. We have no bullet. Need get more."

His vocabulary was improved, but still lamentable.

"Stop the engine," said the nearest Taliban guard. He wore dirty robes, and had a semi-automatic pointed at the South African's head. Other men stood behind the line of oil drums, weapons at the ready.

"Shit," Clement had a bad feeling. "Here we go again."

Jhalal switched off the ignition. "It's probably nothing. A routine check." They all knew he would have to get them out of this. Asuto's Arabic might be poor, but Clement's was non-existent.

Clement said, "It's because I'm American."

"It may not be you."

But of course it was.

The Taliban leader stepped back, so the truck door could open, and told them to get out.

They all stepped down.

Jhalal tried reason. "Brother, our journey is most urgent."

"Throw down your arms."

They had near-empty pistols in their belts. The camp really was running out of ammunition.

"But my brother . . ."

"Now!"

Jhalal translated.

They obeyed. Their guns lay in the dirt. Jhalal said: "Have you heard of Prince Kamal?"

"A Saudi lap-dog, feared only by cowards. What of him?"

Jhalal said: "He is no dog. You risk his anger." This brigand must not be told what no outsider knew. There must be no mention of the camp, or what went on there. Jhalal hoped the Prince's name was enough to make these clods remove their barricade and let the truck through. He said: "We serve the Prince."

It was not to be.

The leader gestured at Clement. "And this God-cursed American. He, too, belongs to Kamal?"

"Prince Kamal. Yes, this man is a vital member of our . . . group."

"he speaks our tongue?"

"Sadly, no."

There was a cold silence. The leader did not like this situation. Neither did his followers by the look of them – and things seemed ready to get ugly. Jhalal and Asuto looked ready to defend Clement, but had only their bare hands. It was an uneven fight with only one possible result.

All three of them would die.

Clement did not want conflict. He recalled the words of Heathcote: "Always fight as a last resort." and "Never gamble against lousy odds."

They were made to raise their hands and stand by the oil drums, two Taliban men searching them roughly. Jhalal held the eye of the leader, and said: "Will you contact the Prince?"

The headman considered. "I have a cell phone," he said. "If Kamal has one, give me the number."

"Ah," said Jhalal, and his heart sank. Because the Prince did not allow cell phones at the quarry site, and kept his own number secret. Prince Kamal had learned his lesson in Iran when Heathcote's sniper team was captured. H knew the Americans had a whole apparatus listening for calls in this region. Jhalal sighed. He was beaten. His life, and the lives of his two friends, now hung on the whim of a murderous thug in this god-forsaken place. All they could do was trust in Allah.

Clement was bound and gagged, and forced to his knees in the roadway. This was a plain, dirt track, surrounded by high, stone escarpment on either side. Beyond that lay two uphill slopes that became sheer rock, then went on, ever upwards, to form a jagged mountain range. No stranger knew what lay between these peaks and valleys, with their swirling air currents – and a few trickles of stream that kept this meager country alive. The whole region was a natural fortress, holding off all intruders for a thousand years; from crusading knights to the Red-Coats of the British Empire. As recently as the 1980's these wild, scruffy-looking fighters defeated a modern-day Soviet Army. The Russians had failed to subdue this tiny, ferocious country.

The Americans were still trying.

Now a cell phone was produced by the leader of these mountain men, and a call made, but not to Prince Kamal.

A rapid conversation took place, and Jhalal translated for his two companions:

Transport was being summoned, and it must be close by, because whoever was coming had said ten minutes.

There followed a silence. Both sides glared at each other and waited. It had been less than ten minutes, when two jeeps, rusting and dilapidated, pulled up with a clatter of faulty valve adjustment. At a distance, both vehicles looked American, but close up they were cheap, shoddy imitations, churned out by prison-like factories in the former Soviet Union.

Thousands were abandoned here by the Russians.

The drivers, two squat-looking brutes, wore the usual dirty turban and ragged burnoose, and had bandoleers of ammunition slung across their chests. Each had a rifle within easy reach.

Their eyes never left the hillsides, as three strangers were loaded in behind them under guard. Clement, wrists tightly bound, was put into the back of one Jeep, between the brigands' leader and another man.

Jhalal and Asuto were in the other vehicle.

Clement thought: If I live through this – I'm a lucky man. Then the Jeep leapt forward, a metal seat jarred his spine – and they were soon racing along the narrow, bumpy ravine at breakneck speed.

The camp truck stayed behind, under the watchful eyes of the remaining Taliban at the check-point.

Both Jeeps were, of course, home in under ten minutes.

Clement was covered in bruises.

Local Taliban headquarters was little more than a stone hut. The walls appeared unsteady, there were gaps in the corrugated iron roof, some big enough to let in rain or sun, depending on the weather. It was so small that more men lay, sat or lounged around outside than could ever get inside.

The Jeeps parked, and Clement was untied, while their guards chased even more people out, so that the prisoners were left alone inside with their captors.

The Taliban chief again pointed at Clement. "Why is this man in a place where no American can be?"

He looked to Jhalal for an answer.

"It is secret."

"Then reveal it." This with a snarl.

"I will not."

"You will, my knife is sharp."

"To speak is forbidden. Do what you must."

"Forbidden by whom? Your Prince?"

"Far mightier than you believe."

"And why is Prince Kamal in my territory?"

Jhalal looked away. "I cannot say."

"Then you die in this room."

Jhalal shrugged. "Then it is written."

"You die so easily?"

Jhalal glanced at Asuto. "We are all three sworn to die, and soon. Kill even one of us, and pay a bloody price."

That finally made an impression.

"Where is this Prince?"

"At our camp."

"Where is that?"

"At the old quarry."

"Ah, this you may tell me."

"The quarry will tell you nothing. You must speak with the Prince. How else will you find him?"

"I know only one quarry. It is hours from here."

"If you are wise, you will go."

"What will Prince Kamal say to me?"

"Allah will decide."

"What do you think Kamal will say?"

"Whatever it is, you should listen." Jhalal looked calmly at his captors. "He does not tolerate fools."

"And who tells me this? What is your name?"

"Jhalal."

"No other name?"

"Not for you."

"And these other two?"

"Have no names at all."

"You risk much, Jhalal,"

"Trust me, so do you."

"You go too far –"

Jhalal exploded. "No, you go too far!" Clement was surprised by the Iraqi's anger, whether pretended or real – and although Clement had no idea what was being said.

Jhalal wagged a finger at his adversary, and raised his voice until it was heard outside, and faces peered in through the open doorway. "You dung-eaters defy God's will! Our is a holy quest, and yet you keep us from it in this godless place! Tomorrow heads will roll. Your families will be tortured and killed, and each of you here will end this life begging for death. Prince Kamal is not a kindly man. He is no dog, as you may think, but his teeth are terrible."

Jhalal looked the Taliban leader straight in the eye. "And I say it is you who goes too far."

The other Taliban gave each other meaningful looks. Their mood had changed. Resolve was lacking; there was no denying it.

Jhalal said: "Forget this, my brother. We pretend this never happened, and you return us to our truck."

"No," said the leader doggedly. "You bring an enemy here, and violate the passes. That is no small matter. Your prince cannot be phoned, and it is too far to drive. We have a Mullah in Khyber al Makrit. I will consult him. He will decide." The headman glanced at his men. They nodded agreement. He had been clever. Mentioning the Mullah had got them back on track.

Jhalal translated for his two companions, and while he saw no cause for panic, he did say the future looked bleak.

Clement groaned inwardly.

Jhalal hung his head. Arguing their case had got him nowhere, and now a religious zealot in Khyber al Makrit would decide their fate. Looking bleak was something of an understatement.

Especially for Clement.

The Taliban leader said: "I leave now. My men will hold you here."

Clearly he could not be talked out of it.

He turned and left the hut.

His men remained.

Clement saw hatred in their faces.

This was going to be a rough ride.

He resolved to show a brave front. Thinking about Shahanna would surely help. They had awoken in each other's arms this morning. It must have happened by chance, sometime in the night, and they leaped apart like scolded cats. Then they had laughed at each other, silently, in the early dawn. Clement chuckled at the memory, and his guards exchanged astonished looks. He realized they must wonder what he found so amusing, given his fate when their leader returned. It crossed his mind to laugh in their faces, but he restrained himself. He had enough bruises already.

The silence became oppressive.

The guard in charge finally said something to Jhalal. As a result, everyone trooped out into the fresh air. Permission was given to sit on the large rocks strewn everywhere, some of them fallen from the crumbling headquarters.

Clement looked around him. The number of guards had multiplied with the move outside. Every Afghan in sight watched the prisoners with the eyes of a hawk. Life here was none too exciting, and three intruders, one of whom might be shot, had lifted these brigands' spirits.

So here Clement sat – surrounded by enemies who would like nothing better than to shoot him now. He glanced over at Jhalal, who was ignoring the tension, at least on the surface. Jhalal was a good man in a tight spot. But Asuto looked hostile, and eager for a confrontation. He would fight, rather than submit to the judgement of any Mullah from Khyber al Makrit. Clement regretted that the African was here at all. Asuto was not like Jhalal. He was a menace. His kind of shoot-first strategy would not work here, and they were all still alive due to pure luck. Asuto lacked the subtlety to see this, and might well start a fight at any minute. Poor Arabic had prevented him from asserting his authority since their truck was stopped, and Clement thanked his stars for that, and the fact that these hill bandits would never believe a black foreigner was in charge of this expedition; let alone the senior man back at camp. Clement decided that all these factors had saved everyone, including Jhalal and himself, from Asuto

Kenyatta.

Clement thought about Prince Kamal. Whatever the outcome today, the Prince would hit the roof; even if they survived. A delay in bringing ammunition was enough to get all three of them beheaded. Clement came close to laughing hysterically at this, but stifled the impulse.

Asuto and Jhalal suddenly stood up.

The headman's Jeep was coming back.

Barely half an hour had passed.

Everyone in sight was getting up. The Taliban leader drove up to Jhalal, making no attempt to get out of the Jeep. He said: "Get in. I'm letting you all go."

They drove away seconds later.

The second Jeep tagged on behind.

The headman was a changed character. He said very little on the way back to his checkpoint and their truck, but what he did say was respectful. He drove like a man in a trance, apologizing more than once during the journey. When they parted – he actually saluted, although it was not very military, and he used the wrong hand. No one saluted him back.

The supply truck was soon on its way to Khyber al Makrit, its occupants light-headed with relief. They had no idea why fortune had smiled so brightly, and it would never be explained. All three agreed that Allah was indeed great; especially later, when they discovered Prince Kamal was dead.

The truth behind their rescue was very simple: The Taliban leader never reached Khyber al Makrit or its Mullah. He didn't get far from his headquarters at all. He had not driven a mile when a tall man with a piercing gaze materialized in the roadway and stopped him. The man introduced himself as Hassan.

Hassan had stared into his eyes . . .

~ ~ ~

Heathcote said: "That's definitely Clement. The one talking to Jhalal – and that other one must be the South African. Looks like they've been disarmed; that's a pistol on the ground, but I don't see any physical injury. The guys holding them are local Taliban. They have rocket launchers and a few old Russian automatics."

He sat looking at satellite shots of Clement's capture. There were also pictures of Taliban headquarters and the eventual release of all three men – all taken in infra-red from an altitude close to outer-space. Definition on the screen was grainy. The sun had been low in the sky.

Heathcote was addressing a young Lab-Tech who controlled the images with mouse and keyboard, and the two of them were watching alone, in the basement of the Federal building where they both worked.

The technician said: "That checkpoint is in what we call the Stronghold. A no-go zone close to the border. Nearest town is Khyber al Makrit, a small speck of a place not even shown on certain maps. But it is a Jihadist hot-spot. That's where Clement's truck went, after the Taliban let them go."

"Well, at least you found that truck, and my guys. And now you've found them, you'll find Prince Kamal and his new camp. That's our top priority. Has your wonder satellite got any shots of that?"

"Not yet."

"Clement and Jhalal didn't return there?"

"We lost transmission."

Heathcote made a face. He was so tired of hearing

that. He said: "Let me see a large-scale scan."

The photographic down-load filled a 54 inch flat screen monitor on the wall in front of them. It showed what looked like the surface of the Moon from a great height, but was actually both sides of the Pakistan-Afghan frontier – including the so-called Stronghold region.

Picture scale was too large to show much detail.

Heathcote ignored the rules down here, just as he did everywhere else, and lit a cigarette. He said: "Go smaller – and show heat images."

The technician pressed a button. Pink blobs, depicting life-forms, appeared on fuzzy pictures taken nearer the ground. Heathcote thought: "Come on, Prince Kamal. You're out there somewhere. What rock are you hiding under?" There had been no word from either Hassan or Henry Archer for days, and Heathcote was anxious enough to be looking at satellite shots.

He scowled at the huge, map-like picture. It moved over Khyber al Makrit, and kept going. This was again filmed during early morning or just before sunset, because long, eerie shadows fell across the ground. Heathcote watched, but saw nothing that looked remotely like a camp. Then a landmark captured his attention. It was a small, circular lake that was clearly man-made. Too symmetrical for Mother Nature. Heathcote asked the Lab-Tech to zoom in. "What's that?" he said; then waited, while the youngster looked up his file data.

Heathcote was relieved to have found Clement. There was danger; the capture and release pictures proved that. This caused Heathcote, not for the first time, to question the wisdom of this mission. Naturally there was always danger. It was necessary to this work, but these breaks in communication, with Hassan, Clement and Shahanna off the radar, were nerve-wracking. Heathcote had served with George Clement, Bo's father, and part of Heathcote's fear was having to make that dreadful phone-call, explaining the loss of Beauregard Clement.

Those calls were the worst part of the job.

Heathcote's technician said: "It's a re-activated quarry."

"What?"

The Lab-Tech said it again: "The lake – it's an old quarry. Says here that it was recently re-opened."

No way, thought Heathcote. No one would re-start a quarry; not with a war raging around it. American shellfire, the daylight bombing and drone raids, would simply be too disruptive – not to mention life-threatening. A terrorist camp, though, that was different. The quarry made a great shelter – from shells and bombing, and satellites that swooped overhead.

He said: "Kid, if that quarry's back in business – I'm a ballet dancer."

"Yes, sir."

Any idea how we find out?"

The tech hesitated; then he said: "Close-ups, sir."

Heathcote nodded. This was a bright young man. Christ, these days they all were. Heathcote knew he shouldn't poke fun at him, but it was hard not to. He said: "Exactly right. We need good close-ups."

He was about ready to call this a day.

But the kid had his own agenda. He pushed another button. The image on-screen faded, and another, more detailed photo took its place – showing that ruin of a Taliban headquarters where Clement and the others were detained on their way to Khyber al Makrit. Then the Lab-Tech switched over to heat image, and it revealed the usual host of pink blobs moving around.

The building crawled with enemy rebels.

Inside and outside.

The technician said: "Sir, this place is, by our own definition, a prime target for a Predator drone. One missile will take them all out. It's an identified hostile target behind enemy lines, and it meets all the criteria for a strike. I mean, you couldn't really miss if you tried."

It made perfect sense.

"My boy," said Heathcote. "You're destined for stardom. Your parents must be so proud. I don't like no-go zones, and hitting that rat-hole will be payback for the shit they did to Clement. I like the way you think."

"I try, sir. I'm a big fan of Clement."

"Me, too, son. Me too."

Heathcote lit another cigarette and inhaled deeply, filling his lungs. He knew he was killing himself, but the addiction was strong, and his zest for life had gone since his wife died. A sad excuse, perhaps, but Heathcote told himself it was the only one he had. He inhaled deeply again, and be damned.

They viewed more film but saw nothing of interest. Finally the big screen blacked out as the download ended. Heathcote still suspected that quarry. They ran the footage again, but the satellite had been flying too far north of the pit and lake to see more than the silhouette of excavated mounds. It might be the new camp; it might not. The Lab-Tech turned off the equipment.

Heathcote said: "I want to see their pubic hair. How long?"

The youngster looked at his watch. "About ten hours. Our next Ozone-Bird is on the wrong side of the world."

"Okay. Go home and get some sleep."

"Yes, sir. Goodnight."

"Goodnight. See you tomorrow.'

Heathcote locked up behind both of them and went off to the camp-bed that now stood permanently in one corner of his office.

~ ~ ~

The Lab-Tech's name was Kyle Fairchild. Heathcote looked it up before returning to the film room, because he was sick of calling him, Son, or Kid. The file said Fairchild was pretty much a genius.

Heathcote made his way down there at close to the ten hour mark, to find that the younger man arrived some time ago – and had everything up and running. Fresh coffee and muffins were on a T. V. Table next to where Heathcote sat the night before. Fairchild was humming softly, as he adjusted knobs and dials.

Heathcote eased into his chair. "Good morning. Are we winning the war on terror? He looked over the muffins and picked one with blueberries. The coffee was hot when he tried it.

Fairchild looked up. "I'm re-running yesterday – looking for a good place to start surveillance of the quarry. Today's download hasn't begun yet."

They both looked at the over-sized screen.

That fuzzy Afghan moonscape came up, and solidified.

There were buildings, mostly hovels, in the foreground.

Heathcote said: "Where's that again?"

"Khyber al Makrit."

"Right. That's where Clement and his buddies ended up. Okay, so how far can that Chevy of theirs go on a tank of gas?"

"About two hundred miles."

"That's your circle then. We need low and precise."

Fairchild nodded. "Yes, sir. I told the operators that last night."

"Good man." Heathcote finished his muffin, and fought off the urge to fish for a cigarette.

They both waited.

The screen began playing Clement's capture and release.

The display eventually went blank.

They waited some more.

Then the new download started up: Drab sand and rocks and pebbles came into focus, as their eye-in-the-sky swept low, magnification at its highest setting, over a flat stretch of land near Khyber al Makrit. Heathcote shifted in his seat, impatient to get to the quarry site.

A narrow gully came next, banked by a mountain on each side. A dirt strip of road snaked through between them. Fairchild said: "That's it. We're close to that checkpoint where they got stopped."

"I hope we follow the road."

"Don't worry, sir. I gave instructions. That truck they were driving has no cross country ability."

"You truly are a genius, Fairchild."

"Thank you, sir. I've always thought so."

The camera backtracked the road all the way along the ravine, until passing over the row of oil cans and the men that guarded it. Heathcote noted with satisfaction that the focus was diamond sharp.

Someone at the Satellite Center was very good.

The road, and the camera, straightened out a little as they swept back out into a more level countryside.

The next phase of the journey seemed to last forever: Endless miles of nothing, interrupted only once, by a camel train with ungainly, wrapped bundles that probably contained at least one illegal substance. After that, one length of cart-track turned into another, until Heathcote wanted to scream. He caved in, and fell back on nicotine, the smoke soothing his nerves.

An outcrop of palm trees came up, followed by several more. Then, suddenly, as if springing out of the ground, the outer rim of a deep, partially re-dug pit came into view; with the same dirt-heaps the camera captured yesterday.

Heathcote leaned forward to see.

The camera appeared to slow down. It didn't, but the remote operator on duty knew what he was looking for, and was angling the lens to prolong its coverage of this scene. With this kind of expert rotation, the satellite could film the same spot for about ten minutes.

The wooden hut came up, then the edge of the lake. Now the shot panned back, showing the entire water surface and its surroundings. People could be seen for the first time: Some in groups, performing activities one would expect – like gymnastics, or the cleaning of weapons. There was also an open kitchen, with cooks, and some yards away, one terrorist yelling at another, angrily waving his arms.

The picture shifted elsewhere.

Now came the pay-off. Clement walked on camera, like a multiple Oscar winner whose appearance completes the night. Heathcote came to his feet, almost cheering. He turned to Fairchild with a pleased grin, and said: "He's fine. We got him!"

Fairchild laughed. "Damned if we didn't, sir."

The horizon was already changing. Clement was gone, along with the quarry and everything around it. Fairchild noted the co-ordinates, phoned the Center to request two satellite flyovers daily, always at low level, and always with direct feed. Then he hung up and looked expectantly at his boss.

Heathcote said: "Come on, I know this twenty-four hour Titty Bar. I'll buy you a drink."

The next day they received Henry Archer's latest signal. Prince Kamal was dead of a heart attack, and the Tribunal, in the form of its one surviving Al Qaeda General, had placed Asuto Kenyatta in command.

CHAPTER FOURTEEN

KATHY LESTER WAS EXUBERANT.

She was in the White House, despite her irrational, last-minute fear of being turned away at the gates. Now she and a female security-escort were walking down the corridor to where Century News had set up its temporary Interview-Studio. Not many reporters had been where Kathy Lester was about to go.

When Scott Anderson offered this assignment, Kathy was nervous, overwhelmed at the thought of talking to the leader of the free world, and sure she'd somehow screw it up, perhaps forgetting to ask a vital question, or asking something that she shouldn't, or having her lipstick on crooked. She nearly ruined her career by turning it down. But her inner voice pointed out how stupid that would be. And certainly by taking this on, Kathy Lester had become a reporter of tremendous stature, almost overnight.

It would take guts, Kathy had decided in Scott Anderson's office. Well, Kathy had guts, and she craved stardom, and everything else that came with it. Why else would she work for an old creep like Scott Anderson in the first place? So she had agreed to do this interview, and knew that was the right decision when her co-hosts on the morning show were so jealous they refused to discuss it. A six-figure bonus from Scott Anderson was the cherry on the cake. Every morning she plugged the upcoming Presidential Interview on the talk-show, which drove her co-stars insane.

Sometimes life is perfect.

Scott Anderson took his time revealing what the thrust of this interview should be, but finally, as the day drew near, a script of questions and possible answers landed on her desk. The content delighted her. Kathy Lester was not going to interview the President of the United States so much as destroy him. The Iranian-nukes issue was making his poll numbers plummet, and Kathy's job was to finish him off. Events had overtaken this presidency, with North Korea and Iran launching a nuclear strike at America by joint proxy. There was absolutely no defense against this, unless the bombs were found and disarmed. The chances of that were non-existent. Lucifer intended to topple President Christiansen once and for all, and Kathy had been primed accordingly. Opportunities like this only came once.

Tonight was hers.

She imagined how her victim felt, right now, surrounded by cameras and special lighting that had been set up earlier. He would be sweating from the heat of those bulbs, because she had arrived fifteen minutes late, to prolong his discomfort – acting on Scott Anderson's advice. The President would also be wondering what questions Kathy would ask, which should make him sweat even more. Viewers reacted badly to nervous-looking politicians in disarray, and Century News relied on such tactics. Kathy, by comparison, was as cool, fresh as a daisy, and ready to come out swinging. Tonight the President was dead meat, and when his party lost its majority in the mid-term elections, Kathy Lester would get the credit.

And another six-digit bonus.

She was wearing an original Christian Dior, purchased

for the occasion. She had charged it, private-jetting over to Paris, and Scott Anderson was happy to pay. He knew what this program was worth in ratings, and had doubled Century's advertising-rates for the entire evening. Tonight Lucifer's Bentley contained champagne and roses, and drove Kathy right up to the White House steps. This demonstrated that Scott Anderson had a talent for the overstated, and more money than should be legal. A lifetime of such luxury beckoned Kathy, and fired her imagination, as she finally reached the makeshift studio where tonight's slaughter was to take place. Then Scott Anderson called to wish her luck and bumped her up to twenty million a year.

Kathy Lester was ready for battle.

And almost unlimited wealth.

She joined her film-crew in front of a gilt-trimmed, white door, while the Secret Service lady went inside.

~ ~ ~

Soon the cameras were rolling.

"Mr. President . . . Good evening."

"Good evening to you, Kathy."

"Thank you for interrupting what I know is a busy schedule."

The red light on Camera One blinked reassuringly at Kathy Lester. They were going out live, on the President's insistence. Century News had agreed immediately, and regarded it as a stupid move he would soon regret.

Kathy and the President did the politeness dance for somewhat longer than was customary – as a slow-burning antagonism built up between them. But on the surface, both of them remained charm personified; until the President ended it with the poetic gallantry of a seasoned wordsmith, yet again welcoming her and Century News to the White House.

Kathy watched him, thinking: Your ass is mine.

Without pausing for Kathy to speak, he smiled for the camera, and for the viewers at home, and said he was ready for her first question. Even as a fledgling Senator, he had been acknowledged as a beguiling speaker, and now, as he turned to face her, Kathy had a twinge of doubt. The man's charisma was evident. He wore a jogging suit, and looked younger and more handsome than his fifty years would suggest. He seemed comfortable under the glaring studio lights, without a trace of sweat, and Kathy wondered briefly if this interview was going to backfire on her.

This meat did not look very dead.

And it had a determined look on its face.

She said: "President Christiansen, these are climactic times and people are worried about the future."

Thus began her script.

The camera swiveled onto the President, and she prayed for him to say something really dumb right away. Scott Anderson's writers said he would, and they had worked on Kathy's response for days.

She felt more confident. Iranian nukes were waiting in the wings, poised to take center stage and steal the show. Kathy just had to wait for Christiansen to answer on America's future, and then pull the trigger. The future spelled his downfall, Century's best minds were all agreed on that. Whatever this left-wing President said next would condemn him in the eyes of the electorate.

If all else failed Kathy Lester was ready to prompt him. For example, she'd been told to ask: "What about North

Korea? They have the bomb and their nuclear program goes on completely unchecked with no action from us." That was calculated to floor any President – just as it always had. Then Kathy would tie-in Iran and squeeze his nuts in a vice. But Korea was second-string-stuff. Right now her job was to challenge him on Iran and see where it went from there.

The President began briskly. "You say the future – but you really mean this rumor of Iran having US bound missiles."

What was this? Was he trying to diffuse the issue by mentioning it before she did? Well, that wouldn't save him. Kathy was sure of that.

"It's not a rumor, sir."

The President ignored that. "Kathy, we are the most powerful country this world has ever seen. We have cutting-edge technology – other nations rent or buy surveillance satellites from us. We also have more than enough military resources and technology for response to any nuclear threat. I assure you that we are well aware of this situation and constantly monitoring it. The Ayatollah knows that. We are also trying to get a resolution from the United Nations."

"The so-called 'Rogue Nation' mandate?" said Kathy Lester., very pleased that the President was unintentionally on script. The United Nations was a favorite punching bag for the right-wing media, and Century's top analysts had prepped Kathy for exactly this conversation.

"Correct," said the President. "The world is not our private Kingdom. We do not have an empire – despite what many people claim. Better to work with the international body set up for that purpose. We need the backing of other countries, and the United Nations gives us that."

"So you're saying we do nothing. Let the U. N. Handle it?" This was going even better than Century projected. He was digging his own grave.

"On the world stage, yes. And the press should cover that, and keep out of top secret matters. Let me, and our Intelligence and Military, do what we do – out of the spotlight. A network like yours should not report every move we make on the seven o' clock news. It defeats our purpose and feeds information to America's enemies. They watch television, too."

Kathy was not ready for that, and she sat, searching for words. Nowhere in her script did it suggest that the President might take this route. He'd just accused Century News of aiding the enemy, for God's sake. What did she say to that?

The President went on: "You just stated that nuclear bombs from Iran are more than a rumor. That's outrageous! My White House has not said that publicly – neither has the Iranian government! We are still negotiating for U. N. Inspectors to go in and see for themselves. So where is Century News getting its information? You, Kathy, and your world-wide organization, have been blabbing about this sensitive topic for weeks; which is intolerable for me and our Intelligence agencies. It simply has to stop. Century News is becoming a threat to national security."

A ghastly pause followed.

A President never took on a reporter like this.

Kathy felt she had to fight back. She said: "So you

blame the media for your failure to solve this problem?"

"That's just what I mean – that's how your network covers the news: Making it up as you go along. In a few seconds, Kathy, you say there's a problem, and I'm not solving it. Statements that hugely affect public opinion – statements that have caused widespread panic since you made them on your morning news-show. The only reason I agreed to this interview was to set the record straight. Folks need to know the truth; not what your boss wants them to believe."

"So we're lying, Mr. President?" Kathy didn't know what else to say, but felt she was on safe ground. Iran had purchased the weapons, and Christiansen could not deny that on national television. Kathy Lester would feel a lot better, however, once she got this son-of-a-bitch back on script.

"No offense, Kathy. But I do wonder about your sources."

She felt relieved. This ground was even safer. "They're impeccable, Mr. President. But I can't reveal them, you know that."

The fact was these sources were in China and North Korea, and if she knew that and said so, Kathy's career was over. Scott Anderson's connections over there were more secret than anything being discussed tonight, and the President was smart enough to have worked that out.

He said: "Of course you won't reveal them, because either they don't exist, or your sources are enemies of the United States. Reliable informants on this issue live in Beijing, Seoul and Tehran. Your boss's involvement over there amounts to betraying this country. That's not protected by freedom of speech. So, either he's making this stuff up, or he's a traitor. Hard to say which is worse."

My God, thought Kathy Lester. The script was useless now.

The President continued: "Americans expect me to run the country and protect them – and they expect you to cover that as news reporters. They don't confuse the two, as your owner, Mr. Anderson, does. He constantly tries to run this country, by shaping public opinion. Scott Anderson constructs the news as he sees fit; then tells his viewers what to think about it. On your show, Kathy, you use a lot of clever phrases, like: "Well, people are saying . . ." or "Some people think . . ." or "That's not what I'm hearing . . ." This implies that unless a viewer accepts what you say he's out of line with mainstream, informed opinion. It's a useful trick that saves you naming a source, because there isn't one. You just speak with Scott Anderson's voice."

Kathy Lester was at her wit's end. She had to get this conversation back on track. "Let's stay with Iran, Mr. President,"

She got lucky. The schmuck actually agreed. "Why not?" he said. "I've made my point. What's your next question?"

Kathy's heart leaped in her chest. Just a few words to deny his allegations, and she would be back on script again. "Mr. President, it's not enough to hide behind national security – or to blame the man who pays my salary. You can't shift responsibility onto Century News, or the United Nations or anyone else. The American people need to know what you're doing, as our Commander-in-Chief, about this threat from Iran. You have troops in the region. You have ships. You have aircraft – either unmanned, or flown by our heroic pilots. What's your course of action?"

The question hung in the air.

Then he said, "At the moment, absolutely nothing."

Kathy Lester could not believe he said that. Far from making excuses, he was leaving himself wide open; just as Century analysts had predicted. Kathy didn't need to decide what to say next. It was all written down for her. There was no saving this guy now. She quickly moved in for the kill.

She began gently enough. "So you have no battle plan. No strategy."

The President bridled. He seemed to recognize the gaping, black hole opening up at his feet. "I didn't say that," he said.

"Then what are you saying, Mr. President?" she said. "You propose to do – what was it? – 'absolutely nothing' but when I press the issue that's not what you said. Which is it, sir? If you have some grand design, tell us about it. And if not, 'fess up – so we can elect a President who knows what the Dickens he's doing."

Christiansen seemed to welcome the silence. So did Kathy Lester. The longer he went without speaking, the more hesitant and indecisive he looked, and that was always curtains for any politician. She thought: Take your time, sweetie. Momma's got you on the ropes – you're screwed."

Playing to the camera, she said: Mr. President, would you like me to repeat the question?"

"No, thank you." He looked disturbingly confident. "Ms. Lester, you have asked a straight question – indeed, you seem unable to stop asking it again and again – so I will give you a straight answer."

"Whenever you're ready, Mr. President."

He looked hard at her, then back at the camera. "We are at war," he began. "We have been for years, and our fellow countrymen know it. Hundreds of thousands of our soldiers are fighting on foreign soil, in harm's way – and constantly under attack. Our enemies believe America is becoming the next evil empire, and they'll stop at nothing to bring us down. That is why we're at war. Sadly, our allies don't stand completely behind us, either."

Then he explained his Iran strategy – breaking a silence that had lasted weeks. There were nuclear strike submarines on alert in the Red Sea and the Mediterranean. They were accompanied by three aircraft carriers, similarly armed, ready to launch at Iran – or any other hostiles in the region. "Normally a President does not speak of such things," Christiansen said. "They are better handled through diplomacy – behind the scenes – but tonight you have forced my hand."

Kathy Lester thought: My boss set a trap, and you blundered into it like a dumb kid. You have just breached national security, during a coast to coast broadcast. She said coldly: "Too much information, Mr. President. As you said yourself, our enemies watch TV." Wouldn't that include Iran?" She felt and looked triumphant.

"Oh, Iran already knows about it. We warned them in writing through the British Consulate there, a week ago – and their Foreign Minister was cautioned face to face, at a private meeting in Istanbul, by our Secretary of state."

This was the moment when Kathy Lester would have pulled the plug, cutting off transmission, but they were going out live, just as the president had stipulated, and she couldn't.

Clearly he had the situation well in hand.

Viewers would see that right away.

American missiles were now aimed directly at Tehran.

And they had been for a week.

She said: "Oh, really?" and a sick feeling built up in her stomach. She was pretty sure she'd lost this round, if not the entire fight.

Before she could recover, the President was talking. "There's something else I'd like to say – If Scott Anderson wishes to lead this great country of ours, he needs to run for President, instead of using outright lies, innuendo and propaganda to make people think a certain way. He's made television his own political weapon – and he answers to absolutely no one. It's everything Adolf Hitler ever dreamed of. And it's very dangerous, for us and the rest of the world, and it needs to stop."

President Christiansen looked squarely at Kathy Lester. "Do you have any more questions?"

Kathy said she did, but knew they were routine, winding down kind of questions. The main battle was over.

Her sick feeling was growing worse.

She was losing.

This slippery eel had beaten her.

The interview ran twenty agonizing minutes more.

Then they smiled brittle smiles and said goodnight to each other, and to America watching at home.

~ ~ ~

Kathy Lester got back into the limousine with a heavy heart. She was scared of Scott Anderson at the best of times, and she dreaded to think what his reaction to this fiasco would be. She flounced into the back seat and snapped at the driver to take her straight to the hotel. There was no point in returning to Century's Washington studio, because not only was Kathy sure she no longer had a job, but there were dark tales of what happened to those who failed Scott Anderson.

She had been hearing them for years.

But if she went to the hotel, his platinum card would allow her to get drunk, and hopefully laid, in one of the best places in town. One last fling before Kathy went into the job dumpster. She'd stop at the hotel bar, and start there. This was a very expensive Dior, and the regency was full of pretty young men with an eye for money, eager to help her out of this dress for a price. Scott Anderson would pay for that, too. Upscale toy-boys always took credit cards.

And they put out like stallions.

That was what Kathy Lester needed tonight.

She could face reality tomorrow.

~ ~ ~

Lucifer was waiting for her in the bar.

He was in a trendy, pinewood booth, installed against a thick wall of greenish glass bricks, placed there to set off two copper-colored sculptures that dwarfed everything else in sight. He did not look pleased. He saw Kathy Lester and called out to her in that reedy, cracked voice he had, asking her to come and join him. She did as she was told. Anderson stopped a waiter and ordered two whisky sours. Kathy never drank those, but he hadn't asked. That seemed to be the point. They both waited for the drinks to arrive, but even when they did, Anderson still didn't speak.

She sipped her drink, dearly wanting to drain its contents. But she stayed ladylike and aloof, barely tasting it.

He was watching her.

"Mr. Anderson. I'm so sorry . . ."

He said, "What the hell happened?"

She didn't answer because he already knew. The greatest interview of her life had got away from her. She knew she didn't have to tell him that. He had been watching, and had seen it for himself. She decided, Fuck you, Scott Anderson! She gulped the rest of her drink and set down the empty glass.

He snapped his fingers for another.

"What happened?" he repeated.

He clearly wanted an answer. This question was not going to go away. She took a deep breath. "He ambushed me with a personal attack on you. Presidents just don't do that on television. Christiansen caught me totally unawares, precisely as his goddamn speech writers intended. His advisers were better than ours, and I got the shit kicked out of me."

"And?"

"Then he beat our script again, revealing his Iranian strategy to the world when our guys said he could never do that and survive. Well, they were wrong. Right after the show, our focus groups and pollsters said America stands with him a hundred percent. I might as well have stayed at home."

Anderson grunted. "So Angel Eyes won; and you lost."

"Angel Eyes?" She had heard the expression before, but it still puzzled her.

Lucifer bared cigar-stained teeth. "My pet name for the President."

"Well, like I said – I'm sorry . . . but yes, he wiped the

floor with me."

Scott Anderson sighed. "I'd say that he did." Then he snarled into his raised glass: "But our pompous, know-nothing writers, who get paid a king's ransom; they let you and me down." Anderson's words were slightly muffled, echoing into an ice-filled tumbler, but his anger was unmistakable.

Things didn't look good for those writers.

Kathy said: "That may be, but I was there. It was up to me to think on my feet. Instead I got creamed. I know I'm fired – and I deserve it."

"You're not fired."

"I let him slip through my fingers . . ."

"You're not fired."

"Please don't play with me. I've watched you do it before. You told that Austrian studio head he wasn't fired, when Bruno Schwenk died and their reporters were scooped by another channel. When he got your letter, firing him anyway, he jumped off the top floor. He couldn't tell his wife they were going to lose everything. Well, I'm not Austrian, and I don't believe you."

Anderson shrugged. "That was supposed to be a secret. I paid the wife a fortune to keep it quiet."

"Well, someone talked, and I don't . . ." As Kathy spoke, the mix in her drink, or something, began to burn her mouth, like fire. She broke off in mid-sentence, afraid she would choke.

Lucifer grinned. The drink was burning her: he saw the pain on her face. It was hell-fire. He stared into her glass, and added amphetamines, for good measure. Kathy Lester didn't know it, but she was in for a rough night.

He was not going to fire her.

He had promised.

But that was all he promised.

He made his grin a warm smile. "I'll give you a letter, saying you won't be fired."

Kathy looked confused. The drugs were kicking in, and although her mouth and throat must be calming down, her thoughts were getting muddled. She frowned. "I don't get it. You hand me the interview of the year, and I screw it up. You bush-whack me here, when I come looking for meaningless sex – but you're not mad at me and I'm not fired. What the hell are you doing here? Don't say I have to fuck you tonight. I just got rid of your fat boy, Lewin Smith!" Suddenly Kathy was feeling the alcohol, and with a sweep of one hand, she slammed her glass sideways. It skidded, but did not fall or break. She gave a faint hiccup.

There, Kathy thought tipsily. Now you have to fire me and get this bullshit over with. I should be having my third orgasm under a handsome young god by now. She decided to goad Scott Anderson a bit further – before she went off to have intercourse with someone stupid.

At least it wouldn't be him.

She stood up shakily. "Now if you don't mind – I'm off to find someone who can go all night." Her tone implied Anderson could not.

He actually laughed. "Don't let me keep you."

"Do I really still have a job."

"Yes – probably for the rest of your life."

The implications of that went over her head. She said: "Well, I hope so. I'm sorry about tonight."

"I know you are. Have a good evening."

"Thanks. I intend to." She meant to say something witty about needing a condom, but the words slipped away in a fog. She swayed as she turned away. "If you need me, I shall be briefly at the bar."

But for some reason, Kathy Lester walked straight past the bar and went to her room . . .

~ ~ ~

Lucifer smoked a cigar, which no one seemed to find objectionable, and enjoyed a third whiskey sour. Kathy Lester had failed him and that was intolerable. Now he had to make an example of her.

He picked one of the waiters, not quite at random.

He called him over, ordered yet another drink – and stared into two increasingly vacant eyes for several moments.

The man was around thirty, not as young as the woman who just left would have liked, but good looking and strong, with a muscular build from working out, which was essential for what he was about to do to Kathy Lester.

How pleasing that this waiter was an almost pure soul. Lucifer enjoyed exploiting the wicked, but he preferred to destroy the good.

The waiter received a generous tip and left.

Satanically speaking, he was now armed and dangerous.

~ ~ ~

There was a discrete knock at her door. Kathy Lester was not only irritated, but half undressed and befuddled. She had succumbed fast to the drugs, and her gait was a little unsteady, as she walked to the door.

"Who is it?"

"Bar delivery. The gentleman sent up a bottle."

She frowned. Please thank him, but it's very late and I couldn't possibly drink anything else."

"Sorry, Ma'am," the waiter said. "He said you would say that, but he insists."

Kathy Lester could imagine. Anderson had probably browbeaten this guy, and slipped him a hundred.

She'd take the bottle and dump it.

"Just a minute,"

She thought, Boy, my head feels funny, She went off and put on a terry robe with the hotel logo. Then she unbolted the door and let him in. "This is stupid – I'm ready for bed." She heard how drunk she sounded as she said it.

A buff looking Adonis swept into the room. "Where do you want this?" It was Dom Perignon.

And the waiter was quite attractive,

A tad mature for her taste; but better than nothing.

"Oh, I don't care . . . just put it on the table." The room seemed to tip sideways, and her head suddenly cleared.

There was a sudden heat in her loins.

Her use of the word "I" had triggered a response in her and the waiter. It was a trick Lucifer always found amusing. "People use the word "I" all the time. Kathy Lester had said it twice in sixty seconds. Now she was becoming sexually excited and the waiter was looking at her strangely. It was evident that he had an erection.

They were both under Lucifer's spell.

He ripped off her robe and she let him, snaking both arms around his neck. They kissed in a fierce, animal way, their mouths locked together, as she stripped of his shirt and unfastened his pants.

Soon they were naked on the bed, groping at each other's bodies like teenagers in the back of a car. Kathy heard him mutter, "Oh, my God," again and again, and she was aware of her own voice screaming, between deep grunts of pleasure, as the waiter thrust his hand back and forth between her thighs. Her reaction was astonishing, even to her, as the two of them thrashed about on the covers.

Then she was stride him, experiencing more pleasure as she swigged champagne from the open bottle.

He said, "That's right – don't stop. Just keep moving like that."

There was a symphony in her head. She removed her lips from the bottle. "You're just what I . . . oh, fuck!" she finished wildly.

She let the bottle fall, and he responded vigorously.

She felt a pain that was all too enjoyable. His strength was evident, as he thrust into her. The champagne had increased her need.

It was meant to.

It was laced with a product of Columbia.

~ ~ ~

Sometime later he stood over her. Kathy peered up at him woozily. He said, "You were great for me. How was it for you?"

"Oh, God. He was predictable – and stupid.

"Fantastic,' she said into a dark, endless tunnel. Her lips felt as though they were blocks of cement.

This was the final phase.

Kathy went into a semi-trance.

He padded away from the bed and came back with a butcher knife that Lucifer had silently told him to steal from the kitchen.

He laid the implement on the bed and straddled her. Then he began to masturbate. His movements were wooden, and his eyes glazed.

He ejaculated onto her breasts.

Now came the end. Kathy came wide awake as he raised the knife, suddenly seeing what was happening. He was afraid she would cry out, or struggle – so he cut her throat with a downward, slashing motion. Kathy's eyeballs rolled up, and she fell back dead. He struck at her many times, lacerating the pale flesh of her stomach, groin and thighs. There was a lot of blood.

"All right," he told Kathy's corpse. "Let's make you smaller."

He started to chop her up.

It took every ounce of his strength, but he finally got it done. The stench of blood filled the room. He was caked in it. The knife slid from his fingers and fell to the floor.

Lucifer drifted in through a wall. "Good boy," he said. "A pity there's no death penalty in New York. I'd love to watch you fry."

Without moving, the devil caused bloody writing to appear on the walls, mirrors, and on the sliding glass doors to the balcony. The word 'Pig" featured several times, and the word "Whore". Lucifer retrieved the knife and put it in the young man's hand. "Do it now," he said.

The waiter cut his own throat.

~ ~ ~

Heathcote yawned. He had spent all-night down here in the basement, looking at flyover-shots of Prince Kamal's campsite disguised as a quarry. He and Fairchild had made it their nightly routine, coming down here while others slept, reviewing the latest satellite pictures as they came in. It usually took a couple of hours, including discussion and analysis of what they saw. Then they both went home for some sleep. But the satellite lens had captured little of interest for days. That was; until tonight.

Tonight had been different.

Around mid-afternoon over Afghanistan the camera caught Shahanna out in the open. Not only that, but they had a very clear shot of what she was doing. Fairchild had easily picked her out on their large screen. She sat in a canvas chair with one leg crossed over the other. Magnification was boosted enough to show the pattern on her camouflage pants.

Shahanna was writing on yellow note-pad in her lap. That caused Heathcote to shout to Fairchild, who froze the frame and began enhancing to a point that would have been unthinkable a few years before. Within seconds, from half a world away, they were seeing Prince Kamal's last order, dictated shortly before he died, although of course they didn't know that, because it was still in Arabic. Shahanna was writing it down for them, with a cheap ball-point pen. She'd already filled half a page.

Shahanna was very smart. Knowing Heathcote was probably watching, she had come outside in case a sky-cam passed overhead. The message she was re-working must be important. She was taking quite a risk.

They waited until she stopped writing.

Now they needed a translator.

Fairchild did not need to be told. He got on his phone and woke up a lot of people. Sometime later, a disheveled Farsi speaker was ushered into the viewing room. He was a Kurd who ran a convenience store in Alexandria. He had been press-ganged by FBI men who told him what he did tonight would make him a hero. They also said he would go to jail if he ever talked about it.

They re-ran the Shahanna footage for him.

What he translated was a shock. Prince Kamal had ordered another small-scale attack on US soil within days, and here was Shahanna sounding the alarm; on a sunny afternoon in the quarry pit – under the gaze of cutting edge technology that she hoped was watching.

Fortunately it was.

Fairchild was a craftsman. He pushed buttons and twisted dials, holding the lens on Shahanna until they had everything. The camera stayed focused on her notepad until the satellite lost her. No other person, or location, in the campsite had been photographed for the data base today.

Hard copies were printed out. The Kurdish gentleman soon produced an accurate translation. It turned out that not only was this a short term mission, but already under way. Trainees from Kamal's camp had been sent to carry it out, instead of using activists resident in the United States. The reason, going by Shahanna's notes, was that all of these trainees were borderline cases. This was a make-or-break test. Those that succeeded in America, and flew home safely, would take part in Prince Kamal's full-scale nuclear attack.

It was a death sentence either way. At least two would not survive the current mission in any case. The drivers of the suicide vehicles – two stolen cars packed with enough C-4 to do incredible damage.

None of the names meant much, as far as Heathcote could tell from what was on file. They were all first-timers, which after all was why they were being tested. To make things worse, the FBI had no reliable photos – making the infiltrators harder to catch. Heathcote saw immediately that such an attack had every chance of success, due to the random nature of its planning.

Heathcote sent their Kurdish translator away with enough cash to guarantee his silence, in case threats didn't work. Then he said to Fairchild: "Show me the last seven days of tapes. Let's see everything our dead Prince did last week. You never know. He might give something away."

Heathcote did not hold out much hope. He was talking about discarded footage already analyzed and rejected, either for poor quality, or because the content was not useful.

Fairchild moved his mouse on its pad.

The rim of the quarry flipped into focus.

Then a lot of open ground.

 Next the lake and Prince Kamal's hut.

The were no people shots; no movement of any kind – and Heathcote almost told Fairchild to stop: This was pointless.

Fairchild switched to the next day.

And the next day after that . . .

There was a lot of movement, over several days – Recruits in training, trying out various combat techniques, from Karate to firing every kind of weapon at every kind of target or just strolling around, not doing much of anything. Last week there had been so much footage of prayers and mealtimes, that the satellite schedule was altered to avoid them. Now the program recorded only regular coverage of everyday events in the camp, which was what Fairchild showed now, but with most of the material scanned, there was still no sign of Prince Kamal. Fairchild apologized, as he brought up video from six days ago.

At first there was more empty quarry.

Then the Prince came out of his hut, but all you could see was the top of his head. Fairchild used a calculator, then he made an adjustment to get low trajectory at an acute angle. Digital enhancement began filling in anything the high-altitude lenses had missed. Suddenly Prince Kamal's face swung up at Heathcote, clearly recognizable in the dawn light. The Prince sauntered arrogantly to the water's edge.

A short line of men and women knelt there, waiting for him.

Fairchild enhanced the shot even more, raising an eyebrow at Heathcote, who silently punched the air.

This looked like a swearing-in ceremony.

It was. As lip-readers would later confirm, the terrorists, one after the other, took an oath of obedience, recited their final will, and said their prayers – with Prince Kamal standing over them like some satanic high-priest. Nearly half of them did this, before the satellite moved off.

How had this been overlooked?

Fatigue and the need to hurry.

And the top of a head not being very interesting.

Until you looked again, a week later.

It looked to Heathcote as if they had found the attack team just before they left for America. There were small piles of western-style baggage nearby, and everyone on their knees wore western clothing. Heathcote did some quick mental arithmetic. The could be in America within three days of these pictures being taken. And they were taken six days ago.

The motherfuckers were already here.

This time it was Heathcote who rushed for the phone.

He called every international airport on the Eastern Seaboard of the United States, reasoning that this was as far as the terrorists could get in the time elapsed. Heathcote spoke to the Director of security at each likely destination. Then he called the corresponding police department and spoke to them. Each conversation was the same: He gave a last-minute warning, and requested an e-mail address where photos could be sent as soon as Fairchild had them downloaded. It was all he could do in the time he had.

Fairchild had produced head-shots of all of them by the time Heathcote got off the phone. Homicidal maniacs of both sexes in close-up. The exposure was not that great, but it would do. US Customs officers were used to looking at lousy passport pictures. These would be a challenge.

Heathcote told Fairchild to e-mail them to all the addresses on the list and went back upstairs to his office.

He stopped at the canteen and picked up a calorie-laden breakfast: Scrambled eggs, sausage, bacon and grits, all liberally sprinkled with Tabasco sauce. He set it on his desk, turned on the T. V. News and ate as he watched.

Heathcote caught the lead story: Little more than a replay of last night's Oval Office interview, showing highlights consisting of the President's best, show-stopping sound-bites, as he demolished that lady reporter and her boss. But that was not the big news to this story. This morning Kathy Lester had been found murdered in her hotel room. There was hate-filled daubing everywhere in blood, and a male hotel employee was found, also dead, at her bedside. The Hyatt Regency Hotel chain had so far refused to comment.

Heathcote flipped channels, hoping either to escape

the story, or find coverage that was less sensational.

No such luck. Every network had it, and was in an insane feeding frenzy. All that was missing were lurid pictures of the crime-scene, or some suggestion that the President had done it; although it was said, several times, that the White House had expressed deep regret at the news. More tidbits and rumors were added by the minute, served up gaily as breaking-news by rivals of Kathy Lester, like vultures devouring a creature they had not liked very much.

No one seemed to mourn her passing.

Heathcote switched it off.

His food was cold and unfinished.

He sat gathering his thoughts. Nothing in the news coverage affected him or his problems, but he felt repulsed by what the world had become.

Heathcote checked his watch. It was sunrise in the Afghan hills. The first satellite sweep was due at any moment, and although it might well yield nothing, he felt he ought to return to the basement and watch. With Prince Kamal's impromptu attacks coming at any time, the smallest clue might be helpful. Shahanna sat in plain sight yesterday, so he could read what she wrote.

Maybe she'd do it again today.

Heathcote abandoned his breakfast and went downstairs. Fairchild had read his mind, and the equipment was ready.

Dawn had broken in Afghanistan. Heathcote felt drained. When was the last time he slept for more than an hour or two? He knew he pushed himself too hard, but that was what he got paid for. He was expected to have updates on the President's desk, twice a day. He also managed a vast intelligence network, and kept abreast of all that happened in the world. In between he must save America from this lunatic Saudi Prince. Heathcote took his seat.

No coffee or muffins today.

Afghan dawn plus fifteen. The download was now overdue. There might be a good reason, but that wouldn't help, if Heathcote had to inform his boss, Richard Powell, that technical difficulty had delayed transmission. Last time, Powell had been furious that the President was kept waiting. "This isn't the Space Shuttle, Heathcote. Get your rinky-dink program under control – or I'll cancel it!"

Therefore if there was a satellite glitch, at this, the very worst of moments, how did Heathcote keep Powell off his back? Simply lie to the bastard? Honesty had certainly not worked last time. Heathcote considered, wishing he had some coffee. Then, suddenly, he knew the answer: Re-show yesterday's pictures.

Only Heathcote and Fairchild had seen them.

Richard Powell need never know, and Shahanna's bomb-warning would blow his mind. Heathcote gnawed at a cuticle on his thumb, going over the deception in his mind. It had to be foolproof.

But at dawn plus nineteen, he was saved. The screen came to life, and a sweep-over of the Afghan quarry began, regrettably late, but extremely clear. Heathcote could hear Fairchild's gasp of relief from clear across the room.

Human figures appeared right away.

Shahanna was center screen, walking with Asuto Kenyatta. She wore a stylish pair of denims, making her look slightly overdressed in that setting. The African was flexing his fingers and arms, like a prize-fighter waiting to step in the ring. Heathcote was struck by the obvious physical strength of the man. Did he work out? Was there a gymnasium in this training camp? Of course not. Asuto Kenyatta was in superb condition from fighting, killing and surviving all his life.

Shahanna looked wary of him.

Heathcote had a sudden urge to call out to her. He wanted to ask where Clement was. Why was she alone with Kamal's executioner?

Shahanna said something to. Something that would be lip-read and transcribed for Heathcote later. Asuto's eyes flashed, registering what she said, but he did not reply. Now a third figure entered the screen-shot. A shady looking white man, interrupting the pair, his hands spread in apology. It was the Canadian national filmed at the previous camp. Here, as there, he taught advanced-level English. Hassan had described him as a spineless lackey. The man spoke to Kenyatta, who ignored him and moved on. Shahanna followed him, giving the tutor a scathing look.

Heathcote was amused at the man's hurt expression. These Muslims who hired his services would despise him as an infidel, and even more as one who betrayed his country. That was clearly how Kenyatta felt. Shahanna, whose views on such matters were well known, simply hated him for being there at all.

Heathcote looked at the screen and the length of Asuto's shadow. This download had started late, and because satellites always moved at the same pace, twenty minutes had been lost. Shadows lengthen slowly with the sun on the horizon, but shrink rapidly as it rises. This was already happening. Heathcote checked the digital time-clock at the foot of the screen and saw he had ten minutes left.

They were running out of time.

And Shahanna was clearly not sending any message. How could she, standing out there with Kenyatta? That was understandable. But Heathcote always felt better if he at least saw Clement, just to know he was alive and well. His capture and detainment on the way to Khyber al Makrit had been harrowing to watch. Besides, Shahanna was far better protected with her partner on hand.

That was the whole idea.

Heathcote asked Fairchild to program a lower angle, just like yesterday, but more pronounced. That would help, but not much. It might gain thirty seconds, but it was all they could do.

This satellite sweep was proving worthless.

Fairchild made the adjustment. Shahanna and Asuto became first blurry . . . then larger and clearer, as magnification changed.

The shot widened. Shahanna and Kenyatta went away, and a skinny Afghan filled the screen, stirring something in a large iron pot. Smoke billowed, and hot coals glowed red in a wide circle on the sand. Heathcote sighed. This was all very scenic, but still of no use whatsoever.

Fairchild got busy with his mouse-pad.

There were forty seconds left.

The picture changed again. Now they saw Jhalal, crawling out of a tent. He was looking up at someone, and talking. Fairchild broadened the picture, to see who it was. The image clarified to show . . . Clement! He'd lost some weight, but otherwise looked healthy. For Heathcote, it made the delay worthwhile, and Fairchild whooped aloud.

It was a heady moment.

Then a very tall Arab crawled out to join them – and for some reason Heathcote remembered what Hassan looked like, remembered hiring him, and a whole lot of other things that had escaped him before. All three American operatives stood breathing in the cool, early morning air, but not for long, because the satellite resumed its course, making them smaller before losing them altogether.

The camera, several times higher now, took in the waters of the bottomless lake; then crossed the mid-section of the quarry. Then more tents, growing smaller, and more people standing around, waiting for whatever was stewing in that iron pot. A little way off, one man urinated on the ground.

Next came the quarry's edge.

Then the landscape that surrounded the quarry.

By now it all looked tiny.

Heathcote said to the youngster: "Shut it down."

He had seen Clement and felt better. The screen blanked off and the ceiling lights came on. Fairchild logged off the satellite. There was no point paying for computer-time they were not going to use. The two men walked together to the door.

As he turned out the lights, Heathcote said: "Great job."

"Nothing more from Shahanna," the younger man said ruefully.

They went out and entered the main elevator. They got out at ground level, and that was where they parted. Fairchild was going home. Heathcote was off to get another breakfast and work through the day, warning whoever needed to know about the bomb attacks he expected.

Heathcote reached the foyer and looked around. The security guards stood at their posts. They looked like subway attendants with gold badges, their barriers constantly in use. Barred turnstiles protected by Plexiglas shields.

The lobby was jammed with people waiting to get out, and the new shift threading through them to get in. Identity cards were being scrutinized and swiped by the guards. Outside, through the glass doors, Heathcote saw three men getting out of a taxi, while a fourth man paid the driver. Then the cab pulled away. A few yards further on, another taxi sat empty, waiting for passengers. The outside gate-guards were used to that, and would have waved it through. Heathcote looked at the driver. He was swarthy-looking, and his hands shook. Heathcote swore, and yelled a warning.

One of Prince Kamal's bombers was waiting to die.

Heathcote ran toward the outside doors.

He yelled at the guards to clear the area.

A woman screamed, and everyone stampeded, jostling each other in their panic, and crowding the tubular barriers.

Heathcote got outside and advanced on the taxi. It blew up as he approached. The car appeared to stagger, in a roar of flame. Pieces of metal catapulted everywhere from the explosion. The noise was thunderous, and terrifying.

Heathcote was blasted back into a wall. His head struck the concrete. He felt a dull pain, and blood trickling from his ears. He had bitten his tongue, and a salty taste filled his mouth, as that began to bleed as well. He got up and walked unsteadily back to what was left of the entrance way. Blood was spattered in a wide arc on the ground. Probably all that was left of the driver.

The empty cab lay in charred and twisted fragments.

The glass doors of the building had shattered, and jagged pieces crunched under foot. Inside, people were injured and others were tending them.

Prince Kamal had struck from the grave.

CHAPTER FIFTEEN

SHAHANNA FELT ON EDGE. The Fourth of July was now only ten days away, and they could ship out at any time. All six teams were waiting nervously, and everyone, including her, had been fitted for an airline uniform. Hers was an Air France tunic, complete with skirt and cap.

None of those who bombed Washington yesterday were coming back. The drivers of both vehicles were blown up; the others were shot at the scene or arrested later, when they tried to fly home. They might get a death sentence in about ten years, given the way America ran its legal system.

Shahanna wanted them dead today.

She wanted them to rot in hell. At least their airline uniforms would never be worn now. Several of the six teams here had lost potential members. News of the bombings had come quickly. The ground floor of Heathcote's building was badly damaged, and while no one was killed, many were injured by flying glass and debris. The second vehicle, even more heavily laden with explosive, had destroyed part of CIA Headquarters in Langley. Much of the structure was rubble, and some two hundred people had lost their lives, with even more in hospital.

Shahanna felt terrible. Her warning was too late. Or the reaction too slow. Either from her or at headquarters. Not one life had been saved. And wasn't that why she and Clement were doing this – to protect Americans?

~ ~ ~

She was thinking this, as she walked beside Asuto Kenyatta – making the morning rounds as if he were the Prince. Getting the top job had changed Asuto overnight. It was as if he took on all the arrogance of Kamal himself.

"You seem unwell,' he said.

She knew she didn't care if she had leprosy. She looked away, to avoid his eye, and said, "What do you mean?"

"You're not yourself today. You can't even walk straight; you keep tripping over rocks. You did not come to prayers to give thanks for our successes in Alexandria and Langley. Whatever is the matter? Our own sacrifice is coming . Are you having second thoughts, Sorya?"

No, she thought. It's those bombings. I have friends in both places and God knows how many of them are dead. That's what's wrong, you pompous pig. "It's nothing," she said. "My time of the month." Now she was on safe ground. Women were weak in the eyes of Muslim men like him.

"Ah, I see," Asuto said in a clipped tone.

He looked slightly embarrassed.

She almost giggled. This was certainly how to handle him. "When do we leave?," she asked casually. My jacket and hat insignia are Air France. Am I going to a French city?" Her guess was Montreal, the French Canadian capital of Quebec. A good place for airline crew to cross the US border.

"All in good time, Sorya." This new, haughty manner of his was hard to take. She kept her face blank.

Asuto said, "Only I know for now. It's better that way."

She wanted to scream. He was every bit as secretive as

his predecessor. And that was not all. Training was complete and six teams selected; so why were they still in an overheated Afghan quarry, instead of relaxing by a swimming pool in Cairo or Tunis? Here there was little to do but eat, sleep and wait for the next meal – or the next sleep. Everyone was dying of nervous tension. All because Asuto Kenyatta was as cheap as the Prince, saving money for the Saudis as if it was his own. Did he think they might reward him? Suddenly her dislike of this surly man almost drowned her. Why not just kill him, here and now, and have done with it? He was famously ready to die in America, so why wait? With him gone this entire mission would be put on hold. Shahanna had a pistol on her belt, and they were alone.

But she couldn't shoot him out in the open, with so many people close enough to hear the noise.

She dug her fingernails into her palms, and got control of herself. She said: "Why don't you and I go hunting for game?" It was worth a try. This suggestion had worked pretty well with Prince Kamal.

"Hunting is not safe. These hill brigands don't want us here. They were ready to kill your Mr. Keller. All three of us were in danger, and it was Allah that saved us – His name be praised."

"He's not my Mr. Keller."

Asuto did not respond, but his eyes took on a sly look.

She decided to ignore that. "I'm not afraid to go hunting."

"Who spoke of fear?"

"I think we need to go. Our food is awful."

"Unhappily true. But there is too much at stake – to risk a bullet for the cooking pot."

"You drive – and I'll shoot back at them."

Surprisingly, and completely out of character, Asuto burst out laughing. "I truly believe you would."

Shahanna felt she had the upper hand. Maybe she could kill him after all. She thought, Hunting is the answer. I'll shoot you in the head and say you wandered off. Everybody will think you died in a quicksand. She looked away from him, as if Asuto could read her mind. Her head would end up on a stake.

But she wanted to do this.

Life might go back to normal, without Kenyatta.

So she should go ahead.

She said impulsively: "Let's get the Range Rover. Fuck the Taliban."

He scowled at her. "I dislike foul language."

She had made a mistake. "Forgive me," she said. "But I hate to be in their power. Why don't we go and be done with it?"

His face froze, as if she had insulted him. "I am in the power of no one. Certainly not the Taliban. Go and get us some guns: Two rifles; one shotgun. You give me no peace, woman."

She had finally said the right thing. You never knew with this imbecile. She decided not to push it. "Yes, Asuto. I apologize for my rudeness."

It was just like talking to Prince Kamal.

She ran off dutifully.

Hassan was there, alone, when she looked in his tent. She said: "Get the other two. I'm taking Asuto hunting, and I'm going to kill him. Follow us in the truck, at a distance, in case I mess it up or something goes wrong – and don't try to talk me out of it. He killed a lot of

Americans yesterday."

She ran off again.

When she struggled over to the late Prince's hunting vehicle, loaded down with weaponry, Kenyatta was at the wheel. She said: "Let me drive. You're a better shot, and we might see something on the way."

She put the guns in the back.

He said: "On the way? Where are we going?"

She hesitated. "I don't know." It sounded silly, even to her.

He grunted. "When we first arrived, the Prince and I scouted the area. I know the perfect place."

She could have hugged herself. Asuto was so determined to lead, he was making it easy for her. Shahanna wanted to laugh. Instead, she said: "How wonderful. Off to the hunt!"

"The hunt pleases Allah," he said. "And I am a killer of lions.'

She gave him a sunny smile. "Yes, so you are.'

He got out on the driver's side to let her in.

Then they heard the convoy.

They both looked towards the ravine beyond the entrance to the quarry. A dust cloud swirled over the first bus as it broke, or appeared to break, straight though the rocky wall. It was painted gray, and followed by two more, both identical in color. They were old American school buses with the windows smashed out, each one a dilapidated oven in this heat. They sounded like tractors roaring across a field. All three had a Red Crescent painted on the side – the Arab equivalent of the Red Cross – designating it as some kind of emergency medical vehicle.

They lined up at the lake's edge, and then the three

engines died, one by one, until there was silence again.

The African left Shahanna in the Range Rover and went off to greet whoever was on board. No one had got out. She realized that any chance of killing him was lost. Had she been capable of it? Shahanna still wasn't sure, but now her hunting trip would not take place and she would never know. Shahanna sighed. These buses had to show up sometime, but did it have to be right now? She gave them a measuring look. Obviously they were the cheapest transport available. It would be a miracle if any of them started again. She silently cursed Prince Kamal. This was so typical of him, and now getting out of here was going to be pure hell. She opened the car door, shading her eyes to see better, and moved toward the buses.

Behind her, alerted by the sound of engines, Gabriel read Shahanna's mind.

Hassan came level with her, and said: "Those buses are for us."

She turned. "Prince Kamal having the last laugh."

Clement and Jhalal joined them, and they all stood looking at the buses, which were finally emptying out. Men in green overalls joined Kenyatta on the ground. Some wore white coats with stethoscopes round their necks, looking like doctors and medical orderlies. Shahanna realized that was to fool anyone who stopped these buses on their way out of Afghanistan.

A thick-set Saudi in his fifties was talking to Asuto. Plainly a soldier, even from a distance but disguised as a doctor. It was General Makhud – Shahanna recognized him from her stay at the Saudi royal palace. Army Chief of Staff and last surviving Tribunal member. That left him in charge of this mission with full authority of the Saudi

King. It was Makhud who found this quarry-camp for Prince Kamal.

Hassan and Jhalal pushed forward through a crowd that had gathered to look at the newcomers and their buses. Most people realized that their passport out of here had arrived. They also wanted to hear what General Makhud had to say. Shahanna followed Hassan. Clement joined her.

She knew they were both thinking the same thing: If the camp vacated now, with no warning, how could Hassan tell Heathcote? And with another sniper team out there somewhere, with orders to remove General Makhud, shouldn't Heathcote know he was right here with Asuto Kenyatta, another prime target?

There was another question: How could these buses leave Afghanistan without going back to Iran, which Prince Kamal left in disgrace? The only other way out was even worse: through American held Afghanistan. It was the wrong way if you were in a hurry, and Muslim extremists were an endangered species, hunted not only by American troops, but also the French and British. Three buses from nowhere would be stopped at every checkpoint. Was General Makhud really that stupid?

Shahanna said: Where the hell is he taking us?"

Clement shrugged. "It doesn't matter," he said in a low voice. "We can't lose. If everyone makes it, we're right there with them. If they don't, and they get caught, our side wins, and you and I get to go home. Either way, this Makhud is no Prince Kamal. He'll probably get rid of Asuto."

Shahanna decided he was right. She shot a glance at him. Why did he always see the big picture, and she sometimes didn't?

~ ~ ~

Gabriel knew what to do. His power level was up. He must return to America, see Heathcote and bring him up to date. Besides, Gabriel needed to know what was going on in Washington, and, just as importantly, what Lucifer was up to in New York. For that to happen, the situation here must be stabilized. Gabriel knew Shahanna was thinking to kill Asuto and postpone the whole attack. but Gabriel knew Heathcote's strategy: All six terrorist teams must go to America. Otherwise the nukes would simply stay at sea, or be hidden on land, until another group was trained to use them.

Removing Asuto was a bad idea.

The South African must lead this attack.

 And fail.

Gabriel stood with the other three, at the edge of an enthusiastic crowd that had formed around General Makhud and the buses. Jhalal said he remembered the General from the Tribunal, when he and Asuto Kenyatta were recruited. Hassan nodded absently. Gabriel knew who the General was. The most cunning demon that Lucifer ever smuggled into the Saudi palace. Gabriel had already read the General's mind: He was here to take Kenyatta's place, and about to make it public. All six suicide teams would answer to the General himself.

The King had decreed it.

Gabriel thought quickly. Should events be allowed to take their course, with Asuto fired, should Gabriel intervene and kill this fat demon before it said something publicly.

Asuto was a disastrous leader. Gabriel, in his role as

Hassan, had seen plenty evidence of that. Therefore the question answered itself.

It was desirable to have Kenyatta in command. His rawness made him hot-headed and his decisions were flawed. His lack of control created an advantage for those trying to prevent the attack. General Makhud apparently agreed with Gabriel, and he was ready to make it official. Asuto's promotion had been hasty and short-sighted, awarded during the after-shock of losing Prince Kamal.

Now the Saudi king had sent an old dog to take over. His most faithful general, a man who got results. Kenyatta, on the other hand, was an outsider with no leadership skills, no friends and no Prince Kamal around to save him. He wasn't even an Arab. No wonder the king wanted him gone. This mission was a matter of Saudi prestige. Kamal's forced flight from Iran had embarrassed the king, forcing him to beg the Afghans for use of this old quarry.

Equally humiliating was having an unknown African in charge. Asuto would be lucky to keep his head. The King wanted him handed over to the Taliban to do with as they wished. That was in the General's mind.

Gabriel would not allow that.

He must keep Asuto in place, for all the reasons the Saudis wanted him gone. But the angel must act quickly.

General Makhud must die.

Right here and now.

Gabriel decided to use theatrics. Instead of a standard heart attack, this would appear to be an assassin's bullet. To convince both this crowd and the devil in New York. Lucifer was watching for demons who had heart attacks, and he must never know that Gabriel was here.

The US Army would take the blame.

The angel pointed a finger, his hand low and out of sight.

Makhud staggered forward, as if struck in the back of his head by a high caliber projectile. His skull shattered, with blood streaming down the remains of his face. His eyes glazed, and he dropped like a stone. There was a whip-crack of sound, as Gabriel produced the effect of a far-off sniper's rifle. The crowd fell back, but Asuto Kenyatta took a tentative step, as if to render first-aid, then stopped, seeing that it was hopeless. The general's brains were scattered glistening on the ground, the frontal lobes completely ripped away.

He was well beyond medical help.

Kenyatta barked some orders, and people hastened to obey. Everyone was armed, and most of the crowd went into a defensive position – aiming every gun in the direction from which the shot must have come. It soon became apparent there was no target, and people began to lower their weapons. General Makhud was picked up and carried away. He was heavy, and it took several men to lift him.

Everyone began talking at once.

Most thought the assassin was at least a mile away.

Gabriel left the scene.

No one saw him go. Even without a spell, the camp was so distracted that he could have marched away with a brass band.

By the time things calmed down in the quarry, an elegantly dressed Englishman named Henry Archer was on a plane to Washington.

~ ~ ~

From his D. C. hotel room, it took one phone call.

Heathcote immediately sent a car.

Gabriel handed him a report on the current situation, with the usual story that it came from Hassan, smuggled here by Henry Archer in a diplomatic bag. Heathcote was sold on this report before he read it, being desperate for an up-date, and most impressed with Hassan as a source. The report's main point was this:

Those buses meant the camp was history.

Revenge of Islam had started.

The report basically said the clock was ticking.

Heathcote agreed. Departure for America must take place now. This was no great surprise with the Fourth of July so close. A long, drawn-out journey, at least at the start, was to be expected. Prince Kamal's quarry was far from highways and train tracks, with airports non-existent in every direction.

And the report became a plan:

Those on the ground – Clement and the others – would keep Heathcote informed as they traveled, as best they could. Heathcote said, "This Hassan is a miracle worker. Without him we'd be up shit's creek. He'll get word through."

Henry Archer expressed every confidence that Hassan would, explaining that the two of them had worked together before. The Englishman didn't mention the shooting of General Makhud. Best to let that news filter through later, because Heathcote was no fool, and knew there was no American sniper team, which, in turn, raised questions that really had no answer.

Heathcote got up from his desk and approached a wall covered in maps. They all showed the area in question, between Turkey and the Russian Steppes. He selected one, and pin-pointed a spot with his finger. "The satellite loses the quarry here. Now they're leaving, that's a problem. Tracking three buses on dirt tracks and passes overhung by rocks is bad enough, but this guy Asuto knows where he's going, while we don't have a clue." Removing his finger, Heathcote swung it far to the East. "This is my best guess." Now he jabbed the same finger down at another spot – halfway across the map. He had started and finished in only one country.

Gabriel already knew the destination, from reading Makhud's thoughts, and here was Heathcote reading them, too. His sweeping curve indicated Russia, bordering directly on Afghanistan, and his finger had come to rest on Moscow, a lot further East. Heathcote was exactly right. It was an inspired guess, but not surprising, because he and Makhud were in the same business on opposing sides. One significant difference, of course, was that Heathcote was still alive.

And not a demon.

That made two differences.

Makhud's plan was sound. Moscow was the perfect jumping off point for the whole of Europe, and Asuto could filter his people through a dozen western airports before they flew to America, moving in teams, or in ones and twos.

Tracking them would not be easy.

But it must be done.

Again Heathcote asked about Hassan.

Again Henry Archer reassured him.

Together they calculated time and distance. Moscow lay more than two thousand miles from the Afghan quarry. How long for Asuto to get there? Difficult to say, because this journey could not be made by bus — that would take weeks, and Asuto did not have weeks. He had to switch to a faster form of transport. And were they all going to travel together through Afghanistan and Russia? Split up in Moscow, before flying to Europe? Heathcote decided they'd stay together until they got through Russia. Asuto would not want them out of his sight.

Gabriel agreed, knowing that to be correct — but unable to say so because mind reading was not an acceptable explanation.

They guessed the journey would take five days. That gave Heathcote time to get enough of his people to Moscow. It was also the shortest time they thought Asuto could possibly manage.

Gabriel left the meeting more confident than Heathcote, because he was making the journey at Asuto's side, and would know what was going on. Heathcote would just have to sweat it out.

The Angel of Death had no time for airline flight. Asuto might already be on the move. Gabriel couldn't see him waiting to bury General Makhud. New York, and the devil, would therefore have to wait. The angel threw himself into the vortex, hurtling towards the quarry with a slight feeling of nausea as his power drained away. Crossing the world for a second time was taking its toll.

He became Hassan as he hit the ground.

It was almost sunset.

He made the third bus by seconds. The sorry-looking convoy wound its way across the rock-bed quarry floor, diesels roaring and clattering in disarray. Grey-black fumes hung in the air like a shroud.

Revenge of Islam was saying goodbye to the quarry.

~ ~ ~

Shahanna and Clement sat at the front of the lead bus, looking out at darkening mountains, and the occasional glimmer of light from a village as they passed it by. They were all posing as refugees or wounded, evacuating after the latest American bombing raids. These happened every day, so it was easy to invent one.

Three busloads of human garbage, moving slowly across stony landscape to avoid further bloodshed. It was a good cover story, promising to evoke sympathy in anybody who intercepted them with a view to a search.

Few would disagree that this rugged part of the Pashtun Triangle offered little advantage to man or beast. But for these buses it had two assets: It was a far flung, primitive location in which very few N. A. T. O. Troops were to be found. And it was a region with no registration of births, deaths or marriages. Identification was largely unheard of, and nomads roamed freely and unchecked.

Fleeing as refugees was a masterstroke.

And close to foolproof.

Shahanna was glad not to be one of the phony casualties that almost filled each bus. Most of her fellow passengers were either disguised as stretcher cases or walking wounded, wearing filthy bandages dipped in cow blood. These became stiff when dry, chafing the skin and attracting flies. But it was expected that this, and the worsening smell, would convince any U. N. Soldiers.

Everyone on board wore the burnoose and peasant robes; except for Asuto, who stood out with his darker skin and overgrown, bushy curls. This giveaway hair was only partly hidden by a locally-made, flat sheepskin cap. No one knew who he would say he was, if questioned. They just hoped he got away with it. Any foreign soldier who tried to arrest Asuto was bound to die. The African had a gun and a knife, and would certainly use them. He had refused to give them up, even to Jhalal and Hassan. Everyone else was unarmed, and made convincing victims. Asuto Kenyatta, on the other hand, looked like what he was: a vicious killer.

Shahanna hoped they would not be stopped, that the night would pass peacefully and no one would see if she fell asleep on Clement and snuggled into him. She smiled to herself, imagining them making love on the smooth, satin sheets of that bed in New York. The thought of it made her wet.

Throughout this journey, she would not even think about Revenge of Islam. Just shut it out of her mind. She began to fantasize about sex with Clement. Closing her eyes, she told herself: Not the real thing, but better than nothing. It would begin with a kiss. She imagined herself pressing against him, and felt the familiar warmth rising through her body. It was easy to envision what came next: Both of them undressing; peeling off their clothing, Shahanna seducing him with a light, feathery touch, first here, then there, until desire overcame them both and they clung together in a furious embrace. Then she would give herself to him.

She knew he had a great body, and imagined how he would make love. He might lick gently at her parted thighs; then move a little higher. Just thinking of it, Shahanna felt a wave of passion engulf her. Now she imagined arousing him. Running her fingers down his chest and stomach, lingering around his groin, using her nails to tantalize and inflame him.

Opening her eyes, Shahanna turned to look at him. She did not dare speak. Her voice would be full of desire, and someone might hear. She looked at him in the special way she developed in the camp, her face blank, drinking him in but not letting it show. Now he turned to look at her, and she sensed that he felt her naked lust. That feeling lasted one, fleeting moment. Then the bus slowed and there was a shout from the driver. Using the foul-mouthed cursing of the hills, he swung the wheel hard. Air-brakes hissed, the bus lurched to a stop, and slammed people almost out of their seats. The driver was still cursing, using even more vulgar phrases. His passengers came wide awake and paid attention.

Some laughed at what the man was saying.

He was a hefty looking and tall, and robustly formed for a man in these parts. He leaned to thrust his head out of the window, and insulted the mother of someone standing below.

That someone replied, in a melodic, foreign tongue.

Shahanna sighed.

They had been stopped by the French.

She stood up and called to the driver: "Let me up there. I speak their tongue."

He nodded, pushed a button, and the front doors folded open with a hydraulic gasp. A French paratrooper came aboard. An Armor-Lite machine gun swung from his shoulder, and he wore a pale blue beret. A young Lieutenant, with a clipped moustache and twinkling brown eyes. He looked tall and slender, stooping slightly to come aboard. His armband said: "U. N." in large, white letters.

As if there were any doubt.

The driver ignored him. This Moroccan woman had

volunteered, and the bulky Arab turned to her now, an unspoken question on his face. Shahanna replied with an unspoken answer. The driver shrugged, and passed the Lieutenant to jump off the bus. Shahanna realized he wouldn't be of any further use. He vanished in the dark. She was on her own.

She approached the Frenchman. She thought: What do I do? Deceive him, or give the game away?

It was strange. An American ally, almost a fellow countryman to her, and she had to mislead him, shielding the very terrorists she meant to defeat. Her other option was to blurt out the truth and hope he had enough U. N. Troops to overwhelm three busloads of trained desert fighters. Shahanna seriously doubted that. Besides, arresting Asuto and his people was a short term solution. She had got over her impulse to kill him. The nuclear devices were already on their way to America, and in two months another six teams could be ready. Al Qaeda had unlimited money, and endless volunteers for training. Clement and Hassan had explained all this when General Makhud got shot, asking her to see the big picture, Shahanna had seen it.

The Frenchman looked enquiringly at her. She said, "Bonsoir, M'sieur. Puis je vous aider?"

(Good evening, sir. Can I help you?)

He looked greatly relieved. "Mais, merci, Mademoiselle. Bien sur!"

(Why, thank you, Miss. Most certainly.)

All eyes were on Shahanna. She realized she was now responsible for the lives of everyone; most of all this unwitting French Lieutenant. She took a deep mental breath.

Time for her hard luck story.

Her smile was captivating as she continued in French. "These buses belong to the Swiss Red Cross, and the Egyptian Red Crescent." It was not true, but there was no way to disprove it in the middle of the night. "These refugees are under the protection of both organizations. We have documents if you wish." This was true: Their paperwork came from the most expert forgers.

The Lieutenant waved that off with an airy hand, unwilling to read anything not written in French. He looked up and down the bus, noting the pitiful appearance of almost everyone, seeing that many of them wore bandages, and were groaning in pain. His next words revealed that he had a questioning mind. He said: "Why are so many hurt?"

The perfect question. Shahanna said: "You bombed us by mistake."

Now he looked troubled. "When did this happen?"

"Four nights ago,"

There my sweet little Frenchman. I've played the guilt card. General Makhud was more clever than you. Now you believe you wiped out an innocent village, causing injury and death, and they've been trying for days to get to safety, and you're holding them up. If this didn't work, nothing would.

As long as he didn't wonder about children.

There weren't any.

But the Frenchman was taken in. He asked Shahanna to translate for everyone that the convoy could be on its way. She was thrilled to pass that on, and let it show in her face and in her voice. Then, as the French officer got off and the driver got on, she made her way back to clement, feeling like a conquering hero.

Merde! she thought. I have magical powers!

No search. No close inspection of anyone; no serious interrogation; not even many questions – how on earth had she got away with it? Perhaps the Lieutenant's gratitude because she spoke French. Maybe it was just pure luck. Whatever the reason she hoped she could do it again.

~ ~ ~

They approached the Russian border at first light, after another night on the road. There were towers, floodlights, and serious looking soldiers with fur hats and automatic sub-machine guns.

There was no border control on the Afghan side.

But this was Russia, paranoid and hostile, landmines and barbed wire fencing everywhere. Shahanna's first thought was to tell the driver to go back. But more armed men appeared out of the growing dawn. All three buses were ringed by Red Army troops, attack dogs and clicking rifle bolts.

She fought back a sense of panic.

Then a head passed the bus window, and it was Asuto Kenyatta. He was off the bus, and looked ready for trouble.

"Russia?" asked Clement beside her.

Shahanna was so glad to see him awake. "We'll be lucky if they don't shoot us all," she said.

"Where exactly are we?"

"The crossing point."

"What's going on?"

"I pretty much told you. They're pointing guns at us."

"He looked out of the window and saw what she meant.

She said: "Merde! What a way to start the day."

"It'll be okay." He yawned and stretched his arms.

Shahanna had a sudden, dark premonition that something awful was about to happen, and this seemed just the place for it. "Please don't let us die here," she said.

Clement's eyes said he wouldn't.

They also said he was crazy about her.

He said: "We don't speak Russian, Neither does Asuto. Let him handle it; he can't make things any worse than we would. And he's as tough as they are."

Shahanna managed a smile. "Okay." She looked outside. "He's already talking to them, showing our papers and being the alpha-dog. They're saluting. Somebody high-up in Moscow must know who we are."

"Let's hope so. We don't want to get bogged down here."

Shahanna withdrew inside herself. She shrank into her own world, with her own thoughts, to conquer here fear. After a few minutes the formula seemed to work. Russia was outside, and Clement was inside, with her. Feeling a lot better, she said: "Wake me when it's over." Then she tried to sleep.

It was not to be.

She heard the doors open. The driver said something or other.

The reply was harsh and impatient.

Booted feet stomped onto the bus.

This was not a kindly French Lieutenant.

Shahanna opened her eyes to look. There were four of them, guns at the ready, as threatening as that Frenchman had been charming, and completely on edge, whereas he had been calm. They wore fur hats. They looked trigger-happy. They were young, scruffy looking, and they moved like street bullies, with a false swagger. The first one was already halfway down the aisle.

All their eyes were on Clement.

"*Stoi!*"

(Halt!)

It was a Russian officer, thank God, framed in the door. His fur hat was flecked with a gray that looked like wolf. An animal he resembled himself, with his stubble of a beard, and narrow, slanting blue eyes. The butt of an unlit cheroot protruded from one corner of his mouth.

He was a Major, and he, too, was looking at Clement.

He spoke rapid-fire Russian, and his men turned and withdrew. He let them off the bus, then came down the aisle himself. He was an extremely tall man, and had to hunch down, in order to maneuver.

With no hesitation he approached Clement and stopped in front of him. He said in passable English: "You are the American."

It was not a question.

Shahanna said: "He's a refugee. We all are."

The Major ignored that. "The rest of you are cleared for entry into our country. But this man . . . we have small . . . problem. This man goes with me."

"No!" Shahanna was beset by terror. If they took Clement, she'd never see him again. She grabbed his arm, willing him not to move. She wanted to smother him with kisses, to promise him that everything was alright, because this was just a dream. But Shahanna did none of these things, because Clement gently removed her hand from his arm and stood up. Then, moving quickly, he was past her and followed the crouching Major outside. Neither man looked back.

~ ~ ~

Clement felt strange, not sure why he stood up or why he was leaving the safety of the bus. As they both got off, the Russian Major turned and the eyes of the two men met. Something passed between them. Actually more of a feeling than a look, but Clement suddenly felt safer and more secure. Like being protected by a friend. It was almost as if he knew this Russian Major.

~ ~ ~

The Russian Major was Gabriel. His premonition of Clement's imprisonment and torture had returned, more frequent and stronger since General Makhud's three buses came within sight of the former Soviet border. It was here that Clement would suffer and possibly die. Gabriel sensed Prince Kamal's hand in this: His jealousy and resentment of Clement had been undeniable, especially when it came to "Sorya". That much was clear to Gabriel. Most likely Asuto Kenyatta had been given special instructions. Clement was to be handed over to Russia, who would give him back to Afghanistan, where he could be executed for espionage. This was how things were done in this region. Therefore Gabriel had become a wolfish looking Russian Major.

And got Clement out of there.

A residual image of Hassan, asleep on the third bus, had been left behind to cover Gabriel's absence. Right now that bus was being boarded by Russian soldiers, most of whom needed a bath.

Gabriel and Clement were by now a safe distance away, fast approaching the border crossing. The angel turned to Clement as they walked. In English that was suddenly flawless, he said casually, "Heathcote says hello."

Clement was completely taken aback. "Jesus! This is dangerous!"

"Not for you. Not anymore."

Clement thought a moment. "You mean there was danger, but you've got me out of it. How does Heathcote know our route? Oh, wait – the satellite."

No, Heathcote played no part, thought Gabriel. Just as well, because the satellite had missed all three buses, two dawns in a row. His brother Michael had said so after a quick trip to Alexandria.

Aloud, Gabriel said: "My regiment mans this checkpoint. I will take you across. You can rejoin your friends on the other side." It was, of course, not Gabriel's regiment, but everyone in it would think so, by the time he reached the red and white poles of the frontier station.

He felt Clement's confusion and fear. It could not be helped. The appalling vision of beatings and broken bones must not come true. What Prince Kamal did to Shahanna was bad enough.

Gabriel would not be that careless again.

They entered the arc-lights, approaching the steel and armored glass of a guard hut, and more men in uniform coats and fur hats. These were not young, but they could have done with a wash.

Gabriel said: "This is it."

"What do we do?"

"You, nothing. Wait here."

Gabriel strode forward, making his face a sinister mask. His latest version of a Russian officer was hard bitten and mean – calculated to intimidate years of training and discipline out of these men. A wolf[s smile, turning to an angry snarl when needed, should go a long way.

Sarcasm, obscenities and threats would do the rest.

They saw him and lined up outside, adjusting uniform and equipment. The wolf closed in for the kill. Gabriel walked behind them, dissatisfied with one man's shoulder patches, and the webbing belt of another.

They stared straight ahead.

"Which of you dogs is in charge?" asked Gabriel. He came around to face them from the front.

"I am, Major."

Gabriel planted himself in front of the speaker.

"Name and rank, you filthy pig."

"Corporal Urakin." The man's gaze was steady. He had the high, pronounced cheekbones and dark eyes of a Cossack, undeniable – even with his hair cropped, no beard – and here, far from his grassy steppes. His expression said, Think you're a hot shot? I don't

"Listen to me, Urakin," said Gabriel. "I'm the devil, and I'll make you drink your own piss."

Gabriel spat, and the man looked away.

Russians believe in the devil just as they believe in God. Gabriel could see that the Cossack was afraid. In Urakin's home village, if anyone said he was the evil one, he was believed and ostracized, possibly attacked and killed. Now the corporal changed his tone. "May I ask, sir, what does the Major require?"

Gabriel gestured toward Clement, a few feet away. "That bus passenger works secretly for Mother Russia. I need his verbal report. That will take a while. The others suspect nothing, because I arrested him. You will search each bus thoroughly and take your time. Take care not to find anything; they're cleared by Moscow. There will be no violence, damage, or anything like that. Just make it look good, and make it last. Is that clear?"

"Yes, Major." Urakin stamped his feet and turned to his men. He became a different man. A model soldier. He took a deep breath, and barked at the others: "You heard the Commander! Shape up, and do as he says!"

They slammed their feet together.

The buses would be here for hours.

Gabriel could live with that. It was the price of having Clement safely in Russia. Whatever might have happened with the juvenile-delinquent soldiers who boarded the first bus had been avoided. Gabriel was in no hurry.

Minutes later, the Russian Major led Clement under the raised pole dividing two countries and two cultures, while Corporal Urakin and his squad moved off, stone-faced, in the direction of the buses from Afghanistan. They marched in perfect step. They had their orders, and they would follow them.

CHAPTER SIXTEEN

ON THE LARGEST MAP adorning Heathcote's wall, two dissecting red lines divided the Pacific and Atlantic, and all the oceans in between. One struck down through the South China Sea and japan, cutting Australia in half. A second line ran left to right; below the Gulf of Mexico, Europe, Africa, India and China, cutting the world in half. Everything east of Sicily was by now disregarded, due to the time lost. It was less effective to chase a ship from behind – in the direction it was going. The best chance was to come at it head on, so Heathcote's search was taking place mainly from West to East, with a little North to South thrown in. By this method, he should avoid missing the two Korean freighters altogether.

But he needed a sighting quickly.

Even as he sat, willing the map to save him, his mind was on other, more pressing matters. He recalled Henry Archer's advice: Find those fleeing buses within twenty-four hours, or forget them and switch to staking-out Moscow.

And forty-eight hours had come and gone.

The satellite had failed to find that convoy.

Heathcote couldn't delay any longer.

He remembered something else Henry Archer said: The six teams would probably make Moscow sometime this week. Heathcote had little time to get his watchers in place. His European move, while costly in funds and personnel, must be made now. It involved a huge operation. Every available agent must be sent; not only to

Moscow, but every city in Europe with flights to and from America or Russia. An expensive gamble, in money and FBI agents, and it had to pay off.Otherwise the game was over.

Heathcote had about five hundred men and women in reserve, and hoped it was enough. They were young and inexperienced for the most part. And his old-timers were hardly top drawer. Still, they were what he had, and it was time to send them in. Every agent had satellite shots of the terrorists – including the three working undercover for Heathcote. His surveillance teams would watch every European arrival gate, and check every passenger, especially those traveling in airline uniform from Moscow, where some of Heathcote's watchers should have spotted them first.

Determined to ignore the terrible odds against him, Heathcote began yet another round of phone calls.

And missed yet another lunch.

~ ~ ~

The search at the Russian frontier lasted four hours.

A Russian named Janko Petrovich introduced himself to Asuto Kenyatta while their luggage was being reloaded onto the buses.

He was very tall, and looked a little like Hassan.

And a little like a wolf.

His first name, he said, was pronounced Yanko.

They shook hands, and Petrovich said: "We'll soon get you going again. My job is to smooth the way to Moscow."

"Praise Allah," said the African. "Someone who speaks English. One of my men was taken into custody. Can you get him released?"

Petrovich nodded reassuringly, and smiled as if this

problem were already solved. He said: "Robert Henry Keller, United States citizen, is waiting for you on the other side. He has been questioned, found blameless, and allowed to go. I paid a small fee, of course. That's how it's done here."

Gabriel suspected that protecting Clement here at the border was not enough. To avoid further incident, he would escort Asuto's assortment of monsters all the way to the Russian capital. Trouble seemed to find Clement, and that brush with the border guards was just another example. Gabriel's Russian Major had fixed that problem – but similar problems were certain to follow.

Janko Petrovich was the answer.

The last suitcases and packages were stuffed into the luggage space of the three buses. Asuto shouted for everyone to get back on board, seeming much relieved by the presence of Janko Petrovich. Gabriel smiled, knowing the African vaguely remembered hiring a Russian guide, although the details somehow escaped him. Hassan was erased from Asuto's mind, and everyone else's, including the angel's three special charges who belonged to Heathcote. Hassan would return, just as before, once they reached Moscow with Clement still in one piece.

Minutes later the buses pulled onto the main highway to Moscow. One look at the sign showing the kilometers to MOCKBA – Moscow in the Russian alphabet – said that it was too far for a bus – even one in good condition, which these were not. Then Asuto announced that they would soon transfer to a train. The journey would still take three days, two of them crossing a part of Russia every bit as primitive as Afghanistan. For Gabriel it meant three days of much needed rest. Three days restoring his power, just when he was most likely to need it. But the seats in these buses consisted of hard planks that had long ago replaced the original upholstery, and Gabriel, sitting next to Asuto Kenyatta, hoped the railway was not much further.

Asuto said: "Thank you for returning our Mr. Keller. You must have very good connections."

Gabriel shrugged. "People I work for have connections."

Kenyatta's respect showed on his face. He assumed Petrovich was Russian Mafia, just as Gabriel knew he would.

Soon the buses bumped over rusted iron tracks embedded in the highway. Shortly after that they turned and took a side road. Then they bumped along some more, and came to a stop. The name of the station, a railroad siding really, was a mouthful, even if you spoke Russian. Gabriel doubted if anyone who didn't live nearby had even heard of the place. Prince Kamal had stuck his pin in a very empty portion of the map. He found the original nowhere.

Then they saw the train.

It was something out of Doctor Zhivago.

Asuto took one look at it and said: "Allah save us all."

"Indeed," said Janko Petrovich.

They studied the carriages, for want of a better word, although 'cattle cars' would have done just as well.

Kenyatta slid open a plank door and shouted, "Come on!"

More doors slid back.

A dreadful stench came from the straw-covered floors.

Prince Kamal had stiffed them again.

Kenyatta sent for Clement and Petrovich. He said, "I

want you two with me at all times. If anything goes wrong, you, Mr. Petrovich, will advise me and make the problem go away. We will certainly need to bribe officials of one kind or another. I expect you to handle that. As for you, Mr. Keller, you get arrested too often. I want you with me just in case."

Both men agreed.

All three entered the musty carriage and sat in line on a flimsy, sacking-covered bench seat. Others, behind them on the mud-cake of a platform, clambered aboard and came to sit opposite. They were soon rolling through a countryside so vast that it seemed to have no horizon. Occasional peasants appeared and disappeared, as they plowed the sweeping expanse of rock-strewn earth. They were all that moved on the unrelenting emptiness of the Russian Steppe.

Kenyatta began to nod off, his chin tucked into his chest. But before he did so, he said, "Wake me if anything happens. I'm a light sleeper."

It was not true; at least not today. He snored, and could not be diverted from it. Nor could he be woken up. Most snoring follows a certain rhythm, to which others can adjust. Not so Asuto Kenyatta. He stopped at odd intervals, and spluttered and changed tempo, often with a disturbing rasp at the back of his throat. His companions tried hard to ignore it. Clement had once read that snoring was a sign of unhappiness. He decided the African lived in a private hell – and next to him, in the form of Janko Petrovich, the Angel Gabriel was thinking the same thing.

Clement saw only one solution.

He moved to the end of the car.

Petrovich and the others soon followed.

~ ~ ~

Lucifer was out shopping for real estate in New Jersey.

Trump Tower overflowed with demons, making his penthouse there less desirable, and his nearby brownstone was also losing its appeal. Both were high-maintenance and expensive, and the parks and streets were plagued by homeless people and petty crime, ruining what was once an exclusive and secluded part of Manhattan. The devil had had enough. This morning, after breakfast, he sent for the Rolls and ordered his driver over the Marazano Bridge and out of New York.

Lucifer liked the countryside. A home out here would be relaxing, and protect him from unwelcome visitors. It was unlikely the homeless would be found in any significant number. And there was something else: Hordes of angels had recently been staking-out his Town house, in the air and in the trees and on the ground. Some were even posing as the homeless he so reviled. Their goodness polluted the very air he breathed. He hoped moving away would deter them. If it didn't, a legion of demons could be unleashed into the rural quiet of New Jersey. Lucifer couldn't do that where he lived now. And his two hell-spawned gargoyles were no longer enough. In any case an unearthly battle for Park West or Rockefeller Plaza was out of the question.

Too many people about.

The devil consulted his realty list. Their first stop was the large, vacant estate of an ex-champion boxer, whose hangers-on milked him for seventy million dollars and left him with nothing but an unpaid mortgage. Lucifer smiled with satisfaction. He knew the fighter's manager, and his promoter, and all their dirty secrets. Evidence of wrongdoing existed; much of it involving mismanagement of this boxer. The Promoter had a lien on the estate that amounted to an illegal conflict of interest, because the boxer had declared bankruptcy on this man's advice, and could sell only with his permission. That was fraud and double dealing. People regularly went to jail for less. And Century News could make enough fuss to get the promoter an extended sentence. The man's legal advisers would be aware of that, when it was revealed that Lucifer had it all documented. That would bring the price down nicely.

The Rolls arrived, after a leisurely drive on country roads, the last few empty of traffic altogether.

The elegant car made virtually no sound as it slowed to go under a stone archway; then it glided past well-tended lawns dotted with statues, rose trees and ornamental ponds with gushing fountains.

The outside of the house was garish and ostentatious, so was the inside. Everything would have to be gutted and redone. The swimming pool was worse: built in the form of a boxing-glove, and painted black and gold. Lucifer was hugely disappointed. He was soon shaking the hand of a pretty sales-representative and taking her card, but he had already crossed the house off his list. Renovations would cost a small fortune. No matter how low the asking price.

He almost bought the next property on sight.

It was surrounded by forty acres of woodland, and a lake clear enough to see its salmon, dappled in sunlight, as they basked around the smooth rounded rocks forming the shallows. Lucifer liked fishing, and this was far more convenient than his over-sized fishing yacht, putting to sea twice a year if he was lucky, at an expense that boggled the mind. Out here, with his own private nursery, he could catch breakfast, lunch or dinner every day if he wished. All for the price of a few worms, or whatever it was that salmon ate.

It also had an empty stable and a paddock: Enough room and board for a dozen horses. The young man Lucifer was about to become was an accomplished rider already. This got better and better. The swimming pool was encased in glass, with a profusion of palm trees, tropical flowers of every variety, and dozens of rare, exotic birds. It was also in an acceptable greenish blue.

Then there was the house itself. It was a three-story, modernized Elizabethan mansion. Some sixty rooms were restored to their original condition, but with heating and plumbing brought up to date. The entire house was a step into history. The devil talked to the owner and the owner's authorized agent. They offered him first refusal for a period of three months. He agreed, but didn't ask the price. He didn't have to. It would be like buying Buckingham Palace, the Tower of London and the Crown Jewels. But Lucifer had to have it, and that was all that mattered.

He would still visit the other real estate listings, but this was the one. The devil could continue to rule America, from here; at least for whatever time America and its citizens had left.

Prophecy held that there was to be a final conflict between Lucifer and Gabriel, with the forces of angels and demons tearing at one another in blind fury. Lucifer was sure he could win, given this as the battlefield.

Deciding to buy made time less important. Now he could break for lunch.

He told his driver where to go.

It was in the hills that passed for mountains here, close to the Pennsylvania State line. They parked in front of leaded bay windows and ivy-covered walls. The Inn was called Ye Olde Coachman, and built shortly after the house Lucifer liked so much. His driver ate hot-dogs in the car, while Lucifer enjoyed lobster bisque and a roast Cornish Game Hen inside. He ate it all with his customary Burgundy, followed by Cognac and a cigar. The staff fawned on him, while the manager asked several times if everything was satisfactory. Lucifer finally sent him away. Then, in a fit of mean spiritedness, the devil left an insulting tip.

Lucifer viewed millionaire residences all afternoon. Nothing matched up to the one with the lake and stables. He could have made a deal for it on the spot, but delay worked in his favor, and was, in fact, essential. In three months, Lucifer would make a bid for the property that no one else in the Tri-State area could possibly afford, but by that time, the devil would be him in a brand-new, younger man's body, with much of America blown to pieces by Al Qaeda and the Free Patriot Militia.

Then Gabriel could bring it on.

Lucifer told his driver to take him home.

As the Rolls paused before Lucifer's wrought iron gates, the car's custom-installed phone rang, and when he answered, a voice said, "This is Dietrich."

Lucifer had forgotten their appointment. This was a demon indeed. One time head of Century Tower security, the Horseman of War throughout the centuries. That was why he now commanded the Free Patriot Militia. Lucifer's secret paramilitary army was soon to play a part in the end of the world.

The devils said: "Where are you?"

"In your suite at Century Tower?"

Lucifer had the driver turn around, The Rolls made a dignified U-turn, and was soon speeding through the garment district. They got to the Century building in a few minutes. It was towering, hence the name, and clad completely with mirrored glass. The Rolls dropped Lucifer at the steps to the main entrance.

Dietrich was waiting in the executive suite, drinking Lucifer's favorite single malt with his feet up on the desk.

The devil said, "Make yourself at home."

The feet swung onto the floor, and Dietrich vacated Lucifer's chair. He knew just where the line was, and took pleasure in never quite crossing it. Dietrich also knew how dangerous Lucifer was, having witnessed punishment more grisly than that visited upon Kathy Lester. Dietrich had often carried out such crimes on Lucifer's direct order. This made Dietrich valuable, but the devil always made it clear that this could change at any time.

Lucifer's Horseman of War was last of the Apocalyptic four. The other three were dead, slaughtered in the last high-level skirmish with Gabriel. Both the devil and Dietrich were lucky to survive.

Nick-named the Lizard, Dietrich looked grotesquely malevolent in human form. His appearance was recently altered to protect him from the Angel Gabriel. Of course it didn't work, but this demon who once looked like a brutish ex-Nazi with sandy hair was now a brutish Latino, with reptilian eyes and swarthy features, his hair slicked-back in a gleaming black pony tail. His suits were always expensive, mostly imported silk. He was wearing one now; it was double breasted. had a silvery sheen, and a ten thousand dollar price tag.

He said: "You're scotch is excellent."

It was another attempt to bait Lucifer; they both knew Dietrich couldn't resist it. The two of them had been sparring this way since Lucifer called this demon forth from the dark side, when time began. The strife between them was eternal, and in his twisted way the devil enjoyed it.

They both sat down, Lucifer at his desk and his visitor opposite him in a black, calfskin swivel-chair. The devil poured himself a large slug of whiskey, saying: "I hope your Neo-Nazis are ready." At the same time, as so often before, he silently vowed that Dietrich would pay for his insolence.

"They're always ready, Said Dietrich. "Just say where to send them, and what they have to do."

Lucifer knew this was no empty promise. Dietrich could deliver twenty thousand armed men, equipped with tanks and howitzers, and deliver them just like that, with no advanced notice. Telling him in advance was Lucifer's way of insulting him, as payment for those feet on the desk, and stealing forbidden scotch.

The devil said: "I need two hundred men at a hundred airports, on a given date."

Dietrich didn't blink. "And the date?"

"Third of July. The eve of America's birthday."

"That can be done. Are you ready to bankroll their travel and expenses for three days, because that's how long it will take to get them in position, and then I have to pay them. They won't fight for free." It did not escape Lucifer that Dietrich was saying this about those claiming to be die-hard patriots.

Lucifer lit a cigar and slid the box across to Dietrich. They were Cuban – best quality, from the devil's private stock. Fidel Castro, until he died, had been a favored vassal. The devil said, "Money's never an issue. You know that, so name a figure. Just make sure they're all in place on time."

Dietrich selected a cigar while he did the math. "Thirty million, possibly more. I'll have an exact price by next week."

"Thirty Million?"

"I wouldn't cheat you."

Of course he would.

The devil said: "I know that, but thirty million seems low, even to me, and you still don't know what I want them to do. How can you quote so low – without asking a single question? Have you become psychic?"

"No. I know how you operate. One hundred airports, on one specific day? That means a concentrated attack on America. Most of my men are going to die, possibly all of them. Either way I keep the money. Survivors won't come after me for payment. They'll be on the run."

"I forgot how clever you are."

Dietrich looked pleased with himself, and made a concession without being told, He said: "I'll use crack troops – no rookies, no weirdos – no one with a criminal record. That improves their chance of getting where they're going. We don't want someone recognized and stopped by the cops. That would wreck everything."

Dietrich had made no attempt to light his cigar, and Lucifer, having never offered him one before, knew why: The demon was suspicion, fearing poison. Lucifer lit one just like it, and said: "Why kill you now, when I need you most?"

That was good enough for Dietrich. He picked up the cigar and used a match from a box on the devil's desk. Today he was safe, But they both knew the devil might well get rid of him in the future.

Dietrich said: "What happens at a hundred airports?"

The devil said: "Bombard everything with artillery, then storm whatever aircraft and public buildings remain standing. Kill everyone in sight. It's a diversion to protect something scheduled the next day. Both events, staged so close together, will disrupt the whole country. Lucifer paused, trying to remember something else. "Oh, yes. All rental cars to be shelled in their parking lots. Those vehicles are a chunk of the US economy. Let it be the day of the exploding gas tank."

"Dietrich said, "Possibly ten million cars. I look forward to seeing that."

Lucifer reached into a drawer, removed a foolscap folder, and handed it across the desk. The Lizard opened it, and two sheets of typing slid into his hand. "Two lists," said Lucifer. "One names the airports to attack. The second page lists six airports you leave alone. They get it on Independence Day – from somebody else."

"Somebody else. Who?"

"Muslims."

"Arabs?"

Lucifer became impatient. "Of course Arabs. Who else would carry out nuclear strikes against America?"

Dietrich laughed. "Any number of countries, if they thought they could get away with it."

Lucifer was forced to smile. "True – but fortunately for us, these Muslims don't care if they get away with it."

"Why are you doing this? It won't destroy the world."

"America is the world. It's economic structure will be destroyed, and its financial base gone. Global banks, from London to Tokyo, will fail. Two towers explode on Wall Street – and the US economy is crippled, and takes a decade to recover. This will be far worse."

Dietrich was impressed. "You *are* destroying the world."

It was Lucifer's turn to laugh. "America will be like Germany in 1945. Everything important will be gone. This country is too big to operate with road and rail. Besides, they haven't developed either one. Highways and bridges collapse, trains move at a snail pace, and their oil supply will be cut off. The Saudi King will pull the plug. So will all the others. Plenty of new customers in Europe and Asia, whose economies will recover with the United States out of the picture. It's all agreed in advance. What would America use for fuel? That sandy crap they get from shale?"

"Then how is the rest of the world destroyed?"

"Oh, I give Europe and China ten years, once I start on them."

"How's that?"

The devil thought how wonderful it would be to have a young, strong body again, buying homes in various parts of the world, as he had in centuries past. The mansion in New Jersey was only part of his plan. Bruno Schwenk died leaving two beautiful houses in the Austrian alps, and the devil had representatives scouting for places in the coastal regions of Southern India.

"I'll relocate," he said blithely.

He rose and walked across to a panoramic window,

turning his back to look out at New York's boxy skyline.

Dietrich saw that the meeting was at an end. He got up and left, taking his cigar with him. His future, listening to Lucifer, had just become rather misty. On the street outside, waiting for a cab, Dietrich knew only one thing:

He was going to make war on America.

~ ~ ~

This Petrovich is good," announced Asuto Kenyatta. "People can't do enough to please him." He was speaking to Shahanna, and they were stopped at a run-down fuel depot, where the train's coal and water were being replenished.

He stood with Sorya on another flattened mound of earth functioning as a railroad platform. "The Russian Mafia has a long arm. The station master bowed when he spoke to him, and shopkeepers acted the same way, when he took me to get food for everyone. Petrovich is like a king."

"The food was good," said Sorya.

"I refused the pork."

"I'd have eaten anything but lamb. Or yellow rice."

Kenyatta frowned. "You trouble me," he said. He gave her a pious look. "Such meat is unclean."

"I like bacon – crispy, American style."

"Yes, that is what troubles me."

"You allow Hasheesh," Sorya's chin jutted defiantly. "You let others drink vodka, or whisky. Robb Keller eats hamburger, the filthiest of meats, but you don't rebuke him. You bully me for being a woman. Don't deny it, it's true – a five thousand year tradition. You're taught to treat us badly, and you do."

Asuto sighed. He refused to argue. Women were

inferior, with wickedness in their souls. So was it written. It was as simple as that. How dare Sorya speak this way to him? Perhaps he should beat her.

She said: "This Russian and Robb Keller can do no wrong in your eyes – because they're men."

Kenyatta decided to shut her up. "You are treated just like a man, Sorya. You are on this mission, because Prince Kamal picked you over many others, mostly men. Soon you will die like a man, when we strike, but the whole world will know you're a woman. What more do you want?"

"Information."

"What do you mean?" This sudden change of direction took him by surprise.

He saw she was ready to pounce. She said: "Tell me where I'm going. France or somewhere else? My uniform is French. And where are the others going?" Shahanna fixed him with a defiant stare.

Asuto was taken aback. She did not fear him, although he had power of life or death over her. That much was clear. He wondered if Sorya was the spy Prince Kamal believed to be among them. It seemed very possible. She turned up out of the blue with an American lover. Prince Kamal had accepted her out of pure lust. And if Sorya was a spy, so was Rob Keller. Kenyatta knew it didn't really matter. There was no means of communication between here and Moscow. Any spy had no access to radio or telephone. Or any way to send a message to anyone. After that Sorya would be on a plane. She was to be killed during the flight by two women on her team, together with Keller, on orders from Prince Kamal before his death. Failing that Sorya and Rob Keller would die in a nuclear blast.

Along with Asuto and millions of Americans.

Based on this logic, Kenyatta decided to tell her what she wanted to know. He said she was going to Frankfurt.

He refused to say anything else.

CHAPTER SEVENTEEN

THE MESSAGE, MARKED TOP SECRET, was placed on Heathcote's desk by courier three days later. It was from Hassan. They were in Moscow. Hassan was a team leader, and his team, including Clement, Shahanna and Jhalal, would be flying into Frankfurt within twenty-four hours. Heathcote's war machine, on both sides of the Atlantic went into action.

In Russia, Prince Kamal's machine was ready for anything.

~ ~ ~

Shahanna was excited to be in Moscow. Their hotel was somehow linked with Tolstoy, and named for him, but the desk clerk spoke no English, and Petrovich, who might have explained, was suddenly gone. This meant Shahanna would never hear the story of the famous Russian writer and this grimy hotel tucked away on a narrow side street. All the same, the sense of history was overwhelming.

This was the Russia of the Tsars; of Lenin and of Stalin. This city had defeated Napoleon. A city of composers, painters and ballet dancers. The first city where Hitler's armies faltered, beaten off by men and women with picks and shovels, who leaped out of hastily dug trenches with their children at their feet – and fought against German tanks. And they won. The Panzer generals retreated and went around them, and Moscow was saved.

This was a city of women. They suffered all its wars, nursing it back to life when war ended, their men mostly dead, lost fighting at the front. It fell to women to rebuild, to run the factories and workplaces, to clear away the rubble from the bombing, and drive tractors on the farms. Russian women, like others across Europe, raised their children in craters in the ground that used to be their homes. Many lived from the black market, or sold their bodies for food. Shahanna admired them, and identified with them. This was their city. She would have been shocked to hear that German and Austrian women, like the mother of Bruno Schwenk, did the same. The tutors at Shahanna's expensive French college had not concerned themselves with German suffering. The war was Germany's fault.Shahanna just wanted to drink in Moscow. She stood at a window, from where she could glimpse Gorky Park, dotted with people strolling idly in their summer clothes. The Russian capital was city of legends, of myths, and of dreams and disappointments. Hitler came close to destroying it, Communism came even closer, and now it was the oligarchs who abused their wealth and power.

But Moscow was still here.

Populated by thinkers aware of their inherent freedom.

And the wisdom of their history.

Immediately below Shahanna's window, the lanes of traffic seemed constantly at a standstill. Car ownership had exploded along with overpopulation of the Russian capital. A succession of politicians and police chiefs had failed to resolve this, or to rid themselves of Moscow's new elite: An underworld of cocaine-dealing gangsters, immune to law and order, utterly ruthless and feared. They routinely killed anyone in their way. The thought of this reminded Shahanna of Janko Petrovich. She wondered where he went. Asuto and Clement said he was Russian Mafia. He vanished shortly after arrival in Moscow, so she decided they were probably right.

Hassan helped her from the train in Moscow's main station, although she couldn't recall seeing him for days. It had been a happy reunion. Hassan was always a comforting presence. She felt somehow safer with him around.

Shahanna was the only one with a room to herself, an unexpected kindness from Asuto that she failed to understand. The rest of her team were sharing rooms, with some sleeping on the floor. Other teams were in other hotels. And somewhere across town, in yet another hotel, one with five stars and a page in the guide book, was Asuto Kenyatta himself.

She hoped he'd stay there.

She decided to try on her airline uniform, which was waiting on her bed when she arrived. It fitted well, so perfectly creased that she took it off again, to keep it that way. Then she took a bath because there was no shower. The Soviet Union had not built them into hotels of this vintage. As she soaked her thoughts drifted to the five others down the hall. Her whole team was on this floor. There were three she knew well, Asuto having put her on Hassan's team with Clement and Jhalal. The rest were fanatical Jihadis she knew only by sight, or from Prince Kamal's files.

Shahanna stepped out of the tub and dried off with a towel. Her hair was wet, and she left it loose, to dry. Then she changed back into her jeans, which she'd washed in the bath and hung outside on the balcony. She did not put on a bra. Only one had survived the desert, and that was reserved for her Air France uniform. She smiled at the thought that she would soon be back in America, then the smile faded as she remembered why she was going.

She left her room once her hair had dried. Her stomach demanded food. The train made no stops today, and there had been nothing to eat. Shahanna guessed everybody else was as hungry as her. She went down the hall to see what the others had to say. There was no Yellow Pages in her room, and she doubted Russians had such a thing. Hassan always seemed to find his way around in strange places, almost as if he'd been there before. She would try him first.

She knocked on his door. Clement let her in, and she didn't dare show how pleased she was to see him. No one seemed to be watching, but she had got used to being careful. Sure enough, inside, sitting on a couch, were a man and woman she didn't know. Men are easy enough to fool, but females are another matter. A woman can spot sexual attraction a mile away. Shahanna wished she could warn Clement, who looked at her with adoration, but even a whisper might alert this mystery woman. Shahanna shot Clement a venomous look instead.

Clement got the message, and she marched right past him.

Hassan was watching Russian television. Shahanna asked herself why. Surely he didn't understand it. Then it dawned on her: Maybe he did, and had decided to keep it from Asuto and Petrovich. Why not? He spoke English, and several Arab dialects, and once, when Shahanna forgot herself and called the Prince something vulgar in French, Hassan had laughed. There seemed to be more to this good-natured Iraqi than met the eye.

He saw her and came to his feet, greeting her warmly and inviting her to sit with him. She took the chair next to his. She explained why she had come, and suggested that as this hotel had no restaurant, not even a bar, they all go out together and find a place that looked good. Shahanna realized as she spoke that she was just dying to try Russian cooking.

She felt upbeat and curious. He was a chance to do something exciting, instead of skulking around, completely on edge about being a spy and a terrorist, with enemies on all side. Shahanna was in the mood to shop for slinky clothes, go dancing with Clement and take him back to her room under everyone's nose.

A good meal out would be a good start.

And if the whole team, Hassan's was the standard twelve, went out to eat tonight, she and Clement would get a good look at them, and if Hassan was on form, they could get a message to Heathcote. At least a list of names going to Frankfurt. That, and a chance to be with Clement, made the prospect of an evening with a bunch of fanatics and sickos easier to take.

She and Hassan went room to room, inviting suggestions, and any hope of eating local cuisine soon evaporated. Nobody wanted Russian food, or anything Russian at all. They wanted the kind of food they were used to – and some of them complained about having to go out and get it.

Hassan found a nightclub that served dinner. It was Turkish-owned; all silks and expensive rugs. Its belly dancers were visibly nubile young things, flirting with the male guests, and they were doubtless for hire. The atmosphere seemed authentic, as Hassan's people filed in.

A band played drums, flutes and tambourines in a corner, and a buxom lady in chiffon was slithering her way across an embroidered carpet.

Several tables were moved together to accommodate Hassan's unexpectedly large party.

A handsome young Turk brought menus. "Good evening. Welcome to Ali Baba's." he said, in the soft speech of Istanbul.

Before anyone else could respond, a rat-faced terrorist called Nazir snapped his fingers. "Bring some wine, and tea – and send some of those girls over. Do you have any vodka?"

"This is a God-fearing house. We don't serve alcohol, and our girls come only if they choose." The waiter looked affronted. Everyone knew that not serving alcohol was just a lie to put Nazir in his place.

Hassan said: "Just bring tea. And advise me what dishes to order. The recipes you are famed for. Your reputation brought me here."

That settled it for the whole team. Hassan had all the money.

The waiter was charmed. "We offer figs, dates and olives to begin, at no charge. I will bring it myself."

"Perfect. Everyone is very hungry," Hassan said. He slipped a hundred dollar bill into the waiter's hand.

"Coming right away, sir." The young man hurried off.

Hassan looked at Nazir. The offender looked down, absorbed with the whiteness of the table cloth, and nervously crumpling his napkin. But before Hassan could speak, the waiter was back with a large tray. "This is curd soup, our cook's own recipe." He set it down in the midst of them. "Also complimentary. The dried fruit and olives are on the way."

"You are most kind," said Hassan.

The waiter bowed and left. Shahanna handed out bowls of soup; then she tried her own. It was good, tasting strongly of cumin, onions and garlic – with flakes of chicken for flavor. Gleaming, yellow pools of oil floated on top, and the curd was mixed with yogurt, giving it a rich, creamy texture. A plate of Pita bread came, and everyone began tearing off chunks for dipping. The menus still lay untouched, Hassan told the waiter to serve whatever he liked – except for lamb.

Then, very sparingly, he sipped at his soup,

The man next to Shahanna introduced himself as Ishmael Mansou. Despite his dark hair and skin, he looked more European than Arab, and he spoke German, which was why he was bound for Frankfurt. He soon began talking about duty to the sacred Islamic cause, avoiding sensitive detail but revealing perfect teeth every time he opened his mouth. Ishmael had spent time in America. Shahanna knew that from his file. Some aspects of life there had clearly appealed to him. His smile was a perfect example of the Hollywood style of dental-work. Yet the day after tomorrow, Ishmael would assist in the killing of thousands of innocent Americans, he and his gleaming smile melting with them in a searing blast ten miles wide.

Shahanna found him revolting. He grew up among the Tuareg, a tribe of roaming, warlike nomads who traditionally herded their massive flocks across a thousand square miles burning sand. They raided other tribes and caravans foolish enough to cross their part of the Sahara. Ishmael was just as deadly with bow or rifle, on horseback or on foot. At Prince Kamal's first camp, Ishmael had stabbed a man during a practice knife fight, blaming his victim for being too slow.

The Prince had agreed.

The man died two days later.

Henceforth Ishmael became the Prince's executioner, hacking off heads for display on stakes, or setting fire to victims of the Prince's disapproval, lighting up the night and filling the campsite with their screams. Among those in the training camp, Ishmael was hated and feared.

A woman opposite him spoke next. She was the woman from an hour ago, sitting on Hassan's couch. "We have not met, Sorya," she said. "My name is Ashirad." Her voice was cold and menacing, her eyes hostile.

Shahanna knew the name; not the face. Now she put them together. Ashirad's file had described a crazed vixen devoted to Islam, cruel and clever, a killer who used a knife to the stomach, looking into her victim's eyes as they died. Shahanna could hardly bring herself to look at Ashirad. She was small-built to be so deadly, but you sensed it in her, even here at dinner.

Shahanna reached across to shake her hand. "I know your reputation," she said. "I'm proud to meet you."

Her hand was ignored. Ashirad pulled a face. "I'm sick of all the waiting. I'm sick of Iran and Afghanistan, and now this God-cursed place. I'm sick of foreigners and their putrid food and the way they look at us. Thank God we're eating here tonight, and not some Russian flea-pit, with beets and cabbage and smelly waitresses. I hate everything about this country."

Shahanna had discretely withdrawn her hand. "Don't worry. We'll soon be out of here, and flying West to our take-off point."

"Do you know where that is?"

This could be a trap. Asuto Kenyatta may have ordered this woman to ask exactly that question. Shahanna said: "No, not yet." Apparently, it was still not generally known that this team was flying to America from Germany.

Ashirad looked even more discontented. She turned to Hassan. "You're our team leader. Asuto must have told you."

"Of course he did." Hassan's annoyance showed in his face. Everyone at the table paid attention. Not only was Ashirad breaking security, her rudeness insulted Hassan to his face. They wondered how he would react.

"And will you tell me?" she said aggressively.

"Not yet." His tone was measured, but still dismissive enough to tell Ashirad not to ask again.

She looked ready to argue, but common sense made her concentrate on her soup. Shahanna reached for some salt, and looked around the table until she spotted the only other woman in their group.

Shahanna remembered this one's record and knew her by sight. Mahata was good to look at, and getting attention from the men. A slim Somali woman in her late twenties, with high cheekbones and the eyes of a cat. Her hair was cut close to the head, her skin gleaming and dark. Mahata could not pass for European, even if she spoke German or French, which she did not. This woman was as African as the desert flowers where she came from.

Mahata, like Ishmael, had killed a man during training, with a stranglehold that took three men to break it. Her victim had made unwelcome advances the night before, and died for it. Mahata was as mean as a snake. Although not an executioner for Prince Kamal, she would have done it if asked. Shahanna hated women like her and Ashirad. Mahata was the perfect female terrorist, one who used sexuality to get by a sentry post, or through customs, and this week, to evade the FBI in America. That was Prince Kamal's thinking when he recruited her. The Prince's file said Mahata hated men. It also said she was a lesbian.

Shahanna felt out of her depth. Only two women on Hassan's team, and she was no match for either of them. How long would she last in a knife fight with Ashirad? Or any kind of fight with Mahata? She may soon be obliged to deal with these two. Clement and Jhalal, not to mention Hassan, would shrink from it. Kamal's trainers said it was a male instinct. It came down to this: Two absolutely lethal females against a raw beginner with not one kill to her name. Shahanna decided not to worry. Fighting for her life had been increasingly likely for months.

She could live with it.

Across from Mahata sat a man Shahanna knew by reputation. She had glimpsed him at both training camps, and at the border when Russian soldiers searched the buses, but she had never actually met him, and had fervently hoped she never would. This man was Sharif Bakhar, like Hassan and Jhalal he was Iraqi, but had nothing else in common with either of them. Both men avoided him. Sharif Bakhar was despised throughout the Arab world, and for good reason. He was an ex-colonel who served in Saddam Hussein's infamous Palace Guard.

Bakhar was stern-faced and forbidding, and well into his forties. He wore a bushy mustache that covered his upper lip. A typical Saddam look-alike of the type that thrived in the Iraqi Army. For his age he was wiry and fit, and unlikely to spread at the midriff. This man had easily made the transition from soldier to terrorist. His field of expertise was artillery and explosives.

In the first Gulf War, Sharif Bakhar was the youngest Colonel in Saddam's army, and responsible for one of its most shameful episodes. By age twenty-four he commanded gun batteries that fired a special kind of shell. This shell resembled a garbage can filled with poison gas.

In Northern Iraq – with American support promised and expected – there was a Kurdish uprising at the end of the war. No Americans ever came. The guns of Colonel Bakhar moved up, and the bombardment began. It went on for months. Using Anthrax, encased in those clumsy, trash-can containers, they exterminated a million Kurdish men, women and children.

Half the population was wiped out.

George Bush Senior did nothing.

If this were not bad enough, Sharif Bakhar and his men conducted the clean-up that followed. They went in and butchered those the shells left alive. Survivors were put to death in a frenzy of blood-letting. Women were raped, despite the scabs and bleeding sores that Anthrax had left on their bodies. No one was shot, or killed humanely. People were sliced to pieces alive, and left to rot on the ground. Children and babies fared no better.

Thinking of it, Shahanna pushed her soup away.

And now Sharif Bakhar was here, a fugitive from the International War Crimes Commission, but a celebrity at this table tonight. And tomorrow, as a disciple of Prince Kamal and Al Qaeda, Sharif Bakhar would wear the uniform of a Lufthansa pilot and fly off to slay more defenseless millions, this time in the United States. Unless somebody stopped him.

Someone beyond Bakhar reached for bread. It was Azul, a convict the Saudi court pardoned on condition he enlisted for Afghanistan. From there, like Jhalal and Asuto, he was selected by Prince Kamal and the tribunal. Azul Ghutir was diagnosed in prison, before his release, as criminally insane. There was the only thing that set him apart from his companions:

No psychiatrist had analyzed them.

Azul's eyes had a glassy look, and his unwashed hair was a stringy mass of greasy locks. He paid no attention to those around him, who they were, or what was said. He sat as though mesmerized, stirring his soup with a finger.

Next to Azul was Mustafa Ben Abhat. Shahanna knew that name from constantly updating his file. Early on Kamal wanted to fail this man, yet another head to bleed onto the sand. Mustafa was bumbling and hopeless. His tutors despaired of him. How had he fooled the tribunal?

His days were clearly numbered.

Then a change took place. Maybe some instinct warned him, or voices spoke in his head, urging him to save himself. In any case a miracle occurred and Mustafa improved, almost overnight. He was suddenly a star pupil and impressed everyone. Now Ben Abhat could shoot a bull's-eye at two hundred paces and reassemble a detonator. He could draw a map of all six target cities. When the final test results came in, he had passed with great marks in combat initiative, leadership, courage and resourcefulness. His ability to kill got the highest rating.

He was instantly put on a team.

Fragrant main dishes arrived from Ali Baba's kitchen.

There was no lamb, and everyone clapped. Shahanna took the lid off a platter. Chicken and rice, smothered in a creamy onion marinade and fresh herbs. It was perfectly browned and smelled delicious. Another cover came off to reveal stuffed, steamed aubergines, cooked in a tomato and coriander sauce with pepper and cardoman seeds on top. Shahanna was thrilled to see food not cooked on an open fire. More bread was brought, then a long, silver salver of couscous, again delighting Shahanna, because it originated in the Moroccan region of North Africa, where she grew up.

The natural pecking order came into play, as everyone reached for everything at once; a case of devil take the hindmost.

The last dish was a wooden plank, containing six spitted rabbits, It took two men to carry it in. The carcasses had been rubbed with salt, and turned over charcoal all day. One waiter put his end down sharply, and meat actually fell off the bone, exposing more than one small set of ribs.

The garlic aroma was mouthwatering.

"That one's for me," said Nazir, pointing rudely. "I trapped rabbits as a boy. My mother cooked them just like that."

There was some argument, and he got half a rabbit. Everyone's mother had cooked just like that, except Shahanna's. He family had lived by the sea, and she preferred fish to this dark meat she had never seen, and suddenly did not want to eat. She said: "Give mine to Nazir."

He gave her a crafty, self-satisfied smile. "Bless you, Sorya. May Allah reward your generous spirit."

"Eat and be well, Nazir." *May Allah curse you to hell.*

Nazir was a Saudi. Shahanna wished his mother had poisoned him. His file said he had killed his wife and her lover by burning them alive. Then he tied the bodies together, and had them thrown off a cliff. Nazir came from a rich family, and a deal was made with the palace. One more murderer went to Afghanistan.

Now he was here.

Shahanna ate chicken and rice, and looked around. There was a new face, almost opposite her, next to Ashirad. He was a mystery, and his name escaped her. Strangely she hadn't noticed him until now. (It was as if he hadn't been there.) She began to study him more closely.

He was slim and tall, even sitting down. About Hassan's height, as far as she could tell. He had pleasant, even honest look, unlike those around him. He spoke Arabic with a high-class drawl, but even though his skin was brown, he made a strange Arab. For one thing, his eyes were a startling blue.

So who was he?

She leaned across and asked him.

"We haven't met," he said. "I'm Prince Kamal's cousin, Hakim."

She saw no resemblance at all. "Why are you joining us?"

"I speak French," he said, "Like you, Sorya. You grew up with it, in Morocco. I went to the Sorbonne, in Paris."

There was something strange here. Did he know she attended the Sorbonne? He sounded as if he was reciting from memory. Then it hit her – this Hakim had probably read her file, given his family connection. He was a member of the Saudi royal household. He had not visited either camp, or ridden the train through Russia; but now he was on the team. Was this Kama's replacement, sent by the King? Was he their new leader, or sent to die with them? Obviously he had arrived today, flying in from God-knew-where on a first class ticket.

"Well, hello," said Shahanna. "So Prince Kamal was your cousin . . . Oh, wait . . . are you a Prince? Do we call you Your Highness?"

People stopped eating to listen.

He laughed. "I'm a nobody. The bastard son of a lowly Emir. Kamal was barely a cousin, and the King is no relation at all. Sending me here is His Majesty's answer to the annoyance of my being alive. I may not return. That is why I'm here. To go boom-boom with the rest of you."

She tried to absorb this. It didn't make sense.

She said: "Are you a believer?"

"You mean Islam – the Holy Jihad?"

"Yes."

"Then, no. I'm just a convenient sacrifice."

No one was eating now. All heads had turned.

"Ashirad said: "And who is to kill you?"

He smiled. "America."

Shahanna suddenly understood. "You've angered the King. This is your sentence: To die with us."

"Precisely."

"What did you do?" said Shahanna.

Around the table you could have heard a pin drop.

"I slept with his European mistress. Stupid, I know, but I can't resist a beautiful woman. He found us in bed at an apartment he pays for. She said their affair was over, but she was lying – I should have known better."

Shahanna had to hide her smile.

Ashirad was not smiling. "And now we're stuck with you. Can you at least use a gun?"

"Yes, I was in the Army. A sharpshooter on the Palace Guard. That's how I met Margot, that's her name. She's Hungarian. The king gave me a choice, either come here, or face a firing squad at home. I was shackled under guard on the plane, and I can never come back. Your attack is perfect – it's a one-way trip."

Ishmael sneered at him. "We should send you back to – ."

Hassan cut him off. "You're staying, Hakim. Ours is a holy Jihad. I won't throw away an extra man. You will work with Sorya and the American, Robb Keller ." Hassan pointed them out. "We have a uniform for you, and hand-baggage with a non-scan pistol. Sorya will tell you what to do."

How strange, thought Shahanna. A Saudi black-sheep shows up, to join a mission that took years to plan and cost a fortune. A palace guard hardly qualifies, but suddenly he's to die with the rest of us. Why would the king risk so much for a man he could have executed on the spot? And why did Hassan put him with her and Clement? Something was going on, but what?

~ ~ ~

Gabriel read her thoughts. She was suspicious, but the pieces didn't quite fit. He hoped nobody else was that smart. Hakim was another angel, summoned by Gabriel to help. Revenge of Islam was here and Hassan would have his hands full. Besides, Gabriel had other obligations, some of which might take him to New York and elsewhere at any second. Recruiting Sephius – Hakim's real name – made sense. Hassan's group needed a constant angel presence for obvious reasons; not least of which was to protect Shahanna and Clement.

Gabriel knew about Prince Kamal's death order based on his suspicions about Sorya and her American boyfriend. Gabriel guessed an attempt would be made before they reached America.

That attempt must fail.

Gabriel made one of his mental shifts, and the mood around the table changed. People began talking. Hakim faded into the background, as dishes were passed, more were served and conversation became more friendly than a short time ago. Meanwhile, the music and dancing never stopped.

It was like a family gathering.

For violent delusional lunatics.

An hour later, some left the restaurant, and others stayed – either drinking, or trying to get a belly dancer to sleep with them or both things at once. Shahanna drew Clement aside, as the others they were following approached a Taxi-stand. "I need to talk to you."

"Okay." His brow wrinkled slightly. "What's the matter?"

She was afraid of being overheard. Ashirad stood at the curb, looking in their direction. Shahanna lowered her voice. "Nothing's wrong. I want you to come to my room."

He said: "Are you serious? I mean, I'd love that, but they watch us – Asuto has several of them on it – I'm sure of that. That Ashirad is looking at us now. Your room is not a good idea."

"Screw Asuto and Ashirad," she said. "What can they do? Shoot us for fucking? Anything happens, there'll be Russian cops all over the place, and Revenge of Islam is busted. Asuto can't risk that. It makes tonight my last chance to seduce you. Then off we go to certain death."

She gave him an exaggerated wink.

Shahanna was determined. She had hoped it would happen in America, when they got back and life returned to normal, but they might not make it back. This thought, like her desire for Clement, could not be denied any longer.

She took his arm and they walked together to an empty cab. When they drove off, Ashirad was still there, a malevolent look on her face. Clement gave the driver the name of their hotel.

~ ~ ~

When her bedroom door closed, Clement put his arms around her. "I was wrong," he said. "Your room was a good idea, the best you ever had."

Shahanna smiled up at him. She hoped that heavy, drawn out meal had not made him drowsy. She had energetic demands to make.

Clement said: "You're sure about this?"

"Very."

"Then so am I." He kissed her, for a very long time, on the mouth, and something powerful descended over both of them.

Eventually she said: "No one kisses like that."

"So how was it – not bad?" He laughed softly.

"You know exactly . . . how it was." She steered him over to the bed, and collapsed them both onto it.

As he unzipped her jeans, she said: "Hurry! Be quick!"

He chuckled. "I thought slow was better – or is fast a French thing?"

"No. You're making me wet."

"And?"

"I have no panties on – and I can't wash these jeans again."

They both subsided in laughter as she helped him undress her. Soon they were both naked.

The first time was almost savage, and quick.

Afterwards, Shahanna said dreamily: "I love you very much."

"Me, too. It's too bad."

She smiled at him. "It's wonderful."

"Yes. Now stop talking."

He kissed her passionately, exploring her with his hands.

She moaned.

"You're so beautiful," he whispered. He slide a hand down her stomach, and made her wet all over again.

She began to breathe heavily.

He gently bit her nipples, first one; then the other.

He shoved his fingers into her, moving the back and forth, hard.

Her back arched,

Her mouth came open in a silent scream.

He slid downward, and his head moved between her thighs; he used his tongue; it flickered gently and lightly, like a flame. Shahanna moaned again, thrusting herself up at him, spreading her legs wide.

She finally begged him to stop, and enter her.

"She gasped, when he did.

They writhed slowly together, breathing harshly.

She said, "Do it harder."

He obeyed.

Their movements became more rapid, faster and

faster, until she cried: "Oh, yes! Don't stop! Oh, God – do it more!"

Finally she shuddered, and her body relaxed.

He kept going. She began to move under him, and they started again.

His nails dug into her buttocks.

Unable to hold back, she bucked against him, panting hard. Their bodies were slick with sweat. She growled, deep in her throat. "Oh, yes! Make it hurt!"

He thrust harder, losing control.

She closed her eyes. "Harder! Aah . . . yes. Oh, God you really know how to fuck!"

Later, he said, "Where did you learn to talk so dirty?"

She grinned. "I read a lot of books."

"Well, your command of disgusting English is perfect."

He ran one finger idly over her stomach.

She said: "Bo . . ."

"Yes?"

Bo . . . please!"

"What?"

"Please do it again. Hard and fast!"

"Yes, my love."

He rolled her onto her back.

He knelt and parted her thighs.

She kissed him fiercely, then said: "Now! Inside me! I want it now!"

He entered her again.

"Merde," she groaned. "I've wanted this so long."

Building slowly, their motion became frantic. She thrust her head back with a groan of ecstasy. A scream started in her throat.

He covered her mouth with his, afraid they might be

heard. He said hoarsely" "It's okay, don't stop. Just don't yell out."

She climaxed, and it went on for some time.

They finally went limp in each other's arms, and she raised her had to caress his cheek. Contentment filled their world, and neither of them could move or speak. They lay still, perfect with each other, for what seemed like forever. Finally, she said: "I knew it would be like that."

He looked at her. "You're the woman of my dreams."

That's what I was thinking."

That made him smile.

She said, "It's only nine-thirty. This is not over yet."

Her hand slipped down to his pelvis.

~ ~ ~

The day after the Alexandria explosion, Heathcote was back at work. He skipped breakfast, replacing it with coffee and cigarettes, glad that this floor was undamaged by the catastrophe he failed to prevent downstairs.

Navy doctors at Bethesda Hospital had stopped trying to keep him there after an hour of argument. He was determined to leave, and they let him. They had failed to stop him smoking in his room, and weren't too sorry to see him go. Heathcote rushed back to work in clothes that were stained and torn.

Now he sat, needing to build a wall around America.

He re-read Shahanna's terrorist profiles, forwarded to him by Henry Archer and the Brits. It was a study in detail. There was even a description of the Turkish restaurant they ate in.

And a list of everyone going to Frankfurt.

Good girl, he thought. Always using your head.

But he knew he needed more. Where were the other

teams going? What American city, of the targeted six, was each team bound for? Heathcote's surveillance people would have to determine that, as Asuto's attack squads flew out of Moscow. Without knowing at least some of that, Heathcote had little chance of success. The terrorists must not only be shadowed, but hemmed in, until the nukes appeared. Then Heathcote's operatives would swoop.

Heathcote thought it all through again, and felt more optimistic. He was ready to brief the President.

Using a secure cell phone, he called the White House and asked for the official who arranged his appointments.

Heathcote identified himself and said, "There's something urgent. Could I come right away?"

They sent a helicopter.

He was soon sitting in the Oval Office.

The President looked tense, and reminded Heathcote that the Fourth of July was only two days away.

"Sir, I have four very reliable agents on the inside. Two Iraqis and an American male and female. They're part of one of the Al Qaeda teams in Moscow, ready to fly out any minute. I have all European destinations covered. The team we penetrated is going into Frankfurt Rhine-Main airport, just outside Frankfurt. Others are bound for Paris, Rome and London. From there they will embark for the United States, and make their way to the target-cities."

The president looked unconvinced.

He said, "Can you really get them all? In two days?"

"It's better than it sounds, sir. Hassan's team is posing as Air France or Lufthansa crew – that makes them recognizable and easy to track. The other teams will be dressed the same way. Their uniforms, whatever airline they're from, will give them away. We're lucky they're not moving as individuals, pretending to be doctors, typists or businessmen. Those uniforms are Prince Kamal's biggest mistake. I have enough watchers in Western Europe to intercept them all, and follow wherever they go after that. The terrorists won't even smell them."

"But no one gets detained?"

"No, sir. Not yet. I have people at every significant airport. Both over here and over there. They're in place and waiting."

"You still mean to arrest them here."

"Yes, Mr. President. Once we have those nukes, we bag the lot of them. Take every team into custody. As I said in my memo, sir, they're meeting the weapons at the airports where they intend to set them off. We don't move in until then."

"And those weapons? They're still on the water?"

"Yes. Mr. President. But the sea search is near complete. The area of ocean not yet checked by satellite is growing smaller – those two freighters have to be very close, which actually helps us. I have every hope of getting them both, very soon."

The President hunched at his desk. "I hope we've got this right. The stakes could not be higher."

"I'm no gambler, sir. I only play if I'm sure to win."

The President hesitated. "Well, we absolutely can't afford to lose. I do think your plan makes sense. And I trust you to carry it out."

Heathcote breathed more easily.

They began talking in general terms, discussing their deployed forces on land, sea and in the air, and what technology those forces could bring to bear. Then one of several phones rang. The President picked it up, covering the mouthpiece. He said he was sorry they didn't have more time. The Secretary of State was on his way. Heathcote got up and they shook hands across the desk. Heathcote left.

He needed a drink, maybe a couple of drinks.

Instead he got back in the helicopter.

CHAPTER EIGHTEEN

ASUTO KENYATTA SPENT THAT NIGHT in Moscow alone.

After three days on a train, he was not only tired, but sick of his companions. He had no wish to go out. His desire for women was limited, and sex-for-sale was most of what Moscow had to offer. It was, after all, ruled by corrupt politicians and organized crime.

He had housed all six teams, including the one he led himself, in run-down hotels all around the city. He gave final instructions to the other five leaders, then silently said goodbye to them forever. Asuto would use tonight to get them out of his system. Forget they ever existed. His overall leadership role had ended. He had no interest in their well-being, and if any were caught in Moscow, he didn't want to be involved. He would hide out at the Hilton until he joined his own team tomorrow.

Asuto expected some of the terrorist units to be caught.

They would be tortured.

Better to die when the bombs went off.

His mind switched to his hatred for the Saudis. Once the details of these attacks came out, as was inevitable, the Saudi future looked bleak. The thought pleased Asuto. Their involvement in 9/11 would resurface, and America would take its revenge. That alone was worth dying for. For Asuto honor was sacred. He hated the Saudis and any other sand dwellers who dared call him a monkey to his face. No Arab had ever treated him well except Jhalal, a good man but still a hated Arab. They were as evil as America itself. Asuto was confident that, as payment the Fourth of July, the Great Satan would obliterate the desert lands with air-strikes.Praise Allah. Let it be so.

Asuto ate alone in his suite on the top floor, eating sparingly as he always did. He was unable to choose between rice or soup; so he ordered both, but hardly touched them. Instead he sat silently gloating. America had no idea he was coming, but very soon the name Asuto Kenyatta would be on everyone's lips.

Asuto drank only the water served with his meal. Then later, herbal tea. After that he went to bed.

CHAPTER NINETEEN

CLEMENT, IN BLUE TUNIC AND CAP with Lufthansa insignia, set down his overnight bag and studied the departure board in Moscow's largest European terminal hall. There were four flights scheduled for Frankfurt, all leaving by mid-morning.

He noted the flight numbers and turned away.

Shahanna and Hassan were waiting nearby – an attractive Air France stewardess standing with her Captain. The rest of the team sat in a drawn out row, a short distance away. Their uniforms represented either the French or German national airlines – in an almost identical dark blue.

Breakfast had been consumed here at the airport. It was hurried, and expensive, the food as bad as the coffee. Nobody could finish either, and the waiter was ill-tempered and rude.

Asuto Kenyatta was not answering his phone, according to Ashirad, who had tried to reach him twice. Clement doubted the African had slept in. More likely his plane, and his team, had already taken off. No one commented on what Ashirad said, but Shahanna had quietly told Clement she hoped Asuto and his entire band of murderers got arrested. As she said this, Clement saw Hassan look at her sharply, although he could not possibly have heard – but even if he had, better him than Ashirad.

Now Clement needed a booking desk. Any airline would do. First he walked over to Shahanna and Hassan. They listened to his flight information, and then they all looked around. Hassan finally spotted the Air France ticket counters, and Shahanna led the way. Clement fetched the others; then stayed at the back of the group, with those who did not speak French.They were all booked for space available, by a Russian blonde spooning soup out of a plastic cup. A yellow tag on her chest said she spoke Russian, French and English. She didn't speak the last two very well, so Shahanna used a mixture of both. There were no seats on any Air France flight taking off today, but one Lufthansa aircraft was only half full. Hassan turned it down, because only Ishmael spoke German, and two others beside Clement wore that uniform. The plane's regular flight crew might be suspicious if these supposed fellow countrymen stayed silent during a six hour flight, even when addressed in their own language.

So much for having Ishmael on the team.

Hassan's next option was Swissair: no good for the same reason. Most Swiss speak French and German, and among cabin crew, that had to be a given. Added to which, this Frankfurt flight was two seats short.

The answer, after much keyboard clicking, was Scandinavian Air Services. They had more than enough room, would speak only Swedish or English, and their flight left for Frankfurt in an hour. Shahanna thanked the Air France attendant with a quick smile; then Hassan's group headed for yet another check-in counter.

Scandinavian Airways, said a polite young lady from Stockholm, could certainly get them all on the same flight to Germany, but not sitting together. They'd be spread throughout the tourist section in twos and threes, with one of them on a folding seat outside the pilot cabin. Was that okay?

Shahanna conferred with Hassan.

They agreed that it was.

As Clement checked in his bag, he turned to Shahanna. "How about something to read? That booth over there has English language newspapers and magazines. Let's take a look. We have an hour to kill."

They both knew this was a last chance to talk alone.

They told Hassan where they were going. He said: "Try not to be too long. The others might notice."

Clement wondered exactly how much Hassan knew.

They bought a copy of Newsweek and The Washington Post. Then they sat in an empty row of those gray, contoured seats found in departure halls everywhere. Two airline crew blocked from view by a cell phone plug-in station and a young Russian woman selling glasses of piping hot tea from an urn on her cart. Clement felt safe from prying ears or eyes.

As if reading aloud from Newsweek, he said, "That Ashirad is a viper. She and the other girl are up to something – and I think it concerns us."

"I'm sure you're right. I sensed it, too."

"What do we do?"

She frowned into her newspaper. "Nothing. I told you last night: Screw both of them."

"Well, you be careful. They're both killers."

"They all are – except for Hassan and Jhalal. You and I had better go back."

They stood up. She said: "Do you love me?"

Her eyes said, and love fucking me?

"Beyond all reason." A look passed between them; then they strolled back to join Hassan.

They passed Sharif Bakhar on the way. He was trying

to get a Russian vending machine to accept Afghan coins.

"The baby killer," muttered Clement.

"I look at him and see bloody corpses."

"Me, too."

They hurried past.

Hassan stood talking to a young hostess from Scandinavian Airlines. He looked concerned.

Take off was delayed. A small bird had been sucked into an air-intake on landing, causing slight damage to one engine. A repair was in hand, but would take a while. This lady would keep them informed, but for now, she offered food vouchers, a smile and an apology.

Sharif Bakhar came back and sat down. Clement noted with amusement that he was empty-handed. His foreign coins must not have worked. A Russian vending machine had won the day.

Shahanna noticed it, too, but her response was more practical. Nudging Clement, she said: "Want a Coke?"

He felt her sudden excitement. "God, yes! They sell it here, don't they? He felt in his pocket. "I don't have any change, shit!"

"Don't worry – I do." She hurried off, rattling it in her hand.

Coca Cola was banned in Prince Kamal's camps. Clement hadn't seen a can in months. It amazed him how badly he wanted one now. He could already taste it. Tiny bubbles, stinging his tongue.

The very thought signaled a return to civilization. He sat waiting for Shahanna, like a child waiting for Christmas. He tried to read Newsweek, but that didn't help. He was desperate for a soda.

Then there she stood, the love of his life, with one,

familiar red and white can in each hand . . .

Then the Swedish hostess came back.

More smiles. More apology.

It was going to take longer than expected.

She went away, and Clement thought they might as well be back in America, with airport grid-lock, and delayed departures for any number of reasons.

Coca Cola cans were emptied, and the latest American news consumed from cover to cover. Two hours went by, seeming an eternity. Every time Hassan looked at his watch, it seemed time went slower and slower. The whole team's mood was grim. Shahanna made several more trips to the vending machines, with contributions from those with the right cash.

Clement went to the restroom to shave.

Looking in the mirror, wishing those Swedish mechanics would hurry up, he ran his razor across one cheek. A disheveled Russian stopped behind him, in overalls and a cloth cap, swigging vodka from the bottle and talking to himself. Clement watched the man's reflection, in case he needed to defend himself.

There was no need to worry.

"Nastrovya!"

The drunk toasted Clement's back before shuffling on. He arrived at a porcelain receptacle on the wall, rested his head against the tiles and urinated onto the floor. Clement put away his shaving kit, hurriedly dried his hands and face, and strode for the exit.

The air was better outside.

The hall was filling up. Two tourist charters, each with better than two hundred passengers, were lining up at the flight gates, their luggage in a disorderly heap at their feet.

Russians had become like all other Europeans: They loved to travel. One party was going to the Greek Islands, the other to Spain. Chasing the sun was as popular here as anywhere else. Clement was sick of the sun.

They'd be on a beach tomorrow.

He would not.

As he joined the others again, he saw the Swedish hostess talking to Hassan. The last half hour had done the trick. The plane was ready, and their flight would be called soon.

Clement went to the departure board, hoping to watch it change and relieve his boredom. The

The display did not change. Scandinavian still showed a delay.

He stood there, frustration mounting.

Then their flight was called.

At the same time the digital board in front of him changed to reflect that S. A. S. 282 was boarding at Gate 10.

Clement returned to the others.

Three hours of waiting melted away.

CHAPTER TWENTY

IT WAS JULY 1ST.

Two days before their deadline, assembled regiments of the Free Patriot Militia began moving into position. There were enough of them, with enough heavy armament, to give the US Army a serious fight. They were soon strung out in columns across the Continental United States, using the highways where they could, marching over fields and open ground where they could not, taking tanks, trucks and light armored cannon with them. Shoulder-launched rockets filled the trucks, with field-kitchens stacked in front to conceal them.

Everyone was moving at a cracking pace.

Dietrich was on the East Coast, flying a Comanche helicopter with false military markings. He and his second-in-command in the West, who was also hopping from state to state in an identical machine, were supervising from the air.

The passage of such large numbers of troops drew a lot of attention. But as they moved through towns and cities, it was explained as a rehearsal for the Fourth of July. Those who saw them on the highway assumed it was an Army maneuver, and not one witness, over a two day period, found it worth reporting to anyone. This allowed them to spread across the United States like an undetected virus.

Most units passed themselves off, quite falsely, as detachments of state or national guard – and that, too, was accepted everywhere by townsfolk and farmer alike.

Dietrich fully understood America's affection for its military, and he knew how to exploit it in a situation like this. Dietrich himself was covering thousands of square miles, and burned a tank of gas every hour.So did his partner in the West.

Lucifer had asked the impossible, and Dietrich came through for him, mobilizing every unit at his disposal, and every man in it, except those considered moronic, or with a criminal record. Dietrich had kept that promise.

He had also tripled his price, and Lucifer paid it.

In gold bullion.

They both knew the dollar was finished.

Or would be after tomorrow.

Dietrich was hovering up over Interstate 95, watching a long, winding column of good ole boys from North Carolina, working their way towards the Mason Dixon Line, where they would divide into forces of two hundred; then split up, heading for specified airports. They drove an assortment of Humvees, trucks and Jeeps, all painted in blotchy grey and green – displaying a Free patriot flag on every antenna. And so they marched, boots crunching the rhythm and gear-boxes humming the tune.

Their attack area stretched from Rayleigh, their home-state capital, to Richmond, around the southern tip of Virginia. They had already dropped off one assault group near Durham, who would while away their time in bars or truck-stops, until they received the signal from Dietrich.

Then they would move on Atlanta.

Well to the north of them, two whole divisions had left the Appalachians and were spread over New Jersey, Pennsylvania and Delaware – where one target would be Dover Air Force Base: of concern to Dietrich due to its ability to move large numbers of genuine US troops at short notice. It was Lucifer's one military objective, and Dietrich estimated his own casualties at a hundred percent.

But his fee increased.

In case he was wrong.

Lucifer agreed, but had stipulated that a force of six thousand, armed with tanks and heavy artillery, be deployed in this north eastern region. These Appalachian divisions were equipped with large amounts of costly ex-military hardware – hoarded over many years – which was why they were chosen.

North of them lay New York City, but the Free Patriot Militia was not going there. That told Dietrich something. Kennedy Airport was being saved for the 4th of July itself. The Arab terrorists he was covering for would hit it on Independence Day. Lucifer always did have a sense of drama. Dietrich had guessed the six Al Qaeda targets using the same logic: If the Free Patriots were not attacking, then the Muslim terrorists were. Dietrich was impressed by the cities selected. All perfect for a nuclear strike. Dietrich had worked out where the six weapons came from. It was obvious. The Iran-nukes were all over the media.

It didn't bother Dietrich that America would be eradicated. He hated mortals, and their ridiculous countries; this one more than any other. So proud of itself, and declining faster than ancient Rome. The Romans lasted a thousand years. America barely managed two hundred.

But there were plenty of other nations to exploit, divide and rule. Lucifer and all his demons would up-stakes and move somewhere else. Once in a new body, there was nothing to stop the devil setting up shop in India, China, or anywhere else with a future. The Germans were doing well again, and might bear watching. The devil was known to be looking for another Austrian Fuehrer.

Leaving America suited Dietrich just fine.

He hated the food.

Dietrich banked the Comanche hard left, and the column of soldiers disappeared and changed to a forest of tree-tops flanking the highway. He kicked in the Turbo-thrust and raced North.

He shot across beautiful grassland dotted with bright colored, leafy woods. Farm buildings and gas-stations came and went as he swept low, staying below any radar that was watching. Two hundred miles an hour was exhilarating at low altitude, and Dietrich whooped aloud. He was streaking in a wide, diversionary loop, to avoid Washington D. C. and its Air Force protected suburbs.

His intercom crackled. "Dietrich, where the hell are you?"

It was Lucifer, naturally, and Dietrich considered not answering at all. This was the third call today, and it was barely noon. The flood of last minute orders was endless. Dietrich reached for the volume switch, to turn it up, and accidentally lost his grip on the steering. The helicopter careened to the right, the tail swung up, and his altitude began to drop alarmingly. He fought with the controls, steering left and pulling back on the stick with all his strength. The treetops below became a whirl of green and browns, and came up to meet him at dizzying speed. He was suddenly afraid he might become the cause of a major forest fire.

Lucifer said, "Dietrich! I know you can hear me!"

Dietrich gritted his teeth and hauled on the stick.

After several nerve wracking seconds, to his relief, it came all the way back to the edge of his seat.

The nose came up, the trees disappeared, and blue sky filled the convex windshield in front of him. He had never been so pleased to see anything.

He took a quick bearing, and adjusted his course.

Lucifer shouted something indistinct.

Dietrich grabbed the microphone and pushed "Transmit".

He gave his position, and that of the troops he'd seen, which were now the troops to his South, and asked Lucifer bluntly what he wanted. There was no point in being polite. The devil had been foul tempered all morning, and sounded furious now. Dietrich would not mention the near-crash, or that thanks to Lucifer he had missed death by a hundred feet.

"What do I want?" screamed Lucifer. "I want your fucking attention!"

Damn, thought Dietrich. If he shouts any louder, they'll hear him in the White House. He turned the volume back down.

Lucifer, now less loud, shouted "Dietrich!"

Dietrich switched to transmit, held the button down, and said dryly that Lucifer had his attention. He pushed receive and waited.

Lucifer cursed for a full minute.

Dietrich listened, then decided to defend himself after all. "I had quite a problem up here," he said.

"Oh?"

"Nearly went down in a ball of flame. I was startled,

and lost control." He did not add that Lucifer was to blame.

"Never mind that." The devil sounded impatient. "When do you expect to be at Ronald Reagan?"

He meant the airport.

"We surround it at noon tomorrow." Lucifer knew that; it was written into the battle plans. Three thousand men were moving down from Maryland for that purpose. Dietrich checked his watch, and saw that they would cross into Northern Virginia very soon. The same group would be wiping out Dover Air Force base. Dietrich quoted the schedule from memory.

Lucifer snorted. "I know when they should be there – I'm asking if they will."

Dietrich realized he'd better check. When Lucifer got like this he was impossible. There was no pleasing him. You did what he said without argument. Not only that, you did it right away.

Dietrich said he'd find out and call Lucifer back. He broke the connection and tuned to another frequency. It took a while to get through.

The Maryland Commander was retired Army. His report was precise, and matter of fact: On course and dead on time. They would be at Ronald Reagan in compliance with orders: 0200 hours tomorrow . . . had anything changed?

No, nothing had.

Dietrich told him to stand by, and called Lucifer back. "On time," he said. "If anything, they'll be early." He knew this commander was a hard-driving fanatic, who would march his men to death rather than fail. "That son of a bitch might have them there tonight."

Lucifer was reassured. "Tell him," he said. "To kill anyone in military uniform, but no airline personnel. Some of our Mid-Eastern brethren may be at Reagan on the 4th, dressed as aircrew or ground workers. They need plenty of genuine airline people alive, to act as cover.

"I'll pass that on," Dietrich said. He cut the connection.

The Maryland Commander was completely unfazed. Anyone in airline uniform gets a free pass. Got it. How about regular civilians? Fair game?"

"Why not?" Dietrich was amused. "Sweet of you to ask. We don't want you killing anyone without permission. You might go to hell."

The Marylander said something that sounded like motherfucker, with his hand over the handset.

"Yes, I am," said Dietrich. "And my boss is worse; so do your goddamn job – and watch your mouth."

There was silence. Then: "Roger that. We'll kill 'em all."

There was a click. Maryland had hung up.

Dietrich pulled off his headset.

He took a compass bearing and turned more into the sun. He donned a pair of expensive sunglasses and a ball cap, and put the headset back on. Then he switched to another frequency.

"Come in, Bald Eagle," said Dietrich. "Can you hear me?" His deputy, the demon he was calling, was clear across the country.

He clicked 'Receive' and got nothing but static.

He was about to give up when, suddenly, the whistles and pops eased up enough for him to catch a word or two.

A voice said, ". . . ald Eagle . . . come in."

Nothing more.

Dietrich cursed. He fiddled with knobs, thinking that fifty thousand dollars did not buy the technology it used to.

"Say again, Bald Eagle!" Dietrich pressed the red button for automatic Megahertz adjustment.

Bald Eagle was cloaked in silence, flying somewhere high over the rocky landscape of Arizona. His name was Wesley Slater, a rodeo promoter whose friends had no idea he was a demon of some note. They called him "Cowboy". His barbecues were famous, and people clamored for invitations.

Now Wes Slater's western twang came through clearly. "Dietrich, you cocksucker! If you can hear this – say so!" The climate in Arizona was dry. So was Cowboy's sense of humor.

Only he could say cocksucker to Dietrich.

Dietrich didn't laugh. He was in a hurry. "Give position and rate of progress."

"Near Phoenix. I got three prongs out – all makin' good speed."

Dietrich was pleased but not surprised. Three motorized columns were specified in the plan, and the highways out there were always empty. Column One was making for the municipal airport outside Phoenix. They were almost there, and would be deploying tanks and infantry soon. Column Two would cross into New Mexico, turning for Albuquerque and Santa Fe. They had not only tanks, Humvees and foot-soldiers, but heavy artillery as well. It was overkill, but Dietrich gave value for money. He was sending in enough fire power to lay both targets flat. The third column was smaller, and already wheeling back the other way, striking for Oklahoma City. The airport there was the size of a chicken coop, and little or no fighting was expected. The Free Patriot's goal was to turn it into a huge crater.

Slater had six other divisions in his command, already divided into units of fighting strength and going their separate ways, through tough, south-western terrain, towards a variety of spread-out destinations. Dietrich asked for, and received, an updated report on all of them.

Cowboy's artillery units were where they should be, and on time. From the West Virginia regiments, to those moving down from Minnesota. Most Airports in that part of the country would be hammered into rubble.

Slater said: "What about California. How come we're only hitting chickenshit places like Pasadena, and Palm Springs?"

Dietrich had no time for this. Cowboy's major weakness was asking questions. Dietrich felt a flash of anger. "Orders," he said. He pulled back on his stick, swerving to miss a telephone pylon, hidden by a rise in the ground. He grunted with effort, and said, "Just stick to the program, and stop trying to think." Dietrich also thought it foolish not to take care of Los Angeles or San Diego with the kind of manpower and weaponry they had at their disposal, but he wasn't about to say so. Maybe L. A. and the Navy yards in San Diego were getting nuked tomorrow.

He said, "Just do it, asshole! Am I clear?"

Slater said: "Clear. Roger and out."

Dietrich brought up a tiny local airfield on his G. P. S. It was time to refuel and take a nap.

And so it went for the next ten hours; as he flew up

and down his portion of the largest target area ever conceived. He and Wes Slater were attacking more ground than the D-Day Invasion. Dietrich took savage pleasure in it, grinning as he raced back and forth. He stopped only for gas or food, still tracking his convoys; then moved on to do it again somewhere else. The whole time came a flood of absurd phone calls from Lucifer, who never slept, and was never satisfied. . .

The first signal came from Baltimore, just after midnight.

"Attack troops ready."

It was now the third of July.

Dietrich marked Baltimore off his list, and waited.

Soon the calls were coming thick and fast.

After Baltimore came Tallahassee, then Savannah, and Atlanta, followed by smaller cities and towns. Some of the names were barely known to Dietrich. There was no pattern to it, and no logic when it came to North or South. More and more units took up position, and Dietrich continued to update his list. He had to rely on verbal reports, a visual check at night being impossible – even using infra-red. Not only were his troops scattered in all directions, but it was dark, and Dietrich could not risk any low level flying. Radio calls kept coming in, and he landed in a field to listen, logging everything, and eating a beef sandwich and drinking a beer. The devil didn't make contact. He was calling on the dark power to increase mightily over the next two days The most obscene and loathsome rituals were taking place in Century Tower.

Daylight finally came.

Dietrich took to the air with most of his list checked off. The only major objective left was Newark

International, in New Jersey. Newark airport was being held back until later today, for good reason. It was so close to JFK That the two targets almost counted as one. Newark, if attacked too soon, would act as an early warning system. As soon as the powers-that-be thought the Big Apple itself was again under attack, all hell would break loose. The National Guard would be called in immediately – and if that were to happen, Dietrich wanted it at the end of today's battle, rather than the beginning. His Newark units were therefore biding their time.

Dietrich flew north and watched for radar blips. These roads were free of his people, and the screen stayed clear, except for the occasional freight-truck, or a family of campers pulling a trailer behind them. There were no cops; it was way too early for radar traps, and Dietrich had his divisions safely past this point; so he didn't bother to scan for patrol cars. He soon reached Interstate 95 and followed its sinewy path to the Pennsylvania border; then he cut across country, looking for Pittsburgh and its smoke stacks as he scrutinized the horizon.

The dark silhouette of the city came up first, then the foul stench of the factories found him. He flattened his course and circled slowly West, looking for runways and a watchtower. They eventually came up on his right. He saw his men, at battalion strength, ready to advance at the appointed hour. They had left the highway several miles back, to approach from open country. They were lying low as ordered, and no one knew they were there. Their artillery was in place, shells stacked neatly by each heavy gun, the gunners ready to fire. It looked text book perfect.

Damn, thought Dietrich, we're going to get away with it.

He wheeled off, without making radio contact, and set a course for Philadelphia. He was there in twenty minutes.

Philadelphia was different. The airport was surrounded by highways, overpasses and exit-ramps. Here, two Free patriot brigades had split up into motorized platoons and left the road at chosen points. Now they ringed the wired fence of the airport at carefully spaced intervals. Several squads had moved up to cover the terminal buildings from the front. Unlike the others, they had no tanks, because there was not that much to knock down. But they had artillery, and when the shelling stopped, everyone would converge on the area they had blasted clear.

Dietrich flew over them and kept going.

Ploughed fields whipped beneath him, and for a while he saw only painted barns and the occasional tractor.

He glanced at the fuel gauge and saw the needle past red. He thought, one hour in the air is not enough. I needed extra tanks. His G. P. S. showed no suitable fueling place for thirty miles. He reduced speed and hoped he made it. The last thing he needed was to crash-land here. He thought of how Lucifer would take the news, and laughed crazily. It would be better to die in the crash. He flew on for twenty-five miles, and the fuel gauge showed completely empty.

The engine-note became unstable. Dirt in the fuel line was being sucked through, clogging the injectors. Dietrich knew he'd be lucky to make two more miles, and he had to make four. He searched the ground for a likely meadow, but it was all plowed, bumpy soil, and completely isolated. Go down here and he'd be stranded, and on foot. Dietrich kept on flying, stubbornly making for the airfield, ignoring the fuel gauge, determined to find that airfield or die.

He reached it on fumes and air.

The fuel pumps were open despite the early hour, with a young attendant on duty, watching as Dietrich touched down.

The demon handed him a wad of cash. "Got jet-cleaner fluid?"

"Sure do. You on empty?"

"Zip. Zero. Nada. I'm way beyond empty." Dietrich thought: Damned hayseed. Just fill me up!"

He said nothing and handed over his gas-tank key. He thought: If I piss this guy off, he'll take forever, and I don't have the time. Hard to make my next check-in as it is. That means have to go back to Philadelphia or miss the attack. That's the toughest one, and I have to be there in case they fuck it up.

Eventually a buzzer sounded, and his tanks were full.

It came to fifteen hundred dollars.

"You gave me two thousand," said the attendant. "I'll get your change."

"Keep it," said Dietrich.

He swung up into the cockpit again. He started the rotors, waving the attendant back, then took off laughing, with the young man scrambling clear. The supercharger kicked in at the flip of a switch, and Dietrich streaked for Philadelphia, expending high octane as he went.

~ ~ ~

The shelling had begun.

Philadelphia's airport was shrouded in smoke.

Dietrich killed his speed; then hovered, five hundred yards away. The gunfire was enough to wake the dead, even through Plexiglas, and it could not be long before police and military in the area were called. But the nearest Army post was an hour's drive, and they were not prepared – so it could take hours to respond. Local police could do very little on their own, and by the time any soldiers got here, Philadelphia airport should be wiped out.

SWAT teams might be a nuisance. They were expected to arrive quickly, and get sharpshooters into position, but they would be outgunned and out-manned. It was why Dietrich had supplied hand-held rocket launchers, and any snipers on rooftops, or in ground-based cover, would have a short life-expectancy. They would be blasted to hell, along with whatever they hid behind.

A familiar voice crackled from New York. "Dietrich?"

Dietrich groaned. What now?

Lucifer said: "Has it started?"

"Philadelphia has. We're knocking the crap out of the main buildings – and the runways are pock-marked like the moon. Our guys are waiting for orders to advance, and kill whoever is left. I don't see much resistance. There are plenty of bodies in the rubble."

"Good, good. Anywhere else?"

"Nothing firm yet. I imposed a radio silence, while we get things under way." He wanted to scream at Lucifer, to stop making these insane calls, but caution prevailed and he held his tongue. He said, "I'll be at every site, in the next few hours. You'll hear from me then."

Lucifer was drowned out by gunfire, then became audible again. "Make sure I do, and make sure the news is good. Now patch me through to Slater in Arizona. I want a report from him."

Dietrich did it, glad to be rid of Lucifer, but knowing

he'd soon be back, because due to the time-zone difference, Wesley Slater had nothing to report, which might not go down too well.

Dietrich almost felt sorry for Cowboy.

But didn't.

He set a course for Baltimore, knowing that on the way he'd have to make fuel stops and check on other assault groups. For the rest of today, and throughout tonight,

he would traverse his entire territory more than once. But once his troops began losing, as they eventually must, he would fly back to New York.

Leaving them to their fate.

He transmitted one unit's call-sign. Their commander answered. Dietrich heard explosions in the background, and took that as a good omen. "Tell me how you're doing, and make it fast." This man was long-winded, and Dietrich had things to do.

The Philly Commander kept it short.

They were winning.

A lot of the public were dead.

No Free Patriot losses so far.

It was more of an execution than a battle.

Roger and out.

Dietrich flew over there to take a look. Philadelphia International, when he saw it, looked like a demolition site littered with corpses everywhere you looked. Smoke and blackened rubble completed the picture. What had been a Budget Rental parking-lot was a raging inferno.

That was good enough for Dietrich. He brought the Comanche's nose around and left the scene, and it's bloodshed ehind him. He flew slower, to save on fuel because he was tired of having to stop.

His next stop also looked like a war zone: Baltimore, its large municipal airport engulfed in flame. Armored vehicles moved through dust and debris, with Free Patriots on foot, running beside and behind them. There were even more dead bodies here, and civilian survivors, rooted to the spot, watching with horror until they were rounded up with their hands above their heads.

Five thousand rental cars were burning.

The devil had got his wish.

Dietrich circled above it all, making sure victory was decisive, and this place was out of action. That was most important, because when the counter-attack came, and his men went down, nothing could reverse what they had done.

He headed north again.

He informed Lucifer on the way.

"It's going well," said Dietrich.

"So I see. We're showing it on Century News. Trouble is, our coverage looks like it was done on the cheap. My producers are idiots. I should fire the lot. They knew this was coming. I told them yesterday– and still they didn't send out enough camera crews to do it justice."

Dietrich knew this was pure crap. Century's coverage had to be spectacular; he had seen their choppers, risking their lives to get close, dodging shells and bullets for a better picture. Some of the bodies he'd seen today had to be Century News camera crew. He had seen at least one photographer go down.

Dietrich said something non-committal, and broke the connection.

The gas gauge was again too low to be ignored. Dietrich steered towards a nearby airstrip. At least this one was close. He sped across Amish country outside Lancaster. A small, T-shaped runway came in sight, with one hangar and two or three private aircraft parked outside. Dietrich swung in lower. The Comanche responded to the slightest touch, and he set down like a butterfly on a flower. He got out and looked for someone to fill him up. The pumps were on this side of the hangar, but there was no one around. The place seemed deserted.

He said, "Dammit, where is everybody?"

He walked into the hangar. It was little more than a big shed. Looking left and right, he saw two unattended planes, their engine cowlings on the ground, probably for maintenance or repair.

A voice said, "What do you want?"

The speaker was an old man in brimmed hat and dungarees, a shotgun in his hands. He said, "This is private property. You can't land here." He came closer as he spoke.

"Morning," said Dietrich cheerfully. He took in the distance between him and the shotgun. He'd never make it.

"You . . . Para-Military?" The old man stumbled over the word. He said: "Radio says there's a commotion at the airport, and these Para-guys was involved. A lot of folks bin kilt."

"Who?" said Dietrich. "What are you talking about?"

"Them Free Patriot loonies."

The old grandpaw spat on the concrete floor.

Dietrich swore under his breath. Time was ticking away.

"Get your hands up," said the old man.

"Hold on, there's no need for this." But he raised his

hands.

"Radio said a Comanche helicopter was there."

"I'm regular Army – I haven't been anywhere near the municipal airport. I came from the other direction."

"You be a lying son of a bitch."

Dietrich said, "I have US Army orders."

The man edged closer. "Them hands! Keep 'em up. Don't even twitch."

"Inside pocket, right-hand side," Dietrich said.

The old man made his mistake, eyes going to the flight jacket.

Dietrich inched nearer to him. Every muscle in his body ready.

The man said: "That's not an Army jacket."

"No, it's not," agreed Dietrich. He reached for the gun and punched the old man in the face.

The old man went down, but his grip on the shotgun was incredible. He wrenched it clear as he fell.

Both barrels swung up. "Don't you move," he said.

Dietrich ignored him and took two steps forward, crouching to spring. "You're an old man and you forget things. You've forgotten to cock it." He lunged again.

Gabriel's brother, Michael, stepped back, and straightened up to reveal his true height.

"I forget nothing," said Michael, and fired.

The astonished head of Lucifer's most prominent demon was blown off, leaving a bloody stump.

Michael turned way, dematerializing back into the vortex. He was heading for Arizona. He did not often do the work of Gabriel, but if he did, death came with him. Angels could not stop this airport carnage – it was too late, and Lucifer had somehow increased his power. These airport attacks were like a beast that couldn't be killed. At least Michael had cut off one of its heads.

And Cowboy was next.

~ ~ ~

If there was a God, thought Heathcote, He would smite Richard Powell. A few hours after the surprise attacks on the nation's airports began, the FBI director was already blaming Heathcote.

They both stood in the Oval office, briefing the President on events overall, and suggesting courses of action. Powell wanted to declare a state of emergency and send in drone-strikes, regardless of the civilian lives it cost. He also wanted the President to fire Heathcote.

Powell was indignant, blaming the big ex-marine's department for not seeing this coming.

Heathcote stood silent, accepting the inevitable and awaiting his sentence: The end of a thirty-year career.

"His incompetence, Mr. President, cannot be denied. It's Heathcote's job to sniff out this kind of thing, and he let us down."

"These are hardly terrorists, said the President.

"They are, sir – they're in-bred." It was the latest insider expression.

Christiansen did not understand. He looked inquiringly at Heathcote, who said, "He means 'Home Grown', sir."

"Ah, I see." The President turned back to Powell.

The FBI Director consulted his notes, little more than a copy of the news bulletins on today's 'Civil Unrest' at approximately two hundred airports. 'Civil Unrest' was how Powell had described these events to the Press, and he repeated it now, as if the situation could be helped by using the right phrasing. Director Powell saw himself as a master of spin.

He said, "Heathcote gave us no warning."

The accused stayed silent, offering no defense.

"No warning," repeated Powell. "A force that size, and he didn't notice. They had trucks, guns and tanks; not to mention twenty thousand fully-armed men on the march. The sons of bitches used public roads."

Heathcote said: "That's what fooled everyone. They hid by being out in the open like Army convoys. They became invisible."

"Well, they're not invisible now – they're blasting the hell out of our air transport system. Don't tell us how they did it, Heathcote. We can see that on T. V. Tell us how to fix this shit. Stop pretending none of this has anything to do with you, or your people. What do we fund you for? Why didn't you infiltrate these so-called Free Patriots? You've got undercover agents all over America and the Middle-East."

Richard Powell hid his delight. Given his new lofty position, the devil was paying him to slow down any White House response. Today's events were going well, and Powell was poised to deliver the death-blow. Any defense against Revenge of Islam was doomed, if Heathcote lost his job.

Powell would replace him with an idiot.

Unaware of any of that, but finally ready to speak out, Heathcote said, "We didn't infiltrate the Free Patriots for the same reason we don't control container-traffic coming into our ports – I don't have the budget, or the manpower. Same reason we never built a wall between California and Mexico. It's why I went hat-in-hand, begging for finance to beef-up border and coastal patrols. I have to stop six Korean nukes from getting into the country. I asked action on the Free Patriots three times, Mr. Powell, but you always said no, due to lack of funding. Those memos saying no are in my files and you signed them."

Powell became red in the face. "Don't you dare blame me . . ."

The President intervened. "That's enough. We're not playing this game with the nation in crisis. What I need is analysis and strategy. Nothing else. How do we stop this getting any worse?"

Heathcote said, "Defeat them on the ground. They have limited ammunition; we don't. Air-strikes, drones or smart bombs? All that means too much collateral damage. Ask any Iraqi in Baghdad. Using the Air Force is out. We can't risk killing civilians or first responders, like firefighters or police. A combination of Marines and regular troops is the answer. They encircle these guys in strength and overwhelm them, taking them prisoner as their bullets run out. We have the upper hand already. You just need to give the order, Mr. President."

Powell sneered. "How long will all this take?"

"Not long. They've done their worst already. We just need to mobilize and move against them."

"I agree," said the President. He reached for a phone, and gave some instructions to somebody.

When he hung up, Richard Powell said, "That's fine and good, sir, but what do we do about the chaos and destruction?"

Christiansen said, "Exactly how bad is it?"

Again Heathcote was positive. "Not as bad as feared. Our main six, the airports targeted for tomorrow, were not touched. That tells me this is part of an overall plan. Some places attacked today are in bad shape – but most aren't. These are part-time soldiers; not professional. Destruction is hard to measure and they stopped firing too soon. The bulk of air-traffic can move as normal. At least for the time being. We start urgent repair of everything that's been hit, as soon as we get these Free Patriot lunatics out of there."

Powell said: "I say stop all flights now."

"No," said Heathcote. "That's what we did after 9/11. Big mistake. It brought the country to a standstill, and almost wrecked our economy. For three months after that it was touch and go. Those attacks were meant to cripple us economically, and they almost succeeded. These attacks today, and those tomorrow, are intended to do the same thing. We can't let that happen. Our planes must keep flying."

Powell snorted. "Oh, I'm impressed. This is typical Heathcote – our runways and watchtowers are a shambles. Prince Kamal's deadline, if we can believe Heathcote at all, is tomorrow – and we should just carry on?"

"Stop this!" said the President. "What did I just say, Dick? We all work together on this; I insist on that, and it's my vote that counts. We hold off on airport closure for at least two or three days. They shut down easily enough; it's opening them up again that's difficult. Now let's move on."

The F. B. I. Director saw how the wind was blowing. He cleared his throat. "My suggestion is this: Send in troops to put down this uprising, or whatever it is, as soon as possible. Next save the infra-structure. Call in the National Guard and contractors all over the country and begin rebuilding as soon as the fighting stops. Meantime we face Revenge of Islam as before. Prince Kamal's bombers, and their bombs, are on the way. We have no choice."

It was everything Heathcote had said.

Nothing more, and nothing less.

The President said wryly, "Well said, Dick. Let's get on with it."

He stood up and walked them to the door.

Telling Heathcote to keep up the good work.

CHAPTER TWENTY ONE

HASSAN STOOD AT THE FRONT-DOOR of his Al Qaeda contact in Frankfurt. The rest of his team were waiting at Rhein/Main airport.

As he rang the doorbell,, Gabriel's thoughts were on America. Michael had killed Dietrich in the East, and then Wes Slater in the West, planting the thought in Cowboy's mind to lose height in an empty, perfectly safe, desert sky. His helicopter plunged to the ground and exploded among cactus and rocks, somewhere between Houston and Dallas, creating a fiery spectacle that was seen for miles; along with its plume of spiraling smoke. Dietrich and Slater were a serious loss to the devil.

Gabriel was sorry more was not done, but Lucifer's spear had been blunted. Now Heathcote and the President could get things under control.

And two of Lucifer's top demons were no more. Gabriel was sick of demons. His attack squad, back at the airport, contained eight of them. He intended to change that very soon. The angel pressed the doorbell again, and hoped whoever answered was an ordinary mortal.

She was.

And German-looking, and pretty and blonde.

She answered the door in a Smiley Face tee shirt, wiping sleep from her eyes with a hand holding a toothbrush. Around her neck was neck was a gold cross on a gold chain. She was getting ready for work.

That cross was a good sign.

Gabriel studied her, sensing someone ensnared by evildoers – and yet not quite so innocent herself.

Her eyes focused, and saw Hassan.

Hassan said, "Ulrike?"

He pronounced it in passable German.

She knew who Hassan was. "Come in." She took him into the kitchen, tossing the toothbrush onto a counter. "Please excuse the mess. I asked for today off – because you were coming – but my boss hates me." Her German was high-class and well enunciated. A poor little rich girl.

Gabriel sat down at the table. Choosing a moderate accent of the Middle-East, he said, "You have instructions for me?"

"Yes." She moved to the stove. "Would you like coffee."

"Please." Coffee would allow them time together.

"How do you like it?"

"Black, with sugar. Am I making you late?"

He didn't care if he was.

"No, it's okay. I called and said my car wouldn't start."

Hassan smiled. "So what do I need to know?"

"No. Coffee first. Don't rush me. I want to get it right." But as Ulrike said this, her hands shook and her voice faltered.

Hassan stood up, went over to her, and touched her on the shoulder. "What's the matter?"

She looked at him, and she was crying. She said softly: "The reason you're going to America – it's terrible."

That was encouraging. "Tell me what I need to know."

"You know it's a nuclear attack?"

"Of course. We trained for it."

"Verdammt!"

Gabriel was not sure if she was damning him, or herself, or the situation. He said, You work for these people, knowing what they do, and now you feel guilty? Isn't it a bit late for that?"

She sniffed, fighting off the tears. "Yes."

"Tell me my target city."

"I won't."

Hassan said: "Listen. Things are not what they seem. I promise you, no harm will come to that city."

"I don't believe you."

Then there's nothing more to say."

Gabriel could hypnotize her, but he was pretty sure she needed this chance to save her soul. He sat back down, took out a cell phone and brought up his programmed list of local Al Qaeda members. He flipped down to the number of a demon who controlled this unhappy and misguided young woman.

This demon would now come to Gabriel.

The number answered immediately. The Archangel said, This is Hassan. Yes, I'm here . . . but the girl is not. I had to break in, and I don't know what I'm looking for. How long will it take you to get here? Yes, of course I'll wait. I must know by destination in the United States."

He hung up and put the cell phone away.

He sat in silence for a moment, feeling her eyes upon him. Then she said, "That was clever of you. Now Rashid is coming, isn't he? You told him I wasn't here. Should I leave or stay?"

Hassan said: "Stay until he gets here, in case it's not him – but get dressed in your street clothes."

She poured him some coffee, leaving the pot beside his cup in case he wanted more. Then she went off to change.

When she came back she was quite the junior executive. She had on a smart gray suit under a pleated black gaberdine raincoat with a tie-belt. Ulrike's hair was swept up in a neat bun, her make-up flawless.

Hassan said: "I just called them back."

"Oh, God. They're not coming?"

"They're on their way. I said you came home again – that explains why you're still here when they arrive."

The coffee smelled good. She poured him a second cup, poured one for herself, and sat down next to him.

"I'll tell you which city," she said. "Rashid would make me anyway – he likes hurting women."

"No one will . . ."

She broke in. "You're target is Chicago, O'Hare." She fumbled nervously in her coat pocket, producing cigarettes and lighter. She lit one and inhaled deeply. "Why don't I feel better?"

"You will – trust me."

"No. I give you an American city – and millions die."

He said: "Calm down – it's not as bad as you think. Don't you have to give me something else?"

"Some keys." She went to a kitchen drawer and took out an envelope. They're in here. They all open left-luggage boxes at Rhein/Main, and each one has the name of who gets the clothing and other things left inside."

She gave him the small package.

He shook it. The keys rattled. "Tell me about Rashid."

She shrugged, and sat down again, "He's a big man in the Jihad. Likes to show off how devout he is – always talking about the will of Allah, and the end of the Great Satan. That's what they call America."

Hassan said: "I know. I'm one of them."

She managed a faint smile. Maybe she was feeling better.

"What else?" he said.

She sighed. "Rashid started out as my lover. Then he recruited me. I wasn't very interested in the beginning, it sounded stupid to me, but I loved him and he was great in bed. We made love every night – and he took me to meet people during the day. People important to the cause. They ran night clubs and restaurants mostly, but some owned banks, supermarkets and gas-stations, and other businesses making good money in the Turkish quarter."

"A lot of that money came to Rashid, for Al Qaeda. Sometimes he got millions of Marks, and he took it to his car in a metal case with me on his arm. He promised it was completely safe, carrying a small fortune in the toughest part of Frankfurt. He said no one would dare lay a finger on him, and they never did. The cash went to an account at Deutsche Bank – and from there to another account in Switzerland. God knows what happened to it after that."

"And Rashid? He's not your lover anymore."

"No. He just comes here when he needs me to do something – like giving you your keys and destination."

Car doors were slamming, down in the street. Ulrike went and looked outside. "It's them – it's Rashid."

Soon there was a loud ring on her doorbell.

Ulrike walked down the hallway. She looked through the spy-hole, and came back. "He has one of his thugs with him. What shall I do?" She looked very afraid.

"Let them both in."

Ulrike disappeared. Gabriel sat listening. The doorbell sounded once more; then she opened the door.

Gabriel heard a man's voice. "Is he here?"

Her voice was a whisper. "Ja."

Gabriel read the intent of both visitors. They were here to kill Hassan, but the girl had no idea. They keys were to go to Ashirad – who would then take over as team leader. Instructions from the late Prince Kamal.

Gabriel smiled in the kitchen.

There footsteps were silent as they entered. "Don't stand there gaping, woman. Introduce me to Hassan." Rashid spoke perfect German, with only the slightest accent, and that sounded English, if anything.

Ulrike blushed. "He's at the table."

Hassan stood up.

Rashid stepped forward and shook his hand. "I am Rashid. I have been hoping to meet you."

Gabriel knew they had been ordered to meet him. That was why they used a girl who was having serious second thoughts. They had known Hassan would phone them. That was why he had their number. As a result of all this, the girl would not be tortured. Sometimes things worked out perfectly.

Rashid was tall and handsome, with a moustache. He made his companion, whose name was Yissar, look even uglier than he actually was. Yissar reminded Gabriel of Otto, Karl Jaeger's strong-arm in Kiel. The Muslim version.

They all sat down at the table.

Rashid was a young demon. Yissar was his troll.

Ulrike said brightly: "Some coffee?"

Gabriel thought, One more cup, and I'll throw up. Before the others said anything, he told her, "It's very kind of you, but you're already late for work, and I want to talk to Rashid."

She took the hint, standing up and smoothing down her raincoat. "I'll leave you to it, then." She collected her purse from another room, and told them to lock up when they were done. Then she left for work. With her gone, Rashid got up and made more coffee. While he waited for the water to boil, he said in Pakistani Urdu, "We'll take you back to the airport."

Gabriel thought, You're very smooth, Rashid,

Hassan said, "I'm grateful. Taxis are hard to find."

"Prince Kamal says you are a good man."

Things suddenly fell into place. Rashid's thoughts revealed what Prince Kamal managed to keep hidden, because Gabriel had rarely wondered what he was thinking. It seemed the Prince had decided to clean house, in case Shahanna and Clement were spies after all. The same went for Jhalal and Hassan. None of them would ever get to America.

Gabriel would see about that.

The coffee was ready. Hassan refused. The others drained theirs quickly and stood up. "Rashid said, "I have money for you. We have to stop at my bank to get it."

Gabriel had wondered how they would explain going the wrong way for the airport. The bank was it.

""Well," said Hassan. "Then we'd better get moving."

An engine started outside.

"My Mercedes," said Rashid.

Hassan got to his feet.

He waited to let Yissar go first.

Rashid pushed past them both and made for the front door.

They followed him down to the street.

The Mercedes, long and elegant, sat at the curb, a

misty trail coming from its exhaust. The front passenger door swung open. Rashid got in and spoke to the driver; then indicated that Yissar and Hassan sit together in the back. They got in, and the car pulled away. It was soon following signs for the Autobahn.

Rashid pointed at the driver. "Hassan, this is my friend, Karim. My other friend, Yissar, has a chromium plated pistol pointed at your heart. If that you do anything rash, or refuse to answer my questions, he will pull the trigger, resulting in your death. Now, who is your CIA contact in America? How did they recruit you?"

Gabriel had no answers for him. He couldn't be bothered to lie to these morons. They didn't have long to live, and the joke was they thought they were going to kill him. He decided to pretend that Hassan was confused by the accusations, but fiercely loyal to Prince Kamal.

He said" "Are you sure you have the right Hassan? The prince picked me to lead this team. He never suspected me of anything."

Rashid grinned. "He suspected your relationship with that Moroccan bitch and her boyfriend. When those four American soldiers were captured, it was clear someone had revealed the location of the Iranian camp. It had to be Sorya and her ex-lover, or it had to be you and Jhalal – because you were always with them – and you, Hassan went missing for long periods.

Gabriel was impressed in spite of himself. Prince Kamal had been a good deal smarter than he seemed. Just as well he was gone.

Rashid gave directions to Karim, to a place where they doubtless intended to stop and dispose of Hassan. There was no more mention of Rashid's bank.

Katzenberger Waldt.

It was a forest near Frankfurter Kreuz.

Twenty Kilometers away.

Karim said, "Five minutes on the Autobahn.

Gabriel sat back and relaxed.

Rashid tried again. "Where did you meet Sorya?"

"At the camp. She arrived with His Highness."

A string of other questions were ignored.

This stretch of Autobahn was surprisingly clear. The Mercedes cruised at 130 Kilometers an hour. Trees and fence posts rushed by in a blur. Rashid turned to the driver. "First exit after the Autobahnkreuz." Karim nodded, but the car did not slow down.

Rashid asked more stupid questions.

Hassan said nothing..

Karim braked. Their speed was cut by half, then by even more again, as Karim braked harder, and they entered a winding exit ramp. They were suddenly in a densely treed wood, on a back road with no habitation. Karim whipped around the curves as if still on the Autobahn. One side of the road was a sheer drop of fifty feet. If Gabriel were not immortal he would have been scared to death.

Two side roads and one stack of felled trees came and went, but the Mercedes did not stop. Gabriel could not wait any longer. Whatever Rashid had in mind was taking too long. Hassan had to be at the airport. His Jihadis were waiting. These Frankfurt demons must die now.

And Rashid would finally shut up.

The road straightened out after a curve, with no other traffic in sight. This was the perfect spot. Gabriel waggled one finger, and gave Karim a seizure. The driver slumped forward, head and chest striking the steering wheel, causing the horn to blare loudly, and the car to veer sharply left. Rashid reacted surprisingly quickly. He steered the car with one hand, and pulled Karim upright with the other. He shouted at Yissar to help him. Between them they bundled Karim into the back, while Rashid brought the car under control.

Gabriel waggled his finger again. Two more heart attacks, and the car contained nothing but dead bodies. The angel drifted out as Rashid's lifeless hand pulled the wheel to the right, and the Mercedes tore into the safety rail, showering bright, orange sparks. The big car sped on for another hundred meters, finally plunging with a tearing crash, through steel forged and galvanized in the Ruhr valley. The car somersaulted, and was propelled over the edge by its own weight.

It bounced twice, striking rocks and shingle on the way down. The gasoline-lines ruptured from the impact, and the engine caught fire, shooting orange flame back under pressure through the system, as far as the gas-tank.

Gabriel drifted clear and watched, as the Mercedes catapulted into the tree line below and came to rest upside down.

It exploded in a gusher of flame.

Gabriel said: "Goodbye, Rashid."

Now Ulrike could live in peace.

~ ~ ~

The North Korean Freighter Wai Duc To arrived in Halifax, Nova Scotia on July 2nd. The deck crew moored at an unloading pier and presented a falsified cargo manifest to the Harbor Master's representatives when they came on board.

Strangely, for this was a courteous, hospitable city, these port officials were neither smiling or friendly as the examined the paperwork, and examined it far more thoroughly than expected. They asked to see the Captain. He came, bringing a Filipino steward who understood English. The Captain was informed that his ship was under quarantine, and subject to search. He remained unruffled, having transferred three large crates to another vessel – ten miles out to sea.

The Iranian nukes were gone.

An FBI team arrived within hours. Heathcote was with them, having taken charge from the moment they all landed in Canada. They were all hand-picked, and they were either anti-terrorist or anti-drug. The two abilities Heathcote needed, given this situation. His anti-drug teams knew how to search, and his counter-terrorist operatives knew how to interrogate.

Heathcote had a black belt in both.

They searched the holds of the ship from bow to stern. At the same time groups of F. B. I. drug interdiction agents, aided by Canadian and American coast guard and police units, went over every inch of the deck. They had three canines with handlers. These dogs were trained to detect the space-age packaging required for the storage, preservation or transport of fissionable material. They were German shepherds, flown in from a nuclear research facility in Nevada. They barked furiously, at one specific location near the port side, apparently smelling traces of something, but no cargo of any kind was anywhere in sight. Heathcote was undeterred, telling the dog handlers to keep going. If their animals couldn't find the Korean weapons, nobody would.

And nobody did.

They found nothing.

By mid-afternoon the ship had been taken apart from top to bottom.

Then they did it again.

Again nothing.

It would be getting dark soon, and Heathcote called it off. He walked disgustedly down the metal gang-plank, aware he had been duped. The cargo was somewhere else. Probably transferred to a smaller vessel, not too far out to sea. Giant, dockside cranes dominated the harbor, mocking him and his search party as they came ashore. All was still, as they walked to their cars, save for lights coming on in scattered buildings. Water lapped gently beyond the jetty, the sea shimmering, its ripples receding into the gloomy twilight.

Heathcote drove in a rented Ford, and used a borrowed cell-phone. He caught the Harbor Master at his evening meal. Heathcote spoke, he explained, with the authority of the Canadian Prime Minister, obtained for the visiting investigators by the President of the United States. The Korean ship was to be impounded, the Captain and crew arrested and put in jail. Police were on their way.

Heathcote called their main precinct. He introduced himself to a desk-sergeant and gave him a heads up.

No one was to have access to the prisoners; no lawyers, no food, nothing to drink. They were to be stripped to their underwear and kept in individual cells. No shoes and no central heating. Let them spend an uncomfortable night in fear; then Heathcote's people would turn them inside out.

He hung up, assured that everything would be carried

out to the letter. Heathcote felt encouraged. Clearly he had more clout in Nova Scotia than he did at home. He soon heard police sirens nearing the docks, and a string of black vans, windows barred, went rushing by within minutes.

Heathcote went to his hotel and checked in, hoping to catch a few hours' sleep. He wanted to be at least half awake, and half alert, when questioning the North Koreans in the morning.

There was an e-mail from Mexico waiting for him at the front desk. It came from the team he had sent to find the southbound Korean freighter. They had found it, and it was empty. Again the nuclear devices had been unloaded at sea before docking, onto any one of a thousand fishing craft in the area. Heathcote's man-in-charge down there was asking for instructions.

Heathcote sent a cable back: Hold captain and crew at all costs. Sweat them until somebody talks.

Then he went to his room.

He imagined two fishing boats entering US waters from extreme north and south under full power. He called his coastguard contacts. They said it was hopeless, but they would try. Every seagoing vessel they had would try.

He phoned the Border Patrol for helicopter coverage, then alerted northern and southern Air Force squadrons as well.

They said a night search was a waste of time. Their radar instruments could miss a small enough fishing boat. Heathcote said fuck that. This was why God invented the infra-red lens in the first place. Just get out there and find the goddamned nukes! But he knew they were right. It was hopeless. Looking for two fishing boats was worse than looking for two freighters. Heathcote still had to try. He invoked the name of President Christiansen, and that settled it.

The helicopters took to the air.

So did Air Force jet-fighters and spotter planes.

His room phone started ringing. It was a conference call. The President, the cabinet and the Chiefs of Staff wanted to talk to him. Heathcote gave up any thought of sleep. The aide he spoke to put him on hold, so he grabbed his notes and sat on the bed, holding the receiver to his ear.

He imagined their reaction to what he had to say.

There was an acoustic hum, accompanied by a low hiss of electronic echo as he listened, which then became an unnerving silence. Finally the telephone came abruptly to life, and somebody spoke. It was the President, his tone businesslike and reassuring, as it always was.

It steadied Heathcote nerves.

As he expected, they wanted an update on what was going on, and would he start with the airport attacks. Heathcote was encouraged. This gave him some good news to start with. Thousands of insurgents, he said – those calling themselves the Free Patriot Militia – were either dead, taken prisoner, or fleeing on all fronts. For thirty-six hours, local law enforcement and National Guard divisions had performed miracles, backed by regular Army, Marines and Reserves. They had subdued the uprising. Every occupied airport had by now surrendered.

Repair work was already under way, and many scheduled flights would resume across the country tomorrow morning. The civil death-toll was not as high as feared, but still substantial, and represented a national disaster of forbidding scale. The Free Patriot Militia had been captured in droves. Charges were being brought at Federal and State level, and the militants would face the death penalty without exception. Those on the run would be caught. They were easy to spot, armed and dressed as they were, and they had no public sympathy whatsoever. Large and small groups were already being pointed out to the authorities.

There was quiet at the Washington end.

Until Heathcote invited questions. Then the response was that of parrots in a cage, but the President drowned them out, saying time was pressing and they should move on. Mr. Heathcote had covered the main facts, and the State Department would issue a press release in the morning. Any outstanding questions should be answered then. Heathcote was glad to be over the first hurdle, but the next subject, the Al Qaeda nukes and their unknown whereabouts, would be much harder.

He consulted his notes and took a deep breath. Then he reported the seizure of two North Korean freighters, and their lack of cargo, knowing there would be hard questions when he finished, with nothing the President could do to help him.

There was no way to make this look good.

Heathcote outlined the situation, and as they listened, he sensed their outrage and disbelief, but he battled on, hoping he imagined it. He could have left out the worst part: like two fishing boats being almost invisible, or that the bombs could already be ashore, but he didn't. President Christiansen valued honesty, Heathcote knew, and so he withheld nothing.

He was right about their response. They attacked him. It was hard to hear the best minds in Washington doubt his ability, his judgment and his chances of success. He was tempted to tell them all to go to hell. He longed to shout down the phone, "Get somebody else, if they can do better!" But he remained calm, and explained the situation again, in terms of what could be done and what could not. He concluded by saying the odds were actually in his favor.

Six groups of terrorists against all of America's might.

They reluctantly accepted that.

And that brought him to the next topic. He had saved the Fourth of July for last. He tossed his notes aside and gripped the receiver. Heathcote knew what he must say, and reading it would not make it any better. There was only one way to tell this. They may as well hear his own, frank assessment.

He began with Prince Kamal's terror squads – as newsrooms around the world might soon be calling them. He told of them leaving Afghanistan; then crossing Russia and spending a night in Moscow; from there they flew on to Frankfurt, Paris, London and other destinations, having broken down into smaller groups. They were under close surveillance by Heathcote's army of FBI agents, and would remain so, until they got to the United States. The threat was contained. Heathcote knew where they all were, and pretty much where they were going. Those six bombs must be found, and Asuto's teams were the only link. They were supposed to receive them by tomorrow – and that was all Heathcote had to work with for now. He told his Washington audience he would soon know more. Interrogation of the two North Korean ship crews was bound to produce something.

Heathcote hoped it was true.

He paused, then continued:

The target cities were on full alert. None of them had been attacked by the Free Patriots, and that spoke for itself.

He recited the list into the phone, although everyone already knew it. JFK was first, and then the others: Chicago . . . Miami . . . Houston . . . Washington DC. And finally, Los Angeles and San Diego, the only significant targets in California, everything else already bombarded by the Patriot Militia. Revenge of Islam was committed to those six airports, they had nowhere else to go.

Those listening finally grasped the logic of his strategy. As Heathcote spoke there were murmurs of approval. Discontent was fading,

Heathcote stopped talking and the President thanked him and wished him luck. There were echoes of this from the others. Then the White House speaker phone ceased humming and the line went dead.

Now Heathcote stood alone.

Sleep was impossible.

He smoked cigarettes all night.

CHAPTER TWENTY TWO

A 747 OUT OF FRANKFURT was flying at twenty-thousand feet.

It was an American Airlines flight to London, and Hassan's entire team was on board. From there, they'd go on to Chicago, flying with British Airways on yet another space-available booking.

Jhalal was on edge. Like everyone else, he had picked up a gun and other items , including some unexpected clothing, from a left luggage box in the Frankfurt Departure Hall. It was a jacket and pants unlike the Lufthansa uniform he wore now. He was dying to change into it, because after two days in the same clothes, Jhalal smelled bad and felt disgusting.

But this new outfit was no good yet. He couldn't put it on until the final leg of the journey. These clothes had nothing to do with an airline. They had come from Chicago, O'Hare, with markings that said he worked there as ground crew. The whole team would pose as airport workers. but they all had the same problem: They must wait, putting on the uniform under a raincoat, shortly before landing in Chicago. This must be done in the restrooms, and only when the moment was right. That moment was still hours away. Jhalal stared at the floor, and tried to ignore his own stink. A good thing he had a window seat to himself.

This was only Jhalal's second flight ever. He sat with his face averted, to escape the attention of passersby, certain that he could never pass for German, if anyone looked too closely. Some passenger would expose him, pointing a finger and shouting: "That man is a terrorist!" So far it hadn't happened, but the journey wasn't over yet. The Iraqi shifted in his seat, silently cursing Prince Kamal.

They barely touched down at Heathrow, before they were in the air again, this time headed for O'Hare.

This flight lasted just under eight hours, and again, Jhalal endured it in solitary misery. When they landed in London, things went quicker than in Frankfurt. No birds in jet-intakes, no smiling Swedish lady giving Jhalal and his companions furtive glances. Jhalal was afraid some other team member might suspect what he and Hassan already knew – they were under FBI surveillance, and had been since reaching Germany. British Airways had been tipped off, and this rather special aircraft was being rushed through on purpose.

As a result everything went smoothly and they took off on time. The main thing, for Jhalal, was being able to wash and change. His turn was next. Ashirad and Mahata had gone into the tiny steel closet of a toilet first, and were still there fifteen minutes later, by Jhalal's watch.

When he got up and tried the door, strange bumping sounds came from the other side, accompanied by grunts, moaning and other sounds indicating that sex was taking place. Jhalal thought both women insane, but had no wish to confront them. Both were ill-tempered and unpredictable.

He went back to his seat, glaring angrily at the door.

~ ~ ~

Shahanna sat watching, two rows back. She knew it was Jhalal's turn, being very conscious of the long delay, needing the toilet for another reason. Shahanna had to pee, and she wished Jhalal had dragged those two women out of there. But Jhalal failed her, by retreating, and now she was desperate.

She would ask for help.

Sharif Bakhar had the seat behind her, and he was startled when she popped up and spoke to him.

"How's your bladder?" she said.

"Disgusting woman," he said. "guard your tongue."

Shahanna felt hopeless. That was the answer most of them would give. Maybe her phrasing was poor, but none of these devout Muslim men would discuss this subject with a woman.

That didn't solve her problem. Every second spent squirming in her seat was an eternity. She became afraid of wetting herself. She giggled, at how Sharif Bakhar would react to that. She stared out at the layered clouds, and her discomfort eased up a little. Then she remembered Hassan, offered up a short prayer, and went to find him. There must be a toilet at his end of the plane.

There were two but they were occupied. However she did find Hassan, relaxed and reading the New York Times. Page one was taken up completely by the defeat of the Free Patriots, and asked, in a blaring headline, if the danger was over or just beginning? Both Hassan and "Sorya" knew the answer to that. It was why they were here. He looked up and smiled when she sat next to him.

She explained her problem, ashamed to say something so personal, although telling Sharif Bakhar didn't bother her at all. Telling Hassan made her feel impure. And yet she realized, even as she told him, her urge to urinate was greatly reduced. Hassan somehow having done this flashed into her mind, making her wonder at her own foolishness. But it was a minor miracle.

"Feeling better?" he asked.

It was as if he knew . . .

Yes, she told him. But she still had to change her clothes.

Hassan got to his feet. "Follow me."

He strode off between twin rows of seats, in the direction of a bathroom occupied by a pair of tiresome Arab women. Shahanna's mouth went dry. She sensed trouble with both these she-monsters, who would certainly blame her for Hassan's intervention. But she followed obediently.

Hassan spoke over his shoulder. "Leave this to me," he said. "They won't hurt you. That's a promise."

She thought, Reading my mind again?

They stood at the bathroom door.

Hassan knocked loudly.

"Go away!" It was Mahata's voice, sounding breathless. "Piss in a bottle. If I open this door you'll be sorry."

Gabriel reached out and gripped the metal handle. It turned, and the door swung open. He said, "They must have forgotten to lock it."

Shahanna thought that unlikely. And hadn't he made a strange gesture with his other hand?

"Shut that door!" screamed Ashirad. They both stood, naked, revealed in the widening gap. Their faces were flushed, and Shahanna realized in a flash what these two had been doing. If it was anybody else, she would have laughed. But it was them. And there was hate in Ashirad's eyes, as she glimpsed Sorya, half-hidden by Hassan's distinctive height.

Mahata glared at her, too, and shouted, "Get out of here!" She made as if to close the door, but Hassan stuck his foot in the gap. When Mahata saw who he was, her face changed, and she stopped pushing at the door. She said, "A thousand pardons, Hassan. We're just leaving." There was movement behind her, and a rustle of clothing. Hassan pulled the door shut, and waited outside with Shahanna.

She thought, Now what?

Minutes passed.

The door opened again, and the two women emerged looking sheepish. The looks they gave Shahanna froze her blood.

She thought, I'm as good as dead.

Hassan won't save me next time.

~ ~ ~

Heathcote dozed off towards dawn, and the phone rang.

He heaved out of his armchair to answer it, patting his shirt pocket for American cigarettes with the other hand. He yawned at the voice on the other end. "Yes, okay. I'm coming right away."

It was time for the North Koreans.

The Canadian calling him sounded old-style cop. "We'll get these fucks to talk, sir. I promise you that."

Heathcote thanked him and hung up, knowing he needed men like that to succeed. Men like that, and the goodwill of that man's boss, who was as yet an unknown quantity. Was he old-style cop, too, or a fucking menace, like Richard Powell? Whatever he turned out to be could make or break Heathcote.

Heathcote put on the same crumpled jacket he threw on the floor a few hours ago. He phoned one of his senior men. "Get everyone over to Police Headquarters – and bring our Korean speakers with you. I'll be there soon."

There were no taxis on the street. He started walking in the direction he needed to go. Eventually a cab came in sight and drew up next to him. "Where to, eh?" Heathcote told him and got in.

Daylight broke as they drove. A million diamonds danced on the bright waters of the harbor, where the driver turned sharply, and whisked them towards the municipal district. Ten minutes later Heathcote entered the office of the Canadian in charge of any chance Heathcote might have to squeeze his North Korean prisoners until the name of a fishing boat popped out.

John Hearst, according to his desk plaque, was a full Inspector of Police. By the look of him, good at his job from doing it a long time. He had on a suit more rumpled than Heathcote's, and a face resembling John Wayne. Best of all his ashtray was full of cigarette stubs.

Heathcote liked him already.

He said: "Inspector Hearst, if you have time, I thought we could use a few moments on our own."

He smiled as he sat down opposite his host, whose office was littered with files and papers; just like Heathcote's.

~ ~ ~

Inspector Hearst smiled back. This was the American who had everyone shitting bricks. The Commissioner had called Hearst, followed by the Mayor and some Border officer in the Mounties, who spouted enough heroic bullshit to last the inspector a very long time. Then finally, a call came from the Canadian Prime Minister, and Inspector Hearst finally took these callers seriously, because everyone had said pretty much the same thing:

Give this Heathcote whatever he wants.

And do it before he asks.

Inspector Hearst had got it.

Now he said: "What can I do for you, sir?"

"Well, stop calling me sir. The name's Brad."

"Brad. What else?"

"Can I smoke?"

"Sure, go ahead." He pushed the ashtray nearer.

He certainly seemed obliging enough.

Heathcote lit a Camel and offered one to Hearst, who lit it with a gold lighter and inhaled slowly. He said, "Now, what can I really do for you?"

"Bend some rules," said Heathcote, thinking, Are you ready to help me do what it takes? Even bad things? Aloud, he said, "I need to tell you stuff that's top secret. Is that a problem?"

"Not for me."

"Okay." Heathcote was inclined to trust this man. "You know about the chaos at our airports. Well, it gets worse. Within twenty-four hours, three nuclear devices from that cargo ship will go off in our largest urban areas – so will another three coming in through Mexico. They were all unloaded offshore."

"So that's it. We wondered about that search. Asked for by your State Department. It was top priority."

"Now you know. This is a threat of some magnitude. Every second we spend on those Koreans is probably worth a human life – an American life. Our time is running out. I've come to ask how you feel if certain guidelines get pushed aside. These fuckers will not be read their rights."

"You want to get rough."

It wasn't a question.

"Extremely." Heathcote felt the self-loathing rise in his throat. He swallowed it, and waited for Hearst to speak.

The Inspector leaned forward. "Let me put it this way: You have a blank check here. It's like a poker hand. You have four aces. Such an attack on your country will not be tolerated by my country. Some big fish have made it clear that you have a free hand, but on a personal note, I'll go even further: If those Koreans downstairs brought this evil to your door, I'll watch you shoot every one of them, and re-load your gun when you run out of bullets. Do I make myself clear?"

Heathcote was so relieved he couldn't speak.

Inspector Hearst said, "You're in charge. Do whatever it takes."

"Thank you," said Heathcote. "He said a silent prayer of thanks, and let his breath out slowly.

He had one final favor to ask. "I'll need your best interrogators."

"They're yours. To work with your men?"

"No. Keep them separate. Techniques vary, and your guys and mine will do better with their regular partners. Speed is essential. The bombs are moving as we speak. I was thinking teams of two, if you agree."

"That's certainly how we do it." Hearst spread his hands and smiled. "Anything else you want?"

"Just to get started. Oh . . . and thank you. I can't tell

you how much I appreciate your help."

Hearst smiled again. "Don't mention it. We're neighbors."

He walked around the desk to shake Heathcote's hand. It was a heartfelt gesture. It said he understood terrorism, nuclear weapons and the urgency of this. It said he knew Heathcote was a good man in a tough spot.

It said Hearst was a good man himself.

He went back and sat down. Then he made some phone calls, assigning detectives to Heathcote. When he hung up, the two leaders discussed what needed doing, how to do it, and how many pairs they had to work with.

Today would be a long day.

Half an hour later, Hearst took Heathcote down to a hastily assembled operations room. More than thirty interrogators were waiting. Most stood and sat within easy reach of the interview rooms on this floor, others close to the elevators. There were other rooms and cells on the upper levels. Overnight each had been equipped with two-way mirrors, movement-activated cameras and recording devices for both audio and video equipment. As Hearst put it to Heathcote, they had everything Canadian cops watched on American TV. The room buzzed with police talk, and smelled of aftershave. Heathcote felt quite at home.

A dozen Korean interpreters sat off in a corner.

Hearst made a short speech, accompanied by a round of introductions. Heathcote retained as many of the names and faces as he could. A dozen or so detectives sounded French when speaking English, and he tried hard to pronounce their names correctly. They had volunteered from nearby Quebec.

Eventually it was his turn to speak.

The expertise of everyone in this room was needed, Heathcote said, as he told them how these North Koreans were to be treated. There was little time. Every question had to count. Every morsel of information squeezed out. If anyone felt reluctant about a tough, hands on approach, they ought to leave now, and Heathcote would understand. Violence was offensive, and against God. It made Heathcote feel sick.

No one moved.

Heathcote thanked them.

They split up in groups, and the Korean ship's officers were brought in, wearing only their skivvies and shoes, as instructed. This included the Captain, who was quickly pointed out to Heathcote.

Heathcote said, "I'll take him myself."

This was the eight hundred pound gorilla.

The man who knew everything.

Regular crew would be interviewed here, and upstairs, because there were so many of them, and a number of detectives and FBI entered the elevators. Their expressions said it was game-time, and they knew it.

Heathcote took two of his men from Alexandria, and the Korean Captain, into a cell. A translator followed them. They all sat around a steel table bolted to the floor. One of the FBI men turned on a recorder-camera, noting time and date. The North Korean Commander was breathing hard, not surprising, given his situation, and his eyes darted from one captor to another.

Heathcote thought, This fucker's scared shitless.

This was soon proved wrong.

The interpreter, a slightly built, Canadian-born Korean in his thirties, sat next to the prisoner. He introduced himself to the Captain in their own language.

The Captain spat in his face.

Heathcote finally understood. This was all planned. The Captain was acting under orders. He was scared, as Heathcote had seen, but he was also playing a part: Playing for time, allowing the nuclear weapons to make their way into American waters, to be picked up and transported inland.

The translator was given a tissue.

He wiped the spittle off his cheek.

Heathcote asked the Captain his name.

The interpreter repeated it in a subdued voice.

This time there was no spitting.

The Captain slapped the interpreter across the face.

The two FBI men grabbed his arms and cuffed him.

Heathcote said: "This isn't working. He's fucking with us. We have to get control, or he'll keep this up all day."

He knew his men understood that.

The translator looked angry but confused.

Heathcote stood up. The Captain stared defiantly at him. The American walked slowly around the table — producing a near-empty pack of Camels and removing one, placing it between his lips as he went. Heathcote stood before the handcuffed prisoner, lighting the cigarette; then he drew on it, hard, several times, until it glowed redly. He saw the Captain's face change. The hostility left, and fear took its place, as he eyed the cigarette like a cornered rat. He was a coward after all. That would help. Heathcote took the cigarette and held it close to the man's eye. Then he told the interpreter to say there would be no more spitting, slapping, or bad behavior of any kind. Heathcote waited, as every word was translated.

The Captain hissed like a snake.

But his eyes never left that cigarette. Now Heathcote repeated his original question, and this time they got his name. Then he told them his home port.

He was cracking.

But it was taking too long.

CHAPTER TWENTY THREE

IT WAS SHAHANNA'S TURN to become a Chicago airport worker by changing in the restroom. They were an hour from O'Hare. She was second to last. Last was Hassan, seated at the back. Shahanna glared at a toilet that seemed like a curse on them all. A curse placed by God, or Prince Kamal. She couldn't decide which.

When not in use for lesbian sex, it was occupied by a sporadic but never-ending stream of passengers. Using it to switch clothes was the worst idea Prince Kamal ever had. Shahanna stood up with her carry-on from Left-luggage in Frankfurt. Thanks to Heathcote's intervention, it was not searched at any stage of the journey. She made her way down the aisle.

The sign on the door said: VACANT. Shahanna went inside, slid the bolt and bent over to unzip her bag on the floor. The cubicle was cramped and faintly smelly. This was going to be difficult.

She took out an apron, skirt and striped cap. Apparently she was a cafeteria waitress at Chicago's international airport, because the blouse that came next had a name-tag. Her name was Maria Sanchez.

She took off her Air France uniform and stood in her underwear. There was a knock on the door. She called out: "Just a minute," as she struggled into a hip-hugging brown skirt.

The knock came again, and a voice hissed: "It's urgent!"

Shahanna recognized Ashirad's voice, and nearly died of fright. Then she tried to bluff it out. "Who is it?"

The door was rattled from outside and a screw dropped from the bolt. Ashirad must have loosened it when it was her turn to get changed. The door slammed inwards and two pairs of hands seized Shahanna. Her throat was suddenly in a death grip. Now the door was kicked shut. She choked, trying to scream, but no sound came. She kicked out wildly and wriggled partly free. Her neck was released, and she bit someone's arm, but a fist struck the side of her face, bouncing her head off the metal wall. Now Ashirad stood before her, ready with another punch.

It never came.

The door opened again, and suddenly Hassan had Ashirad from behind. There was a retching sound; then she sagged against the wall and slid to the floor. She stayed there, not breathing. Hassan stepped past Shahanna and pointed at Mahata, who clutched her chest and sank to her knees. Her face bore a tortured expression, brown eyes blank and unfocused.

Both women were dead.

Gabriel knew without looking. This turn of events would have to be dealt with. But first he helped Shahanna get dressed, talking quietly the whole time to lessen the shock. Then he sent her back to her seat.

What he had to do would not take long.

First he dissolved the women's Chicago uniforms, then, out of thin air, he conjured high-priced tourist attire:

Designer pants, blouses and head-scarfs, and the brand-name purses only carried by rich women.

Working quickly, he arranged both corpses and scattered the clothes randomly on the floor, as if done carelessly, in a fit of passion. He was thinking of them naked in here before. He rolled Mahata onto her back, spread her legs, knees bent, feet flat on the floor. He placed Ashirad in a kneeling crouch, face down, her head upon Mahata's thigh. The diagram was easy enough to follow.

The odds for two heart attacks are astronomical, but no one would worry about that. Two women died having sex. Policemen and forensic experts have a morbid sense of humor. This would cloud their thinking when they came on board. Later this would infect everyone, including the media. Hassan and the others would be long gone before people stopped snickering. Gabriel looked around to make sure he had everything right. There must be no trace of Shahanna.

He closed the door behind him and went back down the plane, his Chicago outfit miraculously appearing on his lofty frame. He sat down, crossed his legs and went back to reading his magazine.

He did not have to wait long.

A fat lady opened the door and screamed.

On landing they were held up for hours.

~ ~ ~

They all wore raincoats through Immigration. Gabriel stood first in line, looking relaxed, holding his customs declaration form. Behind him stood Clement, filling out his own, using a pen borrowed from Shahanna, who had stated she had no contraband, and signed to that effect.

Just like Hassan before her.

Every conspirator had their coat buttoned to the neck, but so did a lot of other people, and no one paid much attention.

Gabriel had made it rain outside.

The soon-to-be airport staff stayed close together. Jhalal stood talking quietly to Hakim, who was really the Angel Sephius. The rest formed a silent clump behind Hakim, and looked nervous. The removal of Ashirad and Mahata had left only five bombers not working for Heathcote. Closest were Ishmael, Crazy Azul and Mustafa Ben Abhat, with Nazir and Sharif Bakhar at the back.

The women's' deaths did not go over well. No one was buying the heart attack story, and the hard-liners were close to revolt. Ishmael and Nazir had to be dragged off the plane – determined to stay and find out what happened.

The killings panicked the passengers. The idea of two dead, nude females terrified them. Flight attendants ran back and forth, calming people and consulting the pilots, one of whom called ahead to Chicago. Gabriel noted that the cabin crew were painstakingly respectful. The words 'lesbian' or 'sex' were never used. Not by the hostesses, and not by those flying the plane.

But passengers are human. The lady who found the bodies talked, and her story expanded as it passed from seat to seat. Rumor became fact, and spread quickly. Ashirad and her partner were soon an Olympic event. Leather masks and straps were mentioned. Even a horsewhip. It was said that the moaning, screaming and carrying on could be heard in the First-Class compartment.

No mention was made of Hassan or Shahanna. Gabriel

had imposed a mind-block, and no connection was made between the dead women and his team. The two deceased were remembered as having traveled alone, and when the police boarded in Chicago, that was what they were told.

The Customs line suddenly moved.

Hassan's team was next.

It was Hassan's turn to show his passport. He walked towards the stern-looking lady who occupied the control booth. Gabriel looked her in the eye, and she became all smiles. Then she stamped his entry visa without really looking at it, and wished him a nice day in a rather dreamy voice.

Then she waved him through.

She waved them all through.

Gabriel had considered letting the undesirables in his team be arrested. After all, Heathcote's FBI spotters were all over the place, but he dismissed the idea as being less than these terrorists deserved. He had decided, standing in the customs line, to kill them all. Here in the airport. Gabriel just needed to remove them from the gaze of those same spotters of Heathcote's.

This idea had been born in Moscow.

It would be enacted today.

Ashirad and Mahata had been a good start.

~ ~ ~

Hassan led everyone to the baggage area, where they stood between the gondolas, as if waiting for suitcases, but leaving empty-handed, in twos and threes, whenever they got the chance.

The FBI watchers did not react to this; nor did they immediately follow. They had orders to keep back, and not interfere. This made Hassan's surviving terrorists feel safe, giving them a sense of having got away with it.

They strode confidently into the main airport.

Raincoats came off in alcoves and washrooms. Chicago airport gained nine new workers, while Lufthansa and Air France lost nine aircrew. Soon they were out in the open beyond the security barriers, the operators of which ignored them, because of the way they were dressed.

Gabriel had a choice to make: Who among his genuine terrorists should die first? Who was to have the next seizure? Then, suddenly, taking in the unlimited vastness of O'Hare, he came up with a way of killing them all at once – because the order they died in was irrelevant. It had more to do with architecture.

As with many a modern-day airport complex, Chicago International's main hall was based on circular design and construction. Starting at any point – on any floor – if you kept walking, you finished up back there again. All roads, and in this case there was only one, led back to your starting point.

With this in mind, Gabriel called his team together, and sent them off, singly and at intervals, to meet him on the other side of this huge circular walkway. Heathcote's people and Hakim set off in a clockwise direction. The rest were sent the other way.

Now Gabriel had them divided.

Those who would live and those who would die.

This main terminal was near empty, which helped no end. Gabriel waited, giving his quarry a start and watching actual cleaners and ground staff begin their day. Book store employees began pulling up shutters; candy vendors polished display cases, and a whole lot of people dressed like Gabriel were sweeping, emptying trash or vacuuming carpets and furniture.

Gabriel was the only one doing nothing.

It was time for his kind of clean-up.

He took a quick look around, to make sure no FBI were in attendance, reacting to him or the movement of his people. He needn't have worried. Heathcote's orders were very specific: Hassan's group in particular was to have a free hand, and a lot of room to move in; therefore the watchers were hanging back, and the disappearance of an entire team had taken place unhindered.

No one was watching Hassan.

Gabriel vanished, drifting halfway up to the towering ceiling; then he shot forward at a fast enough rate to catch his prey quickly.

The five who must now die.

In as many minutes.

~ ~ ~

Nazir's stride was short; because he was short. He was dressed as a security guard, but the gun on his hip was issued by Prince Kamal; not the airport authority. Nazir had its holster flap open.

Gabriel landed on the carpeted floor, materializing behind this man who was first because he walked slowly. The Angel of Death fell into step behind Nazir, keeping a short distance between them. This section of corridor was as empty as the main hall. Any FBI trackers were well behind, and out of sight.

Nazir did not look round.

Gabriel flexed and got ready.

He began closing the gap.

This shift of pace, or some slight sound, finally alerted Nazir. He looked over his shoulder, saw Hassan, and stopped to let him catch up. Gabriel reached him. Putting a finger to his lips, and indicated that they should walk on. As expected, Nazir lumbered off again at his slow-moving pace.

Increasing his ace, Gabriel closed in for the kill. This death would not be quick, or painless; none of them would. Gabriel made the decision days ago: No merciful seizures; no easy departures into the void. These monsters didn't deserve it; they were all going to suffer.

Gabriel was feeling vengeful.

Nazir had burned a man and woman alive, his wife and her lover. Then he hurled them off a cliff to satisfy his honor. His actions ever since had been equally depraved and violent, when dealing with his own enemies, or those of Al Qaeda. But what had brought him to Chicago was pure evil. Nazir thrilled at the prospect of wiping out a city this size. His dying would reflect this.

Without warning Gabriel thrust his hand into Nazir's heart. The pain must have been excruciating, because the Arab screamed and fell to his knees, eyes bulging. His executioner sank down with him.

The Angel of Death knelt, as if trying to render first aid. This helped to conceal the writhing and the blood. Gabriel inserted an unpleasant memory into Nazir's brain: His dead wife and her lover, naked, and in the throes of passion. The images were vivid. The wronged husband could even hear their cries. They were making love for the last time. In Nazir's bed. The woman was astride the man, spread-legged, her breasts bouncing as she moved. A moan of pleasure came from her lips.

Although in agony, Nazir was enraged all over again, all these years later, tears of rage and pain in his eyes.

Gabriel detected no remorse; only pride and anger. In his last, dying moments, Nazir's only thought was to murder his wife and her lover again in an even more hideous manner. Gabriel removed his hand from Nazir's rib-cage and made the death-motion, one finger outstretched. Starting now and building slowly, the final heart tremors set in, causing the victim's body to convulse and shake. Gabriel massaged Nazir's upper body, as if easing his suffering, but this gave the spell strength, bringing death ever closer.

There were shouts of alarm behind them.

Gabriel heard voice and footsteps. He turned and saw two groups of travelers: Three old men in Hawaiian shirts to his left, and a family of four, complete with an airport baggage-cart, coming up on the other side. Both groups were either yelling or gaping, open-mouthed.

A security guard hurried up, no doubt alerted that a colleague had been taken ill. He knelt beside Gabriel and said he would take over. Then he bent down and began to breathe into Nazir's mouth.

Gabriel stood up, releasing his hold on the dying Arab's mind. Looking down, he saw the light of life leaving Nazir's eyes. The Archangel tried to feel sorrow, or pity, but could not. He threw one, final thought, and ended it.

Another demon left the mortal world.

The body that housed it shuddered, and died.

Gabriel wanted to be gone. Nazir was dead. The crowd was becoming a throng, and the angel was getting hemmed in. He began to move through them, repeatedly excusing himself, until he finally broke clear.

The angel looked back. All attention was on Nazir, and his new, would-be rescuer, still applying the kiss of life.

Two FBI observers arrived and observed the throng. The rest of the hallway was empty. Gabriel became invisible, and went flying off in search of whoever came next.

He passed over a considerable area. There were small groups of people, and the odd person on their own, but no sign of those he was after. Gabriel wondered if he had missed someone, and thought of turning back. Then, surprisingly, he saw two of them together.

Ishmael Mansou and Sharif Bakhar.

Ishmael had stopped to admire four young girls who were killing time between flights, flipping through the clothing rack of an open-fronted fashion store. Bakhar had caught up with Ishmael. This complicated things for Gabriel – although both men were distracted by the girls, which made killing them easier.

The complication was the girls.

Like any killer, Gabriel disliked witnesses.

He materialized behind the two Arabs. They were openly discussing the physical attributes of the women in extremely vulgar terms, in the raw language of the bazaar: This one had nicely formed breasts; this one had good buttocks and a flat belly; the third had a perfect body but a plain face; while the last was a red-head, and probably the best in bed.

Gabriel cleared his throat.

They spun round together, recognized Hassan, and took on the look of two guilty schoolboys. The Archangel clamped each of them by the shoulder. They looked terrified. Gabriel allowed deadly energy to flow through his hands.

Both their hearts stopped beating.

As he died, Sharif Bakhar's Kurdish victims paraded

before his eyes. Bloated, gassed torsos danced a mocking jig, eyes burning with accusation and hatred. Sharif Bakhar took this with him into the darkness: visions of raped women, disemboweled children —and the corpses of their menfolk, with heads and limbs lopped off. Sharif Bakhar's last moments were a living hell.

Gabriel wished he could do more.

At the same time, Ishmael revisited the men and women he had shot, stabbed and violated as a young man, attacking and burning other Tuareg encampments with the rest of his clan, flaying their hapless victims, taking only their flocks, leaving only their bones to bleach in the sun.

The dying Taureg's mind filled with more recent crimes, those committed in Iran and Afghanistan. Ishmael had beheaded, burned alive and tortured any failing trainees. All on the lunatic orders of Prince Kamal.

Now their death screams echoed in Ishmael's head.

And then he died.

Now only Gabriel held the corpses upright: A sober-looking airport employee helping two co-workers who looked drunk. The awkward trio wove its way down the hallway, leaving fashion boutique and female shoppers behind. The two dead bodies bobbed comically, like badly-stringed puppets.

The four young women didn't even notice.

Gabriel made for an expanse of window that ran from ceiling to floor, providing a panoramic view of the runways, and groups of aircraft waiting for take-off. There was a bench, centered against this giant piece of glass, and in the middle of that, the remains of someone's lunch – a half-eaten burger left in its open Styrofoam container, along with an abandoned can of Sprite.

These items were just what Gabriel needed.

He sat the bodies down, one on either side of the leftovers – a couple of airport workers on their meal break. Their eyes were open, their faces calm, and no one would suspect anything for a while. Gabriel did some elementary arithmetic: Now there were only two more terrorists to go.

Crazy Azul and Mustafa Ben Abhat.

Gabriel became one with the air, and sped off to find them. He had no time to fill the brains of these last two with last-minute nightmares. He had wasted time on the first three, but found it gratifying.

Their fear had been his justice.

Azul was suddenly below and slightly ahead, dressed as an electrician. Gabriel kept going, flying straight over him and delivering death on the move. Azul fell to the ground, causing people nearby to run to the spot.

Gabriel went faster.

Up ahead, he saw what he hoped was Mustafa Ben Abhat trying to get through a cluster of Japanese businessmen. Gabriel closed in. It was Ben Abhat. The invisible angel streaked across the intervening gap, swooping down. Gabriel hit the ground and solidified at the same time. Right in front of his man.

This was the last one. Now Gabriel did not have to rush things. Ben Abhat wore a surprised look, seeing Hassan come out of nowhere, in a place where he was not supposed to be. The Arab's eyes looked wary.

Gabriel grimaced. This was the coward, the man so afraid of Prince Kamal he became a textbook terrorist. Mustafa Ben Abhat had agreed to slaughter everyone in Chicago, and die with them, because he was terrified of the

Prince, and having his head on a stake.

Now death had found Abhat earlier than expected.

The only thing missing was the stake.

~ ~ ~

At the age of twelve. Mustafa betrayed his best friend. The other boy was a year older and belonged to a local gang of thieves. They picked pockets in the market, or stole camels and livestock, or robbed travelers who strayed too close to the village. They were strictly small-fry, paying tribute to the local Mosque from whatever they took. Then, one day they waylaid the wrong horseman. A nobleman, leaving a prostitute's house at dawn, was relieved of his mount, his clothes and a considerable sum in gold coins. The boys had no idea who he was.

Retribution soon came. A small army descended on the village. Young men and boys were lined up, and most of the culprits identified. A few, like Abhat's friend, were hiding in the village well.

Without ceremony, those caught had one hand lopped off. The bleeding stumps were burned and coated with pitch. The screaming was unimaginable. Abhat, who had nothing to do with the crime, was so scared that he fainted. When he came around, his fate had been decided, and his hand was on the chopping block. Without hesitation he gave the names and whereabouts of his friend and the rest of the gang. A rope was thrown down the well and they reluctantly clambered out. Then they were strangled for trying to escape justice. Mustafa Abhat was let go.

It began a pattern.

The local Mosque was fundamentalist. Its Imam was a harsh man, dedicated to rooting out and punishing the slightest sin. He fed on informants, and easily recruited young Mustafa, offering protection from the parents of the dead boys. An alliance was formed, and Mustufa went to work, spying out any hint of wrongdoing and exposing it. He got a lot of offenders arrested, maimed or killed. Radical Islam embraced him with open arms, making him untouchable.

He remained highly valued, until massive losses of manpower, in Afghanistan and Iraq, forced them to send him into battle. Mustafa was paralyzed by his own cowardice, and cast about for a way to escape the fighting. What he came up with was a big gamble. Mustufa Abhat appeared before Prince Kamal's Tribunal, lying in his teeth about being prepared to die, intending to betray Revenge of Islam as soon as he got to America. This was his intention now, trudging through this Infidel airport, looking for a policeman to take him into custody.

Seconds later his sightless eyes bulged at the high ceiling, arms and legs in disarray on well-trodden carpet, after the Angel of Death squeezed the life out of him and left the body lying there.

Gabriel, ready to rejoin the forces of Heathcote, had simply dusted himself down and walked off.

Four fake terrorists were waiting for Hassan.

~ ~ ~

Shahanna felt anxious, and she could tell that Clement was also on edge. Jhalal chewed nervously at a fingernail, and Hakim, the cousin of Prince Kamal, kept looking up and down the walkway in both directions. Then Hassan walked around a curve and into sight.

They all stood a little straighter as he approached.

When he joined them, Shahanna thought how haggard

he looked. All the same, she felt better now he was here. Her companions relaxed, too. When Hassan spoke, it was in that quiet, measured tone of his. "The others won't be coming," he said.

Hakim gave a short laugh. The rest looked puzzled.

"I killed them," Hassan said bluntly.

Shahanna and the others absorbed this. It took a moment, but everyone seemed relieved.

She certainly was.

Hassan's next words were equally welcome. "This airport can look after itself," he said. "We're leaving.'

He explained about the FBI teams, the camera surveillance, and other measures Heathcote had taken at the targeted airports. There were even military snipers on hand. And if a nuclear weapon showed up in Chicago, there was no longer a Revenge of Islam team to receive it. Whoever brought it in would be arrested and held. Hassan seemed very confident, and Shahanna felt she may have misjudged his mood just now. He had nothing but good news.

She said: "Where are we going?"

"New York," answered Hassan.

But first," said Gabriel in his own voice, "We need to talk."

Shahanna had a peculiar feeling. Hassan had changed. It was his voice more than anything – it had become deeper, and reverberating. The change in his looks was more subtle: Less like an Arab and more . . . maybe spiritual was the word. Still basically the same person – although, if anything, even taller.

Then things got very weird.

Chicago airport, and its furnishings, fell away, leaving

all five of them suspended in blue sky, a light mist of cloud swirling around their feet. It looked just like Shahanna's childhood picture of Heaven.

And that was not all that was strange.

Hakim was no longer Hakim. He had also gained height, and he and Hassan, this new Hassan, now had giant feathered wings, and a dim, golden glow around their heads. It was incredible, but it could not be argued.

Hassan was not what he seemed.

Nor was his friend, Hakim.

Gabriel said: "You are all good souls. Don't be afraid – just listen."

Jhalal had paled. He said, "Are you . . ."

"My name is Gabriel. I'm also your friend, Hassan."

Jhalal looked confused. He said: "How can this be?"

Shahanna said: "Some sort of hallucination?"

Gabriel smiled. "It's hard for you to understand, Jhalal. Your friend Hassan is a memory I gave you. He does not really exist."

Clement said: "Is this a dream?"

"No."

Hakim cleared his throat. The wings fluttered at his back. "Time is short," he said. "Gabriel must go to New York. He has to go now, and we're going with him. Then it gets complicated. He will take us to JFK, and leave us there to find Asuto Kenyatta and stop him. Gabriel has a bone to pick with someone on Park Avenue. But before that he has things to do in Washington DC. Look at it this way: He'll be solving one set of problems while we solve another."

Shahanna groaned. "Not another plane ride!"

Hakim smiled. "No," he said. "We'll be going by . . .

other means. Close your eyes and trust us."

"No way," said Clement. "I'm not going anywhere. Neither is Shahanna or Jhalal."

Shahanna said: "I'll go."

Hassan was her friend, whatever else he was.

Clement hesitated. "This is crazy . . ."

"Who . . ?" began Jhalal.

"Who are we?" Gabriel said. He looked vaguely embarrassed. "We're what you call angels."

"But you're something else," said Clement.

"Angels is close enough." Gabriel pointed to the clouds at their feet. "This is an illusion, a deception really. We wanted your attention, and the biblical stuff never fails. Most of you believe in Heaven."

"And your wings?"

"Oh . . . well, yes. We do have them."

Hakim said, "My real name is Sephius."

As he said this, there was a kind of jolt, and suddenly they were back at Chicago O'Hare – just as before.

Shahanna was inclined to trust them. What they said was probably true, although she had no idea why she thought that. It seemed to her that anyone who could grow wings and show four people Heaven could do anything. These two angels, or whoever they were, certainly had amazing powers.

Gabriel looked at her. "Do you trust me?"

She nodded that she did.

That meant Clement would, too.

Jhalal said: "I also . . . trust you."

"Why?" Gabriel looked surprised.

"Because I stood on a cloud."

"That will do," said Gabriel. "But I told you none of

that was real – Sephius and I made you see it. However, what happens next will be very real. I need you to believe in the unbelievable. I need you to believe we're in New York when I snap my fingers. Can you do that?"

All three mortals looked doubtful.

Sephius said: "Close your eyes and leave this to us. When we get there, you'll have no more questions."

Three pairs of eyes closed.

The world seemed to tilt.

~ ~ ~

Shahanna's eyes opened again, at JFK International.

In Overseas Departures.

Hassan looked like Hassan. Hakim was Hakim. Shahanna suddenly understood why they were here, and what came next. Clement's face said he knew, too. A glance at Jhalal told the same story.

They were here to kill Asuto's team.

She felt dizzy, and her skin was tingling. She had no idea how they got to New York. It was as if a section of her memory was blocked off. But she had no more questions. Had somebody told her that?

Common sense said Asuto Kenyatta was already here. He had chosen his squad with the greatest care, each one fanatic, well-trained and ready to kill in a split second. Each one skilled with gun, knife or bare hands.

They must be stopped at any cost.

Hassan shepherded his team into a corner, clear of the security cameras. Shahanna said to him: "They're already here."

"They are. We were late leaving Frankfurt." The Archangel felt guilty. In no time at all he'd be Gabriel again, and invisible, leaving these mortals with Sephius for protection. And Sephius was not staying long.

Clement looked around. "So where are they likely to be?" he said, as if expecting to see Asuto, brandishing a bomb. "They're dressed like us, but their uniforms will say New York – Kennedy Airport." He took off his name-tag and ripped the O'Hare patches from his sleeves. Now he was just a man in dungarees. Hassan nodded to the others, and they did the same.

Jhalal said, "This won't be easy. We don't know where to look."

"You'll find them," said Hassan. "Asuto hasn't the sense to hide."

Jhalal looked at him. "What about you,' he said.

"I have to go."

"Go where?"

"No time to tell you."

"You are Hassan, my friend since childhood. We have come this far, and now you leave us. Why is that?"

Hassan smiled. "The will of Allah."

Jhalal would never argue with that. Shahanna thought Hassan was very clever to have said it. But she, too, wished he would stay.

Clement offered Hassan his hand. "Good luck," he said. "With whatever you're doing."

Gabriel shook it, and turned to Shahanna. "Look after him," he said. "You're the crack shot with a pistol."

Shahanna blew him a kiss. Hassan's cheek was too high to reach. "We'll do just fine," she said.

Jhalal's eyes had never left Hassan. "Salaam Alaikum," he said.

"Alaikum Salaam."

And Hassan walked away.

~ ~ ~

Shahanna was first to move off, looking for enemies as she went. She saw, from the corner of her eye, that the others were doing the same. Hakim appeared beside her. She decided to state the obvious. "We have to kill them."

He shrugged. "It must be done or your whole world changes." Sephius did not add that he was leaving within the hour. She and Clement had a destiny that must be faced by them alone. So did Jhalal, whose fate would be decided very soon. Hakim would vanish at that point.

Shahanna glanced at her companions, knowing had heard everything. They had no problem with killing. Jhalal had killed before. Shahanna wasn't sure about Clement but he spent a lot of time preparing for it. Shahanna herself was the weak link, and knew it. She hated the very idea.

She looked across at Jhalal, and spoke in Arabic.

"What did you say?" asked Clement.

She looked at him. "I said I guess we kill them."

Shahanna wished this wasn't happening, but it was, and Clement stepped into an alcove and loaded his handgun.

She looked around, but still saw no trace of Asuto. She said: "Are we sure they're in this terminal?" Hakim said, "Absolutely." He was looking at all the flying angels that Shahanna couldn't see.

Clement returned, his firearm put away. He said, "They're definitely here. One of Kenyatta's women just came out of the ladies room with a mop and bucket. She was the star of my physics class."

Shahanna sighed, accepting reality. There was no avoiding a fight. She glanced quickly at Jhalal, one thing lingering in her mind. Asuto Kenyatta was Jhalal's friend, and had been for months. Maybe that feeling was mutual. Today Asuto had to die, quite possibly at the hand of Jhalal. She looked again at the Iraqi, trying to read his face. His expression showed nothing, and she could hardly ask him.

Then Jhalal spoke.

"The Monkey," he said. "You can leave to me."

CHAPTER TWENTY FOUR

THE KOREAN CAPTAIN HELD OUT longer than expected.

"No missiles," he told Heathcote and his men through the translator. "Carry only electric circuits." It went on for over an hour. Eventually the interpreter announced that the prisoner would say nothing further, and wanted a lawyer. The Captain's face was defiant.

Heathcote silently cursed the man and whoever had briefed him on the American legal system. The translator, who clearly mistrusted the North Korean's answers, stared furiously at him, as they waited for Heathcote to respond.

Heathcote said this was not an official hearing; there would be no judge or jury, either now or later. And no lawyer. If the Captain did not talk, he would get a military hearing under the Terrorism Act, and transfer to a foreign prison. The only judge here was Heathcote. The accused faced jail overseas for years, with no rights, no hope of a trial, and no hope of release. Did he really want that?

The prisoner's mouth became a thin line. He grunted out his previous statement again.

Heathcote understood.

Whoever bought this man paid a lot.

And his family already had the money.

Heathcote saw no alternative. He had to let his men loose on this guy. He nodded at one of them, and left the room.He closed that cell door and went a few cells further, lighting up another Camel on the way. He wondered how to act with a regular crew member. Should he appear friendly or hostile? Or a combination of both?

Two Canadian detectives had been assigned to the next cell, and had been working their Korean for a while. Heathcote opened the door and decided to keep his options open. No matter what orders the crew had, some would give the game away. Some always did. Certain clues would come to light, be they large or small. The trick was, getting them all to assemble the Jig-Saw puzzle they represented. It was the third of July, but some things can't be rushed.

Heathcote viewed the suspect: A surly-looking fellow with a shaved head and angry eyes. Was he a lowly merchant seaman who hated the Communist system? Would he turn informer? Maybe he resented the Captain for some reason, and wanted to spill the beans. At first glance it didn't look likely, and if not, Heathcote must move on until he found the right man.

Someone ready to talk.

Heathcote sat down on the Canadian side of the table. The North Korean and his interpreter were on the other.

Keeping his voice low, one of the detectives said it was hopeless. This guy said he was a bosun's mate, but did nothing but make political speeches condemning Capitalism. It seemed possible he was secret police, put on board to spy on everyone else. Heathcote agreed, and made up his mind: A hard-liner party man might know something important. Heathcote needed to break him quickly. Forget taking things slowly. Sometimes breaking the rules was the only way to go.

Heathcote got up and walked slowly around behind

his victim, taking a ball-point pen from his inside pocket. He clicked on it, exposing a sharp steel point; then jammed it squarely into the Korean's inner ear.

There was a piercing scream, and the man bucked in his chair, striking both knees on the table. The Canadian policemen did not react at all. Just sat there as if nothing had happened.

The translator looked shocked.

Heathcote said: "Keep on him. I'll be back soon."

He went out, picked another cell and found a scene like the one he just left, except the prisoner was talking too fast for translation, with tears running down his cheeks. He was a cook, and no more than eighteen years old. Heathcote said, "Tell him it's all right. Nothing bad is going to happen. Christ, he's pissed himself."

The interpreter relayed this.

Leaving out the stained pants.

Heathcote asked the boy his name. The cook looked at him in pure terror. One of the detectives said, "That scream from next door didn't help."

Heathcote thought it probably did.

He said: "Get him anything he wants – Food, drink, or cigarettes – and say I'm offering asylum in the United States to anyone who knows anything." Then he left the room.

Vinegar or honey.

Whatever it took.

As soon as Heathcote entered the next cell, he knew fortune had smiled on him. The face confronting him was not fanatical, or scared: It showed the self-assurance of a criminal who had done this many times before. The Korean's skin had the pallid look of one who has served several terms in prison. It might take some clever footwork from Heathcote, but if anyone was going to say what happened to the ship's forbidden cargo, this was the man.

He smiled and offered the prisoner a Camel.

Then he said he'd be back and went out.

Heathcote tried one more cell on this floor, after which he would hit the elevators. He found two of his FBI interrogators, one male, one female, and watched them at work for a while. A plump, moon-faced Korean in his forties was being questioned. It went on for some time, and it was going nowhere.

"Outside," said Heathcote to his people.

They trooped out behind him, a veteran agent from the Serious Crime Division, and his partner, a young woman with less than a year on the job. She said, "Is anything wrong?"

Heathcote grunted. "Everything," he said. "You keep smiling at him and crossing your legs – and you're showing so much cleavage I'm surprised he hasn't asked for your hand in marriage."

She was not smiling now.

Heathcote said: "Go and have some coffee."

It was not a request. She took off on her high heels, clicking along the passageway, her head held defiantly high.

The two men went back inside the cell.

"What's his name?" asked Heathcote, sitting down opposite him.

The agent didn't know, and picked up the file, but the interpreter answered for him: "It's Wuc Lai."

Heathcote memorized the name and offered Wuc Lai a cigarette. The suspect took one, but stared past the two

American policemen.

It remained unlit.

Heathcote said, "Tell him he has sixty seconds."

There was an exchange in rapid Korean.

The Translator said, "Sixty seconds. Then what?"

"We clip electrodes on his balls, and fry his manhood," said Heathcote. "That's why we sent the woman away. Translate exactly."

Quietly, he told his man to fetch some convincing equipment. There must be some apparatus in this building that looked capable of electronic torture. The FBI man nodded and left the cell.

He was a man on a mission.

Heathcote hoped he found something quickly. He lit the North Korean's cigarette, but made no attempt at conversation. The prisoner puffed nervously, inhaling as if his life depended on it, but he didn't speak, either.

They sat for several minutes.

Heathcote said, "What happened to the nukes?"

The fat man mumbled something unintelligible. Heathcote leaned forward and knocked the cigarette out of his mouth. "Talk English! I know you can. Your eyes move every time one of us speaks."

"Okay," the man muttered. "No need for rough stuff." His use of slang, accented but fluent, came as a surprise. Probably this man had translated for the Captain when they docked. Heathcote cursed his inability, and that of the Canadians, to tell Filipinos from Koreans.

That's better," said Heathcote, keeping his tone matter of fact. "You've spent time in the States. Now tell me what I want to know."

The chubby prisoner shrugged. "What's it worth?"

"Your balls. Come on, scumbag. The clock is ticking."

"I want asylum."

"Who doesn't? We have seventy guys like you, all wanting the same thing. Lucky man is the first one to talk. I need the name of the off-loading vessel, with its course and destination. It's up to you."

"It was a fishing boat, very fast."

"We guessed that. What else?" Heathcote sensed there was a limit to what this man knew. "What's it called. Where's it going?"

I didn't see the name. I was below."

Not the interpreter, then.

The man looked desperate. He said, "I don't know their course. That's a secret."

"But you saw the nukes."

"Yes."

"And it was a fast sport-fishing boat."

"Yes. The crew was American. I heard them talking."

"But not their destination?"

"Afraid not."

He clearly knew nothing else.

The door opened, and the FBI agent came in empty-handed. Heathcote told him to sit down. No need for electrodes, Heathcote said, and the girl could come back. The agent dialed her on his cell phone.

Heathcote said, "Get a statement from this clown."

Then he left.

He went back next door. The habitual criminal was no better. He tried to trade what little he knew, but it was exactly what the fat Filipino had said. it was obviously what the whole crew knew, and would not bring American citizenship. Heathcote had struck out twice.

His luck was turning bad.

He gritted his teeth and left the room.

~ ~ ~

The time factor was killing him. At this rate he could not hope to interview more than this one floor. He called a reliable agent and sent him upstairs with instructions to get tough with every suspect up there.

Heathcote returned to the crying cook. The boy's answers came quickly. Captain and crew were American, on a sixty footer with a turbo-charged diesel. The youngster heard it when the boat peeled away with the nukes on board. He had been at the stern, throwing chicken bones over the side. He could not read a name, but he recognized the word "Maine" next to a mud-smeared registration.

He said they headed south.

No surprise there.

Heathcote still needed more.

~ ~ ~

Heathcote went back to the North Korean Captain. The one man guaranteed to know all the answers. He must be made to talk. The odds were not good, but the stakes were enormous. Heathcote took out his Walther automatic and opened the cell door. He saw a change had taken place. The Korean had bruises on his face.

Heathcote placed his gun on the table.

The Captain stared at it.

Heathcote addressed the interpreter. "I have three questions. He refuses to answer he dies. Translate that exactly."

"Sir," protested the interpreter. "you can't do that."

Heathcote gestured at his two Washington agents.

"They will confirm that I can."

The FBI men played along. They both nodded. One of them leaned over, picked up the gun and handed it back to Heathcote, who pointed it at the Captain's head. His aim was rock steady.

The translator explained the situation to the prisoner.

Heathcote said, "Name of the fishing boat?"

The question was translated.

There was no answer.

"The boat's destination?"

Again nothing.

Heathcote knew what he had to do. So did his men. He lowered the gun barrel and squeezed a shot into the Captain's thigh. The interpreter leaped up, aghast, as the man screamed and crashed to the floor. The suspect rolled on his side, moaning. Blood oozed from the wound. Heathcote moved to stand over him and pressed the gun to his head. "Now, the name of the boat."

The Captain whimpered softly. No translation needed. Heathcote cocked his automatic and got ready to fire. The Captain's eyes squeezed tightly shut, and his head jerked, as he tried vainly to pull away.

But he mumbled a few words.

Heathcote said, "What did he say?"

"He says – don't shoot. He'll tell you."

"Get him a doctor," said Heathcote.

One agent hurried from the room. A doctor came, and began cleaning the wound in search of the bullet. It was then that the Captain finally opened up. "The boat was called "No Problem". A sixty foot luxury cruiser, rigged for sport fishing and registered in the State of Maine. This confirmed what the young cook said. Heathcote would see that he got accepted for citizenship. Meanwhile the Captain admitted he had not spoken directly to the American Captain, and didn't know his name. The man had held safely off, as the bombs were loaded separately by dinghy, yelling orders at a crew of four. With the cargo on board, "No Problem" took off without saying goodbye.

Heathcote repeated question two and added a third.

"Where's she bound? Where are the bombs hidden?"

She was headed for her home port, a small town on the coast of Maine called New Harbor; thereby avoiding the Canadian land border, but risking American Coast Guard and shore patrols. Heathcote looked up New Harbor on a map. It was six hundred miles away. Everyone checked the time and did the same calculation. They sent for Inspector Hearst, who soon had people on phone, Fax and Email, because, even cruising non-stop and flat out, "No Problem" was still on the water, with a fair way to go. Heathcote and Hearst high-fived each other.

With prompting, the now bandaged Korean Captain answered the third question: The nukes were hidden in specially made lead casing, hanging under the vessel from a rigid steel cable attached to the keel. This slowed the boat down, but kept her safe from search.

Until now.

Heathcote had won some time.

The Korean Captain went to hospital in an ambulance. Eyebrows were raised at the nature of his wound, but a few words from the Canadian police took care of that. It went in the record as a hunting accident.

Heathcote got an urgent call from Mexico. The second Korean freighter had come up empty. A Joint-Agency task force was tearing it apart, and the crew had been taken into custody. It was a replay of Canada, with a captain unwilling to talk, but an entire crew seeking asylum. They were ready to tell all. The Senior agent in charge was named Alex Cory. He promised to call Heathcote back as soon as they had a clear picture. Then he hung up.

It took less than an hour.

This fast-boat was called "Samurai Sword". Another high speed vessel, seventy feet long and designed to skip along the surface. However, her cargo was also submerged and would slow her down. Her goal was a deserted stretch of California coastline called Baja Chica.

~ ~ ~

A US Navy frigate stopped "Samurai Sword" on the open sea. An armed boarding party conducted a search and sent divers down. They came back up in five minutes, and bobbed in the water. One of them held up two fingers of one hand. "There are only two bombs," he said.

Prince Kamal had thwarted them.

There was a third speedboat, and doubtless a fourth on the northern route, each with one bomb and slipping through the net. This was Prince Kamal's insurance policy. It meant five nuclear devices were out there and on the move. Even worse, the names of the two extra boats were unknown.

A ship to shore call went from the Navy Frigate to Senior Agent Cory. He asked that the crew of "Samurai Sword" be helicoptered to San Diego.

"Aye, sir," said a young female Navy Lieutenant. She hung up and dialed a Navy Rescue squadron. They sent a chopper at top speed.

The suspects were in the air an hour later.

So was Senior Agent Cory.

~ ~ ~

Again the Captain was American. His crew was Mexican, and none of them had papers.

Agent Cory was a tall, gangling Texan with unruly hair and perfect nose, lips and teeth.

Most women went to bed with him on the first date,

Most men did not understand why.

When he reported to a Desk-Sergeant of Military Police on San Diego Naval Base, he was directed to a row of airy, open-fronted cells with their bars painted white. Five pairs of eyes rotated miserably to him, one cell having been allocated to each prisoner. The captain, who looked more angry than miserable, was housed at the far end. His face was dark from sea and sun.

Cory asked if any M. P. spoke Spanish.

A guard said most of those on gate duty did.

Two of them were fetched.

But Cory started with the boat's Skipper. It had worked in Vancouver; it might work here. Cory stood in front of the man's cell and offered him a cigarette through the bars. It was haughtily refused. This was California. No one smoked anymore. Alex Cory lit one for himself, and said, "Who took that last bomb? What kind of boat, and where is it going?"

He got no answer.

He had it repeated in Spanish.

With the same result.

The Mexicans weren't talking, either.

"Alright, fine," said Cory. He spoke to one of the M P's. "Is there a room I could use somewhere, with a couple of you on guard?" The MP said there was. "Good," said Cory.

Then bring these pricks one at a time. He pointed at the American captain. "Start with him."

The Captain's name was Hank Irwin. His driver's license said he was thirty-eight years old and revealed him as a resident of Orange County. Cory had gone through the man's wallet, and set it on the table between them. The interrogation room was a cell in an empty block, and two guards watched over Cory and Irvin through the bars. There were no other witnesses.

Irwin was manacled to a table. The cell door was opened and Cory moved inside to stand opposite him.

Cory said, "You're in deep shit, Hank. Just for the terror and conspiracy charges, you'll get a death sentence if we push it. And as for smuggling nuclear warheads into the United States . . . Hell, I can take you outside, right now, and hang you myself. No one is going to say shit."

"Go fuck yourself."

Agent Cory had no way of knowing, but Hank Irwin was inhabited by a demon, and had been since his teens. Hank Irvin was not a nice man, and this had been noticed early on by the dark forces. In the years since then, he'd been possessed by increasingly malignant spirits. They turned Hank Irwin into a dangerous psychopath. The one in him now entertained itself with foul-language.

"Fuck your mother, too," Hank cackled, and slapped his thigh.

Cory's cell-phone rang. He answered it.

It was Heathcote.

Some distance north of New Harbor, Maine, the Captain of "No Problem" was telling the FBI and Coastguard nothing; the good news being that with his two warheads captured, the number of missing bombs was only two.

One in the North and one in the South.

Cory said he understood, and hung up. He looked at Hank Irwin, who was grinning at his own cleverness.

Cory sighed. He asked an MP to lend him his side arm. It was handed through the bars with the safety lock on. Cory tucked the gun in his waistband. Hank Irwin shielded his face, raising chained hands in mock horror

This was a mistake.

Thinking quickly, Cory leaned forward, seized one of the man's fingers and snapped it like a twig.

Irwin bellowed and crashed backwards onto the floor. He rolled away from Cory and swiped at him with his good hand, cursing and shouting in fury. His punch flailed empty air.

The MP's stared fixedly ahead.

Cory got Irwin upright and back into his chair.

Cory's mother, just grossly insulted, flashed into his mind. She would not approve of what he'd done, or what he might do next. Cory shook his head to make her go away. Mom didn't have to save America.

The Captain sucked at his finger. It was broken behind the knuckle, and turning a rainbow of colors. He winced as his teeth scraped bone, but did not utter a sound. This was a bad sign; Irwin was still not going to talk.

Cory got ready for Plan B.

He had the MP's remove everything Irwin was wearing below the waist. After a struggle, and more roars of pain, they took off his jeans and underwear, leaving crotch and genitals exposed.

Humiliation replaced fury on the Captain's face.

For the first time ever, Agent Cory pointed a gun at

someone, and it was aimed for a man's private parts. Keeping the self-disgust off his face, he said, "Name the other boat or lose the family jewels."

It only took five seconds.

"I can't tell you!" spluttered Irwin. "They'll kill me."

Cory knew he meant the shit-head terrorists who hired him.

He said, "Never mind them. I shoot you in the balls and you die right here within minutes.." Cory wondered if he could do it.

"You can't. There are witnesses."

Cory lowered his gun for a moment. "Gentlemen," he said to the MP's. Why don't you take a walk. It's time for your break."

They saluted and left.

Irwin uttered a choking curse. "You won't get away with this!"

"The hell I won't," said Cory. "Everyone on this base knows why you're here. The guys here fight and die for America. They'd throw your dead body in a ditch and not give a damn. And I won't, either."

Cory realized he meant every word.

Hank Irwin saw that, too. "Okay," he said. "Put the gun away and I'll tell you."

Cory kept the gun trained, unwavering. "Go ahead," he said, not sure if he had succeeded. The Captain had given in too quickly. He was about to make something up. This proved true almost immediately. Irwin said the second boat, heading south with a missile on-board, was called "Triple Ripple". She was going for Los Angeles, where she would lose herself among a thousand boats just like her.

Triple Ripple's cargo would destroy LA and its airport.

"I hope," said Cory. "you're not jerking me around." He squeezed an imaginary shot into Irwin's hairy scrotum. "We don't find that boat pretty quick, your balls are gone."

The prisoner winced, his courage evaporating.

"Okay," he said. "Maybe not Triple Ripple. That's my cousin's boat. The one you want is "Sea Rustler". She's identical to mine, and heading for L. A. Harbor."

Cory ran down the hallway to a phone.

~ ~ ~

The Coastguard put out bulletins immediately. Two nukes left was two too many. A lot of speedy fishing cruisers got stopped and searched in case "Sea Rustler" was another false name. The other fugitive boat, making its escape somewhere off the coast of Maine, had no name at all.

The L. A. calls came in one after another. "Not the boat in question. Legitimate fishing party. No cables, or anything else, under the hull."

Cory drank two pots of coffee and waited.

The next call began with, "Sir, we have your package in custody."

Cory tensed. "Who is this?"

Coastguard Lieutenant Dawson, sir. I'm using a cell phone from the Coastguard Cutter Arapaho, and this is not a secure line."

Sharp kid, thought Cory. Careful what he says.

"Roger that," he said. "But you have "Sea Rustler" and its cargo?"

"Yes, sir. We surely do."

Cory was delighted. "Let me speak to your Captain."

There was a short silence. "Uh . . . that would be me, sir."

Cory gave an embarrassed laugh. "Christ, I'm sorry, Captain. Either you guys are getting younger, or I'm getting old; that's all. He laughed again, and said the joke was on him. "What are your orders?"

Tow them to our home port, sir."

Cory did not ask where that was. Revenge of Islam could be listening in. Hackers and phone tapping had become an art-form throughout the Middle East. He said, "I want them under close guard. Shoot and only ask questions if somebody lives. That's the deal. Understood?"

"Yes, sir. We've all seen their cargo."

Cory thought, This kid is good. Two years out of college, by the sound of him.

He said, "First Command?"

"Yes, sir."

We're proud of you. Tell your crew – we're proud of them, too."

The Lieutenant thanked him and cut the connection.

The southern nukes were all in custody.

~ ~ ~

The north was different.

One bomb was still out there on the loose.

Heathcote called New Harbor.

"Any luck with boat number six?"

A Maine Coast Guard Commander said, "Afraid not. This crew is not talking."

Heathcote looked at his watch, and asked for one of his men.

An Agent called Kraft came on the line.

Heathcote said, "Have you tried muscle?

He knew he could not get to New Harbor before the last fugitive boat, and the last nuclear bomb, vanished forever. It had to be somewhere on the East Coast.

Kraft said, "Nothing worked. I'm sure they don't know. Two of our guys beat more than one of them unconscious."

They both said goodbye and hung up.

About an hour later, Heathcote phoned the President from Police Headquarters in Vancouver.

"One nuke still unaccounted for," he said bluntly.

The president told him to come home.

~ ~ ~

Two hours later a sixty foot Aqua-Master slipped into a little used inlet twenty miles below Winter Harbor. The captain dropped anchor two hundred yards off shore and sent down two men with wet-suits and air-tanks. The bomb came on deck while a motorized skiff sped out from shore. It was the final phase. The last of the North Korean nukes was conveyed to the beach and up a steep pathway to a to a helio-jet belonging to a businessman from Yemen. The aircraft stood waiting on a piece of open ground with its hatchway raised. The package went in behind the pilots, and they wheeled away into the sky – flying straight for New York.

They would be there by morning.

CHAPTER TWENTY FIVE

"BLEND IN."

That was Asuto Kenyatta's order to his group of well-assorted phony airport employees. "Don't attract attention."

Then he had them fan out.

It didn't help; there were so few people about that spreading out made his team even more visible and easy to spot. Yesterday's airport attacks had booked passengers running scared. JFK was nearly deserted, with thousands of last-minute cancelations. Some were phoned in, but a lot of people simply hadn't shown up. Incoming flights from overseas were bringing customers in sporadic waves, but for most of the day the world's busiest air terminals would be virtually empty. It took America's biggest carriers, like Delta, Continental and American by surprise. Heathcote's warning to shut down on July 4th had been largely ignored, in spite of the Free Patriot attacks. The airlines refused to accept that kind of financial loss. The sparse crowds surprised Asuto Kenyatta, too, and made him nervous.

His team was even more exposed than anticipated.

~ ~ ~

The FBI watchers loved it.

Agent Six said, "Second Floor Mezzanine. Report."

Two of them in sight," murmured Agent One into everyone's earpiece. "Jaguar and Gazelle."

"What are they doing?" asked Six, checking his coded list. Jaguar and Gazelle were Arun Shatah and Shachti Bhoudin.

A middle-aged man and a younger woman.

With a female agent watching them.

"They're doing nothing," said One quietly. "Fifty yards apart."

Agent Six sipped coffee from a plastic cup. He was far above the Mezzanine, in an empty air-control office that had been taken out of service for a day. He was dark haired, cleanly shaven, and had a lot of experience at this kind of thing. It was going well, but he knew better than to relax for a second. The expected terrorists were all here, matching the list in his hand, and each one was being observed by two, three or even four agents. It was a textbook operation, with the subjects passed from one watcher to the next. This lessened the chance of surveillance being detected. Agent One could be seen through an extremely large window from where Six was sitting. She was dressed as a bag lady, and as she spoke to Agent Six, it looked like she was mumbling to herself.

Six called another agent.

"Baggage Hall. Do you still have Zebra and Lioness?"

The terrorists were operating in loose knit pairs. Zebra's real name was Ahmed Mustafa.

Agent Ten, another female, young and brunette, came back with a slight crackle in his headset. "Yes, Zebra's a porter, so this is a good hide-out for him. He takes incoming passengers and their bags to the front-doors; then directs them outside to the curb. He's making good tips."

"And Lioness?" That was Ahmed's wife, Allaya Mustafa.

"She's got a mop from somewhere. She keeps well clear of Zebra but they check up on each other. She moves around by cleaning the floor; he does it with luggage. As a pair they're very professional"

So are you, thought Agent Six.

With few exceptions, everyone under his control was impressive, including a small army of sharpshooters – holed up in the underground parking lot on Heathcote's orders. They had volunteered from the ranks of navy seals, marines, special forces and airborne rangers. Agent Six couldn't use them in the terminal, in case passengers got caught in the crossfire, and he worried about using them if terrorists got out on the runways. If a plane or fuel truck got hit, the result would be catastrophic. But Agent Six did have helicopters on hand, in case these marksmen were needed.

He addressed his whole team. "Everyone on station?"

They all confirmed but Agent Seven. Agent Six asked those working near Seven if they knew anything.

"Eight reporting. I have visual on Nine and Ten. Seven told us he was going to the restroom."

All four of them were covering the baggage hall.

"Report when he's back."

"Roger," said Agent Eight.

Six spoke to someone else. "Bookings," he said. What have you got?"

They had split the departure halls into sections, with names like 'Bookings' and 'Check In' for clarity, and to confuse anyone using a cell phone scanner. Security was something of a fetish for Agent Six. He did not want his people exposed. They were all armed, in case snipers were not enough. The problem was, Kenyatta's team were mastershots. The FBI watchers were not.

Agent Twelve answered from Bookings. He was an old, grizzled veteran by FBI standards, at forty one. "We had two until just now, but we've gained another two from nowhere. Two pairs where we just had one. Jackal and Monkey are still on my right. The new guys came in from the left."

Jackal was Asuto Kenyatta. Monkey a female called Rama Khabulah. Asuto was listed as leader of Revenge of Islam, and this group in particular.

Agent Six was exasperated. "Oh, that's great! Who are they, and why didn't you tell me? And which team lost them without telling me?"

There was silence.

Agent Six sighed. Two of his squads had screwed up, and did not want to admit it. Even if they did, there was nothing to be done. It was not as if a reprimand would help put it right. They must pay better attention.

He hated mistakes like this.

He said, "Forget it. Agent Twelve, identify your new arrivals."

Agent Twelve spoke. "Cobra and Leopard," he said apologetically. "They should be with Agent Four."

Abeh Hassimi and Jemyma Ramuf-Hayad.

Agent Six said, "What happened, Four?"

More silence.

"Agent Four?"

"We lost them."

He was a hot-shot graduate from Princeton. He

belonged the right clubs, wore the right clothes and had outstanding family connections. All this had convinced him that he knew it all, and deserved a higher rank. Agent Six graded him poorly, and, looking back on it, probably made things worse by teaming him with Agent Five, the older agent who was experienced but lacked initiative and drive. The intended balance between the two was not being achieved.

Agent Four was a snotty little shit.

Six decided to let it go. Every terrorist in this airport was a threat, no matter who was watching them, and making a big deal about this would waste valuable time. Agent Six said, "Twelve, report on both pairs, starting with Jackal and Monkey. How far apart are they? Has anyone made contact?"

He was worried about the bomb showing up.

Agent Twelve said, "Both pairs are working separately, dressed as electricians, pretending to take fuse boxes apart."

"That's new. When were you planning to tell me?"

"Sorry, Boss. No outsider has gone near them." Twelve sounded resentful. This was ready to get out of hand. Surveillance was all about discipline. Agent Six said, "Shape up, guys. They're here to destroy New York."

There were grunts of agreement. They all got it.

Asuto Kenyatta was one dangerous fucker.

His file said so.

Agents Twelve and Four actually said they got it.

"Okay," said Six. "Let's stay sharp."

He threw his empty coffee cup away and walked downstairs to look at the book display outside a gift shop. The young female agent who was his assistant followed at a distance. Agent Six bought a cheap novel, sat in a plastic chair and pretended to read a few pages while surveying the departure hall.

Agent Twelve checked in. Cobra and Leopard were eating McDonald's on a bench, sticking close together; same thing with Leopard and Monkey. Agent Twelve wondered if something might happen once the food was gone. Six wondered, too, and told Twelve to keep his eyes open. Then he told Four and Five to get over there and help. They had lost Cobra and Leopard. Now they could have them back.

He addressed Agent Sixteen. "Report."

Agent Sixteen was the best operative on this assignment; she was a good-looking thirty five and working alone disguised as a hooker. Her biggest problem was keeping male passengers away.

She said, "Rhino and Pelican still in sight."

Chirati A' Mumta and Abu Ben Assef.

"Any action?" asked Agent Six.

"No. They ignore each other. She sits down occasionally, and he's walking around with a broom, doing nothing. Agent Six knew this woman, Chirati, was new to the group, an outsider they picked up in Frankfurt. Her file said so. It also said Chirati and Abu Ben Assef did not get along. It seemed Asuto Kenyatta had a twisted sense of humor, putting them together.

Another watcher said, "Cougar and Mustang haven't moved. Two security guards just went by, and the targets never blinked." These were Rhangi Abdul and Mufassa Korani. Two young, well-muscled street thugs.

Agent Six grudgingly admired Prince Kamal. His infiltrators were disciplined and well-trained. They knew how to act low-key, even if they stood out like a sore thumb due to a lack of passengers expected to hide them. It was cleverly done. They simply imitated the behavior of genuine airport workers. There was a lot of doing not much going on, and these terrorists fitted right in.

Agent two broke in. "We have a new face."

Agent Six gripped his novel, hard. This was the last thing he expected or wanted

to hear. A 'Face' indicated a name listed as any member of any Revenge of Islam team. Unlikely that this one belonged to Asuto. Why would he or she just walk in? Agent Six was dying to know.

He asked the obvious. "Who is it?"

Agent Two hesitated. "I think it's Clement."

Six was dumbfounded. That didn't make any sense. Clement was a friendly, for a start, and spent months penetrating Prince Kamal's project in-country. He was accepted and fully-trained, but he'd been seen boarding a plane for Chicago with his team-mates. Why was he here? Where were the others Heathcote had embedded? They were on the same flight as Clement.

He said calmly, "Clement is listed for Chicago."

"I know, but it's him . . . that's all I'm say . . . Jesus Christ!"

"Agent Two? What is it?"

"Three more faces. Standing by the restrooms."

"Who?"

"Shahanna and Jhalal, as large as life. And this tall stranger; he matches Hassan's description of the new guy, Hakim. We don't have a picture. Hassan didn't send one, but he's in uniform, like the other two."

"For Chicago, right?"

"No badges. Shahanna's a waitress, could be working anywhere."

"And the men?"

"Plain denim. They look like mechanics."

Agent Six thought rapidly. "Okay, okay. These are our guys. Remember that and don't use their names again. That's an order."

Agent Twelve sounded hesitant. "Sorry, Six, but we have no code-names for them, because. . ."

"I know. They should be in Chicago."

"How about Face One, Two, Three and Four?"

Six agreed, numbering in the order these friendlies showed up, with Clement as One and Hakim being Four. The main thing was, his circuit of watchers would not use real names again, and that would do for now. The senior agent did wonder what the hell was going on. Not knowing was troublesome, and he hoped Clement would soon reveal why he had come here – by his actions.

And where was Hassan?

Wasn't he this team's leader?

Agent Six made a decision. "Make no contact," he said. "We might compromise whatever their doing and place them in danger. There's a reason they're here; we just don't know what it is. These four agents were in place for months, working to stop this Revenge of Islam madness. We don't want to jeopardize that."

Nobody argued with that.

He said, "Agents Two and Three, a loose tail at a distance – and I mean loose, and distant. At least fifty yards, and hand them over to Agents Four and Five in ten minutes. They eventually swap with another pair, and so on. I don't want you noticed by Clement, his people, or by our targets."

He knew this was a pain in the ass. It complicated things for everyone, and made their job that much harder.

Agent Two said, "Roger Six, we're on it. All our Faces are moving over towards Departures. We will follow."

~ ~ ~

Hakim, standing in for the Archangel Gabriel, spotted both agents as soon as the tail began, but said nothing to his companions. Two and Three noticed this, and reported that the new man seemed unconcerned. An FBI presence was expected, and therefore no big deal. Either that, or Hakim was unsure, and keeping quiet for now. This caused both watchers to drop back even further, just in case. From there they appeared to be looking at anything except the group from Chicago.

Agent Six said, "Did the others see you?"

"I'm not sure."

"Is that Two?"

"Yes."

"Three, what do you think?"

"Clement did. He looked right at me, and said something to Shahanna, but she didn't react."

"Because he told her not to?"

"Probably."

They were ignoring the ban on real names, but Agent Six realized that keeping track of "Face" numbers was too complicated.

He let some of his frustration show. "Not a good start. You can't stake out our own guys without getting blown in seconds."

Agent Four said nothing.

Agent Two said, "Clement saw nothing. Sure, he

looked our way but there was no recognition. Hakim was different; he must have x-ray vision. We're both Salvation Army, shaking a can. No one ever spots us."

That was true, and Agent Six backed off. These two were good at what they did. He said, "Okay, keep tabs on them from deep field, for their safety and yours."

Asuto Kenyatta would know Clement in a second.

All hell would break loose.

Clement and party were well ahead, said Agent Three. They might be heading for the fast-food area, the restrooms or baggage carousels. They were setting a fast pace and their Salvation Army escort hurried to keep up.

Six pictured it in his mind. Clement leading his group like a mother duck, and the two FBI watchers scampering behind. Agent Six could have laughed, were the situation not so serious. Agent Three reported everything in a monotone, oblivious to everything except his targets.

Suddenly he said, "Shit, they're splitting up! What do we do, Boss?"

An elderly lady stopped and gave Agent Three a disapproving look. What was the Salvation Army coming to? Agent Four hastily apologized for his partner, who was now listening intently to his headset.

Agent Six was saying, "How are they splitting – into pairs, or what?"

"Yeah, looks like it. Two and two."

"Okay, stay with them. You each take a pair. Keep in touch; so I can track it and pass them to someone else."

Agent Six threw his book angrily into a trash can, as he made his way back to his temporary office. Now he had two men diverted from their main mission. That was two men not tracking Asuto Kenyatta and his band of murderers.

Added to which both Two and Three were now working alone. The protection an FBI agent gets from his partner was lost.

Agent Three took Shahanna and Clement, checking in as he did so. He said they were moving randomly, as if looking for something. Agent Four confirmed that he had Hakim and Jhalal; and had changed direction with them. Jhalal was following signs for the bathroom, most likely where he was going.

Agent Six regained his desk and got to work. He called Heathcote and told him what was going on. The arrival of Clement was seen as good news, but the reason was a puzzle. Heathcote didn't understand it, either. He agreed the watchers should stay well back and let things develop. Agent Six said goodbye and called up all his operatives. He wanted an update.

No noticeable changes, they said. Kenyatta's crew was killing time, clearly waiting for the bomb. They had remained in place, moving around for effect, but not straying far from their original position. Suddenly Agent Twelve spoke, dropping his voice to barely a whisper. "Monkey's closing in on me. He and Jackal have stopped work on the fuse box, and Jackal went to the men's room. Now Monkey is drinking a Coke ... sitting down ... oh, fuck ... three seats from me. I'm standing up and walking away."

Agent Six said, "Someone get in that toilet after Jackal. I want to know if he pisses or shits, and if he washes his hands. Get a man in there now!"

Agent Twelve replied. "Okay, Boss. Eleven going in now."

There was a faint noise of hurried steps in every headset, then Agent Eleven said softly, "I'm walking away. Jackal just came back out. He must have been checking the place was empty."

Several agents began tracking Asuto Kenyatta, passing him on every so often. The voices changed, but Agent Six had details of the South African's progress, as he made his way back to Agent Twelve, who was waiting for him, not too far from a Somalian woman terrorist code-named Monkey.

Everyone relaxed slightly.

Then Clement and Shahanna entered the area.

Eleven and Twelve both called it in.

"Get back!', said Agent Four, still tailing Clement and his female partner. Jackal has seen them ... and ducked out of sight."

"Did they see him?" Agent Six wanted to know.

"No, they were looking the wrong way."

All headsets went silent, as everyone tried to figure it out.

Clement and Shahanna were sitting ducks.

Why was Jackal hiding?

Kenyatta kept furtive eye on Sorya and Rob Keller. The burly African had slipped behind a pillar as soon as he saw them. There was no denying it; they were here. Exactly where they were not supposed to be.

Asuto was not that surprised.

"We have spies," Prince Kamal had said. "I fear it may be the two I recruited in Paris – Sorya and her American boyfriend. If they do anything strange or unexpected, either in Europe or America, you kill them. Also their Iraqi friends, Hassan and Jhalal. The woman Mahata has the same orders." Mahata was dead in Chicago. Asuto didn't know that, but Sorya was a traitor. Her presence New York confirmed that. Killing her would be a pleasure.

And anyone with her.

Starting with Rob Keller.

It sounded easy, when Prince Kamal explained it. Asuto realized immediately that the opposite was true. To do this publicly, in an airport, was out of the question. He must somehow get his victims alone and out of sight. That might be impossible. And it was not as if he had nothing else to do.

A nuclear weapon was on its way.

Millions of New-Yorkers must be obliterated.

Sorya and her American could wreck everything. Asuto considered a moment; then backed away from his hiding place until it was safe to turn and walk away. He would take care of those two later.

His priority was the bomb.

Without that Asuto would fail.

And everything became nothing.

The detonator was already here, spirited through American customs by Chirati in a Jordanian diplomatic bag, repeating the miracle she performed in Frankfurt. Chirati was the detonator operator, and her zero hour was very close. That was why Asuto Kenyatta retreated, and Sorya was allowed to live.

At least for now.

Agent Eleven watched him go, and called it in.

Agent Six said, Stay on him, wherever he goes. Clement and his guys are not the focus here. That African knows how and when the bomb is coming in. He's bound to be nervous as a cat, so don't get too close."

Agent Six knew about Chirati. He also knew that five other detonator experts had been arrested, all around the country.

Asuto Kenyatta was ignorant of that fact.

~ ~ ~

Clement told Shahanna to take a look around. "You were Kamal's contact person. You dealt with the teams, you know everyone by sight. If you recognize anyone we find a way to take them out. Shoot if you have to, but it's best avoided. Gunfire will alert Asuto and the others."

They were walking past the baggage carousels.

He added gently, "Remember any names?"

She frowned. "Let's see. The two Mustafas – man and wife – then that guy Rama Kabullah ... who else? ... Oh, yes – a woman called Chirati something or other, and her boyfriend, Abu Ben Assef. They trained in Germany; I've never seen them. She's here to detonate the device. He's her protection."

"That's five. Any more?"

She slowed her stride. "Give me a minute, Okay? Yes, I forgot Ranghi Abdul and a guy named Mufassa. Then there was another female – Shachti. I don't remember the second name. That's only eight, but adding Asuto makes nine. The rest may come to me later."

"Nine is plenty," said Clement. "More than enough."

"Chacti is important; she sets off the bomb."

"You're right," said Clement. "I was to activate ours, with Mahata as my back up. She died in the toilet attacking you, just before we landed in Chicago. Then Hassan killed everybody and brought us here."

Clement wondered where Chirati was. Eliminating her

would save a lot of trouble.

Five minutes ago, ironically, he had walked right past her. Her back was turned to him as she played the role of a cleaning lady, polishing the same piece of floor she shined an hour ago.

Now, looking around and seeing no likely terrorists. Clement took a deep breath. He asked Shahanna the question he had avoided since they arrived. What do you think happened to the rest of our team? How could Hassan do it so quickly? Especially with them spaced at least a hundred yards apart."

Shahanna shrugged. "I accept what I see,"

"And what do you think you saw?"

"I saw Hassan kill two women in a toilet."

"I know. Sorry for bringing this up."

Shahanna said. "It's okay. I'm not upset; I was amazed. He did it so fast, without even touching them. Just pointed his finger."

"And that's how they died?"

"That's exactly how they died."

Clement thought, This is too weird.

But he believed her, for want of a better explanation. Once you accepted that it was easier to believe that Hassan's entire terrorist group was obliterated by a pointing finger. Clement realized that was how Shahanna saw it, and he couldn't disagree. Maybe Hassan used some kind of laser.

Clement said, "I guess you're right. You saw what you saw. Best forget it until this thing with Asuto is over."

"And Hakim?"

"A rich clown. Hassan is his personal hit-man."

A feeble joke, intended to lighten the mood.

Shahanna laughed despite herself. "It would be funnier if Hassan hadn't killed so many people, even terrible people like them. He's not the man we knew in the camps. I have no idea how he got us to New York."

"True." Clement was suddenly tired of talking about this. Even more than before, he regretted bringing it up.

Shahanna said, "You want me to shut up."

She was smiling.

"Yes," he said, smiling back. "Find me Asuto Kenyatta, or this Chirati, and I'll be your personal hit-man."

He hoped this conversation was over.

They had walked the entire length of the baggage hall.

They turned and started back.

"Okay," she said. Her face relaxed, and she seemed satisfied. She gave him one of her squeezes.

They passed some reservation desks, with few passengers lining up, and followed signs that said, "Car Rental" and "Restaurants and Departure Gates".

In their pockets, each of them held a gun.

~ ~ ~

Asuto Kenyatta watched them go. He had been following, very carefully, but now he slipped away and found Chirati. When they were alone and it was safe, he spoke in a subdued voice. "Something must have happened," he said. "Part of another team is here and I have no idea why. They may be working against us."

She shrugged. "Then eliminate them." She sounded disinterested. Her boyfriend, Abu, took care of things like this.

Asuto was not looking for advice.

Clement and the others must be killed. He knew that. But the bomb was due any minute. A gun battle in the world's largest airport was unthinkable until Asuto had it in his possession.

He told Chirati that.

Then he left before he strangled her.

~ ~ ~

Everything, except for what was actually said, was relayed to Agent Six by his FBI watchers.

Jackal (Asuto) and Rhino (Chirati) were furtively discussing something, probably the sighting of Clement and Shahanna – who were again headed for Departures, looking around as they went. No one used code-names for either American; it seemed pointless when Jackal knew they were here. Agent Six was too preoccupied to notice – frantically trying to make sense of it all.

Two things were obvious:

Clement was searching for Asuto.

Asuto did not want to be found.

That meant they were enemies, and Asuto knew it. The thing was – did Clement? He was walking around in the open with Shahanna. Was that because he believed there was no danger, or were they trying to flush the intruders out?

Agent Six was interrupted in mid-thought.

"Our guys have stopped," said Agent Twelve. He spoke in the low-monotone they all used with a target in sight, even though this was Clement."

"Why? Did something happen?" said Agent Six.

Twelve sounded uncertain. "Shahanna may have recognized Cobra. Hard to tell from here."

At that moment, the pair resumed walking.

Nothing had happened.

Shahanna had not seen Abeh Hassimi.

He'd had a lucky escape.

Twelve waited to be sure; then reported in.

Agent Six was relieved. He said, "False alarm, everybody. Stay cool."

He went down to the main foyer, bought a sports magazine and pretended to read it. He doubted that he fooled anyone, having done the same thing about twenty minutes ago, but trying to outguess Clement and Asuto was nerve-wracking. Agent Six felt better down here in the middle of things. He could see several watchers, which meant several terrorists were also nearby.

His female second in command walked up and handed him a sketch of everyone's whereabouts, compiled from watcher reports as they came in. Every one of Kenyatta's fanatics was listed, with their location highlighted in pink. The FBI surveillance squads were shown with the terrorists for whom they were responsible. Heathcote's people, led by Clement, were marked as on the move.

Hassan still seemed to be missing.

Agent Six looked at his deputy. "Clement's objective is a mystery we can't solve." He folded the map and put it in his wallet. "I see two groups stalking each other. If they engage, I want our side to win. I wish I knew how to help Clement now – and avoid that altogether.

Agent Two broke in. "Hakim and Jhalal are looking directly at me. Can anyone take them?"

"Are you blown?" asked Agent Six.

A short pause.

"Negative, Now they're staring at someone else."

Agent Six said, "Four, you're nearest. Can you see them?"

"Yeah, I got 'em."

"What do you make of it?"

"Same as the other two – they're looking all around."

Agent Six swore softly. This distraction was pulling him away from the main task. Every minute it got worse. He turned to his assistant. "Get me Heathcote again," he said grimly. "He needs to make a decision."

She dialed on her phone. "Yes, sir."

"Get him; then give the phone to me"

"Sir, the line's busy."

Now Agent Six swore out loud.

~ ~ ~

In a depressed part of Missouri, one small township was thriving, defying a world of unemployment and food stamps. In Woodward, Missouri, life was indeed good. There was meat on the table, and the church was full on Sunday. So were the collection plates. All due to a modest-sized, privately owned factory that employed most of the population. A specialized company, making for a specialized market – and exporting to any foreign country with an airline industry.

Maston Aluminum & Castor changed their name to MastaCast in the late 1980's. They manufactured invalid-chairs that conformed to federal law governing air transport in America. Dimensions, height and width were in strict compliance, measured in feet and inches, which put most foreign competition out of the running. US requirements were met for material, structure, electrics, and mobility of the finished product. A MastaCast wheelchair was a technical wonder when it came off the production line. They stood in rows at every airport across the nation.

About half were destroyed on July 3rd.

Commerce is a cycle, but after the name-change, when small business struggled in a weakening economy, MastaCast not only remained afloat; they prospered. Overseas sales rose astronomically each year, saving their workforce from the unemployment line. The MastaCast profit sheet stayed in the black, and their boardroom rewarded itself with raises verging on criminal.

Factory wages stayed the same.

Around this time a miracle occurred. The firm's greatest financial triumph of all time came out of the blue. It put MastaCast on even more solid ground and promised a future paved in gold. Board members could now look forward to a period of expansion and security. Their benefactor was the Kingdom of Saudi Arabia. And the magician who performed this miracle was a Saudi Prince.

Prince Kamal visited the plant, immaculately dressed, on a whirlwind trip from a business meeting in New York. His name was lost on the Chairman of MastaCast but the enormous check he wrote was not. Prince Kamal was charming and well-spoken; he was also generous. He ordered twenty thousand of their De-Luxe model, with a modification to the lower frame and suspension that all but doubled the price. It made the contract worth over thirty million dollars. The MastaCast sales director all but swooned. Kamal wanted an aluminum container installed, large enough to take a moderate-sized piece of luggage, and concealed by thick canvass to deter theft and prevent sliding. Designers at MastaCast thought it a nice touch, never considering the security aspect of such a hidden compartment at an airport. Why should they? The goods were all going abroad. But the world is always smaller than it seems. Six of these custom chairs, with two spares, wound up in a rented garage in Philadelphia. The back of each was marked with the name of a different US airport.

They were now bomb transporters.

One of these was driven up to the passenger unloading bay at JFK in a red van at 10: 30 am on the Fourth of July. At the wheel sat what looked to be a blond American of Swedish or German descent. He shared the cab with two swarthy passengers. All three were wearing sunglasses on a cloudy day.

The van had a valid sticker on its windshield, confirming the owner as a disabled driver.

Aziz Damiri was one of those rare Assyrians with blond hair and blue eyes. He was never taken for an Arab. One reason why Aziz had been chosen. He'd also lost a leg and parts of his spine to an American land mine on the Afghan Plain. That, and his hatred of America, was the other reason.

Aziz was expert at driving his special wheelchair.

He had practiced for weeks.

He had made out his will and testament. At a mosque, this morning, witnessed by two Muslim clerics.

Now Aziz was helped into the wheelchair by his two minders, who did not have blue eyes or blond hair, and kept glancing nervously about, as if afraid of being noticed. They looked like Olympic weight-lifters, and worked fast.

"Go with Allah," said one of them in desert Arabic, as they pushed him through JFK's automatic doors. "Speak only to Asuto." They left him near the entrance, and drove away in the van.

The bomb had been delivered.

Aziz did not move right away. He took stock of his surroundings, comparing them to a map drawn in his head. He had studied the JFK interior for weeks; he knew where Lufthansa and Hertz were located, or where to find the Food Court. All of these places were landmarks the way to those Aziz was looking for: Asuto Kenyatta and eleven other Muslim martyrs.

He soon worked it out.

The wheelchair turned abruptly to match his course.

A security man noticed Aziz, and came over to him. His uniform consisted of a blue shirt with eagle and star badges on the sleeves. Wide yellow stripes on black pants. Aziz felt his heart pounding in his chest. He was not sure if the man was a policeman. Was this over before it began? He saw the holster on a thick leather belt.

"Sir, do you need assistance?"

Aziz understood. His two "friends" dumped him and took off. That would seem strange to an American. This one was concerned because Aziz was crippled. Someone to pity. Cripples were put to death where Aziz came from. Only volunteering for Revenge of Islam had saved him and five others.

Those five were in F. B. I. custody.

Aziz smiled at his would-be savior. "I'm fine, thank you, sir. No help needed." He had been taught to speak like a Scandinavian tourist.

He pushed a button to start the chair. It rolled forward gently. Aziz didn't want to look like he was trying to escape.

He began to sweat, all the same.

"Need directions?" asked the officer politely.

"Thanks but I know where I'm going."

"Oh?"

Now the nosy bastard sounded suspicious.

Aziz stopped the chair, anxious to reassure him. If not here was a pistol on top of the bomb.

He invented a lie. "I have a brochure in Swedish, with a map."

Would this dolt demand to see it?

Aziz hoped not.

"You're very kind," he said. "A nice welcome to New York."

Amazingly, the man reached and shook his hand.

"Enjoy your stay."

With that he turned and left.

~ ~ ~

Aziz waited, to be sure; then he rolled forward again. Banks of reception desks, from every airline, began to come up on his far right. Aziz was looking for Delta. That was where he would make contact with Revenge Of Islam. He had a ticket to Minnesota St. Paul, and could show it if asked.

Naturally he wouldn't be using it.

This was Aziz Damiri's last day on earth.

A female voice came over the speaker system. "Passenger Clement, please go to a white courtesy phone."\The name meant nothing to Aziz, or anyone here who knew Rob Keller. This was an emergency measure agreed by Heathcote and Agent Six during their first conversation. A safe way to contact Clement.

The security official was no longer in sight.

Aziz increased speed.

Destiny was waiting.

~ ~ ~

Asuto was torn by indecision. Chirati had said it: Kill Clement and anybody with him. Thanks to her, everybody was aware of Prince Kamal's death order. The majority wanted it carried out. Asuto found it difficult to argue; Hassan and his friends had been under suspicion since Afghanistan. Now Sorya and Keller had crossed the line and given themselves away. Even worse, Jhalal was here with a tall Arab stranger. Both Mustafas had seen this and reported it.

Chirati had shrugged. "We kill them, too." she said.

It was not that simple. Asuto had two major problems. The Revenge of Islam came first regardless. And while Asuto relished executing Sorya and her lover, Jhalal was his friend, and that was unfortunate.

Asuto was afraid he had to kill him.

~ ~ ~

He was still working not far from Chirati. He went over to where she was tirelessly cleaning nothing. Asuto said, "No sign of our delivery man?"

"Not yet."

"He's overdue by a few minutes. He has yellow hair and blue eyes, and he's using a wheelchair. Keep your eyes open."

Chirati knew all that. She said, "Can't see him if he's not here."

She sounded annoyed.

Asuto ignored her tone of voice. "Let's hope he comes soon."

The appeal for Clement was repeated, droning across the Departure Hall. Neither terrorist paid it any attention. The name had no meaning.

"Ten minutes," said Chirati. "That's all it takes. No need to unload the bomb. I'll thread the detonator cable through the frame of the wheelchair. Then I hook up three wires and boom!"

She had practiced a thousand times.

"Ten minutes?" said Asuto.

"Maybe only five. Once I run my program, the explosion will be immediate and devastating. This whole place is Ground Zero. No more New York – and not much New Jersey. That's what our experts say."

Her tone was matter of fact enough to convince him. Worrying about her was the last thing he needed, on top of everything else. The bomb being overdue was bad enough on its own. But a part of him still wondered how Chirati would react once it was time to die. Suicide bombers often backed out at the last second. Asuto prayed to Allah that this woman was not one of those.

A thought occurred to him.

"What made you volunteer?"

She answered calmly, but her eyes took on a black, burning look. "My family lived in Hamburg," she said. In a condemned tenement owned by the local German slumlord. No smoke alarms, extinguishers, or any of that. A gang of Skinheads burned it down one night. My parents, brothers and sisters all died in the flames. Nothing left of them but a pile of ashes.

"You escaped?"

"No one escaped. I was back in Beirut, visiting friends and people who used to be our neighbors." She turned her back. The brass railing she began polishing was already gleaming.

They didn't speak again for some time.

~ ~ ~

When Aziz Damiri rolled into view, Asuto grasped Chirati by the shoulder. She whipped around, startled.

Then she saw what he saw and understood.

Their moment had come.

In the most expensive wheelchair of all time.

The Assyrian, for his part, had seen Asuto and was making a bee-line for him. But he moved slowly, looking at everything and everyone. A bored passenger, interested only in passing some time.

He had been trained for this moment.

Chirati nodded at Asuto. "I'll get the others," she said quietly.

She was following the plan. Once the weapon arrived, and Asuto satisfied himself that the serial number was correct, his entire team must gather where the device was to be triggered, and form a defensive circle.

No one must get through it.

That was why they had x-ray proof Belgian automatic s.

They would protect both Chirati and the wheelchair with their lives, which were anyway forfeit. They had nothing to lose, and would slaughter anybody who came near them.

As she walked away, Asuto started worrying about something else. Sorya and her boyfriend were in this immediate area. That fact made him nervous all over again, as he moved discretely towards Aziz Damiri.

The bomb carrier had played his part.

Americans would die by the million.

The thought of that revived Asuto's inner demon.

~ ~ ~

A chorus of FBI watchers signaled Chirati's departure. Voices battled to be heard in the ear-piece of Agent Six. He told everyone to shut up and quietly told his assistant to activate the assembled sharpshooters. They should come up to ground level and fan out; just as a precaution. All weapons to be kept out of sight. Agent Six still had misgivings, but Chirati was alone, and out in the open. There might be an opportunity to shoot her. One single shot from a silenced sniper's rifle makes little noise, and should go unnoticed. Taking out Chirati was worth the risk.

Agent Six asked what she was doing now.

Several voices answered.

Rhino was taking the escalator up to the second level.

Two watchers slipped onto it, some way behind her, carrying computer cases and wearing blue suits.

She didn't look back, and hurried away when she reached flat ground.

Agent Six said softly, "Careful now."

The fifty yard rule had gone unheeded. Agents Seven and Eight were only twenty feet away from Rhino.

They wheeled away from each other when they got to the top, following Chirati from both left and right, dropping back as they did so.

Something's happening," said Agent Three, coming from the opposite direction. "She just passed Cobra, and nodded to him. She kept on walking, but now Cobra and Leopard are following. They're well back and separated. All three of them are going somewhere together."

His voice became a murmur. "They're passing me. Now I see Seven and Eight, coming towards me. You got 'em, boys. I'm out."

Agent Three recognized the significance of what he had seen. Agent Six realized it, too. Abeh Hassimi and Jemyma had just been activated. They were following

Chirati to some prearranged destination.

The bomb must have arrived.

Agent Five chimed in. "Rhino is walking past Zebra; he and Lioness are getting to their feet. Now they're following."

The two Mustafas had joined the others.

~ ~ ~

"This may be it."

Agent Six said it calmly, but his adrenalin was pumping hard enough for him to feel it. He told everyone to stay alert, and instructed the military marksmen to remain downstairs for now. More than ever he needed to speak to Heathcote. He turned to his assistant. "Try the other number – the private one."

"I already did, sir. It's an unlisted domestic phone. He's not home at this time of day. His office line is busy, and his cell is not active. Want me to call our switchboard in Alexandria, and have them break in?"

"Yes, for Christ's sake!" said Agent Six angrily. It was not her fault, but the cards seemed stacked against him at the worst time. Clement was ignoring appeals to come to the phone, and the bomb could go off at any minute.

Even as he thought this, things got slightly worse. Sulkily, with a phone to her ear, she handed him a note. He read it and wanted to scream. Clement had spoken to Agent Two. He said stay the fuck away, and stop calling. He was gone before the watcher could say a word.

Agent Six felt control slipping through his hands and that scared him. "God help us," he muttered. Then he gritted his teeth, forcing his mind to clear.

This was the whole point of his life – happening now, in real time, in the course of the next few minutes. His fingernails dug into his palms. That steadied him. He thought rapidly. It came down to two things: He must have sight of the bomb before taking any action. And every terrorist must be accounted for and under surveillance. His watchers must forget Clement and his people, friendly or otherwise. They weren't supposed to be here; so why waste personnel?

He issued appropriate orders.

His assistant helped to make the calls. Then her phone rang. "Director Heathcote, sir." She gave him her phone. He covered it, and thanked her.

It was an apology.

They both knew it.

Heathcote's voice resonated in his ear. "Agent Cooper. What's up?"

Agent Six took a deep breath. Then, as accurately as possible, given the tangle of facts, he explained the situation and asked for Heathcote's opinion. What should they do next?

For a moment the Intel Director said nothing. Agent Six knew this was a time for action. Take the initiative and overwhelm the enemy before they got together in strength. But that nuke distorted the equation – and that was what Heathcote, like Agent Six, was trying to figure out. Agent Six had every confidence in the Director. This would soon be reinforced, and embrace Clement, when Heatchcote revealed that Chicago airport was littered with dead terrorists.

But for now Heathcote seemed deep in thought.

The silence continued.

When the decision came, Agent Six was not disappointed. "Take a few out, said Heathcote." Arrest all those Chirati hasn't reached yet. Make them disappear. She and Asuto won't know if they're lost, taking a leak, or shot dead by Clement. Every one you get is a bonus. Our four Chicago survivors are going up against Asuto's whole gang; so you'll be doing Clement a favor."

Heathcote added, "This Asuto, their leader, he gets your best people. He's the key to this. Lose him we lose the bomb."

Agent Six began relaying orders.

Heathcote wished him luck and cut the connection.

~ ~ ~

The watchers went into action. Any terrorist not yet activated by Rhino was to be arrested now. Every agent had a weapon drawn but out of sight, its silencer screwed in place. Deadly force was authorized if necessary. The detail assigned to Jackal, or Asuto Kenyatta, was doubled from two to four. Agent Six cautioned them to keep safely clear. Asuto must suspect nothing.

He and his bomb were the golden prize.

Protecting Clement was no longer a priority. He and the others were virtually on their own; it simply couldn't be helped. Agent Six had told those concerned to withdraw. Clement had asked for a clear field. Now he had it. The FBI working JFK would not get in Clement's way, but might fail to help if he got in trouble. This went against the grain, but there it was.

Agent Six spoke to everyone on his circuit.

The arrests were to start now.

He didn't have to tell them twice. They'd been dying for this. Agent Six listened, as Jaguar and Gazelle were whisked away at gunpoint. "Someone get Monkey and Pelican," he said. They should be easy meat. Their partners are Rhino and Jackal; so they're both on their own."

Aroon Mumta and Chachti Bhoudin had been first. Now it was the turn of Abu Ben Assef and Rama Kabullah. Agent Six waited, while as his operatives closed in. He went down his list of code names, looking for more.

He said, "Who's taking Cougar and Mustang?"

Ranghi Abdul and Mufassa Kerami.

There was a dull *whoomp* in his earpiece.

After a short pause, Agent Twelve said, "That's me, and Ten. "I'm afraid Mustang is dead."

Six understood. "Okay, get them both out of there. You know what to do."

There were fire and rescue trucks in the unloading zone. They'd been there all morning, ready for incidents like this. Agent Six was glad he thought of it. Again he listened in, as Cougar and Mustang were removed.

One upright; one horizontal.

The next report, from Agent Four, was bad news. Monkey could not be touched. Rama Khabullah had seen Rhino descending the elevator, others from the group at her back. For her part Chirati also had Monkey in full view. Agents Four and Eight turned and made themselves scarce.

It was the first failure.

Within seconds Monkey hooked up with Chirati.

Agent Six shook it off. He focused on the capture of Pelican. It went very quickly. Abu Ben Assef did not see it coming. Suddenly not just two, but four guns were aimed at his chest. He never had a chance. Chirati's unprotected partner was taken out to his own private ambulance in handcuffs. A full SWAT team was waiting inside to convey him to Ryker's Island.

They had taken out five.

Almost cutting Asuto's force in half.

Agent Six congratulated everyone.

A pity Monkey got away, but this was a huge victory. They had got so many. Only one fatal shot fired and it caused no attention. This was spectacular even by the standard set by Agent Six.

But it would be nice to know where Clement was.

Then Agent Twelve spoke up.

"Jackal's moving."

"Moving where?" Agent Six tensed up. This was the Chess King.

Twelve hesitated. "Looks like ... He's stopped again. He's seen Rhino and the others – they're headed straight for him. He's turned back. Now he's walking over to a blond guy in a wheelchair."

"He's what?"

"A tourist, by the look of him. Why would Jackal ... Oh, no. This is not a tourist. He's moved next to Jackal and they're on the way to Rhino."

Agent Six knew instantly.

" Christ! It's the fucking bomb!"

Another voice cut in. It was Agent Ten. "Jhahal has just walked into this situation. He's on his own. Am I the only one seeing him?"

Other agents spoke up. They were indeed seeing Jhalal, and, like Agent Ten, they watched him spot Asuto and back away.

~ ~ ~

Asuto had seen Jhalal. He quickly told Chirati and the others not to look in that direction. Asuto would deal with this. Aziz was introduced and handed over to Chirati until

Asuto came back. They understood, and left in a straggly line for the detonation point, Chirati and Aziz in the lead. Asuto walked directly away from where Jhalal had stood before he disappeared.

Chirati was more than capable of setting things up with a reduced crew she had.

But where were the rest? Asuto had a feeling that Jhalal, working with Rob Keller and Sorya, was involved in their going missing.

Asuto knew without looking that Jhalal was following him. Anyone with their training would. The trick now was to lure him into an alcove, or other place out of sight. Once there the rest would be easy. Asuto patted the shape of long-pointed dagger hidden in his clothes. Like his Belgian automatic, it was made from undetectable material, and came through customs with no trouble. He touched it briefly again, reminding himself that Jhalal was no longer his friend,

Asuto kept walking.

Jhalal followed him.

Asuto stepped behind a pillar, giving Jhalal every chance to see him, then waiting for the Iraqi to catch up. The African drew back into shadow, able to observe his victim but blocking himself from sight.

Jhalal kept on coming.

Then, out of the blue, another figure joined him. Asuto was startled; the man was far too tall for an Arab, but had the look of the desert about him. He and Jhalal crossed the gap between them and Asuto's hiding place, exchanging a few words on the way. No doubt they thought they had him cornered.

Then two strange things happened.

Jhalal drew his gun.

And Hakim suddenly wasn't there.

Asuto was baffled, but drew his knife as he saw Jhalal framed in the glare of JFK's ceiling lights, realizing the Iraqi saw nothing but dark and shadow. The drama unfolded with lightning speed. Asuto jack-knifed and lunged, thrusting hard for the abdomen. The elongated blade slid in easily, going low and deep. Asuto completed the move by ripping upwards.

Jhalal's intestines slithered to the floor..

He died instantly.

Asuto wiped the knife clean and put it away. He dragged Jhalal into an alcove behind the pillar, and stepped into the open. He half expected to face the Iraqi's tall companion. He needn't have worried.

Hakim was gone.

It had been Jhalal's time.

CHAPTER TWENTY SIX

LUCIFER WAS STILL LIVING in his New York brownstone, although papers were signed on the New Jersey mansion, and he could take possession any day. He was pleased, and celebrating both that and the chaos caused everywhere by the Free Patriot Militia. Half the country was in total panic.

And that was not all. His new physical body was delivered and ready. The young fool from South America was drugged and lying unconscious in another room. Lucifer could now renew himself. Even more cause for gloating and celebration. But the devil's pleasure was not complete, and he was descending into a dark mood, drinking himself into a stupor.

Because everything else was going wrong.

The country was a shambles; that was true. Most airports were devastated and people from coast to coast were nervous and afraid to travel. But rebuilding had already begun. Even worse, Lucifer could not trigger Armageddon. Despite all the damage from shellfire, today's headlines said airports were being made safe, and those North Korean bombs – with which Century News had terrified America for weeks – were captured as they came ashore. The nuclear crisis was over. Lucifer knew this was partly bluff. That last speedboat had got through; then a helicopter completed the journey inland. By now the bomb was somewhere in a wheelchair, ready to do its work. Lucifer's Arab contacts said it was coming to New York.Let it come, he thought moodily. I'm nuclear-proof;

so is this house and the young Brazilian upstairs. I've always disliked this sludge-bucket of a town. I can't wait to see it gone.

There was no more wine. He found some Tequila and took a slug from the bottle. His balance was a little unsteady. He liked to get drunk; it made him even meaner and gave rise to all kinds of wickedness. Lucifer adored fire, tempest and flood, but a bloody war, with millions of casualties, pleased him like nothing else. Mounds of rotting corpses fed his blackened soul.

The Twentieth Century was a triumph, with two major wars destroying more than half the world, followed by one in Vietnam and more in the Middle East. The 1900's were more enjoyable than this century, although a nuclear weapon that wiped out Manhattan would improve things no end.

The aftermath had such promise. Millions would die. which was lovely in its way, but twice as many would be burned and maimed. Their suffering, dreadful and drawn out, would be a delight. Diseases would soon begin to spread, bringing even more death. Best of all, of course, would be the radioactive fall-out. It would carry on the wind across much of the United States. It would be the nuclear accident that had miraculously never happened in America, despite the huge stockpiles the Pentagon insisted upon. The victims of radiation would go blind, their skin sliding off in rubbery folds. Their hair would fall out in clumps and every breath become an agony. Then they would slowly die. Thinking of all this, Lucifer produced a drunken laugh.

Things might work out after all.

He could introduce a few features from that

enormously satisfying Second World War. The aftermath had been Lucifer's masterpiece. Most cities were reduced to rubble, and millions who survived the bombing faced starvation without much shelter or heat. This gave rise to a thriving black market. Poverty was widespread and people scavenged for items to trade. Some made it through the winter; many did not. Spring arrived and governments began to recover. Roads and buildings were being rebuilt. Commerce was still struggling; shortages of every kind brought on severe rationing, causing petty and organized crime to prosper. Lucifer threw in a thriving market in illegal drugs, alcohol and sex.

Then he sat back and let it happen.

Sodom and Gomorrah followed.

Today's America was halfway there already. With three hundred million guns in the country, the effect of yesterday's shelling and today's vaporization of the North East should turn America back into the Wild West. Paranoia, rifles and automatic weapons would make 1950's Europe look like Disneyland. And what followed would be a virtual replay of the Civil War. Morality would break down, brutality would rule, and Lucifer would reign supreme.

A New Age of Rape and Pillage.

The devil laughed again. This time at his liquor-induced cleverness. The bottle of Tequila was kicking in.

No more living in America full-time. Its glitzy luxury would be gone; so what was the point? With a newly acquired and nuke-proof mansion in New Jersey Lucifer could come and go as he pleased, setting up shop in several other carefully selected nations at once. This had always been planned, and that gorgeous Brazilian body upstairs suddenly made it possible. Brazil itself was on the list for obvious reasons. Russia, Germany and India also qualified. Moscow was a cesspit of organized crime – in the grasp of the most brutal government in history. Army tanks and machine guns patrolled the streets; order was maintained by arrest without warning. Execution and torture were the norm, and prison camps in the Gulag were overflowing.

The devil couldn't wait to live there.

Cities in India were hard to choose from. The slum areas were deplorable, but the microchip industry had turned the place into Silicone Valley. Lucifer had contracted to buy one luxury apartment, and two palaces built during British rule. Both of these had Polo fields, which tickled him no end. His Brazilian replacement had quite a reputation for horsemanship.

Germany was special. Despite the sad loss of Bruno Schwenk, the prospect of a Fourth Reich was fast becoming reality. Austria had never failed Lucifer yet. A third likely Fuehrer had been recruited by Gerhardt Hof, and already secured a seat in an increasingly right wing Assembly of Representatives. As a springboard to a renewed alliance with Germany, Vienna was ideal. Its tangled web of influence had dominated Central Europe since ancient times, stretching from Rhine to Danube, and deep into Russia. Lucifer wanted to move there now. When his new Austrian Fuehrer rose high enough on the steps of power, Lucifer would smooth his path into a united Fatherland. Until then he must be schooled in the evil arts and the casting of spells.

The devil didn't even know this one's name.

It didn't matter.

Germans were extremely reliable.

They'd march again.

Dietrich was no more, neutralized by the Archangel Michael, at least for now. The Horseman of War was essential to a Nazi revival, and Lucifer knew he must create him yet again. Exactly when depended on how quickly Lucifer could bring Europe to a boil. Satisfied, and smugly hopeful once more, the devil went off to one of several bathrooms and vomited up tequila. Feeling refreshed, he headed for an upper floor. The rest of the night would be spent droning the vilest of forbidden incantations to invoke the creatures of darkness.

Their power was infinite.

New York would be gone by dawn.

~ ~ ~

Lung Chiang received a lengthy text from Lucifer. The Chinese angel read it with a rising sense of horror.

His mind screamed at him: I will not do this; I cannot do this; I don't dare do this. A crime against any Archangel is a crime against Heaven itself. Lucifer must be out of his mind.

He orders the death of Gabriel.

A sin punished by fire. I won't do it. Lucifer is failing; it could not be more clear. His grand design for crippling America seems to have succeeded at no better than half strength thus far. Should he fail today, attempting to devastate New York City and the east coast; then all his scheming comes to nothing. Armageddon in America will never come to fruition.

And I refuse to help him.

I will not perish by flame so he may live.

Heaven would hunt me down.

And there would be no forgiveness.

The Chinese angel, still deep in thought and thoroughly shaken, moved outside to his orchid garden. He calmed himself, and began clipping delicately with a tiny pair of pruning shears, a leaf here, and a bloom there.

The time to break with the devil was now.

But Chiang lacked the courage to do it.

The knowledge depressed him, and he went back indoors. He opened an ornately painted screen door to enter the house, and got a shock. The red lacquered floor crawled with serpents, coiling into tangled masses everywhere. They smothered the furniture and hung from the walls and ceiling. They were of all sizes, some gargantuan and some tiny, and most of them were deadly.

It was a message.

From the King of Serpents.

~ ~ ~

Lung Chiang stepped back, closed the door and went back to his exotic flowers, knowing the snakes would be gone when he returned. He began to rethink his position. Terrified as Lung Chiang might be of the forces of Heaven; the devil was vengeful and a thousand times worse. He must be kept at bay. Better to concoct a way to rid the world of Gabriel, present it to Lucifer, and then try to avoid carrying it out. It would have to be a plan to first isolate the Angel of Death; then somehow ensnare and destroy him while he was unprotected. After much thought, and tending of orchids, Lung Chiang saw this as his only way out.

So how best to go after Gabriel?

At least in theory.

Chiang knew he must deliver quickly. Events in

America would be impacted, just as they were reaching crisis-point. He dusted his hands, put away the pruning implement and returned to his house. He entered cautiously, glad to see that everything was back in order and the snakes were gone, just as expected. He took a near-scolding Japanese style bath and put on a fresh silk robe.

This helped him think.

He sat cross-legged on silk matting woven for a courtier during the Yuan dynasty. He closed his eyes, seeking a solution that might not end his existence. Part of it came to him immediately: Both Gabriel and Lucifer must be deceived. They must each be told a credible lie, and should Gabriel survive; then the lies told to Lucifer had better be really good. Was Gabriel in New York? Lung Chiang hoped so. Otherwise the Archangel would be really hard to find.

Unless, realized Lung Chiang in a blinding breakthrough of a thought. Unless one went through Michael.

Oh, yes. Oh, exceedingly yes. Michael was the answer. He knew where his brother was at all times, and would do anything to protect him. And Michael was easy to find. He was fearless. He didn't hide. Or go missing for days, like Gabriel. Michael could be found in seconds by means of telepathy. He didn't trust Lung Chiang, but convince him Gabriel was in danger, and that could be overcome.

Now, mused Chiang. What do I tell Michael?

He wrinkled his brow. There was something he had heard days ago, on the angel grapevine. What was it? Scraps of gossip fluttered here and there all the time; most of it unreliable but often something useful came along. The rumor he was thinking of eluded him, but he'd heard it more than once.

Then it fell into place. One of the Fallen had a dark secret he was willing to reveal for cash, two days ago. A secret involving Lucifer. Chiang showed little interest until the angel, still hoping for payment, blurted that the devil had killed a young virgin, and her partly dismembered corpse was in his house. Lung Chiang attached little significance to such a disclosure. Lucifer did these things all the time, and the Chinese angel promptly forgot about it. What made it memorable, was that an Angel Herald had witnessed the butchery and confirmed the story.

That made it credible.

Heraldic angels never lie.

He added that a young, semi-conscious male lay in Lucifer's attic, placed upon a pentacle and guarded by gibbering demons.

An undeniable truth to impart to Michael. The devil might be embarked on any one of a thousand atrocities, but for Lung Chiang this one must threaten Gabriel's very existence. Michael's lie took a while to perfect. Finally, after much polishing, even Lung Chiang believed it.

He went back outside, this time to his rock garden. Then he squatted down on the ground and pictured Michael in his mind.

O, Michael, kindred angel spirit . . . hear me . . .

~ ~ ~

Michael was not fooled for a moment.

Lung Chiang was lying. He was a deceiver. The Chinese angel spoke with Lucifer's tongue; therefore it was the devil talking to Michael. This was not a cunning trap. It was glaringly transparent. The devil meant to somehow ambush Gabriel; it couldn't be more obvious if Lung Chiang had said so.

This had not been a warning.

It was a baited hook.

Michael knew about the virgin. Also the young Brazilian. Two stories doing the rounds. But Lung Chiang was no longer skilled in the dark arts, and his explanations were full of holes, sounding just like the falsehoods they were. The devil meant to take Gabriel's life. Pure and simple. Michael was convinced of that, but reacted with caution. He suggested that Lucifer was simply renewing himself, as he did occasionally, when his current body was worn out, and no longer of use. The Chinese angel argued poetically, insisting that Gabriel was in mortal danger. At least, Michael thought, they were both agreed about that. Finally Lung Chiang left, with no idea what the Archangel Michael was thinking.

Michael recognized this as a serious crisis, but what action should he take? There was more at stake than Gabriel's life. The movement of the heavens was bringing great change; a final conflict between good and evil. it was why the devil was so active, with his make-or-break onslaught on America. This had not entirely succeeded – due to the efforts of Gabriel and the hordes of angels at Century Tower, the White House, US airports and other key locations. But Lucifer's scheme had not exactly failed, either. America's fate was being decided now, at the world's busiest airline destination, by terrorists on one side and FBI agents on the other.

Michael must be very careful.

His first impulse was to tell his brother, who was not in New York, as everyone believed, but in Washington D.

C. – to speak directly with President Christiansen, the unawakened angel in the Oval Office.

Gabriel would react swiftly.

His answer was always to confront Lucifer.

That worried Michael. His brother must not be put at risk, or diverted from his visit to the White House. No, decided Michael, involving Gabriel was unwise. He would charge straight into Lucifer's trap.

Which could end in disaster.

Michael sighed. He came to the conclusion he knew he would all along, a decision already in his mind as he listened to Lung Chiang's lies, designed to isolate the Angel of Death, making him vulnerable. Michael made that decision now. He would handle this himself. The devil must be confronted in New York.

Michael snapped his fingers and vanished.

~ ~ ~

Gabriel should have seen this coming.

An angel had brought disturbing news of Michael. Disturbing enough for Gabriel to abandon his intention to visit President Christiansen and rush to New York. The angel horde surrounding Lucifer's Brownstone in Manhattan had seen Michael enter, drifting through an outside wall. Gabriel's brother was alone and unattended by angel escort. He had not greeted any of the angel's guarding the devil's mansion. Michael ignored them, and was inside before they had time to react.

Gabriel materialized on the steps of Lucifer's gated Brownstone, beyond reach of its high-tech cameras and motion detectors. The narrow roadway on which the mansion stood was deserted

New York boiled in the July heat under an overcast

sky.

There was no outward sign of anyone home.

Curtains were drawn and the hump-backed troll who monitored the cameras was not at his post. Gabriel sensed the presence of both his brother and Lucifer. The blanket of angels – there to restrict the devil's power – was gone. And as far as Gabriel could tell, that had only just happened. Lucifer must have found some way to expel them and used it. He wouldn't want Michael protected.

Nor did he want witnesses.

Apparently.

Gabriel threw a thought, directed solely at Michael, and asked what was going on. Seconds later he felt a weak but responsive mind probe. He saw a misty image of Michael with one finger pressed to his lips.

Good, thought Gabriel.

Michael knows I'm here but Lucifer doesn't.

Gabriel waited.

More faint words eventually came. Michael was blocking Lucifer from his mind. That made his thought pattern weak, and difficult to read. His frustration at Gabriel's coming here was obvious; Michael considered it a serious mistake, although made with the best intentions.

"What is Lucifer up to?" asked Gabriel.

Michael's obvious disgust made his words hard to follow. He told falteringly of a human heart, lying in its own blood on a stone altar. A grisly pentacle was daubed on the floor of Lucifer's attic in the same watery fluid. Lucifer squatted in it, naked, mumbling spells and incantations. He'd been doing it for hours, and seemed in a trance; though he might be faking, hoping to entrap Gabriel.

"Are you nearby, Michael?"

Yes, was the muted response. Beside the altar, said Michael, the corpse of a young girl, the one providing the heart, hung half out of its coffin. Lucifer hacked her open to remove the organ from her chest, shattering the ribs with a cleaver. Her dress still gaped open at the front; with the jagged bone-ends protruding. Considerable force must have been used, but bruising at her throat suggested she was strangled to death beforehand. Lucifer's skin was blood-streaked.

He had performed this ritual himself.

The devil had looked up only once, upon Michael's arrival. Lucifer pointed one, gnarled finger, paralyzing the Archangel's wings, arms and legs, then went back to his chanting. Michael thought it no coincidence that he was left alive. Lucifer wanted the Angel of Death; Michael was the bait.

And Gabriel had come.

The scheme had worked, or so the devil would believe. Gabriel would have been here soon anyway.

He had plans for Lucifer.

Gabriel made a split-second decision. And in that split-second, he manifested at his brother's side. At first glance the situation did not seem too serious. Michael was standing upright but unable to move, having been paralyzed as he approached Lucifer. The devil's old, shriveled body crouched not far away, in his obscenity of a pentacle, summoning the dark power in a high, reedy voice. He had not paused or looked up since Gabriel arrived. All the same Michael's eyes darted in that direction.

Gabriel looked over there, and evaluated what he saw.

Lucifer knelt, scrawny ribs showing through paper-like skin. His head was bowed, wispy remnants of hair plastered down by sweat mingled with the girl's blood. The Angel of death felt a familiar fury that he fought to control. Michael's life depended on it.

But Lucifer had become this filthy, disgusting creature.

It was time for him to die.

~ ~ ~

The death of Jhalal had gone unnoticed.

Asuto Kenyatta moved into the open, knife safely concealed. He had killed Jhalal without remorse. His Iraqi friend no longer existed. This Jhalal was a traitor, a threat to Revenge of Islam; nothing more. Any semblance of friendship ended today, when Jhalal showed up in a place he had no right to be.

Prince Kamal's orders were clear: Sorya, Rob Keller and their friends must be eliminated, and while something must have gone wrong in Chicago – all four of them could die just as well here in New York.

And Jhalal was a good start.

Asuto felt exhilarated and went off in search his team. He looked around for Sorya, but saw no sign of her, Rob Keller or the light-skinned Arab who had somehow managed to replace Hassan.

There were more tourists than before. The departure lounge had filled up – with a number of flights checking in at the same time. Americans were proving braver than they seemed earlier. No matter; they could be incinerated here or in their homes. It was all the same to Asuto Kenyatta.

But the crowd slowed him down.

With his team nowhere in sight.

Asuto began to lose his temper. He pushed a man out of the way and tried to clear himself a path. He knew where he was going but too many travelers, most with luggage, were hemming him in.

Killing Jhalal had wasted valuable time.

He thought fast. How to scatter this crowd? These people must get out of his way willingly. Asuto could not force them. They were too many, and Revenge of Islam was in motion and must not be compromised. Hurting and killing people was impossible in this situation. Asuto had a sudden memory of a lion attack at the edge of his village, while he was guarding goats as a child. Two lionesses, and a shaggy-maned male, dashed from a thicket and took down one of his flock at lightning speed. Without pausing, or slowing down, they pounced on another one. The other boys ran away, shouting, "Lions, lions!" but Asuto stood his ground; furious at the loss of two goats and afraid of the beating to come.

He scooped up a few rocks and hurled them at the three lions. By pure chance he struck one of the females on her flank, drawing blood. The lions ran off, and Asuto was declared a hero. He was not scolded for the dead goats; the village awarded him his first spear, and a feast was held.

That spear killed a lion six years later.

Asuto cursed the swarming sea of airline passengers and the answer came to him. He was on the wrong side of a flock of goats. He must somehow panic them, just as those other boys and goats had panicked. Asuto must become three lions, and stampede these infidels in every direction.

He pushed those closest away, shouting that he had a

bomb set to go off in twenty seconds.

This was what they feared since they arrived, and their nerves were at breaking point. They scattered like a startled herd. Their luggage lay in a wide abandoned strip, where it fell as they threw it aside. All Kenyatta had to do was run through it and keep running. The way was clear, and his team could not be far away, but he saw frightened passengers talking to security men and pointing at him.

Ahead of Asuto was an escalator, and on the right, a narrow corridor of pillars that turned into a shadowy tunnel connecting this passenger hall to the next. That was where Chirati and the others had gone. He ran into the dark opening and picked up speed, his muscular legs pumping like pistons.

~ ~ ~

Behind him Shahanna and Clement emerged from hiding, having watched him, and his staged bomb threat from the sidelines. They saw him go; then turned to nod at each other in agreement.

They trotted after him.

~ ~ ~

"Not yet," said Clement between breaths. "Go slow. He will lead us to the others. We don't know who some of them are, and they may have the bomb. If they do I shoot Asuto and you kill this Chirati woman. Our agents must be watching them. Hopefully they'll join in."

They slowed their pace but kept Kenyatta in sight. He ran out of the tunnel and into the next passenger hall. He did not pause or look back, but ran on in a straight line. Asuto knew where he was going.

What remained of his team came into view.

Clement noticed one was in a wheelchair. A blond man

who was never in any of Prince Kamal's camps.

Clement felt a rush of adrenaline.

That had to be the bomb carrier.

Two security guards hurried past Shahanna. The first bumped her slightly; then swerved to avoid Clement. He called back, "Sorry, Ma'am!" Shahanna managed to say, "That's okay," before both men were gone.

Clement and Shahanna ran faster. He said, "Forget about Chirati. My target is Asuto, but you get the wheelchair guy. He's got the bomb." Clement sounded matter of fact, as if it hardly mattered. He didn't want to spook her.

They both knew she was the better shot.

Clement looked ahead and stopped running. Shahanna slowed and did the same.

Asuto had joined his group.

He looked agitated, telling them something. All eyes turned toward Clement and Shahanna, but then something else became apparent.

The two security guards were closing in, yelling, with guns drawn. Asuto and his people faced this new threat, each taking a shooting stance in a blur of motion, pistols braced in both hands. Both guards were shouting at them to surrender. It was Chirati who replied. She shot each man calmly between the eyes, and watched their bodies fall before she lowered her weapon.

No one had noticed Clement and Shahanna.

Asuto gave an order, and they all ran.

~ ~ ~

Clement stood rooted to the spot. He regretted not joining the battle, but the odds were dreadful. Six more guns, not even counting Chirati or the wheelchair guy.

Now some instinct moved Clement forward, as the terrorists made for the exit doors leading out onto the runways.

The wheelchair brought up the rear.

With a gunman on either side.

Shahanna fell in step with Clement, both holding back as he pondered what to do. If they took the offensive now, or Asuto happened to look back, neither of them was likely to survive.

No one looked back.

The reason lay ahead, blocking the main doors. Three more uniformed guards at a security barrier. Asuto's people stormed it in force. There was a rapid exchange of fire; Ahmed Mustafa went down, shot through the heart, but it was no contest. Not one guard survived; their bodies lay riddled with bullets, the armored barricade hanging in pierced, worthless shreds. The whole thing was over almost at once. Asuto, and what remained of Revenge of Islam, leaped over and through the corpses and wreckage. The first pair ran out into daylight, once the massive doors swung open. All the terrorists followed in short order, forming an organized group as they ran.

They veered left, and were soon out of sight.

Those doors gaped open, sucking in humidity from outside. The lack of sound was ominous. Clement went cautiously forward, Shahanna at his side, until they reached the elongated threshold. He peered out at a section of runway. He looked to the left, and his quarry was in plain view, a hundred yards away. They stood facing outwards in a circle, close to a parked Boeing 707. Their guns were aimed, cocked and unwavering, ready to stave off any attack, defending the bomb and its handicapped carrier, safely inside this defensive ring. Next to Aziz and his wheelchair stood Chirati, responsible for detonating the device. She received equal protection, being equally vital to the mission. Clement and Shahanna knew this from their own training.

The Chicago bomb carrier had never arrived.

But Clement was to activate the detonator.

Of course he wouldn't.

Now he turned to Shahanna. "Back inside. We need to think."

They both withdrew. There was no way to cross that open ground without being seen and shot to pieces. The thought of it had them whispering, for fear of being heard. Neither of them had any ideas. Clement told Shahanna to keep back, and went to look outside again, this time to his right.

A small baggage train stood, empty and unattended with carts attached, not far from the doorway in which he crouched. The key was in the ignition, a numbered tag dangling from it. This to Clement was a gift from God. Here was some fire-cover that moved. This electric train could take him and Shahanna where they needed to go, but they were two against six, and he'd seen Asuto's people shoot. He went back and asked Shahanna, who said it was a great idea – as long as she drove. Clement didn't think of arguing; there was no time.

And she would never give in.

~ ~ ~

Hunched down like a crab, Shahanna scrambled across to the first cart behind the caterpillar that pulled them all. Keeping it between her and the bomb-team, she inched along to the towing engine; then crept inside, still crouched almost flat. She felt, rather than heard Clement jump aboard a cart. A nearby jet turbine had started up – and the whine of its intake drowned out everything else. Shahanna was not distracted. Keeping low to the floor, she switched on and wrestled the gear shift into drive. The vehicle jolted into motion, followed jerkily by half a dozen carts.

The passenger jet dropped its noise level; then stopped, and Shahanna heard the tires of her vehicle swishing on the tarmac. A quick, stolen glance told her she was going the right way. Revenge of Islam's last stand lay directly ahead. As she bobbed her head back down, she saw other heads turning to look.

Asuto's had been among them.

A sudden shadow made her look up. The wing of a large plane appeared to pass overhead, as the baggage train slipped through beneath it. Now she heard Asuto, as he yelled for whoever was driving to keep clear. Shahanna did not slow down, or change course. She just kept coming up on them. Then came a hail of bullets. That told her she was close enough.

She peered out.

She was on top of Kenyatta, near enough to run him down. He bounded back and shot at her. His team held formation, and continued firing at her, too. Shahanna ducked away, slewed to her right and braked hard. She and her caravan of carts came to a stop. Awkwardly, in the cramped cabin, she drew her gun. It was long-barreled for accuracy, and she practiced every day.

She crawled out backwards, with the baggage train between her and the enemy, who were no longer shooting but calmly waiting her out. Out of the corner of her eye, she saw Clement doing the same thing. It brought another brief storm of gunfire. Shahanna and Clement had to take cover, until Asuto bellowed in rage at the waste of ammunition. Neither agent was hit, but firing back was impossible.

Shahanna acted in desperation.

She threw herself, bruising knees, elbow and back, under a cart. From there, she could see terrorist feet and legs, but not be seen herself. She raised her pistol, squinting along the sight as she'd been taught. Her breathing regulated. She picked a blue socked ankle and shattered it with her first shot.

Rama Kabullah screamed and fell on his back. Shahanna took careful aim and squeezed, This bullet blew his head apart.

Allya Mustafa bent to look at him. Shahanna could see her chin, and the gaping neck of a blouse. She snapped of a shot that hit below the collarbone, throwing Allya to the ground.

This time Clement delivered the head shot.

Bullets sprayed chips of tarmac up into Shahanna's face. She rolled back to avoid them. Her cart provided excellent cover. Crawling back under the low floor, she tried a shot at scuffed leather shoes and missed.

Clement fired next. There was a roar of pain, and a man's trouser leg ripped open, spraying and dripping blood. The unidentified victim adopted a weird hopping motion, still howling in agony. Clement kept shooting at him, and Shahanna joined in. The other leg was hit, and the terrorist dropped like a stone. It was Abeh Hassimi, and Shahanna shot him dead.

This brought a hail of answering fire; then silence.

There was a scuffle of footsteps, as Asuto and company retreated to an area from where they could see beneath the baggage-carts, and they themselves could take cover.

Shahanna saw the danger at once.

She signaled Clement and they quickly boarded, taking their original places. She started the motor and began to back up, which snaked the train into a curving wall of protection. Next she shifted into "Drive" and the chain of near empty wagons uncoiled and headed back towards safety.

Strangely not a shot was fired at them.

They stopped beside the undercarriage of another large Boeing. Both its tires and landing gear were massive, dominating this section of the aircraft, and offering a perfect shield and firing point. Clement did not need to be told. He and Shahanna abandoned the baggage train together; then crawled into the shadow of one wing, taking cover behind wheels that dwarfed them. They surveyed the runway, guns at the ready. Nothing. Asuto and the others had gone.

Taking both wheelchair and bomb.

~ ~ ~

A whirring helicopter slowly made itself heard. Agent Six had sent in the Seventh Cavalry. Clement was not surprised. The series of gun battles must have caused quite a stir. Not to mention dead bodies everywhere – of both security guard and terrorist alike. Clement had never met Agent Six, and had no idea who was directing the airport side of this operation; but he knew someone was.

And he was very good.

So were the watchers. Clement had noted close to a dozen, as he and Shahanna meandered back and forth, in search of Asuto. Both male and female agents, very well disguised, and extremely professional. The did not obstruct Clement's group, or give any sign they noticed it's presence. This was true right up to the moment Asuto and Chirati dashed out of the terminal with Clement in pursuit. And now, from the look of it, direct help had arrived. The chopper kept coming, dipped its nose and descended to fifty feet, sweeping down on what Clement guessed was Asuto's new position. Two armed snipers were visible, sighting with high-powered rifles and scopes. Clement followed their aim with his eyes. Asuto was not that far away. His people had taken refuge behind a plane rather like Clement's. Shots came from the helicopter. Then it careened away, banking sharply, then vanished back where it came from.

No one on the ground fired back.

Clement cursed.

They were working on the bomb.

CHAPTER TWENTY SEVEN

LUCIFER BABBLED an ancient lament.

He seemed in a trance-like state.

Gabriel eyed him warily from where he stood with a still paralyzed Michael, some ten yards away. The Angel of Death was alert for any false move or sign of deception, but so far the devil seemed oblivious. He had vacated the pentacle and now crouched, naked and upside down, on the underside of a broad beam that formed the main rafter. Only a self-induced trance kept him from falling.

The young Brazilian lay beside a black altar that loomed over the floor where the pentacle had been drawn. The boy was heavily sedated; beads of sweat stood out on his forehead and chin. Gabriel realized what was happening here. He had suspected it since he arrived. First Michael, then the Angel of Death himself, had interrupted an ancient and satanic ritual.

Lucifer was changing his identity.

And getting a young body.

Gabriel must have arrived faster than the devil had planned for. The ceremony looked half complete, with Lucifer having mistaken how long it lasted, and how soon Gabriel would come for his brother. Due to the tranche devil's thinking ability was limited, and that made him extremely vulnerable. Gabriel had the advantage, and could erase Lucifer's existence here and now.

But he must free Michael first.

That, and only that, held Gabriel back.

He turned toward his brother.

Two naked demons blocked his way. Their skin was so pale and parchment-thin, they barely looked human at all. They had been lurking nearby in case Gabriel showed up. Whether to warn Lucifer or fight off Gabriel was unclear. He decided probably both. It really didn't matter. They would be dead in seconds. Gabriel was not feeling merciful, and he had very little time.

The nearest one was a stumpy legged gray-hair with bulbous eyes, a sagging belly and bad teeth. The other was scrawny, picking at filthy nails with a long dagger. His eyes were blood red, and he had the look of an overgrown rat.

Gabriel advanced on them.

Angered, they stood their ground, hissing and snapping, both squarely in front of Michael, black access to him.

Gabriel called softly to his brother. "Michael, can you hear me?"

A change in Michael's eyes said he could.

The demons moved closer together. They knew about Gabriel, and what he did to creatures of their kind. The fat one snarled aggressively, exposing those rotted fangs. He would go first, decided Gabriel. He pointed a finger in their direction. "Leave now and live," he said bluntly. Of course he didn't mean it. And their fear of Lucifer was anyway too strong.

Wary, but undeterred, the pair braced for a fight.

Gabriel said, "Last warning – stand aside."

One of Michael's hands moved.

Neither demon did.

Gabriel felt impatient. He wanted them gone. They were the lowest grade, stupid variety of ogre, often used by Lucifer, and easily killed. But should they die this close to the devil, Gabriel realized, it might bring him out of his trance. But the longer Gabriel hesitated, and did nothing, these two demons grew bolder, with Lucifer likely to become Brazilian at any moment.

Michael's other hand moved.

Then an arm.

Gabriel needed to hurry. He opted for a spell. He stared hard at the fatter demon, turning its torso, arms and legs to stone. The creature was transformed into an obscene statue, frozen in its tracks.

The other one saw it happen, and turned away averting his eyes. But this had nothing to do with hypnosis, and Lucifer's warnings. It had to do with divine power. Gabriel snapped his fingers.

Rat-face became a sculpted gargoyle, rooted to the spot. Like his partner, he was paralyzed, and would be for days.

Gabriel moved past them and went to his brother. Michael was far from himself, but visibly recovering. Gabriel embraced him and rocked his upper body, as if to break Lucifer's hold. Gabriel streamed his own power at Michael, uniting their strength. The strength that made them both angels. This was Gabriel's only hope; it was all he could think of. Finally he seized Michael by the shoulders and looked into his eyes. "Brother, can you hear me?"

"Yes, Gabriel." He sounded distant, and faint. His lips barely moved.

"Can you walk, or move your legs?"

Michael spoke more clearly. "I think so. Just give me a moment." Gabriel was encouraged. A moment was all they really needed.

He said, "Let me see you try to walk."

Michael looked at the floorboards, as if eyeing the unsteady deck of a ship.

"Try it," said Gabriel.

Michael took a clumsy step.

Gabriel sighed. He considered snatching Michael and vanishing. Just leave the devil to his own devices. But that was unwise. Michael had not received enough power, and Gabriel had no more to spare. Besides, the new Brazilian version of Lucifer might step out of his coffin with no one here to stop him.

Gabriel must stay.

He told Michael to try again.

Three steps this time; then he sank to his knees, and said, "No good. I can't get my balance."

He struggled up with Gabriel's support.

They took it slowly, step by step, onto a broad, red-carpeted marble staircase. By now Michael was more in control of his limbs, and they started down. The paralysis had receded, Michael's speech was clear, and his facial muscles restored. He took on a more normal look, the numbness fading as his circulation improved. Michael went faster, and he and Gabriel soon reached a lower floor.

Lucifer's voice came from behind them, but this was no longer the rasping voice of an old man.

"Hello, Gabriel."

Both angels turned. Lucifer's boy from Brazil seemed taller standing up. He had stopped on a higher landing. Scott Anderson's replacement wore no clothes, and his body was well-muscled and flawless. Gabriel gave a cold smile. "How very handsome," he said. "I should have destroyed you just now, when I had the chance."

"Yes, indeed," agreed Lucifer. "And now you're out of juice, aren't you? Saving little brother has used it all up."

He had stopped on a higher landing.

""You'd better hope so, Lucifer."

"Ah, but it has – and look at poor Michael. He's all done in."

"He's still worth ten of you."

Gabriel felt a sudden rush of anger. The devil had come close to killing Michael, and now he was joking about it.

Lucifer snickered. "Relax Gabriel. Soon you'll be as helpless as a baby, soiling yourself in human form – no longer an angel at all. I'll turn you into an old lady with Alzheimer's. Think you'll like that?"

Gabriel stepped away from Michael, and assumed his full height. He still dwarfed this new Lucifer, but not as much as he had Scott Anderson. Added to that, the younger version seemed somehow less imposing. Gabriel opted to keep the devil talking and give Michael more time to recover. He said, "Paralyzing me won't be easy. I'm not Michael. You and young hard-body may find that out."

"I'm licking my lips."

It wasn't just sarcasm. The devil darted his tongue from side to side, shaping his perfect features into the image of a serpent.

Then the Brazilian replaced it once more: Fine, sculpted cheekbones, thick black hair, and a smile that couldn't be trusted.

Gabriel knew he had only seconds. He stole a look at

Michael, who gave him the barest nod.

Gabriel slid into Michael's thoughts and told him to make for the street. To save himself. Michael shook his head. Lucifer began to move, gliding down, his feet merely brushing the stairs that separated the three of them. There was no time for a brotherly argument.

Gabriel said, "Let Michael go, and fight it out with me."

The devil paused in-mid-stride, hovering above costly red stair carpet, but there was a cold silence, and a deadly look in his eye.

He was not making any deals.

Acting as one, both angels spread their wings and dived into the stairwell. They sped down past the remaining floors; finally landing in the spacious hallway that gave access to the main door. Michael stumbled as he hit the floor, but he recovered quickly, seeming both agile and alert.

That was at least something.

Then a swishing noise made Gabriel whip around.

Lucifer descended behind them, landing halfway down the last flight of stairs; then walking jauntily down the lower steps. A new-found vigor sounded in his voice, as he said, "Well, we seem to be running away, don't we?" He joined the two archangels on the tiled floor, but at a safe distance.

They were close to the outside door.

He had not ventured far from the stairs.

He grinned. "Now you can both die together."

Gabriel tried the front door. It was not locked. He opened it and walked out into the brightness of the sunlight with Michael at his side. A movement at the security gate caught his eye.

A mailman stood beyond the wrought iron bars, letters for Scott Anderson in his hand. His gaze went from Gabriel to somewhere behind Gabriel, his eyes widening. This meant a naked Lucifer had come outside. Gabriel turned to look. The replacement devil stood on the top step, pointing at the two angels.

They both pointed back.

Michael's aim was steady and unwavering.

"Now it begins," said Gabriel.

~ ~ ~

"So how's it going?" said Heathcote, using his most fatherly tone on Agent Six. "I hear Clement said back off."

"Yes, sir," said Agent Six." He was silent for a moment. When he spoke again he sounded nervous.

"Sir . . . We've been trying to call; your phone was busy."

Heathcote guessed that was his long call to the president. He said, "I understand. No problem."

"it was a problem here for a while, sir. We had a lot going on."

Heathcote didn't like the sound of that. "What happened? Did you round up any terrorists – or did that go badly?"

"We got almost half of them, sir. One dead."

"Damn, that's excellent work, but you don't sound happy . . ."

"Our secondary task was Clement, sir."

"But something went wrong?"

Heathcote looked out of his office window. Marines in camouflage were checking workers in at the main gate. Everyone had to walk half a mile from where they parked their car. Security bollards – filled with sand or water – blocked every access road from every direction. Heathcote sighed. Whatever had happened to his America – the land of the free?

"Sir?"

Agent Six had been talking, but strain and lack of sleep were taking their toll on Heathcote. He hardly understood a word.

He said, "I'm sorry. What did you say?"

"I said I'm afraid we lost them, sir."

Heathcote took a deep breath. "Lost who? Asuto Kenyatta and his survivors; or Clement and his people?"

There was a pause.

"Both, sir."

Heathcote controlled a rising panic. "You lost them all?"

"It was confused situation, sir. First we found your guy, Jhalal. He'd been stabbed to death."

"Jesus Christ! When were you going to tell me that? I make a check-in phone call, and you have a disaster on your hands! What else happened?"

"They just . . . ran out of our vision, sir."

"What do you mean? Who did?"

Agent Six sounded fraught. "All of them . . . Kenyatta's crowd took off running, and Clement and the girl went after them. My guys lost them. They had orders to keep back, stay out of the way."

Heathcote swallowed his frustration. "I see, " he said. And are you trying to find them?"

"They're leaving quite a trail. Airport Police report shooting at a Security barrier. Revenge of Islam killed everyone in sight; then Kenyatta led them out among refueling aircraft. Your two agents followed."

"Clement and Shahanna?"

"Yes, sir."

Heathcote gritted his teeth. "So they're on their own. The two of them."

"I have Marksman closing in, sir. By helicopter."

"I would hope so. They need to zero in and open fire. Take these Revenge of Islam vermin out on sight."

"They will, sir. They'll also protect Clement and the girl, and I've sent out half my people on the ground to do the same."

"Get the fuckers with the bomb."

"Yes, sir. We saw the wheelchair it came in."

"Kill anybody that goes near it."

"Understood," said Agent Six. "I'm leaving to join my men, sir."

"Keep in touch. This line will be kept open."

A click, and Heathcote was gone.

~ ~ ~

Clement cursed the lack of cover afforded by a Jumbo Jet. And the limited field of vision. His knees ached from squatting behind one of the wheels. Shahanna couched with him, unable to see any better. They squinted through a nest of cables and wiring attached to the landing gear. Fifty yards away, several tell-tale pairs of feet could be seen below the underbelly of another giant aircraft. At least that hadn't changed. The bottom half of the wheelchair was also visible.

Shahanna said, "What do we do? It's hard to see but they're well in range."

"Fire at their feet. Same as before."

He checked his automatic was loaded, and counted his

remaining clips. Shahanna copied him.

She said her heart was pounding.

Clement looked at her. "You were astonishing. Shot two of them to my one."

"Luck. At very short range."

Clement had seen her aiming parallel to the ground; she must have wrists of steel.

"Not luck, my lovely. You have a natural gift."

Shahanna grinned. "It was luck. I closed my eyes."

"Are you serious?"

She laughed. "No, now shut up while I shoot somebody."

She moved to see across the tarmac, her head at an angle, inches from Clement's. For a moment they both saw the same thing. She peeked over the aircraft tire, then rose to brace gun and forearm against solid rubber. Shahanna made a barely visible, head-on target, blending with her surroundings.

Her front sight was set for fifty yards.

Clement positioned himself to give covering fire.

There was plenty to aim at. Still in view under the other plane, multiple pairs of feet moved back and forth. The wheelchair was stationary. The bomb must have been removed, and was in play. Asuto had one objective. Everything over there was coming together; they had the expertise, the weapon, and the means to set it off. It was safe to assume they were about to kill New York.

Clement heard footsteps behind him.

He and Shahanna were suddenly surrounded by F. B. I. agents waving badges and I. D. cards. Most of them wore disguises. Agent Six, his suit-jacket left behind in haste, introduced himself as Senior Agent Harris. Shahanna said something vile in Arabic and lowered her gun.

Harris gave swift commands, directing his agents to take cover at various vantage points. As they moved into place a hail of bullets came from the plane commandeered by Asuto Kenyatta. The terrorist fire was deadly and accurate at such short range. Three agents went down, one shot in the head, two others in the back and chest. Then a female was shot dead, trying to pull one of the wounded to safety. Agent Six and his people took cover.

The firing stopped.

It was a stand-off.

No one was going anywhere.

Agent Six had his pretty assistant dial Heathcote. It would not be a happy phone call.

Then the helicopter swept in again, and all hell broke loose.

Four men with high-powered rifles were now framed in each doorway, and ropes were lowered toward the ground. Presumably for more fighting men to scramble down. Someone in Asuto's group fired and killed two snipers instantly. Now a cascade of bullets raked the helicopter, as other terrorists joined in. Jagged holes appeared in the nose and sides of the helicopter. The cockpit and engine casing were also struck. The chopper pilot had no choice. For the second time he retreated, dragging a cat's cradle of useless descent ropes behind him.

Clement let events wash past him, intent on moving pairs of Revenge of Islam feet. Asuto and everyone else seemed to be taking up their previous positions. Two sets of feet faced Clement, the owners standing guard as wheelchair man and detonator woman did their work.

Detonation must be close.

It was likely that Asuto was one of the guards.

Clement conveyed that to Shahanna and Harris. Before they could comment the female assistant handed Clement her boss's cell phone.

"Director Heathcote," she said. "He wants to talk to you."

There was relief in Heathcote's voice. He said, "Bo Clement, thank God you and Shahanna made it back!" He paused, then he said, "I was really sorry to hear the news about Jhalal."

Clement was stunned.

"Sir . . . what about Jhalal? Did something happen?"

"Oh, Jesus!" said Heathcote. "You didn't know . . . He was found stabbed to death, half an hour ago."

Clement tried to take that in his stride, and did not succeed. Shahanna asked him what was wrong. He put Heathcote on hold, then told her what the director had said. She, too, looked devastated.

There was no time to discuss it. Clement brought his boss back on the line, giving details of events on the tarmac, including Shahanna's sharpshooting, two failed helicopter probes, and the casualties to the FBI watchers working for Senior Agent Harris. Clement ended by explaining the layout of this area and the positions occupied by him, Shahanna, Harris and his agents – and the terrorists.

"Any visible targets?" said Heathcote. Can you kill them from where you are?" Clement realized the director had it pictured in his mind, and he was asking the only important question.

"They've stopped moving around, leaving two gunmen

to fend us off. At first we could see their feet. Not anymore; Asuto got smart."

"Maybe you could . . ."

A turbo-prop started up.

Silently cursing the screaming engine noise, Clement pressed the phone to his ear. "Sir . . . are you still there?"

But the connection was dead.

Clement handed the phone back. He looked at his watch. How long had they been working on that bomb? Had they started a count-down? Once that began, Clement knew there were only fifteen minutes to go; he had memorized it in Afghanistan with everyone else.

Asuto had been there twice that long, but coping with two helicopter interventions had occupied most of that time. It was safest to assume they were halfway to activation,, and the blast was twenty minutes away.

Very little time, given this situation.

A frontal attack in force seemed the best idea, but Clement rejected it. If it was obvious to him; it would be obvious to Asuto – who would have assigned everyone to guard against that, except his two technicians.

Clement needed to outmaneuver Asuto.

He looked around, determined to think of something.

The noisy jet was turning, pivoting on its front wheel, and suddenly the light in Clement's mind came on. He knew what to do. At least he fervently prayed that he did. Turning to Senior Agent Harris, Clement asked if he had a number for the main control tower.

Agent Six said he did.

Clement told him to call them.

~ ~ ~

Asuto trained his gun on the place where he last saw

FBI movement. This was all he could do. There were no longer an American in sight, and he could have howled with frustration. And to make things worse, Chirati's computerized detonator mechanism was taking far too long to set up.

Aziz Pali, seated in his chair above the warhead, was working steadily and seemed to know what he was doing, but he and Chirati had never worked together before, and it was clear to Asuto they were having trouble.

Chirati was an expert shot, one reason she was recruited, and her performance on leaving the departure hall had been impressive, killing those security men efficiently, and without a thought. Out here, however, she was proving a disappointment. Technically she was clumsy and slow, and she seemed disheartened by the loss of half the team, including her lover – shot to death at the security barrier. Chirati had not been the same since. Her boyfriend's death, and the other missing team members, left her with less protection while she connected fuses and electrodes.

Chirati seemed acutely aware of that.

Asuto was furious with her.

Her task called for accuracy and speed, especially with a sizable force of FBI only meters away. Rob Keller and Sorya were among them. Asuto had seen them board the baggage train, and watched as they obliterated half his force. This confirmed their being spies, as Prince Kamal predicted. No doubt they were feeding the FBI information. May Allah wither their tongues.

Jemyma knelt beside him, her gun on the ground, cleaning a light bullet wound to Allaya Mustafa's leg. It was nothing serious and the bleeding had stopped. Asuto growled with displeasure, knowing it was a waste of time. This entire area was now ground zero, with the explosion taking place at any time. He needed both these women watching the FBI, up here in the firing line, fingers on the trigger for the few seconds of life they had left. He said this gruffly to Jemyma, seeing her hands shake, as she applied a bandage to little more than a scratch.

He turned away and yelled at Chirati to hurry up.

She was kneeling, hunched over a terminal board, and jerked spasmodically at the sound of his voice. This made her drop her pliers. Asuto cursed out loud. Aziz Pali leaned down to pick them up, and gave them back with a smile. It calmed her, and she returned to consulting her wiring diagram. Her hair fell across her face, and she brushed it back. Asuto knew she did this about once a minute.

Her task was tantalizingly close to finished.

Bomb and detonator were now programmed, and compatible, but the wiring was taking twice as long as it should. The vital wiring linked both devices through terminals welded on the wheelchair frame today, in a rented garage in Jersey City. If Chirati's connections were not perfect, the bomb and its firing mechanism could not communicate. The attempt would abort. That was Asuto's greatest fear. Why did everything have to be digital with its own robot built in? A simple three-pronged socket would have exploded the bomb by now.

Chirati glanced back.

Asuto glowered at her. He saw that her face was dripping sweat, her hair again stuck to her forehead and most of one cheek. She shook it free. As he studied her their eyes met, and she cringed like a rabbit in a trap. To avoid making things worse Asuto gave her a smile of encouragement. It didn't work. She knew he must be furious, and dropped her eyes. Aziz Pali swiveled to look at Auto, and gave a warning shake of his head.

Asuto swore in Bantu. He raised his gun and cocked it; then aimed it at Chirati's head, his meaning unmistakable. "Finish now! There's no more time!" He was incensed enough to kill them both.

He decided to wait another minute, then execute Chirati and have Aziz finish the remaining electrics. But even as Auto was thinking this, she looked up at Aziz and said, "Keyboard, please."

Asuto took his finger off the trigger.

He looked around, expecting another helicopter at any second. He was on edge, as she began the firing sequence. She stopped almost immediately. The keyboard was dead. Asuto cursed louder, this time in English. Aziz took the device, opened it, and examined the insides to see what was wrong. He found a badly seated adapter, prodded it into place with his screwdriver, and seemed satisfied. He handed the keyboard back to Chirati and told her to try again.

She resumed typing.

Asuto said, "How long?"

Chirati: "Two minutes."

Aziz: "Maybe five."

Asuto seethed with frustration. "Which is it?" He raised his pistol for emphasis, knowing Aziz was probably right. "Maybe three," said Chirati over her shoulder. "My fingers are slippery. It's so hot and humid out here."

Asuto did not lower his weapon.

~ ~ ~

"Get on with it, you stupid woman." He very much

wanted the satisfaction of killing her before death claimed everybody here. He stole a glance across at the aircraft sheltering the FBI, and froze for a second. What he saw was disturbing: Rob Keller was on his feet, smiling at whatever another agent, using a cell-phone, was telling him. The other man was also smiling, and nodding his head.

Asuto threw a wild shot at them; then ducked down to escape their answering fire. Aziz told him they were thirty seconds away from ready.

The South African nodded, but his thoughts were on what he just saw. Who were those two Americans talking to?

They had been grinning like baboons.

The turbines of large jet maneuvering nearby suddenly grew even louder, their high-decibel scream doubling in intensity. It forced Asuto and those with him to cover their ears.

He craned to look.

The taxiing aircraft had turned, until its rear jet-ports were directed at the plane with an assortment of terrorists now standing exposed, caught on the wrong side of the fuselage. Two flaming orange exhausts grew larger and larger, as they came relentlessly on, their combined heat destroying everything in its path. Equipment, cable and runway vehicles were melted and vaporized. Fiery hot breath reached out for Asuto, and now he knew what that phone call had been about.

This jet was here to destroy him.

Its bright orange exhausts were searing hot.

Revenge of Islam would die in the flames.

These were Asuto's last thoughts before he became

ashes.

His companions went the same way . . .

. . . so did the very last nuclear bomb.

~ ~ ~

Clement and the others watched it happen.

The main body and undercarriage of the jet hiding the terrorists was scorched black. Metal buckled in the heat; rivets popped; one wing-tip sank to the ground and large portions of the Boeing burst into flames. Then the fuel tanks exploded, scattering blazing debris and showers of everywhere. Some of it rained down on Clement and his companions – and they ran for safety.

From a vantage point closer to the terminal building, they watched the turbulence subside and fire trucks moving in, dowsing the wreckage with chemical foam. The plane that delivered the death-blow had already taxied out of danger.

Clement had been lucky. Air traffic controllers, up in the tower, had understood immediately. Instructions were relayed to a taxiing pilot who also grasped the situation and snapped into action. He swung around until he had the angle right; then reversed at Asuto's position. The backing aircraft, now a fearsome weapon, didn't stop until success was confirmed by the tower.

A Swiss-Air captain had just saved New York.

Even from here, Clement still felt the heat. "It's over," he said.

Somewhere, deep in the wreckage, a melted blob of plastic – all that remained of the keyboard Chirati failed to connect – confirmed his words. The bomb casing and innards had also disintegrated. Not one fragment would be found in the burned out skeleton of the gutted aircraft.

Clement looked at Shahanna and saw she was fighting back tears.

He put a hand on her shoulder. "That was terrible," he said. "I can't imagine how you must feel."

She gave one, massive shudder. "They all deserved it," she said. "I just hate the way they died."

Clement was not sure he did.

It was his country they nearly destroyed.

He asked Agent Harris to lend him his phone. He took it and dialed Heathcote, giving Shahanna a sympathetic smile. He listened to the ring-tone, the events of the last ten minutes bouncing around in his head. He had engineered the death of Kenyatta and the others, without approval, and without consulting anybody. He alone had sentenced them to die. He still believed it was the right thing to do, but he wanted to hear that from Heathcote.

The director was on another call, the operator said. Would Clement hold? He said yes, and was rewarded with soothing music.

Shahanna spoke to him, dabbing her eyes with a tissue. "I'm okay now. I guess I was in shock. Thank God you acted as you did. They had to be stopped."

In the background firemen were still hosing everything down, sending up hissing clouds of steam. The Swiss airliner that incinerated Revenge of Islam was being towed away.

Heathcote came on the line.

He said hello, then listened without interruption, while Clement talked. It was a long and complicated one-way conversation. When it was over, Heathcote had only one question: "Was the bomb neutralized?"

"Nothing left, sir. Agent Harris checked."

"Good. You all did well. I'll tell the president."

Heathcote said goodbye and hung up.

Ambulances were pulling onto the tarmac and stopping. They were here to search for human remains. Clement and Shahanna found themselves gravitating towards them, overcome with a strange urge to see the bodies.

They stepped aside, as stretchers were carried in and loaded with small, blackened lumps that no longer resembled flesh. There was a lot of ashes mixed in. Clement tried in vain to recognize anyone. It was hopeless. One pretzel-like blob was glued to the buckled pieces of a wheelchair, but his identity was anyway a mystery. Then, as what was left of Asuto Kenyatta went by, Clement knew it. Among the grisly fragments a portion of skull and facial bone remained. Even in death Asuto was unmistakable. Some of his slab-like teeth were locked in a snarl. The burly African had left this life as he lived it: defiant and hostile.

Clement realized that Shahanna was trembling.

He took her inside the terminal. Agent Harris judged them both too exhausted for debriefing, and had a car take them to the small, New York hotel that was really an FBI safe house.

This time they both checked into the same room.

Clement gave the front-desk man a government credit card and asked him to buy new clothes for both of them. He joked that their Chicago airport uniforms were not only inappropriate but smelly. He tipped the concierge fifty dollars – being all the American money he had – saying they did not want to be disturbed until morning. The young man, also an FBI agent, refused the cash but did promise to have two complete wardrobes left outside their door, along with some suitable luggage.

~ ~ ~

Clement stood in the tub, closed the plastic curtain and turned on the shower. The water was cold, but he welcomed it. After months of searing desert heat, and the cloying humidity of Chicago and New York, it was heaven-sent relief. Shahanna joined him, and he felt her bare breasts, brushing his skin. They began making passionate love, standing up. Today – like so many days before it – had been filled with horror, and now the two of them blotted that out.

They moved to the bed, and time became a blur, as they went from tenderness to hot desire, then back again, more than once. They lost all sense of reality, and two hours passed, when they finally lay still in each other's arms. Before long Shahanna fell asleep, leaving Clement wide awake and thinking. He relived the all-consuming inferno he and the unleashed at JFK, with one image standing out above the rest. It was the snarling, partial mask of hatred – the horrifying memory of Asuto Kenyatta's charred scrap of a skull.

Other significant memories had been erased. Those of talking to angels, and being whisked by them from Chicago to New York. Now Clement firmly believed that he and Shahanna had made the journey with Jhalal on a regular, scheduled flight. And for the life of him Clement could not remember any more than that. Angels certainly played no part in his thinking.

Hassan was a rapidly fading dream.

CHAPTER TWENTY EIGHT

THE SCENE IN LUCIFER'S COURTYARD was almost comic.

Two very tall men – looking almost like twins – and a younger one with no clothes on; all pointing at each other like gunslingers, under the dumbstruck gaze of a mail man who, only moments ago, had been bored stiff and wondering what his wife had put in his lunch box.

Lucifer advanced down the steps, manifesting a red silken robe as he came. It was cut to show his rippling physique to good advantage. The devil was still as vain as ever, but his eyes were locked on the two archangels, as he came down the steps. Death was in those eyes, and he never faltered.

For him the postman did not exist.

Gabriel felt a sudden shift in the spiritual orbit, knowing instantly that something had happened at JFK. A misty image of Asuto Kenyatta drifted into the consciousness of the Angel of Death. The African was yelling in alarm, and backing away from two great fireballs looming over him from mid-air.

Then the image was gone, Gabriel staggering under the impact of Lucifer's first strike. This, too, took the form of a fireball. It was luminescent, orange and spinning, a flaming orb that smashed into the ground like a thunderbolt, sweeping both angels off their feet.The reborn Lucifer wore a smug look.

He had struck the first blow.

Rising, and standing once more, Gabriel sensed that the devil was not quite settled into his new body, and felt nothing when that cosmic shift reduced his power, just seconds before. Michael must have sensed it, too. He shot his brother a meaningful look. Gabriel, whose power had increased, hoped it was now sufficient to defeat Lucifer, who seemed hell-bent on a fight to the death.

Michael believed firmly in his brother.

They would fight side-by-side; as they always did.

The forces for good had triumphed at Kennedy Airport, and Gabriel decided the outcome here would be the same.

Lucifer was in high spirits. He had whooped when the fireball landed. Creating one, and a successful first shot, made him feel invincible. He quickly launched another, this time at Michael, who easily avoided it. A second scorched hole appeared in the crazy paving on which they all now stood. Lucifer inched closer, keeping a wary eye on Gabriel, who was circling to his right.

The mail man whistled in disbelief.

Then he went off in search of a cop.

He would not find one.

Three powerful minds had seen to that.

~ ~ ~

Without warning Gabriel went from circling to attacking. He created a fireball of his own; then aimed and fired in a split-second. It hurtled at Lucifer's head, intended to twist at the end of its path, striking viciously from behind. An angel spell contained in the fire would damage the devil's nervous system.

Virtually destroying his brain.

Lucifer ducked as it hit, reducing the effect, but his mouth hung slackly open, and he seemed to have lost his bearings as he staggered back. He fought hard to recover, and his face took on a more normal look.

But not as normal as before.

His demeanor was noticeably vacant, reaction and movement slightly slower. He barely avoided a dual bombardment by the two angels. One leg was dragging, and his eyes, when he straightened up, were staring wildly.

Lucifer's cockiness was gone, and his amusement with it. What might have started as a game had grown deadly serious. The devil was in a fight for his life. Both angels advanced, forcing him to back away.

Gabriel thought, He's groggy. Finish him now.

He sent the thought to Michael, and they closed in from opposite sides. They each created a fireball and threw together. Twin lightning bolts struck Lucifer, engulfing him in searing flame. The impact was powerful, doubled in force. It knocked the devil back several feet. Then smoke and fire fell away, as the fireballs faded, and he slapped at his smoldering robe, muttering curses. His hair was visibly scorched as he turned away and ran back up the steps. Blistered lumps of scalp showed through the bare patches. Lucifer stumbled inside the house and disappeared.

Both angels ran after him, then stopped, as a naked demon emerged from the front door. He was joined by two more, one of them female. Their bodies were slick with sweat, either from depraved sexual activity, or some satanic ritual Gabriel didn't like to think about. He recognized the woman who flirted with him at the Bunch of Grapes, where he first met Clement and Shahanna. Her looks were suffering, now she was a fully-fledged demon in her own right. Her face was lined and pinched, her voluptuousness descending rapidly into scrawny, premature old age. Without warning she spat a tongue of flame at Michael, aiming for his head. Gabriel made a quick hand-gesture and stopped the flimsy projectile in mid-flight.

It evaporated.

She scampered down the steps, screaming, "Kill them! Kill them both!"

Gabriel chose not to destroy her. She had been drunk that night in Washington, and was drunk now. He ignored her for the other two.

Both had battle-scars; they had fought angels before. It showed in the surefooted way they moved and the look in their eyes. These two worked together often, and had no fear of Gabriel.

Every step they took said so.

Now they split up, keeping well clear of the woman; it not only made them hard to attack, but made her an unskilled and easy target, intended to distract either Gabriel or Michael.

It didn't work.

The female was not that important.

Pursuing Lucifer was.

Gabriel faked a throw at the one on his left. The demon didn't duck or flinch. He said, "Angel of Death – your kind is finished."

He spat flame at Michael.

Both angels pointed, and snuffed it out.

Michael sent a fire-bolt at the demons throat, breaking its head off at the neck. The torso fell sideways down the steps.

The female ran screeching into the house.

One demon remained.

"Step aside," said Gabriel.

He gave it a few seconds to make up its mind. He was repaid by an obscene belch. The creature's mouth opened wide, and emitted a burning, gaseous sulfur ball. It flew at Gabriel with incredible speed.

"Leave it to me!" shouted Michael, knowing his brother needed to conserve power. He raised one hand, causing the flaming projectile to pause in the air, then catapult back at the demon who created it.

The demon died.

The two angels entered the devil's house, knowing that one way or the other, this would be the last time.

~ ~ ~

Lucifer made it to the third floor. Fearful thoughts were overpowering him. What was wrong? His renewed energy should have killed them both. Instead they came close to killing him. His brand new body was damaged, youthful power draining away, and there was little time to repair it because the double doors slammed downstairs, and the stench of angels re-entered the house.

Lucifer forced himself upward, determined to reach the attic and its resources of evil before Gabriel caught up with him. As he finally stumbled into his lair, the burned traces of silken robe dissolved and fell away. He made for the center of the pentacle and knelt before the grisly adornments of his altar. The virgin's blackened heart gleamed at him, draped with the entrails of a large rat.

A quick but powerful spell healed all bodily injury.

Juanito Diaz, the boy from Brazil, was back in business.

Lucifer snapped his fingers, and now he was dressed in a yellow tracksuit with black stripes. The devil rose, left the attic and descended the stairs, looking for sign of Gabriel as he passed each floor. Lucifer finally found both angels, watching television from an open doorway that led into his ground floor den.

The TV screen told it all. Shown live from JFK: A close-up of a mangled scrap of wheelchair, half buried in plane parts and rubble.

Revenge of Islam had failed.

Lucifer stood on the bottom stair, straining to see.

The newscaster confirmed it. The plot by Muslim extremists, involving a nuclear weapon, had been foiled by the FBI. Millions of lives had been saved. The commentary droned on and on. The footage ended with one jet aircraft backing into another on the ground, turning terrorists and bomb into mostly vapor.

Lucifer felt sick.

Not out of sympathy for dead demons and Arabs.

But for his beautiful Armageddon.

~ ~ ~

Gabriel and Michael turned to face him, having known all along he was there. He sprang away, landing cat-footed on carpeting that had cost a fortune. An impressive leap that put a distance of twenty feet or so between them.

Juanito Diaz was as agile and fit as before.

The spells Lucifer cast had worked.

The devil brought up one hand, ready to unleash a series of fireballs. Both angels saw this, and went into a defensive crouch. Lucifer switched from fireballs to something else, twirling one finger and focusing his gaze on Michael.

"Death," said Lucifer, "beckons." With that, he drew a circle in mid-air with his finger, then tightened it, like a noose.

Michael clutched at his throat.

More tightening, and he began to choke.

Lucifer stole a look at Gabriel, wanting him distracted by this, so he might more easily be attacked.

The devil brought his will to bear: *Come on, Gabriel. Don't look at me; look at him.* He tightened the noose again, causing Michael to fight for breath.

Gabriel still looked at Lucifer.

It was not a distracted look.

Michael was making hoarse sounds, each attempt to inhale an excruciating agony. Lucifer squeezed, closing his imaginary loop like a steel band.

Suddenly the air was electric, as Gabriel assaulted him with an anger delivered from Heaven itself. An awesome power had been released. The sheer fury of it forced the devil to release Michael and defend himself. Flinging up both hands to protect his head, he turned and ran away. This gave Gabriel an opening.

A gigantic fireball struck Lucifer from behind.

He tottered, and fell in a smoking heap.

The angels moved in on him.

All the back and forth from Chicago, Washington D C and New York had drained Gabriel. The devil was still a match for him, even with divine help. He and Michael were aware of it, and approached their prey with caution.

Lucifer scrambled to his feet and snarled.

The Angel of Death knew he had the momentum, but he must act quickly. Before the devil realized what was happening, Gabriel again invoked a power far mightier than his own, bowing his head and asking for help. The answer was immediate. There was a blinding flash of white light.

Lucifer screamed and collapsed.

Gabriel knew he had been answered.

A whole world had changed in seconds, and it was changed forever.

Michael stirred the devil with his foot. Lucifer rolled over, his ashen face showing shock and surprise. "You can't do this," he said, but his words ended in a choking cough. The devil went into convulsions, arms and legs flailing, and drumming on the floor. Then his muscles gave out and he sank, immobilized, and lay still.

Gabriel leaned over him. There was a pulse, and signs of breathing. Gabriel would have wished Lucifer dead, but Heaven had other plans. The devil was paralyzed, but fully conscious and aware of his surroundings.

And so it was ordained for all eternity.

That was Lucifer's punishment.

Far more terrible than death.

The Angel of Death saw pain in those wild, staring eyes, as it dawned on Lucifer what the future held in store. His existence had been made nothing. Captivity in his new body was all he would ever know. The cruelty of it matched that of Lucifer himself, and showed the depth of Heaven's anger.

Gabriel and Michael turned away.

Then the house began to shake.

Seconds later the luxury brownstone was collapsing, with great slabs of masonry falling down, the doomed structure raining bricks, wood, dust and debris that used to be Lucifer's sanctuary. None of this harmed him; he was protected, and his fate sealed. The two angels left him there. They walked outside, unscathed by the tumbling destruction all around them, becoming invisible as they went.

Sirens could be heard approaching.

Onlookers were already running up and gawking.

An ambulance drove over tangled wrought iron fencing and into the courtyard. It stopped just short of the rubble. Black and white patrol cars swerved in behind it, police officers leaping out and mounting the chipped and broken steps where a sizable mansion had stood. Everything was knocked flat. As if on cue, the collapse had stopped, but not a wall remained, barely a brick attached to mortar. There was, however, a convenient path to where Lucifer lay. He was unable to move but parts of him could be seen. A variety of uniformed figures picked their way towards him. Yellow tape was being stretched around the property.

Michael and Gabriel looked at each other, and flitted away unseen.

That ambulance would take Lucifer where he needed to go.

~ ~ ~

Gabriel landed in the streets of Heaven. Michael had gone home to Budapest. The Angel of Death was here to rest, and seek advice from other archangels in this holy place: An unspeakably high elevation in the mountains of Tibet. Throughout the angel world it was called Heaven. This earthly version was a tiny village with less than thirty buildings; even counting the temple, a bathhouse and two religious shrines. Gabriel had come here to replenish himself in the sky of the world.

Before seeing President Christiansen.

And then meting out justice to Lung Chang.

~ ~ ~

President Christian was in the White House dining room, sharing a lunchtime sandwich with his wife, Dawn. She brushed imaginary off the tablecloth and said, "You had better get going," as she always did if he attended a function against her wishes, and today was no exception.

Dawn was a Native American, and liked to joke that she was as stubborn as the tribes that survived the White Man. She and Christiansen were childhood sweethearts, and their home in Wisconsin was on tribal land.

It was twenty-four hours since the saving of New York.

"Richard Powell is head of the FBI. He had a very good day," the president said, trying to placate her.

"He's an arrogant pig."

"That's got nothing to do with it." He swallowed a last mouthful before reaching for his napkin.

She stood up to clear the plates. "Rubbish."

"I have to present this medal," said Christiansen.

"Doesn't mean I have to like it."

The president finished his iced tea. It was refreshing. He recalled Summer picnics in Wisconsin, when they were courting. Was that really thirty years ago?

He put his glass down. His wife continued clearing up, noisily, in order to show her displeasure. "She said, "Powell is unworthy of you, and his job."

"That's not the point, my dearest."

'My dearest' always broke her down. She said, "Go to your party." She grinned at him, because her anger was fake, and she adored him.

"It's hardly a party," he said.

Dawn shrugged. She'd said her piece, and despite having defended the FBI head, Christiansen knew she was right. This afternoon the wrong man would be honored, the true heroes being a couple of dozen of Powell's agents, and the man he spent a lot of his time trying to fire – Bradley Heathcote.

Reading his thoughts, Dawn said, "That Heathcote should get a medal."

Her husband sighed. "Yes, I know."

Two secret servicemen entered the room. President and First Lady walked arm in arm to the open door and stopped.

Christiansen kissed her cheek. "I'll be back before you know it."

"You still have to learn tomorrow's speech."

"I know. And I will." With that he was gone and the door closed.

~ ~ ~

The president quickened his stride. The elevator was waiting; he and the secret service rode down to the ground floor. Then came the line of gleaming black cars, then more secret servicemen and a cavalcade of motorcycle outriders. The signal was given and they all glided down the driveway.

Christiansen would be glad when this was over.

He sat back in leather upholstery, deciding what to do and say when they reached the FBI building. He saw, as the White House gates opened, that a mass of people had gathered at the roadside, waving flags and cheering. In contrast to the gloomy city of two days ago, the capital had come alive, ready to celebrate survival and a better tomorrow. As always Americans had bounced back. They had walked, pedaled and driven here in their thousands. According to Secret Service reports, they stood fifty deep along several city blocks.

The presidential column swept past them.

The crowd began to sing.

It was the Star Spangled Banner.

Christiansen's favorite bodyguard, sitting opposite, muttered to his partner, "Now the Feds will be unbearable. They're getting all the credit."

The president had been thinking the same thing, but thinking it about Richard Powell.

He said, "Ask the driver to slow down. These folks deserve a wave and a smile; not a glimpse of me streaking by like a racehorse."

The body guard nodded and gave the order.

The people understand, thought the president, as they slowed to little more than a crawl. The nation is reborn, and they feel it. Christiansen pushed a button and lowered the window. People were shouting from the crowd.

"Great job, Mr. President!"

"God bless America!"

This went on for only a few seconds. Then there was silence in the president's head, as if a knife had cut across his senses. He felt a little strange.

Then things got downright weird.

The car and everything else in sight vanished.

President Christiansen was alone, standing in the sky.

~ ~ ~

It had all gone away. No car; no bodyguards; no motorcycle escort. And no more Washington D. C. The sky surrounding the president was azure blue, and almost devoid of cloud. He knew he must be dreaming, but hadn't he been driving to Richard Powell's award ceremony? Weren't there thousands of onlookers just seconds ago? And didn't he feel perfectly normal and wide awake?

What on Earth was going on?

Then the angel showed up.

Amazingly, it smiled and spoke, introducing itself as the Angel Gabriel, and the President of the United States began to wonder about that sandwich he just ate with his wife. What the angel said next was startling.

Gabriel shook his head. "It's not the Tuna."

Apparently he read minds.

"Then this is a dream," said the president. "What does it mean?"

The angel did not answer that.

"Let's take a walk." Gabriel offered his hand.

The president grasped it firmly. This was surely a dream; he had fallen asleep in the car. Then, with a chill of fear, it struck him that he might have died. Wasn't Gabriel the Angel of Death. Church on Sundays seemed a long time ago, but Christiansen felt certain about that name – Gabriel, the horn blower.

Had he come to blow for a president?

Were they really here, walking through the sky?

"It's no dream," said Gabriel. "And you're very much alive. I am here because I have something important to tell you."

"Where are we?" said the president.

Gabriel laughed. "My fake portrayal of Heaven," he said frankly.

President Christiansen still suspected bad Mayonnaise.

"So what's important?" he said.

"Angels really exist," said Gabriel. "You're an unawakened one."

The president's face showed disbelief, but he'd heard this before, from his wife's uncle, a Blackfoot, a native American as she was. Uncle Aaron wore the medicine shirt. He was a shaman, and his words carried a lot of weight.

This made Christiansen think.

Now Gabriel slipped a vision into his mind. A small ante-room in the FBI building on E-Street. The president himself stood erect, pinning a medal on Richard Powell to the applause of selected dignitaries in the background. Every television network and cable news channel was filming the event.

The President stepped back.

Powell's award glinted on his chest.

Gabriel said, "This will happen soon."

The president knew that much already.

"I was on my way there."

The vision continued. He saw himself begin his speech of congratulation. At the same time, Gabriel's voice sounded in his head. "Look at Mr. Powell."

At first nothing happened.

Then the FBI Director's hand flew to his heart. He staggered, abruptly enough that the president stopped mid-speech, showing great concern. Powell fell to his knees, then collapsed full-length on the floor. People looked on in alarm – others ran forward to try and help him.

"Remember this," said Gabriel.

Richard Powell was coughing up blood. Strangely it looked black. The cameras kept turning and captured it all.

They kept turning until Richard Powell fell back dead. Only Gabriel and the president, standing in an unreal blue sky, saw what else happened in that ante-room. It was the Angel Gabriel, causing the heart attack by pointing; then ending it with a snap of his fingers.

Gabriel turned to President Christiansen. "When this happens, remember what I have told you. You are an angel, and need to know it."

Then the Angel of Death was gone.

The president did not react.

He looked thoughtful.

EPILOGUE

LUNG CHIANG SENSED the assassins coming.

They were angels, headed by Gabriel, and Michael.

It was evening, the Hour of the Horse, and Chiang was feasting on the tiny spiced tongues of river ducks. A glistening morsel was balanced between ivory chopsticks, when his enjoyment was overshadowed by the presence of the Angel of Death and his accursed brother.

Chang stopped eating and sat back.

He called softly through an open doorway.

A guard appeared from the garden surrounding the house, and was told of the danger. This guard, like all those on duty, was a fallen angel. Since the failed attack on America, Chiang was marked for death by Heaven, and he was taking no chances. The guard hurried off to organize a defense.

Lung Chiang sat with his eyes closed. The intrusion was entirely silent, but he felt the movement outside. There were no footsteps. Angels do not impact the ground as they walk; they glide just above it. Chiang relied on a well-defined mind-picture of Gabriel's party closing in on his own defenders.

The archangels were outnumbered. Dozens of Chiang's Fallen moved into place and had them surrounded.

Chiang knew this would avail him nothing.

The conflict was terrifyingly brief, and fierce. The number slain by Gabriel alone guaranteed the outcome.

In no time at all Chiang's side had lost.

He composed himself.

Gabriel had come. He had been expected for days. Lucifer was either destroyed or imprisoned by heavenly decree. This was widely known, and left scant hope for the likes of Lung Chiang, especially in light of the trap he had set by sending Michael and Gabriel to New York. A lot of demons and fallen angels had died or disappeared already. Those holding high position in government, not only in America but all over the world. It was a clear sign that the devil's rein had ended.

Lung Chiang knew this was the end.

He resumed eating, but the food was cold. Duck fat formed tasteless globules in his mouth and he set the bowl aside.

A voice spoke from the bamboo doorway.

A blood-drenched guard, begging his master to save him. Chang advised him to drown himself in the river. The overweight tong leader laughed harshly, dismissing the wounded fighter with a wave of the hand. As he had feared all along, where Gabriel was concerned, guards were useless.

Chiang emptied a cup of sake, stood up and lumbered off to his sleeping quarters. A servant slipped into the room behind him, hastening to pull the shades and light a pair of delicately shaded lamps on cabinets beside the bed. Lung Chang had little patience for any of this tonight, and told the man to leave. The figure did not move. Then it occurred to Chiang that this was no servant. He knelt at the foot of the bed and looked up into the eyes of Gabriel. There was no argument or discussion. The Angel of Death raised a hand.

That hand, and this room, were the last thing Chang ever saw.

Except for the fireball that killed him.

~ ~ ~

Lucifer was in torment.

The strait-jacket cut into his shoulders, arms and back. He could not cry out. Gabriel had taken away his power of speech.

This ward was for the criminally insane; the deceptively handsome young man from Brazil was its latest inmate. From the next bed and old man, also strapped down, babbled incessantly. The room was ripe with the smell of urine. This was the devil's Hell on Earth. All light bulbs had been removed, creating night. In eight hours they would be replaced, creating day. At the end of a row of twenty beds, tiny fragments of light showed under the door of the attendant's midget office. The attendant was asleep and would not wake up until breakfast.

This nightmare was eternal; it would never end. The Brazilian was registered as a John Doe. Every few years he would be shuffled to another mental facility and admitted. This would disguise the fact that he never aged, and never recovered from the coma that doctors attributed to his condition. Lucifer's brain squirmed at the thought that he would never move or speak again. He had been condemned to century after century of eternal nothing.

Two nurses stopped by to check on his vital signs, whispering and laughing at some silly joke. They were pretty, even in semi-darkness, and their presence filled Lucifer with desire. He raged at his inability to speak, let alone touch them, now that he was so young and attractive.

One of them undid his strait jacket and lifted the skimpy hospital robe he wore underneath it exposing chest, stomach and groin. Her fingers brushed his skin as she attached electrical sensors to read his heart-rate. This almost drove the devil out of his mind, but he fought for control, knowing this was Gabriel's design, and events like this would torture him every day. Year after year, and century after century. Heaven had not only defeated him, but devised the perfect revenge.

Lucifer uttered a scream that no one could hear.

~ ~ ~

Washington D. C., 6th July. Televised at 8: oopm Eastern Time.

This was not the speech written for the president, but it was the one he gave, and the one history would remember:

My fellow Americans,

Today we are free in the true sense of the word. Two days ago, when we celebrate our nation's birth, we triumphed over an enemy who came closer to victory than bears thinking about. Today the world is different. You know it, and I know it. The air is pure, the sun shines brighter. There are many, like me, who choose to believe that the hand of evil has been lifted from us.

My phone has not stopped ringing. Congratulations and good wishes keep pouring in from all over the world. There is also surprising news of the death of national leaders, both here and overseas; others simply vanished overnight. This has affected countries great and small. Those who perpetuated war, hunger and suffering are gone. It saddens me to say they probably won't be missed.

Those of us still in office have a renewed sense of

brotherhood, and a commitment to move our nations forward together. Over and over, during a conversation with one of my foreign counterparts, I heard the same words: unity, peace and friendship. There is a new light shining on us all.

The nuclear age is ended. Disposal of the world's weapons arsenals have already begun, and the days of fossil fuels are also numbered. We have known for decades that our energy must come from other sources, like solar power, wind and hydro-electricity. There will be an international conference in Paris in one week, with everyone attending and given a chance to speak. There will not be much negotiation; everyone has stated a desire to sign on behalf of their population.

Our world has a new sense of purpose. As President of the United States, I vow to protect America, and ensure the future that beckons us. Every world leader I spoke to is willing to do the same.

America is the shining city on the hill. It always has been, and there is nobody on Earth that doesn't know it. God give us strength and wisdom to remember who we are, and why we were founded. Men and women everywhere hold those truths, as set out in our Declaration of Independence, to be self-evident. That why they come by the million, seeking the freedom we promise.

And so, my fellow Americans, I ask for your help to fulfill that promise; for them and for each and every one of us.

We can, and I assure you – we will.

Goodnight, and God bless you all. God bless America!

This speech was shown on all US network and cable channels, and social media feeds on every continent.

It went over very well.

~ ~ ~

A small white dot hissed angrily on the darkened TV screen.

Shahanna sat up with a yawn, pulling at her tousled hair until it looked acceptable in the mirror opposite.

She had dreamed of angels and demons, for three nights running, and no longer bothered to wonder why. The dreams resembled memories. They faded as she woke up, and were soon gone like smoke and mist.

As she got out of bed the TV sprang back to life. It was the same news channel as last night, when she and Clement watched the president's speech. It filled the room with the picture and chirpy commentary from a Century News lady. Shahanna noted that the woman's legs were no longer crossed due to the tightness of her skirt. Century seemed to be experiencing the same revolution as everybody else.

The screen changed.

Now it showed a replay of President Christiansen's speech.

Clement woke up, rubbing his eyes, and they watched it again together. Shahanna found herself mesmerized for a second time.

The camera switched to live coverage from high above Rockefeller Plaza. All the streets were jammed with people. People dancing; people singing; people laughing and hugging strangers; many toasting each other with bottles or paper cups. New York was bursting with energy.

They had danced all night in Times Square.

They were dancing in Queens.

They were dancing in the Bronx.

They were dancing from Memphis to Detroit.

From the Outer Banks to Honolulu.

Shahanna reached for her clothes. Clement handed her a clingy, chiffon blouse and said, "Are you thinking what I'm thinking?"

She nodded. "We should go down there. We're so close."

He agreed with a smile.

"Get your pants on," she said.

They showered and got dressed.

He said, ""I want to see people who aren't terrorists."

Shahanna had on tight jeans, with her midriff bare.

"I want to belly-dance across Manhattan," she said.

"Then you shall."

They ran downstairs. The hotel was surrounded by an ocean of people, and it took an effort to cross the street. The mood of the crowd was even more buoyant than it looked on TV.

"This is my kind of party," said Clement.

"New York, I love you!" shouted Shahanna.

They got onto Fifth Avenue, bought some high-priced wine and headed for Central Park. The crowd was even thicker. A newspaper lay trampled underfoot. The headline said: President Says War is Whack! Shahanna saw a small boy mouthing the words as he read it. All around her, the noise was deafening, singing and shouting condensed into one mammoth roar. She grabbed Clement's hand and let him steer here wherever they were going.

At the park he turned in through the trees.

A path led between well-tended lawns.

They sat on the grass by a flower bed, enjoying the temporary solitude. Everyone, it seemed, had joined the masses behind them. She and Clement sat without speaking, until the child appeared.

"Oh," cried Shahanna. "How cute!"

It was a little girl, blonde, in a pink dress.

She held a posy of flowers.

She toddled over and held them out to Shahanna.

"Oh, no, sweetie," said Clement. "Someone gave those to you . . ."

Sunlight flashed upon the girl's hair, looking like a halo. She put the flowers into Shahanna's hand. Her mouth was that of a cherub, her eyes the brightest blue. "For Shahanna," she said firmly.

That startled them both.

Shahanna said gently, "Did someone send you to me?"

The child nodded.

"Do you know their name?"

She nodded again.

Shahanna could think of no one. "A man or woman?"

The girl skipped away, laughing. "My name is Gabriella," she said.

Then she vanished before their eyes.

After a moment, Clement said, "I don't understand."

Shahanna smiled and hugged him.

"I think you do," she said.

Thank you for reading.
Please review this book. Reviews help others find Absolutely Amazing eBooks and inspire us to keep providing these marvelous tales.

If you would like to be put on our email list to receive updates on new releases, contests, and promotions, please go to AbsolutelyAmazingEbooks.com and sign up.

ABOUT THE AUTHOR

Arndt Schorr was born in Europe of British and German descent. He was raised and educated in both countries, speaks English German and French. He met and married his American wife in Augsburg, Germany, and moved to the United States in 1996. They have two grown up children and live in Key West, FL. This book is the culmination of forty years of writing short stories and novels in Europe and America. It is the second title in Arndt Schorr's new series, The Fourth Angel War.

ABSOLUTELY AMAZING eBOOKS

NewAtlantianLibrary.com
or AbsolutelyAmazingeBooks.com
or AA-eBooks.com